F. SCOTT FITZGERALD

THE SHORT STORIES OF F. SCOTT FITZGERALD

EDITED AND WITH A PREFACE BY
MATTHEW J. BRUCCOLI

SCRIBNER PAPERBACK FICTION
PUBLISHED BY SIMON & SCHUSTER
NEW YORK LONDON TORONTO SYDNEY TOKYO SINGAPORE

SCRIBNER PAPERBACK FICTION
Simon & Schuster Inc.
Rockefeller Center
1230 Avenue of the Americas
New York, NY 10020

First Scribner Paperback Fiction Edition 1995

SCRIBNER PAPERBACK FICTION and design
are trademarks of Simon & Schuster Inc.

Manufactured in the United States of America

5   7   9   10   8   6   4

Library of Congress Cataloging-in-Publication Data
Fitzgerald, F. Scott (Francis Scott), 1896–1940.
[Short stories. Selections]
The short stories of F. Scott Fitzgerald/edited and with a preface by
Matthew J. Bruccoli.
p.   cm.
1. Bruccoli, Matthew Joseph, 1931–   II. Title.
PS3511.I9A6   1989
813'.52—dc20   89-6351   CIP

ISBN 0-684-80445-X

Balance of copyrights appear on page 776

*The editor and publisher dedicate this volume
in memory of Scottie Fitzgerald Smith*

CONTENTS

◆

FOREWORD

◆

"MY WHOLE THEORY of writing I can sum up in one sentence. An author ought to write for the youth of his own generation, the critics of the next, and the schoolmasters of ever afterward." So proclaimed the young Scott Fitzgerald in the first flush of success at the appearance of *This Side of Paradise* in 1920. How magnificently—if, sad to say, posthumously—he fulfilled that ideal. His all too brief literary career—a dozen years of commercial and critical success followed by distractions and disappointments—ended in 1940 when he suffered a fatal heart attack at the age of forty-four. He was hard at work on the Hollywood novel he hoped would restore his literary fortunes, *The Last Tycoon*. At the time of his death his books were not, as was later supposed, out of print with his publisher. The truth is sadder: they were all in stock at our warehouse and listed in the catalogue, but there were no orders.

Now, a half century later, more copies of F. Scott Fitzgerald's books are ordered each year than were sold cumulatively throughout his entire lifetime. His novels and short stories are taught in virtually every high school and college across the country. This new, comprehensive collection of Fitzgerald's best short fiction is being published some seventy years—a biblical lifespan—after the author's first novel was accepted by my great-grandfather in 1919. I am struck by the realization that three generations (and namesakes) later I was the first of our family to have been introduced to Fitzgerald's work in the *classroom*. My grandfather, Fitzgerald's friend and publisher for the latter half of his career, died on the eve of the author's reappraisal and subsequent revival that gained momentum through the Fifties and has continued in full force down to the present time. It was my father who was to preside over Fitzgerald's literary apotheosis, a publishing phenomenon perhaps unprecedented in modern American letters. Through him I had the good fortune to meet and work with the author's talented and generous daughter, Scottie, and her collaborator and advisor, Matthew J. Bruccoli, whose prolific scholarship and infectious enthusiasm have long fanned the flames of Fitzgerald studies.

The day I met Professor Bruccoli fifteen years ago I asked what had prompted him to devote the lion's share of his scholarship to Fitzgerald. He told me exactly how it happened. One Sunday afternoon in 1949 Bruccoli, then a high school student, was driving with his family along the Merritt Parkway from Connecticut to New York City when he heard a dramatization of "The Diamond as Big as the Ritz" on the car radio. He later went to a library to find the story; the librarian had never heard of Scott Fitzgerald. But finally he managed to locate a copy—"and I never stopped reading Fitzgerald."

There is something magical about F. Scott Fitzgerald. Much has been written—and dramatized—about the Jazz Age personas and syncopated lives of Scott and Zelda. But the real magic lies embedded in his prose and it is perhaps nowhere more pervasive than in the amazing range and versatility of his short stories: the best sparkle with greater luster than ever in this new collection that displays them afresh in their proper literary and biographical settings. Each tale partakes of its creator's poetic imagination, his dramatic vision, his painstaking (if virtuosic and seemingly effortless) craftsmanship. Each bears Fitzgerald's distinctive hallmark, the indelible stamp of grace.

Fitzgerald once claimed to his agent Harold Ober that "good stories write themselves—bad ones have to be written." Yet a decade later he confessed that "there is no use of me trying to rush things." Even during his most prolific stages, he noted, "I could not turn out more than 8–9 top-price stories a year." The secret of success was not to be found in original themes. In his own view there were but "two basic stories of all times—*Cinderella* and *Jack the Giant Killer*—the charm of women and the courage of men." Nor should we look to the "booze and inspiration" school of thought, as he dubbed it: "You do not," he argued, "produce a short story for the *Saturday Evening Post* on a bottle." (Fitzgerald did, however, admit to writing his first novel with the aid of a liquid "stimulant"—Coca-Cola!) Some clues to his creative craftsmanship may be gleaned from his instructive if sometimes professorial letters to his daughter: "Stories are best written in either one jump or three, according to length. The three-jump story should be done on three successive days, then a day or so for revise and off she goes. This of course is the ideal. . . ." Still, he cautioned her, "nobody ever became a writer just by wanting to be one. If you have anything to say, anything you feel nobody has ever said before, you have got to feel it so desperately that you will find some way to say it that nobody has ever found before, so that the thing you have to say and the way of saying it blend as one matter—as indissolubly as if they were conceived together."

In the last year of his life Fitzgerald pondered in a poignant letter to his wife, Zelda, then hospitalized in an asylum, the loss of his former success in the genre: "It's odd that my old talent for the short story vanished. It was partly that times changed, editors changed, but part of it was tied up somehow with you and me—the happy ending. Of course every third story had some other ending, but essentially I got my public with stories of young love. I must have had a powerful imagination to project it so far and so often into the past." The key to Fitzgerald's enduring and elusive enchantment lies, I believe, in the power of his romantic imagination to transfigure his characters and settings—and indeed the very shape and sound of his prose. I shall never forget that evening train ride from Princeton to Philadelphia on which I first read "The Diamond as Big as the Ritz": a commute was converted into a fantastic voyage. And I can still see Anson Hunter, "The Rich Boy," whose self-conscious superiority will forever, in my eyes, embellish the gilded lobby of New York's Plaza Hotel. Fitzgerald's stories transform their external geography as thoroughly as the realm within. The ultimate effect, once the initial reverberations of imagery and language have subsided, transcends the bounds of fiction.

—CHARLES SCRIBNER III

PREFACE

◆

Mostly, we authors repeat ourselves—that's the
truth. We have two or three great and moving
experiences in our lives—experiences so great
and so moving that it doesn't seem at the time
that anyone else has been so caught up and
pounded and dazzled and astonished and beaten
and broken and rescued and illuminated and
rewarded and humbled in just that way ever
before.

Then we learn our trade, well or less well,
and we tell our two or three stories—each time
in a new disguise—maybe ten times, maybe a
hundred, as long as people will listen.

—"One Hundred False Starts,"
Saturday Evening Post (4 March 1933)

F. SCOTT FITZGERALD's short stories remain a misunderstood and
underrated aspect of his career. They have been dismissed as hackwork and
condemned for impeding his serious work. Certainly they are uneven; but
Fitzgerald's best stories are among the best in American literature.*

Fitzgerald's stories now require two approaches. One should try to read
them as though for the first time as they originally appeared—for the pleasure
of their style, wit, warmth, and versatility. They should also be read in
terms of their role in the canon of a great writer. Fitzgerald was partly
responsible for the continuing difficulty in properly assaying his stories.
After an initial period of exuberance at what seemed instant celebrity and
easy money, he came to resent the financial necessity of writing stories and

---

* The Fitzgerald story canon includes some 160 published stories, including his school
writings. (The "some" is necessitated by the borderline essay/fiction pieces.) Breakdowns:
thirty-eight professional stories published before *The Great Gatsby* (1925); fifty-five between
Gatsby and *Tender Is the Night* (1934); sixty-four during the Twenties; fifty-eight during the
Thirties.

the creative energy they drained from his novels. Fitzgerald's disparagement of his stories has persuaded critics to classify most of them as facile pot-boilers. But his bitterness was generated by the effort—not the ease—of writing fiction for the mass-circulation magazines. In the mid-Thirties, when Fitzgerald was having great difficulty in satisfying this market, he wrote in his *Notebooks:* "I have asked a lot of my emotions—one hundred and twenty stories. The price was high, right up with Kipling, because there was one little drop of something not blood, not a tear, not my seed, but me more intimately than these, in every story, it was the extra I had. Now it has gone and I am just like you now."[1] During this period of discouragement he explained to his agent, Harold Ober, that "all my stories are conceived like novels, require a special emotion, a special experience—so that my readers, if such there be, know that each time it'll be something new, not in form, but in substance (it'd be better for me if I could write pattern stories but the pencil just goes dead on me. . .)."[2] It is meaningful that Fitzgerald assessed his story capacity in terms of their emotional requirements.

Along with facility, Fitzgerald was charged with triviality because his stories did not deal with what critics—especially in the social-conscious Thirties—regarded as significant issues. Fitzgerald addressed this complaint in his introduction to the 1934 Modern Library reprint of *The Great Gatsby:* ". . . I had recently been kidded half haywire by critics who felt that my material was such as to preclude all dealing with mature persons in a mature world. But, my God! it was my material and it was all I had to deal with." There are no degrees of literary worth in material. A writer is his material, and it is as literary as he makes it. Fitzgerald never tried to be, or wanted to be, an experimental or avant-garde writer.

It is necessary to understand Fitzgerald's finances in order to evaluate the influence of his stories on his career. He did not make a fortune. The story income was supposed to provide writing time for novels, but he usually lived from story to story. Fitzgerald never had a blockbuster novel—not even *This Side of Paradise,* which sold 52,000 copies in his lifetime and earned about $15,000 in royalties. *Gatsby* and *Tender Is the Night* were financial failures. In 1929 eight *Post* stories brought Fitzgerald $30,000, while all of his books earned total royalties of $31.77 (including $5.10 for *Gatsby*).

Yet it is misleading to segregate Fitzgerald's stories as merely commercial. He was a professional writer, and everything that a professional gets paid for is commercial work. Fitzgerald was not unusual in combining remunerative magazine work with literary art. Before the time of huge advances and munificent subsidiary-rights deals, prominent novelists supplemented their book incomes with magazine work. Writers live by selling words, and

Fitzgerald competed successfully in the toughest literary marketplace of his time: the high-paying mass-circulation slick-paper magazines. He became identified with the *Saturday Evening Post* where he published sixty-five stories—about 40 percent of his output—reaching a peak price of $4,000 in 1929.* Readers for whom the old *Post* is not even a memory will be surprised by the roster of its contributors, which included Willa Cather, Edith Wharton, William Faulkner, and Thomas Wolfe. The *Post* was the most widely read American magazine during the Twenties (2,750,000 copies per week), and under the editorship of George Horace Lorimer it attempted to shape America's self-image.³ Harold Ober also placed Fitzgerald's work in most of the competing mass-circulation magazines: *Red Book, Liberty, Collier's, Metropolitan,* and *McCall's.* During his lifetime Fitzgerald was far better known and more widely read as a short-story writer than as a novelist.

All these magazines were aimed at family readership, but there is no evidence to support Ernest Hemingway's claim that Fitzgerald admitted he deliberately spoiled stories to make them salable. Although he wrote about the subjects that editors expected from him, his stories were rarely formulaic: "As soon as I feel I am writing to a cheap specification my pen freezes and my talent vanishes over the hill. . . ."⁴ At the top of his form he was able to write popular stories that were honest Fitzgerald stories. His endings were not automatically happy, and he found ways to insert "a touch of disaster." Nonetheless, two masterpieces—"May Day" and "The Diamond as Big as the Ritz"—were too "realistic" or "difficult" for the slicks.

Many aspects of Fitzgerald's life have the structure of fiction, almost as though he were living one of his own stories. His fiction is time-haunted, and it is ironically appropriate that his career breaks into a decade of confidence and a decade of loss. The stories in this volume written after 1929 show Fitzgerald's increasing difficulty in generating the emotional responses for his magazine fiction in an era of personal and national catastrophe. Although his output shrank year by year after 1932, he endeavored to continue providing stories for the *Post* and its siblings, while testing new forms and new material for *Esquire.* Fitzgerald's *Esquire* stories were short-shorts or sketches, without the full development of a conventional magazine story, and some were difficult to classify as stories. Launched in 1934, *Esquire* was a limited-circulation slick monthly with literary ambitions and a flexible editorial policy; it sold for the prohibitive price of 50¢. Its editor, Arnold Gingrich, admired Fitzgerald's prose and accepted almost anything he submitted: but *Esquire* paid him only $250 per piece. Fitzgerald had

---

* To convert the purchasing power of 1929 dollars to 1989 dollars, multiply by at least seven.

forty-five *Esquire* contributions, including the "Crack-Up" essays. After 1937, the year he moved to Hollywood, *Esquire* provided Fitzgerald's only dependable market.

The appellation "a typical Fitzgerald story" is useless. His stories were popular in their time because they were imaginative and surprising—not because they were predictable. If it can be claimed that the patients who read the *Post* in doctors' waiting rooms responded to brilliant prose and narrative control, then that is what made Fitzgerald a successful magazine writer. He was a natural storyteller; his stories are told in an authorial voice that generates reader confidence. Although the stories are heavily plotted and sometimes utilize trick endings, the main function of the plot is to provide a framework for character. Fitzgerald developed a new American figure: the determined girl-woman. Not the cartoon flapper, but the warm, courageous, attractive, and chastely independent young woman competing at life and love for the highest stakes—her future. Fitzgerald treats his aspiring youths, male and female, seriously and judges them rigorously. The didacticism of his stories is sincere: not a sop for the magazine market. He admitted to his daughter, Scottie, in 1939: "Sometimes I wish I had gone along with that gang [musical comedy writers], but I guess I am too much a moralist at heart and really want to preach at people in some acceptable form rather than to entertain them."[5] A favorite Fitzgerald strategy was to end a story with a burst of eloquence or wit that reiterated its themes and expanded its meanings.

A gauge of Fitzgerald's prose is the praise it has elicited from other writers who recognized the difficulty of what he made seem spontaneous. Raymond Chandler commented on the indefinable quality of *charm:* "He had one of the rarest qualities in all literature. . . . the word is charm—charm as Keats would have used it. Who has it today? It's not a matter of pretty writing or clear style. It's a kind of subdued magic, controlled and exquisite, the sort of thing you get from good string quartets."[6] One should be able to feel great writing. There is something extraordinary—even miraculous—in Fitzgerald's prose word by word. James Gould Cozzens came as close as anyone has to explicating this aspect of Fitzgerald's genius:

> a talent for saying not merely the right, the apt, the vivid, or moving thing, but the thing which, having all those qualities, so far transcends your reasonable expectation that you see that it couldn't have been done merely by intelligence, or training, or hard trying, and must simply have been born in a sort of triumphant flash outside the ordinary process of thought.[7]

In every story there were words that branded it a Fitzgerald story.

Fitzgerald did not have two mutually exclusive careers as a magazinist and as a novelist. It was one career, into which all of his work was integrated. Since Fitzgerald perforce wrote stories while he was working on novels, certain "cluster stories" introduce or test themes, settings, and situations that are fully developed in the novel. He routinely "stripped" passages from a story for reuse in a novel. These stories collected here are clearly in the *Gatsby*-cluster: "Winter Dreams," "Dice, Brassknuckles & Guitar," "Absolution," " 'The Sensible Thing,' " and "The Rich Boy" (a post-*Gatsby* work). The stories in this volume that belong to the gestation of *Tender* are: "One Trip Abroad," "Babylon Revisited," "The Bridal Party," "The Swimmers," "Jacob's Ladder," and "The Hotel Child."

Charles Scribner's Sons, Fitzgerald's only publisher during his lifetime, followed each of his novels with a volume of stories: *Flappers and Philosophers* (1920), *Tales of the Jazz Age* (1922), *All the Sad Young Men* (1926), and *Taps at Reveille* (1935)—a total of forty-five stories, twenty-one of which are assembled here. Ostensibly these four collections represent Fitzgerald's selection of his best stories; however, his choices were restricted by the stories available at that time. He did not have enough strong stories for *Tales of the Jazz Age*, but he had too many for *Taps*. Moreover, Fitzgerald had scruples about collecting a story that had been stripped for use in a novel.* He maintained a distinction between magazine and book publication, insisting that inclusion of a story in one of his collections gave it permanence and literary standing. After he incorporated story material (ranging from phrases to paragraphs) into a novel, he declined to reprint that story as it had originally appeared. Either he rewrote the plundered passage or he designated the story as "buried"—not to be reprinted. (But see "A Short Trip Home" and "Babylon Revisited.") In no case did Fitzgerald simply reprint the text of a magazine story.

From its publication by Scribners in 1951—a key year in the Fitzgerald Restoration—Malcolm Cowley's edition of *The Stories of F. Scott Fitzgerald* has been the standard collection and has influenced critical assessment of the story canon, especially in classrooms. Within the restriction of twenty-eight stories, Cowley chose splendidly. Since then, the increasing interest in Fitzgerald has resulted in five volumes of previously uncollected stories.† Now a more inclusive and more representative collection is required. The

---

* These strippings are identified in *The Notebooks of F. Scott Fitzgerald*.

† *Afternoon of an Author* (stories and essays, 1957); *The Pat Hobby Stories* (1962); *The Basil and Josephine Stories* (1973); *Bits of Paradise* (stories by F. Scott and Zelda Fitzgerald, 1973); and *The Price Was High* (1979).

forty-three selections in this volume bring together the classic or core Fitzgerald stories with others that expand the range of his material. Thus, Fitzgerald's extraordinary versatility and control are brilliantly revealed in the fantasy-supernatural stories not collected in Cowley: "The Curious Case of Benjamin Button" (admired by William Faulkner), "A Short Trip Home" (admired by James Thurber), and "One Trip Abroad" (a major story).

A thematic organization could have been imposed on this collection: love and money, North and South, America and Europe, idealism and disillusionment, success and failure, time and mutability. That plan was rejected because his themes overlap in stories. The chronological organization here allows the reader to trace Fitzgerald's magazine work from youthful ebullience through progressively grimmer moods. More usefully, reading these stories in the order of their publication reveals Fitzgerald's delicate sense of history as he evokes the rhythms of the Jazz Age and the Depression. He was not a documentary writer; yet he was a brilliant social historian because of his capacity to convey, through style and point of view, the sense of time and place, the sense of being there. Thus he advised Scottie:

> But when in a freak moment you will want to give the low-down, not the scandal, not the merely *reported* but the *profound* essence of what happened at a prom or after it, perhaps that honesty will come to you—and then you will understand how it is possible to make even a forlorn Laplander *feel* the importance of a trip to Cartier's![8]

Literature is what lasts. Literary history demonstrates that critical reception is an inaccurate forecast of permanent merit. The writings that turn out to be literature are frequently ignored or savaged at the time of their initial publication. In the Twenties the assertion that Fitzgerald's short stories would become classics would have excited incredulity and risibility. The process by which literary works ultimately achieve their proper stature is inexplicable. One lesson provided by F. Scott Fitzgerald's stories is that everything a genius writes partakes of his genius. One hopes there is a second lesson: genius always compells its just recognition.

Textual Note: The stories that Fitzgerald revised for his four collections are published here in those texts. The other stories are reprinted from their original magazine appearances. Typographical errors and punctuation have been silently corrected. Editorial word emendations are stipulated.

—MATTHEW J. BRUCCOLI

·NOTES·

1. "Our April Letter" in *The Notebooks of F. Scott Fitzgerald*, ed. Matthew J. Bruccoli (New York and London: Harcourt Brace Jovanovich/Bruccoli Clark, 1978), p. 131.

2. *As Ever, Scott Fitz——: Letters Between F. Scott Fitzgerald and His Literary Agent Harold Ober, 1919–1940*, ed. Matthew J. Bruccoli and Jennifer Atkinson (Philadelphia and New York: Lippincott, 1972), p. 221.

3. See Jan Cohn, *Creating America: George Horace Lorimer and the Saturday Evening Post* (Pittsburgh: University of Pittsburgh Press, 1989).

4. To Zelda Fitzgerald, 18 May 1940. *The Letters of F. Scott Fitzgerald*, ed. Andrew Turnbull (New York: Scribners, 1963), pp. 117–18.

5. 4 November 1939. *Letters*, p. 63.

6. *Selected Letters of Raymond Chandler*, ed. Frank MacShane (New York: Columbia University Press, 1981), p. 239.

7. Matthew J. Bruccoli, *James Gould Cozzens: A Life Apart* (San Diego: Harcourt Brace Jovanovich, 1983), p. 129.

8. Undated. *The Letters of F. Scott Fitzgerald*, p. 101.

THE SHORT STORIES OF
F. SCOTT FITZGERALD

HEAD AND SHOULDERS

♦

"Head and Shoulders" was the first Fitzgerald story to appear in the Saturday Evening Post *(21 February 1920), but not his first sale—having been preceded by five pieces in* The Smart Set. *He later wrote his agent, Harold Ober: "I was twenty-two [actually twenty-three] when I came to New York and found that you'd sold* Head and Shoulders *to the* Post. *I'd like to get a thrill like that again but I suppose its only once in a lifetime." The $400 fee was one-tenth of what the* Post *would pay for a Fitzgerald story in 1929.*

Originally titled "Nest Feathers," this story was one of a group Fitzgerald wrote in the fall of 1919 after Scribners accepted his first novel, This Side of Paradise. *Fitzgerald's fiction has a curious way of anticipating his life: just as Horace is deflected by marriage from scholarship to entertainment, so would the author of "Head and Shoulders" soon be under pressure to provide literary entertainment after his own marriage to Zelda Sayre in April 1920.*

Fitzgerald selected "Head and Shoulders" for Flappers and Philosophers, *his first story collection, published in 1920.*

♦

IN 1915 Horace Tarbox was thirteen years old. In that year he took the examinations for entrance to Princeton University and received the Grade A—excellent—in Cæsar, Cicero, Vergil, Xenophon, Homer, Algebra, Plane Geometry, Solid Geometry, and Chemistry.

Two years later, while George M. Cohan was composing "Over There," Horace was leading the sophomore class by several lengths and digging out theses on "The Syllogism as an Obsolete Scholastic Form," and during the battle of Château-Thierry he was sitting at his desk deciding whether or not to wait until his seventeenth birthday before beginning his series of essays on "The Pragmatic Bias of the New Realists."

After a while some newsboy told him that the war was over, and he was glad, because it meant that Peat Brothers, publishers, would get out their new edition of "Spinoza's Improvement of the Understanding." Wars were all very well in their way, made young men self-reliant or something, but

Horace felt that he could never forgive the President for allowing a brass band to play under his window on the night of the false armistice, causing him to leave three important sentences out of his thesis on "German Idealism."

The next year he went up to Yale to take his degree as Master of Arts.

He was seventeen then, tall and slender, with near-sighted gray eyes and an air of keeping himself utterly detached from the mere words he let drop.

"I never feel as though I'm talking to him," expostulated Professor Dillinger to a sympathetic colleague. "He makes me feel as though I were talking to his representative. I always expect him to say: 'Well, I'll ask myself and find out.' "

And then, just as nonchalantly as though Horace Tarbox had been Mr. Beef the butcher or Mr. Hat the haberdasher, life reached in, seized him, handled him, stretched him, and unrolled him like a piece of Irish lace on a Saturday-afternoon bargain-counter.

To move in the literary fashion I should say that this was all because when way back in colonial days the hardy pioneers had come to a bald place in Connecticut and asked of each other, "Now, what shall we build here?" the hardiest one among 'em had answered: "Let's build a town where theatrical managers can try out musical comedies!" How afterward they founded Yale College there, to try the musical comedies on, is a story every one knows. At any rate one December, "Home James" opened at the Shubert, and all the students encored Marcia Meadow, who sang a song about the Blundering Blimp in the first act and did a shaky, shivery, celebrated dance in the last.

Marcia was nineteen. She didn't have wings, but audiences agreed generally that she didn't need them. She was a blonde by natural pigment, and she wore no paint on the streets at high noon. Outside of that she was no better than most women.

It was Charlie Moon who promised her five thousand Pall Malls if she would pay a call on Horace Tarbox, prodigy extraordinary. Charlie was a senior in Sheffield, and he and Horace were first cousins. They liked and pitied each other.

Horace had been particularly busy that night. The failure of the Frenchman Laurier to appreciate the significance of the new realists was preying on his mind. In fact, his only reaction to a low, clear-cut rap at his study was to make him speculate as to whether any rap would have actual existence without an ear there to hear it. He fancied he was verging more and more toward pragmatism. But at that moment, though he did not know it, he was verging with astounding rapidity toward something quite different.

The rap sounded—three seconds leaked by—the rap sounded.

"Come in," muttered Horace automatically.

He heard the door open and then close, but, bent over his book in the big armchair before the fire, he did not look up.

"Leave it on the bed in the other room," he said absently.

"Leave what on the bed in the other room?"

Marcia Meadow had to talk her songs, but her speaking voice was like byplay on a harp.

"The laundry."

"I can't."

Horace stirred impatiently in his chair.

"Why can't you?"

"Why, because I haven't got it."

"Hm!" he replied testily. "Suppose you go back and get it."

Across the fire from Horace was another easy-chair. He was accustomed to change to it in the course of an evening by way of exercise and variety. One chair he called Berkeley, the other he called Hume. He suddenly heard a sound as of a rustling, diaphanous form sinking into Hume. He glanced up.

"Well," said Marcia with the sweet smile she used in Act Two ("Oh, so the Duke liked my dancing!"), "Well, Omar Khayyam, here I am beside you singing in the wilderness."

Horace stared at her dazedly. The momentary suspicion came to him that she existed there only as a phantom of his imagination. Women didn't come into men's rooms and sink into men's Humes. Women brought laundry and took your seat in the street-car and married you later on when you were old enough to know fetters.

This woman had clearly materialized out of Hume. The very froth of her brown gauzy dress was an emanation from Hume's leather arm there! If he looked long enough he would see Hume right through her and then he would be alone again in the room. He passed his fist across his eyes. He really must take up those trapeze exercises again.

"For Pete's sake, don't look so critical!" objected the emanation pleasantly. "I feel as if you were going to wish me away with that patent dome of yours. And then there wouldn't be anything left of me except my shadow in your eyes."

Horace coughed. Coughing was one of his two gestures. When he talked you forgot he had a body at all. It was like hearing a phonograph record by a singer who had been dead a long time.

"What do you want?" he asked.

"I want them letters," whined Marcia melodramatically—"them letters of mine you bought from my grandsire in 1881."

Horace considered.

"I haven't got your letters," he said evenly. "I am only seventeen years old. My father was not born until March 3, 1879. You evidently have me confused with some one else."

"You're only seventeen?" repeated Marcia suspiciously.

"Only seventeen."

"I knew a girl," said Marcia reminiscently, "who went on the ten-twenty-thirty when she was sixteen. She was so stuck on herself that she could never say 'sixteen' without putting the 'only' before it. We got to calling her 'Only Jessie.' And she's just where she was when she started—only worse. 'Only' is a bad habit, Omar—it sounds like an alibi."

"My name is not Omar."

"I know," agreed Marcia, nodding—"your name's Horace. I just call you Omar because you remind me of a smoked cigarette."

"And I haven't your letters. I doubt if I've ever met your grandfather. In fact, I think it very improbable that you yourself were alive in 1881."

Marcia stared at him in wonder.

"Me—1881? Why sure! I was second-line stuff when the Florodora Sextette was still in the convent. I was the original nurse to Mrs. Sol Smith's Juliette. Why, Omar, I was a canteen singer during the War of 1812."

Horace's mind made a sudden successful leap, and he grinned.

"Did Charlie Moon put you up to this?"

Marcia regarded him inscrutably.

"Who's Charlie Moon?"

"Small—wide nostrils—big ears."

She grew several inches and sniffed.

"I'm not in the habit of noticing my friends' nostrils."

"Then it was Charlie?"

Marcia bit her lip—and then yawned.

"Oh, let's change the subject, Omar. I'll pull a snore in this chair in a minute."

"Yes," replied Horace gravely, "Hume has often been considered soporific."

"Who's your friend—and will he die?"

Then of a sudden Horace Tarbox rose slenderly and began to pace the room with his hands in his pockets. This was his other gesture.

"I don't care for this," he said as if he were talking to himself—"at all. Not that I mind your being here—I don't. You're quite a pretty little thing, but I don't like Charlie Moon's sending you up here. Am I a laboratory experiment on which the janitors as well as the chemists can make experiments? Is my intellectual development humorous in any way? Do I look like the pictures of the little Boston boy in the comic magazines? Has that callow ass, Moon, with his eternal tales about his week in Paris, any right to——"

"No," interrupted Marcia emphatically. "And you're a sweet boy. Come here and kiss me."

Horace stopped quickly in front of her.

"Why do you want me to kiss you?" he asked intently. "Do you just go round kissing people?"

"Why, yes," admitted Marcia, unruffled. "'At's all life is. Just going round kissing people."

"Well," replied Horace emphatically, "I must say your ideas are horribly garbled! In the first place life isn't just that, and in the second place I won't kiss you. It might get to be a habit and I can't get rid of habits. This year I've got in the habit of lolling in bed until seven-thirty."

Marcia nodded understandingly.

"Do you ever have any fun?" she asked.

"What do you mean by fun?"

"See here," said Marcia sternly, "I like you, Omar, but I wish you'd talk as if you had a line on what you were saying. You sound as if you were gargling a lot of words in your mouth and lost a bet every time you spilled a few. I asked you if you ever had any fun."

Horace shook his head.

"Later, perhaps," he answered. "You see I'm a plan. I'm an experiment. I don't say that I don't get tired of it sometimes—I do. Yet—oh, I can't explain! But what you and Charlie Moon call fun wouldn't be fun to me."

"Please explain."

Horace stared at her, started to speak and then, changing his mind, resumed his walk. After an unsuccessful attempt to determine whether or not he was looking at her Marcia smiled at him.

"Please explain."

Horace turned.

"If I do, will you promise to tell Charlie Moon that I wasn't in?"

"Uh-uh."

"Very well, then. Here's my history: I was a 'why' child. I wanted to see the wheels go round. My father was a young economics professor at Princeton. He brought me up on the system of answering every question I asked him to the best of his ability. My response to that gave him the idea of making an experiment in precocity. To aid in the massacre I had ear trouble—seven operations between the ages of nine and twelve. Of course this kept me apart from other boys and made me ripe for forcing. Anyway, while my generation was laboring through Uncle Remus I was honestly enjoying Catullus in the original.

"I passed off my college examinations when I was thirteen because I couldn't help it. My chief associates were professors, and I took a tremendous pride in knowing that I had a fine intelligence, for though I was unusually gifted I was not abnormal in other ways. When I was sixteen I got tired of being a freak; I decided that some one had made a bad mistake. Still as I'd gone that far I concluded to finish it up by taking my degree of Master of Arts. My chief interest in life is the study of modern philosophy. I am a realist of the School of Anton Laurier—with Bergsonian trimmings—and I'll be eighteen years old in two months. That's all."

"Whew!" exclaimed Marcia. "That's enough! You do a neat job with the parts of speech."

"Satisfied?"

"No, you haven't kissed me."

"It's not in my programme," demurred Horace. "Understand that I don't pretend to be above physical things. They have their place, but——"

"Oh, don't be so darned reasonable!"

"I can't help it."

"I hate these slot-machine people."

"I assure you I—" began Horace.

"Oh, shut up!"

"My own rationality——"

"I didn't say anything about your nationality. You're an Amuricun, ar'n't you?"

"Yes."

"Well, that's O. K. with me. I got a notion I want to see you do something that isn't in your highbrow programme. I want to see if a what-ch-call-em with Brazilian trimmings—that thing you said you were—can be a little human."

Horace shook his head again.

"I won't kiss you."

"My life is blighted," muttered Marcia tragically. "I'm a beaten woman. I'll go through life without ever having a kiss with Brazilian trimmings." She sighed. "Anyways, Omar, will you come and see my show?"

"What show?"

"I'm a wicked actress from 'Home James'!"

"Light opera?"

"Yes—at a stretch. One of the characters is a Brazilian rice-planter. That might interest you."

"I saw 'The Bohemian Girl' once," reflected Horace aloud. "I enjoyed it—to some extent."

"Then you'll come?"

"Well, I'm—I'm——"

"Oh, I know—you've got to run down to Brazil for the week-end."

"Not at all. I'd be delighted to come."

Marcia clapped her hands.

"Goodyforyou! I'll mail you a ticket—Thursday night?"

"Why, I——"

"Good! Thursday night it is."

She stood up and walking close to him laid both hands on his shoulders.

"I like you, Omar. I'm sorry I tried to kid you. I thought you'd be sort of frozen, but you're a nice boy."

He eyed her sardonically.

"I'm several thousand generations older than you are."

"You carry your age well."

They shook hands gravely.

"My name's Marcia Meadow," she said emphatically. " 'Member it—Marcia Meadow. And I won't tell Charlie Moon you were in."

An instant later as she was skimming down the last flight of stairs three at a time she heard a voice call over the upper banister: "Oh, say——"

She stopped and looked up—made out a vague form leaning over.

"Oh, say!" called the prodigy again. "Can you hear me?"

"Here's your connection, Omar."

"I hope I haven't given you the impression that I consider kissing intrinsically irrational."

"Impression? Why, you didn't even give me the kiss! Never fret—so long."

Two doors near her opened curiously at the sound of a feminine voice. A tentative cough sounded from above. Gathering her skirts, Marcia dived wildly down the last flight, and was swallowed up in the murky Connecticut air outside.

Up-stairs Horace paced the floor of his study. From time to time he glanced toward Berkeley waiting there in suave dark-red respectability, an open book lying suggestively on his cushions. And then he found that his circuit of the floor was bringing him each time nearer to Hume. There was something about Hume that was strangely and inexpressibly different. The diaphanous form still seemed hovering near, and had Horace sat there he would have felt as if he were sitting on a lady's lap. And though Horace couldn't have named the quality of difference, there was such a quality— quite intangible to the speculative mind, but real, nevertheless. Hume was radiating something that in all the two hundred years of his influence he had never radiated before.

Hume was radiating attar of roses.

· I I ·

ON Thursday night Horace Tarbox sat in an aisle seat in the fifth row and witnessed "Home James." Oddly enough he found that he was enjoying himself. The cynical students near him were annoyed at his audible appreciation of time-honored jokes in the Hammerstein tradition. But Horace was waiting with anxiety for Marcia Meadow singing her song about a Jazz-bound Blundering Blimp. When she did appear, radiant under a floppity flower-faced hat, a warm glow settled over him, and when the song was over he did not join in the storm of applause. He felt somewhat numb.

In the intermission after the second act an usher materialized beside him, demanded to know if he were Mr. Tarbox, and then handed him a note written in a round adolescent hand. Horace read it in some confusion, while the usher lingered with withering patience in the aisle.

"DEAR OMAR: After the show I always grow an awful hunger. If you want to satisfy it for me in the Taft Grill just communicate your answer to the big-timber guide that brought this and oblige.
Your friend,
MARCIA MEADOW."

"Tell her"—he coughed—"tell her that it will be quite all right. I'll meet her in front of the theatre."

The big-timber guide smiled arrogantly.

"I giss she meant for you to come roun' t' the stage door."

"Where—where is it?"

"Ou'side. Tunayulef. Down ee alley."

"What?"

"Ou'side. Turn to y' left! Down ee alley!"

The arrogant person withdrew. A freshman behind Horace snickered.

Then half an hour later, sitting in the Taft Grill opposite the hair that was yellow by natural pigment, the prodigy was saying an odd thing.

"Do you have to do that dance in the last act?" he was asking earnestly —"I mean, would they dismiss you if you refused to do it?"

Marcia grinned.

"It's fun to do it. I like to do it."

And then Horace came out with a *faux pas*.

"I should think you'd detest it," he remarked succinctly. "The people behind me were making remarks about your bosom."

Marcia blushed fiery red.

"I can't help that," she said quickly. "The dance to me is only a sort of acrobatic stunt. Lord, it's hard enough to do! I rub liniment into my shoulders for an hour every night."

"Do you have—fun while you're on the stage?"

"Uh-huh—sure! I got in the habit of having people look at me, Omar, and I like it."

"Hm!" Horace sank into a brownish study.

"How's the Brazilian trimmings?"

"Hm!" repeated Horace, and then after a pause: "Where does the play go from here?"

"New York."

"For how long?"

"All depends. Winter—maybe."

"Oh!"

"Coming up to lay eyes on me, Omar, or aren't you int'rested? Not as nice here, is it, as it was up in your room? I wish we was there now."

"I feel idiotic in this place," confessed Horace, looking round him nervously.

"Too bad! We got along pretty well."

At this he looked suddenly so melancholy that she changed her tone, and reaching over patted his hand.

"Ever take an actress out to supper before?"

"No," said Horace miserably, "and I never will again. I don't know why I came to-night. Here under all these lights and with all these people laughing and chattering I feel completely out of my sphere. I don't know what to talk to you about."

"We'll talk about me. We talked about you last time."

"Very well."

"Well, my name really is Meadow, but my first name isn't Marcia—it's Veronica. I'm nineteen. Question—how did the girl make her leap to the footlights? Answer—she was born in Passaic, New Jersey, and up to a year ago she got the right to breathe by pushing Nabiscoes in Marcel's tea-room in Trenton. She started going with a guy named Robbins, a singer in the Trent House cabaret, and he got her to try a song and dance with him one evening. In a month we were filling the supper-room every night. Then we went to New York with meet-my-friend letters thick as a pile of napkins.

"In two days we'd landed a job at Divinerries', and I learned to shimmy from a kid at the Palais Royal. We stayed at Divinerries' six months until one night Peter Boyce Wendell, the columnist, ate his milk-toast there. Next morning a poem about Marvellous Marcia came out in his newspaper, and within two days I had three vaudeville offers and a chance at the Midnight Frolic. I wrote Wendell a thank-you letter, and he printed it in his column—said that the style was like Carlyle's, only more rugged, and that I ought to quit dancing and do North American literature. This got me a coupla more vaudeville offers and a chance as an ingénue in a regular show. I took it—and here I am, Omar."

When she finished they sat for a moment in silence, she draping the last skeins of a Welsh rabbit on her fork and waiting for him to speak.

"Let's get out of here," he said suddenly.

Marcia's eyes hardened.

"What's the idea? Am I making you sick?"

"No, but I don't like it here. I don't like to be sitting here with you."

Without another word Marcia signalled for the waiter.

"What's the check?" she demanded briskly. "My part—the rabbit and the ginger ale."

Horace watched blankly as the waiter figured it.

"See here," he began, "I intended to pay for yours too. You're my guest."

With a half-sigh Marcia rose from the table and walked from the room. Horace, his face a document in bewilderment, laid a bill down and followed her out, up the stairs and into the lobby. He overtook her in front of the elevator and they faced each other.

"See here," he repeated, "you're my guest. Have I said something to offend you?"

After an instant of wonder Marcia's eyes softened.

"You're a rude fella," she said slowly. "Don't you know you're rude?"

"I can't help it," said Horace with a directness she found quite disarming. "You know I like you."

"You said you didn't like being with me."

"I didn't like it."

"Why not?"

Fire blazed suddenly from the gray forests of his eyes.

"Because I didn't. I've formed the habit of liking you. I've been thinking of nothing much else for two days."

"Well, if you—"

"Wait a minute," he interrupted. "I've got something to say. It's this: in six weeks I'll be eighteen years old. When I'm eighteen years old I'm coming up to New York to see you. Is there some place in New York where we can go and not have a lot of people in the room?"

"Sure!" smiled Marcia. "You can come up to my 'partment. Sleep on the couch, if you want to."

"I can't sleep on couches," he said shortly. "But I want to talk to you."

"Why, sure," repeated Marcia—"in my 'partment."

In his excitement Horace put his hands in his pockets.

"All right—just so I can see you alone. I want to talk to you as we talked up in my room."

"Honey boy," cried Marcia, laughing, "is it that you want to kiss me?"

"Yes," Horace almost shouted. "I'll kiss you if you want me to."

The elevator man was looking at them reproachfully. Marcia edged toward the grated door.

"I'll drop you a post-card," she said.

Horace's eyes were quite wild.

"Send me a post-card! I'll come up any time after January first. I'll be eighteen then."

And as she stepped into the elevator he coughed enigmatically, yet with a vague challenge, at the ceiling, and walked quickly away.

· III ·

HE WAS THERE AGAIN. She saw him when she took her first glance at the restless Manhattan audience—down in the front row with his head bent a bit forward and his gray eyes fixed on her. And she knew that to him they were alone together in a world where the high-rouged row of ballet faces and the massed whines of the violins were as imperceivable as powder on a marble Venus. An instinctive defiance rose within her.

"Silly boy!" she said to herself hurriedly, and she didn't take her encore.

"What do they expect for a hundred a week—perpetual motion?" she grumbled to herself in the wings.

"What's the trouble, Marcia?"

"Guy I don't like down in front."

During the last act as she waited for her specialty she had an odd attack of stage fright. She had never sent Horace the promised post-card. Last night she had pretended not to see him—had hurried from the theatre immediately after her dance to pass a sleepless night in her apartment, thinking—as she had so often in the last month—of his pale, rather intent face, his slim, boyish figure, the merciless, unworldly abstraction that made him charming to her.

And now that he had come she felt vaguely sorry—as though an unwonted responsibility was being forced on her.

"Infant prodigy!" she said aloud.

"What?" demanded the negro comedian standing beside her.

"Nothing—just talking about myself."

On the stage she felt better. This was her dance—and she always felt that the way she did it wasn't suggestive any more than to some men every pretty girl is suggestive. She made it a stunt.

> *"Uptown, downtown, jelly on a spoon,*
> *After sundown shiver by the moon."*

He was not watching her now. She saw that clearly. He was looking very deliberately at a castle on the back drop, wearing that expression he had worn in the Taft Grill. A wave of exasperation swept over her—he was criticising her.

> *"That's the vibration that thr-ills me,*
> *Funny how affection fi-lls me,*
> *Uptown, downtown——"*

Unconquerable revulsion seized her. She was suddenly and horribly conscious of her audience as she had never been since her first appearance. Was that a leer on a pallid face in the front row, a droop of disgust on one young girl's mouth? These shoulders of hers—these shoulders shaking—were they hers? Were they real? Surely shoulders weren't made for this!

> *"Then—you'll see at a glance*
> *I'll need some funeral ushers with St. Vitus dance*
> *At the end of the world I'll——"*

The bassoon and two cellos crashed into a final chord. She paused and poised a moment on her toes with every muscle tense, her young face looking out dully at the audience in what one young girl afterward called "such a curious, puzzled look," and then without bowing rushed from the stage. Into the dressing-room she sped, kicked out of one dress and into another, and caught a taxi outside.

Her apartment was very warm—small, it was, with a row of professional pictures and sets of Kipling and O. Henry which she had bought once from a blue-eyed agent and read occasionally. And there were several chairs which matched, but were none of them comfortable, and a pink-shaded lamp with blackbirds painted on it and an atmosphere of rather stifled pink throughout. There were nice things in it—nice things unrelentingly hostile to each other, offsprings of a vicarious, impatient taste acting in stray moments. The worst was typified by a great picture framed in oak bark of Passaic as seen from the Erie Railroad—altogether a frantic, oddly extravagant, oddly penurious attempt to make a cheerful room. Marcia knew it was a failure.

Into this room came the prodigy and took her two hands awkwardly.

"I followed you this time," he said.

"Oh!"

"I want you to marry me," he said.

Her arms went out to him. She kissed his mouth with a sort of passionate wholesomeness.

"There!"

"I love you," he said.

She kissed him again and then with a little sigh flung herself into an armchair and half lay there, shaken with absurd laughter.

"Why, you infant prodigy!" she cried.

"Very well, call me that if you want to. I once told you that I was ten thousand years older than you—I am."

She laughed again.

"I don't like to be disapproved of."

"No one's ever going to disapprove of you again."

"Omar," she asked, "why do you want to marry me?"

The prodigy rose and put his hands in his pockets.

"Because I love you, Marcia Meadow."

And then she stopped calling him Omar.

"Dear boy," she said, "you know I sort of love you. There's something about you—I can't tell what—that just puts my heart through the wringer every time I'm round you. But, honey—" She paused.

"But what?"

"But lots of things. But you're only just eighteen, and I'm nearly twenty."

"Nonsense!" he interrupted. "Put it this way—that I'm in my nineteenth year and you're nineteen. That makes us pretty close—without counting that other ten thousand years I mentioned."

Marcia laughed.

"But there are some more 'buts.' Your people——"

"My people!" exclaimed the prodigy ferociously. "My people tried to make a monstrosity out of me." His face grew quite crimson at the enormity of what he was going to say. "My people can go way back and sit down!"

"My heavens!" cried Marcia in alarm. "All that? On tacks, I suppose."

"Tacks—yes," he agreed wildly—"on anything. The more I think of how they allowed me to become a little dried-up mummy——"

"What makes you think you're that?" asked Marcia quietly—"me?"

"Yes. Every person I've met on the streets since I met you has made me jealous because they knew what love was before I did. I used to call it the 'sex impulse.' Heavens!"

"There's more 'buts,' " said Marcia.

"What are they?"

"How could we live?"

"I'll make a living."

"You're in college."

"Do you think I care anything about taking a Master of Arts degree?"

"You want to be Master of Me, hey?"

"Yes! What? I mean, no!"

Marcia laughed, and crossing swiftly over sat in his lap. He put his arm round her wildly and implanted the vestige of a kiss somewhere near her neck.

"There's something white about you," mused Marcia, "but it doesn't sound very logical."

"Oh, don't be so darned reasonable!"

"I can't help it," said Marcia.

"I hate these slot-machine people!"

"But we——"

"Oh, shut up!"

And as Marcia couldn't talk through her ears she had to.

· I V ·

HORACE AND MARCIA were married early in February. The sensation in academic circles both at Yale and Princeton was tremendous. Horace Tarbox, who at fourteen had been played up in the Sunday magazines sections of metropolitan newspapers, was throwing over his career, his chance of being a world authority on American philosophy, by marrying a chorus girl—they made Marcia a chorus girl. But like all modern stories it was a four-and-a-half-day wonder.

They took a flat in Harlem. After two weeks' search, during which his idea of the value of academic knowledge faded unmercifully, Horace took a position as clerk with a South American export company—some one had told him that exporting was the coming thing. Marcia was to stay in her show for a few months—anyway until he got on his feet. He was getting a hundred and twenty-five to start with, and though of course they told him it was only a question of months until he would be earning double that, Marcia refused even to consider giving up the hundred and fifty a week that she was getting at the time.

"We'll call ourselves Head and Shoulders, dear," she said softly, "and the shoulders'll have to keep shaking a little longer until the old head gets started."

"I hate it," he objected gloomily.

"Well," she replied emphatically, "your salary wouldn't keep us in a tenement. Don't think I want to be public—I don't. I want to be yours. But I'd be a half-wit to sit in one room and count the sunflowers on the wall-paper while I waited for you. When you pull down three hundred a month I'll quit."

And much as it hurt his pride, Horace had to admit that hers was the wiser course.

March mellowed into April. May read a gorgeous riot act to the parks and waters of Manhattan, and they were very happy. Horace, who had no habits whatsoever—he had never had time to form any—proved the most adaptable of husbands, and as Marcia entirely lacked opinions on the subjects that engrossed him there were very few joltings and bumpings. Their minds moved in different spheres. Marcia acted as practical factotum, and Horace lived either in his old world of abstract ideas or in a sort of triumphantly earthy worship and adoration of his wife. She was a continual source of astonishment to him—the freshness and originality of her mind, her dynamic, clear-headed energy, and her unfailing good humor.

And Marcia's co-workers in the nine-o'clock show, whither she had transferred her talents, were impressed with her tremendous pride in her husband's mental powers. Horace they knew only as a very slim, tight-lipped, and immature-looking young man, who waited every night to take her home.

"Horace," said Marcia one evening when she met him as usual at eleven, "you looked like a ghost standing there against the street lights. You losing weight?"

He shook his head vaguely.

"I don't know. They raised me to a hundred and thirty-five dollars to-day, and——"

"I don't care," said Marcia severely. "You're killing yourself working at night. You read those big books on economy——"

"Economics," corrected Horace.

"Well, you read 'em every night long after I'm asleep. And you're getting all stooped over like you were before we were married."

"But, Marcia, I've got to——"

"No, you haven't, dear. I guess I'm running this shop for the present, and I won't let my fella ruin his health and eyes. You got to get some exercise."

"I do. Every morning I——"

"Oh, I know! But those dumb-bells of yours wouldn't give a consumptive two degrees of fever. I mean real exercise. You've got to join a gymnasium. 'Member you told me you were such a trick gymnast once that they tried to get you out for the team in college and they couldn't because you had a standing date with Herb Spencer?"

"I used to enjoy it," mused Horace, "but it would take up too much time now."

"All right," said Marcia. "I'll make a bargain with you. You join a gym and I'll read one of those books from the brown row of 'em."

" 'Pepys' Diary'? Why, that ought to be enjoyable. He's very light."

"Not for me—he isn't. It'll be like digesting plate glass. But you been telling me how much it'd broaden my lookout. Well, you go to a gym three nights a week and I'll take one big dose of Sammy."

Horace hesitated.

"Well——"

"Come on, now! You do some giant swings for me and I'll chase some culture for you."

So Horace finally consented, and all through a baking summer he spent three and sometimes four evenings a week experimenting on the trapeze in Skipper's Gymnasium. And in August he admitted to Marcia that it made him capable of more mental work during the day.

"*Mens sana in corpore sano,*" he said.

"Don't believe in it," replied Marcia. "I tried one of those patent medicines once and they're all bunk. You stick to gymnastics."

One night in early September while he was going through one of his contortions on the rings in the nearly deserted room he was addressed by a meditative fat man whom he had noticed watching him for several nights.

"Say, lad, do that stunt you were doin' last night."

Horace grinned at him from his perch.

"I invented it," he said. "I got the idea from the fourth proposition of Euclid."

"What circus he with?"

"He's dead."

"Well, he must of broke his neck doin' that stunt. I set here last night thinkin' sure you was goin' to break yours."

"Like this!" said Horace, and swinging onto the trapeze he did his stunt.

"Don't it kill your neck an' shoulder muscles?"

"It did at first, but inside of a week I wrote the *quod erat demonstrandum* on it."

"Hm!"

Horace swung idly on the trapeze.

"Ever think of takin' it up professionally?" asked the fat man.

"Not I."

'Good money in it if you're willin' to do stunts like 'at an' can get away with it."

"Here's another," chirped Horace eagerly, and the fat man's mouth dropped suddenly agape as he watched this pink-jerseyed Prometheus again defy the gods and Isaac Newton.

The night following this encounter Horace got home from work to find a rather pale Marcia stretched out on the sofa waiting for him.

"I fainted twice to-day," she began without preliminaries.

"What?"

"Yep. You see baby's due in four months now. Doctor says I ought to have quit dancing two weeks ago."

Horace sat down and thought it over.

"I'm glad, of course," he said pensively—"I mean glad that we're going to have a baby. But this means a lot of expense."

"I've got two hundred and fifty in the bank," said Marcia hopefully, "and two weeks' pay coming."

Horace computed quickly.

"Including my salary, that'll give us nearly fourteen hundred for the next six months."

Marcia looked blue.

"That all? Course I can get a job singing somewhere this month. And I can go to work again in March."

"Of course nothing!" said Horace gruffly. "You'll stay right here. Let's see now—there'll be doctor's bills and a nurse, besides the maid. We've got to have some more money."

"Well," said Marcia wearily, "I don't know where it's coming from. It's up to the old head now. Shoulders is out of business."

Horace rose and pulled on his coat.

"Where are you going?"

"I've got an idea," he answered. "I'll be right back."

Ten minutes later as he headed down the street toward Skipper's Gymnasium he felt a placid wonder, quite unmixed with humor, at what he was going to do. How he would have gaped at himself a year before! How every one would have gaped! But when you opened your door at the rap of life you let in many things.

The gymnasium was brightly lit, and when his eyes became accustomed to the glare he found the meditative fat man seated on a pile of canvas mats smoking a big cigar.

"Say," began Horace directly, "were you in earnest last night when you said I could make money on my trapeze stunts?"

"Why, yes," said the fat man in surprise.

"Well, I've been thinking it over, and I believe I'd like to try it. I could work at night and on Saturday afternoons—and regularly if the pay is high enough."

The fat man looked at his watch.

"Well," he said, "Charlie Paulson's the man to see. He'll book you inside of four days, once he sees you work out. He won't be in now, but I'll get hold of him for to-morrow night."

The fat man was as good as his word. Charlie Paulson arrived next night and put in a wondrous hour watching the prodigy swoop through the air in amazing parabolas, and on the night following he brought two large men with him who looked as though they had been born smoking black cigars and talking about money in low, passionate voices. Then on the succeeding Saturday Horace Tarbox's torso made its first professional appearance in a gymnastic exhibition at the Coleman Street Gardens. But though the audience numbered nearly five thousand people, Horace felt no nervousness. From his childhood he had read papers to audiences—learned that trick of detaching himself.

"Marcia," he said cheerfully later that same night, "I think we're out of the woods. Paulson thinks he can get me an opening at the Hippodrome, and that means an all-winter engagement. The Hippodrome, you know, is a big——"

"Yes, I believe I've heard of it," interrupted Marcia, "but I want to know about this stunt you're doing. It isn't any spectacular suicide, is it?"

"It's nothing," said Horace quietly. "But if you can think of any nicer way of a man killing himself than taking a risk for you, why that's the way I want to die."

Marcia reached up and wound both arms tightly round his neck.

"Kiss me," she whispered, "and call me 'dear heart.' I love to hear you say 'dear heart.' And bring me a book to read to-morrow. No more Sam Pepys, but something trick and trashy. I've been wild for something to do all day. I felt like writing letters, but I didn't have anybody to write to."

"Write to me," said Horace. "I'll read them."

"I wish I could," breathed Marcia. "If I knew words enough I could write you the longest love-letter in the world—and never get tired."

But after two more months Marcia grew very tired indeed, and for a row of nights it was a very anxious, weary-looking young athlete who walked out before the Hippodrome crowd. Then there were two days when his place was taken by a young man who wore pale blue instead of white, and got very little applause. But after the two days Horace appeared again, and those who sat close to the stage remarked an expression of beatific happiness on that young acrobat's face, even when he was twisting breathlessly in the air in the middle of his amazing and original shoulder swing. After that performance he laughed at the elevator man and dashed up the stairs to the flat five steps at a time—and then tiptoed very carefully into a quiet room.

"Marcia," he whispered.

"Hello!" She smiled up at him wanly. "Horace, there's something I want you to do. Look in my top bureau drawer and you'll find a big stack of paper. It's a book—sort of—Horace. I wrote it down in these last three months while I've been laid up. I wish you'd take it to that Peter Boyce Wendell who put my letter in his paper. He could tell you whether it'd be a good book. I wrote it just the way I talk, just the way I wrote that letter to him. It's just a story about a lot of things that happened to me. Will you take it to him, Horace?"

"Yes, darling."

He leaned over the bed until his head was beside her on the pillow, and began stroking back her yellow hair.

"Dearest Marcia," he said softly.

"No," she murmured, "call me what I told you to call me."

"Dear heart," he whispered passionately—"dearest, dearest heart."

"What'll we call her?"

They rested a minute in happy, drowsy content, while Horace considered.

"We'll call her Marcia Hume Tarbox," he said at length.

"Why the Hume?"

"Because he's the fellow who first introduced us."

"That so?" she murmured, sleepily surprised. "I thought his name was Moon."

Her eyes closed, and after a moment the slow, lengthening surge of the bedclothes over her breast showed that she was asleep.

Horace tiptoed over to the bureau and opening the top drawer found a heap of closely scrawled, lead-smeared pages. He looked at the first sheet:

SANDRA PEPYS, SYNCOPATED

By Marcia Tarbox

He smiled. So Samuel Pepys had made an impression on her after all. He turned a page and began to read. His smile deepened—he read on. Half an hour passed and he became aware that Marcia had waked and was watching him from the bed.

"Honey," came in a whisper.

"What, Marcia?"

"Do you like it?"

Horace coughed.

"I seem to be reading on. It's bright."

"Take it to Peter Boyce Wendell. Tell him you got the highest marks in Princeton once and that you ought to know when a book's good. Tell him this one's a world beater."

"All right, Marcia," said Horace gently.

Her eyes closed again and Horace crossing over kissed her forehead— stood there for a moment with a look of tender pity. Then he left the room.

All that night the sprawly writing on the pages, the constant mistakes in spelling and grammar, and the weird punctuation danced before his eyes. He woke several times in the night, each time full of a welling chaotic sympathy for this desire of Marcia's soul to express itself in words. To him there was something infinitely pathetic about it, and for the first time in months he began to turn over in his mind his own half-forgotten dreams.

He had meant to write a series of books, to popularize the new realism as Schopenhauer had popularized pessimism and William James pragmatism.

But life hadn't come that way. Life took hold of people and forced them into flying rings. He laughed to think of that rap at his door, the diaphanous shadow in Hume, Marcia's threatened kiss.

"And it's still me," he said aloud in wonder as he lay awake in the darkness. "I'm the man who sat in Berkeley with temerity to wonder if that rap would have had actual existence had my ear not been there to hear it. I'm still that man. I could be electrocuted for the crimes he committed.

"Poor gauzy souls trying to express ourselves in something tangible. Marcia with her written book; I with my unwritten ones. Trying to choose our mediums and then taking what we get—and being glad."

· V ·

"Sandra Pepys, Syncopated," with an introduction by Peter Boyce Wendell, the columnist, appeared serially in *Jordan's Magazine*, and came out in book form in March. From its first published instalment it attracted attention far and wide. A trite enough subject—a girl from a small New Jersey town coming to New York to go on the stage—treated simply, with a peculiar vividness of phrasing and a haunting undertone of sadness in the very inadequacy of its vocabulary, it made an irresistible appeal.

Peter Boyce Wendell, who happened at that time to be advocating the enrichment of the American language by the immediate adoption of expressive vernacular words, stood as its sponsor and thundered his indorsement over the placid bromides of the conventional reviewers.

Marcia received three hundred dollars an instalment for the serial publication, which came at an opportune time, for though Horace's monthly salary at the Hippodrome was now more than Marcia's had ever been, young Marcia was emitting shrill cries which they interpreted as a demand for country air. So early April found them installed in a bungalow in Westchester County, with a place for a lawn, a place for a garage, and a place for everything, including a sound-proof impregnable study, in which Marcia faithfully promised Mr. Jordan she would shut herself up when her daughter's demands began to be abated, and compose immortally illiterate literature.

"It's not half bad," thought Horace one night as he was on his way from the station to his house. He was considering several prospects that had opened up, a four months' vaudeville offer in five figures, a chance to go back to Princeton in charge of all gymnasium work. Odd! He had once intended to go back there in charge of all philosophic work, and now he had not even been stirred by the arrival in New York of Anton Laurier, his old idol.

The gravel crunched raucously under his heel. He saw the lights of his sitting-room gleaming and noticed a big car standing in the drive. Probably Mr. Jordan again, come to persuade Marcia to settle down to work.

She had heard the sound of his approach and her form was silhouetted against the lighted door as she came out to meet him.

"There's some Frenchman here," she whispered nervously. "I can't pronounce his name, but he sounds awful deep. You'll have to jaw with him."

"What Frenchman?"

"You can't prove it by me. He drove up an hour ago with Mr. Jordan, and said he wanted to meet Sandra Pepys, and all that sort of thing."

Two men rose from chairs as they went inside.

"Hello, Tarbox," said Jordan. "I've just been bringing together two celebrities. I've brought M'sieur Laurier out with me. M'sieur Laurier, let me present Mr. Tarbox, Mrs. Tarbox's husband."

"Not Anton Laurier!" exclaimed Horace.

"But, yes. I must come. I have to come. I have read the book of Madame, and I have been charmed"—he fumbled in his pocket—"ah, I have read of you too. In this newspaper which I read to-day it has your name."

He finally produced a clipping from a magazine.

"Read it!" he said eagerly. "It has about you too."

Horace's eye skipped down the page.

"A distinct contribution to American dialect literature," it said. "No attempt at literary tone; the book derives its very quality from this fact, as did 'Huckleberry Finn.' "

Horace's eyes caught a passage lower down; he became suddenly aghast —read on hurriedly:

"Marcia Tarbox's connection with the stage is not only as a spectator but as the wife of a performer. She was married last year to Horace Tarbox, who every evening delights the children at the Hippodrome with his won-drous flying-ring performance. It is said that the young couple have dubbed themselves Head and Shoulders, referring doubtless to the fact that Mrs. Tarbox supplies the literary and mental qualities, while the supple and agile shoulders of her husband contribute their share to the family fortunes.

"Mrs. Tarbox seems to merit that much-abused title—'prodigy.' Only twenty——"

Horace stopped reading, and with a very odd expression in his eyes gazed intently at Anton Laurier.

"I want to advise you—" he began hoarsely.

"What?"

"About raps. Don't answer them! Let them alone—have a padded door."

BERNICE BOBS
HER HAIR

◆

"Bernice Bobs her Hair" was Fitzgerald's fourth Saturday Evening Post *story (1 May 1920) and provided the subject for the dust-jacket illustration when it was collected in* Flappers and Philosophers. *It occupies an important position in the Fitzgerald canon as a witty early treatment of a characteristic subject that he would later examine more seriously: the competition for social success and the determination with which his characters—especially the young women—engage in it. The story was based on the detailed memo Fitzgerald wrote his younger sister, Annabel, advising her how to achieve popularity with boys: "Cultivate deliberate physical grace." (See the complete letter in* Correspondence of F. Scott Fitzgerald, *pp. 15–18.) Fitzgerald had some difficulty bringing "Bernice" to salable form; he cut some three thousand words and rewrote to "inject a snappy climax."*

◆

AFTER DARK on Saturday night one could stand on the first tee of the golf-course and see the country-club windows as a yellow expanse over a very black and wavy ocean. The waves of this ocean, so to speak, were the heads of many curious caddies, a few of the more ingenious chauffeurs, the golf professional's deaf sister—and there were usually several stray, diffident waves who might have rolled inside had they so desired. This was the gallery.

The balcony was inside. It consisted of the circle of wicker chairs that lined the wall of the combination clubroom and ballroom. At these Saturday-night dances it was largely feminine; a great babel of middle-aged ladies with sharp eyes and icy hearts behind lorgnettes and large bosoms. The main function of the balcony was critical. It occasionally showed grudging admiration, but never approval, for it is well known among ladies over thirty-five that when the younger set dance in the summer-time it is with the very worst intentions in the world, and if they are not bombarded with stony eyes stray couples will dance weird barbaric interludes in the corners, and the more popular, more dangerous, girls will sometimes be kissed in the parked limousines of unsuspecting dowagers.

But, after all, this critical circle is not close enough to the stage to see the actors' faces and catch the subtler byplay. It can only frown and lean, ask questions and make satisfactory deductions from its set of postulates, such as the one which states that every young man with a large income leads the life of a hunted partridge. It never really appreciates the drama of the shifting, semicruel world of adolescence. No; boxes, orchestra-circle, principals, and chorus are represented by the medley of faces and voices that sway to the plaintive African rhythm of Dyer's dance orchestra.

From sixteen-year-old Otis Ormonde, who has two more years at Hill School, to G. Reece Stoddard, over whose bureau at home hangs a Harvard law diploma; from little Madeleine Hogue, whose hair still feels strange and uncomfortable on top of her head, to Bessie MacRae, who has been the life of the party a little too long—more than ten years—the medley is not only the center of the stage but contains the only people capable of getting an unobstructed view of it.

With a flourish and a bang the music stops. The couples exchange artificial, effortless smiles, facetiously repeat "*la*-de-*da-da* dum-*dum*," and then the clatter of young feminine voices soars over the burst of clapping.

A few disappointed stags caught in midfloor as they had been about to cut in subsided listlessly back to the walls, because this was not like the riotous Christmas dances—these summer hops were considered just pleasantly warm and exciting, where even the younger marrieds rose and performed ancient waltzes and terrifying fox trots to the tolerant amusement of their younger brothers and sisters.

Warren McIntyre, who casually attended Yale, being one of the unfortunate stags, felt in his dinner-coat pocket for a cigarette and strolled out onto the wide, semidark veranda, where couples were scattered at tables, filling the lantern-hung night with vague words and hazy laughter. He nodded here and there at the less absorbed and as he passed each couple some half-forgotten fragment of a story played in his mind, for it was not a large city and every one was Who's Who to every one else's past. There, for example, were Jim Strain and Ethel Demorest, who had been privately engaged for three years. Every one knew that as soon as Jim managed to hold a job for more than two months she would marry him. Yet how bored they both looked, and how wearily Ethel regarded Jim sometimes, as if she wondered why she had trained the vines of her affection on such a wind-shaken poplar.

Warren was nineteen and rather pitying with those of his friends who hadn't gone East to college. But, like most boys, he bragged tremendously about the girls of his city when he was away from it. There was Genevieve Ormonde, who regularly made the rounds of dances, house-parties, and football games at Princeton, Yale, Williams, and Cornell; there was black-eyed Roberta Dillon, who was quite as famous to her own generation as Hiram Johnson or Ty Cobb; and, of course, there was Marjorie Harvey, who besides having a fairylike face and a dazzling, bewildering tongue was already justly celebrated for having turned five cart-wheels in succession during the last pump-and-slipper dance at New Haven.

Warren, who had grown up across the street from Marjorie, had long been "crazy about her." Sometimes she seemed to reciprocate his feeling with a faint gratitude, but she had tried him by her infallible test and informed him gravely that she did not love him. Her test was that when she was away from him she forgot him and had affairs with other boys. Warren found this discouraging, especially as Marjorie had been making little trips all summer, and for the first two or three days after each arrival home he saw great heaps of mail on the Harveys' hall table addressed to her in various masculine handwritings. To make matters worse, all during the month of August she had been visited by her cousin Bernice from Eau Claire, and it seemed impossible to see her alone. It was always necessary to hunt round and find some one to take care of Bernice. As August waned this was becoming more and more difficult.

Much as Warren worshipped Marjorie, he had to admit that Cousin Bernice was sorta dopeless. She was pretty, with dark hair and high color, but she was no fun on a party. Every Saturday night he danced a long arduous duty dance with her to please Marjorie, but he had never been anything but bored in her company.

"Warren"—a soft voice at his elbow broke in upon his thoughts, and he turned to see Marjorie, flushed and radiant as usual. She laid a hand on his shoulder and a glow settled almost imperceptibly over him.

"Warren," she whispered, "do something for me—dance with Bernice. She's been stuck with little Otis Ormonde for almost an hour."

Warren's glow faded.

"Why—sure," he answered half-heartedly.

"You don't mind, do you? I'll see that you don't get stuck."

"'Sall right."

Marjorie smiled—that smile that was thanks enough.

"You're an angel, and I'm obliged loads."

With a sigh the angel glanced round the veranda, but Bernice and Otis were not in sight. He wandered back inside, and there in front of the women's dressing-room he found Otis in the center of a group of young men who were convulsed with laughter. Otis was brandishing a piece of timber he had picked up, and discoursing volubly.

"She's gone in to fix her hair," he announced wildly. "I'm waiting to dance another hour with her."

Their laughter was renewed.

"Why don't some of you cut in?" cried Otis resentfully. "She likes more variety."

"Why, Otis," suggested a friend, "you've just barely got used to her."

"Why the two-by-four, Otis?" inquired Warren, smiling.

"The two-by-four? Oh, this? This is a club. When she comes out I'll hit her on the head and knock her in again."

Warren collapsed on a settee and howled with glee.

"Never mind, Otis," he articulated finally. "I'm relieving you this time."

Otis simulated a sudden fainting attack and handed the stick to Warren.

"If you need it, old man," he said hoarsely.

No matter how beautiful or brilliant a girl may be, the reputation of not being frequently cut in on makes her position at a dance unfortunate. Perhaps boys prefer her company to that of the butterflies with whom they dance a dozen times an evening, but youth in this jazz-nourished generation is temperamentally restless, and the idea of foxtrotting more than one full fox trot with the same girl is distasteful, not to say odious. When it comes to several dances and the intermissions between she can be quite sure that a young man, once relieved, will never tread on her wayward toes again.

Warren danced the next full dance with Bernice, and finally, thankful for the intermission, he led her to a table on the veranda. There was a moment's silence while she did unimpressive things with her fan.

"It's hotter here than in Eau Claire," she said.

Warren stifled a sigh and nodded. It might be for all he knew or cared. He wondered idly whether she was a poor conversationalist because she got no attention or got no attention because she was a poor conversationalist.

"You going to be here much longer?" he asked, and then turned rather red. She might suspect his reasons for asking.

"Another week," she answered, and stared at him as if to lunge at his next remark when it left his lips.

Warren fidgeted. Then with a sudden charitable impulse he decided to try part of his line on her. He turned and looked at her eyes.

"You've got an awfully kissable mouth," he began quietly.

This was a remark that he sometimes made to girls at college proms when they were talking in just such half dark as this. Bernice distinctly jumped. She turned an ungraceful red and became clumsy with her fan. No one had ever made such a remark to her before.

"Fresh!"—the word had slipped out before she realized it, and she bit her lip. Too late she decided to be amused, and offered him a flustered smile.

Warren was annoyed. Though not accustomed to have that remark taken seriously, still it usually provoked a laugh or a paragraph of sentimental banter. And he hated to be called fresh, except in a joking way. His charitable impulse died and he switched the topic.

"Jim Strain and Ethel Demorest sitting out as usual," he commented.

This was more in Bernice's line, but a faint regret mingled with her relief as the subject changed. Men did not talk to her about kissable mouths, but she knew that they talked in some such way to other girls.

"Oh, yes," she said, and laughed. "I hear they've been mooning round for years without a red penny. Isn't it silly?"

Warren's disgust increased. Jim Strain was a close friend of his brother's, and anyway he considered it bad form to sneer at people for not having money. But Bernice had had no intention of sneering. She was merely nervous.

· II ·

WHEN MARJORIE and Bernice reached home at half after midnight they said good night at the top of the stairs. Though cousins, they were not intimates. As a matter of fact Marjorie had no female intimates—she considered girls stupid. Bernice on the contrary all through this parent-arranged visit had rather longed to exchange those confidences flavored with giggles and tears that she considered an indispensable factor in all feminine intercourse. But in this respect she found Marjorie rather cold; felt somehow the same difficulty in talking to her that she had in talking to men. Marjorie never giggled, was never frightened, seldom embarrassed, and in fact had very few of the qualities which Bernice considered appropriately and blessedly feminine.

As Bernice busied herself with tooth-brush and paste this night she wondered for the hundredth time why she never had any attention when she was away from home. That her family were the wealthiest in Eau Claire; that her mother entertained tremendously, gave little dinners for her daughter before all dances and bought her a car of her own to drive round in, never occurred to her as factors in her home-town social success. Like most girls she had been brought up on the warm milk prepared by Annie Fellows Johnston and on novels in which the female was beloved because of certain mysterious womanly qualities, always mentioned but never displayed.

Bernice felt a vague pain that she was not at present engaged in being popular. She did not know that had it not been for Marjorie's campaigning she would have danced the entire evening with one man; but she knew that even in Eau Claire other girls with less position and less pulchritude were given a much bigger rush. She attributed this to something subtly unscrupulous in those girls. It had never worried her, and if it had her mother would have assured her that the other girls cheapened themselves and that men really respected girls like Bernice.

She turned out the light in her bathroom, and on an impulse decided to go in and chat for a moment with her aunt Josephine, whose light was still on. Her soft slippers bore her noiselessly down the carpeted hall, but hearing voices inside she stopped near the partly opened door. Then she caught her own name, and without any definite intention of eavesdropping lingered— and the thread of the conversation going on inside pierced her consciousness sharply as if it had been drawn through with a needle.

"She's absolutely hopeless!" It was Marjorie's voice. "Oh, I know what you're going to say! So many people have told you how pretty and sweet she is, and how she can cook! What of it? She has a bum time. Men don't like her."

"What's a little cheap popularity?"

Mrs. Harvey sounded annoyed.

"It's everything when you're eighteen," said Marjorie emphatically. "I've done my best. I've been polite and I've made men dance with her, but they just won't stand being bored. When I think of that gorgeous coloring wasted on such a ninny, and think what Martha Carey could do with it—oh!"

"There's no courtesy these days."

Mrs. Harvey's voice implied that modern situations were too much for her. When she was a girl all young ladies who belonged to nice families had glorious times.

"Well," said Marjorie, "no girl can permanently bolster up a lame-duck visitor, because these days it's every girl for herself. I've even tried to drop her hints about clothes and things, and she's been furious—given me the funniest looks. She's sensitive enough to know she's not getting away with much, but I'll bet she consoles herself by thinking that she's very virtuous and that I'm too gay and fickle and will come to a bad end. All unpopular girls think that way. Sour grapes! Sarah Hopkins refers to Genevieve and Roberta and me as gardenia girls! I'll bet she'd give ten years of her life and her European education to be a gardenia girl and have three or four men in love with her and be cut in on every few feet at dances."

"It seems to me," interrupted Mrs. Harvey rather wearily, "that you ought to be able to do something for Bernice. I know she's not very vivacious."

Marjorie groaned.

"Vivacious! Good grief! I've never heard her say anything to a boy except that it's hot or the floor's crowded or that she's going to school in New York next year. Sometimes she asks them what kind of car they have and tells them the kind she has. Thrilling!"

There was a short silence, and then Mrs. Harvey took up her refrain:

"All I know is that other girls not half so sweet and attractive get partners. Martha Carey, for instance, is stout and loud, and her mother is distinctly common. Roberta Dillon is so thin this year that she looks as though Arizona were the place for her. She's dancing herself to death."

"But, mother," objected Marjorie impatiently, "Martha is cheerful and awfully witty and an awfully slick girl, and Roberta's a marvellous dancer. She's been popular for ages!"

Mrs. Harvey yawned.

"I think it's that crazy Indian blood in Bernice," continued Marjorie. "Maybe she's a reversion to type. Indian women all just sat round and never said anything."

"Go to bed, you silly child," laughed Mrs. Harvey. "I wouldn't have told you that if I'd thought you were going to remember it. And I think most of your ideas are perfectly idiotic," she finished sleepily.

There was another silence, while Marjorie considered whether or not convincing her mother was worth the trouble. People over forty can seldom be permanently convinced of anything. At eighteen our convictions are hills from which we look; at forty-five they are caves in which we hide.

Having decided this, Marjorie said good night. When she came out into the hall it was quite empty.

· III ·

WHILE MARJORIE was breakfasting late next day Bernice came into the room with a rather formal good morning, sat down opposite, stared intently over and slightly moistened her lips.

"What's on your mind?" inquired Marjorie, rather puzzled.

Bernice paused before she threw her hand-grenade.

"I heard what you said about me to your mother last night."

Marjorie was startled, but she showed only a faintly heightened color and her voice was quite even when she spoke.

"Where were you?"

"In the hall. I didn't mean to listen—at first."

After an involuntary look of contempt Marjorie dropped her eyes and became very interested in balancing a stray corn-flake on her finger.

"I guess I'd better go back to Eau Claire—if I'm such a nuisance." Bernice's lower lip was trembling violently and she continued on a wavering note: "I've tried to be nice, and—and I've been first neglected and then insulted. No one ever visited me and got such treatment."

Marjorie was silent.

"But I'm in the way, I see. I'm a drag on you. Your friends don't like me." She paused, and then remembered another one of her grievances. "Of course I was furious last week when you tried to hint to me that that dress was unbecoming. Don't you think I know how to dress myself?"

"No," murmured Marjorie less than half-aloud.

"What?"

"I didn't hint anything," said Marjorie succinctly. "I said, as I remember, that it was better to wear a becoming dress three times straight than to alternate it with two frights."

"Do you think that was a very nice thing to say?"

"I wasn't trying to be nice." Then after a pause: "When do you want to go?"

Bernice drew in her breath sharply.

"Oh!" It was a little half-cry.

Marjorie looked up in surprise.

"Didn't you say you were going?"

"Yes, but——"

"Oh, you were only bluffing!"

They stared at each other across the breakfast-table for a moment. Misty waves were passing before Bernice's eyes, while Marjorie's face wore that rather hard expression that she used when slightly intoxicated undergraduates were making love to her.

"So you were bluffing," she repeated as if it were what she might have expected.

Bernice admitted it by bursting into tears. Marjorie's eyes showed boredom.

"You're my cousin," sobbed Bernice. "I'm v-v-visiting you. I was to stay a month, and if I go home my mother will know and she'll wah-wonder——"

Marjorie waited until the shower of broken words collapsed into little sniffles.

"I'll give you my month's allowance," she said coldly, "and you can spend this last week anywhere you want. There's a very nice hotel——"

Bernice's sobs rose to a flute note, and rising of a sudden she fled from the room.

An hour later, while Marjorie was in the library absorbed in composing one of those non-committal, marvellously elusive letters that only a young girl can write, Bernice reappeared, very red-eyed and consciously calm. She cast no glance at Marjorie but took a book at random from the shelf and sat down as if to read. Marjorie seemed absorbed in her letter and continued writing. When the clock showed noon Bernice closed her book with a snap.

"I suppose I'd better get my railroad ticket."

This was not the beginning of the speech she had rehearsed up-stairs, but as Marjorie was not getting her cues—wasn't urging her to be reasonable; it's all a mistake—it was the best opening she could muster.

"Just wait till I finish this letter," said Marjorie without looking round. "I want to get it off in the next mail."

After another minute, during which her pen scratched busily, she turned round and relaxed with an air of "at your service." Again Bernice had to speak.

"Do you want me to go home?"

"Well," said Marjorie, considering, "I suppose if you're not having a good time you'd better go. No use being miserable."

"Don't you think common kindness——"

"Oh, please don't quote 'Little Women'!" cried Marjorie impatiently. "That's out of style."

"You think so?"

"Heavens, yes! What modern girl could live like those inane females?"

"They were the models for our mothers."

Marjorie laughed.

"Yes, they were—not! Besides, our mothers were all very well in their way, but they know very little about their daughters' problems."

Bernice drew herself up.

"Please don't talk about my mother."

Marjorie laughed.

"I don't think I mentioned her."

Bernice felt that she was being led away from her subject.

"Do you think you've treated me very well?"

"I've done my best. You're rather hard material to work with."

The lids of Bernice's eyes reddened.

"I think you're hard and selfish, and you haven't a feminine quality in you."

"Oh, my Lord!" cried Marjorie in desperation. "You little nut! Girls like you are responsible for all the tiresome colorless marriages; all those ghastly inefficiencies that pass as feminine qualities. What a blow it must be when a man with imagination marries the beautiful bundle of clothes that he's been building ideals round, and finds that she's just a weak, whining, cowardly mass of affectations!"

Bernice's mouth had slipped half open.

"The womanly woman!" continued Marjorie. "Her whole early life is occupied in whining criticisms of girls like me who really do have a good time."

Bernice's jaw descended farther as Marjorie's voice rose.

"There's some excuse for an ugly girl whining. If I'd been irretrievably ugly I'd never have forgiven my parents for bringing me into the world. But you're starting life without any handicap—" Marjorie's little fist clinched. "If you expect me to weep with you you'll be disappointed. Go or stay, just as you like." And picking up her letters she left the room.

Bernice claimed a headache and failed to appear at luncheon. They had a matinée date for the afternoon, but the headache persisting, Marjorie made explanation to a not very downcast boy. But when she returned late in the afternoon she found Bernice with a strangely set face waiting for her in her bedroom.

"I've decided," began Bernice without preliminaries, "that maybe you're right about things—possibly not. But if you'll tell me why your friends aren't—aren't interested in me I'll see if I can do what you want me to."

Marjorie was at the mirror shaking down her hair.

"Do you mean it?"

"Yes."

"Without reservations? Will you do exactly what I say?"

"Well, I——"

"Well nothing! Will you do exactly as I say?"

"If they're sensible things."

"They're not! You're no case for sensible things."

"Are you going to make—to recommend——"

"Yes, everything. If I tell you to take boxing-lessons you'll have to do it. Write home and tell your mother you're going to stay another two weeks."

"If you'll tell me——"

"All right—I'll just give you a few examples now. First, you have no ease of manner. Why? Because you're never sure about your personal appearance. When a girl feels that she's perfectly groomed and dressed she can forget that part of her. That's charm. The more parts of yourself you can afford to forget the more charm you have."

"Don't I look all right?"

"No; for instance, you never take care of your eyebrows. They're black and lustrous, but by leaving them straggly they're a blemish. They'd be beautiful if you'd take care of them in one-tenth the time you take doing nothing. You're going to brush them so that they'll grow straight."

Bernice raised the brows in question.

"Do you mean to say that men notice eyebrows?"

"Yes—subconsciously. And when you go home you ought to have your teeth straightened a little. It's almost imperceptible, still——"

"But I thought," interrupted Bernice in bewilderment, "that you despised little dainty feminine things like that."

"I hate dainty minds," answered Marjorie. "But a girl has to be dainty in person. If she looks like a million dollars she can talk about Russia, ping-pong, or the League of Nations and get away with it."

"What else?"

"Oh, I'm just beginning! There's your dancing."

"Don't I dance all right?"

"No, you don't—you lean on a man; yes, you do—ever so slightly. I noticed it when we were dancing together yesterday. And you dance standing up straight instead of bending over a little. Probably some old lady on the side-line once told you that you looked so dignified that way. But except with a very small girl it's much harder on the man, and he's the one that counts."

"Go on." Bernice's brain was reeling.

"Well, you've got to learn to be nice to men who are sad birds. You look as if you'd been insulted whenever you're thrown with any except the most popular boys. Why, Bernice, I'm cut in on every few feet—and who does most of it? Why, those very sad birds. No girl can afford to neglect them. They're the big part of any crowd. Young boys too shy to talk are the very best conversational practice. Clumsy boys are the best dancing practice. If you can follow them and yet look graceful you can follow a baby tank across a barb-wire sky-scraper."

Bernice sighed profoundly, but Marjorie was not through.

"If you go to a dance and really amuse, say, three sad birds that dance with you; if you talk so well to them that they forget they're stuck with you, you've done something. They'll come back next time, and gradually so many sad birds will dance with you that the attractive boys will see there's no danger of being stuck—then they'll dance with you."

"Yes," agreed Bernice faintly. "I think I begin to see."

"And finally," concluded Marjorie, "poise and charm will just come. You'll wake up some morning knowing you've attained it, and men will know it too."

Bernice rose.

"It's been awfully kind of you—but nobody's ever talked to me like this before, and I feel sort of startled."

Marjorie made no answer but gazed pensively at her own image in the mirror.

"You're a peach to help me," continued Bernice.

Still Marjorie did not answer, and Bernice thought she had seemed too grateful.

"I know you don't like sentiment," she said timidly.

Marjorie turned to her quickly.

"Oh, I wasn't thinking about that. I was considering whether we hadn't better bob your hair."

Bernice collapsed backward upon the bed.

· I V ·

ON THE FOLLOWING Wednesday evening there was a dinner-dance at the country club. When the guests strolled in Bernice found her place-card with a slight feeling of irritation. Though at her right sat G. Reece Stoddard, a most desirable and distinguished young bachelor, the all-important left held only Charley Paulson. Charley lacked height, beauty, and social shrewdness, and in her new enlightenment Bernice decided that his only qualification to be her partner was that he had never been stuck with her. But this feeling of irritation left with the last of the soup-plates, and Marjorie's specific instruction came to her. Swallowing her pride she turned to Charley Paulson and plunged.

"Do you think I ought to bob my hair, Mr. Charley Paulson?"

Charley looked up in surprise.

"Why?"

"Because I'm considering it. It's such a sure and easy way of attracting attention."

Charley smiled pleasantly. He could not know this had been rehearsed. He replied that he didn't know much about bobbed hair. But Bernice was there to tell him.

"I want to be a society vampire, you see," she announced coolly, and went on to inform him that bobbed hair was the necessary prelude. She added that she wanted to ask his advice, because she had heard he was so critical about girls.

Charley, who knew as much about the psychology of women as he did of the mental states of Buddhist contemplatives, felt vaguely flattered.

"So I've decided," she continued, her voice rising slightly, "that early next week I'm going down to the Sevier Hotel barber-shop, sit in the first chair, and get my hair bobbed." She faltered, noticing that the people near her had paused in their conversation and were listening; but after a confused second Marjorie's coaching told, and she finished her paragraph to the vicinity at large. "Of course I'm charging admission, but if you'll all come down and encourage me I'll issue passes for the inside seats."

There was a ripple of appreciative laughter, and under cover of it G. Reece Stoddard leaned over quickly and said close to her ear: "I'll take a box right now."

She met his eyes and smiled as if he had said something surpassingly brilliant.

"Do you believe in bobbed hair?" asked G. Reece in the same undertone.

"I think it's unmoral," affirmed Bernice gravely. "But, of course, you've either got to amuse people or feed 'em or shock 'em." Marjorie had culled this from Oscar Wilde. It was greeted with a ripple of laughter from the men and a series of quick, intent looks from the girls. And then as though she had said nothing of wit or moment Bernice turned again to Charley and spoke confidentially in his ear.

"I want to ask you your opinion of several people. I imagine you're a wonderful judge of character."

Charley thrilled faintly—paid her a subtle compliment by overturning her water.

Two hours later, while Warren McIntyre was standing passively in the stag line abstractedly watching the dancers and wondering whither and with whom Marjorie had disappeared, an unrelated perception began to creep slowly upon him—a perception that Bernice, cousin to Marjorie, had been cut in on several times in the past five minutes. He closed his eyes, opened them and looked again. Several minutes back she had been dancing with a visiting boy, a matter easily accounted for; a visiting boy would know no better. But now she was dancing with some one else, and there was Charley Paulson headed for her with enthusiastic determination in his eye. Funny —Charley seldom danced with more than three girls an evening.

Warren was distinctly surprised when—the exchange having been effected—the man relieved proved to be none other than G. Reece Stoddard himself. And G. Reece seemed not at all jubilant at being relieved. Next time Bernice danced near, Warren regarded her intently. Yes, she was pretty, distinctly pretty; and to-night her face seemed really vivacious. She had that look that no woman, however histrionically proficient, can successfully counterfeit—she looked as if she were having a good time. He liked the way she had her hair arranged, wondered if it was brilliantine that made it glisten so. And that dress was becoming—a dark red that set off her shadowy eyes and high coloring. He remembered that he had thought her pretty when she first came to town, before he had realized that she was dull. Too bad she was dull—dull girls unbearable—certainly pretty though.

His thoughts zigzagged back to Marjorie. This disappearance would be like other disappearances. When she reappeared he would demand where she had been—would be told emphatically that it was none of his business. What a pity she was so sure of him! She basked in the knowledge that no other girl in town interested him; she defied him to fall in love with Genevieve or Roberta.

Warren sighed. The way to Marjorie's affections was a labyrinth indeed. He looked up. Bernice was again dancing with the visiting boy. Half unconsciously he took a step out from the stag line in her direction, and hesitated. Then he said to himself that it was charity. He walked toward her—collided suddenly with G. Reece Stoddard.

"Pardon me," said Warren.

But G. Reece had not stopped to apologize. He had again cut in on Bernice.

That night at one o'clock Marjorie, with one hand on the electric-light switch in the hall, turned to take a last look at Bernice's sparkling eyes.

"So it worked?"

"Oh, Marjorie, yes!" cried Bernice.

"I saw you were having a gay time."

"I did! The only trouble was that about midnight I ran short of talk. I had to repeat myself—with different men of course. I hope they won't compare notes."

"Men don't," said Marjorie, yawning, "and it wouldn't matter if they did—they'd think you were even trickier."

She snapped out the light, and as they started up the stairs Bernice grasped the banister thankfully. For the first time in her life she had been danced tired.

"You see," said Marjorie at the top of the stairs, "one man sees another man cut in and he thinks there must be something there. Well, we'll fix up some new stuff to-morrow. Good night."

"Good night."

As Bernice took down her hair she passed the evening before her in review. She had followed instructions exactly. Even when Charley Paulson cut in for the eighth time she had simulated delight and had apparently been both interested and flattered. She had not talked about the weather or Eau Claire or automobiles or her school, but had confined her conversation to me, you, and us.

But a few minutes before she fell asleep a rebellious thought was churning drowsily in her brain—after all, it was she who had done it. Marjorie, to be sure, had given her her conversation, but then Marjorie got much of her conversation out of things she read. Bernice had bought the red dress, though she had never valued it highly before Marjorie dug it out of her trunk—and her own voice had said the words, her own lips had smiled, her own feet had danced. Marjorie nice girl—vain, though—nice evening—nice boys— like Warren—Warren—Warren—what's-his-name—Warren——

She fell asleep.

· V ·

TO BERNICE the next week was a revelation. With the feeling that people really enjoyed looking at her and listening to her came the foundation of self-confidence. Of course there were numerous mistakes at first. She did not know, for instance, that Draycott Deyo was studying for the ministry; she was unaware that he had cut in on her because he thought she was a quiet, reserved girl. Had she known these things she would not have treated him to the line which began "Hello, Shell Shock!" and continued with the bathtub story—"It takes a frightful lot of energy to fix my hair in the summer—there's so much of it—so I always fix it first and powder my face and put on my hat; then I get into the bathtub, and dress afterward. Don't you think that's the best plan?"

Though Draycott Deyo was in the throes of difficulties concerning baptism by immersion and might possibly have seen a connection, it must be admitted that he did not. He considered feminine bathing an immoral subject, and gave her some of his ideas on the depravity of modern society.

But to offset that unfortunate occurrence Bernice had several signal successes to her credit. Little Otis Ormonde pleaded off from a trip East and elected instead to follow her with a puppylike devotion, to the amusement of his crowd and to the irritation of G. Reece Stoddard, several of whose afternoon calls Otis completely ruined by the disgusting tenderness of the glances he bent on Bernice. He even told her the story of the two-by-four and the dressing-room to show her how frightfully mistaken he and every one else had been in their first judgment of her. Bernice laughed off that incident with a slight sinking sensation.

Of all Bernice's conversation perhaps the best known and most universally approved was the line about the bobbing of her hair.

"Oh, Bernice, when you goin' to get the hair bobbed?"

"Day after to-morrow maybe," she would reply, laughing. "Will you come and see me? Because I'm counting on you, you know."

"Will we? You know! But you better hurry up."

Bernice, whose tonsorial intentions were strictly dishonorable, would laugh again.

"Pretty soon now. You'd be surprised."

But perhaps the most significant symbol of her success was the gray car of the hypercritical Warren McIntyre, parked daily in front of the Harvey house. At first the parlor-maid was distinctly startled when he asked for Bernice instead of Marjorie; after a week of it she told the cook that Miss Bernice had gotta holda Miss Marjorie's best fella.

And Miss Bernice had. Perhaps it began with Warren's desire to rouse jealousy in Marjorie; perhaps it was the familiar though unrecognized strain of Marjorie in Bernice's conversation; perhaps it was both of these and something of sincere attraction besides. But somehow the collective mind of the younger set knew within a week that Marjorie's most reliable beau had made an amazing face-about and was giving an indisputable rush to Marjorie's guest. The question of the moment was how Marjorie would take it. Warren called Bernice on the 'phone twice a day, sent her notes, and they were frequently seen together in his roadster, obviously engrossed in one of those tense, significant conversations as to whether or not he was sincere.

Marjorie on being twitted only laughed. She said she was mighty glad that Warren had at last found some one who appreciated him. So the younger set laughed, too, and guessed that Marjorie didn't care and let it go at that.

One afternoon when there were only three days left of her visit Bernice was waiting in the hall for Warren, with whom she was going to a bridge party. She was in rather a blissful mood, and when Marjorie—also bound for the party—appeared beside her and began casually to adjust her hat in the mirror, Bernice was utterly unprepared for anything in the nature of a clash. Marjorie did her work very coldly and succinctly in three sentences.

"You may as well get Warren out of your head," she said coldly.

"What?" Bernice was utterly astounded.

"You may as well stop making a fool of yourself over Warren McIntyre. He doesn't care a snap of his fingers about you."

For a tense moment they regarded each other—Marjorie scornful, aloof; Bernice astounded, half-angry, half-afraid. Then two cars drove up in front of the house and there was a riotous honking. Both of them gasped faintly, turned, and side by side hurried out.

All through the bridge party Bernice strove in vain to master a rising uneasiness. She had offended Marjorie, the sphinx of sphinxes. With the most wholesome and innocent intentions in the world she had stolen Marjorie's property. She felt suddenly and horribly guilty. After the bridge game, when they sat in an informal circle and the conversation became general, the storm gradually broke. Little Otis Ormonde inadvertently precipitated it.

"When you going back to kindergarten, Otis?" some one had asked.

"Me? Day Bernice gets her hair bobbed."

"Then your education's over," said Marjorie quickly. "That's only a bluff of hers. I should think you'd have realized."

"That a fact?" demanded Otis, giving Bernice a reproachful glance.

Bernice's ears burned as she tried to think up an effectual come-back. In the face of this direct attack her imagination was paralyzed.

"There's a lot of bluffs in the world," continued Marjorie quite pleasantly. "I should think you'd be young enough to know that, Otis."

"Well," said Otis, "maybe so. But gee! With a line like Bernice's——"

"Really?" yawned Marjorie. "What's her latest bon mot?"

No one seemed to know. In fact, Bernice, having trifled with her muse's beau, had said nothing memorable of late.

"Was that really all a line?" asked Roberta curiously.

Bernice hesitated. She felt that wit in some form was demanded of her, but under her cousin's suddenly frigid eyes she was completely incapacitated.

"I don't know," she stalled.

"Splush!" said Marjorie. "Admit it!"

Bernice saw that Warren's eyes had left a ukelele he had been tinkering with and were fixed on her questioningly.

"Oh, I don't know!" she repeated steadily. Her cheeks were glowing.

"Splush!" remarked Marjorie again.

"Come through, Bernice," urged Otis. "Tell her where to get off."

Bernice looked round again—she seemed unable to get away from Warren's eyes.

"I like bobbed hair," she said hurriedly, as if he had asked her a question, "and I intend to bob mine."

"When?" demanded Marjorie.

"Any time."

"No time like the present," suggested Roberta.

Otis jumped to his feet.

"Good stuff!" he cried. "We'll have a summer bobbing party. Sevier Hotel barber-shop, I think you said."

In an instant all were on their feet. Bernice's heart throbbed violently.

"What?" she gasped.

Out of the group came Marjorie's voice, very clear and contemptuous.

"Don't worry—she'll back out!"

"Come on, Bernice!" cried Otis, starting toward the door.

Four eyes—Warren's and Marjorie's—stared at her, challenged her, defied her. For another second she wavered wildly.

"All right," she said swiftly, "I don't care if I do.

An eternity of minutes later, riding down-town through the late afternoon beside Warren, the others following in Roberta's car close behind, Bernice had all the sensations of Marie Antoinette bound for the guillotine in a tumbrel. Vaguely she wondered why she did not cry out that it was all a mistake. It was all she could do to keep from clutching her hair with both hands to protect it from the suddenly hostile world. Yet she did neither. Even the thought of her mother was no deterrent now. This was the test supreme of her sportsmanship; her right to walk unchallenged in the starry heaven of popular girls.

Warren was moodily silent, and when they came to the hotel he drew up at the curb and nodded to Bernice to precede him out. Roberta's car emptied a laughing crowd into the shop, which presented two bold plate-glass windows to the street.

Bernice stood on the curb and looked at the sign, Sevier Barber-Shop. It was a guillotine indeed, and the hangman was the first barber, who, attired in a white coat and smoking a cigarette, leaned nonchalantly against the first chair. He must have heard of her; he must have been waiting all week, smoking eternal cigarettes beside that portentous, too-often-mentioned first chair. Would they blind-fold her? No, but they would tie a white cloth round her neck lest any of her blood—nonsense—hair—should get on her clothes.

"All right, Bernice," said Warren quickly.

With her chin in the air she crossed the sidewalk, pushed open the swinging screen-door, and giving not a glance to the uproarious, riotous row that occupied the waiting bench, went up to the first barber.

"I want you to bob my hair."

The first barber's mouth slid somewhat open. His cigarette dropped to the floor.

"Huh?"

"My hair—bob it!"

Refusing further preliminaries, Bernice took her seat on high. A man in the chair next to her turned on his side and gave her a glance, half lather, half amazement. One barber started and spoiled little Willy Schuneman's monthly haircut. Mr. O'Reilly in the last chair grunted and swore musically in ancient Gaelic as a razor bit into his cheek. Two bootblacks became wide-eyed and rushed for her feet. No, Bernice didn't care for a shine.

Outside a passer-by stopped and stared; a couple joined him; half a dozen small boys' noses sprang into life, flattened against the glass; and snatches of conversation borne on the summer breeze drifted in through the screen-door.

"Lookada long hair on a kid!"

"Where'd yuh get 'at stuff? 'At's a bearded lady he just finished shavin'."

But Bernice saw nothing, heard nothing. Her only living sense told her that this man in the white coat had removed one tortoise-shell comb and then another; that his fingers were fumbling clumsily with unfamiliar hair-pins; that this hair, this wonderful hair of hers, was going—she would never again feel its long voluptuous pull as it hung in a dark-brown glory down her back. For a second she was near breaking down, and then the picture before her swam mechanically into her vision—Marjorie's mouth curling in a faint ironic smile as if to say:

"Give up and get down! You tried to buck me and I called your bluff. You see you haven't got a prayer."

And some last energy rose up in Bernice, for she clinched her hands under the white cloth, and there was a curious narrowing of her eyes that Marjorie remarked on to some one long afterward.

Twenty minutes later the barber swung her round to face the mirror, and she flinched at the full extent of the damage that had been wrought. Her hair was not curly, and now it lay in lank lifeless blocks on both sides of her suddenly pale face. It was ugly as sin—she had known it would be ugly as sin. Her face's chief charm had been a Madonna-like simplicity. Now that was gone and she was—well, frightfully mediocre

—not stagy; only ridiculous, like a Greenwich Villager who had left her spectacles at home.

As she climbed down from the chair she tried to smile—failed miserably. She saw two of the girls exchange glances; noticed Marjorie's mouth curved in attenuated mockery—and that Warren's eyes were suddenly very cold.

"You see"—her words fell into an awkward pause—"I've done it."

"Yes, you've—done it," admitted Warren.

"Do you like it?"

There was a half-hearted "Sure" from two or three voices, another awkward pause, and then Marjorie turned swiftly and with serpentlike intensity to Warren.

"Would you mind running me down to the cleaners?" she asked. "I've simply got to get a dress there before supper. Roberta's driving right home and she can take the others."

Warren stared abstractedly at some infinite speck out the window. Then for an instant his eyes rested coldly on Bernice before they turned to Marjorie.

"Be glad to," he said slowly.

· VI ·

BERNICE DID NOT fully realize the outrageous trap that had been set for her until she met her aunt's amazed glance just before dinner.

"Why, Bernice!"

"I've bobbed it, Aunt Josephine."

"Why, child!"

"Do you like it?"

"Why, Ber-nice!"

"I suppose I've shocked you."

"No, but what'll Mrs. Deyo think to-morrow night? Bernice, you should have waited until after the Deyos' dance—you should have waited if you wanted to do that."

"It was sudden, Aunt Josephine. Anyway, why does it matter to Mrs. Deyo particularly?"

"Why, child," cried Mrs. Harvey, "in her paper on 'The Foibles of the Younger Generation' that she read at the last meeting of the Thursday Club she devoted fifteen minutes to bobbed hair. It's her pet abomination. And the dance is for you and Marjorie!"

"I'm sorry."

"Oh, Bernice, what'll your mother say? She'll think I let you do it."

"I'm sorry."

Dinner was an agony. She had made a hasty attempt with a curling-iron, and burned her finger and much hair. She could see that her aunt was both worried and grieved, and her uncle kept saying, "Well, I'll be darned!" over and over in a hurt and faintly hostile tone. And Marjorie sat very quietly, intrenched behind a faint smile, a faintly mocking smile.

Somehow she got through the evening. Three boys called; Marjorie disappeared with one of them, and Bernice made a listless unsuccessful attempt to entertain the two others—sighed thankfully as she climbed the stairs to her room at half past ten. What a day!

When she had undressed for the night the door opened and Marjorie came in.

"Bernice," she said, "I'm awfully sorry about the Deyo dance. I'll give you my word of honor I'd forgotten all about it."

"'Sall right," said Bernice shortly. Standing before the mirror she passed her comb slowly through her short hair.

"I'll take you down-town to-morrow," continued Marjorie, "and the hairdresser'll fix it so you'll look slick. I didn't imagine you'd go through with it. I'm really mighty sorry."

"Oh, 'sall right!"

"Still it's your last night, so I suppose it won't matter much."

Then Bernice winced as Marjorie tossed her own hair over her shoulders and began to twist it slowly into two long blond braids until in her cream-colored negligée she looked like a delicate painting of some Saxon princess. Fascinated, Bernice watched the braids grow. Heavy and luxurious they were, moving under the supple fingers like restive snakes—and to Bernice remained this relic and the curling-iron and a to-morrow full of eyes. She could see G. Reece Stoddard, who liked her, assuming his Harvard manner and telling his dinner partner that Bernice shouldn't have been allowed to go to the movies so much; she could see Draycott Deyo exchanging glances with his mother and then being conscientiously charitable to her. But then perhaps by to-morrow Mrs. Deyo would have heard the news; would send round an icy little note requesting that she fail to appear—and behind her back they would all laugh and know that Marjorie had made a fool of her; that her chance at beauty had been sacrificed to the jealous whim of a selfish girl. She sat down suddenly before the mirror, biting the inside of her cheek.

"I like it," she said with an effort. "I think it'll be becoming."

Marjorie smiled.

"It looks all right. For heaven's sake, don't let it worry you!"

"I won't."

"Good night, Bernice."

But as the door closed something snapped within Bernice. She sprang dynamically to her feet, clinching her hands, then swiftly and noiselessly crossed over to her bed and from underneath it dragged out her suitcase. Into it she tossed toilet articles and a change of clothing. Then she turned to her trunk and quickly dumped in two drawerfuls of lingerie and summer dresses. She moved quietly, but with deadly efficiency, and in three-quarters of an hour her trunk was locked and strapped and she was fully dressed in a becoming new travelling suit that Marjorie had helped her pick out.

Sitting down at her desk she wrote a short note to Mrs. Harvey, in which she briefly outlined her reasons for going. She sealed it, addressed it, and laid it on her pillow. She glanced at her watch. The train left at one, and she knew that if she walked down to the Marborough Hotel two blocks away she could easily get a taxicab.

Suddenly she drew in her breath sharply and an expression flashed into her eyes that a practised character reader might have connected vaguely with the set look she had worn in the barber's chair—somehow a development of it. It was quite a new look for Bernice—and it carried consequences.

She went stealthily to the bureau, picked up an article that lay there, and turning out all the lights stood quietly until her eyes became accustomed to the darkness. Softly she pushed open the door to Marjorie's room. She heard the quiet, even breathing of an untroubled conscience asleep.

She was by the bedside now, very deliberate and calm. She acted swiftly. Bending over she found one of the braids of Marjorie's hair, followed it up with her hand to the point nearest the head, and then holding it a little slack so that the sleeper would feel no pull, she reached down with the shears and severed it. With the pigtail in her hand she held her breath. Marjorie had muttered something in her sleep. Bernice deftly amputated the other braid, paused for an instant, and then flitted swiftly and silently back to her own room.

Down-stairs she opened the big front door, closed it carefully behind her, and feeling oddly happy and exuberant stepped off the porch into the moonlight, swinging her heavy grip like a shopping-bag. After a minute's brisk walk she discovered that her left hand still held the two blond braids. She laughed unexpectedly—had to shut her mouth hard to keep from emitting an absolute peal. She was passing Warren's house now, and on the impulse she set down her baggage, and swinging the braids like pieces of rope flung them at the wooden porch, where they landed with a slight thud. She laughed again, no longer restraining herself.

"Huh!" she giggled wildly. "Scalp the selfish thing!"

Then picking up her suitcase she set off at a half-run down the moonlit street.

THE ICE PALACE

◆

"The Ice Palace" appeared in the 22 May 1920 issue of the Saturday Evening Post *and was collected in* Flappers and Philosophers. *It was the first of a group of stories in which Fitzgerald examined the cultural as well as social differences between the North and South. "It is a grotesquely pictorial country as I found out long ago, and as Mr. Faulkner has since abundantly demonstrated," he commented in 1940. Fitzgerald was particularly aware of the influence of the South on its women—a concern that was reinforced by his marriage to an Alabama belle.*

◆

THE SUNLIGHT dripped over the house like golden paint over an art jar, and the freckling shadows here and there only intensified the rigor of the bath of light. The Butterworth and Larkin houses flanking were intrenched behind great stodgy trees; only the Happer house took the full sun, and all day long faced the dusty road-street with a tolerant kindly patience. This was the city of Tarleton in southernmost Georgia, September afternoon.

Up in her bedroom window Sally Carrol Happer rested her nineteen-year-old chin on a fifty-two-year-old sill and watched Clark Darrow's ancient Ford turn the corner. The car was hot—being partly metallic it retained all the heat it absorbed or evolved—and Clark Darrow sitting bolt upright at the wheel wore a pained, strained expression as though he considered himself a spare part, and rather likely to break. He laboriously crossed two dust ruts, the wheels squeaking indignantly at the encounter, and then with a terrifying expression he gave the steering-gear a final wrench and deposited self and car approximately in front of the Happer steps. There was a plaintive heaving sound, a death-rattle, followed by a short silence; and then the air was rent by a startling whistle.

Sally Carrol gazed down sleepily. She started to yawn, but finding this quite impossible unless she raised her chin from the window-sill, changed her mind and continued silently to regard the car, whose owner sat brilliantly if perfunctorily at attention as he waited for an answer to his signal. After a moment the whistle once more split the dusty air.

"Good mawnin'."

With difficulty Clark twisted his tall body round and bent a distorted glance on the window.

"'Tain't mawnin', Sally Carrol."

"Isn't it, sure enough?"

"What you doin'?"

"Eatin' 'n apple."

"Come on go swimmin'—want to?"

"Reckon so."

"How 'bout hurryin' up?"

"Sure enough."

Sally Carrol sighed voluminously and raised herself with profound inertia from the floor, where she had been occupied in alternately destroying parts of a green apple and painting paper dolls for her younger sister. She approached a mirror, regarded her expression with a pleased and pleasant languor, dabbed two spots of rouge on her lips and a grain of powder on her nose, and covered her bobbed corn-colored hair with a rose-littered sunbonnet. Then she kicked over the painting water, said, "Oh, damn!"— but let it lay—and left the room.

"How you, Clark?" she inquired a minute later as she slipped nimbly over the side of the car.

"Mighty fine, Sally Carrol."

"Where we go swimmin'?"

"Out to Walley's Pool. Told Marylyn we'd call by an' get her an' Joe Ewing."

Clark was dark and lean, and when on foot was rather inclined to stoop. His eyes were ominous and his expression somewhat petulant except when startlingly illuminated by one of his frequent smiles. Clark had "a income"—just enough to keep himself in ease and his car in gasolene—and he had spent the two years since he graduated from Georgia Tech in dozing round the lazy streets of his home town, discussing how he could best invest his capital for an immediate fortune.

Hanging round he found not at all difficult; a crowd of little girls had grown up beautifully, the amazing Sally Carrol foremost among them; and they enjoyed being swum with and danced with and made love to in the flower-filled summery evenings—and they all liked Clark immensely. When feminine company palled there were half a dozen other youths who were always just about to do something, and meanwhile were quite willing to join him in a few holes of golf, or a game of billiards, or the consumption

of a quart of "hard yella licker." Every once in a while one of these contemporaries made a farewell round of calls before going up to New York
or Philadelphia or Pittsburgh to go into business, but mostly they just stayed
round in this languid paradise of dreamy skies and firefly evenings and noisy
niggery street fairs—and especially of gracious, soft-voiced girls, who were
brought up on memories instead of money.

The Ford having been excited into a sort of restless resentful life Clark
and Sally Carrol rolled and rattled down Valley Avenue into Jefferson Street,
where the dust road became a pavement; along opiate Millicent Place, where
there were half a dozen prosperous, substantial mansions; and on into the
down-town section. Driving was perilous here, for it was shopping time;
the population idled casually across the streets and a drove of low-moaning
oxen were being urged along in front of a placid street-car; even the shops
seemed only yawning their doors and blinking their windows in the sunshine
before retiring into a state of utter and finite coma.

"Sally Carrol," said Clark suddenly, "it a fact that you're engaged?"

She looked at him quickly.

"Where'd you hear that?"

"Sure enough, you engaged?"

" 'At's a nice question!"

"Girl told me you were engaged to a Yankee you met up in Asheville last
summer."

Sally Carrol sighed.

"Never saw such an old town for rumors."

"Don't marry a Yankee, Sally Carrol. We need you round here."

Sally Carrol was silent a moment.

"Clark," she demanded suddenly, "who on earth shall I marry?"

"I offer my services."

"Honey, you couldn't support a wife," she answered cheerfully. "Anyway, I know you too well to fall in love with you."

" 'At doesn't mean you ought to marry a Yankee," he persisted.

"S'pose I love him?"

He shook his head.

"You couldn't. He'd be a lot different from us, every way."

He broke off as he halted the car in front of a rambling, dilapidated house.
Marylyn Wade and Joe Ewing appeared in the doorway.

" 'Lo, Sally Carrol."

"Hi!"

"How you-all?"

"Sally Carrol," demanded Marylyn as they started off again, "you engaged?"

"Lawdy, where'd all this start? Can't I look at a man 'thout everybody in town engagin' me to him?"

Clark stared straight in front of him at a bolt on the clattering windshield.

"Sally Carrol," he said with a curious intensity, "don't you like us?"

"What?"

"Us down here?"

"Why, Clark, you know I do. I adore all you boys."

"Then why you gettin' engaged to a Yankee?"

"Clark, I don't know. I'm not sure what I'll do, but—well, I want to go places and see people. I want my mind to grow. I want to live where things happen on a big scale."

"What you mean?"

"Oh, Clark, I love you, and I love Joe here, and Ben Arrot, and you-all, but you'll—you'll——"

"We'll all be failures?"

"Yes. I don't mean only money failures, but just sort of—of ineffectual and sad, and—oh, how can I tell you?"

"You mean because we stay here in Tarleton?"

"Yes, Clark; and because you like it and never want to change things or think or go ahead."

He nodded and she reached over and pressed his hand.

"Clark," she said softly, "I wouldn't change you for the world. You're sweet the way you are. The things that'll make you fail I'll love always—the living in the past, the lazy days and nights you have, and all your carelessness and generosity."

"But you're goin' away?"

"Yes—because I couldn't ever marry you. You've a place in my heart no one else ever could have, but tied down here I'd get restless. I'd feel I was—wastin' myself. There's two sides to me, you see. There's the sleepy old side you love; an' there's a sort of energy—the feelin' that makes me do wild things. That's the part of me that may be useful somewhere, that'll last when I'm not beautiful any more."

She broke off with characteristic suddenness and sighed, "Oh, sweet cooky!" as her mood changed.

Half closing her eyes and tipping back her head till it rested on the seat-back she let the savory breeze fan her eyes and ripple the fluffy curls of her bobbed hair. They were in the country now, hurrying between tangled growths of bright-green coppice and grass and tall trees that sent sprays of foliage to hang a cool welcome over the road. Here and there they passed a battered negro cabin, its oldest white-haired inhabitant smoking a corncob pipe beside the door, and half a dozen scantily clothed pickaninnies parading tattered dolls on the wild-grown grass in front. Farther out were lazy cotton-fields, where even the workers seemed intangible shadows lent by the sun to the earth, not for toil, but to while away some age-old tradition in the golden September fields. And round the drowsy picturesqueness, over the trees and shacks and muddy rivers, flowed the heat, never hostile, only comforting, like a great warm nourishing bosom for the infant earth.

"Sally Carrol, we're here!"

"Poor chile's soun' asleep."

"Honey, you dead at last outa sheer laziness?"

"Water, Sally Carrol! Cool water waitin' for you!"

Her eyes opened sleepily.

"Hi!" she murmured, smiling.

· II ·

IN NOVEMBER Harry Bellamy, tall, broad, and brisk, came down from his Northern city to spend four days. His intention was to settle a matter that had been hanging fire since he and Sally Carrol had met in Asheville, North Carolina, in midsummer. The settlement took only a quiet afternoon and an evening in front of a glowing open fire, for Harry Bellamy had everything she wanted; and, besides, she loved him—loved him with that side of her she kept especially for loving. Sally Carrol had several rather clearly defined sides.

On his last afternoon they walked, and she found their steps tending half-unconsciously toward one of her favorite haunts, the cemetery. When it came in sight, gray-white and golden-green under the cheerful late sun, she paused, irresolute, by the iron gate.

"Are you mournful by nature, Harry?" she asked with a faint smile.

"Mournful? Not I."

"Then let's go in here. It depresses some folks, but I like it."

They passed through the gateway and followed a path that led through a wavy valley of graves—dusty-gray and mouldy for the fifties; quaintly carved with flowers and jars for the seventies; ornate and hideous for the nineties, with fat marble cherubs lying in sodden sleep on stone pillows, and great impossible growths of nameless granite flowers. Occasionally they saw a kneeling figure with tributary flowers, but over most of the graves lay silence and withered leaves with only the fragrance that their own shadowy memories could waken in living minds.

They reached the top of a hill where they were fronted by a tall, round headstone, freckled with dark spots of damp and half grown over with vines.

"Margery Lee," she read; "1844–1873. Wasn't she nice? She died when she was twenty-nine. Dear Margery Lee," she added softly. "Can't you see her, Harry?"

"Yes, Sally Carrol."

He felt a little hand insert itself into his.

"She was dark, I think; and she always wore her hair with a ribbon in it, and gorgeous hoop-skirts of alice blue and old rose."

"Yes."

"Oh, she was sweet, Harry! And she was the sort of girl born to stand on a wide, pillared porch and welcome folks in. I think perhaps a lot of men went away to war meanin' to come back to her; but maybe none of 'em ever did."

He stooped down close to the stone, hunting for any record of marriage.

"There's nothing here to show."

"Of course not. How could there be anything there better than just 'Margery Lee,' and that eloquent date?"

She drew close to him and an unexpected lump came into his throat as her yellow hair brushed his cheek.

"You see how she was, don't you, Harry?"

"I see," he agreed gently. "I see through your precious eyes. You're beautiful now, so I know she must have been."

Silent and close they stood, and he could feel her shoulders trembling a little. An ambling breeze swept up the hill and stirred the brim of her floppidy hat.

"Let's go down there!"

She was pointing to a flat stretch on the other side of the hill where along the green turf were a thousand grayish-white crosses stretching in endless, ordered rows like the stacked arms of a battalion.

"Those are the Confederate dead," said Sally Carrol simply.

They walked along and read the inscriptions, always only a name and a date, sometimes quite indecipherable.

"The last row is the saddest—see, 'way over there. Every cross has just a date on it, and the word 'Unknown.' "

She looked at him and her eyes brimmed with tears.

"I can't tell you how real it is to me, darling—if you don't know."

"How you feel about it is beautiful to me."

"No, no, it's not me, it's them—that old time that I've tried to have live in me. These were just men, unimportant evidently or they wouldn't have been 'unknown'; but they died for the most beautiful thing in the world—

the dead South. You see," she continued, her voice still husky, her eyes glistening with tears, "people have these dreams they fasten onto things, and I've always grown up with that dream. It was so easy because it was all dead and there weren't any disillusions comin' to me. I've tried in a way to live up to those past standards of noblesse oblige—there's just the last remnants of it, you know, like the roses of an old garden dying all round us—streaks of strange courtliness and chivalry in some of these boys an' stories I used to hear from a Confederate soldier who lived next door, and a few old darkies. Oh, Harry, there was something, there was something! I couldn't ever make you understand, but it was there."

"I understand," he assured her again quietly.

Sally Carrol smiled and dried her eyes on the tip of a handkerchief protruding from his breast pocket.

"You don't feel depressed, do you, lover? Even when I cry I'm happy here, and I get a sort of strength from it."

Hand in hand they turned and walked slowly away. Finding soft grass she drew him down to a seat beside her with their backs against the remnants of a low broken wall.

"Wish those three old women would clear out," he complained. "I want to kiss you, Sally Carrol."

"Me, too."

They waited impatiently for the three bent figures to move off, and then she kissed him until the sky seemed to fade out and all her smiles and tears to vanish in an ecstasy of eternal seconds.

Afterward they walked slowly back together, while on the corners twilight played at somnolent black-and-white checkers with the end of day.

"You'll be up about mid-January," he said, "and you've got to stay a month at least. It'll be slick. There's a winter carnival on, and if you've never really seen snow it'll be like fairy-land to you. There'll be skating and skiing and tobogganing and sleigh-riding, and all sorts of torchlight parades on snow-shoes. They haven't had one for years, so they're going to make it a knock-out."

"Will I be cold, Harry?" she asked suddenly.

"You certainly won't. You may freeze your nose, but you won't be shivery cold. It's hard and dry, you know."

"I guess I'm a summer child. I don't like any cold I've ever seen."

She broke off and they were both silent for a minute.

"Sally Carrol," he said very slowly, "what do you say to—March?"

"I say I love you."

"March?"

"March, Harry."

· III ·

ALL NIGHT in the Pullman it was very cold. She rang for the porter to ask for another blanket, and when he couldn't give her one she tried vainly, by squeezing down into the bottom of her berth and doubling back the bedclothes, to snatch a few hours' sleep. She wanted to look her best in the morning.

She rose at six and sliding uncomfortably into her clothes stumbled up to the diner for a cup of coffee. The snow had filtered into the vestibules and covered the floor with a slippery coating. It was intriguing, this cold, it crept in everywhere. Her breath was quite visible and she blew into the air with a naïve enjoyment. Seated in the diner she stared out the window at white hills and valleys and scattered pines whose every branch was a green platter for a cold feast of snow. Sometimes a solitary farmhouse would fly by, ugly and bleak and lone on the white waste; and with each one she had an instant of chill compassion for the souls shut in there waiting for spring.

As she left the diner and swayed back into the Pullman she experienced a surging rush of energy and wondered if she was feeling the bracing air of which Harry had spoken. This was the North, the North—her land now!

"Then blow, ye winds, heigho!
A-roving I will go,"

she chanted exultantly to herself.

"What's 'at?" inquired the porter politely.

"I said: 'Brush me off.' "

The long wires of the telegraph-poles doubled; two tracks ran up beside the train—three—four; came a succession of white-roofed houses, a glimpse of a trolley-car with frosted windows, streets—more streets—the city.

She stood for a dazed moment in the frosty station before she saw three fur-bundled figures descending upon her.

"There she is!"

"Oh, Sally Carrol!"

Sally Carrol dropped her bag.

"Hi!"

A faintly familiar icy-cold face kissed her, and then she was in a group of faces all apparently emitting great clouds of heavy smoke; she was shaking hands. There were Gordon, a short, eager man of thirty who looked like an amateur knocked-about model for Harry, and his wife, Myra, a listless lady with flaxen hair under a fur automobile cap. Almost immediately Sally Carrol thought of her as vaguely Scandinavian. A cheerful chauffeur adopted her bag, and amid ricochets of half-phrases, exclamations, and perfunctory listless "my dears" from Myra, they swept each other from the station.

Then they were in a sedan bound through a crooked succession of snowy streets where dozens of little boys were hitching sleds behind grocery wagons and automobiles.

"Oh," cried Sally Carrol, "I want to do that! Can we, Harry?"

"That's for kids. But we might——"

"It looks like such a circus!" she said regretfully.

Home was a rambling frame house set on a white lap of snow, and there she met a big, gray-haired man of whom she approved, and a lady who was like an egg, and who kissed her—these were Harry's parents. There was a breathless indescribable hour crammed full of half-sentences, hot water, bacon and eggs and confusion; and after that she was alone with Harry in the library, asking him if she dared smoke.

It was a large room with a Madonna over the fire-place and rows upon rows of books in covers of light gold and dark gold and shiny red. All the chairs had little lace squares where one's head should rest, the couch was just comfortable, the books looked as if they had been read—some—and Sally Carrol had an instantaneous vision of the battered old library at home, with her father's huge medical books, and the oil-paintings of her three great-uncles, and the old couch that had been mended up for forty-five years and was still luxurious to dream in. This room struck her as being neither attractive nor particularly otherwise. It was simply a room with a lot of fairly expensive things in it that all looked about fifteen years old.

"What do you think of it up here?" demanded Harry eagerly. "Does it surprise you? Is it what you expected, I mean?"

"You are, Harry," she said quietly, and reached out her arms to him.

But after a brief kiss he seemed anxious to extort enthusiasm from her.

"The town, I mean. Do you like it? Can you feel the pep in the air?"

"Oh, Harry," she laughed, "you'll have to give me time. You can't just fling questions at me."

She puffed at her cigarette with a sigh of contentment.

"One thing I want to ask you," he began rather apologetically; "you Southerners put quite an emphasis on family, and all that—not that it isn't quite all right, but you'll find it a little different here. I mean—you'll notice a lot of things that'll seem to you sort of vulgar display at first, Sally Carrol; but just remember that this is a three-generation town. Everybody has a father, and about half of us have grandfathers. Back of that we don't go."

"Of course," she murmured.

"Our grandfathers, you see, founded the place, and a lot of them had to take some pretty queer jobs while they were doing the founding. For instance, there's one woman who at present is about the social model for the town; well, her father was the first public ash man—things like that."

"Why," said Sally Carrol, puzzled, "did you s'pose I was goin' to make remarks about people?"

"Not at all," interrupted Harry; "and I'm not apologizing for any one either. It's just that—well, a Southern girl came up here last summer and said some unfortunate things, and—oh, I just thought I'd tell you."

Sally Carrol felt suddenly indignant—as though she had been unjustly spanked—but Harry evidently considered the subject closed, for he went on with a great surge of enthusiasm.

"It's carnival time, you know. First in ten years. And there's an ice palace they're building now that's the first they've had since eighty-five. Built out of blocks of the clearest ice they could find—on a tremendous scale."

She rose and walking to the window pushed aside the heavy Turkish portières and looked out.

"Oh!" she cried suddenly. "There's two little boys makin' a snow man! Harry, do you reckon I can go out an' help 'em?"

"You dream! Come here and kiss me."

She left the window rather reluctantly.

"I don't guess this is a very kissable climate, is it? I mean, it makes you so you don't want to sit round, doesn't it?"

"We're not going to. I've got a vacation for the first week you're here, and there's a dinner-dance to-night."

"Oh, Harry," she confessed, subsiding in a heap, half in his lap, half in the pillows, "I sure do feel confused. I haven't got an idea whether I'll like it or not, an' I don't know what people expect, or anythin'. You'll have to tell me, honey."

"I'll tell you," he said softly, "if you'll just tell me you're glad to be here."

"Glad—just awful glad!" she whispered, insinuating herself into his arms in her own peculiar way. "Where you are is home for me, Harry."

And as she said this she had the feeling for almost the first time in her life that she was acting a part.

That night, amid the gleaming candles of a dinner-party, where the men seemed to do most of the talking while the girls sat in a haughty and expensive aloofness, even Harry's presence on her left failed to make her feel at home.

"They're a good-looking crowd, don't you think?" he demanded. "Just look round. There's Spud Hubbard, tackle at Princeton last year, and Junie

Morton—he and the red-haired fellow next to him were both Yale hockey captains; Junie was in my class. Why, the best athletes in the world come from these States round here. This is a man's country, I tell you. Look at John J. Fishburn!"

"Who's he?" asked Sally Carrol innocently.

"Don't you know?"

"I've heard the name."

"Greatest wheat man in the Northwest, and one of the greatest financiers in the country."

She turned suddenly to a voice on her right.

"I guess they forgot to introduce us. My name's Roger Patton."

"My name is Sally Carrol Happer," she said graciously.

"Yes, I know. Harry told me you were coming."

"You a relative?"

"No, I'm a professor."

"Oh," she laughed.

"At the university. You're from the South, aren't you?"

"Yes; Tarleton, Georgia."

She liked him immediately—a reddish-brown mustache under watery blue eyes that had something in them that these other eyes lacked, some quality of appreciation. They exchanged stray sentences through dinner, and she made up her mind to see him again.

After coffee she was introduced to numerous good-looking young men who danced with conscious precision and seemed to take it for granted that she wanted to talk about nothing except Harry.

"Heavens," she thought, "they talk as if my being engaged made me older than they are—as if I'd tell their mothers on them!"

In the South an engaged girl, even a young married woman, expected the same amount of half-affectionate badinage and flattery that would be accorded a débutante, but here all that seemed banned. One young man, after getting well started on the subject of Sally Carrol's eyes, and how they had allured him ever since she entered the room, went into a violent confusion when he found she was visiting the Bellamys—was Harry's fiancée. He seemed to feel as though he had made some risqué and inexcusable blunder, became immediately formal, and left her at the first opportunity.

She was rather glad when Roger Patton cut in on her and suggested that they sit out a while.

"Well," he inquired, blinking cheerily, "how's Carmen from the South?"

"Mighty fine. How's—how's Dangerous Dan McGrew? Sorry, but he's the only Northerner I know much about."

He seemed to enjoy that.

"Of course," he confessed, "as a professor of literature I'm not supposed to have read Dangerous Dan McGrew."

"Are you a native?"

"No, I'm a Philadelphian. Imported from Harvard to teach French. But I've been here ten years."

"Nine years, three hundred an' sixty-four days longer than me."

"Like it here?"

"Uh-huh. Sure do!"

"Really?"

"Well, why not? Don't I look as if I were havin' a good time?"

"I saw you look out the window a minute ago—and shiver."

"Just my imagination," laughed Sally Carrol. "I'm used to havin' everythin' quiet outside, an' sometimes I look out an' see a flurry of snow, an' it's just as if somethin' dead was movin'."

He nodded appreciatively.

"Ever been North before?"

"Spent two Julys in Asheville, North Carolina."

"Nice-looking crowd, aren't they?" suggested Patton, indicating the swirling floor.

Sally Carrol started. This had been Harry's remark.

"Sure are! They're—canine."

"What?"

She flushed.

"I'm sorry; that sounded worse than I meant it. You see I always think of people as feline or canine, irrespective of sex."

"Which are you?"

"I'm feline. So are you. So are most Southern men an' most of these girls here."

"What's Harry?"

"Harry's canine distinctly. All the men I've met to-night seem to be canine."

"What does 'canine' imply? A certain conscious masculinity as opposed to subtlety?"

"Reckon so. I never analyzed it—only I just look at people an' say 'canine' or 'feline' right off. It's right absurd, I guess."

"Not at all. I'm interested. I used to have a theory about these people. I think they're freezing up."

"What?"

"I think they're growing like Swedes—Ibsenesque, you know. Very gradually getting gloomy and melancholy. It's these long winters. Ever read any Ibsen?"

She shook her head.

"Well, you find in his characters a certain brooding rigidity. They're righteous, narrow, and cheerless, without infinite possibilities for great sorrow or joy."

"Without smiles or tears?"

"Exactly. That's my theory. You see there are thousands of Swedes up here. They come, I imagine, because the climate is very much like their own, and there's been a gradual mingling. There're probably not half a dozen here to-night, but—we've had four Swedish governors. Am I boring you?"

"I'm mighty interested."

"Your future sister-in-law is half Swedish. Personally I like her, but my theory is that Swedes react rather badly on us as a whole. Scandinavians, you know, have the largest suicide rate in the world."

"Why do you live here if it's so depressing?"

"Oh, it doesn't get me. I'm pretty well cloistered, and I suppose books mean more than people to me anyway."

"But writers all speak about the South being tragic. You know—Spanish señoritas, black hair and daggers an' haunting music."

He shook his head.

"No, the Northern races are the tragic races—they don't indulge in the cheering luxury of tears."

Sally Carrol thought of her graveyard. She supposed that that was vaguely what she had meant when she said it didn't depress her.

"The Italians are about the gayest people in the world—but it's a dull subject," he broke off. "Anyway, I want to tell you you're marrying a pretty fine man."

Sally Carrol was moved by an impulse of confidence.

"I know. I'm the sort of person who wants to be taken care of after a certain point, and I feel sure I will be."

"Shall we dance? You know," he continued as they rose, "it's encouraging to find a girl who knows what she's marrying for. Nine-tenths of them think of it as a sort of walking into a moving-picture sunset."

She laughed, and liked him immensely.

Two hours later on the way home she nestled near Harry in the back seat.

"Oh, Harry," she whispered, "it's so co-old!"

"But it's warm in here, darling girl."

"But outside it's cold; and oh, that howling wind!"

She buried her face deep in his fur coat and trembled involuntarily as his cold lips kissed the tip of her ear.

· I V ·

THE FIRST WEEK of her visit passed in a whirl. She had her promised toboggan-ride at the back of an automobile through a chill January twilight. Swathed in furs she put in a morning tobogganing on the country-club hill; even tried skiing, to sail through the air for a glorious moment and then land in a tangled laughing bundle on a soft snow-drift. She liked all the winter sports, except an afternoon spent snow-shoeing over a glaring plain under pale yellow sunshine, but she soon realized that these things were for children—that she was being humored and that the enjoyment round her was only a reflection of her own.

At first the Bellamy family puzzled her. The men were reliable and she liked them; to Mr. Bellamy especially, with his iron-gray hair and energetic dignity, she took an immediate fancy, once she found that he was born in Kentucky; this made of him a link between the old life and the new. But toward the women she felt a definite hostility. Myra, her future sister-in-law, seemed the essence of spiritless conventionality. Her conversation was so utterly devoid of personality that Sally Carrol, who came from a country where a certain amount of charm and assurance could be taken for granted in the women, was inclined to despise her.

"If those women aren't beautiful," she thought, "they're nothing. They just fade out when you look at them. They're glorified domestics. Men are the center of every mixed group."

Lastly there was Mrs. Bellamy, whom Sally Carrol detested. The first day's impression of an egg had been confirmed—an egg with a cracked, veiny voice and such an ungracious dumpiness of carriage that Sally Carrol felt that if she once fell she would surely scramble. In addition, Mrs. Bellamy seemed to typify the town in being innately hostile to strangers. She called Sally Carrol "Sally," and could not be persuaded that the double name was anything more than a tedious ridiculous nickname. To Sally Carrol this shortening of her name was like presenting her to the public half clothed. She loved "Sally Carrol"; she loathed "Sally." She knew also that Harry's mother disapproved of her bobbed hair; and she had never dared smoke down-stairs after that first day when Mrs. Bellamy had come into the library sniffing violently.

Of all the men she met she preferred Roger Patton, who was a frequent visitor at the house. He never again alluded to the Ibsenesque tendency of the populace, but when he came in one day and found her curled upon the sofa bent over "Peer Gynt" he laughed and told her to forget what he'd said—that it was all rot.

And then one afternoon in her second week she and Harry hovered on the edge of a dangerously steep quarrel. She considered that he precipitated it entirely, though the Serbia in the case was an unknown man who had not had his trousers pressed.

They had been walking homeward between mounds of high-piled snow and under a sun which Sally Carrol scarcely recognized. They passed a little girl done up in gray wool until she resembled a small Teddy bear, and Sally Carrol could not resist a gasp of maternal appreciation.

"Look! Harry!"

"What?"

"That little girl—did you see her face?"

"Yes, why?"

"It was red as a little strawberry. Oh, she was cute!"

"Why, your own face is almost as red as that already! Everybody's healthy here. We're out in the cold as soon as we're old enough to walk. Wonderful climate!"

She looked at him and had to agree. He was mighty healthy-looking; so was his brother. And she had noticed the new red in her own cheeks that very morning.

Suddenly their glances were caught and held, and they stared for a moment at the street-corner ahead of them. A man was standing there, his knees bent, his eyes gazing upward with a tense expression as though he were about to make a leap toward the chilly sky. And then they both exploded into a shout of laughter, for coming closer they discovered it had been a ludicrous momentary illusion produced by the extreme bagginess of the man's trousers.

"Reckon that's one on us," she laughed.

"He must be a Southerner, judging by those trousers," suggested Harry mischievously.

"Why, Harry!"

Her surprised look must have irritated him.

"Those damn Southerners!"

Sally Carrol's eyes flashed.

"Don't call 'em that!"

"I'm sorry, dear," said Harry, malignantly apologetic, "but you know what I think of them. They're sort of—sort of degenerates—not at all like the old Southerners. They've lived so long down there with all the colored people that they've gotten lazy and shiftless."

"Hush your mouth, Harry!" she cried angrily. "They're not! They may be lazy—anybody would be in that climate—but they're my best friends, an' I don't want to hear 'em criticised in any such sweepin' way. Some of 'em are the finest men in the world."

"Oh, I know. They're all right when they come North to college, but of all the hangdog, ill-dressed, slovenly lot I ever saw, a bunch of small-town Southerners are the worst!"

Sally Carrol was clinching her gloved hands and biting her lip furiously.

"Why," continued Harry, "there was one in my class at New Haven, and we all thought that at last we'd found the true type of Southern aristocrat, but it turned out that he wasn't an aristocrat at all—just the son of a Northern carpetbagger, who owned about all the cotton round Mobile."

"A Southerner wouldn't talk the way you're talking now," she said evenly.

"They haven't the energy!"

"Or the somethin' else."

"I'm sorry, Sally Carrol, but I've heard you say yourself that you'd never marry——"

"That's quite different. I told you I wouldn't want to tie my life to any of the boys that are round Tarleton now, but I never made any sweepin' generalities."

They walked along in silence.

"I probably spread it on a bit thick, Sally Carrol. I'm sorry."

She nodded but made no answer. Five minutes later as they stood in the hallway she suddenly threw her arms round him.

"Oh, Harry," she cried, her eyes brimming with tears, "let's get married next week. I'm afraid of having fusses like that. I'm afraid, Harry. It wouldn't be that way if we were married."

But Harry, being in the wrong, was still irritated.

"That'd be idiotic. We decided on March."

The tears in Sally Carrol's eyes faded; her expression hardened slightly.

"Very well—I suppose I shouldn't have said that."

Harry melted.

"Dear little nut!" he cried. "Come and kiss me and let's forget."

That very night at the end of a vaudeville performance the orchestra played "Dixie" and Sally Carrol felt something stronger and more enduring than her tears and smiles of the day brim up inside her. She leaned forward gripping the arms of her chair until her face grew crimson.

"Sort of get you, dear?" whispered Harry.

But she did not hear him. To the spirited throb of the violins and the inspiring beat of the kettledrums her own old ghosts were marching by and on into the darkness, and as fifes whistled and sighed in the low encore they seemed so nearly out of sight that she could have waved good-by.

> *"Away, away,*
> *Away down South in Dixie!*
> *Away, away,*
> *Away down South in Dixie!"*

· V ·

IT WAS A particularly cold night. A sudden thaw had nearly cleared the streets the day before, but now they were traversed again with a powdery wraith of loose snow that travelled in wavy lines before the feet of the wind, and filled the lower air with a fine-particled mist. There was no sky—only a dark, ominous tent that draped in the tops of the streets and was in reality a vast approaching army of snowflakes—while over it all, chilling away the comfort from the brown-and-green glow of lighted windows and muffling the steady trot of the horse pulling their sleigh, interminably washed the north wind. It was a dismal town after all, she thought—dismal.

Sometimes at night it had seemed to her as though no one lived here— they had all gone long ago—leaving lighted houses to be covered in time by tombing heaps of sleet. Oh, if there should be snow on her grave! To be beneath great piles of it all winter long, where even her headstone would be a light shadow against light shadows. Her grave—a grave that should be flower-strewn and washed with sun and rain.

She thought again of those isolated country houses that her train had passed, and of the life there the long winter through—the ceaseless glare through the windows, the crust forming on the soft drifts of snow, finally the slow, cheerless melting, and the harsh spring of which Roger Patton had told her. Her spring—to lose it forever—with its lilacs and the lazy sweetness it stirred in her heart. She was laying away that spring—afterward she would lay away that sweetness.

With a gradual insistence the storm broke. Sally Carrol felt a film of flakes melt quickly on her eyelashes, and Harry reached over a furry arm and drew down her complicated flannel cap. Then the small flakes came in skirmish-line, and the horse bent his neck patiently as a transparency of white appeared momentarily on his coat.

"Oh, he's cold, Harry," she said quickly.

"Who? The horse? Oh, no, he isn't. He likes it!"

After another ten minutes they turned a corner and came in sight of their destination. On a tall hill outlined in vivid glaring green against the wintry sky stood the ice palace. It was three stories in the air, with battlements and embrasures and narrow icicled windows, and the innumerable electric lights inside made a gorgeous transparency of the great central hall. Sally Carrol clutched Harry's hand under the fur robe.

"It's beautiful!" he cried excitedly. "My golly, it's beautiful, isn't it! They haven't had one here since eighty-five!"

Somehow the notion of there not having been one since eighty-five oppressed her. Ice was a ghost, and this mansion of it was surely peopled by those shades of the eighties, with pale faces and blurred snow-filled hair.

"Come on, dear," said Harry.

She followed him out of the sleigh and waited while he hitched the horse. A party of four—Gordon, Myra, Roger Patton, and another girl—drew up beside them with a mighty jingle of bells. There were quite a crowd already, bundled in fur or sheepskin, shouting and calling to each other as they moved through the snow, which was now so thick that people could scarcely be distinguished a few yards away.

"It's a hundred and seventy feet tall," Harry was saying to a muffled figure beside him as they trudged toward the entrance; "covers six thousand square yards."

She caught snatches of conversation: "One main hall"—"walls twenty to forty inches thick"—"and the ice cave has almost a mile of—"—"this Canuck who built it——"

They found their way inside, and dazed by the magic of the great crystal walls Sally Carrol found herself repeating over and over two lines from "Kubla Khan":

> "It was a miracle of rare device,
> A sunny pleasure-dome with caves of ice!"

In the great glittering cavern with the dark shut out she took a seat on a wooden bench, and the evening's oppression lifted. Harry was right—it was beautiful; and her gaze travelled the smooth surface of the walls, the blocks for which had been selected for their purity and clearness to obtain this opalescent, translucent effect.

"Look! Here we go—oh, boy!" cried Harry.

A band in a far corner struck up "Hail, Hail, the Gang's All Here!" which echoed over to them in wild muddled acoustics, and then the lights suddenly went out; silence seemed to flow down the icy sides and sweep over them. Sally Carrol could still see her white breath in the darkness, and a dim row of pale faces over on the other side.

The music eased to a sighing complaint, and from outside drifted in the full-throated resonant chant of the marching clubs. It grew louder like some paean of a viking tribe traversing an ancient wild; it swelled—they were coming nearer; then a row of torches appeared, and another and another, and keeping time with their moccasined feet a long column of gray-mackinawed figures swept in, snowshoes slung at their shoulders, torches soaring and flickering as their voices rose along the great walls.

The gray column ended and another followed, the light streaming luridly this time over red toboggan caps and flaming crimson mackinaws, and as they entered they took up the refrain; then came a long platoon of blue and white, of green, of white, of brown and yellow.

"Those white ones are the Wacouta Club," whispered Harry eagerly. "Those are the men you've met round at dances."

The volume of the voices grew; the great cavern was a phantasmagoria of torches waving in great banks of fire, of colors and the rhythm of soft-leather steps. The leading column turned and halted, platoon deployed in front of platoon until the whole procession made a solid flag of flame, and then from thousands of voices burst a mighty shout that filled the air like a crash of thunder, and sent the torches wavering. It was magnificent, it was tremendous! To Sally Carrol it was the North offering sacrifice on some mighty altar to the gray pagan God of Snow. As the shout died the band struck up again and there came more singing, and then long reverberating cheers by each club. She sat very quiet listening while the staccato cries rent the stillness; and then she started, for there was a volley of explosion, and great clouds of smoke went up here and there through the cavern—the flashlight photographers at work—and the council was over. With the band at their head the clubs formed in column once more, took up their chant, and began to march out.

"Come on!" shouted Harry. "We want to see the labyrinths down-stairs before they turn the lights off!"

They all rose and started toward the chute—Harry and Sally Carrol in the lead, her little mitten buried in his big fur gantlet. At the bottom of the chute was a long empty room of ice, with the ceiling so low that they had to stoop—and their hands were parted. Before she realized what he intended Harry had darted down one of the half-dozen glittering passages that opened into the room and was only a vague receding blot against the green shimmer.

"Harry!" she called.

"Come on!" he cried back.

She looked round the empty chamber; the rest of the party had evidently decided to go home, were already outside somewhere in the blundering snow. She hesitated and then darted in after Harry.

"Harry!" she shouted.

She had reached a turning-point thirty feet down; she heard a faint muffled answer far to the left, and with a touch of panic fled toward it. She passed another turning, two more yawning alleys.

"Harry!"

No answer. She started to run straight forward, and then turned like lightning and sped back the way she had come, enveloped in a sudden icy terror.

She reached a turn—was it here?—took the left and came to what should have been the outlet into the long, low room, but it was only another glittering passage with darkness at the end. She called again, but the walls gave back a flat, lifeless echo with no reverberations. Retracing her steps she turned another corner, this time following a wide passage. It was like the green lane between the parted waters of the Red Sea, like a damp vault connecting empty tombs.

She slipped a little now as she walked, for ice had formed on the bottom of her overshoes; she had to run her gloves along the half-slippery, half-sticky walls to keep her balance.

"Harry!"

Still no answer. The sound she made bounced mockingly down to the end of the passage.

Then on an instant the lights went out, and she was in complete darkness. She gave a small, frightened cry, and sank down into a cold little heap on the ice. She felt her left knee do something as she fell, but she scarcely noticed it as some deep terror far greater than any fear of being lost settled upon her. She was alone with this presence that came out of the North, the dreary loneliness that rose from ice-bound whalers in the Arctic seas, from smokeless, trackless wastes where were strewn the whitened bones of adventure. It was an icy breath of death; it was rolling down low across the land to clutch at her.

With a furious, despairing energy she rose again and started blindly down the darkness. She must get out. She might be lost in here for days, freeze to death and lie embedded in the ice like corpses she had read of, kept perfectly preserved until the melting of a glacier. Harry probably thought she had left with the others—he had gone by now; no one would know until late next day. She reached pitifully for the wall. Forty inches thick, they had said—forty inches thick!

"Oh!"

On both sides of her along the walls she felt things creeping, damp souls that haunted this palace, this town, this North.

"Oh, send somebody—send somebody!" she cried aloud.

Clark Darrow—he would understand; or Joe Ewing; she couldn't be left here to wander forever—to be frozen, heart, body, and soul. This her—this Sally Carrol! Why, she was a happy thing. She was a happy little girl. She liked warmth and summer and Dixie. These things were foreign—foreign.

"You're not crying," something said aloud. "You'll never cry any more. Your tears would just freeze; all tears freeze up here!"

She sprawled full length on the ice.

"Oh, God!" she faltered.

A long single file of minutes went by, and with a great weariness she felt her eyes closing. Then some one seemed to sit down near her and take her face in warm, soft hands. She looked up gratefully.

"Why, it's Margery Lee," she crooned softly to herself. "I knew you'd come." It really was Margery Lee, and she was just as Sally Carrol had known she would be, with a young, white brow, and wide, welcoming eyes, and a hoop-skirt of some soft material that was quite comforting to rest on.

"Margery Lee."

It was getting darker now and darker—all those tombstones ought to be repainted, sure enough, only that would spoil 'em, of course. Still, you ought to be able to see 'em.

Then after a succession of moments that went fast and then slow, but seemed to be ultimately resolving themselves into a multitude of blurred rays converging toward a pale-yellow sun, she heard a great cracking noise break her new-found stillness.

It was the sun, it was a light; a torch, and a torch beyond that, and another one, and voices; a face took flesh below the torch, heavy arms raised her, and she felt something on her cheek—it felt wet. Some one had seized her and was rubbing her face with snow. How ridiculous—with snow!

"Sally Carrol! Sally Carrol!"

It was Dangerous Dan McGrew; and two other faces she didn't know.

"Child, child! We've been looking for you two hours! Harry's half-crazy!"

Things came rushing back into place—the singing, the torches, the great shout of the marching clubs. She squirmed in Patton's arms and gave a long low cry.

"Oh, I want to get out of here! I'm going back home. Take me home"
—her voice rose to a scream that sent a chill to Harry's heart as he came

racing down the next passage—"to-morrow!" she cried with delirious, un-restrained passion—"To-morrow! To-morrow! To-morrow!"

· VI ·

THE WEALTH of golden sunlight poured a quite enervating yet oddly comforting heat over the house where day long it faced the dusty stretch of road. Two birds were making a great to-do in a cool spot found among the branches of a tree next door, and down the street a colored woman was announcing herself melodiously as a purveyor of strawberries. It was April afternoon.

Sally Carrol Happer, resting her chin on her arm, and her arm on an old window-seat, gazed sleepily down over the spangled dust whence the heat waves were rising for the first time this spring. She was watching a very ancient Ford turn a perilous corner and rattle and groan to a jolting stop at the end of the walk. She made no sound, and in a minute a strident familiar whistle rent the air. Sally Carrol smiled and blinked.

"Good mawnin'."

A head appeared tortuously from under the car-top below.

"'Tain't mawnin', Sally Carrol."

"Sure enough!" she said in affected surprise. "I guess maybe not."

"What you doin'?"

"Eatin' green peach. 'Spect to die any minute."

Clark twisted himself a last impossible notch to get a view of her face.

"Water's warm as a kettla steam, Sally Carrol. Wanta go swimmin'?"

"Hate to move," sighed Sally Carrol lazily, "but I reckon so."

THE OFFSHORE PIRATE

♦

"The Offshore Pirate" (29 May 1920) was Fitzgerald's third Saturday Evening Post *appearance during that month and demonstrates his rapid development as a versatile fiction writer. It is the first story that develops Fitzgerald's recurring plot idea of a heroine won by her lover's performance of an extraordinary deed.*

The story had originally ended with the weak explanation that it was all Ardita's dream. Fitzgerald rewrote the conclusion to emphasize the storyness of the story: "The last line takes Mr. Lorimer [the editor of the Post*] at his word. Its one of the best lines I've ever written." "The Offshore Pirate" was collected in* Flappers and Philosophers.

♦

THIS UNLIKELY story begins on a sea that was a blue dream, as colorful as blue-silk stockings, and beneath a sky as blue as the irises of children's eyes. From the western half of the sky the sun was shying little golden disks at the sea—if you gazed intently enough you could see them skip from wave tip to wave tip until they joined a broad collar of golden coin that was collecting half a mile out and would eventually be a dazzling sunset. About half-way between the Florida shore and the golden collar a white steam-yacht, very young and graceful, was riding at anchor and under a blue-and-white awning aft a yellow-haired girl reclined in a wicker settee reading The Revolt of the Angels, by Anatole France.

She was about nineteen, slender and supple, with a spoiled alluring mouth and quick gray eyes full of a radiant curiosity. Her feet, stockingless, and adorned rather than clad in blue-satin slippers which swung nonchalantly from her toes, were perched on the arm of a settee adjoining the one she occupied. And as she read she intermittently regaled herself by a faint application to her tongue of a half-lemon that she held in her hand. The other half, sucked dry, lay on the deck at her feet and rocked very gently to and fro at the almost imperceptible motion of the tide.

The second half-lemon was well-nigh pulpless and the golden collar had grown astonishing in width, when suddenly the drowsy silence which enveloped the yacht was broken by the sound of heavy footsteps and an elderly man topped with orderly gray hair and clad in a white-flannel suit appeared at the head of the companionway. There he paused for a moment until his eyes became accustomed to the sun, and then seeing the girl under the awning he uttered a long even grunt of disapproval.

If he had intended thereby to obtain a rise of any sort he was doomed to disappointment. The girl calmly turned over two pages, turned back one, raised the lemon mechanically to tasting distance, and then very faintly but quite unmistakably yawned.

"Ardita!" said the gray-haired man sternly.

Ardita uttered a small sound indicating nothing.

"Ardita!" he repeated. "Ardita!"

Ardita raised the lemon languidly, allowing three words to slip out before it reached her tongue.

"Oh, shut up."

"Ardita!"

"What?"

"Will you listen to me—or will I have to get a servant to hold you while I talk to you?"

The lemon descended slowly and scornfully.

"Put it in writing."

"Will you have the decency to close that abominable book and discard that damn lemon for two minutes?"

"Oh, can't you lemme alone for a second?"

"Ardita, I have just received a telephone message from the shore——"

"Telephone?" She showed for the first time a faint interest.

"Yes, it was——"

"Do you mean to say," she interrupted wonderingly, " 'at they let you run a wire out here?"

"Yes, and just now——"

"Won't other boats bump into it?"

"No. It's run along the bottom. Five min——"

"Well, I'll be darned! Gosh! Science is golden or something—isn't it?"

"Will you let me say what I started to?"

"Shoot!"

"Well, it seems—well, I am up here——" He paused and swallowed several times distractedly. "Oh, yes. Young woman, Colonel Moreland has called up again to ask me to be sure to bring you in to dinner. His son Toby has come all the way from New York to meet you and he's invited several other young people. For the last time, will you——"

"No," said Ardita shortly, "I won't. I came along on this darn cruise with the one idea of going to Palm Beach, and you knew it, and I absolutely refuse to meet any darn old colonel or any darn young Toby or any darn old young people or to set foot in any other darn old town in this crazy state. So you either take me to Palm Beach or else shut up and go away."

"Very well. This is the last straw. In your infatuation for this man—a man who is notorious for his excesses, a man your father would not have allowed to so much as mention your name—you have reflected the demi-monde rather than the circles in which you have presumably grown up. From now on——"

"I know," interrupted Ardita ironically, "from now on you go your way and I go mine. I've heard that story before. You know I'd like nothing better."

"From now on," he announced grandiloquently, "you are no niece of mine. I——"

"O-o-o-oh!" The cry was wrung from Ardita with the agony of a lost soul. "Will you stop boring me! Will you go 'way! Will you jump overboard and drown! Do you want me to throw this book at you!"

"If you dare do any——"

Smack! The Revolt of the Angels sailed through the air, missed its target by the length of a short nose, and bumped cheerfully down the companionway.

The gray-haired man made an instinctive step backward and then two cautious steps forward. Ardita jumped to her five feet four and started at him defiantly, her gray eyes blazing.

"Keep off!"

"How dare you!" he cried.

"Because I darn please!"

"You've grown unbearable! Your disposition——"

"You've made me that way! No child ever has a bad disposition unless it's her family's fault! Whatever I am, you did it."

Muttering something under his breath her uncle turned and, walking forward, called in a loud voice for the launch. Then he returned to the awning, where Ardita had again seated herself and resumed her attention to the lemon.

"I am going ashore," he said slowly. "I will be out again at nine o'clock to-night. When I return we will start back to New York, where I shall turn you over to your aunt for the rest of your natural, or rather unnatural, life."

He paused and looked at her, and then all at once something in the utter childishness of her beauty seemed to puncture his anger like an inflated tire, and render him helpless, uncertain, utterly fatuous.

"Ardita," he said not unkindly, "I'm no fool. I've been round. I know men. And, child, confirmed libertines don't reform until they're tired—and then they're not themselves—they're husks of themselves." He looked at her as if expecting agreement, but receiving no sight or sound of it he continued. "Perhaps the man loves you—that's possible. He's loved many women and he'll love many more. Less than a month ago, one month, Ardita, he was involved in a notorious affair with that red-haired woman, Mimi Merril; promised to give her the diamond bracelet that the Czar of Russia gave his mother. You know—you read the papers."

"Thrilling scandals by an anxious uncle," yawned Ardita. "Have it filmed. Wicked clubman making eyes at virtuous flapper. Virtuous flapper conclusively vamped by his lurid past. Plans to meet him at Palm Beach. Foiled by anxious uncle."

"Will you tell me why the devil you want to marry him?"

"I'm sure I couldn't say," said Ardita shortly. "Maybe because he's the only man I know, good or bad, who has an imagination and the courage of his convictions. Maybe it's to get away from the young fools that spend their vacuous hours pursuing me around the country. But as for the famous Russian bracelet, you can set your mind at rest on that score. He's going to give it to me at Palm Beach—if you'll show a little intelligence."

"How about the—red-haired woman?"

"He hasn't seen her for six months," she said angrily. "Don't you suppose I have enough pride to see to that? Don't you know by this time that I can do any darn thing with any darn man I want to?"

She put her chin in the air like the statue of France Aroused, and then spoiled the pose somewhat by raising the lemon for action.

"Is it the Russian bracelet that fascinates you?"

"No, I'm merely trying to give you the sort of argument that would appeal to your intelligence. And I wish you'd go 'way," she said, her temper rising again. "You know I never change my mind. You've been boring me for three days until I'm about to go crazy. I won't go ashore! Won't! Do you hear? Won't!"

"Very well," he said, "and you won't go to Palm Beach either. Of all the selfish, spoiled, uncontrolled, disagreeable, impossible girls I have——"

Splush! The half-lemon caught him in the neck. Simultaneously came a hail from over the side.

"The launch is ready, Mr. Farnam."

Too full of words and rage to speak, Mr. Farnam cast one utterly condemning glance at his niece and, turning, ran swiftly down the ladder.

· II ·

FIVE O'CLOCK rolled down from the sun and plumped soundlessly into the sea. The golden collar widened into a glittering island; and a faint breeze that had been playing with the edges of the awning and swaying one of the dangling blue slippers became suddenly freighted with song. It was a chorus of men in close harmony and in perfect rhythm to an accompanying sound of oars cleaving the blue waters. Ardita lifted her head and listened.

> *"Carrots and peas,*
> *Beans on their knees,*
> *Pigs in the seas,*
> *Lucky fellows!*
> *Blow us a breeze,*
> *Blow us a breeze,*
> *Blow us a breeze,*
> *With your bellows."*

Ardita's brow wrinkled in astonishment. Sitting very still she listened eagerly as the chorus took up a second verse.

> *"Onions and beans,*
> *Marshalls and Deans,*
> *Goldbergs and Greens*
> *And Costellos.*
> *Blow us a breeze,*
> *Blow us a breeze,*
> *Blow us a breeze,*
> *With your bellows."*

With an exclamation she tossed her book to the deck, where it sprawled at a straddle, and hurried to the rail. Fifty feet away a large rowboat was approaching containing seven men, six of them rowing and one standing up in the stern keeping time to their song with an orchestra leader's baton.

> *"Oysters and rocks,*
> *Sawdust and socks,*
> *Who could make clocks*
> *Out of cellos?—"*

The leader's eyes suddenly rested on Ardita, who was leaning over the rail spellbound with curiosity. He made a quick movement with his baton and the singing instantly ceased. She saw that he was the only white man in the boat—the six rowers were negroes.

"Narcissus ahoy!" he called politely.

"What's the idea of all the discord?" demanded Ardita cheerfully. "Is this the varsity crew from the county nut farm?"

By this time the boat was scraping the side of the yacht and a great hulking negro in the bow turned around and grasped the ladder. Thereupon the leader left his position in the stern and before Ardita had realized his intention he ran up the ladder and stood breathless before her on the deck.

"The women and children will be spared!" he said briskly. "All crying babies will be immediately drowned and all males put in double irons!"

Digging her hands excitedly down into the pockets of her dress Ardita stared at him, speechless with astonishment.

He was a young man with a scornful mouth and the bright blue eyes of a healthy baby set in a dark sensitive face. His hair was pitch black, damp and curly—the hair of a Grecian statue gone brunette. He was trimly built, trimly dressed, and graceful as an agile quarter-back.

"Well, I'll be a son of a gun!" she said dazedly.

They eyed each other coolly.

"Do you surrender the ship?"

"Is this an outburst of wit?" demanded Ardita. "Are you an idiot—or just being initiated to some fraternity?"

"I asked you if you surrendered the ship."

"I thought the country was dry," said Ardita disdainfully. "Have you been drinking finger-nail enamel? You better get off this yacht!"

"What?" The young man's voice expressed incredulity.

"Get off the yacht! You heard me!"

He looked at her for a moment as if considering what she had said.

"No," said his scornful mouth slowly; "no, I won't get off the yacht. You can get off if you wish."

Going to the rail he gave a curt command and immediately the crew of the rowboat scrambled up the ladder and ranged themselves in line before him, a coal-black and burly darky at one end and a miniature mulatto of four feet nine at the other. They seemed to be uniformly dressed in some sort of blue costume ornamented with dust, mud, and tatters; over the shoulder of each was slung a small, heavy-looking white sack, and under their arms they carried large black cases apparently containing musical instruments.

"'Ten-*shun!*" commanded the young man, snapping his own heels together crisply. "Right *driss!* Front! Step out here, Babe!"

The smallest negro took a quick step forward and saluted.

"Yas-suh!"

"Take command, go down below, catch the crew and tie 'em up—all except the engineer. Bring him up to me. Oh, and pile those bags by the rail there."

"Yas-suh!"

Babe saluted again and wheeling about motioned for the five others to gather about him. Then after a short whispered consultation they all filed noiselessly down the companionway.

"Now," said the young man cheerfully to Ardita, who had witnessed this last scene in withering silence, "if you will swear on your honor as a flapper—which probably isn't worth much—that you'll keep that spoiled little mouth of yours tight shut for forty-eight hours, you can row yourself ashore in our rowboat."

"Otherwise what?"

"Otherwise you're going to sea in a ship."

With a little sigh as for a crisis well passed, the young man sank into the settee Ardita had lately vacated and stretched his arms lazily. The corners of his mouth relaxed appreciatively as he looked round at the rich striped awning, the polished brass, and the luxurious fittings of the deck. His eye fell on the book, and then on the exhausted lemon.

"Hm," he said, "Stonewall Jackson claimed that lemon-juice cleared his head. Your head feel pretty clear?"

Ardita disdained to answer.

"Because inside of five minutes you'll have to make a clear decision whether it's go or stay."

He picked up the book and opened it curiously.

"The Revolt of the Angels. Sounds pretty good. French, eh?" He stared at her with new interest. "You French?"

"No."

"What's your name?"

"Farnam."

"Farnam what?"

"Ardita Farnam."

"Well, Ardita, no use standing up there and chewing out the insides of your mouth. You ought to break those nervous habits while you're young. Come over here and sit down."

Ardita took a carved jade case from her pocket, extracted a cigarette and lit it with a conscious coolness, though she knew her hand was trembling a little; then she crossed over with her supple, swinging walk, and sitting down in the other settee blew a mouthful of smoke at the awning.

"You can't get me off this yacht," she said steadily; "and you haven't got very much sense if you think you'll get far with it. My uncle'll have wirelesses zigzagging all over this ocean by half past six."

"Hm."

She looked quickly at his face, caught anxiety stamped there plainly in the faintest depression of the mouth's corners.

"It's all the same to me," she said, shrugging her shoulders. " 'Tisn't my yacht. I don't mind going for a coupla hours' cruise. I'll even lend you that book so you'll have something to read on the revenue boat that takes you up to Sing Sing."

He laughed scornfully.

"If that's advice you needn't bother. This is part of a plan arranged before I ever knew this yacht existed. If it hadn't been this one it'd have been the next one we passed anchored along the coast."

"Who are you?" demanded Ardita suddenly. "And what are you?"

"You've decided not to go ashore?"

"I never even faintly considered it."

"We're generally known," he said, "all seven of us, as Curtis Carlyle and his Six Black Buddies, late of the Winter Garden and the Midnight Frolic."

"You're singers?"

"We were until to-day. At present, due to those white bags you see there, we're fugitives from justice, and if the reward offered for our capture hasn't by this time reached twenty thousand dollars I miss my guess."

"What's in the bags?" asked Ardita curiously.

"Well," he said, "for the present we'll call it—mud—Florida mud."

· III ·

WITHIN TEN MINUTES after Curtis Carlyle's interview with a very frightened engineer the yacht Narcissus was under way, steaming south through a balmy tropical twilight. The little mulatto, Babe, who seemed to have Carlyle's implicit confidence, took full command of the situation. Mr. Farnam's valet and the chef, the only members of the crew on board except the engineer, having shown fight, were now reconsidering, strapped securely to their bunks below. Trombone Mose, the biggest negro, was set busy with a can of paint obliterating the name Narcissus from the bow, and substituting the name Hula Hula, and the others congregated aft and became intently involved in a game of craps.

Having given orders for a meal to be prepared and served on deck at seven-thirty, Carlyle rejoined Ardita, and, sinking back into his settee, half closed his eyes and fell into a state of profound abstraction.

Ardita scrutinized him carefully—and classed him immediately as a romantic figure. He gave the effect of towering self-confidence erected on a slight foundation—just under the surface of each of his decisions she discerned a hesitancy that was in decided contrast to the arrogant curl of his lips.

"He's not like me," she thought. "There's a difference somewhere."

Being a supreme egotist Ardita frequently thought about herself; never having had her egotism disputed she did it entirely naturally and with no detraction from her unquestioned charm. Though she was nineteen she gave the effect of a high-spirited precocious child, and in the present glow of her youth and beauty all the men and women she had known were but driftwood on the ripples of her temperament. She had met other egotists—in fact she found that selfish people bored her rather less than unselfish people—but as yet there had not been one she had not eventually defeated and brought to her feet.

But though she recognized an egotist in the settee next to her, she felt none of that usual shutting of doors in her mind which meant clearing ship for action; on the contrary her instinct told her that this man was somehow completely pregnable and quite defenseless. When Ardita defied convention—and of late it had been her chief amusement—it was from an intense desire to be herself, and she felt that this man, on the contrary, was preoccupied with his own defiance.

She was much more interested in him than she was in her own situation, which affected her as the prospect of a matinée might affect a ten-year-old child. She had implicit confidence in her ability to take care of herself under any and all circumstances.

The night deepened. A pale new moon smiled misty-eyed upon the sea, and as the shore faded dimly out and dark clouds were blown like leaves along the far horizon a great haze of moonshine suddenly bathed the yacht and spread an avenue of glittering mail in her swift path. From time to time there was the bright flare of a match as one of them lighted a cigarette, but except for the low undertone of the throbbing engines and the even wash of the waves about the stern the yacht was quiet as a dream boat star-bound through the heavens. Round them flowed the smell of the night sea, bringing with it an infinite languor.

Carlyle broke the silence at last.

"Lucky girl," he sighed, "I've always wanted to be rich—and buy all this beauty."

Ardita yawned.

"I'd rather be you," she said frankly.

"You would—for about a day. But you do seem to possess a lot of nerve for a flapper."

"I wish you wouldn't call me that."

"Beg your pardon."

"As to nerve," she continued slowly, "it's my one redeeming feature. I'm not afraid of anything in heaven or earth."

"Hm, I am."

"To be afraid," said Ardita, "a person has either to be very great and strong—or else a coward. I'm neither." She paused for a moment, and eagerness crept into her tone. "But I want to talk about you. What on earth have you done—and how did you do it?"

"Why?" he demanded cynically. "Going to write a movie about me?"

"Go on," she urged. "Lie to me by the moonlight. Do a fabulous story."

A negro appeared, switched on a string of small lights under the awning, and began setting the wicker table for supper. And while they ate cold sliced chicken, salad, artichokes, and strawberry jam from the plentiful larder below, Carlyle began to talk, hesitatingly at first, but eagerly as he saw she was interested. Ardita scarcely touched her food as she watched his dark young face—handsome, ironic, faintly ineffectual.

He began life as a poor kid in a Tennessee town, he said, so poor that his people were the only white family in their street. He never remembered any white children—but there were inevitably a dozen pickaninnies streaming in his trail, passionate admirers whom he kept in tow by the vividness of his imagination and the amount of trouble he was always getting them in and out of. And it seemed that this association diverted a rather unusual musical gift into a strange channel.

There had been a colored woman named Belle Pope Calhoun who played the piano at parties given for white children—nice white children that would have passed Curtis Carlyle with a sniff. But the ragged little "poh white" used to sit beside her piano by the hour and try to get in an alto with one of those kazoos that boys hum through. Before he was thirteen he was picking up a living teasing ragtime out of a battered violin in little cafés round Nashville. Eight years later the ragtime craze hit the country, and he took six darkies on the Orpheum circuit. Five of them were boys he had grown up with; the other was the little mulatto, Babe Divine, who was a wharf nigger round New York, and long before that a plantation hand in Bermuda, until he stuck an eight-inch stiletto in his master's back. Almost before Carlyle realized his good fortune he was on Broadway, with offers of engagements on all sides, and more money than he had ever dreamed of.

It was about then that a change began in his whole attitude, a rather curious, embittering change. It was when he realized that he was spending the golden years of his life gibbering round a stage with a lot of black men. His act was good of its kind—three trombones, three saxophones, and Carlyle's flute—and it was his own peculiar sense of rhythm that made all the difference; but he began to grow strangely sensitive about it, began to hate the thought of appearing, dreaded it from day to day.

They were making money—each contract he signed called for more—but when he went to managers and told them that he wanted to separate from his sextet and go on as a regular pianist, they laughed at him and told him he was crazy—it would be an artistic suicide. He used to laugh afterward at the phrase "artistic suicide." They all used it.

Half a dozen times they played at private dances at three thousand dollars a night, and it seemed as if these crystallized all his distaste for his mode of livelihood. They took place in clubs and houses that he couldn't have gone into in the daytime. After all, he was merely playing the rôle of the eternal monkey, a sort of sublimated chorus man. He was sick of the very smell of the theatre, of powder and rouge and the chatter of the greenroom, and the patronizing approval of the boxes. He couldn't put his heart into it any more. The idea of a slow approach to the luxury of leisure drove him wild. He was, of course, progressing toward it, but, like a child, eating his ice-cream so slowly that he couldn't taste it at all.

He wanted to have a lot of money and time, and opportunity to read and play, and the sort of men and women round him that he could never have—the kind who, if they thought of him at all, would have considered him rather contemptible; in short he wanted all those things which he was beginning to lump under the general head of aristocracy, an aristocracy which it seemed almost any money could buy except money made as he was making it. He was twenty-five then, without family or education or any promise that he would succeed in a business career. He began speculating wildly, and within three weeks he had lost every cent he had saved.

Then the war came. He went to Plattsburg, and even there his profession followed him. A brigadier-general called him up to headquarters and told him he could serve the country better as a band leader—so he spent the war entertaining celebrities behind the line with a headquarters band. It was not so bad—except that when the infantry came limping back from the trenches he wanted to be one of them. The sweat and mud they wore seemed only one of those ineffable symbols of aristocracy that were forever eluding him.

"It was the private dances that did it. After I came back from the war the old routine started. We had an offer from a syndicate of Florida hotels. It was only a question of time then."

He broke off and Ardita looked at him expectantly, but he shook his head.

"No," he said, "I'm not going to tell you about it. I'm enjoying it too much, and I'm afraid I'd lose a little of that enjoyment if I shared it with any one else. I want to hang on to those few breathless, heroic moments when I stood out before them all and let them know I was more than a damn bobbing, squawking clown."

From up forward came suddenly the low sound of singing. The negroes had gathered together on the deck and their voices rose together in a haunting melody that soared in poignant harmonics toward the moon. And Ardita listened in enchantment.

> "Oh down—
>   Oh down,
> Mammy wanna take me downa milky way,
> Oh down—
>   Oh down,
> Pappy say to-morra-a-a-ah!
> But mammy say to-day,
> Yes—mammy say to-day!"

Carlyle sighed and was silent for a moment, looking up at the gathered host of stars blinking like arc-lights in the warm sky. The negroes' song had died away to a plaintive humming and it seemed as if minute by minute the brightness and the great silence were increasing until he could almost hear the midnight toilet of the mermaids as they combed their silver dripping curls under the moon and gossiped to each other of the fine wrecks they lived in on the green opalescent avenues below.

"You see," said Carlyle softly, "this is the beauty I want. Beauty has got to be astonishing, astounding—it's got to burst in on you like a dream, like the exquisite eyes of a girl."

He turned to her, but she was silent.

"You see, don't you, Anita—I mean, Ardita?"

Again she made no answer. She had been sound asleep for some time.

· I V ·

IN THE DENSE sun-flooded noon of next day a spot in the sea before them resolved casually into a green-and-gray islet, apparently composed of a great granite cliff at its northern end which slanted south through a mile of vivid coppice and grass to a sandy beach melting lazily into the surf. When Ardita, reading in her favorite seat, came to the last page of The Revolt of the Angels, and slamming the book shut looked up and saw it, she gave a little cry of delight, and called to Carlyle, who was standing moodily by the rail.

"Is this it? Is this where you're going?"

Carlyle shrugged his shoulders carelessly.

"You've got me." He raised his voice and called up to the acting skipper: "Oh, Babe, is this your island?"

The mulatto's miniature head appeared from round the corner of the deck-house.

"Yas-suh! This yeah's it."

Carlyle joined Ardita.

"Looks sort of sporting, doesn't it?"

"Yes," she agreed; "but it doesn't look big enough to be much of a hiding-place."

"You still putting your faith in those wirelesses your uncle was going to have zigzagging round?"

"No," said Ardita frankly. "I'm all for you. I'd really like to see you make a get-away."

He laughed.

"You're our Lady Luck. Guess we'll have to keep you with us as a mascot—for the present, anyway."

"You couldn't very well ask me to swim back," she said coolly. "If you do I'm going to start writing dime novels founded on that interminable history of your life you gave me last night."

He flushed and stiffened slightly.

"I'm very sorry I bored you."

"Oh, you didn't—until just at the end with some story about how furious you were because you couldn't dance with the ladies you played music for."

He rose angrily.

"You have got a darn mean little tongue."

"Excuse me," she said, melting into laughter, "but I'm not used to having men regale me with the story of their life ambitions—especially if they've lived such deathly platonic lives."

"Why? What do men usually regale you with?"

"Oh, they talk about me," she yawned. "They tell me I'm the spirit of youth and beauty."

"What do you tell them?"

"Oh, I agree quietly."

"Does every man you meet tell you he loves you?"

Ardita nodded.

"Why shouldn't he? All life is just a progression toward, and then a recession from, one phrase—'I love you.' "

Carlyle laughed and sat down.

"That's very true. That's—that's not bad. Did you make that up?"

"Yes—or rather I found it out. It doesn't mean anything especially. It's just clever."

"It's the sort of remark," he said gravely, "that's typical of your class."

"Oh," she interrupted impatiently, "don't start that lecture on aristocracy again! I distrust people who can be intense at this hour in the morning. It's a mild form of insanity—a sort of breakfast-food jag. Morning's the time to sleep, swim, and be careless."

Ten minutes later they had swung round in a wide circle as if to approach the island from the north.

"There's a trick somewhere," commented Ardita thoughtfully. "He can't mean just to anchor up against this cliff."

They were heading straight in now toward the solid rock, which must have been well over a hundred feet tall, and not until they were within fifty yards of it did Ardita see their objective. Then she clapped her hands in delight. There was a break in the cliff entirely hidden by a curious overlapping of rock, and through this break the yacht entered and very slowly traversed a narrow channel of crystal-clear water between high gray walls. Then they were riding at anchor in a miniature world of green and gold, a gilded bay smooth as glass and set round with tiny palms, the whole resembling the mirror lakes and twig trees that children set up in sand piles.

"Not so darned bad!" cried Carlyle excitedly. "I guess that little coon knows his way round this corner of the Atlantic."

His exuberance was contagious, and Ardita became quite jubilant.

"It's an absolutely sure-fire hiding-place!"

"Lordy, yes! It's the sort of island you read about."

The rowboat was lowered into the golden lake and they pulled ashore.

"Come on," said Carlyle as they landed in the slushy sand, "we'll go exploring."

The fringe of palms was in turn ringed in by a round mile of flat, sandy country. They followed it south and brushing through a farther rim of tropical vegetation came out on a pearl-gray virgin beach where Ardita kicked off her brown golf shoes—she seemed to have permanently abandoned stockings—and went wading. Then they sauntered back to the yacht, where the indefatigable Babe had luncheon ready for them. He had posted a lookout on the high cliff to the north to watch the sea on both sides, though he doubted if the entrance to the cliff was generally known—he had never even seen a map on which the island was marked.

"What's its name," asked Ardita—"the island, I mean?"

"No name 'tall," chuckled Babe. "Reckin she jus' island, 'at's all."

In the late afternoon they sat with their backs against great boulders on the highest part of the cliff and Carlyle sketched for her his vague plans. He was sure they were hot after him by this time. The total proceeds of the coup he had pulled off, and concerning which he still refused to enlighten her, he estimated as just under a million dollars. He counted on lying up here several weeks and then setting off southward, keeping well outside the usual channels of travel, rounding the Horn and heading for Callao, in Peru. The details of coaling and provisioning he was leaving entirely to Babe, who, it seemed, had sailed these seas in every capacity from cabin-boy aboard a coffee trader to virtual first mate on a Brazilian pirate craft, whose skipper had long since been hung.

"If he'd been white he'd have been king of South America long ago," said Carlyle emphatically. "When it comes to intelligence he makes Booker T. Washington look like a moron. He's got the guile of every race and nationality whose blood is in his veins, and that's half a dozen or I'm a liar. He worships me because I'm the only man in the world who can play better ragtime than he can. We used to sit together on the wharfs down on the New York water-front, he with a bassoon and me with an oboe, and we'd blend minor keys in African harmonics a thousand years old until the rats would crawl up the posts and sit round groaning and squeaking like dogs will in front of a phonograph."

Ardita roared.

"How you can tell 'em!"

Carlyle grinned.

"I swear that's the gos——"

"What you going to do when you get to Callao?" she interrupted.

"Take ship for India. I want to be a rajah. I mean it. My idea is to go up into Afghanistan somewhere, buy up a palace and a reputation, and then after about five years appear in England with a foreign accent and a mysterious past. But India first. Do you know, they say that all the gold in the world drifts very gradually back to India. Something fascinating about that to me. And I want leisure to read—an immense amount."

"How about after that?"

"Then," he answered defiantly, "comes aristocracy. Laugh if you want to—but at least you'll have to admit that I know what I want—which I imagine is more than you do."

"On the contrary," contradicted Ardita, reaching in her pocket for her cigarette case, "when I met you I was in the midst of a great uproar of all my friends and relatives because I did know what I wanted."

"What was it?"

"A man."

He started.

"You mean you were engaged?"

"After a fashion. If you hadn't come aboard I had every intention of slipping ashore yesterday evening—how long ago it seems—and meeting him in Palm Beach. He's waiting there for me with a bracelet that once belonged to Catharine of Russia. Now don't mutter anything about aristocracy," she put in quickly. "I liked him simply because he had had an imagination and the utter courage of his convictions."

"But your family disapproved, eh?"

"What there is of it—only a silly uncle and a sillier aunt. It seems he got into some scandal with a red-haired woman named Mimi something—it was frightfully exaggerated, he said, and men don't lie to me—and anyway I didn't care what he'd done; it was the future that counted. And I'd see to that. When a man's in love with me he doesn't care for other amusements. I told him to drop her like a hot cake, and he did."

"I feel rather jealous," said Carlyle, frowning—and then he laughed. "I guess I'll just keep you along with us until we get to Callao. Then I'll lend you enough money to get back to the States. By that time you'll have had a chance to think that gentleman over a little more."

"Don't talk to me like that!" fired up Ardita. "I won't tolerate the parental attitude from anybody! Do you understand me?"

He chuckled and then stopped, rather abashed, as her cold anger seemed to fold him about and chill him.

"I'm sorry," he offered uncertainly.

"Oh, don't apologize! I can't stand men who say 'I'm sorry' in that manly, reserved tone. Just shut up!"

A pause ensued, a pause which Carlyle found rather awkward, but which Ardita seemed not to notice at all as she sat contentedly enjoying her cigarette and gazing out at the shining sea. After a minute she crawled out on the rock and lay with her face over the edge looking down. Carlyle, watching her, reflected how it seemed impossible for her to assume an ungraceful attitude.

"Oh, look!" she cried. "There's a lot of sort of ledges down there. Wide ones of all different heights."

He joined her and together they gazed down the dizzy height.

"We'll go swimming to-night!" she said excitedly. "By moonlight."

"Wouldn't you rather go in at the beach on the other end?"

"Not a chance. I like to dive. You can use my uncle's bathing-suit, only it'll fit you like a gunny sack, because he's a very flabby man. I've got a one-piece affair that's shocked the natives all along the Atlantic coast from Biddeford Pool to St. Augustine."

"I suppose you're a shark."

"Yes, I'm pretty good. And I look cute too. A sculptor up at Rye last summer told me my calves were worth five hundred dollars."

There didn't seem to be any answer to this, so Carlyle was silent, permitting himself only a discreet interior smile.

· V ·

WHEN THE NIGHT crept down in shadowy blue and silver they threaded the shimmering channel in the rowboat and, tying it to a jutting rock, began climbing the cliff together. The first shelf was ten feet up, wide, and furnishing a natural diving platform. There they sat down in the bright moonlight and watched the faint incessant surge of the waters, almost stilled now as the tide set seaward.

"Are you happy?" he asked suddenly.

She nodded.

"Always happy near the sea. You know," she went on, "I've been thinking all day that you and I are somewhat alike. We're both rebels—only for different reasons. Two years ago, when I was just eighteen, and you were——"

"Twenty-five."

"——well, we were both conventional successes. I was an utterly devastating débutante and you were a prosperous musician just commissioned in the army——"

"Gentleman by act of Congress," he put in ironically.

"Well, at any rate, we both fitted. If our corners were not rubbed off they were at least pulled in. But deep in us both was something that made us require more for happiness. I didn't know what I wanted. I went from man to man, restless, impatient, month by month getting less acquiescent and more dissatisfied. I used to sit sometimes chewing at the insides of my mouth and thinking I was going crazy—I had a frightful sense of transiency. I wanted things now—now—now! Here I was—beautiful—I am, aren't I?"

"Yes," agreed Carlyle tentatively.

Ardita rose suddenly.

"Wait a second. I want to try this delightful-looking sea."

She walked to the end of the ledge and shot out over the sea, doubling

up in mid-air and then straightening out and entering the water straight as
a blade in a perfect jack-knife dive.

In a minute her voice floated up to him.

"You see, I used to read all day and most of the night. I began to resent
society——"

"Come on up here," he interrupted. "What on earth are you doing?"

"Just floating round on my back. I'll be up in a minute. Let me tell you.
The only thing I enjoyed was shocking people; wearing something quite
impossible and quite charming to a fancy-dress party, going round with the
fastest men in New York, and getting into some of the most hellish scrapes
imaginable."

The sounds of splashing mingled with her words, and then he heard her
hurried breathing as she began climbing up the side to the ledge.

"Go on in!" she called.

Obediently he rose and dived. When he emerged, dripping, and made the
climb he found that she was no longer on the ledge, but after a frightened
second he heard her light laughter from another shelf ten feet up. There he
joined her and they both sat quietly for a moment, their arms clasped round
their knees, panting a little from the climb.

"The family were wild," she said suddenly. "They tried to marry me off.
And then when I'd begun to feel that after all life was scarcely worth living
I found something"—her eyes went skyward exultantly—"I found some-
thing!"

Carlyle waited and her words came with a rush.

"Courage—just that; courage as a rule of life, and something to cling to
always. I began to build up this enormous faith in myself. I began to see
that in all my idols in the past some manifestation of courage had unconsciously been the thing that attracted me. I began separating courage from
the other things of life. All sorts of courage—the beaten, bloody prize-
fighter coming up for more—I used to make men take me to prize-fights;
the déclassé woman sailing through a nest of cats and looking at them as if
they were mud under her feet; the liking what you like always; the utter
disregard for other people's opinions—just to live as I liked always and to
die in my own way— Did you bring up the cigarettes?"

He handed one over and held a match for her silently.

"Still," Ardita continued, "the men kept gathering—old men and young
men, my mental and physical inferiors, most of them, but all intensely
desiring to have me—to own this rather magnificent proud tradition I'd
built up round me. Do you see?"

"Sort of. You never were beaten and you never apologized."

"Never!"

She sprang to the edge, poised for a moment like a crucified figure against the sky; then describing a dark parabola plunked without a slash between two silver ripples twenty feet below.

Her voice floated up to him again.

"And courage to me meant ploughing through that dull gray mist that comes down on life—not only overriding people and circumstances but overriding the bleakness of living. A sort of insistence on the value of life and the worth of transient things."

She was climbing up now, and at her last words her head, with the damp yellow hair slicked symmetrically back, appeared on his level.

"All very well," objected Carlyle. "You can call it courage, but your courage is really built, after all, on a pride of birth. You were bred to that defiant attitude. On my gray days even courage is one of the things that's gray and lifeless."

She was sitting near the edge, hugging her knees and gazing abstractedly at the white moon; he was farther back, crammed like a grotesque god into a niche in the rock.

"I don't want to sound like Pollyanna," she began, "but you haven't grasped me yet. My courage is faith—faith in the eternal resilience of me —that joy'll come back, and hope and spontaneity. And I feel that till it does I've got to keep my lips shut and my chin high, and my eyes wide— not necessarily any silly smiling. Oh, I've been through hell without a whine quite often—and the female hell is deadlier than the male."

"But supposing," suggested Carlyle, "that before joy and hope and all that came back the curtain was drawn on you for good?"

Ardita rose, and going to the wall climbed with some difficulty to the next ledge, another ten or fifteen feet above.

"Why," she called back, "then I'd have won!"

He edged out till he could see her.

"Better not dive from there! You'll break your back," he said quickly.

She laughed.

"Not I!"

Slowly she spread her arms and stood there swan-like, radiating a pride in her young perfection that lit a warm glow in Carlyle's heart.

"We're going through the black air with our arms wide," she called, "and our feet straight out behind like a dolphin's tail, and we're going to think we'll never hit the silver down there till suddenly it'll be all warm round us and full of little kissing, caressing waves."

Then she was in the air, and Carlyle involuntarily held his breath. He had not realized that the dive was nearly forty feet. It seemed an eternity before he heard the swift compact sound as she reached the sea.

And it was with his glad sigh of relief when her light watery laughter curled up the side of the cliff and into his anxious ears that he knew he loved her.

· VI ·

TIME, having no axe to grind, showered down upon them three days of afternoons. When the sun cleared the port-hole of Ardita's cabin an hour after dawn she rose cheerily, donned her bathing-suit, and went up on deck. The negroes would leave their work when they saw her, and crowd, chuckling and chattering, to the rail as she floated, an agile minnow, on and under the surface of the clear water. Again in the cool of the afternoon she would swim—and loll and smoke with Carlyle upon the cliff; or else they would lie on their sides in the sands of the southern beach, talking little, but watching the day fade colorfully and tragically into the infinite languor of a tropical evening.

And with the long, sunny hours Ardita's idea of the episode as incidental, madcap, a sprig of romance in a desert of reality, gradually left her. She dreaded the time when he would strike off southward; she dreaded all the eventualities that presented themselves to her; thoughts were suddenly troublesome and decisions odious. Had prayers found place in the pagan rituals of her soul she would have asked of life only to be unmolested for a while, lazily acquiescent to the ready, naïf flow of Carlyle's ideas, his vivid boyish imagination, and the vein of monomania that seemed to run crosswise through his temperament and colored his every action.

But this is not a story of two on an island, nor concerned primarily with love bred of isolation. It is merely the presentation of two personalities, and its idyllic setting among the palms of the Gulf Stream is quite incidental. Most of us are content to exist and breed and fight for the right to do both, and the dominant idea, the foredoomed attempt to control one's destiny, is reserved for the fortunate or unfortunate few. To me the interesting thing about Ardita is the courage that will tarnish with her beauty and youth.

"Take me with you," she said late one night as they sat lazily in the grass under the shadowy spreading palms. The negroes had brought ashore their musical instruments, and the sound of weird ragtime was drifting softly over on the warm breath of the night. "I'd love to reappear in ten years as a fabulously wealthy high-caste Indian lady," she continued.

Carlyle looked at her quickly.

"You can, you know."

She laughed.

"Is it a proposal of marriage? Extra! Ardita Farnam becomes pirate's bride. Society girl kidnapped by ragtime bank robber."

"It wasn't a bank."

"What was it? Why won't you tell me?"

"I don't want to break down your illusions."

"My dear man, I have no illusions about you."

"I mean your illusions about yourself."

She looked up in surprise.

"About myself! What on earth have I got to do with whatever stray felonies you've committed?"

"That remains to be seen."

She reached over and patted his hand.

"Dear Mr. Curtis Carlyle," she said softly, "are you in love with me?"

"As if it mattered."

"But it does—because I think I'm in love with you."

He looked at her ironically.

"Thus swelling your January total to half a dozen," he suggested. "Suppose I call your bluff and ask you to come to India with me?"

"Shall I?"

He shrugged his shoulders.

"We can get married in Callao."

"What sort of life can you offer me? I don't mean that unkindly, but seriously; what would become of me if the people who want that twenty-thousand-dollar reward ever catch up with you?"

"I thought you weren't afraid."

"I never am—but I won't throw my life away just to show one man I'm not."

"I wish you'd been poor. Just a little poor girl dreaming over a fence in a warm cow country."

"Wouldn't it have been nice?"

"I'd have enjoyed astonishing you—watching your eyes open on things. If you only wanted things! Don't you see?"

"I know—like girls who stare into the windows of jewelry-stores."

"Yes—and want the big oblong watch that's platinum and has diamonds all round the edge. Only you'd decide it was too expensive and choose one of white gold for a hundred dollars. Then I'd say: 'Expensive? I should say not!' And we'd go into the store and pretty soon the platinum one would be gleaming on your wrist."

"That sounds so nice and vulgar—and fun, doesn't it?" murmured Ardita.

"Doesn't it? Can't you see us travelling round and spending money right and left, and being worshipped by bell-boys and waiters? Oh, blessed are the simple rich, for they inherit the earth!"

"I honestly wish we were that way."

"I love you, Ardita," he said gently.

Her face lost its childish look for a moment and became oddly grave.

"I love to be with you," she said, "more than with any man I've ever met. And I like your looks and your dark old hair, and the way you go over the side of the rail when we come ashore. In fact, Curtis Carlyle, I like all the things you do when you're perfectly natural. I think you've got nerve, and you know how I feel about that. Sometimes when you're around I've been tempted to kiss you suddenly and tell you that you were just an idealistic boy with a lot of caste nonsense in his head. Perhaps if I were just a little bit older and a little more bored I'd go with you. As it is, I think I'll go back and marry—that other man."

Over across the silver lake the figures of the negroes writhed and squirmed in the moonlight, like acrobats who, having been too long inactive, must go through their tricks from sheer surplus energy. In single file they marched, weaving in concentric circles, now with their heads thrown back, now bent over their instruments like piping fauns. And from trombone and saxophone ceaselessly whined a blended melody, sometimes riotous and jubilant, sometimes haunting and plaintive as a death-dance from the Congo's heart.

"Let's dance!" cried Ardita. "I can't sit still with that perfect jazz going on."

Taking her hand he led her out into a broad stretch of hard sandy soil that the moon flooded with great splendor. They floated out like drifting moths under the rich hazy light, and as the fantastic symphony wept and exulted and wavered and despaired Ardita's last sense of reality dropped away, and she abandoned her imagination to the dreamy summer scents of tropical flowers and the infinite starry spaces overhead, feeling that if she opened her eyes it would be to find herself dancing with a ghost in a land created by her own fancy.

"This is what I should call an exclusive private dance," he whispered.

"I feel quite mad—but delightfully mad!"

"We're enchanted. The shades of unnumbered generations of cannibals are watching us from high up on the side of the cliff there."

"And I'll bet the cannibal women are saying that we dance too close, and that it was immodest of me to come without my nose-ring."

They both laughed softly—and then their laughter died as over across the lake they heard the trombones stop in the middle of a bar, and the saxophones give a startled moan and fade out.

"What's the matter?" called Carlyle.

After a moment's silence they made out the dark figure of a man rounding the silver lake at a run. As he came closer they saw it was Babe in a state of unusual excitement. He drew up before them and gasped out his news in a breath.

"Ship stan'in' off sho' 'bout half a mile, suh. Mose, he uz on watch, he say look's if she's done ancho'd."

"A ship—what kind of a ship?" demanded Carlyle anxiously.

Dismay was in his voice, and Ardita's heart gave a sudden wrench as she saw his whole face suddenly droop.

"He say he don't know, suh."

"Are they landing a boat?"

"No, suh."

"We'll go up," said Carlyle.

They ascended the hill in silence, Ardita's hand still resting in Carlyle's as it had when they finished dancing. She felt it clinch nervously from time to time as though he were unaware of the contact, but though he hurt her she made no attempt to remove it. It seemed an hour's climb before they reached the top and crept cautiously across the silhouetted plateau to the edge of the cliff. After one short look Carlyle involuntarily gave a little cry. It was a revenue boat with six-inch guns mounted fore and aft.

"They know!" he said with a short intake of breath. "They know! They picked up the trail somewhere."

"Are you sure they know about the channel? They may be only standing by to take a look at the island in the morning. From where they are they couldn't see the opening in the cliff."

"They could with field-glasses," he said hopelessly. He looked at his wrist-watch. "It's nearly two now. They won't do anything until dawn, that's certain. Of course there's always the faint possibility that they're waiting for some other ship to join; or for a coaler."

"I suppose we may as well stay right here."

The hours passed and they lay there side by side, very silently, their chins in their hands like dreaming children. In back of them squatted the negroes, patient, resigned, acquiescent, announcing now and then with sonorous snores that not even the presence of danger could subdue their unconquerable African craving for sleep.

Just before five o'clock Babe approached Carlyle. There were half a dozen rifles aboard the Narcissus he said. Had it been decided to offer no resistance? A pretty good fight might be made, he thought, if they worked out some plan.

Carlyle laughed and shook his head.

"That isn't a Spic army out there, Babe. That's a revenue boat. It'd be like a bow and arrow trying to fight a machine-gun. If you want to bury those bags somewhere and take a chance on recovering them later, go on and do it. But it won't work—they'd dig this island over from one end to the other. It's a lost battle all round, Babe."

Babe inclined his head silently and turned away, and Carlyle's voice was husky as he turned to Ardita.

"There's the best friend I ever had. He'd die for me, and be proud to, if I'd let him."

"You've given up?"

"I've no choice. Of course there's always one way out—the sure way—but that can wait. I wouldn't miss my trial for anything—it'll be an interesting experiment in notoriety. 'Miss Farnam testifies that the pirate's attitude to her was at all times that of a gentleman.' "

"Don't!" she said. "I'm awfully sorry."

When the color faded from the sky and lustreless blue changed to leaden gray a commotion was visible on the ship's deck, and they made out a group of officers clad in white duck, gathered near the rail. They had field-glasses in their hands and were attentively examining the islet.

"It's all up," said Carlyle grimly.

"Damn!" whispered Ardita. She felt tears gathering in her eyes.

"We'll go back to the yacht," he said. "I prefer that to being hunted out up here like a 'possum."

Leaving the plateau they descended the hill, and reaching the lake were rowed out to the yacht by the silent negroes. Then, pale and weary, they sank into the settees and waited.

Half an hour later in the dim gray light the nose of the revenue boat appeared in the channel and stopped, evidently fearing that the bay might be too shallow. From the peaceful look of the yacht, the man and the girl in the settees, and the negroes lounging curiously against the rail, they evidently judged that there would be no resistance, for two boats were lowered casually over the side, one containing an officer and six bluejackets, and the other, four rowers and in the stern two gray-haired men in yachting flannels. Ardita and Carlyle stood up, and half unconsciously started toward each other. Then he paused and putting his hand suddenly into his pocket he pulled out a round, glittering object and held it out to her.

"What is it?" she asked wonderingly.

"I'm not positive, but I think from the Russian inscription inside that it's your promised bracelet."

"Where—where on earth——"

"It came out of one of those bags. You see, Curtis Carlyle and his Six

Black Buddies, in the middle of their performance in the tea-room of the hotel at Palm Beach, suddenly changed their instruments for automatics and held up the crowd. I took this bracelet from a pretty, overrouged woman with red hair."

Ardita frowned and then smiled.

"So that's what you did! You *have* got nerve!"

He bowed.

"A well-known bourgeois quality," he said.

And then dawn slanted dynamically across the deck and flung the shadows reeling into gray corners. The dew rose and turned to golden mist, thin as a dream, enveloping them until they seemed gossamer relics of the late night, infinitely transient and already fading. For a moment sea and sky were breathless, and dawn held a pink hand over the young mouth of life—then from out in the lake came the complaint of a rowboat and the swish of oars.

Suddenly against the golden furnace low in the east their two graceful figures melted into one, and he was kissing her spoiled young mouth.

"It's a sort of glory," he murmured after a second.

She smiled up at him.

"Happy, are you?"

Her sigh was a benediction—an ecstatic surety that she was youth and beauty now as much as she would ever know. For another instant life was radiant and time a phantom and their strength eternal—then there was a bumping, scraping sound as the rowboat scraped alongside.

Up the ladder scrambled the two gray-haired men, the officer and two of the sailors with their hands on their revolvers. Mr. Farnam folded his arms and stood looking at his niece.

"So," he said, nodding his head slowly.

With a sigh her arms unwound from Carlyle's neck, and her eyes, transfigured and far away, fell upon the boarding party. Her uncle saw her upper lip slowly swell into that arrogant pout he knew so well.

"So," he repeated savagely. "So this is your idea of—of romance. A runaway affair, with a high-seas pirate."

Ardita glanced at him carelessly.

"What an old fool you are!" she said quietly.

"Is that the best you can say for yourself?"

"No," she said as if considering. "No, there's something else. There's that well-known phrase with which I have ended most of our conversations for the past few years—'Shut up!'"

And with that she turned, included the two old men, the officer, and the two sailors in a curt glance of contempt, and walked proudly down the companionway.

But had she waited an instant longer she would have heard a sound from her uncle quite unfamiliar in most of their interviews. He gave vent to a whole-hearted amused chuckle, in which the second old man joined.

The latter turned briskly to Carlyle, who had been regarding this scene with an air of cryptic amusement.

"Well, Toby," he said genially, "you incurable, hare-brained, romantic chaser of rainbows, did you find that she was the person you wanted?"

Carlyle smiled confidently.

"Why—naturally," he said. "I've been perfectly sure ever since I first heard tell of her wild career. That's why I had Babe send up the rocket last night."

"I'm glad you did," said Colonel Moreland gravely. "We've been keeping pretty close to you in case you should have trouble with those six strange niggers. And we hoped we'd find you two in some such compromising position," he sighed. "Well, set a crank to catch a crank!"

"Your father and I sat up all night hoping for the best—or perhaps it's the worst. Lord knows you're welcome to her, my boy. She's run me crazy. Did you give her the Russian bracelet my detective got from that Mimi woman?"

Carlyle nodded.

"Sh!" he said. "She's coming on deck."

Ardita appeared at the head of the companionway and gave a quick involuntary glance at Carlyle's wrists. A puzzled look passed across her face. Back aft the negroes had begun to sing, and the cool lake, fresh with dawn, echoed serenely to their low voices.

"Ardita," said Carlyle unsteadily.

She swayed a step toward him.

"Ardita," he repeated breathlessly, "I've got to tell you the—the truth. It was all a plant, Ardita. My name isn't Carlyle. It's Moreland, Toby Moreland. The story was invented, Ardita, invented out of thin Florida air."

She stared at him, bewildered amazement, disbelief, and anger flowing in quick waves across her face. The three men held their breaths. Moreland, Senior, took a step toward her; Mr. Farnam's mouth dropped a little open as he waited, panic-stricken, for the expected crash.

But it did not come. Ardita's face became suddenly radiant, and with a little laugh she went swiftly to young Moreland and looked up at him without a trace of wrath in her gray eyes.

"Will you swear," she said quietly, "that it was entirely a product of your own brain?"

"I swear," said young Moreland eagerly.

She drew his head down and kissed him gently.

"What an imagination!" she said softly and almost enviously. "I want you to lie to me just as sweetly as you know how for the rest of my life."

The negroes' voices floated drowsily back, mingled in an air that she had heard them sing before.

> *"Time is a thief;*
> *Gladness and grief*
> *Cling to the leaf*
> *As it yellows——"*

"What was in the bags?" she asked softly.

"Florida mud," he answered. "That was one of the two true things I told you."

"Perhaps I can guess the other one," she said; and reaching up on her tiptoes she kissed him softly in the illustration.

MAY DAY

◆

"May Day," Fitzgerald's first great novelette—published during his first year as a professional writer—appeared in July 1920. Fitzgerald presumably sold it directly to Smart Set editors H. L. Mencken and George Jean Nathan without offering it to the Post, or any other magazine, because the material was too strong or realistic for the slicks. "May Day" was the most successful work inspired by Fitzgerald's temporary interest in the school of naturalistic or deterministic fiction. Although it was read by the people Fitzgerald wanted to reach, The Smart Set paid him only $200 for this masterpiece.

"May Day" drew upon Fitzgerald's feelings of failure during the spring of 1919 when he was working for a New York advertising agency. He provided this comment when the story was collected in Tales of the Jazz Age (1922):

> This somewhat unpleasant tale . . . relates a series of events which took place in the spring of the previous year. Each of the three events made a great impression upon me. In life they were unrelated, except by the general hysteria of that spring, which inaugurated the Age of Jazz, but in my story I have tried, unsuccessfully I fear, to weave them into a pattern—a pattern which would give the effect of those months in New York as they appeared to at least one member of what was then the younger generation.

◆

THERE HAD been a war fought and won and the great city of the conquering people was crossed with triumphal arches and vivid with thrown flowers of white, red, and rose. All through the long spring days the returning soldiers marched up the chief highway behind the strump of drums and the joyous, resonant wind of the brasses, while merchants and clerks left their bickerings and figurings and, crowding to the windows, turned their white-bunched faces gravely upon the passing battalions.

Never had there been such splendor in the great city, for the victorious war had brought plenty in its train, and the merchants had flocked thither from the South and West with their households to taste of all the luscious feasts and witness the lavish entertainments prepared—and to buy for their women furs against the next winter and bags of golden mesh and varicolored slippers of silk and silver and rose satin and cloth of gold.

So gaily and noisily were the peace and prosperity impending hymned by the scribes and poets of the conquering people that more and more spenders had gathered from the provinces to drink the wine of excitement, and faster and faster did the merchants dispose of their trinkets and slippers until they sent up a mighty cry for more trinkets and more slippers in order that they might give in barter what was demanded of them. Some even of them flung up their hands helplessly, shouting:

"Alas! I have no more slippers! and alas! I have no more trinkets! May Heaven help me, for I know not what I shall do!"

But no one listened to their great outcry, for the throngs were far too busy—day by day, the foot-soldiers trod jauntily the highway and all exulted because the young men returning were pure and brave, sound of tooth and pink of cheek, and the young women of the land were virgins and comely both of face and of figure.

So during all this time there were many adventures that happened in the great city, and, of these, several—or perhaps one—are here set down.

· I ·

At nine o'clock on the morning of the first of May, 1919, a young man spoke to the room clerk at the Biltmore Hotel, asking if Mr. Philip Dean were registered there, and if so, could he be connected with Mr. Dean's rooms. The inquirer was dressed in a well-cut, shabby suit. He was small, slender, and darkly handsome; his eyes were framed above with unusually long eyelashes and below with the blue semicircle of ill health, this latter effect heightened by an unnatural glow which colored his face like a low, incessant fever.

Mr. Dean was staying there. The young man was directed to a telephone at the side.

After a second his connection was made; a sleepy voice hello'd from somewhere above.

"Mr. Dean?"—this very eagerly—"it's Gordon, Phil. It's Gordon Sterrett. I'm down-stairs. I heard you were in New York and I had a hunch you'd be here."

The sleepy voice became gradually enthusiastic. Well, how was Gordy, old boy! Well, he certainly was surprised and tickled! Would Gordy come right up, for Pete's sake!

A few minutes later Philip Dean, dressed in blue silk pajamas, opened his door and the two young men greeted each other with a half-embarrassed exuberance. They were both about twenty-four, Yale graduates of the year before the war; but there the resemblance stopped abruptly. Dean was blond, ruddy, and rugged under his thin pajamas. Everything about him radiated fitness and bodily comfort. He smiled frequently, showing large and prominent teeth.

"I was going to look you up," he cried enthusiastically. "I'm taking a couple of weeks off. If you'll sit down a sec I'll be right with you. Going to take a shower."

As he vanished into the bathroom his visitor's dark eyes roved nervously around the room, resting for a moment on a great English travelling bag in the corner and on a family of thick silk shirts littered on the chairs amid impressive neckties and soft woollen socks.

Gordon rose and, picking up one of the shirts, gave it a minute examination. It was of very heavy silk, yellow, with a pale blue stripe—and there were nearly a dozen of them. He stared involuntarily at his own shirt-cuffs—they were ragged and linty at the edges and soiled to a faint gray. Dropping the silk shirt, he held his coat-sleeves down and worked the frayed shirt-cuffs up till they were out of sight. Then he went to the mirror and looked at himself with listless, unhappy interest. His tie, of former glory, was faded and thumb-creased—it served no longer to hide the jagged button-holes of his collar. He thought, quite without amusement, that only three years before he had received a scattering vote in the senior elections at college for being the best-dressed man in his class.

Dean emerged from the bathroom polishing his body.

"Saw an old friend of yours last night," he remarked. "Passed her in the lobby and couldn't think of her name to save my neck. That girl you brought up to New Haven senior year."

Gordon started.

"Edith Bradin? That whom you mean?"

" 'At's the one. Damn good looking. She's still sort of a pretty doll—you know what I mean: as if you touched her she'd smear."

He surveyed his shining self complacently in the mirror, smiled faintly, exposing a section of teeth.

"She must be twenty-three anyway," he continued.

"Twenty-two last month," said Gordon absently.

"What? Oh, last month. Well, I imagine she's down for the Gamma Psi dance. Did you know we're having a Yale Gamma Psi dance to-night at Delmonico's? You better come up, Gordy. Half of New Haven'll probably be there. I can get you an invitation."

Draping himself reluctantly in fresh underwear, Dean lit a cigarette and sat down by the open window, inspecting his calves and knees under the morning sunshine which poured into the room.

"Sit down, Gordy," he suggested, "and tell me all about what you've been doing and what you're doing now and everything."

Gordon collapsed unexpectedly upon the bed; lay there inert and spiritless. His mouth, which habitually dropped a little open when his face was in repose, became suddenly helpless and pathetic.

"What's the matter?" asked Dean quickly.

"Oh, God!"

"What's the matter?"

"Every God damn thing in the world," he said miserably. "I've absolutely gone to pieces, Phil. I'm all in."

"Huh?"

"I'm all in." His voice was shaking.

Dean scrutinized him more closely with appraising blue eyes.

"You certainly look all shot."

"I am. I've made a hell of a mess of everything." He paused. "I'd better start at the beginning—or will it bore you?"

"Not at all; go on." There was, however, a hesitant note in Dean's voice. This trip East had been planned for a holiday—to find Gordon Sterrett in trouble exasperated him a little.

"Go on," he repeated, and then added half under his breath, "Get it over with."

"Well," began Gordon unsteadily, "I got back from France in February, went home to Harrisburg for a month, and then came down to New York to get a job. I got one—with an export company. They fired me yesterday."

"Fired you?"

"I'm coming to that, Phil. I want to tell you frankly. You're about the only man I can turn to in a matter like this. You won't mind if I just tell you frankly, will you, Phil?"

Dean stiffened a bit more. The pats he was bestowing on his knees grew perfunctory. He felt vaguely that he was being unfairly saddled with responsibility; he was not even sure he wanted to be told. Though never surprised at finding Gordon Sterrett in mild difficulty, there was something in this present misery that repelled him and hardened him, even though it excited his curiosity.

"Go on."

"It's a girl."

"Hm." Dean resolved that nothing was going to spoil his trip. If Gordon was going to be depressing, then he'd have to see less of Gordon.

"Her name is Jewel Hudson," went on the distressed voice from the bed. "She used to be 'pure,' I guess, up to about a year ago. Lived here in New York—poor family. Her people are dead now and she lives with an old aunt. You see it was just about the time I met her that everybody began to come back from France in droves—and all I did was to welcome the newly arrived and go on parties with 'em. That's the way it started, Phil, just from being glad to see everybody and having them glad to see me."

"You ought to've had more sense."

"I know," Gordon paused, and then continued listlessly. "I'm on my own now, you know, and Phil, I can't stand being poor. Then came this darn girl. She sort of fell in love with me for a while and, though I never intended to get so involved, I'd always seem to run into her somewhere. You can imagine the sort of work I was doing for those exporting people —of course, I always intended to draw; do illustrating for magazines; there's a pile of money in it."

"Why didn't you? You've got to buckle down if you want to make good," suggested Dean with cold formalism.

"I tried, a little, but my stuff's crude. I've got talent, Phil; I can draw— but I just don't know how. I ought to go to art school and I can't afford it. Well, things came to a crisis about a week ago. Just as I was down to about my last dollar this girl began bothering me. She wants some money; claims she can make trouble for me if she doesn't get it."

"Can she?"

"I'm afraid she can. That's one reason I lost my job—she kept calling up the office all the time, and that was sort of the last straw down there. She's got a letter all written to send to my family. Oh, she's got me, all right. I've got to have some money for her."

There was an awkward pause. Gordon lay very still, his hands clenched by his side.

"I'm all in," he continued, his voice trembling. "I'm half crazy, Phil. If I hadn't known you were coming East, I think I'd have killed myself. I want you to lend me three hundred dollars."

Dean's hands, which had been patting his bare ankles, were suddenly quiet—and the curious uncertainty playing between the two became taut and strained.

After a second Gordon continued:

"I've bled the family until I'm ashamed to ask for another nickel."

Still Dean made no answer.

"Jewel says she's got to have two hundred dollars."

"Tell her where she can go."

"Yes, that sounds easy, but she's got a couple of drunken letters I wrote her. Unfortunately she's not at all the flabby sort of person you'd expect."

Dean made an expression of distaste.

"I can't stand that sort of woman. You ought to have kept away."

"I know," admitted Gordon wearily.

"You've got to look at things as they are. If you haven't got money you've got to work and stay away from women."

"That's easy for you to say," began Gordon, his eyes narrowing. "You've got all the money in the world."

"I most certainly have not. My family keep darn close tab on what I spend. Just because I have a little leeway I have to be extra careful not to abuse it."

He raised the blind and let in a further flood of sunshine.

"I'm no prig, Lord knows," he went on deliberately. "I like pleasure— and I like a lot of it on a vacation like this, but you're—you're in awful shape. I never heard you talk just this way before. You seem to be sort of bankrupt—morally as well as financially."

"Don't they usually go together?"

Dean shook his head impatiently.

"There's a regular aura about you that I don't understand. It's a sort of evil."

"It's an air of worry and poverty and sleepless nights," said Gordon, rather defiantly.

"I don't know."

"Oh, I admit I'm depressing. I depress myself. But, my God, Phil, a week's rest and a new suit and some ready money and I'd be like—like I was. Phil, I can draw like a streak, and you know it. But half the time I haven't had the money to buy decent drawing materials—and I can't draw when I'm tired and discouraged and all in. With a little ready money I can take a few weeks off and get started."

"How do I know you wouldn't use it on some other woman?"

"Why rub it in?" said Gordon quietly.

"I'm not rubbing it in. I hate to see you this way."

"Will you lend me the money, Phil?"

"I can't decide right off. That's a lot of money and it'll be darn inconvenient for me."

"It'll be hell for me if you can't—I know I'm whining, and it's all my own fault but—that doesn't change it."

"When could you pay it back?"

This was encouraging. Gordon considered. It was probably wisest to be frank.

"Of course, I could promise to send it back next month, but—I'd better say three months. Just as soon as I start to sell drawings."

"How do I know you'll sell any drawings?"

A new hardness in Dean's voice sent a faint chill of doubt over Gordon. Was it possible that he wouldn't get the money?

"I supposed you had a little confidence in me."

"I did have—but when I see you like this I begin to wonder."

"Do you suppose if I wasn't at the end of my rope I'd come to you like this? Do you think I'm enjoying it?" He broke off and bit his lip, feeling that he had better subdue the rising anger in his voice. After all, he was the suppliant.

"You seem to manage it pretty easily," said Dean angrily. "You put me in the position where, if I don't lend it to you, I'm a sucker—oh, yes, you do. And let me tell you it's no easy thing for me to get hold of three hundred dollars. My income isn't so big but that a slice like that won't play the deuce with it."

He left his chair and began to dress, choosing his clothes carefully. Gordon stretched out his arms and clenched the edges of the bed, fighting back a desire to cry out. His head was splitting and whirring, his mouth was dry and bitter and he could feel the fever in his blood resolving itself into innumerable regular counts like a slow dripping from a roof.

Dean tied his tie precisely, brushed his eyebrows, and removed a piece of tobacco from his teeth with solemnity. Next he filled his cigarette case, tossed the empty box thoughtfully into the waste basket, and settled the case in his vest pocket.

"Had breakfast?" he demanded.

"No; I don't eat it any more."

"Well, we'll go out and have some. We'll decide about that money later. I'm sick of the subject. I came East to have a good time.

"Let's go over to the Yale Club," he continued moodily, and then added with an implied reproof: "You've given up your job. You've got nothing else to do."

"I'd have a lot to do if I had a little money," said Gordon pointedly.

"Oh, for Heaven's sake drop the subject for a while! No point in glooming on my whole trip. Here, here's some money."

He took a five-dollar bill from his wallet and tossed it over to Gordon, who folded it carefully and put it in his pocket. There was an added spot of color in his cheeks, an added glow that was not fever. For an instant before they turned to go out their eyes met and in that instant each found something that made him lower his own glance quickly. For in that instant they quite suddenly and definitely hated each other.

· II ·

FIFTH AVENUE and Forty-fourth Street swarmed with the noon crowd. The wealthy, happy sun glittered in transient gold through the thick windows of the smart shops, lighting upon mesh bags and purses and strings of pearls in gray velvet cases; upon gaudy feather fans of many colors; upon the laces and silks of expensive dresses; upon the bad paintings and the fine period furniture in the elaborate show rooms of interior decorators.

Working-girls, in pairs and groups and swarms, loitered by these windows, choosing their future boudoirs from some resplendent display which included even a man's silk pajamas laid domestically across the bed. They stood in front of the jewelry stores and picked out their engagement rings, and their wedding rings and their platinum wrist watches, and then drifted on to inspect the feather fans and opera cloaks; meanwhile digesting the sandwiches and sundaes they had eaten for lunch.

All through the crowd were men in uniform, sailors from the great fleet anchored in the Hudson, soldiers with divisional insignia from Massachusetts to California, wanting fearfully to be noticed, and finding the great city thoroughly fed up with soldiers unless they were nicely massed into pretty formations and uncomfortable under the weight of a pack and rifle.

Through this medley Dean and Gordon wandered; the former interested, made alert by the display of humanity at its frothiest and gaudiest; the latter reminded of how often he had been one of the crowd, tired, casually fed, overworked, and dissipated. To Dean the struggle was significant, young, cheerful; to Gordon it was dismal, meaningless, endless.

In the Yale Club they met a group of their former classmates who greeted the visiting Dean vociferously. Sitting in a semicircle of lounges and great chairs, they had a highball all around.

Gordon found the conversation tiresome and interminable. They lunched together *en masse*, warmed with liquor as the afternoon began. They were all going to the Gamma Psi dance that night—it promised to be the best party since the war.

"Edith Bradin's coming," said some one to Gordon. "Didn't she used to be an old flame of yours? Aren't you both from Harrisburg?"

"Yes." He tried to change the subject. "I see her brother occasionally. He's sort of a socialistic nut. Runs a paper or something here in New York."

"Not like his gay sister, eh?" continued his eager informant. "Well, she's coming to-night with a junior named Peter Himmel."

Gordon was to meet Jewel Hudson at eight o'clock—he had promised to have some money for her. Several times he glanced nervously at his wrist watch. At four, to his relief, Dean rose and announced that he was going over to Rivers Brothers to buy some collars and ties. But as they left the Club another of the party joined them, to Gordon's great dismay. Dean was in a jovial mood now, happy, expectant of the evening's party, faintly hilarious. Over in Rivers' he chose a dozen neckties, selecting each one after long consultations with the other man. Did he think narrow ties were coming back? And wasn't it a shame that Rivers couldn't get any more Welch Margetson collars? There never was a collar like the "Covington."

Gordon was in something of a panic. He wanted the money immediately. And he was now inspired also with a vague idea of attending the Gamma Psi dance. He wanted to see Edith—Edith whom he hadn't met since one romantic night at the Harrisburg Country Club just before he went to France. The affair had died, drowned in the turmoil of the war and quite forgotten in the arabesque of these three months, but a picture of her, poignant, debonnaire, immersed in her own inconsequential chatter, recurred to him unexpectedly and brought a hundred memories with it. It was Edith's face that he had cherished through college with a sort of detached yet affectionate admiration. He had loved to draw her—around his room had been a dozen sketches of her—playing golf, swimming—he could draw her pert, arresting profile with his eyes shut.

They left Rivers' at five-thirty and paused for a moment on the sidewalk.

"Well," said Dean genially, "I'm all set now. Think I'll go back to the hotel and get a shave, haircut, and massage."

"Good enough," said the other man, "I think I'll join you."

Gordon wondered if he was to be beaten after all. With difficulty he restrained himself from turning to the man and snarling out, "Go on away, damn you!" In despair he suspected that perhaps Dean had spoken to him, was keeping him along in order to avoid a dispute about the money.

They went into the Biltmore—a Biltmore alive with girls—mostly from the West and South, the stellar débutantes of many cities gathered for the dance of a famous fraternity of a famous university. But to Gordon they were faces in a dream. He gathered together his forces for a last appeal, was about to come out with he knew not what, when Dean suddenly excused himself to the other man and taking Gordon's arm led him aside.

"Gordy," he said quickly, "I've thought the whole thing over carefully and I've decided that I can't lend you that money. I'd like to oblige you, but I don't feel I ought to—it'd put a crimp in me for a month."

Gordon, watching him dully, wondered why he had never before noticed how much those upper teeth projected.

"—I'm mighty sorry, Gordon," continued Dean, "but that's the way it is."

He took out his wallet and deliberately counted out seventy-five dollars in bills.

"Here," he said, holding them out, "here's seventy-five; that makes eighty all together. That's all the actual cash I have with me, besides what I'll actually spend on the trip."

Gordon raised his clenched hand automatically, opened it as though it were a tongs he was holding, and clenched it again on the money.

"I'll see you at the dance," continued Dean. "I've got to get along to the barber shop."

"So-long," said Gordon in a strained and husky voice.

"So-long."

Dean began to smile, but seemed to change his mind. He nodded briskly and disappeared.

But Gordon stood there, his handsome face awry with distress, the roll of bills clenched tightly in his hand. Then, blinded by sudden tears, he stumbled clumsily down the Biltmore steps.

· III ·

ABOUT NINE O'CLOCK of the same night two human beings came out of a cheap restaurant in Sixth Avenue. They were ugly, ill-nourished, devoid of all except the very lowest form of intelligence, and without even that animal exuberance that in itself brings color into life; they were lately vermin-ridden, cold, and hungry in a dirty town of a strange land; they were poor, friendless; tossed as driftwood from their births, they would be tossed as driftwood to their deaths. They were dressed in the uniform of the United States Army, and on the shoulder of each was the insignia of a drafted division from New Jersey, landed three days before.

The taller of the two was named Carrol Key, a name hinting that in his veins, however thinly diluted by generations of degeneration, ran blood of some potentiality. But one could stare endlessly at the long, chinless face, the dull, watery eyes, and high cheek-bones, without finding a suggestion of either ancestral worth or native resourcefulness.

His companion was swart and bandy-legged, with rat-eyes and a much-broken hooked nose. His defiant air was obviously a pretense, a weapon of protection borrowed from that world of snarl and snap, of physical bluff and physical menace, in which he had always lived. His name was Gus Rose.

Leaving the café they sauntered down Sixth Avenue, wielding toothpicks with great gusto and complete detachment.

"Where to?" asked Rose, in a tone which implied that he would not be surprised if Key suggested the South Sea Islands.

"What you say we see if we can getta holda some liquor?" Prohibition was not yet. The ginger in the suggestion was caused by the law forbidding the selling of liquor to soldiers.

Rose agreed enthusiastically.

"I got an idea," continued Key, after a moment's thought, "I got a brother somewhere."

"In New York?"

"Yeah. He's an old fella." He meant that he was an elder brother. "He's a waiter in a hash joint."

"Maybe he can get us some."

"I'll say he can!"

"B'lieve me, I'm goin' to get this darn uniform off me to-morra. Never get me in it again, neither. I'm goin' to get me some regular clothes."

"Say, maybe I'm not."

As their combined finances were something less than five dollars, this intention can be taken largely as a pleasant game of words, harmless and consoling. It seemed to please both of them, however, for they reinforced it with chuckling and mention of personages high in biblical circles, adding such further emphasis as "Oh, boy!" "You know!" and "I'll say so!" repeated many times over.

The entire mental pabulum of these two men consisted of an offended nasal comment extended through the years upon the institution—army, business, or poorhouse—which kept them alive, and toward their immediate superior in that institution. Until that very morning the institution had been the "government" and the immediate superior had been the "Cap'n"—from these two they had glided out and were now in the vaguely uncomfortable state before they should adopt their next bondage. They were uncertain, resentful, and somewhat ill at ease. This they hid by pretending an elaborate relief at being out of the army, and by assuring each other that military discipline should never again rule their stubborn, liberty-loving wills. Yet, as a matter of fact, they would have felt more at home in a prison than in this new-found and unquestionable freedom.

Suddenly Key increased his gait. Rose, looking up and following his glance, discovered a crowd that was collecting fifty yards down the street.

Key chuckled and began to run in the direction of the crowd; Rose thereupon also chuckled and his short bandy legs twinkled beside the long, awkward strides of his companion.

Reaching the outskirts of the crowd they immediately became an indistinguishable part of it. It was composed of ragged civilians somewhat the worse for liquor, and of soldiers representing many divisions and many stages of sobriety, all clustered around a gesticulating little Jew with long black whiskers, who was waving his arms and delivering an excited but succinct harangue. Key and Rose, having wedged themselves into the approximate parquet, scrutinized him with acute suspicion, as his words penetrated their common consciousness.

"—What have you got outa the war?" he was crying fiercely. "Look arounja, look arounja! Are you rich? Have you got a lot of money offered you?—no; you're lucky if you're alive and got both your legs; you're lucky if you came back an' find your wife ain't gone off with some other fella that had the money to buy himself out of the war! That's when you're lucky! Who got anything out of it except J. P. Morgan an' John D. Rockerfeller?"

At this point the little Jew's oration was interrupted by the hostile impact of a fist upon the point of his bearded chin and he toppled backward to a sprawl on the pavement.

"God damn Bolsheviki!" cried the big soldier-blacksmith who had delivered the blow. There was a rumble of approval, the crowd closed in nearer.

The Jew staggered to his feet, and immediately went down again before a half-dozen reaching-in fists. This time he stayed down, breathing heavily, blood oozing from his lip where it was cut within and without.

There was a riot of voices, and in a minute Rose and Key found themselves flowing with the jumbled crowd down Sixth Avenue under the leadership of a thin civilian in a slouch hat and the brawny soldier who had summarily ended the oration. The crowd had marvellously swollen to formidable proportions and a stream of more non-committal citizens followed it along the sidewalks lending their moral support by intermittent huzzas.

"Where we goin'?" yelled Key to the man nearest him.

His neighbor pointed up to the leader in the slouch hat.

"That guy knows where there's a lot of 'em! We're goin' to show 'em!"

"We're goin' to show 'em!" whispered Key delightedly to Rose, who repeated the phrase rapturously to a man on the other side.

Down Sixth Avenue swept the procession, joined here and there by soldiers and marines, and now and then by civilians, who came up with the inevitable cry that they were just out of the army themselves, as if presenting it as a card of admission to a newly formed Sporting and Amusement Club.

Then the procession swerved down a cross street and headed for Fifth Avenue and the word filtered here and there that they were bound for a Red meeting at Tolliver Hall.

"Where is it?"

The question went up the line and a moment later the answer floated back. Tolliver Hall was down on Tenth Street. There was a bunch of other sojers who was goin' to break it up and was down there now!

But Tenth Street had a faraway sound and at the word a general groan went up and a score of the procession dropped out. Among these were Rose and Key, who slowed down to a saunter and let the more enthusiastic sweep on by.

"I'd rather get some liquor," said Key as they halted and made their way to the sidewalk amid cries of "Shell hole!" and "Quitters!"

"Does your brother work around here?" asked Rose, assuming the air of one passing from the superficial to the eternal.

"He oughta," replied Key. "I ain't seen him for a coupla years. I been out to Pennsylvania since. Maybe he don't work at night anyhow. It's right along here. He can get us some o'right if he ain't gone."

They found the place after a few minutes' patrol of the street—a shoddy tablecloth restaurant between Fifth Avenue and Broadway. Here Key went inside to inquire for his brother George, while Rose waited on the sidewalk.

"He ain't here no more," said Key emerging. "He's a waiter up to Delmonico's."

Rose nodded wisely, as if he'd expected as much. One should not be surprised at a capable man changing jobs occasionally. He knew a waiter once—there ensued a long conversation as they walked as to whether waiters made more in actual wages than in tips—it was decided that it depended on the social tone of the joint wherein the waiter labored. After having given each other vivid pictures of millionaires dining at Delmonico's and throwing away fifty-dollar bills after their first quart of champagne, both men thought privately of becoming waiters. In fact, Key's narrow brow was secreting a resolution to ask his brother to get him a job.

"A waiter can drink up all the champagne those fellas leave in bottles," suggested Rose with some relish, and then added as an afterthought, "Oh, boy!"

By the time they reached Delmonico's it was half past ten, and they were surprised to see a stream of taxis driving up to the door one after the other and emitting marvelous, hatless young ladies, each one attended by a stiff young gentleman in evening clothes.

"It's a party," said Rose with some awe. "Maybe we better not go in. He'll be busy."

"No, he won't. He'll be o'right."

After some hesitation they entered what appeared to them to be the least elaborate door and, indecision falling upon them immediately, stationed themselves nervously in an inconspicuous corner of the small dining-room in which they found themselves. They took off their caps and held them in their hands. A cloud of gloom fell upon them and both started when a door at one end of the room crashed open, emitting a comet-like waiter who streaked across the floor and vanished through another door on the other side.

There had been three of these lightning passages before the seekers mustered the acumen to hail a waiter. He turned, looked at them suspiciously, and then approached with soft, catlike steps, as if prepared at any moment to turn and flee.

"Say," began Key, "say, do you know my brother? He's a waiter here."

"His name is Key," annotated Rose.

Yes, the waiter knew Key. He was up-stairs, he thought. There was a big dance going on in the main ballroom. He'd tell him.

Ten minutes later George Key appeared and greeted his brother with the utmost suspicion; his first and most natural thought being that he was going to be asked for money.

George was tall and weak chinned, but there his resemblance to his brother ceased. The waiter's eyes were not dull, they were alert and twinkling, and his manner was suave, in-door, and faintly superior. They exchanged formalities. George was married and had three children. He seemed fairly interested, but not impressed by the news that Carrol had been abroad in the army. This disappointed Carrol.

"George," said the younger brother, these amenities having been disposed of, "we want to get some booze, and they won't sell us none. Can you get us some?"

George considered.

"Sure. Maybe I can. It may be half an hour, though."

"All right," agreed Carrol, "we'll wait."

At this Rose started to sit down in a convenient chair, but was hailed to his feet by the indignant George.

"Hey! Watch out, you! Can't sit down here! This room's all set for a twelve o'clock banquet."

"I ain't goin' to hurt it," said Rose resentfully. "I been through the delouser."

"Never mind," said George sternly, "if the head waiter seen me here talkin' he'd romp all over me."

"Oh."

The mention of the head waiter was full explanation to the other two; they fingered their overseas caps nervously and waited for a suggestion.

"I tell you," said George, after a pause, "I got a place you can wait; you just come here with me."

They followed him out the far door, through a deserted pantry and up a pair of dark winding stairs, emerging finally into a small room chiefly furnished by piles of pails and stacks of scrubbing brushes, and illuminated by a single dim electric light. There he left them, after soliciting two dollars and agreeing to return in half an hour with a quart of whiskey.

"George is makin' money, I bet," said Key gloomily as he seated himself on an inverted pail. "I bet he's making fifty dollars a week."

Rose nodded his head and spat.

"I bet he is, too."

"What'd he say the dance was of?"

"A lot of college fellas. Yale College."

They both nodded solemnly at each other.

"Wonder where that crowda sojers is now?"

"I don't know. I know that's too damn long to walk for me."

"Me too. You don't catch me walkin' that far."

Ten minutes later restlessness seized them.

"I'm goin' to see what's out here," said Rose, stepping cautiously toward the other door.

It was a swinging door of green baize and he pushed it open a cautious inch.

"See anything?"

For answer Rose drew in his breath sharply.

"Doggone! Here's some liquor I'll say!"

"Liquor?"

Key joined Rose at the door, and looked eagerly.

"I'll tell the world that's liquor," he said, after a moment of concentrated gazing.

It was a room about twice as large as the one they were in—and in it was prepared a radiant feast of spirits. There were long walls of alternating bottles set along two white covered tables; whiskey, gin, brandy, French and Italian vermouths, and orange juice, not to mention an array of syphons and two great empty punch bowls. The room was as yet uninhabited.

"It's for this dance they're just starting," whispered Key; "hear the violins playin'? Say, boy, I wouldn't mind havin' a dance."

They closed the door softly and exchanged a glance of mutual comprehension. There was no need of feeling each other out.

"I'd like to get my hands on a coupla those bottles," said Rose emphatically.

"Me too."

"Do you suppose we'd get seen?"

Key considered.

"Maybe we better wait till they start drinkin' 'em. They got 'em all laid out now, and they know how many of them there are."

They debated this point for several minutes. Rose was all for getting his hands on a bottle now and tucking it under his coat before any one came into the room. Key, however, advocated caution. He was afraid he might get his brother in trouble. If they waited till some of the bottles were opened it'd be all right to take one, and everybody'd think it was one of the college fellas.

While they were still engaged in argument George Key hurried through the room and, barely grunting at them, disappeared by way of the green baize door. A minute later they heard several corks pop, and then the sound of cracking ice and splashing liquid. George was mixing the punch.

The soldiers exchanged delighted grins.

"Oh, boy!" whispered Rose.

George reappeared.

"Just keep low, boys," he said quickly. "I'll have your stuff for you in five minutes."

He disappeared through the door by which he had come.

As soon as his footsteps receded down the stairs, Rose, after a cautious look, darted into the room of delights and reappeared with a bottle in his hand.

"Here's what I say," he said, as they sat radiantly digesting their first drink. "We'll wait till he comes up, and we'll ask him if we can't just stay here and drink what he brings us—see. We'll tell him we haven't got any place to drink it—see. Then we can sneak in there whenever there ain't nobody in that there room and tuck a bottle under our coats. We'll have enough to last us a coupla days—see?"

"Sure," agreed Rose enthusiastically. "Oh, boy! And if we want to we can sell it to sojers any time we want to."

They were silent for a moment thinking rosily of this idea. Then Key reached up and unhooked the collar of his O. D. coat.

"It's hot in here, ain't it?"

Rose agreed earnestly.

"Hot as hell."

· I V ·

SHE WAS STILL quite angry when she came out of the dressing-room and crossed the intervening parlor of politeness that opened onto the hall— angry not so much at the actual happening which was, after all, the merest commonplace of her social existence, but because it had occurred on this particular night. She had no quarrel with herself. She had acted with that correct mixture of dignity and reticent pity which she always employed. She had succinctly and deftly snubbed him.

It had happened when their taxi was leaving the Biltmore—hadn't gone half a block. He had lifted his right arm awkwardly—she was on his right side—and attempted to settle it snugly around the crimson fur-trimmed opera cloak she wore. This in itself had been a mistake. It was inevitably more graceful for a young man attempting to embrace a young lady of whose acquiescence he was not certain, to first put his far arm around her. It avoided that awkward movement of raising the near arm.

His second *faux pas* was unconscious. She had spent the afternoon at the hairdresser's; the idea of any calamity overtaking her hair was extremely repugnant—yet as Peter made his unfortunate attempt the point of his elbow had just faintly brushed it. That was his second *faux pas*. Two were quite enough.

He had begun to murmur. At the first murmur she had decided that he was nothing but a college boy—Edith was twenty-two, and anyhow, this dance, first of its kind since the war, was reminding her, with the accelerating rhythm of its associations, of something else—of another dance and another man, a man for whom her feelings had been little more than a sad-eyed, adolescent mooniness. Edith Bradin was falling in love with her recollection of Gordon Sterrett.

So she came out of the dressing-room at Delmonico's and stood for a second in the doorway looking over the shoulders of a black dress in front of her at the groups of Yale men who flitted like dignified black moths around the head of the stairs. From the room she had left drifted out the heavy fragrance left by the passage to and fro of many scented young beauties—rich perfumes and the fragile memory-laden dust of fragrant powders. This odor drifting out acquired the tang of cigarette smoke in the hall, and then settled sensuously down the stairs and permeated the ballroom where the Gamma Psi dance was to be held. It was an odor she knew well, exciting, stimulating, restlessly sweet—the odor of a fashionable dance.

She thought of her own appearance. Her bare arms and shoulders were powdered to a creamy white. She knew they looked very soft and would gleam like milk against the black backs that were to silhouette them tonight.

The hairdressing had been a success; her reddish mass of hair was piled and crushed and creased to an arrogant marvel of mobile curves. Her lips were finely made of deep carmine; the irises of her eyes were delicate, breakable blue, like china eyes. She was a complete, infinitely delicate, quite perfect thing of beauty, flowing in an even line from a complex coiffure to two small slim feet.

She thought of what she would say to-night at this revel, faintly prestiged already by the sounds of high and low laughter and slippered footsteps, and movements of couples up and down the stairs. She would talk the language she had talked for many years—her line—made up of the current expressions, bits of journalese and college slang strung together into an intrinsic whole, careless, faintly provocative, delicately sentimental. She smiled faintly as she heard a girl sitting on the stairs near her say: "You don't know the half of it, dearie!"

And as she smiled her anger melted for a moment, and closing her eyes she drew in a deep breath of pleasure. She dropped her arms to her side until they were faintly touching the sleek sheath that covered and suggested her figure. She had never felt her own softness so much nor so enjoyed the whiteness of her own arms.

"I smell sweet," she said to herself simply, and then came another thought—"I'm made for love."

She liked the sound of this and thought it again; then in inevitable succession came her new-born riot of dreams about Gordon. The twist of her imagination which, two months before, had disclosed to her her unguessed desire to see him again, seemed now to have been leading up to this dance, this hour.

For all her sleek beauty, Edith was a grave, slow-thinking girl. There was a streak in her of that same desire to ponder, of that adolescent idealism that had turned her brother socialist and pacifist. Henry Bradin had left Cornell, where he had been an instructor in economics, and had come to New York to pour the latest cures for incurable evils into the columns of a radical weekly newspaper.

Edith, less fatuously, would have been content to cure Gordon Sterrett. There was a quality of weakness in Gordon that she wanted to take care of; there was a helplessness in him that she wanted to protect. And she wanted someone she had known a long while, someone who had loved her a long while. She was a little tired; she wanted to get married. Out of a pile of letters, half a dozen pictures and as many memories, and this weariness, she had decided that next time she saw Gordon their relations were going to be changed. She would say something that would change them. There was this evening. This was her evening. All evenings were her evenings.

Then her thoughts were interrupted by a solemn undergraduate with a hurt look and an air of strained formality who presented himself before her and bowed unusually low. It was the man she had come with, Peter Himmel. He was tall and humorous, with horned-rimmed glasses and an air of attractive whimsicality. She suddenly rather disliked him—probably because he had not succeeded in kissing her.

"Well," she began, "are you still furious at me?"

"Not at all."

She stepped forward and took his arm.

"I'm sorry," she said softly. "I don't know why I snapped out that way. I'm in a bum humor to-night for some strange reason. I'm sorry."

"S'all right," he mumbled, "don't mention it."

He felt disagreeably embarrassed. Was she rubbing in the fact of his late failure?

"It was a mistake," she continued, on the same consciously gentle key. "We'll both forget it." For this he hated her.

A few minutes later they drifted out on the floor while the dozen swaying, sighing members of the specially hired jazz orchestra informed the crowded ballroom that "if a saxophone and me are left alone why then two is compan-ee!"

A man with a mustache cut in.

"Hello," he began reprovingly. "You don't remember me."

"I can't just think of your name," she said lightly—"and I know you so well."

"I met you up at—" His voice trailed disconsolately off as a man with very fair hair cut in. Edith murmured a conventional "Thanks, loads—cut in later," to the *inconnu*.

The very fair man insisted on shaking hands enthusiastically. She placed him as one of the numerous Jims of her acquaintance—last name a mystery. She remembered even that he had a peculiar rhythm in dancing and found as they started that she was right.

"Going to be here long?" he breathed confidentially.

She leaned back and looked up at him.

"Couple of weeks."

"Where are you?"

"Biltmore. Call me up some day."

"I mean it," he assured her. "I will. We'll go to tea."

"So do I—Do."

A dark man cut in with intense formality.

"You don't remember me, do you?" he said gravely.

"I should say I do. Your name's Harlan."

"No-ope. Barlow."

"Well, I knew there were two syllables anyway. You're the boy that played the ukulele so well up at Howard Marshall's house party."

"I played—but not——"

A man with prominent teeth cut in. Edith inhaled a slight cloud of whiskey. She liked men to have had something to drink; they were so much more cheerful, and appreciative and complimentary—much easier to talk to.

"My name's Dean, Philip Dean," he said cheerfully. "You don't remember me, I know, but you used to come up to New Haven with a fellow I roomed with senior year, Gordon Sterrett."

Edith looked up quickly.

"Yes, I went up with him twice—to the Pump and Slipper and the Junior prom."

"You've seen him, of course," said Dean carelessly. "He's here to-night. I saw him just a minute ago."

Edith started. Yet she had felt quite sure he would be here.

"Why, no, I haven't——"

A fat man with red hair cut in.

"Hello, Edith," he began.

"Why—hello there——"

She slipped, stumbled lightly.

"I'm sorry, dear," she murmured mechanically.

She had seen Gordon—Gordon very white and listless, leaning against the side of a doorway, smoking and looking into the ballroom. Edith could see that his face was thin and wan—that the hand he raised to his lips with a cigarette was trembling. They were dancing quite close to him now.

"—They invite so darn many extra fellas that you—" the short man was saying.

"Hello, Gordon," called Edith over her partner's shoulder. Her heart was pounding wildly.

His large dark eyes were fixed on her. He took a step in her direction. Her partner turned her away—she heard his voice bleating——

"—but half the stags get lit and leave before long, so——"

Then a low tone at her side.

"May I, please?"

She was dancing suddenly with Gordon; one of his arms was around her; she felt it tighten spasmodically; felt his hand on her back with the fingers spread. Her hand holding the little lace handkerchief was crushed in his.

"Why Gordon," she began breathlessly.

"Hello, Edith."

She slipped again—was tossed forward by her recovery until her face

touched the black cloth of his dinner coat. She loved him—she knew she
loved him—then for a minute there was silence while a strange feeling of
uneasiness crept over her. Something was wrong.

Of a sudden her heart wrenched, and turned over as she realized what it
was. He was pitiful and wretched, a little drunk, and miserably tired.

"Oh——" she cried involuntarily.

His eyes looked down at her. She saw suddenly that they were blood-
streaked and rolling uncontrollably.

"Gordon," she murmured, "we'll sit down; I want to sit down."

They were nearly in mid-floor, but she had seen two men start toward
her from opposite sides of the room, so she halted, seized Gordon's limp
hand and led him bumping through the crowd, her mouth tight shut, her
face a little pale under her rouge, her eyes trembling with tears.

She found a place high up on the soft-carpeted stairs, and he sat down
heavily beside her.

"Well," he began, staring at her unsteadily, "I certainly am glad to see
you, Edith."

She looked at him without answering. The effect of this on her was
immeasurable. For years she had seen men in various stages of intoxication,
from uncles all the way down to chauffeurs, and her feelings had varied
from amusement to disgust, but here for the first time she was seized with
a new feeling—an unutterable horror.

"Gordon," she said accusingly and almost crying, "you look like the
devil."

He nodded. "I've had trouble, Edith."

"Trouble?"

"All sorts of trouble. Don't you say anything to the family, but I'm all
gone to pieces. I'm a mess, Edith."

His lower lip was sagging. He seemed scarcely to see her.

"Can't you—can't you," she hesitated, "can't you tell me about it, Gordon? You know I'm always interested in you."

She bit her lip—she had intended to say something stronger, but found
at the end that she couldn't bring it out.

Gordon shook his head dully. "I can't tell you. You're a good woman.
I can't tell a good woman the story."

"Rot," she said, defiantly. "I think it's a perfect insult to call any one a
good woman in that way. It's a slam. You've been drinking, Gordon."

"Thanks." He inclined his head gravely. "Thanks for the information."

"Why do you drink?"

"Because I'm so damn miserable."

"Do you think drinking's going to make it any better?"

"What you doing—trying to reform me?"

"No; I'm trying to help you, Gordon. Can't you tell me about it?"

"I'm in an awful mess. Best thing you can do is to pretend not to know me."

"Why, Gordon?"

"I'm sorry I cut in on you—it's unfair to you. You're pure woman—and all that sort of thing. Here, I'll get some one else to dance with you."

He rose clumsily to his feet, but she reached up and pulled him down beside her on the stairs.

"Here, Gordon. You're ridiculous. You're hurting me. You're acting like a—like a crazy man——"

"I admit it. I'm a little crazy. Something's wrong with me, Edith. There's something left me. It doesn't matter."

"It does, tell me."

"Just that. I was always queer—little bit different from other boys. All right in college, but now it's all wrong. Things have been snapping inside me for four months like little hooks on a dress, and it's about to come off when a few more hooks go. I'm very gradually going loony."

He turned his eyes full on her and began to laugh, and she shrank away from him.

"What *is* the matter?"

"Just me," he repeated. "I'm going loony. This whole place is like a dream to me—this Delmonico's—"

As he talked she saw he had changed utterly. He wasn't at all light and gay and careless—a great lethargy and discouragement had come over him. Revulsion seized her, followed by a faint, surprising boredom. His voice seemed to come out of a great void.

"Edith," he said, "I used to think I was clever, talented, an artist. Now I know I'm nothing. Can't draw, Edith. Don't know why I'm telling you this."

She nodded absently.

"I can't draw, I can't do anything. I'm poor as a church mouse." He laughed, bitterly and rather too loud. "I've become a damn beggar, a leech on my friends. I'm a failure. I'm poor as hell."

Her distaste was growing. She barely nodded this time, waiting for her first possible cue to rise.

Suddenly Gordon's eyes filled with tears.

"Edith," he said, turning to her with what was evidently a strong effort at self-control, "I can't tell you what it means to me to know there's one person left who's interested in me."

He reached out and patted her hand, and involuntarily she drew it away.

"It's mighty fine of you," he repeated.

"Well," she said slowly, looking him in the eye, "any one's always glad to see an old friend—but I'm sorry to see you like this, Gordon."

There was a pause while they looked at each other, and the momentary eagerness in his eyes wavered. She rose and stood looking at him, her face quite expressionless.

"Shall we dance?" she suggested, coolly.

—Love is fragile—she was thinking—but perhaps the pieces are saved, the things that hovered on lips, that might have been said. The new love words, the tendernesses learned, are treasured up for the next lover.

· V ·

PETER HIMMEL, escort to the lovely Edith, was unaccustomed to being snubbed; having been snubbed, he was hurt and embarrassed, and ashamed of himself. For a matter of two months he had been on special delivery terms with Edith Bradin, and knowing that the one excuse and explanation of the special delivery letter is its value in sentimental correspondence, he had believed himself quite sure of his ground. He searched in vain for any reason why she should have taken this attitude in the matter of a simple kiss.

Therefore when he was cut in on by the man with the mustache he went out into the hall and, making up a sentence, said it over to himself several times. Considerably deleted, this was it:

"Well, if any girl ever led a man on and then jolted him, she did—and she has no kick coming if I go out and get beautifully boiled."

So he walked through the supper room into a small room adjoining it, which he had located earlier in the evening. It was a room in which there were several large bowls of punch flanked by many bottles. He took a seat beside the table which held the bottles.

At the second highball, boredom, disgust, the monotony of time, the turbidity of events, sank into a vague background before which glittering cobwebs formed. Things became reconciled to themselves, things lay quietly on their shelves; the troubles of the day arranged themselves in trim formation and at his curt wish of dismissal, marched off and disappeared. And with the departure of worry came brilliant, permeating symbolism. Edith became a flighty, negligible girl, not to be worried over; rather to be laughed at. She fitted like a figure of his own dream into the surface world forming about him. He himself became in a measure symbolic, a type of the continent bacchanal, the brilliant dreamer at play.

Then the symbolic mood faded and as he sipped his third highball his imagination yielded to the warm glow and he lapsed into a state similar to floating on his back in pleasant water. It was at this point that he noticed that a green baize door near him was open about two inches, and that through the aperture a pair of eyes were watching him intently.

"Hm," murmured Peter calmly.

The green door closed—and then opened again—a bare half inch this time.

"Peek-a-boo," murmured Peter.

The door remained stationary and then he became aware of a series of tense intermittent whispers.

"One guy."

"What's he doin'?"

"He's sittin' lookin'."

"He better beat it off. We gotta get another li'l' bottle."

Peter listened while the words filtered into his consciousness.

"Now this," he thought, "is most remarkable."

He was excited. He was jubilant. He felt that he had stumbled upon a mystery. Affecting an elaborate carelessness he arose and walked around the table—then, turning quickly, pulled open the green door, precipitating Private Rose into the room.

Peter bowed.

"How do you do?" he said.

Private Rose set one foot slightly in front of the other, poised for fight, flight, or compromise.

"How do you do?" repeated Peter politely.

"I'm o'right."

"Can I offer you a drink?"

Private Rose looked at him searchingly, suspecting possible sarcasm.

"O'right," he said finally.

Peter indicated a chair.

"Sit down."

"I got a friend," said Rose, "I got a friend in there." He pointed to the green door.

"By all means let's have him in."

Peter crossed over, opened the door and welcomed in Private Key, very suspicious and uncertain and guilty. Chairs were found and the three took their seats around the punch bowl. Peter gave them each a highball and offered them a cigarette from his case. They accepted both with some diffidence.

"Now," continued Peter easily, "may I ask why you gentlemen prefer to lounge away your leisure hours in a room which is chiefly furnished, as far as I can see, with scrubbing brushes. And when the human race has progressed to the stage where seventeen thousand chairs are manufactured on every day except Sunday—" he paused. Rose and Key regarded him vacantly. "Will you tell me," went on Peter, "why you choose to rest yourselves on articles intended for the transportation of water from one place to another?"

At this point Rose contributed a grunt to the conversation.

"And lastly," finished Peter, "will you tell me why, when you are in a building beautifully hung with enormous candelabra, you prefer to spend these evening hours under one anemic electric light?"

Rose looked at Key; Key looked at Rose. They laughed; they laughed uproariously; they found it was impossible to look at each other without laughing. But they were not laughing with this man—they were laughing at him. To them a man who talked after this fashion was either raving drunk or raving crazy.

"You are Yale men, I presume," said Peter, finishing his highball and preparing another.

They laughed again.

"Na-ah."

"So? I thought perhaps you might be members of that lowly section of the university known as the Sheffield Scientific School."

"Na-ah."

"Hm. Well, that's too bad. No doubt you are Harvard men, anxious to preserve your incognito in this—this paradise of violet blue, as the newspapers say."

"Na-ah," said Key scornfully, "we was just waitin' for somebody."

"Ah," exclaimed Peter, rising and filling their glasses, "very interestin'. Had a date with a scrublady, eh?"

They both denied this indignantly.

"It's all right," Peter reassured them, "don't apologize. A scrublady's as good as any lady in the world. Kipling says 'Any lady and Judy O'Grady under the skin.' "

"Sure," said Key, winking broadly at Rose.

"My case, for instance," continued Peter, finishing his glass. "I got a girl up here that's spoiled. Spoildest darn girl I ever saw. Refused to kiss me; no reason whatsoever. Led me on deliberately to think sure I want to kiss you and then plunk! Threw me over! What's the younger generation comin' to?"

"Say tha's hard luck," said Key—"that's awful hard luck."

"Oh, boy!" said Rose.

"Have another?" said Peter.

"We got in a sort of fight for a while," said Key after a pause, "but it was too far away."

"A fight?—tha's stuff!" said Peter, seating himself unsteadily. "Fight 'em all! I was in the army."

"This was with a Bolshevik fella."

"Tha's stuff!" exclaimed Peter, enthusiastic. "That's what I say! Kill the Bolshevik! Exterminate 'em!"

"We're Americuns," said Rose, implying a sturdy, defiant patriotism.

"Sure," said Peter. "Greatest race in the world! We're all Americuns! Have another."

They had another.

· VI ·

AT ONE O'CLOCK a special orchestra, special even in a day of special orchestras, arrived at Delmonico's, and its members, seating themselves arrogantly around the piano, took up the burden of providing music for the Gamma Psi Fraternity. They were headed by a famous flute-player, distinguished throughout New York for his feat of standing on his head and shimmying with his shoulders while he played the latest jazz on his flute. During his performance the lights were extinguished except for the spotlight on the flute-player and another roving beam that threw flickering shadows and changing kaleidoscopic colors over the massed dancers.

Edith had danced herself into that tired, dreamy state habitual only with débutantes, a state equivalent to the glow of a noble soul after several long highballs. Her mind floated vaguely on the bosom of her music; her partners changed with the unreality of phantoms under the colorful shifting dusk, and to her present coma it seemed as if days had passed since the dance began. She had talked on many fragmentary subjects with many men. She had been kissed once and made love to six times. Earlier in the evening different undergraduates had danced with her, but now, like all the more popular girls there, she had her own entourage—that is, half a dozen gallants had singled her out or were alternating her charms with those of some other chosen beauty; they cut in on her in regular, inevitable succession.

Several times she had seen Gordon—he had been sitting a long time on the stairway with his palm to his head, his dull eyes fixed at an infinite speck on the floor before him, very depressed, he looked, and quite drunk—but Edith each time had averted her glance hurriedly. All that seemed long ago;

her mind was passive now, her senses were lulled to trance-like sleep; only
her feet danced and her voice talked on in hazy sentimental banter.

But Edith was not nearly so tired as to be incapable of moral indignation
when Peter Himmel cut in on her, sublimely and happily drunk. She gasped
and looked up at him.

"Why, *Peter!*"

"I'm a li'l' stewed, Edith."

"Why, Peter, you're a *peach*, you are! Don't you think it's a bum way
of doing—when you're with me?"

Then she smiled unwillingly, for he was looking at her with owlish sentimentality varied with a silly spasmodic smile.

"Darlin' Edith," he began earnestly, "you know I love you, don't you?"

"You tell it well."

"I love you—and I merely wanted you to kiss me," he added sadly.

His embarrassment, his shame, were both gone. She was a mos' beautiful
girl in whole worl'. Mos' beautiful eyes, like stars above. He wanted to
'pologize—firs', for presuming try to kiss her; second, for drinking—but
he'd been so discouraged 'cause he had thought she was mad at him—

The red-fat man cut in, and looking up at Edith smiled radiantly.

"Did you bring any one?" she asked.

No. The red-fat man was a stag.

"Well, would you mind—would it be an awful bother for you to—to
take me home to-night?" (this extreme diffidence was a charming affectation
on Edith's part—she knew that the red-fat man would immediately dissolve
into a paroxysm of delight).

"Bother? Why, good Lord, I'd be darn glad to! You know I'd be darn
glad to."

"Thanks *loads!* You're awfully sweet."

She glanced at her wrist-watch. It was half-past one. And, as she said
"half-past one" to herself, it floated vaguely into her mind that her brother
had told her at luncheon that he worked in the office of his newspaper until
after one-thirty every evening.

Edith turned suddenly to her current partner.

"What street is Delmonico's on, anyway?"

"Street? Oh, why Fifth Avenue, of course."

"I mean, what cross street?"

"Why—let's see—it's on Forty-fourth Street."

This verified what she had thought. Henry's office must be across the
street and just around the corner, and it occurred to her immediately that
she might slip over for a moment and surprise him, float in on him, a

shimmering marvel in her new crimson opera cloak and "cheer him up." It was exactly the sort of thing Edith revelled in doing—an unconventional, jaunty thing. The idea reached out and gripped at her imagination—after an instant's hesitation she had decided.

"My hair is just about to tumble entirely down," she said pleasantly to her partner; "would you mind if I go and fix it?"

"Not at all."

"You're a peach."

A few minutes later, wrapped in her crimson opera cloak, she flitted down a side-stairs, her cheeks glowing with excitement at her little adventure. She ran by a couple who stood at the door—a weak-chinned waiter and an over-rouged young lady, in hot dispute—and opening the outer door stepped into the warm May night.

· VII ·

THE OVER-ROUGED young lady followed her with a brief, bitter glance—then turned again to the weak-chinned waiter and took up her argument.

"You better go up and tell him I'm here," she said defiantly, "or I'll go up myself."

"No, you don't!" said George sternly.

The girl smiled sardonically.

"Oh, I don't, don't I? Well, let me tell you I know more college fellas and more of 'em know me, and are glad to take me out on a party, than you ever saw in your whole life."

"Maybe so——"

"Maybe so," she interrupted. "Oh, it's all right for any of 'em like that one that just ran out—God knows where *she* went—it's all right for them that are asked here to come or go as they like—but when I want to see a friend they have some cheap, ham-slinging, bring-me-a-doughnut waiter to stand here and keep me out."

"See here," said the elder Key indignantly, "I can't lose my job. Maybe this fella you're talkin' about doesn't want to see you."

"Oh, he wants to see me all right."

"Anyways, how could I find him in all that crowd?"

"Oh, he'll be there," she asserted confidently. "You just ask anybody for Gordon Sterrett and they'll point him out to you. They all know each other, those fellas."

She produced a mesh bag, and taking out a dollar bill handed it to George.

"Here," she said, "here's a bribe. You find him and give him my message. You tell him if he isn't here in five minutes I'm coming up."

George shook his head pessimistically, considered the question for a moment, wavered violently, and then withdrew.

In less than the allotted time Gordon came down-stairs. He was drunker than he had been earlier in the evening and in a different way. The liquor seemed to have hardened on him like a crust. He was heavy and lurching —almost incoherent when he talked.

" 'Lo, Jewel," he said thickly. "Came right away. Jewel, I couldn't get that money. Tried my best."

"Money nothing!" she snapped. "You haven't been near me for ten days. What's the matter?"

He shook his head slowly.

"Been very low, Jewel. Been sick."

"Why didn't you tell me if you were sick. I don't care about the money that bad. I didn't start bothering you about it at all until you began neglecting me."

Again he shook his head.

"Haven't been neglecting you. Not at all."

"Haven't! You haven't been near me for three weeks, unless you been so drunk you didn't know what you were doing."

"Been sick, Jewel," he repeated, turning his eyes upon her wearily.

"You're well enough to come and play with your society friends here all right. You told me you'd meet me for dinner, and you said you'd have some money for me. You didn't even bother to ring me up."

"I couldn't get any money."

"Haven't I just been saying that doesn't matter? I wanted to see *you*, Gordon, but you seem to prefer your somebody else."

He denied this bitterly.

"Then get your hat and come along," she suggested.

Gordon hesitated—and she came suddenly close to him and slipped her arms around his neck.

"Come on with me, Gordon," she said in a half whisper. "We'll go over to Devineries' and have a drink, and then we can go up to my apartment."

"I can't, Jewel,——"

"You can," she said intensely.

"I'm sick as a dog!"

"Well, then, you oughtn't to stay here and dance."

With a glance around him in which relief and despair were mingled,

Gordon hesitated; then she suddenly pulled him to her and kissed him with soft, pulpy lips.

"All right," he said heavily. "I'll get my hat."

· VIII ·

WHEN EDITH CAME OUT into the clear blue of the May night she found the Avenue deserted. The windows of the big shops were dark; over their doors were drawn great iron masks until they were only shadowy tombs of the late day's splendor. Glancing down toward Forty-second Street she saw a commingled blur of lights from the all-night restaurants. Over on Sixth Avenue the elevated, a flare of fire, roared across the street between the glimmering parallels of light at the station and streaked along into the crisp dark. But at Forty-fourth Street it was very quiet.

Pulling her cloak close about her Edith darted across the Avenue. She started nervously as a solitary man passed her and said in a hoarse whisper—"Where bound, kiddo?" She was reminded of a night in her childhood when she had walked around the block in her pajamas and a dog had howled at her from a mystery-big back yard.

In a minute she had reached her destination, a two-story, comparatively old building on Forty-fourth, in the upper window of which she thankfully detected a wisp of light. It was bright enough outside for her to make out the sign beside the window—the *New York Trumpet*. She stepped inside a dark hall and after a second saw the stairs in the corner.

Then she was in a long, low room furnished with many desks and hung on all sides with file copies of newspapers. There were only two occupants. They were sitting at different ends of the room, each wearing a green eye-shade and writing by a solitary desk light.

For a moment she stood uncertainly in the doorway, and then both men turned around simultaneously and she recognized her brother.

"Why, Edith!" He rose quickly and approached her in surprise, removing his eye-shade. He was tall, lean, and dark, with black, piercing eyes under very thick glasses. They were far-away eyes that seemed always fixed just over the head of the person to whom he was talking.

He put his hands on her arms and kissed her cheek.

"What is it?" he repeated in some alarm.

"I was at a dance across at Delmonico's, Henry," she said excitedly, "and I couldn't resist tearing over to see you."

"I'm glad you did." His alertness gave way quickly to a habitual vagueness. "You oughtn't to be out alone at night though, ought you?"

The man at the other end of the room had been looking at them curiously, but at Henry's beckoning gesture he approached. He was loosely fat with little twinkling eyes, and, having removed his collar and tie, he gave the impression of a Middle-Western farmer on a Sunday afternoon.

"This is my sister," said Henry. "She dropped in to see me."

"How do you do?" said the fat man, smiling. "My name's Bartholomew, Miss Bradin. I know your brother has forgotten it long ago."

Edith laughed politely.

"Well," he continued, "not exactly gorgeous quarters we have here, are they?"

Edith looked around the room.

"They seem very nice," she replied. "Where do you keep the bombs?"

"The bombs?" repeated Bartholomew, laughing. "That's pretty good—the bombs. Did you hear her, Henry? She wants to know where we keep the bombs. Say, that's pretty good."

Edith swung herself onto a vacant desk and sat dangling her feet over the edge. Her brother took a seat beside her.

"Well," he asked, absent-mindedly, "how do you like New York this trip?"

"Not bad. I'll be over at the Biltmore with the Hoyts until Sunday. Can't you come to luncheon to-morrow?"

He thought a moment.

"I'm especially busy," he objected, "and I hate women in groups."

"All right," she agreed, unruffled. "Let's you and me have luncheon together."

"Very well."

"I'll call for you at twelve."

Bartholomew was obviously anxious to return to his desk, but apparently considered that it would be rude to leave without some parting pleasantry.

"Well"—he began awkwardly.

They both turned to him.

"Well, we—we had an exciting time earlier in the evening."

The two men exchanged glances.

"You should have come earlier," continued Bartholomew, somewhat encouraged. "We had a regular vaudeville."

"Did you really?"

"A serenade," said Henry. "A lot of soldiers gathered down there in the street and began to yell at the sign."

"Why?" she demanded.

"Just a crowd," said Henry, abstractedly. "All crowds have to howl.

They didn't have anybody with much initiative in the lead, or they'd probably have forced their way in here and smashed things up."

"Yes," said Bartholomew, turning again to Edith, "you should have been here."

He seemed to consider this a sufficient cue for withdrawal, for he turned abruptly and went back to his desk.

"Are the soldiers all set against the Socialists?" demanded Edith of her brother. "I mean do they attack you violently and all that?"

Henry replaced his eye-shade and yawned.

"The human race has come a long way," he said casually, "but most of us are throw-backs; the soldiers don't know what they want, or what they hate, or what they like. They're used to acting in large bodies, and they seem to have to make demonstrations. So it happens to be against us. There've been riots all over the city to-night. It's May Day, you see."

"Was the disturbance here pretty serious?"

"Not a bit," he said scornfully. "About twenty-five of them stopped in the street about nine o'clock, and began to bellow at the moon."

"Oh"— She changed the subject. "You're glad to see me, Henry?"

"Why, sure."

"You don't seem to be."

"I am."

"I suppose you think I'm a—a waster. Sort of the World's Worst Butterfly."

Henry laughed.

"Not at all. Have a good time while you're young. Why? Do I seem like the priggish and earnest youth?"

"No—" She paused, "—but somehow I began thinking how absolutely different the party I'm on is from—from all your purposes. It seems sort of—of incongruous, doesn't it?—me being at a party like that, and you over here working for a thing that'll make that sort of party impossible ever any more, if your ideas work."

"I don't think of it that way. You're young, and you're acting just as you were brought up to act. Go ahead—have a good time?"

Her feet, which had been idly swinging, stopped and her voice dropped a note.

"I wish you'd—you'd come back to Harrisburg and have a good time. Do you feel sure that you're on the right track——"

"You're wearing beautiful stockings," he interrupted. "What on earth are they?"

"They're embroidered," she replied, glancing down. "Aren't they cunning?" She raised her skirts and uncovered slim, silk-sheathed calves. "Or do you disapprove of silk stockings?"

He seemed slightly exasperated, bent his dark eyes on her piercingly.

"Are you trying to make me out as criticizing you in any way, Edith?"

"Not at all——"

She paused. Bartholomew had uttered a grunt. She turned and saw that he had left his desk and was standing at the window.

"What is it?" demanded Henry.

"People," said Bartholomew, and then after an instant: "Whole jam of them. They're coming from Sixth Avenue."

"People?"

The fat man pressed his nose to the pane.

"Soldiers, by God!" he said emphatically. "I had an idea they'd come back."

Edith jumped to her feet, and running over joined Bartholomew at the window.

"There's a lot of them!" she cried excitedly. "Come here, Henry!"

Henry readjusted his shade, but kept his seat.

"Hadn't we better turn out the lights?" suggested Bartholomew.

"No. They'll go away in a minute."

"They're not," said Edith, peering from the window. "They're not even thinking of going away. There's more of them coming. Look—there's a whole crowd turning the corner of Sixth Avenue."

By the yellow glow and blue shadows of the street lamp she could see that the sidewalk was crowded with men. They were mostly in uniform, some sober, some enthusiastically drunk, and over the whole swept an incoherent clamor and shouting.

Henry rose, and going to the window exposed himself as a long silhouette against the office lights. Immediately the shouting became a steady yell, and a rattling fusillade of small missiles, corners of tobacco plugs, cigarette-boxes, and even pennies beat against the window. The sounds of the racket now began floating up the stairs as the folding doors revolved.

"They're coming up!" cried Bartholomew.

Edith turned anxiously to Henry.

"They're coming up, Henry."

From down-stairs in the lower hall their cries were now quite audible.

"—God damn Socialists!"

"Pro-Germans! Boche-lovers!"

"Second floor, front! Come on!"

"We'll get the sons——"

The next five minutes passed in a dream. Edith was conscious that the clamor burst suddenly upon the three of them like a cloud of rain, that there was a thunder of many feet on the stairs, that Henry had seized her arm and drawn her back toward the rear of the office. Then the door opened and an overflow of men were forced into the room—not the leaders, but simply those who happened to be in front.

"Hello, Bo!"

"Up late, ain't you?"

"You an' your girl. Damn *you!*"

She noticed that two very drunken soldiers had been forced to the front, where they wobbled fatuously—one of them was short and dark, the other was tall and weak of chin.

Henry stepped forward and raised his hand.

"Friends!" he said.

The clamor faded into a momentary stillness, punctuated with mutterings.

"Friends!" he repeated, his far-away eyes fixed over the heads of the crowd, "you're injuring no one but yourselves by breaking in here to-night. Do we look like rich men? Do we look like Germans? I ask you in all fairness——"

"Pipe down!"

"I'll say you do!"

"Say, who's your lady friend, buddy?"

A man in civilian clothes, who had been pawing over a table, suddenly held up a newspaper.

"Here it is!" he shouted. "They wanted the Germans to win the war!"

A new overflow from the stairs was shouldered in and of a sudden the room was full of men all closing around the pale little group at the back. Edith saw that the tall soldier with the weak chin was still in front. The short dark one had disappeared.

She edged slightly backward, stood close to the open window, through which came a clear breath of cool night air.

Then the room was a riot. She realized that the soldiers were surging forward, glimpsed the fat man swinging a chair over his head—instantly the lights went out, and she felt the push of warm bodies under rough cloth, and her ears were full of shouting and trampling and hard breathing.

A figure flashed by her out of nowhere, tottered, was edged sideways, and of a sudden disappeared helplessly out through the open window with a frightened, fragmentary cry that died staccato on the bosom of the clamor. By the faint light streaming from the building backing on the area Edith had a quick impression that it had been the tall soldier with the weak chin.

Anger rose astonishingly in her. She swung her arms wildly, edged blindly toward the thickest of the scuffling. She heard grunts, curses, the muffled impact of fists.

"Henry!" she called frantically, "Henry!"

Then, it was minutes later, she felt suddenly that there were other figures in the room. She heard a voice, deep, bullying, authoritative; she saw yellow rays of light sweeping here and there in the fracas. The cries became more scattered. The scuffling increased and then stopped.

Suddenly the lights were on and the room was full of policemen, clubbing left and right. The deep voice boomed out:

"Here now! Here now! Here now!"

And then:

"Quiet down and get out! Here now!"

The room seemed to empty like a wash-bowl. A policeman fast-grappled in the corner released his hold on his soldier antagonist and started him with a shove toward the door. The deep voice continued. Edith perceived now that it came from a bull-necked police captain standing near the door.

"Here now! This is no way! One of your own sojers got shoved out of the back window an' killed hisself!"

"Henry!" called Edith, "Henry!"

She beat wildly with her fists on the back of the man in front of her; she brushed between two others; fought, shrieked, and beat her way to a very pale figure sitting on the floor close to a desk.

"Henry," she cried passionately, "what's the matter? What's the matter? Did they hurt you?"

His eyes were shut. He groaned and then looking up said disgustedly——

"They broke my leg. My God, the fools!"

"Here now!" called the police captain. "Here now! Here now!"

· IX ·

"CHILDS', FIFTY-NINTH STREET," at eight o'clock of any morning differs from its sisters by less than the width of their marble tables or the degree of polish on the frying-pans. You will see there a crowd of poor people with sleep in the corners of their eyes, trying to look straight before them at their food so as not to see the other poor people. But Childs', Fifty-ninth, four hours earlier is quite unlike any Childs' restaurant from Portland, Oregon, to Portland, Maine. Within its pale but sanitary walls one finds a noisy medley of chorus girls, college boys, débutantes, rakes, *filles de joie* —a not unrepresentative mixture of the gayest of Broadway, and even of Fifth Avenue.

In the early morning of May the second it was unusually full. Over the marble-topped tables were bent the excited faces of flappers whose fathers owned individual villages. They were eating buckwheat cakes and scrambled eggs with relish and gusto, an accomplishment that it would have been utterly impossible for them to repeat in the same place four hours later.

Almost the entire crowd were from the Gamma Psi dance at Delmonico's except for several chorus girls from a midnight revue who sat at a side table and wished they'd taken off a little more make-up after the show. Here and there a drab, mouse-like figure, desperately out of place, watched the butterflies with a weary, puzzled curiosity. But the drab figure was the exception. This was the morning after May Day, and celebration was still in the air.

Gus Rose, sober but a little dazed, must be classed as one of the drab figures. How he had got himself from Forty-fourth Street to Fifty-ninth Street after the riot was only a hazy half-memory. He had seen the body of Carrol Key put in an ambulance and driven off, and then he had started up town with two or three soldiers. Somewhere between Forty-fourth Street and Fifty-ninth Street the other soldiers had met some women and disappeared. Rose had wandered to Columbus Circle and chosen the gleaming lights of Childs' to minister to his craving for coffee and doughnuts. He walked in and sat down.

All around him floated airy, inconsequential chatter and high-pitched laughter. At first he failed to understand, but after a puzzled five minutes he realized that this was the aftermath of some gay party. Here and there a restless, hilarious young man wandered fraternally and familiarly between the tables, shaking hands indiscriminately and pausing occasionally for a facetious chat, while excited waiters, bearing cakes and eggs aloft, swore at him silently, and bumped him out of the way. To Rose, seated at the most inconspicuous and least crowded table, the whole scene was a colorful circus of beauty and riotous pleasure.

He became gradually aware, after a few moments, that the couple seated diagonally across from him, with their backs to the crowd, were not the least interesting pair in the room. The man was drunk. He wore a dinner coat with a dishevelled tie and shirt swollen by spillings of water and wine. His eyes, dim and bloodshot, roved unnaturally from side to side. His breath came short between his lips.

"He's been on a spree!" thought Rose.

The woman was almost if not quite sober. She was pretty, with dark eyes and feverish high color, and she kept her active eyes fixed on her companion with the alertness of a hawk. From time to time she would lean and whisper intently to him, and he would answer by inclining his head heavily or by a particularly ghoulish and repellent wink.

Rose scrutinized them dumbly for some minutes, until the woman gave him a quick, resentful look; then he shifted his gaze to two of the most conspicuously hilarious of the promenaders who were on a protracted circuit of the tables. To his surprise he recognized in one of them the young man by whom he had been so ludicrously entertained at Delmonico's. This started him thinking of Key with a vague sentimentality, not unmixed with awe. Key was dead. He had fallen thirty-five feet and split his skull like a cracked cocoanut.

"He was a darn good guy," thought Rose mournfully. "He was a darn good guy, o'right. That was awful hard luck about him."

The two promenaders approached and started down between Rose's table and the next, addressing friends and strangers alike with jovial familiarity. Suddenly Rose saw the fair-haired one with the prominent teeth stop, look unsteadily at the man and girl opposite, and then begin to move his head disapprovingly from side to side.

The man with the blood-shot eyes looked up.

"Gordy," said the promenader with the prominent teeth, "Gordy."

"Hello," said the man with the stained shirt thickly.

Prominent Teeth shook his finger pessimistically at the pair, giving the woman a glance of aloof condemnation.

"What'd I tell you Gordy?"

Gordon stirred in his seat.

"Go to hell!" he said.

Dean continued to stand there shaking his finger. The woman began to get angry.

"You go way!" she cried fiercely. "You're drunk, that's what you are!"

"So's he," suggested Dean, staying the motion of his finger and pointing it at Gordon.

Peter Himmel ambled up, owlish now and oratorically inclined.

"Here now," he began as if called upon to deal with some petty dispute between children. "Wha's all trouble?"

"You take your friend away," said Jewel tartly. "He's bothering us."

"What's 'at?"

"You heard me!" she said shrilly. "I said to take your drunken friend away."

Her rising voice rang out above the clatter of the restaurant and a waiter came hurrying up.

"You gotta be more quiet!"

"That fella's drunk," she cried. "He's insulting us."

"Ah-ha, Gordy," persisted the accused. "What'd I tell you." He turned to the waiter. "Gordy an' I friends. Been tryin' help him, haven't I, Gordy?"

Gordy looked up.

"Help me? Hell, no!"

Jewel rose suddenly, and seizing Gordon's arm assisted him to his feet.

"Come on, Gordy!" she said, leaning toward him and speaking in a half whisper. "Let's us get out of here. This fella's got a mean drunk on."

Gordon allowed himself to be urged to his feet and started toward the door. Jewel turned for a second and addressed the provoker of their flight.

"I know all about *you!*" she said fiercely. "Nice friend, you are, I'll say. He told me about you."

Then she seized Gordon's arm, and together they made their way through the curious crowd, paid their check, and went out.

"You'll have to sit down," said the waiter to Pete after they had gone.

"What's 'at? Sit down?"

"Yes—or get out."

Peter turned to Dean.

"Come on," he suggested. "Let's beat up this waiter."

"All right."

They advanced toward him, their faces grown stern. The waiter retreated.

Peter suddenly reached over to a plate on the table beside him and picking up a handful of hash tossed it into the air. It descended as a languid parabola in snowflake effect on the heads of those near by.

"Hey! Ease up!"

"Put him out!"

"Sit down, Peter!"

"Cut out that stuff!"

Peter laughed and bowed.

"Thank you for your kind applause, ladies and gents. If some one will lend me some more hash and a tall hat we will go on with the act."

The bouncer bustled up.

"You've gotta get out!" he said to Peter.

"Hell, no!"

"He's my friend!" put in Dean indignantly.

A crowd of waiters were gathering. "Put him out!"

"Better go, Peter."

There was a short struggle and the two were edged and pushed toward the door.

"I got a hat and a coat here!" cried Peter.

"Well, go get 'em and be spry about it!"

The bouncer released his hold on Peter, who, adopting a ludicrous air of extreme cunning, rushed immediately around to the other table, where he burst into derisive laughter and thumbed his nose at the exasperated waiters.

"Think I just better wait a l'il' longer," he announced.

The chase began. Four waiters were sent around one way and four another. Dean caught hold of two of them by the coat, and another struggle took place before the pursuit of Peter could be resumed; he was finally pinioned after overturning a sugar-bowl and several cups of coffee. A fresh argument ensued at the cashier's desk, where Peter attempted to buy another dish of hash to take with him and throw at policemen.

But the commotion upon his exit proper was dwarfed by another phenomenon which drew admiring glances and a prolonged involuntary "Oh-h-h!" from every person in the restaurant.

The great plate-glass front had turned to a deep creamy blue, the color of a Maxfield Parrish moonlight—a blue that seemed to press close upon the pane as if to crowd its way into the restaurant. Dawn had come up in Columbus Circle, magical, breathless dawn, silhouetting the great statue of the immortal Christopher, and mingling in a curious and uncanny manner with the fading yellow electric light inside.

· X ·

MR. IN AND MR. OUT are not listed by the census-taker. You will search for them in vain through the social register or the births, marriages, and deaths, or the grocer's credit list. Oblivion has swallowed them and the testimony that they ever existed at all is vague and shadowy, and inadmissible in a court of law. Yet I have it upon the best authority that for a brief space Mr. In and Mr. Out lived, breathed, answered to their names and radiated vivid personalities of their own.

During the brief span of their lives they walked in their native garments down the great highway of a great nation; were laughed at, sworn at, chased, and fled from. Then they passed and were heard of no more.

They were already taking form dimly, when a taxicab with the top open breezed down Broadway in the faintest glimmer of May dawn. In this car sat the souls of Mr. In and Mr. Out discussing with amazement the blue light that had so precipitately colored the sky behind the statue of Christopher Columbus, discussing with bewilderment the old, gray faces of the early risers which skimmed palely along the street like blown bits of paper on a gray lake. They were agreed on all things, from the absurdity of the bouncer in Childs' to the absurdity of the business of life. They were dizzy with the extreme maudlin happiness that the morning had awakened in their glowing souls. Indeed, so fresh and vigorous was their pleasure in living that they felt it should be expressed by loud cries.

"Ye-ow-ow!" hooted Peter, making a megaphone with his hands—and Dean joined in with a call that, though equally significant and symbolic, derived its resonance from its very inarticulateness.

"Yo-ho! Yea! Yoho! Yo-buba!"

Fifty-third Street was a bus with a dark, bobbed-hair beauty atop; Fifty-second was a street cleaner who dodged, escaped, and sent up a yell of, "Look where you're aimin'!" in a pained and grieved voice. At Fiftieth Street a group of men on a very white sidewalk in front of a very white building turned to stare after them, and shouted:

"Some party, boys!"

At Forty-ninth Street Peter turned to Dean. "Beautiful morning," he said gravely, squinting up his owlish eyes.

"Probably is."

"Go get some breakfast, hey?"

Dean agreed—with additions.

"Breakfast and liquor."

"Breakfast and liquor," repeated Peter, and they looked at each other, nodding. "That's logical."

Then they both burst into loud laughter.

"Breakfast and liquor! Oh, gosh!"

"No such thing," announced Peter.

"Don't serve it? Ne'mind. We force 'em serve it. Bring pressure bear."

"Bring logic bear."

The taxi cut suddenly off Broadway, sailed along a cross street, and stopped in front of a heavy tomb-like building in Fifth Avenue.

"What's idea?"

The taxi-driver informed them that this was Delmonico's.

This was somewhat puzzling. They were forced to devote several minutes to intense concentration, for if such an order had been given there must have been a reason for it.

"Somep'm 'bouta coat," suggested the taxi-man.

That was it. Peter's overcoat and hat. He had left them at Delmonico's. Having decided this, they disembarked from the taxi and strolled toward the entrance arm in arm.

"Hey!" said the taxi-driver.

"Huh?"

"You better pay me."

They shook their heads in shocked negation.

"Later, not now—we give orders, you wait."

The taxi-driver objected; he wanted his money now. With the scornful condescension of men exercising tremendous self-control they paid him.

Inside Peter groped in vain through a dim, deserted check-room in search of his coat and derby.

"Gone, I guess. Somebody stole it."

"Some Sheff student."

"All probability."

"Never mind," said Dean, nobly. "I'll leave mine here too—then we'll both be dressed the same."

He removed his overcoat and hat and was hanging them up when his roving glance was caught and held magnetically by two large squares of cardboard tacked to the two coat-room doors. The one on the left-hand door bore the word "In" in big black letters, and the one on the right-hand door flaunted the equally emphatic word "Out."

"Look!" he exclaimed happily——

Peter's eyes followed his pointing finger.

"What?"

"Look at the signs. Let's take 'em."

"Good idea."

"Probably pair very rare an' valuable signs. Probably come in handy."

Peter removed the left-hand sign from the door and endeavored to conceal it about his person. The sign being of considerable proportions, this was a matter of some difficulty. An idea flung itself at him, and with an air of dignified mystery he turned his back. After an instant he wheeled dramatically around, and stretching out his arms displayed himself to the admiring Dean. He had inserted the sign in his vest, completely covering his shirt front. In effect, the word "In" had been painted upon his shirt in large black letters.

"Yoho!" cheered Dean. "Mister In."

He inserted his own sign in like manner.

"Mister Out!" he announced triumphantly. "Mr. In meet Mr. Out."

They advanced and shook hands. Again laughter overcame them and they rocked in a shaken spasm of mirth.

"Yoho!"

"We probably get a flock of breakfast."

"We'll go—go to the Commodore."

Arm in arm they sallied out the door, and turning east in Forty-fourth Street set out for the Commodore.

As they came out a short dark soldier, very pale and tired, who had been wandering listlessly along the sidewalk, turned to look at them.

He started over as though to address them, but as they immediately bent on him glances of withering unrecognition, he waited until they had started unsteadily down the street, and then followed at about forty paces, chuckling to himself and saying "Oh, boy!" over and over under his breath, in delighted, anticipatory tones.

Mr. In and Mr. Out were meanwhile exchanging pleasantries concerning their future plans.

"We want liquor; we want breakfast. Neither without the other. One and indivisible."

"We want both 'em!"

"Both 'em!"

It was quite light now, and passers-by began to bend curious eyes on the pair. Obviously they were engaged in a discussion, which afforded each of them intense amusement, for occasionally a fit of laughter would seize upon them so violently that, still with their arms interlocked, they would bend nearly double.

Reaching the Commodore, they exchanged a few spicy epigrams with the sleepy-eyed doorman, navigated the revolving door with some difficulty, and then made their way through a thinly populated but startled lobby to the dining-room, where a puzzled waiter showed them an obscure table in a corner. They studied the bill of fare helplessly, telling over the items to each other in puzzled mumbles.

"Don't see any liquor here," said Peter reproachfully.

The waiter became audible but unintelligible.

"Repeat," continued Peter, with patient tolerance, "that there seems to be unexplained and quite distasteful lack of liquor upon bill of fare."

"Here!" said Dean confidently, "let me handle him." He turned to the waiter—"Bring us—bring us—" he scanned the bill of fare anxiously. "Bring us a quart of champagne and a—a—probably ham sandwich."

The waiter looked doubtful.

"Bring it!" roared Mr. In and Mr. Out in chorus.

The waiter coughed and disappeared. There was a short wait during which they were subjected without their knowledge to a careful scrutiny by the headwaiter. Then the champagne arrived, and at the sight of it Mr. In and Mr. Out became jubilant.

"Imagine their objecting to us having champagne for breakfast—jus' imagine."

They both concentrated upon the vision of such an awesome possibility, but the feat was too much for them. It was impossible for their joint imaginations to conjure up a world where any one might object to any one else having champagne for breakfast. The waiter drew the cork with an enormous *pop*—and their glasses immediately foamed with pale yellow froth.

"Here's health, Mr. In."

"Here's same to you, Mr. Out."

The waiter withdrew; the minutes passed; the champagne became low in the bottle.

"It's—it's mortifying," said Dean suddenly.

"Wha's mortifying?"

"The idea their objecting us having champagne breakfast."

"Mortifying?" Peter considered. "Yes, tha's word—mortifying."

Again they collapsed into laughter, howled, swayed, rocked back and forth in their chairs, repeating the word "mortifying" over and over to each other—each repetition seeming to make it only more brilliantly absurd.

After a few more gorgeous minutes they decided on another quart. Their anxious waiter consulted his immediate superior, and this discreet person gave implicit instructions that no more champagne should be served. Their check was brought.

Five minutes later, arm in arm, they left the Commodore and made their way through a curious, staring crowd along Forty-second Street, and up Vanderbilt Avenue to the Biltmore. There, with sudden cunning, they rose to the occasion and traversed the lobby, walking fast and standing unnaturally erect.

Once in the dining-room they repeated their performance. They were torn between intermittent convulsive laughter and sudden spasmodic discussions of politics, college, and the sunny state of their dispositions. Their watches told them that it was now nine o'clock, and a dim idea was born in them that they were on a memorable party, something that they would remember always. They lingered over the second bottle. Either of them had only to mention the word "mortifying" to send them both into riotous gasps. The dining-room was whirring and shifting now; a curious lightness permeated and rarefied the heavy air.

They paid their check and walked out into the lobby.

It was at this moment that the exterior doors revolved for the thousandth time that morning, and admitted into the lobby a very pale young beauty with dark circles under her eyes, attired in a much-rumpled evening dress. She was accompanied by a plain stout man, obviously not an appropriate escort.

At the top of the stairs this couple encountered Mr. In and Mr. Out.

"Edith," began Mr. In, stepping toward her hilariously and making a sweeping bow, "darling, good morning."

The stout man glanced questioningly at Edith, as if merely asking her permission to throw this man summarily out of the way.

" 'Scuse familiarity," added Peter, as an afterthought. "Edith, good-morning."

He seized Dean's elbow and impelled him into the foreground.

"Meet Mr. In, Edith, my bes' frien'. Inseparable. Mr. In and Mr. Out."

Mr. Out advanced and bowed; in fact, he advanced so far and bowed so low that he tipped slightly forward and only kept his balance by placing a hand lightly on Edith's shoulder.

"I'm Mr. Out, Edith," he mumbled pleasantly, "S'misterin Misterout."

" 'Smisterinanout," said Peter proudly.

But Edith stared straight by them, her eyes fixed on some infinite speck in the gallery above her. She nodded slightly to the stout man, who advanced bull-like and with a sturdy brisk gesture pushed Mr. In and Mr. Out to either side. Through this alley he and Edith walked.

But ten paces farther on Edith stopped again—stopped and pointed to a short, dark soldier who was eying the crowd in general, and the tableau of Mr. In and Mr. Out in particular, with a sort of puzzled, spell-bound awe.

"There," cried Edith. "See there!"

Her voice rose, became somewhat shrill. Her pointing finger shook slightly.

"There's the soldier who broke my brother's leg."

There were a dozen exclamations; a man in a cutaway coat left his place near the desk and advanced alertly; the stout person made a sort of lightning-like spring toward the short, dark soldier, and then the lobby closed around the little group and blotted them from the sight of Mr. In and Mr. Out.

But to Mr. In and Mr. Out this event was merely a particolored iridescent segment of a whirring, spinning world.

They heard loud voices; they saw the stout man spring; the picture suddenly blurred.

Then they were in an elevator bound skyward.

"What floor, please?" said the elevator man.

"Any floor," said Mr. In.

"Top floor," said Mr. Out.

"This is the top floor," said the elevator man.

"Have another floor put on," said Mr. Out.

"Higher," said Mr. In.

"Heaven," said Mr. Out.

· XI ·

IN A BEDROOM of a small hotel just off Sixth Avenue Gordon Sterrett awoke with a pain in the back of his head and a sick throbbing in all his veins. He looked at the dusky gray shadows in the corners of the room and at a raw place on a large leather chair in the corner where it had long been in use. He saw clothes, dishevelled, rumpled clothes on the floor and he smelt stale cigarette smoke and stale liquor. The windows were tight shut. Outside the bright sunlight had thrown a dust-filled beam across the sill— a beam broken by the head of the wide wooden bed in which he had slept. He lay very quiet—comotose, drugged, his eyes wide, his mind clicking wildly like an unoiled machine.

It must have been thirty seconds after he perceived the sunbeam with the dust on it and the rip on the large leather chair that he had the sense of life close beside him, and it was another thirty seconds after that before he realized that he was irrevocably married to Jewel Hudson.

He went out half an hour later and bought a revolver at a sporting goods store. Then he took a taxi to the room where he had been living on East Twenty-seventh Street, and leaning across the table that held his drawing materials, fired a cartridge into his head just behind the temple.

THE JELLY-BEAN

◆

"The Jelly-Bean" was written as a sequel to "The Ice Palace." When the Post declined it, Fitzgerald changed the names but refused to provide a happy ending. The story was published in the October 1920 Metropolitan Magazine, as part of a six-story deal which brought Fitzgerald a raise from $500 to $900 per story.

Fitzgerald provided this comment when he collected "The Jelly-Bean" in Tales of the Jazz Age:

> *This is a Southern story, with the scene laid in the small city of Tarleton, Georgia. I have a profound affection for Tarleton, but somehow whenever I write a story about it I receive letters from all over the South denouncing me in no uncertain terms. "The Jelly Bean" . . . drew its full share of these admonitory notes.*
>
> *It was written under strange circumstances shortly after my first novel was published, and, moreover, it was the first story in which I had a collaborator. For, finding that I was unable to manage the crap-shooting episode, I turned it over to my wife, who, as a Southern girl, was presumably an expert on the technique and terminology of that great sectional pastime.*

◆

JIM POWELL was a Jelly-bean. Much as I desire to make him an appealing character, I feel that it would be unscrupulous to deceive you on that point. He was a bred-in-the-bone, dyed-in-the-wool, ninety-nine three-quarters per cent Jelly-bean and he grew lazily all during Jelly-bean season, which is every season, down in the land of the Jelly-beans well below the Mason-Dixon line.

Now if you call a Memphis man a Jelly-bean he will quite possibly pull a long sinewy rope from his hip pocket and hang you to a convenient telegraph-pole. If you call a New Orleans man a Jelly-bean he will probably grin and ask you who is taking your girl to the Mardi Gras ball. The particular

Jelly-bean patch which produced the protagonist of this history lies somewhere between the two—a little city of forty thousand that has dozed sleepily
for forty thousand years in southern Georgia, occasionally stirring in its
slumbers and muttering something about a war that took place sometime,
somewhere, and that everyone else has forgotten long ago.

Jim was a Jelly-bean. I write that again because it has such a pleasant
sound—rather like the beginning of a fairy story—as if Jim were nice. It
somehow gives me a picture of him with a round, appetizing face and all
sorts of leaves and vegetables growing out of his cap. But Jim was long and
thin and bent at the waist from stooping over pool-tables, and he was what
might have been known in the indiscriminating North as a corner loafer.
"Jelly-bean" is the name throughout the undissolved Confederacy for one
who spends his life conjugating the verb to idle in the first person
singular—I am idling, I have idled, I will idle.

Jim was born in a white house on a green corner. It had four weather-
beaten pillars in front and a great amount of lattice-work in the rear that
made a cheerful criss-cross background for a flowery sun-drenched lawn.
Originally the dwellers in the white house had owned the ground next door
and next door to that and next door to that, but this had been so long ago
that even Jim's father scarcely remembered it. He had, in fact, thought it a
matter of so little moment that when he was dying from a pistol wound got
in a brawl he neglected even to tell little Jim, who was five years old and
miserably frightened. The white house became a boarding-house run by a
tight-lipped lady from Macon, whom Jim called Aunt Mamie and detested
with all his soul.

He became fifteen, went to high school, wore his hair in black snarls,
and was afraid of girls. He hated his home where four women and one old
man prolonged an interminable chatter from summer to summer about what
lots the Powell place had originally included and what sort of flowers would
be out next. Sometimes the parents of little girls in town, remembering Jim's
mother and fancying a resemblance in the dark eyes and hair, invited him
to parties, but parties made him shy and he much preferred sitting on a
disconnected axle in Tilly's Garage, rolling the bones or exploring his mouth
endlessly with a long straw. For pocket money, he picked up odd jobs, and
it was due to this that he stopped going to parties. At his third party little
Marjorie Haight had whispered indiscreetly and within hearing distance that
he was a boy who brought the groceries sometimes. So instead of the two-
step and polka, Jim had learned to throw any number he desired on the
dice and had listened to spicy tales of all the shootings that had occurred in
the surrounding country during the past fifty years.

He became eighteen. The war broke out and he enlisted as a gob and polished brass in the Charleston Navy-yard for a year. Then, by way of variety, he went North and polished brass in the Brooklyn Navy-yard for a year.

When the war was over he came home. He was twenty-one, his trousers were too short and too tight. His buttoned shoes were long and narrow. His tie was an alarming conspiracy of purple and pink marvellously scrolled, and over it were two blue eyes faded like a piece of very good old cloth long exposed to the sun.

In the twilight of one April evening when a soft gray had drifted down along the cottonfields and over the sultry town, he was a vague figure leaning against a board fence, whistling and gazing at the moon's rim above the lights of Jackson Street. His mind was working persistently on a problem that had held his attention for an hour. The Jelly-bean had been invited to a party.

Back in the days when all the boys had detested all the girls, Clark Darrow and Jim had sat side by side in school. But, while Jim's social aspirations had died in the oily air of the garage, Clark had alternately fallen in and out of love, gone to college, taken to drink, given it up, and, in short, become one of the best beaux of the town. Nevertheless Clark and Jim had retained a friendship that, though casual, was perfectly definite. That afternoon Clark's ancient Ford had slowed up beside Jim, who was on the sidewalk and, out of a clear sky, Clark had invited him to a party at the country club. The impulse that made him do this was no stranger than the impulse which made Jim accept. The latter was probably an unconscious ennui, a half-frightened sense of adventure. And now Jim was soberly thinking it over.

He began to sing, drumming his long foot idly on a stone block in the sidewalk till it wobbled up and down in time to the low throaty tune:

> *"One mile from Home in Jelly-bean town,*
> *Lives Jeanne, the Jelly-bean Queen.*
> *She loves her dice and treats 'em nice;*
> *No dice would treat her mean."*

He broke off and agitated the sidewalk to a bumpy gallop.

"Daggone!" he muttered, half aloud.

They would all be there—the old crowd, the crowd to which, by right of the white house, sold long since, and the portrait of the officer in gray over the mantel, Jim should have belonged. But that crowd had grown up together into a tight little set as gradually as the girls' dresses had lengthened inch by inch, as definitely as the boys' trousers had dropped suddenly to their ankles. And to that society of first names and dead puppy-loves

Jim was an outsider—a running mate of poor whites. Most of the men knew him, condescendingly; he tipped his hat to three or four girls. That was all.

When the dusk had thickened into a blue setting for the moon, he walked through the hot, pleasantly pungent town to Jackson Street. The stores were closing and the last shoppers were drifting homeward, as if borne on the dreamy revolution of a slow merry-go-round. A street-fair farther down made a brilliant alley of vari-colored booths and contributed a blend of music to the night—an oriental dance on a calliope, a melancholy bugle in front of a freak show, a cheerful rendition of "Back Home in Tennessee" on a hand-organ.

The Jelly-bean stopped in a store and bought a collar. Then he sauntered along toward Soda Sam's, where he found the usual three or four cars of a summer evening parked in front and the little darkies running back and forth with sundaes and lemonades.

"Hello, Jim."

It was a voice at his elbow—Joe Ewing sitting in an automobile with Marylyn Wade. Nancy Lamar and a strange man were in the back seat.

The Jelly-bean tipped his hat quickly.

"Hi, Ben—" then, after an almost imperceptible pause—"How y' all?"

Passing, he ambled on toward the garage where he had a room up-stairs. His "How y' all" had been said to Nancy Lamar, to whom he had not spoken in fifteen years.

Nancy had a mouth like a remembered kiss and shadowy eyes and blue-black hair inherited from her mother who had been born in Budapest. Jim passed her often in the street, walking small-boy fashion with her hands in her pockets and he knew that with her inseparable Sally Carrol Hopper she had left a trail of broken hearts from Atlanta to New Orleans.

For a few fleeting moments Jim wished he could dance. Then he laughed and as he reached his door began to sing softly to himself:

> *"Her Jelly Roll can twist your soul,*
> *Her eyes are big and brown,*
> *She's the Queen of the Queens of the Jelly-beans—*
> *My Jeanne of Jelly-bean Town."*

· II ·

At NINE-THIRTY Jim and Clark met in front of Soda Sam's and started for the Country Club in Clark's Ford.

"Jim," asked Clark casually, as they rattled through the jasmine-scented night, "how do you keep alive?"

The Jelly-bean paused, considered.

"Well," he said finally, "I got a room over Tilly's garage. I help him some with the cars in the afternoon an' he gives it to me free. Sometimes I drive one of his taxies and pick up a little thataway. I get fed up doin' that regular though."

"That all?"

"Well, when there's a lot of work I help him by the day—Saturdays usually—and then there's one main source of revenue I don't generally mention. Maybe you don't recollect I'm about the champion crap-shooter of this town. They make me shoot from a cup now because once I get the feel of a pair of dice they just roll for me."

Clark grinned appreciatively.

"I never could learn to set 'em so's they'd do what I wanted. Wish you'd shoot with Nancy Lamar some day and take all her money away from her. She will roll 'em with the boys and she loses more than her daddy can afford to give her. I happen to know she sold a good ring last month to pay a debt."

The Jelly-bean was non-committal.

"The white house on Elm Street still belong to you?"

Jim shook his head.

"Sold. Got a pretty good price, seein' it wasn't in a good part of town no more. Lawyer told me to put it into Liberty bonds. But Aunt Mamie got so she didn't have no sense, so it takes all the interest to keep her up at Great Farms Sanitarium."

"Hm."

"I got an old uncle up-state an' I reckin I kin go up there if ever I get sure enough pore. Nice farm, but not enough niggers around to work it. He's asked me to come up and help him, but I don't guess I'd take much to it. Too doggone lonesome——" He broke off suddenly. "Clark, I want to tell you I'm much obliged to you for askin' me out, but I'd be a lot happier if you'd just stop the car right here an' let me walk back into town."

"Shucks!" Clark grunted. "Do you good to step out. You don't have to dance—just get out there on the floor and shake."

"Hold on," exclaimed Jim uneasily. "Don't you go leadin' me up to any girls and leavin' me there so I'll have to dance with 'em."

Clark laughed.

"'Cause," continued Jim desperately, "without you swear you won't do that I'm agoin' to get out right here an' my good legs goin' carry me back to Jackson Street."

They agreed after some argument that Jim, unmolested by females, was to view the spectacle from a secluded settee in the corner where Clark would join him whenever he wasn't dancing.

So ten o'clock found the Jelly-bean with his legs crossed and his arms conservatively folded, trying to look casually at home and politely uninterested in the dancers. At heart he was torn between overwhelming self-consciousness and an intense curiosity as to all that went on around him. He saw the girls emerge one by one from the dressing-room, stretching and pluming themselves like bright birds, smiling over their powdered shoulders at the chaperones, casting a quick glance around to take in the room and, simultaneously, the room's reaction to their entrance—and then, again like birds, alighting and nestling in the sober arms of their waiting escorts. Sally Carrol Hopper, blonde and lazy-eyed, appeared clad in her favorite pink and blinking like an awakened rose. Marjorie Haight, Marylyn Wade, Harriet Cary, all the girls he had seen loitering down Jackson Street by noon, now, curled and brilliantined and delicately tinted for the overhead lights, were miraculously strange Dresden figures of pink and blue and red and gold, fresh from the shop and not yet fully dried.

He had been there half an hour, totally uncheered by Clark's jovial visits which were each one accompanied by a "Hello, old boy, how you making out?" and a slap at his knee. A dozen males had spoken to him or stopped for a moment beside him, but he knew that they were each one surprised at finding him there and fancied that one or two were even slightly resentful. But at half past ten his embarrassment suddenly left him and a pull of breathless interest took him completely out of himself—Nancy Lamar had come out of the dressing-room.

She was dressed in yellow organdie, a costume of a hundred cool corners, with three tiers of ruffles and a big bow in back until she shed black and yellow around her in a sort of phosphorescent lustre. The Jelly-bean's eyes opened wide and a lump arose in his throat. For a minute she stood beside the door until her partner hurried up. Jim recognized him as the stranger who had been with her in Joe Ewing's car that afternoon. He saw her set her arms akimbo and say something in a low voice, and laugh. The man laughed too and Jim experienced the quick pang of a weird new kind of pain. Some ray had passed between the pair, a shaft of beauty from that sun that had warmed him a moment since. The Jelly-bean felt suddenly like a weed in a shadow.

A minute later Clark approached him, bright-eyed and glowing.

"Hi, old man," he cried with some lack of originality. "How you making out?"

Jim replied that he was making out as well as could be expected.

"You come along with me," commanded Clark. "I've got something that'll put an edge on the evening."

Jim followed him awkwardly across the floor and up the stairs to the locker-room where Clark produced a flask of nameless yellow liquid.

"Good old corn."

Ginger ale arrived on a tray. Such potent nectar as "good old corn" needed some disguise beyond seltzer.

"Say, boy," exclaimed Clark breathlessly, "doesn't Nancy Lamar look beautiful?"

Jim nodded.

"Mighty beautiful," he agreed.

"She's all dolled up to a fare-you-well to-night," continued Clark. "Notice that fellow she's with?"

"Big fella? White pants?"

"Yeah. Well, that's Ogden Merritt from Savannah. Old man Merritt makes the Merritt safety razors. This fella's crazy about her. Been chasing after her all year.

"She's a wild baby," continued Clark, "but I like her. So does everybody. But she sure does do crazy stunts. She usually gets out alive, but she's got scars all over her reputation from one thing or another she's done."

"That so?" Jim passed over his glass. "That's good corn."

"Not so bad. Oh, she's a wild one. Shoots craps, say, boy! And she do like her highballs. Promised I'd give her one later on."

"She in love with this—Merritt?"

"Damned if I know. Seems like all the best girls around here marry fellas and go off somewhere."

He poured himself one more drink and carefully corked the bottle.

"Listen, Jim, I got to go dance and I'd be much obliged if you just stick this corn right on your hip as long as you're not dancing. If a man notices I've had a drink he'll come up and ask me and before I know it it's all gone and somebody else is having my good time."

So Nancy Lamar was going to marry. This toast of a town was to become the private property of an individual in white trousers—and all because white trousers' father had made a better razor than his neighbor. As they descended the stairs Jim found the idea inexplicably depressing. For the first time in his life he felt a vague and romantic yearning. A picture of her began to form in his imagination—Nancy walking boylike and debonnaire along the street, taking an orange as tithe from a worshipful fruit-dealer, charging a dope on a mythical account at Soda Sam's, assembling a convoy of beaux and then driving off in triumphal state for an afternoon of splashing and singing.

The Jelly-bean walked out on the porch to a deserted corner, dark between the moon on the lawn and the single lighted door of the ballroom. There he found a chair and, lighting a cigarette, drifted into the thoughtless reverie that was his usual mood. Yet now it was a reverie made sensuous by the night and by the hot smell of damp powder puffs, tucked in the fronts of low dresses and distilling a thousand rich scents to float out through the open door. The music itself, blurred by a loud trombone, became hot and shadowy, a languorous overtone to the scraping of many shoes and slippers.

Suddenly the square of yellow light that fell through the door was obscured by a dark figure. A girl had come out of the dressing-room and was standing on the porch not more than ten feet away. Jim heard a low-breathed "doggone" and then she turned and saw him. It was Nancy Lamar.

Jim rose to his feet.

"Howdy?"

"Hello—" she paused, hesitated and then approached. "Oh, it's—Jim Powell."

He bowed slightly, tried to think of a casual remark.

"Do you suppose," she began quickly, "I mean—do you know anything about gum?"

"What?"

"I've got gum on my shoe. Some utter ass left his or her gum on the floor and of course I stepped in it."

Jim blushed, inappropriately.

"Do you know how to get it off?" she demanded petulantly. "I've tried a knife. I've tried every damn thing in the dressing-room. I've tried soap and water—and even perfume and I've ruined my powder-puff trying to make it stick to that."

Jim considered the question in some agitation.

"Why—I think maybe gasolene——"

The words had scarcely left his lips when she grasped his hand and pulled him at a run off the low veranda, over a flower bed and at a gallop toward a group of cars parked in the moonlight by the first hole of the golf course.

"Turn on the gasolene," she commanded breathlessly.

"What?"

"For the gum of course. I've got to get it off. I can't dance with gum on."

Obediently Jim turned to the cars and began inspecting them with a view to obtaining the desired solvent. Had she demanded a cylinder he would have done his best to wrench one out.

"Here," he said after a moment's search. "Here's one that's easy. Got a handkerchief?"

"It's up-stairs wet. I used it for the soap and water."

Jim laboriously explored his pockets.

"Don't believe I got one either."

"Doggone it! Well, we can turn it on and let it run on the ground."

He turned the spout; a dripping began.

"More!"

He turned it on fuller. The dripping became a flow and formed an oily pool that glistened brightly, reflecting a dozen tremulous moons on its quivering bosom.

"Ah," she sighed contentedly, "let it all out. The only thing to do is to wade in it."

In desperation he turned on the tap full and the pool suddenly widened sending tiny rivers and trickles in all directions.

"That's fine. That's something like."

Raising her skirts she stepped gracefully in.

"I know this'll take it off," she murmured.

Jim smiled.

"There's lots more cars."

She stepped daintily out of the gasolene and began scraping her slippers, side and bottom, on the running board of the automobile. The Jelly-bean contained himself no longer. He bent double with explosive laughter and after a second she joined in.

"You're here with Clark Darrow, aren't you?" she asked as they walked back toward the veranda.

"Yes."

"You know where he is now?"

"Out dancin', I reckin."

"The deuce. He promised me a highball."

"Well," said Jim, "I guess that'll be all right. I got his bottle right here in my pocket."

She smiled at him radiantly.

"I guess maybe you'll need ginger ale though," he added.

"Not me. Just the bottle."

"Sure enough?"

She laughed scornfully.

"Try me. I can drink anything any man can. Let's sit down."

She perched herself on the side of a table and he dropped into one of the wicker chairs beside her. Taking out the cork she held the flask to her lips and took a long drink. He watched her fascinated.

"Like it?"

She shook her head breathlessly.

"No, but I like the way it makes me feel. I think most people are that way."

Jim agreed.

"My daddy liked it too well. It got him."

"American men," said Nancy gravely, "don't know how to drink."

"What?" Jim was startled.

"In fact," she went on carelessly, "they don't know how to do anything very well. The one thing I regret in my life is that I wasn't born in England."

"In England?"

"Yes. It's the one regret of my life that I wasn't."

"Do you like it over there."

"Yes. Immensely. I've never been there in person, but I've met a lot of Englishmen who were over here in the army, Oxford and Cambridge men—you know, that's like Sewanee and University of Georgia are here—and of course I've read a lot of English novels."

Jim was interested, amazed.

"D' you ever hear of Lady Diana Manners?" she asked earnestly.

No, Jim had not.

"Well, she's what I'd like to be. Dark, you know, like me, and wild as sin. She's the girl who rode her horse up the steps of some cathedral or church or something and all the novelists made their heroines do it afterwards."

Jim nodded politely. He was out of his depths.

"Pass the bottle," suggested Nancy. "I'm going to take another little one. A little drink wouldn't hurt a baby.

"You see," she continued, again breathless after a draught. "People over there have style. Nobody has style here. I mean the boys here aren't really worth dressing up for or doing sensational things for. Don't you know?"

"I suppose so—I mean I suppose not," murmured Jim.

"And I'd like to do 'em an' all. I'm really the only girl in town that has style."

She stretched out her arms and yawned pleasantly.

"Pretty evening."

"Sure is," agreed Jim.

"Like to have boat," she suggested dreamily. "Like to sail out on a silver lake, say the Thames, for instance. Have champagne and caviare sandwiches along. Have about eight people. And one of the men would jump overboard to amuse the party and get drowned like a man did with Lady Diana Manners once."

"Did he do it to please her?"

"Didn't mean drown himself to please her. He just meant to jump overboard and make everybody laugh."

"I reckin they just died laughin' when he drowned."

"Oh, I suppose they laughed a little," she admitted. "I imagine she did, anyway. She's pretty hard, I guess—like I am."

"You hard?"

"Like nails." She yawned again and added, "Give me a little more from that bottle."

Jim hesitated but she held out her hand defiantly.

"Don't treat me like a girl," she warned him. "I'm not like any girl *you* ever saw." She considered. "Still, perhaps you're right. You got—you got old head on young shoulders."

She jumped to her feet and moved toward the door. The Jelly-bean rose also.

"Good-bye," she said politely, "good-bye. Thanks, Jelly-bean."

Then she stepped inside and left him wide-eyed upon the porch.

· III ·

AT TWELVE O'CLOCK a procession of cloaks issued single file from the women's dressing-room and, each one pairing with a coated beau like dancers meeting in a cotillion figure, drifted through the door with sleepy happy laughter—through the door into the dark where autos backed and snorted and parties called to one another and gathered around the water-cooler.

Jim, sitting in his corner, rose to look for Clark. They had met at eleven; then Clark had gone in to dance. So, seeking him, Jim wandered into the soft-drink stand that had once been a bar. The room was deserted except for a sleepy negro dozing behind the counter and two boys lazily fingering a pair of dice at one of the tables. Jim was about to leave when he saw Clark coming in. At the same moment Clark looked up.

"Hi, Jim!" he commanded. "C'mon over and help us with this bottle. I guess there's not much left, but there's one all around."

Nancy, the man from Savannah, Marylyn Wade, and Joe Ewing were lolling and laughing in the doorway. Nancy caught Jim's eye and winked at him humorously.

They drifted over to a table and arranging themselves around it waited for the waiter to bring ginger ale. Jim, faintly ill at ease, turned his eyes on Nancy, who had drifted into a nickel crap game with the two boys at the next table.

"Bring them over here," suggested Clark.

Joe looked around.

"We don't want to draw a crowd. It's against club rules."

"Nobody's around," insisted Clark, "except Mr. Taylor. He's walking up and down like a wild-man trying to find out who let all the gasolene out of his car."

There was a general laugh.

"I bet a million Nancy got something on her shoe again. You can't park when she's around."

"O Nancy, Mr. Taylor's looking for you!"

Nancy's cheeks were glowing with excitement over the game. "I haven't seen his silly little flivver in two weeks."

Jim felt a sudden silence. He turned and saw an individual of uncertain age standing in the doorway.

Clark's voice punctuated the embarrassment.

"Won't you join us, Mr. Taylor?"

"Thanks."

Mr. Taylor spread his unwelcome presence over a chair. "Have to, I guess. I'm waiting till they dig me up some gasolene. Somebody got funny with my car."

His eyes narrowed and he looked quickly from one to the other. Jim wondered what he had heard from the doorway—tried to remember what had been said.

"I'm right to-night," Nancy sang out, "and my four bits is in the ring."

"Faded!" snapped Taylor suddenly.

"Why, Mr. Taylor, I didn't know you shot craps!" Nancy was overjoyed to find that he had seated himself and instantly covered her bet. They had openly disliked each other since the night she had definitely discouraged a series of rather pointed advances.

"All right, babies, do it for your mamma. Just one little seven." Nancy was *cooing* to the dice. She rattled them with a brave underhand flourish, and rolled them out on the table.

"Ah-h! I suspected it. And now again with the dollar up."

Five passes to her credit found Taylor a bad loser. She was making it personal, and after each success Jim watched triumph flutter across her face. She was doubling with each throw—such luck could scarcely last.

"Better go easy," he cautioned her timidly.

"Ah, but watch this one," she whispered. It was eight on the dice and she called her number.

"Little Ada, this time we're going South."

Ada from Decatur rolled over the table. Nancy was flushed and half-hysterical, but her luck was holding. She drove the pot up and up, refusing to drag. Taylor was drumming with his fingers on the table, but he was in to stay.

Then Nancy tried for a ten and lost the dice. Taylor seized them avidly. He shot in silence, and in the hush of excitement the clatter of one pass after another on the table was the only sound.

Now Nancy had the dice again, but her luck had broken. An hour passed. Back and forth it went. Taylor had been at it again—and again and again. They were even at last—Nancy lost her ultimate five dollars.

"Will you take my check," she said quickly, "for fifty, and we'll shoot it all?" Her voice was a little unsteady and her hand shook as she reached to the money.

Clark exchanged an uncertain but alarmed glance with Joe Ewing. Taylor shot again. He had Nancy's check.

"How 'bout another?" she said wildly. "Jes' any bank'll do—money everywhere as a matter of fact."

Jim understood—the "good old corn" he had given her—the "good old corn" she had taken since. He wished he dared interfere—a girl of that age and position would hardly have two bank accounts. When the clock struck two he contained himself no longer.

"May I—can't you let me roll 'em for you?" he suggested, his low, lazy voice a little strained.

Suddenly sleepy and listless, Nancy flung the dice down before him.

"All right—old boy! As Lady Diana Manners says, 'Shoot 'em, Jelly-bean'—My luck's gone."

"Mr. Taylor," said Jim, carelessly, "we'll shoot for one of those there checks against the cash."

Half an hour later Nancy swayed forward and clapped him on the back. "Stole my luck, you did." She was nodding her head sagely.

Jim swept up the last check and putting it with the others tore them into confetti and scattered them on the floor. Someone started singing, and Nancy kicking her chair backward rose to her feet.

"Ladies and gentlemen," she announced. "Ladies—that's you Marylyn. I want to tell the world that Mr. Jim Powell, who is a well-known Jelly-bean of this city, is an exception to a great rule—'lucky in dice—unlucky in love.' He's lucky in dice, and as matter fact I—I *love* him. Ladies and gentlemen, Nancy Lamar, famous dark-haired beauty often featured in the *Herald* as one th' most popular members of younger set as other girls are often featured in this particular case. Wish to announce—wish to announce, anyway, Gentlemen——" She tipped suddenly. Clark caught her and restored her balance.

"My error," she laughed, "she stoops to—stoops to—anyways——
We'll drink to Jelly-bean . . . Mr. Jim Powell, King of the Jelly-beans."

And a few minutes later as Jim waited hat in hand for Clark in the darkness
of that same corner of the porch where she had come searching for gasolene,
she appeared suddenly beside him.

"Jelly-bean," she said, "are you here, Jelly-bean? I think—" and her
slight unsteadiness seemed part of an enchanted dream—"I think you deserve one of my sweetest kisses for that, Jelly-bean."

For an instant her arms were around his neck—her lips were pressed
to his.

"I'm a wild part of the world, Jelly-bean, but you did me a good turn."

Then she was gone, down the porch, over the cricket-loud lawn. Jim saw
Merritt come out the front door and say something to her angrily—saw her
laugh and, turning away, walk with averted eyes to his car. Marylyn and
Joe followed, singing a drowsy song about a Jazz baby.

Clark came out and joined Jim on the steps. "All pretty lit, I guess," he
yawned. "Merritt's in a mean mood. He's certainly off Nancy."

Over east along the golf course a faint rug of gray spread itself across the
feet of the night. The party in the car began to chant a chorus as the engine
warmed up.

"Good-night everybody," called Clark.

"Good-night, Clark."

"Good-night."

There was a pause, and then a soft, happy voice added,

"Good-night, Jelly-bean."

The car drove off to a burst of singing. A rooster on a farm across the
way took up a solitary mournful crow, and behind them a last negro waiter
turned out the porch light. Jim and Clark strolled over toward the Ford,
their shoes crunching raucously on the gravel drive.

"Oh boy!" sighed Clark softly, "how you can set those dice!"

It was still too dark for him to see the flush on Jim's thin cheeks—or to
know that it was a flush of unfamiliar shame.

· I V ·

OVER TILLY'S GARAGE a bleak room echoed all day to the rumble and
snorting down-stairs and the singing of the negro washers as they turned
the hose on the cars outside. It was a cheerless square of a room, punctuated
with a bed and a battered table on which lay half a dozen books—Joe
Miller's "Slow Train thru Arkansas," "Lucille," in an old edition very much

annotated in an old-fashioned hand; "The Eyes of the World," by Harold Bell Wright, and an ancient prayer-book of the Church of England with the name Alice Powell and the date 1831 written on the fly-leaf.

The East, gray when the Jelly-bean entered the garage, became a rich and vivid blue as he turned on his solitary electric light. He snapped it out again, and going to the window rested his elbows on the sill and stared into the deepening morning. With the awakening of his emotions, his first perception was a sense of futility, a dull ache at the utter grayness of his life. A wall had sprung up suddenly around him hedging him in, a wall as definite and tangible as the white wall of his bare room. And with his perception of this wall all that had been the romance of his existence, the casualness, the light-hearted improvidence, the miraculous open-handedness of life faded out. The Jelly-bean strolling up Jackson Street humming a lazy song, known at every shop and street stand, cropful of easy greeting and local wit, sad sometimes for only the sake of sadness and the flight of time—that Jelly-bean was suddenly vanished. The very name was a reproach, a triviality. With a flood of insight he knew that Merritt must despise him, that even Nancy's kiss in the dawn would have awakened not jealousy but only a contempt for Nancy's so lowering herself. And on his part the Jelly-bean had used for her a dingy subterfuge learned from the garage. He had been her moral laundry; the stains were his.

As the gray became blue, brightened and filled the room, he crossed to his bed and threw himself down on it, gripping the edges fiercely.

"I love her," he cried aloud, "God!"

As he said this something gave way within him like a lump melting in his throat. The air cleared and became radiant with dawn, and turning over on his face he began to sob dully into the pillow.

In the sunshine of three o'clock Clark Darrow chugging painfully along Jackson Street was hailed by the Jelly-bean, who stood on the curb with his fingers in his vest pockets.

"Hi!" called Clark, bringing his Ford to an astonishing stop alongside. "Just get up?"

The Jelly-bean shook his head.

"Never did go to bed. Felt sorta restless, so I took a long walk this morning out in the country. Just got into town this minute."

"Should think you *would* feel restless. I been feeling thataway all day——"

"I'm thinkin' of leavin' town," continued the Jelly-bean, absorbed by his own thoughts. "Been thinkin' of goin' up on the farm, and takin' a little that work off Uncle Dun. Reckin I been bummin' too long."

Clark was silent and the Jelly-bean continued:

"I reckin maybe after Aunt Mamie dies I could sink that money of mine in the farm and make somethin' out of it. All my people originally came from that part up there. Had a big place."

Clark looked at him curiously.

"That's funny," he said. "This—this sort of affected me the same way."

The Jelly-bean hesitated.

"I don't know," he began slowly, "somethin' about—about that girl last night talkin' about a lady named Diana Manners—an English lady, sorta got me thinkin'!" He drew himself up and looked oddly at Clark, "I had a family once," he said defiantly.

Clark nodded.

"I know."

"And I'm the last of 'em," continued the Jelly-bean, his voice rising slightly, "and I ain't worth shucks. Name they call me by means jelly—weak and wobbly like. People who weren't nothin' when my folks was a lot turn up their noses when they pass me on the street."

Again Clark was silent.

"So I'm through. I'm goin' to-day. And when I come back to this town it's going to be like a gentleman."

Clark took out his handkerchief and wiped his damp brow.

"Reckon you're not the only one it shook up," he admitted gloomily. "All this thing of girls going round like they do is going to stop right quick. Too bad, too, but everybody'll have to see it thataway."

"Do you mean," demanded Jim in surprise, "that all that's leaked out?"

"Leaked out? How on earth could they keep it secret. It'll be announced in the papers to-night. Doctor Lamar's got to save his name somehow."

Jim put his hands on the sides of the car and tightened his long fingers on the metal.

"Do you mean Taylor investigated those checks?"

It was Clark's turn to be surprised.

"Haven't you heard what happened?"

Jim's startled eyes were answer enough.

"Why," announced Clark dramatically, "those four got another bottle of corn, got tight and decided to shock the town—so Nancy and that fella Merritt were married in Rockville at seven o'clock this morning."

A tiny indentation appeared in the metal under the Jelly-bean's fingers.

"Married?"

"Sure enough. Nancy sobered up and rushed back into town, crying and frightened to death—claimed it'd all been a mistake. First Doctor Lamar went wild and was going to kill Merritt, but finally they got it patched up some way, and Nancy and Merritt went to Savannah on the two-thirty train."

Jim closed his eyes and with an effort overcame a sudden sickness.

"It's too bad," said Clark philosophically. "I don't mean the wedding—reckon that's all right, though I don't guess Nancy cared a darn about him. But it's a crime for a nice girl like that to hurt her family that way."

The Jelly-bean let go the car and turned away. Again something was going on inside him, some inexplicable but almost chemical change.

"Where you going?" asked Clark.

The Jelly-bean turned and looked dully back over his shoulder.

"Got to go," he muttered. "Been up too long; feelin' right sick."

"Oh."

The street was hot at three and hotter still at four, the April dust seeming to enmesh the sun and give it forth again as a world-old joke forever played on an eternity of afternoons. But at half past four a first layer of quiet fell and the shades lengthened under the awnings and heavy foliaged trees. In this heat nothing mattered. All life was weather, a waiting through the hot where events had no significance for the cool that was soft and caressing like a woman's hand on a tired forehead. Down in Georgia there is a feeling—perhaps inarticulate—that this is the greatest wisdom of the South—so after a while the Jelly-bean turned into a poolhall on Jackson Street where he was sure to find a congenial crowd who would make all the old jokes—the ones he knew.

THE CURIOUS CASE
OF BENJAMIN BUTTON

♦

"The Curious Case of Benjamin Button" (Collier's, 27 May 1922) was hard to sell. Fitzgerald later wrote to his agent, Harold Ober: "I know that the magazines want only flapper stories from me—the trouble you had in disposing of Benjamin Button + The Diamond as Big as the Ritz *showed that."*

"Benjamin Button" was Fitzgerald's second published story (preceded by "The Cut-Glass Bowl," 1920) in the fantasy or supernatural mode, in which he wrote a few of his most brilliant stories. Fitzgerald was probably attracted to this form by its tension between romanticism and realism, for the challenge of fantasy is to make impossible events convincing. He provided the genesis for "Benjamin Button" when he collected it in Tales of the Jazz Age:

> *This story was inspired by a remark of Mark Twain's to the effect that it was a pity that the best part of life came at the beginning and the worst part at the end. By trying the experiment upon only one man in a perfectly normal world I have scarcely given his idea a fair trial. Several weeks after completing it, I discovered an almost identical plot in Samuel Butler's "Note-books."*

♦

As LONG ago as 1860 it was the proper thing to be born at home. At present, so I am told, the high gods of medicine have decreed that the first cries of the young shall be uttered upon the anesthetic air of a hospital, preferably a fashionable one. So young Mr. and Mrs. Roger Button were fifty years ahead of style when they decided, one day in the summer of 1860, that their first baby should be born in a hospital. Whether this anachronism had any bearing upon the astonishing history I am about to set down will never be known.

I shall tell you what occurred, and let you judge for yourself.

The Roger Buttons held an enviable position, both social and financial, in ante-bellum Baltimore. They were related to the This Family and the That Family, which, as every Southerner knew, entitled them to membership in that enormous peerage which largely populated the Confederacy. This was their first experience with the charming old custom of having babies— Mr. Button was naturally nervous. He hoped it would be a boy so that he could be sent to Yale College in Connecticut, at which institution Mr. Button himself had been known for four years by the somewhat obvious nickname of "Cuff."

On the September morning consecrated to the enormous event he arose nervously at six o'clock, dressed himself, adjusted an impeccable stock, and hurried forth through the streets of Baltimore to the hospital, to determine whether the darkness of the night had borne in new life upon its bosom.

When he was approximately a hundred yards from the Maryland Private Hospital for Ladies and Gentlemen he saw Doctor Keene, the family physician, descending the front steps, rubbing his hands together with a washing movement—as all doctors are required to do by the unwritten ethics of their profession.

Mr. Roger Button, the president of Roger Button & Co., Wholesale Hardware, began to run toward Doctor Keene with much less dignity than was expected from a Southern gentleman of that picturesque period. "Doctor Keene!" he called. "Oh, Doctor Keene!"

The doctor heard him, faced around, and stood waiting, a curious expression settling on his harsh, medicinal face as Mr. Button drew near.

"What happened?" demanded Mr. Button, as he came up in a gasping rush. "What was it? How is she? A boy? Who is it? What——"

"Talk sense!" said Doctor Keene sharply. He appeared somewhat irritated.

"Is the child born?" begged Mr. Button.

Doctor Keene frowned. "Why, yes, I suppose so—after a fashion." Again he threw a curious glance at Mr. Button.

"Is my wife all right?"

"Yes."

"Is it a boy or a girl?"

"Here now!" cried Doctor Keene in a perfect passion of irritation, "I'll ask you to go and see for yourself. Outrageous!" He snapped the last word out in almost one syllable, then he turned away muttering: "Do you imagine a case like this will help my professional reputation? One more would ruin me—ruin anybody."

"What's the matter?" demanded Mr. Button, appalled. "Triplets?"

"No, not triplets!" answered the doctor cuttingly. "What's more, you can go and see for yourself. And get another doctor. I brought you into the world, young man, and I've been physician to your family for forty years, but I'm through with you! I don't want to see you or any of your relatives ever again! Good-by!"

Then he turned sharply, and without another word climbed into his phaeton, which was waiting at the curbstone, and drove severely away.

Mr. Button stood there upon the sidewalk, stupefied and trembling from head to foot. What horrible mishap had occurred? He had suddenly lost all desire to go into the Maryland Private Hospital for Ladies and Gentlemen —it was with the greatest difficulty that, a moment later, he forced himself to mount the steps and enter the front door.

A nurse was sitting behind a desk in the opaque gloom of the hall. Swallowing his shame, Mr. Button approached her.

"Good-morning," she remarked, looking up at him pleasantly.

"Good-morning. I—I am Mr. Button."

At this a look of utter terror spread itself over the girl's face. She rose to her feet and seemed about to fly from the hall, restraining herself only with the most apparent difficulty.

"I want to see my child," said Mr. Button.

The nurse gave a little scream. "Oh—of course!" she cried hysterically. "Up-stairs. Right up-stairs. Go—*up!*"

She pointed the direction, and Mr. Button, bathed in a cool perspiration, turned falteringly, and began to mount to the second floor. In the upper hall he addressed another nurse who approached him, basin in hand. "I'm Mr. Button," he managed to articulate. "I want to see my——"

Clank! The basin clattered to the floor and rolled in the direction of the stairs. Clank! Clank! It began a methodical descent as if sharing in the general terror which this gentleman provoked.

"I want to see my child!" Mr. Button almost shrieked. He was on the verge of collapse.

Clank! The basin had reached the first floor. The nurse regained control of herself, and threw Mr. Button a look of hearty contempt.

"All *right*, Mr. Button," she agreed in a hushed voice. "Very *well!* But if you *knew* what state it's put us all in this morning! It's perfectly outrageous! The hospital will never have the ghost of a reputation after——"

"Hurry!" he cried hoarsely. "I can't stand this!"

"Come this way, then, Mr. Button."

He dragged himself after her. At the end of a long hall they reached a room from which proceeded a variety of howls—indeed, a room which, in later parlance, would have been known as the "crying-room." They entered. Ranged around the walls were half a dozen white-enameled rolling cribs, each with a tag tied at the head.

"Well," gasped Mr. Button, "which is mine?"

"There!" said the nurse.

Mr. Button's eyes followed her pointing finger, and this is what he saw. Wrapped in a voluminous white blanket, and partially crammed into one of the cribs, there sat an old man apparently about seventy years of age. His sparse hair was almost white, and from his chin dripped a long smoke-colored beard, which waved absurdly back and forth, fanned by the breeze coming in at the window. He looked up at Mr. Button with dim, faded eyes in which lurked a puzzled question.

"Am I mad?" thundered Mr. Button, his terror resolving into rage. "Is this some ghastly hospital joke?"

"It doesn't seem like a joke to us," replied the nurse severely. "And I don't know whether you're mad or not—but that is most certainly your child."

The cool perspiration redoubled on Mr. Button's forehead. He closed his eyes, and then, opening them, looked again. There was no mistake—he was gazing at a man of threescore and ten—a *baby* of threescore and ten, a baby whose feet hung over the sides of the crib in which it was reposing.

The old man looked placidly from one to the other for a moment, and then suddenly spoke in a cracked and ancient voice. "Are you my father?" he demanded.

Mr. Button and the nurse started violently.

"Because if you are," went on the old man querulously, "I wish you'd get me out of this place—or, at least, get them to put a comfortable rocker in here."

"Where in God's name did you come from? Who are you?" burst out Mr. Button frantically.

"I can't tell you *exactly* who I am," replied the querulous whine, "because I've only been born a few hours—but my last name is certainly Button."

"You lie! You're an impostor!"

The old man turned wearily to the nurse. "Nice way to welcome a new-born child," he complained in a weak voice. "Tell him he's wrong, why don't you?"

"You're wrong, Mr. Button," said the nurse severely. "This is your child, and you'll have to make the best of it. We're going to ask you to take him home with you as soon as possible—some time to-day."

"Home?" repeated Mr. Button incredulously.

"Yes, we can't have him here. We really can't, you know?"

"I'm right glad of it," whined the old man. "This is a fine place to keep a youngster of quiet tastes. With all this yelling and howling, I haven't been able to get a wink of sleep. I asked for something to eat"—here his voice rose to a shrill note of protest—"and they brought me a bottle of milk!"

Mr. Button sank down upon a chair near his son and concealed his face in his hands. "My heavens!" he murmured, in an ecstasy of horror. "What will people say? What must I do?"

"You'll have to take him home," insisted the nurse—"immediately!"

A grotesque picture formed itself with dreadful clarity before the eyes of the tortured man—a picture of himself walking through the crowded streets of the city with this appalling apparition stalking by his side. "I can't. I can't," he moaned.

People would stop to speak to him, and what was he going to say? He would have to introduce this—this septuagenarian: "This is my son, born early this morning." And then the old man would gather his blanket around him and they would plod on, past the bustling stores, the slave market— for a dark instant Mr. Button wished passionately that his son was black— past the luxurious houses of the residential district, past the home for the aged. . . .

"Come! Pull yourself together," commanded the nurse.

"See here," the old man announced suddenly, "if you think I'm going to walk home in this blanket, you're entirely mistaken."

"Babies always have blankets."

With a malicious crackle the old man held up a small white swaddling garment. "Look!" he quavered. "*This* is what they had ready for me."

"Babies always wear those," said the nurse primly.

"Well," said the old man, "this baby's not going to wear anything in about two minutes. This blanket itches. They might at least have given me a sheet."

"Keep it on! Keep it on!" said Mr. Button hurriedly. He turned to the nurse. "What'll I do?"

"Go down town and buy your son some clothes."

Mr. Button's son's voice followed him down into the hall: "And a cane, father. I want to have a cane."

Mr. Button banged the outer door savagely. . . .

· II ·

"Good-morning," Mr. Button said, nervously, to the clerk in the Chesapeake Dry Goods Company. "I want to buy some clothes for my child."

"How old is your child, sir?"

"About six hours," answered Mr. Button, without due consideration.

"Babies' supply department in the rear."

"Why, I don't think—I'm not sure that's what I want. It's—he's an unusually large-size child. Exceptionally—ah—large."

"They have the largest child's sizes."

"Where is the boys' department?" inquired Mr. Button, shifting his ground desperately. He felt that the clerk must surely scent his shameful secret.

"Right here."

"Well—" He hesitated. The notion of dressing his son in men's clothes was repugnant to him. If, say, he could only find a *very* large boy's suit, he might cut off that long and awful beard, dye the white hair brown, and thus manage to conceal the worst, and to retain something of his own self-respect—not to mention his position in Baltimore society.

But a frantic inspection of the boys' department revealed no suits to fit the new-born Button. He blamed the store, of course—in such cases it is the thing to blame the store.

"How old did you say that boy of yours was?" demanded the clerk curiously.

"He's—sixteen."

"Oh, I beg your pardon. I thought you said six *hours*. You'll find the youths' department in the next aisle."

Mr. Button turned miserably away. Then he stopped, brightened, and pointed his finger toward a dressed dummy in the window display. "There!" he exclaimed. "I'll take that suit, out there on the dummy."

The clerk stared. "Why," he protested, "that's not a child's suit. At least it *is*, but it's for fancy dress. You could wear it yourself!"

"Wrap it up," insisted his customer nervously. "That's what I want."

The astonished clerk obeyed.

Back at the hospital Mr. Button entered the nursery and almost threw the package at his son. "Here's your clothes," he snapped out.

The old man untied the package and viewed the contents with a quizzical eye.

"They look sort of funny to me," he complained. "I don't want to be made a monkey of——"

"You've made a monkey of me!" retorted Mr. Button fiercely. "Never you mind how funny you look. Put them on—or I'll—or I'll *spank* you."

He swallowed uneasily at the penultimate word, feeling nevertheless that it was the proper thing to say.

"All right, father"—this with a grotesque simulation of filial respect—
"you've lived longer; you know best. Just as you say."

As before, the sound of the word "father" caused Mr. Button to start
violently.

"And hurry."

"I'm hurrying, father."

When his son was dressed Mr. Button regarded him with depression. The
costume consisted of dotted socks, pink pants, and a belted blouse with a
wide white collar. Over the latter waved the long whitish beard, drooping
almost to the waist. The effect was not good.

"Wait!"

Mr. Button seized a hospital shears and with three quick snaps amputated
a large section of the beard. But even with this improvement the ensemble
fell far short of perfection. The remaining brush of scraggly hair, the watery
eyes, the ancient teeth, seemed oddly out of tone with the gayety of the
costume. Mr. Button, however, was obdurate—he held out his hand.
"Come along!" he said sternly.

His son took the hand trustingly. "What are you going to call me, dad?"
he quavered as they walked from the nursery—"just 'baby' for a while? till
you think of a better name?"

Mr. Button grunted. "I don't know," he answered harshly. "I think we'll
call you Methuselah."

· III ·

EVEN AFTER the new addition to the Button family had had his hair cut
short and then dyed to a sparse unnatural black, had had his face shaved
so close that it glistened, and had been attired in small-boy clothes made
to order by a flabbergasted tailor, it was impossible for Mr. Button to
ignore the fact that his son was a poor excuse for a first family baby.
Despite his aged stoop, Benjamin Button—for it was by this name they
called him instead of by the appropriate but invidious Methuselah—was
five feet eight inches tall. His clothes did not conceal this, nor did the
clipping and dyeing of his eyebrows disguise the fact that the eyes underneath were faded and watery and tired. In fact, the baby-nurse who
had been engaged in advance left the house after one look, in a state of
considerable indignation.

But Mr. Button persisted in his unwavering purpose. Benjamin was a
baby, and a baby he should remain. At first he declared that if Benjamin

didn't like warm milk he could go without food altogether, but he was finally prevailed upon to allow his son bread and butter, and even oatmeal by way of a compromise. One day he brought home a rattle and, giving it to Benjamin, insisted in no uncertain terms that he should "play with it," whereupon the old man took it with a weary expression and could be heard jingling it obediently at intervals throughout the day.

There can be no doubt, though, that the rattle bored him, and that he found other and more soothing amusements when he was left alone. For instance, Mr. Button discovered one day that during the preceding week he had smoked more cigars than ever before—a phenomenon which was explained a few days later when, entering the nursery unexpectedly, he found the room full of faint blue haze and Benjamin, with a guilty expression on his face, trying to conceal the butt of a dark Havana. This, of course, called for a severe spanking, but Mr. Button found that he could not bring himself to administer it. He merely warned his son that he would "stunt his growth."

Nevertheless he persisted in his attitude. He brought home lead soldiers, he brought toy trains, he brought large pleasant animals made of cotton, and, to perfect the illusion which he was creating—for himself at least—he passionately demanded of the clerk in the toy-store whether "the paint would come off the pink duck if the baby put it in his mouth." But, despite all his father's efforts, Benjamin refused to be interested. He would steal down the back stairs and return to the nursery with a volume of the "Encyclopædia Britannica," over which he would pore through an afternoon, while his cotton cows and his Noah's ark were left neglected on the floor. Against such a stubbornness Mr. Button's efforts were of little avail.

The sensation created in Baltimore was, at first, prodigious. What the mishap would have cost the Buttons and their kinsfolk socially cannot be determined, for the outbreak of the Civil War drew the city's attention to other things. A few people who were unfailingly polite racked their brains for compliments to give to the parents—and finally hit upon the ingenious device of declaring that the baby resembled his grandfather, a fact which, due to the standard state of decay common to all men of seventy, could not be denied. Mr. and Mrs. Roger Button were not pleased, and Benjamin's grandfather was furiously insulted.

Benjamin, once he left the hospital, took life as he found it. Several small boys were brought to see him, and he spent a stiff-jointed afternoon trying to work up an interest in tops and marbles—he even managed, quite accidentally, to break a kitchen window with a stone from a sling shot, a feat which secretly delighted his father.

Thereafter Benjamin contrived to break something every day, but he did these things only because they were expected of him, and because he was by nature obliging.

When his grandfather's initial antagonism wore off, Benjamin and that gentleman took enormous pleasure in one another's company. They would sit for hours, these two so far apart in age and experience, and, like old cronies, discuss with tireless monotony the slow events of the day. Benjamin felt more at ease in his grandfather's presence than in his parents'—they seemed always somewhat in awe of him and, despite the dictatorial authority they exercised over him, frequently addressed him as "Mr."

He was as puzzled as any one else at the apparently advanced age of his mind and body at birth. He read up on it in the medical journal, but found that no such case had been previously recorded. At his father's urging he made an honest attempt to play with other boys, and frequently he joined in the milder games—football shook him up too much, and he feared that in case of a fracture his ancient bones would refuse to knit.

When he was five he was sent to kindergarten, where he was initiated into the art of pasting green paper on orange paper, of weaving colored maps and manufacturing eternal cardboard necklaces. He was inclined to drowse off to sleep in the middle of these tasks, a habit which both irritated and frightened his young teacher. To his relief she complained to his parents, and he was removed from the school. The Roger Buttons told their friends that they felt he was too young.

By the time he was twelve years old his parents had grown used to him. Indeed, so strong is the force of custom that they no longer felt that he was different from any other child—except when some curious anomaly reminded them of the fact. But one day a few weeks after his twelfth birthday, while looking in the mirror, Benjamin made, or thought he made, an astonishing discovery. Did his eyes deceive him, or had his hair turned in the dozen years of his life from white to iron-gray under its concealing dye? Was the network of wrinkles on his face becoming less pronounced? Was his skin healthier and firmer, with even a touch of ruddy winter color? He could not tell. He knew that he no longer stooped and that his physical condition had improved since the early days of his life.

"Can it be—?" he thought to himself, or, rather, scarcely dared to think.

He went to his father. "I am grown," he announced determinedly. "I want to put on long trousers."

His father hesitated. "Well," he said finally, "I don't know. Fourteen is the age for putting on long trousers—and you are only twelve."

"But you'll have to admit," protested Benjamin, "that I'm big for my age."

His father looked at him with illusory speculation. "Oh, I'm not so sure of that," he said. "I was as big as you when I was twelve."

This was not true—it was all part of Roger Button's silent agreement with himself to believe in his son's normality.

Finally a compromise was reached. Benjamin was to continue to dye his hair. He was to make a better attempt to play with boys of his own age. He was not to wear his spectacles or carry a cane in the street. In return for these concessions he was allowed his first suit of long trousers. . . .

· IV ·

OF THE LIFE of Benjamin Button between his twelfth and twenty-first year I intend to say little. Suffice to record that they were years of normal ungrowth. When Benjamin was eighteen he was erect as a man of fifty; he had more hair and it was of a dark gray; his step was firm, his voice had lost its cracked quaver and descended to a healthy baritone. So his father sent him up to Connecticut to take examinations for entrance to Yale College. Benjamin passed his examination and became a member of the freshman class.

On the third day following his matriculation he received a notification from Mr. Hart, the college registrar, to call at his office and arrange his schedule. Benjamin, glancing in the mirror, decided that his hair needed a new application of its brown dye, but an anxious inspection of his bureau drawer disclosed that the dye bottle was not there. Then he remembered— he had emptied it the day before and thrown it away.

He was in a dilemma. He was due at the registrar's in five minutes. There seemed to be no help for it—he must go as he was. He did.

"Good-morning," said the registrar politely. "You've come to inquire about your son."

"Why, as a matter of fact, my name's Button—" began Benjamin, but Mr. Hart cut him off.

"I'm very glad to meet you, Mr. Button. I'm expecting your son here any minute."

"That's me!" burst out Benjamin. "I'm a freshman."

"What!"

"I'm a freshman."

"Surely you're joking."

"Not at all."

The registrar frowned and glanced at a card before him. "Why, I have Mr. Benjamin Button's age down here as eighteen."

"That's my age," asserted Benjamin, flushing slightly.

The registrar eyed him wearily. "Now surely, Mr. Button, you don't expect me to believe that."

Benjamin smiled wearily. "I am eighteen," he repeated.

The registrar pointed sternly to the door. "Get out," he said. "Get out of college and get out of town. You are a dangerous lunatic."

"I am eighteen."

Mr. Hart opened the door. "The idea!" he shouted. "A man of your age trying to enter here as a freshman. Eighteen years old, are you? Well, I'll give you eighteen minutes to get out of town."

Benjamin Button walked with dignity from the room, and half a dozen undergraduates, who were waiting in the hall, followed him curiously with their eyes. When he had gone a little way he turned around, faced the infuriated registrar, who was still standing in the doorway, and repeated in a firm voice: "I am eighteen years old."

To a chorus of titters which went up from the group of undergraduates, Benjamin walked away.

But he was not fated to escape so easily. On his melancholy walk to the railroad station he found that he was being followed by a group, then by a swarm, and finally by a dense mass of undergraduates. The word had gone around that a lunatic had passed the entrance examinations for Yale and attempted to palm himself off as a youth of eighteen. A fever of excitement permeated the college. Men ran hatless out of classes, the football team abandoned its practice and joined the mob, professors' wives with bonnets awry and bustles out of position, ran shouting after the procession, from which proceeded a continual succession of remarks aimed at the tender sensibilities of Benjamin Button.

"He must be the Wandering Jew!"

"He ought to go to prep school at his age!"

"Look at the infant prodigy!"

"He thought this was the old men's home."

"Go up to Harvard!"

Benjamin increased his gait, and soon he was running. He would show them! He *would* go to Harvard, and then they would regret these ill-considered taunts!

Safely on board the train for Baltimore, he put his head from the window. "You'll regret this!" he shouted.

"Ha-ha!" the undergraduates laughed. "Ha-ha-ha!" It was the biggest mistake that Yale College had ever made. . . .

· V ·

IN 1880 BENJAMIN Button was twenty years old, and he signalized his birthday by going to work for his father in Roger Button & Co., Wholesale Hardware. It was in that same year that he began "going out socially"— that is, his father insisted on taking him to several fashionable dances. Roger Button was now fifty, and he and his son were more and more companionable—in fact, since Benjamin had ceased to dye his hair (which was still grayish) they appeared about the same age, and could have passed for brothers.

One night in August they got into the phaeton attired in their full-dress suits and drove out to a dance at the Shevlins' country house, situated just outside of Baltimore. It was a gorgeous evening. A full moon drenched the road to the lustreless color of platinum, and late-blooming harvest flowers breathed into the motionless air aromas that were like low, half-heard laughter. The open country, carpeted for rods around with bright wheat, was translucent as in the day. It was almost impossible not to be affected by the sheer beauty of the sky—almost.

"There's a great future in the dry-goods business," Roger Button was saying. He was not a spiritual man—his esthetic sense was rudimentary.

"Old fellows like me can't learn new tricks," he observed profoundly. "It's you youngsters with energy and vitality that have the great future before you."

Far up the road the lights of the Shevlins' country house drifted into view, and presently there was a sighing sound that crept persistently toward them—it might have been the fine plaint of violins or the rustle of the silver wheat under the moon.

They pulled up behind a handsome brougham whose passengers were disembarking at the door. A lady got out, then an elderly gentleman, then another young lady, beautiful as sin. Benjamin started; an almost chemical change seemed to dissolve and recompose the very elements of his body. A rigor passed over him, blood rose into his cheeks, his forehead, and there was a steady thumping in his ears. It was first love.

The girl was slender and frail, with hair that was ashen under the moon and honey-colored under the sputtering gas-lamps of the porch. Over her shoulders was thrown a Spanish mantilla of softest yellow, butterflied in black; her feet were glittering buttons at the hem of her bustled dress.

Roger Button leaned over to his son. "That," he said, "is young Hildegarde Moncrief, the daughter of General Moncrief."

Benjamin nodded coldly. "Pretty little thing," he said indifferently. "But when the negro boy had led the buggy away, he added: "Dad, you might introduce me to her."

They approached a group of which Miss Moncrief was the center. Reared in the old tradition, she courtesied low before Benjamin. Yes, he might have a dance. He thanked her and walked away—staggered away.

The interval until the time for his turn should arrive dragged itself out interminably. He stood close to the wall, silent, inscrutable, watching with murderous eyes the young bloods of Baltimore as they eddied around Hildegarde Moncrief, passionate admiration in their faces. How obnoxious they seemed to Benjamin; how intolerably rosy! Their curling brown whiskers aroused in him a feeling equivalent to indigestion.

But when his own time came, and he drifted with her out upon the changing floor to the music of the latest waltz from Paris, his jealousies and anxieties melted from him like a mantle of snow. Blind with enchantment, he felt that life was just beginning.

"You and your brother got here just as we did, didn't you?" asked Hildegarde, looking up at him with eyes that were like bright blue enamel.

Benjamin hesitated. If she took him for his father's brother, would it be best to enlighten her? He remembered his experience at Yale, so he decided against it. It would be rude to contradict a lady; it would be criminal to mar this exquisite occasion with the grotesque story of his origin. Later, perhaps. So he nodded, smiled, listened, was happy.

"I like men of your age," Hildegarde told him. "Young boys are so idiotic. They tell me how much champagne they drink at college, and how much money they lose playing cards. Men of your age know how to appreciate women."

Benjamin felt himself on the verge of a proposal—with an effort he choked back the impulse.

"You're just the romantic age," she continued—"fifty. Twenty-five is too worldly-wise; thirty is apt to be pale from overwork; forty is the age of long stories that take a whole cigar to tell; sixty is—oh, sixty is too near seventy; but fifty is the mellow age. I love fifty."

Fifty seemed to Benjamin a glorious age. He longed passionately to be fifty.

"I've always said," went on Hildegarde, "that I'd rather marry a man of fifty and be taken care of than marry a man of thirty and take care of *him*."

For Benjamin the rest of the evening was bathed in a honey-colored mist. Hildegarde gave him two more dances, and they discovered that they were marvellously in accord on all the questions of the day. She was to go driving with him on the following Sunday, and then they would discuss all these questions further.

Going home in the phaeton just before the crack of dawn, when the first bees were humming and the fading moon glimmered in the cool dew, Benjamin knew vaguely that his father was discussing wholesale hardware.

". . . . And what do you think should merit our biggest attention after hammers and nails?" the elder Button was saying.

"Love," replied Benjamin absent-mindedly.

"Lugs?" exclaimed Roger Button. "Why, I've just covered the question of lugs."

Benjamin regarded him with dazed eyes just as the eastern sky was suddenly cracked with light, and an oriole yawned piercingly in the quickening trees. . . .

· VI ·

WHEN, SIX MONTHS LATER, the engagement of Miss Hildegarde Moncrief to Mr. Benjamin Button was made known (I say "made known," for General Moncrief declared he would rather fall upon his sword than announce it), the excitement in Baltimore society reached a feverish pitch. The almost forgotten story of Benjamin's birth was remembered and sent out upon the winds of scandal in picaresque and incredible forms. It was said that Benjamin was really the father of Roger Button, that he was his brother who had been in prison for forty years, that he was John Wilkes Booth in disguise—and, finally, that he had two small conical horns sprouting from his head.

The Sunday supplements of the New York papers played up the case with fascinating sketches which showed the head of Benjamin Button attached to a fish, to a snake, and, finally, to a body of solid brass. He became known, journalistically, as the Mystery Man of Maryland. But the true story, as is usually the case, had a very small circulation.

However, every one agreed with General Moncrief that it was "criminal" for a lovely girl who could have married any beau in Baltimore to throw herself into the arms of a man who was assuredly fifty. In vain Mr. Roger Button published his son's birth certificate in large type in the Baltimore *Blaze.* No one believed it. You had only to look at Benjamin and see.

On the part of the two people most concerned there was no wavering. So many of the stories about her fiancé were false that Hildegarde refused stubbornly to believe even the true one. In vain General Moncrief pointed out to her the high mortality among men of fifty—or, at least, among men who looked fifty; in vain he told her of the instability of the wholesale hardware business. Hildegarde had chosen to marry for mellowness—and marry she did. . . .

· V I I ·

IN ONE PARTICULAR, at least, the friends of Hildegarde Moncrief were mistaken. The wholesale hardware business prospered amazingly. In the fifteen years between Benjamin Button's marriage in 1880 and his father's retirement in 1895, the family fortune was doubled—and this was due largely to the younger member of the firm.

Needless to say, Baltimore eventually received the couple to its bosom. Even old General Moncrief became reconciled to his son-in-law when Benjamin gave him the money to bring out his "History of the Civil War" in twenty volumes, which had been refused by nine prominent publishers.

In Benjamin himself fifteen years had wrought many changes. It seemed to him that the blood flowed with new vigor through his veins. It began to be a pleasure to rise in the morning, to walk with an active step along the busy, sunny street, to work untiringly with his shipments of hammers and his cargoes of nails. It was in 1890 that he executed his famous business coup: he brought up the suggestion that *all nails used in nailing up the boxes in which nails are shipped are the property of the shippee*, a proposal which became a statute, was approved by Chief Justice Fossile, and saved Roger Button and Company, Wholesale Hardware, more than *six hundred nails every year*.

In addition, Benjamin discovered that he was becoming more and more attracted by the gay side of life. It was typical of his growing enthusiasm for pleasure that he was the first man in the city of Baltimore to own and run an automobile. Meeting him on the street, his contemporaries would stare enviously at the picture he made of health and vitality.

"He seems to grow younger every year," they would remark. And if old Roger Button, now sixty-five years old, had failed at first to give a proper welcome to his son he atoned at last by bestowing on him what amounted to adulation.

And here we come to an unpleasant subject which it will be well to pass over as quickly as possible. There was only one thing that worried Benjamin Button: his wife had ceased to attract him.

At that time Hildegarde was a woman of thirty-five, with a son, Roscoe, fourteen years old. In the early days of their marriage Benjamin had worshipped her. But, as the years passed, her honey-colored hair became an unexciting brown, the blue enamel of her eyes assumed the aspect of cheap crockery—moreover, and most of all, she had become too settled in her ways, too placid, too content, too anemic in her excitements, and too sober in her taste. As a bride it had been she who had "dragged" Benjamin to dances and dinners—now conditions were reversed. She went out socially with him, but without enthusiasm, devoured already by that eternal inertia which comes to live with each of us one day and stays with us to the end.

Benjamin's discontent waxed stronger. At the outbreak of the Spanish-American War in 1898 his home had for him so little charm that he decided to join the army. With his business influence he obtained a commission as captain, and proved so adaptable to the work that he was made a major, and finally a lieutenant-colonel just in time to participate in the celebrated charge up San Juan Hill. He was slightly wounded, and received a medal.

Benjamin had become so attached to the activity and excitement of army life that he regretted to give it up, but his business required attention, so he resigned his commission and came home. He was met at the station by a brass band and escorted to his house.

· V I I I ·

HILDEGARDE, waving a large silk flag, greeted him on the porch, and even as he kissed her he felt with a sinking of the heart that these three years had taken their toll. She was a woman of forty now, with a faint skirmish line of gray hairs in her head. The sight depressed him.

Up in his room he saw his reflection in the familiar mirror—he went closer and examined his own face with anxiety, comparing it after a moment with a photograph of himself in uniform taken just before the war.

"Good Lord!" he said aloud. The process was continuing. There was no doubt of it—he looked now like a man of thirty. Instead of being delighted, he was uneasy—he was growing younger. He had hitherto hoped that once he reached a bodily age equivalent to his age in years, the grotesque phenomenon which had marked his birth would cease to function. He shuddered. His destiny seemed to him awful, incredible.

When he came down-stairs Hildegrade was waiting for him. She appeared annoyed, and he wondered if she had at last discovered that there was something amiss. It was with an effort to relieve the tension between them that he broached the matter at dinner in what he considered a delicate way.

"Well," he remarked lightly, "everybody says I look younger than ever."

Hildegarde regarded him with scorn. She sniffed. "Do you think it's anything to boast about?"

"I'm not boasting," he asserted uncomfortably.

She sniffed again. "The idea," she said, and after a moment: "I should think you'd have enough pride to stop it."

"How can I?" he demanded.

"I'm not going to argue with you," she retorted. "But there's a right way of doing things and a wrong way. If you've made up your mind to be different from everybody else, I don't suppose I can stop you, but I really don't think it's very considerate."

"But, Hildegarde, I can't help it."

"You can too. You're simply stubborn. You think you don't want to be like any one else. You always have been that way, and you always will be. But just think how it would be if every one else looked at things as you do—what would the world be like?"

As this was an inane and unanswerable argument Benjamin made no reply, and from that time on a chasm began to widen between them. He wondered what possible fascination she had ever exercised over him.

To add to the breach, he found, as the new century gathered headway, that his thirst for gayety grew stronger. Never a party of any kind in the city of Baltimore but he was there, dancing with the prettiest of the young married women, chatting with the most popular of the débutantes, and finding their company charming, while his wife, a dowager of evil omen, sat among the chaperons, now in haughty disapproval, and now following him with solemn, puzzled, and reproachful eyes.

"Look!" people would remark. "What a pity! A young fellow that age tied to a woman of forty-five. He must be twenty years younger than his wife." They had forgotten—as people inevitably forget—that back in 1880 their mammas and papas had also remarked about this same ill-matched pair.

Benjamin's growing unhappiness at home was compensated for by his many new interests. He took up golf and made a great success of it. He went in for dancing: in 1906 he was an expert at "The Boston," and in 1908 he was considered proficient at the "Maxixe," while in 1909 his "Castle Walk" was the envy of every young man in town.

His social activities, of course, interfered to some extent with his business, but then he had worked hard at wholesale hardware for twenty-five years and felt that he could soon hand it on to his son, Roscoe, who had recently graduated from Harvard.

He and his son were, in fact, often mistaken for each other. This pleased Benjamin—he soon forgot the insidious fear which had come over him on his return from the Spanish-American War, and grew to take a naïve pleasure in his appearance. There was only one fly in the delicious ointment—he hated to appear in public with his wife. Hildegarde was almost fifty, and the sight of her made him feel absurd. . . .

· IX ·

ONE SEPTEMBER DAY in 1910—a few years after Roger Button & Co., Wholesale Hardware, had been handed over to young Roscoe Button—a man, apparently about twenty years old, entered himself as a freshman at Harvard University in Cambridge. He did not make the mistake of announcing that he would never see fifty again nor did her mention the fact that his son had been graduated from the same institution ten years before.

He was admitted, and almost immediately attained a prominent position in the class, partly because he seemed a little older than the other freshmen, whose average age was about eighteen.

But his success was largely due to the fact that in the football game with Yale he played so brilliantly, with so much dash and with such a cold, remorseless anger that he scored seven touchdowns and fourteen field goals for Harvard, and caused one entire eleven of Yale men to be carried singly from the field, unconscious. He was the most celebrated man in college.

Strange to say, in his third or junior year he was scarcely able to "make" the team. The coaches said that he had lost weight, and it seemed to the more observant among them that he was not quite as tall as before. He made no touchdowns—indeed, he was retained on the team chiefly in hope that his enormous reputation would bring terror and disorganization to the Yale team.

In his senior year he did not make the team at all. He had grown so slight and frail that one day he was taken by some sophomores for a freshman, an incident which humiliated him terribly. He became known as something of a prodigy—a senior who was surely no more than sixteen—and he was often shocked at the worldliness of some of his classmates. His studies seemed harder to him—he felt that they were too advanced. He had heard his classmates speak of St. Midas', the famous preparatory school, at which so many of them had prepared for college, and he determined after his graduation to enter himself at St. Midas', where the sheltered life among boys his own size would be more congenial to him.

Upon his graduation in 1914 he went home to Baltimore with his Harvard diploma in his pocket. Hildegarde was now residing in Italy, so Benjamin went to live with his son, Roscoe. But though he was welcomed in a general way, there was obviously no heartiness in Roscoe's feeling toward him— there was even perceptible a tendency on his son's part to think that Benjamin, as he moped about the house in adolescent mooniness, was somewhat in the way. Roscoe was married now and prominent in Baltimore life, and he wanted no scandal to creep out in connection with his family.

Benjamin, no longer persona grata with the débutantes and younger college set, found himself left much alone, except for the companionship of three or four fifteen-year-old boys in the neighborhood. His idea of going to St. Midas' school recurred to him.

"Say," he said to Roscoe one day, "I've told you over and over that I want to go to prep school."

"Well, go, then," replied Roscoe shortly. The matter was distasteful to him, and he wished to avoid a discussion.

"I can't go alone," said Benjamin helplessly. "You'll have to enter me and take me up there."

"I haven't got time," declared Roscoe abruptly. His eyes narrowed and he looked uneasily at his father. "As a matter of fact," he added, "you'd better not go on with this business much longer. You better pull up short. You better—you better"—he paused and his face crimsoned as he sought for words—"you better turn right around and start back the other way. This has gone too far to be a joke. It isn't funny any longer. You—you behave yourself!"

Benjamin looked at him, on the verge of tears.

"And another thing," continued Roscoe, "when visitors are in the house I want you to call me 'Uncle'—not 'Roscoe,' but 'Uncle,' do you understand? It looks absurd for a boy of fifteen to call me by my first name. Perhaps you'd better call me 'Uncle' *all* the time, so you'll get used to it."

With a harsh look at his father, Roscoe turned away. . . .

· X ·

AT THE TERMINATION of this interview, Benjamin wandered dismally up-stairs and stared at himself in the mirror. He had not shaved for three months, but he could find nothing on his face but a faint white down with which it seemed unnecessary to meddle. When he had first come home from Harvard, Roscoe had approached him with the proposition that he should wear eye-glasses and imitation whiskers glued to his cheeks, and it had seemed for a moment that the farce of his early years was to be repeated. But whiskers had itched and made him ashamed. He wept and Roscoe had reluctantly relented.

Benjamin opened a book of boys' stories, "The Boy Scouts in Bimini Bay," and began to read. But he found himself thinking persistently about the war. America had joined the Allied cause during the preceding month, and Benjamin wanted to enlist, but, alas, sixteen was the minimum age, and he did not look that old. His true age, which was fifty-seven, would have disqualified him, anyway.

There was a knock at his door, and the butler appeared with a letter bearing a large official legend in the corner and addressed to Mr. Benjamin Button. Benjamin tore it open eagerly, and read the enclosure with delight. It informed him that many reserve officers who had served in the Spanish-American War were being called back into service with a higher rank, and it enclosed his commission as brigadier-general in the United States army with orders to report immediately.

Benjamin jumped to his feet fairly quivering with enthusiasm. This was what he had wanted. He seized his cap and ten minutes later he had entered a large tailoring establishment on Charles Street, and asked in his uncertain treble to be measured for a uniform.

"Want to play soldier, sonny?" demanded a clerk, casually.

Benjamin flushed. "Say! Never mind what I want!" he retorted angrily. "My name's Button and I live on Mt. Vernon Place, so you know I'm good for it."

"Well," admitted the clerk, hesitantly, "if you're not, I guess your daddy is, all right."

Benjamin was measured, and a week later his uniform was completed. He had difficulty in obtaining the proper general's insignia because the dealer kept insisting to Benjamin that a nice Y.W.C.A. badge would look just as well and be much more fun to play with.

Saying nothing to Roscoe, he left the house one night and proceeded by train to Camp Mosby, in South Carolina, where he was to command an infantry brigade. On a sultry April day he approached the entrance to the camp, paid off the taxicab which had brought him from the station, and turned to the sentry on guard.

"Get some one to handle my luggage!" he said briskly.

The sentry eyed him reproachfully. "Say," he remarked, "where you goin' with the general's duds, sonny?"

Benjamin, veteran of the Spanish-American War, whirled upon him with fire in his eye, but with, alas, a changing treble voice.

"Come to attention!" he tried to thunder; he paused for breath—then suddenly he saw the sentry snap his heels together and bring his rifle to the present. Benjamin concealed a smile of gratification, but when he glanced around his smile faded. It was not he who had inspired obedience, but an imposing artillery colonel who was approaching on horseback.

"Colonel!" called Benjamin shrilly.

The colonel came up, drew rein, and looked coolly down at him with a twinkle in his eyes. "Whose little boy are you?" he demanded kindly.

"I'll soon darn well show you whose little boy I am!" retorted Benjamin in a ferocious voice. "Get down off that horse!"

The colonel roared with laughter.

"You want him, eh, general?"

"Here!" cried Benjamin desperately. "Read this." And he thrust his commission toward the colonel.

The colonel read it, his eyes popping from their sockets.

"Where'd you get this?" he demanded, slipping the document into his own pocket.

"I got it from the Government, as you'll soon find out!"

"You come along with me," said the colonel with a peculiar look. "We'll go up to headquarters and talk this over. Come along."

The colonel turned and began walking his horse in the direction of headquarters. There was nothing for Benjamin to do but follow with as much dignity as possible—meanwhile promising himself a stern revenge.

But this revenge did not materialize. Two days later, however, his son Roscoe materialized from Baltimore, hot and cross from a hasty trip, and escorted the weeping general, *sans* uniform, back to his home.

· XI ·

IN 1920 ROSCOE BUTTON's first child was born. During the attendant festivities, however, no one thought it "the thing" to mention that the little grubby boy, apparently about ten years of age who played around the house with lead soldiers and a miniature circus, was the new baby's own grandfather.

No one disliked the little boy whose fresh, cheerful face was crossed with just a hint of sadness, but to Roscoe Button his presence was a source of torment. In the idiom of his generation Roscoe did not consider the matter "efficient." It seemed to him that his father, in refusing to look sixty, had not behaved like a "red-blooded he-man"—this was Roscoe's favorite expression—but in a curious and perverse manner. Indeed, to think about the matter for as much as a half an hour drove him to the edge of insanity. Roscoe believed that "live wires" should keep young, but carrying it out on such a scale was—was—was inefficient. And there Roscoe rested.

Five years later Roscoe's little boy had grown old enough to play childish games with little Benjamin under the supervision of the same nurse. Roscoe took them both to kindergarten on the same day and Benjamin found that playing with little strips of colored paper, making mats and chains and curious and beautiful designs, was the most fascinating game in the world. Once he was bad and had to stand in the corner—then he cried—but for the most part there were gay hours in the cheerful room, with the sunlight coming in the windows and Miss Bailey's kind hand resting for a moment now and then in his tousled hair.

Roscoe's son moved up into the first grade after a year, but Benjamin stayed on in the kindergarten. He was very happy. Sometimes when other tots talked about what they would do when they grew up a shadow would cross his little face as if in a dim, childish way he realized that those were things in which he was never to share.

The days flowed on in monotonous content. He went back a third year to the kindergarten, but he was too little now to understand what the bright shining strips of paper were for. He cried because the other boys were bigger than he and he was afraid of them. The teacher talked to him, but though he tried to understand he could not understand at all.

He was taken from the kindergarten. His nurse, Nana, in her starched gingham dress, became the center of his tiny world. On bright days they walked in the park; Nana would point at a great gray monster and say "elephant," and Benjamin would say it after her, and when he was being undressed for bed that night he would say it over and over aloud to her: "Elyphant, elyphant, elyphant." Sometimes Nana let him jump on the bed, which was fun, because if you sat down exactly right it would bounce you up on your feet again, and if you said "Ah" for a long time while you jumped you got a very pleasing broken vocal effect.

He loved to take a big cane from the hatrack and go around hitting chairs and tables with it and saying: "Fight, fight, fight." When there were people there the old ladies would cluck at him, which interested him, and the young ladies would try to kiss him, which he submitted to with mild boredom. And when the long day was done at five o'clock he would go up-stairs with Nana and be fed oatmeal and nice soft mushy foods with a spoon.

There were no troublesome memories in his childish sleep; no token came to him of his brave days at college, of the glittering years when he flustered the hearts of many girls. There were only the white, safe walls of his crib and Nana and a man who came to see him sometimes, and a great big orange ball that Nana pointed at just before his twilight bed hour and called "sun." When the sun went his eyes were sleepy—there were no dreams, no dreams to haunt him.

The past—the wild charge at the head of his men up San Juan Hill; the first years of his marriage when he worked late into the summer dusk down in the busy city for young Hildegarde whom he loved; the days before that when he sat smoking far into the night in the gloomy old Button house on Monroe Street with his grandfather—all these had faded like unsubstantial dreams from his mind as though they had never been.

He did not remember. He did not remember clearly whether the milk was warm or cool at his last feeding or how the days passed—there was only his crib and Nana's familiar presence. And then he remembered nothing. When he was hungry he cried—that was all. Through the noons and nights he breathed and over him there were soft mumblings and murmurings that he scarcely heard, and faintly differentiated smells, and light and darkness.

Then it was all dark, and his white crib and the dim faces that moved above him, and the warm sweet aroma of the milk, faded out altogether from his mind.

THE DIAMOND AS BIG AS THE RITZ

◆

"The Diamond as Big as the Ritz" first appeared in The Smart Set *(June 1922). Originally titled "The Diamond in the Sky," this classic novelette was rejected by the* Post *and other mass-circulation magazines, even after Fitzgerald cut it from twenty thousand words to fifteen thousand. (The amputated words are lost.) He further tightened the story by cutting another eight hundred words when he polished it for his collection* Tales of the Jazz Age. *Editors found it baffling, blasphemous, or objectionably satiric about wealth. The Smart Set paid Fitzgerald only $300 when his* Post *price was $1,500 for a long story. Fitzgerald was discouraged by the editorial reaction to this story "into which I put three weeks real entheusiasm. . . . But by God + Lorimer, I'm going to make a fortune yet." When he collected it in* Tales of the Jazz Age *Fitzgerald explained that "Diamond"*

> *. . . was designed utterly for my own amusement. I was in a mood characterized by a perfect craving for luxury, and the story began as an attempt to feed that craving on imaginary foods.*
>
> *One well-known critic has been pleased to like this extravaganza better than anything I have written. Personally I prefer "The Off-Shore Pirate."*

◆

JOHN T. UNGER came from a family that had been well known in Hades—a small town on the Mississippi River—for several generations. John's father had held the amateur golf championship through many a heated contest; Mrs. Unger was known "from hot-box to hot-bed," as the local phrase went, for her political addresses; and young John T. Unger, who had just turned sixteen, had danced all the latest dances from New York before he put on long trousers. And now, for a certain time, he was to be away from home. That respect for a New England education which is the bane of all provincial places, which drains them yearly of their most promising young men, had seized upon his parents. Nothing would suit them but that he should go to St. Midas' School near Boston—Hades was too small to hold their darling and gifted son.

Now in Hades—as you know if you ever have been there—the names of the more fashionable preparatory schools and colleges mean very little. The inhabitants have been so long out of the world that, though they make a show of keeping up to date in dress and manners and literature, they depend to a great extent on hearsay, and a function that in Hades would be considered elaborate would doubtless be hailed by a Chicago beef-princess as "perhaps a little tacky."

John T. Unger was on the eve of departure. Mrs. Unger, with maternal fatuity, packed his trunks full of linen suits and electric fans, and Mr. Unger presented his son with an asbestos pocket-book stuffed with money.

"Remember, you are always welcome here," he said. "You can be sure, boy, that we'll keep the home fires burning." *much like what*

"I know," answered John huskily. *my parents told*
me as I left...   for school
"Don't forget who you are and where you come from," continued his father proudly, "and you can do nothing to harm you. You are an Unger —from Hades."

So the old man and the young shook hands and John walked away with tears streaming from his eyes. Ten minutes later he had passed outside the city limits, and he stopped to glance back for the last time. Over the gates the old-fashioned Victorian motto seemed strangely attractive to him. His father had tried time and time again to have it changed to something with a little more push and verve about it, such as "Hades—Your Opportunity," or else a plain "Welcome" sign set over a hearty handshake pricked out in electric lights. The old motto was a little depressing, Mr. Unger had thought—but now. . . .

So John took his look and then set his face resolutely toward his destination. And, as he turned away, the lights of Hades against the sky seemed full of a warm and passionate beauty.

St. Midas' School is half an hour from Boston in a Rolls-Pierce motorcar. The actual distance will never be known, for no one, except John T. Unger, had ever arrived there save in a Rolls-Pierce and probably no one ever will again. St. Midas' is the most expensive and the most exclusive boys' preparatory school in the world.

John's first two years there passed pleasantly. The fathers of all the boys were money-kings and John spent his summers visiting at fashionable resorts. While he was very fond of all the boys he visited, their fathers struck him as being much of a piece, and in his boyish way he often wondered at their exceeding sameness. When he told them where his home was they would ask jovially, "Pretty hot down there?" and John would muster a faint smile and answer, "It certainly is." His response would have been heartier had they not all made this joke—at best varying it with, "Is it hot enough for you down there?" which he hated just as much.

In the middle of his second year at school, a quiet, handsome boy named Percy Washington had been put in John's form. The newcomer was pleasant in his manner and exceedingly well dressed even for St. Midas', but for some reason he kept aloof from the other boys. The only person with whom he was intimate was John T. Unger, but even to John he was entirely uncommunicative concerning his home or his family. That he was wealthy went without saying, but beyond a few such deductions John knew little of his friend, so it promised rich confectionery for his curiosity when Percy invited him to spend the summer at his home "in the West." He accepted, without hesitation.

It was only when they were in the train that Percy became, for the first time, rather communicative. One day while they were eating lunch in the dining-car and discussing the imperfect characters of several of the boys at school, Percy suddenly changed his tone and made an abrupt remark.

"My father," he said, "is by far the richest man in the world."

"Oh," said John, politely. He could think of no answer to make to this confidence. He considered "That's very nice," but it sounded hollow and was on the point of saying, "Really?" but refrained since it would seem to question Percy's statement. And such an astounding statement could scarcely be questioned.

"By far the richest," repeated Percy.

"I was reading in the *World Almanac*," began John, "that there was one man in America with an income of over five million a year and four men with incomes of over three million a year, and——"

"Oh, they're nothing." Percy's mouth was a half-moon of scorn. "Catchpenny capitalists, financial small-fry, petty merchants and money-lenders. My father could buy them out and not know he'd done it."

"But how does he——"

"Why haven't they put down *his* income tax? Because he doesn't pay any. At least he pays a little one—but he doesn't pay any on his *real* income."

"He must be very rich," said John simply. "I'm glad. I like very rich people.

"The richer a fella is, the better I like him." There was a look of passionate frankness upon his dark face. "I visited the Schnlitzer-Murphys last Easter. Vivian Schnlitzer-Murphy had rubies as big as hen's eggs, and sapphires that were like globes with lights inside them——"

"I love jewels," agreed Percy enthusiastically. "Of course I wouldn't want any one at school to know about it, but I've got quite a collection myself. I used to collect them instead of stamps."

"And diamonds," continued John eagerly. "The Schnlitzer-Murphys had diamonds as big as walnuts——"

"That's nothing." Percy had leaned forward and dropped his voice to a low whisper. "That's nothing at all. My father has a diamond bigger than the Ritz-Carlton Hotel."

· II ·

THE MONTANA sunset lay between two mountains like a gigantic bruise from which dark arteries spread themselves over a poisoned sky. An immense distance under the sky crouched the village of Fish, minute, dismal, and forgotten. There were twelve men, so it was said, in the village of Fish, twelve somber and inexplicable souls who sucked a lean milk from the almost literally bare rock upon which a mysterious populatory force had begotten them. They had become a race apart, these twelve men of Fish, like some species developed by an early whim of nature, which on second thought had abandoned them to struggle and extermination.

Out of the blue-black bruise in the distance crept a long line of moving lights upon the desolation of the land, and the twelve men of Fish gathered like ghosts at the shanty depot to watch the passing of the seven o'clock train, the Transcontinental Express from Chicago. Six times or so a year the Transcontinental Express, through some inconceivable jurisdiction, stopped at the village of Fish, and when this occurred a figure or so would disembark, mount into a buggy that always appeared from out of the dusk, and drive off toward the bruised sunset. The observation of this pointless and preposterous phenomenon had become a sort of cult among the men of Fish. To observe, that was all; there remained in them none of the vital quality of illusion which would make them wonder or speculate, else a religion might have grown up around these mysterious visitations. But the men of Fish were beyond all religion—the barest and most savage tenets of even Christianity could gain no foothold on that barren rock—so there was no altar, no priest, no sacrifice; only each night at seven the silent concourse by the shanty depot, a congregation who lifted up a prayer of dim, anæmic wonder.

On this June night, the Great Brakeman, whom, had they deified any one, they might well have chosen as their celestial protagonist, had ordained that the seven o'clock train should leave its human (or inhuman) deposit at Fish. At two minutes after seven Percy Washington and John T. Unger disembarked, hurried past the spellbound, the agape, the fearsome eyes of the twelve men of Fish, mounted into a buggy which had obviously appeared from nowhere, and drove away.

After half an hour, when the twilight had coagulated into dark, the silent negro who was driving the buggy hailed an opaque body somewhere ahead of them in the gloom. In response to his cry, it turned upon them a luminous disk which regarded them like a malignant eye out of the unfathomable night. As they came closer, John saw that it was the tail-light of an immense automobile, larger and more magnificent than any he had ever seen. Its body was of gleaming metal richer than nickel and lighter than silver, and the hubs of the wheels were studded with iridescent geometric figures of green and yellow—John did not dare to guess whether they were glass or jewel.

Two negroes, dressed in glittering livery such as one sees in pictures of royal processions in London, were standing at attention beside the car and as the two young men dismounted from the buggy they were greeted in some language which the guest could not understand, but which seemed to be an extreme form of the Southern negro's dialect.

"Get in," said Percy to his friend, as their trunks were tossed to the ebony roof of the limousine. "Sorry we had to bring you this far in that buggy, but of course it wouldn't do for the people on the train or those Godforsaken fellas in Fish to see this automobile."

"Gosh! What a car!" This ejaculation was provoked by its interior. John saw that the upholstery consisted of a thousand minute and exquisite tapestries of silk, woven with jewels and embroideries, and set upon a background of cloth of gold. The two armchair seats in which the boys luxuriated were covered with stuff that resembled duvetyn, but seemed woven in numberless colors of the ends of ostrich feathers.

"What a car!" cried John again, in amazement.

"This thing?" Percy laughed. "Why, it's just an old junk we use for a station wagon."

By this time they were gliding along through the darkness toward the break between the two mountains.

"We'll be there in an hour and a half," said Percy, looking at the clock. "I may as well tell you it's not going to be like anything you ever saw before."

If the car was any indication of what John would see, he was prepared to be astonished indeed. The simple piety prevalent in Hades has the earnest worship of and respect for riches as the first article of its creed—had John felt otherwise than radiantly humble before them, his parents would have turned away in horror at the blasphemy.

They had now reached and were entering the break between the two mountains and almost immediately the way became much rougher.

"If the moon shone down here, you'd see that we're in a big gulch," said Percy, trying to peer out of the window. He spoke a few words into the mouthpiece and immediately the footman turned on a search-light and swept the hillsides with an immense beam.

"Rocky, you see. An ordinary car would be knocked to pieces in half an hour. In fact, it'd take a tank to navigate it unless you knew the way. You notice we're going uphill now."

They were obviously ascending, and within a few minutes the car was crossing a high rise, where they caught a glimpse of a pale moon newly risen in the distance. The car stopped suddenly and several figures took shape out of the dark beside it—these were negroes also. Again the two young men were saluted in the same dimly recognizable dialect; then the negroes set to work and four immense cables dangling from overhead were attached with hooks to the hubs of the great jeweled wheels. At a resounding "Hey-yah!" John felt the car being lifted slowly from the ground—up and up—clear of the tallest rocks on both sides—then higher, until he could see a wavy, moonlit valley stretched out before him in sharp contrast to the quagmire of rocks that they had just left. Only on one side was there still rock—and then suddenly there was no rock beside them or anywhere around.

It was apparent that they had surmounted some immense knife-blade of stone, projecting perpendicularly into the air. In a moment they were going down again, and finally with a soft bump they were landed upon the smooth earth.

"The worst is over," said Percy, squinting out the window. "It's only five miles from here, and our own road—tapestry brick—all the way. This belongs to us. This is where the United States ends, father says."

"Are we in Canada?"

"We are not. We're in the middle of the Montana Rockies. But you are now on the only five square miles of land in the country that's never been surveyed."

"Why hasn't it? Did they forget it?"

"No," said Percy, grinning, "they tried to do it three times. The first time my grandfather corrupted a whole department of the State survey; the second time he had the official maps of the United States tinkered with— that held them for fifteen years. The last time was harder. My father fixed it so that their compasses were in the strongest magnetic field ever artificially set up. He had a whole set of surveying instruments made with a slight

just a little
extravagant

defection that would allow for this territory not to appear, and he substituted them for the ones that were to be used. Then he had a river deflected and he had what looked like a village built up on its banks—so that they'd see it, and think it was a town ten miles farther up the valley. There's only one thing my father's afraid of," he concluded, "only one thing in the world that could be used to find us out."

"What's that?"

Percy sank his voice to a whisper.

"Aeroplanes," he breathed. "We've got half a dozen anti-aircraft guns and we've arranged it so far—but there've been a few deaths and a great many prisoners. Not that we mind *that*, you know, father and I, but it upsets mother and the girls, and there's always the chance that some time we won't be able to arrange it."

Shreds and tatters of chinchilla, courtesy clouds in the green moon's heaven, were passing the green moon like precious Eastern stuffs paraded for the inspection of some Tartar Khan. It seemed to John that it was day, and that he was looking at some lads sailing above him in the air, showering down tracts and patent medicine circulars, with their messages of hope for despairing, rockbound hamlets. It seemed to him that he could see them look down out of the clouds and stare—and stare at whatever there was to stare at in this place whither he was bound— What then? Were they induced to land by some insidious device there to be immured far from patent medicines and from tracts until the judgment day—or, should they fail to fall into the trap, did a quick puff of smoke and the sharp round of a splitting shell bring them drooping to earth—and "upset" Percy's mother and sisters. John shook his head and the wraith of a hollow laugh issued silently from his parted lips. What desperate transaction lay hidden here? What a moral expedient of a bizarre Croesus? What terrible and golden mystery? . . .

The chinchilla clouds had drifted past now and outside the Montana night was bright as day. The tapestry brick of the road was smooth to the tread of the great tires as they rounded a still, moonlit lake; they passed into darkness for a moment, a pine grove, pungent and cool, then they came out into a broad avenue of lawn and John's exclamation of pleasure was simultaneous with Percy's taciturn "We're home."

Full in the light of the stars, an exquisite château rose from the borders of the lake, climbed in marble radiance half the height of an adjoining mountain, then melted in grace, in perfect symmetry, in translucent feminine languor, into the massed darkness of a forest of pine. The many towers, the slender tracery of the sloping parapets, the chiselled wonder of a thousand yellow windows with their oblongs and hectagons and triangles of golden light, the shattered softness of the intersecting planes of star-shine and blue shade, all trembled on John's spirit like a chord of music. On one of the towers, the tallest, the blackest at its base, an arrangement of exterior lights at the top made a sort of floating fairyland—and as John gazed up in warm enchantment the faint acciaccare sound of violins drifted down in a rococo harmony that was like nothing he had ever heard before. Then in a moment the car stopped before wide, high marble steps around which the night air was fragrant with a host of flowers. At the top of the steps two great doors swung silently open and amber light flooded out upon the darkness, silhouetting the figure of an exquisite lady with black, high-piled hair, who held out her arms toward them.

"Mother," Percy was saying, "this is my friend, John Unger, from Hades."

Afterward John remembered that first night as a daze of many colors, of quick sensory impressions, of music soft as a voice in love, and of the beauty of things, lights and shadows, and motions and faces. There was a white-haired man who stood drinking a many-hued cordial from a crystal thimble set on a golden stem. There was a girl with a flowery face, dressed like Titania with braided sapphires in her hair. There was a room where the solid, soft gold of the walls yielded to the pressure of his hand, and a room that was like a platonic conception of the ultimate prism*—ceiling, floor, and all, it was lined with an unbroken mass of diamonds, diamonds of every size and shape, until, lit with tall violet lamps in the corners, it dazzled the eyes with a whiteness that could be compared only with itself, beyond human wish or dream.

Through a maze of these rooms the two boys wandered. Sometimes the floor under their feet would flame in brilliant patterns from lighting below, patterns of barbaric clashing colors, of pastel delicacy, of sheer whiteness, or of subtle and intricate mosaic, surely from some mosque on the Adriatic Sea. Sometimes beneath layers of thick crystal he would see blue or green water swirling, inhabited by vivid fish and growths of rainbow foliage. Then they would be treading on furs of every texture and color or along corridors of palest ivory, unbroken as though carved complete from the gigantic tusks of dinosaurs extinct before the age of man. . . .

Then a hazily remembered transition, and they were at dinner—where each plate was of two almost imperceptible layers of solid diamond between which was curiously worked a filigree of emerald design, a shaving sliced from green air. Music, plangent and unobtrusive, drifted down through far corridors—his chair, feathered and curved insidiously to his back, seemed to engulf and overpower him as he drank his first glass of port. He tried

---

* In his own copy of *Tales of the Jazz Age* Fitzgerald emended "prison" to "prisym."

drowsily to answer a question that had been asked him, but the honeyed luxury that clasped his body added to the illusion of sleep—jewels, fabrics, wines, and metals blurred before his eyes into a sweet mist. . . .

"Yes," he replied with a polite effort, "it certainly is hot enough for me down there."

He managed to add a ghostly laugh; then, without movement, without resistance, he seemed to float off and away, leaving an iced dessert that was pink as a dream. . . . He fell asleep.

When he awoke he knew that several hours had passed. He was in a great quiet room with ebony walls and a dull illumination that was too faint, too subtle, to be called a light. His young host was standing over him.

"You fell asleep at dinner," Percy was saying. "I nearly did, too—it was such a treat to be comfortable again after this year of school. Servants undressed and bathed you while you were sleeping."

"Is this a bed or a cloud?" sighed John. "Percy, Percy—before you go, I want to apologize."

"For what?"

"For doubting you when you said you had a diamond as big as the Ritz-Carlton Hotel."

Percy smiled.

"I thought you didn't believe me. It's that mountain, you know."

"What mountain?"

"The mountain the château rests on. It's not very big, for a mountain. But except about fifty feet of sod and gravel on top it's solid diamond. *One* diamond, one cubic mile without a flaw. Aren't you listening? Say——"

But John T. Unger had again fallen asleep.

· I I I ·

MORNING. As he awoke he perceived drowsily that the room had at the same moment become dense with sunlight. The ebony panels of one wall had slid aside on a sort of track, leaving his chamber half open to the day. A large negro in a white uniform stood beside his bed.

"Good-evening," muttered John, summoning his brains from the wild places.

"Good-morning, sir. Are you ready for your bath, sir? Oh, don't get up—I'll put you in, if you'll just unbutton your pajamas—there. Thank you, sir."

John lay quietly as his pajamas were removed—he was amused and delighted; he expected to be lifted like a child by this black Gargantua who

This is why the land cannot be surveyed.

was tending him, but nothing of the sort happened; instead he felt the bed tilt up slowly on its side—he began to roll, startled at first, in the direction of the wall, but when he reached the wall its drapery gave way, and sliding two yards farther down a fleecy incline he plumped gently into water the same temperature as his body.

He looked about him. The runway or rollway on which he had arrived had folded gently back into place. He had been projected into another chamber and was sitting in a sunken bath with his head just above the level of the floor. All about him, lining the walls of the room and the sides and bottom of the bath itself, was a blue aquarium, and gazing through the crystal surface on which he sat, he could see fish swimming among amber lights and even gliding without curiosity past his outstretched toes, which were separated from them only by the thickness of the crystal. From overhead, sunlight came down through sea-green glass.

"I suppose, sir, that you'd like hot rosewater and soapsuds this morning, sir—and perhaps cold salt water to finish."

The negro was standing beside him.

"Yes," agreed John, smiling inanely, "as you please." Any idea of ordering this bath according to his own meager standards of living would have been priggish and not a little wicked.

The negro pressed a button and a warm rain began to fall, apparently from overhead, but really, so John discovered after a moment, from a fountain arrangement near by. The water turned to a pale rose color and jets of liquid soap spurted into it from four miniature walrus heads at the corners of the bath. In a moment a dozen little paddle-wheels, fixed to the sides, had churned the mixture into a radiant rainbow of pink foam which enveloped him softly with its delicious lightness, and burst in shining, rosy bubbles here and there about him.

"Shall I turn on the moving-picture machine, sir?" suggested the negro deferentially. "There's a good one-reel comedy in this machine to-day, or I can put in a serious piece in a moment, if you prefer it."

"No, thanks," answered John, politely but firmly. He was enjoying his bath too much to desire any distraction. But distraction came. In a moment he was listening intently to the sound of flutes from just outside, flutes dripping a melody that was like a waterfall, cool and green as the room itself, accompanying a frothy piccolo, in play more fragile than the lace of suds that covered and charmed him.

After a cold salt-water bracer and a cold fresh finish, he stepped out and into a fleecy robe, and upon a couch covered with the same material he was rubbed with oil, alcohol, and spice. Later he sat in a voluptuous chair while he was shaved and his hair was trimmed.

"Mr. Percy is waiting in your sitting-room," said the negro, when these operations were finished. "My name is Gygsum, Mr. Unger, sir. I am to see to Mr. Unger every morning."

John walked out into the brisk sunshine of his living-room, where he found breakfast waiting for him and Percy, gorgeous in white kid knickerbockers, smoking in an easy chair.

· I V ·

THIS IS A STORY of the Washington family as Percy sketched it for John during breakfast.

The father of the present Mr. Washington had been a Virginian, a direct descendant of George Washington, and Lord Baltimore. At the close of the Civil War he was a twenty-five-year-old Colonel with a played-out plantation and about a thousand dollars in gold.

Fitz-Norman Culpepper Washington, for that was the young Colonel's name, decided to present the Virginia estate to his younger brother and go West. He selected two dozen of the most faithful blacks, who, of course, worshipped him, and bought twenty-five tickets to the West, where he intended to take out land in their names and start a sheep and cattle ranch.

When he had been in Montana for less than a month and things were going very poorly indeed, he stumbled on his great discovery. He had lost his way when riding in the hills, and after a day without food he began to grow hungry. As he was without his rifle, he was forced to pursue a squirrel, and in the course of the pursuit he noticed that it was carrying something shiny in its mouth. Just before it vanished into its hole—for Providence did not intend that this squirrel should alleviate his hunger—it dropped its burden. Sitting down to consider the situation Fitz-Norman's eye was caught by a gleam in the grass beside him. In ten seconds he had completely lost his appetite and gained one hundred thousand dollars. The squirrel, which had refused with annoying persistence to become food, had made him a present of a large and perfect diamond.

Late that night he found his way to camp and twelve hours later all the males among his darkies were back by the squirrel hole digging furiously at the side of the mountain. He told them he had discovered a rhinestone mine, and, as only one or two of them had ever seen even a small diamond before, they believed him, without question. When the magnitude of his discovery became apparent to him, he found himself in a quandary. The mountain was *a* diamond—it was literally nothing else but solid diamond.

He filled four saddle bags full of glittering samples and started on horseback for St. Paul. There he managed to dispose of half a dozen small stones—when he tried a larger one a storekeeper fainted and Fitz-Norman was arrested as a public disturber. He escaped from jail and caught the train for New York, where he sold a few medium-sized diamonds and received in exchange about two hundred thousand dollars in gold. But he did not dare to produce any exceptional gems—in fact, he left New York just in time. Tremendous excitement had been created in jewelry circles, not so much by the size of his diamonds as by their appearance in the city from mysterious sources. Wild rumors became current that a diamond mine had been discovered in the Catskills, on the Jersey coast, on Long Island, beneath Washington Square. Excursion trains, packed with men carrying picks and shovels, began to leave New York hourly, bound for various neighboring El Dorados. But by that time young Fitz-Norman was on his way back to Montana.

By the end of a fortnight he had estimated that the diamond in the mountain was approximately equal in quantity to all the rest of the diamonds known to exist in the world. There was no valuing it by any regular computation, however, for it was *one solid diamond*—and if it were offered for sale not only would the bottom fall out of the market, but also, if the value should vary with its size in the usual arithmetical progression, there would not be enough gold in the world to buy a tenth part of it. And what could any one do with a diamond that size?

It was an amazing predicament. He was, in one sense, the richest man that ever lived—and yet was he worth anything at all? If his secret should transpire there was no telling to what measures the Government might resort in order to prevent a panic, in gold as well as in jewels. They might take over the claim immediately and institute a monopoly.

There was no alternative—he must market his mountain in secret. He sent South for his younger brother and put him in charge of his colored following—darkies who had never realized that slavery was abolished. To make sure of this, he read them a proclamation that he had composed, which announced that General Forrest had reorganized the shattered Southern armies and defeated the North in one pitched battle. The negroes believed him implicitly. They passed a vote declaring it a good thing and held revival services immediately.

Fitz-Norman himself set out for foreign parts with one hundred thousand dollars and two trunks filled with rough diamonds of all sizes. He sailed for Russia in a Chinese junk and six months after his departure from Montana he was in St. Petersburg. He took obscure lodgings and called immediately upon the court jeweller, announcing that he had a diamond for the Czar. He remained in St. Petersburg for two weeks, in constant danger of being murdered, living from lodging to lodging, and afraid to visit his trunks more than three or four times during the whole fortnight.

On his promise to return in a year with larger and finer stones, he was allowed to leave for India. Before he left, however, the Court Treasurers had deposited to his credit, in American banks, the sum of fifteen million dollars—under four different aliases.

He returned to America in 1868, having been gone a little over two years. He had visited the capitals of twenty-two countries and talked with five emperors, eleven kings, three princes, a shah, a khan, and a sultan. At that time Fitz-Norman estimated his own wealth at one billion dollars. One fact worked consistently against the disclosure of his secret. No one of his larger diamonds remained in the public eye for a week before being invested with a history of enough fatalities, amours, revolutions, and wars to have occupied it from the days of the first Babylonian Empire.

From 1870 until his death in 1900, the history of Fitz-Norman Washington was a long epic in gold. There were side issues, of course—he evaded the surveys, he married a Virginia lady, by whom he had a single son, and he was compelled, due to a series of unfortunate complications, to murder his brother, whose unfortunate habit of drinking himself into an indiscreet stupor had several times endangered their safety. But very few other murders stained these happy years of progress and expansion.

Just before he died he changed his policy, and with all but a few million dollars of his outside wealth bought up rare minerals in bulk, which he deposited in the safety vaults of banks all over the world, marked as bric-à-brac. His son, Braddock Tarleton Washington, followed this policy on an even more tensive scale. The minerals were converted into the rarest of all elements—radium—so that the equivalent of a billion dollars in gold could be placed in a receptacle no bigger than a cigar box.

When Fitz-Norman had been dead three years his son, Braddock, decided that the business had gone far enough. The amount of wealth that he and his father had taken out of the mountain was beyond all exact computation. He kept a note-book in cipher in which he set down the approximate quantity of radium in each of the thousand banks he patronized, and recorded the alias under which it was held. Then he did a very simple thing—he sealed up the mine.

He sealed up the mine. What had been taken out of it would support all the Washingtons yet to be born in unparalleled luxury for generations. His one care must be the protection of his secret, lest in the possible panic attendant on its discovery he should be reduced with all the property-holders in the world to utter poverty.

This was the family among whom John T. Unger was staying. This was the story he heard in his silver-walled living-room the morning after his arrival.

exactly. + he has too keep the secret

· V ·

AFTER BREAKFAST, John found his way out the great marble entrance, and looked curiously at the scene before him. The whole valley, from the diamond mountain to the steep granite cliff five miles away, still gave off a breath of golden haze which hovered idly above the fine sweep of lawns and lakes and gardens. Here and there clusters of elms made delicate groves of shade, contrasting strangely with the tough masses of pine forest that held the hills in a grip of dark-blue green. Even as John looked he saw three fawns in single file patter out from one clump about a half mile away and disappear with awkward gayety into the black-ribbed half-light of another. John would not have been surprised to see a goat-foot piping his way among the trees or to catch a glimpse of pink nymph-skin and flying yellow hair between the greenest of the green leaves.

ONLY IMPRESSED BY THE RICHES.

In some such cool hope he descended the marble steps, disturbing faintly the sleep of two silky Russian wolfhounds at the bottom, and set off along a walk of white and blue brick that seemed to lead in no particular direction.

He was enjoying himself as much as he was able. It is youth's felicity as well as its insufficiency that it can never live in the present, but must always be measuring up the day against its own radiantly imagined future—flowers and gold, girls and stars, they are only prefigurations and prophecies of that incomparable, unattainable young dream.

young mad-times.

Youth, forever dreamy

John rounded a soft corner where the massed rose-bushes filled the air with heavy scent, and struck off across a park toward a patch of moss under some trees. He had never lain upon moss, and he wanted to see whether it was really soft enough to justify the use of its name as an adjective. Then he saw a girl coming toward him over the grass. She was the most beautiful person he had ever seen.

She was dressed in a white little gown that came just below her knees, and a wreath of mignonettes clasped with blue slices of sapphire bound up her hair. Her pink bare feet scattered the dew before them as she came. She was younger than John—not more than sixteen.

"Hello," she cried softly, "I'm Kismine."

She was much more than that to John already. He advanced toward her, scarcely moving as he drew near lest he should tread on her bare toes.

"You haven't met me," said her soft voice. Her blue eyes added, "Oh, but you've missed a great deal!" . . . "You met my sister, Jasmine, last night. I was sick with lettuce poisoning," went on her soft voice, and her eyes continued, "and when I'm sick I'm sweet—and when I'm well."

"You have made an enormous impression on me," said John's eyes, "and I'm not so slow myself"—"How do you do?" said his voice. "I hope you're better this morning."—"You darling," added his eyes tremulously.

John observed that they had been walking along the path. On her suggestion they sat down together upon the moss, the softness of which he failed to determine.

He was critical about women. A single defect—a thick ankle, a hoarse voice, a glass eye—was enough to make him utterly indifferent. And here for the first time in his life he was beside a girl who seemed to him the incarnation of physical perfection.

"Are you from the East?" asked Kismine with charming interest.

"No," answered John simply. "I'm from Hades."

Either she had never heard of Hades, or she could think of no pleasant comment to make upon it, for she did not discuss it further.

"I'm going East to school this fall," she said. "D'you think I'll like it? I'm going to New York to Miss Bulge's. It's very strict, but you see over the weekends I'm going to live at home with the family in our New York house, because father heard that the girls had to go walking two by two."

"Your father wants you to be proud," observed John.

"We are," she answered, her eyes shining with dignity. "None of us has ever been punished. Father said we never should be. Once when my sister Jasmine was a little girl she pushed him down-stairs and he just got up and limped away.

"Mother was—well, a little startled," continued Kismine, "when she heard that you were from—from where you *are* from, you know. She said that when she was a young girl—but then, you see, she's a Spaniard and old-fashioned."

"Do you spend much time out here?" asked John, to conceal the fact that he was somewhat hurt by this remark. It seemed an unkind allusion to his provincialism.

"Percy and Jasmine and I are here every summer, but next summer Jasmine is going to Newport. She's coming out in London a year from this fall. She'll be presented at court."

"Do you know," began John hesitantly, "you're much more sophisticated than I thought you were when I first saw you?"

"Oh, no, I'm not," she exclaimed hurriedly. "Oh, I wouldn't think of being. I think that sophisticated young people are *terribly* common, don't you? I'm not at all, really. If you say I am, I'm going to cry."

She was so distressed that her lip was trembling. John was impelled to protest:

"I didn't mean that; I only said it to tease you."

"Because I wouldn't mind if I *were*," she persisted, "but I'm *not*. I'm very innocent and girlish. I never smoke, or drink, or read anything except poetry. I know scarcely any mathematics or chemistry. I dress *very* simply—in fact, I scarcely dress at all. I think sophisticated is the last thing you can say about me. I believe that girls ought to enjoy their youths in a wholesome way."

"I do, too," said John heartily.

Kismine was cheerful again. She smiled at him, and a still-born tear dripped from the corner of one blue eye.

"I like you," she whispered, intimately. "Are you going to spend all your time with Percy while you're here, or will you be nice to me? Just think— I'm absolutely fresh ground. I've never had a boy in love with me in all my life. I've never been allowed even to *see* boys alone—except Percy. I came all the way out here into this grove hoping to run into you, where the family wouldn't be around."

Deeply flattered, John bowed from the hips as he had been taught at dancing school in Hades.

"We'd better go now," said Kismine sweetly. "I have to be with mother at eleven. You haven't asked me to kiss you once. I thought boys always did that nowadays."

John drew himself up proudly.

"Some of them do," he answered, "but not me. Girls don't do that sort of thing—in Hades."

Side by side they walked back toward the house.

· VI ·

JOHN STOOD facing Mr. Braddock Washington in the full sunlight. The elder man was about forty with a proud, vacuous face, intelligent eyes, and a robust figure. In the mornings he smelt of horses—the best horses. He carried a plain walking-stick of gray birch with a single large opal for a grip. He and Percy were showing John around.

"The slaves' quarters are there." His walking-stick indicated a cloister of marble on their left that ran in graceful Gothic along the side of the mountain.

"In my youth I was distracted for a while from the business of life by a period of absurd idealism. During that time they lived in luxury. For instance, I equipped every one of their rooms with a tile bath."

"I suppose," ventured John, with an ingratiating laugh, "that they used the bathtubs to keep coal in. Mr. Schnlitzer-Murphy told me that once he——"

"The opinions of Mr. Schnlitzer-Murphy are of little importance, I should imagine," interrupted Braddock Washington, coldly. "My slaves did not keep coal in their bathtubs. They had orders to bathe every day, and they did. If they hadn't I might have ordered a sulphuric acid shampoo. I discontinued the baths for quite another reason. Several of them caught cold and died. Water is not good for certain races—except as a beverage."

John laughed, and then decided to nod his head in sober agreement. Braddock Washington made him uncomfortable.

"All these negroes are descendants of the ones my father brought North with him. There are about two hundred and fifty now. You notice that they've lived so long apart from the world that their original dialect has become an almost indistinguishable patois. We bring a few of them up to speak English—my secretary and two or three of the house servants.

"This is the golf course," he continued, as they strolled along the velvet winter grass. "It's all a green, you see—no fairway, no rough, no hazards."

He smiled pleasantly at John.

"Many men in the cage, father?" asked Percy suddenly.

Braddock Washington stumbled, and let forth an involuntary curse.

"One less than there should be," he ejaculated darkly—and then added after a moment, "We've had difficulties."

"Mother was telling me," exclaimed Percy, "that Italian teacher——"

"A ghastly error," said Braddock Washington angrily. "But of course there's a good chance that we may have got him. Perhaps he fell somewhere in the woods or stumbled over a cliff. And then there's always the probability that if he did get away his story wouldn't be believed. Nevertheless, I've had two dozen men looking for him in different towns around here."

"And no luck?"

"Some. Fourteen of them reported to my agent that they'd each killed a man answering to that description, but of course it was probably only the reward they were after——"

He broke off. They had come to a large cavity in the earth about the circumference of a merry-go-round and covered by a strong iron grating. Braddock Washington beckoned to John, and pointed his cane down through the grating. John stepped to the edge and gazed. Immediately his ears were assailed by a wild clamor from below.

"Come on down to Hell!"

"Hello, kiddo, how's the air up there?"

"Hey! Throw us a rope!"

"Got an old doughnut, Buddy, or a couple of second-hand sandwiches?"

"Say, fella, if you'll push down that guy you're with, we'll show you a quick disappearance scene."

"Paste him one for me, will you?"

It was too dark to see clearly into the pit below, but John could tell from the coarse optimism and rugged vitality of the remarks and voices that they proceeded from middle-class Americans of the more spirited type. Then Mr. Washington put out his cane and touched a button in the grass, and the scene below sprang into light.

"These are some adventurous mariners who had the misfortune to discover El Dorado," he remarked.

Below them there had appeared a large hollow in the earth shaped like the interior of a bowl. The sides were steep and apparently of polished glass, and on its slightly concave surface stood about two dozen men clad in the half costume, half uniform, of aviators. Their upturned faces, lit with wrath, with malice, with despair, with cynical humor, were covered by long growths of beard, but with the exception of a few who had pined perceptibly away, they seemed to be a well-fed, healthy lot.

Braddock Washington drew a garden chair to the edge of the pit and sat down.

"Well, how are you, boys?" he inquired genially.

A chorus of execration in which all joined except a few too dispirited to cry out, rose up into the sunny air, but Braddock Washington heard it with unruffled composure. When its last echo had died away he spoke again.

"Have you thought up a way out of your difficulty?"

From here and there among them a remark floated up.

"We decided to stay here for love!"

"Bring us up there and we'll find us a way!"

Braddock Washington waited until they were again quiet. Then he said:

"I've told you the situation. I don't want you here. I wish to heaven I'd never seen you. Your own curiosity got you here, and any time that you can think of a way out which protects me and my interests I'll be glad to consider it. But so long as you confine your efforts to digging tunnels— yes, I know about the new one you've started—you won't get very far. This isn't as hard on you as you make it out, with all your howling for the loved ones at home. If you were the type who worried much about the loved ones at home, you'd never have taken up aviation."

A tall man moved apart from the others, and held up his hand to call his captor's attention to what he was about to say.

"Let me ask you a few questions!" he cried. "You pretend to be a fair-minded man."

"How absurd. How could a man of *my* position be fair-minded toward *you*? You might as well speak of a Spaniard being fair-minded toward a piece of steak."

At this harsh observation the faces of the two dozen steaks fell, but the tall man continued:

"All right!" he cried. "We've argued this out before. You're not a humanitarian and you're not fair-minded, but you're human—at least you say you are—and you ought to be able to put yourself in our place for long enough to think how—how—how——"

"How what?" demanded Washington, coldly.

"—how unnecessary——"

"Not to me."

"Well,—how cruel——"

"We've covered that. Cruelty doesn't exist where self-preservation is involved. You've been soldiers; you know that. Try another."

"Well, then, how stupid."

"There," admitted Washington, "I grant you that. But try to think of an alternative. I've offered to have all or any of you painlessly executed if you wish. I've offered to have your wives, sweethearts, children, and mothers kidnapped and brought out here. I'll enlarge your place down there and feed and clothe you the rest of your lives. If there was some method of producing permanent amnesia I'd have all of you operated on and released immediately, somewhere outside of my preserves. But that's as far as my ideas go."

"How about trusting us not to peach on you?" cried some one.

"You don't proffer that suggestion seriously," said Washington, with an expression of scorn. "I did take out one man to teach my daughter Italian. Last week he got away."

A wild yell of jubilation went up suddenly from two dozen throats and a pandemonium of joy ensued. The prisoners clog-danced and cheered and yodled and wrestled with one another in a sudden uprush of animal spirits. They even ran up the glass sides of the bowl as far as they could, and slid back to the bottom upon the natural cushions of their bodies. The tall man started a song in which they all joined——

*"Oh, we'll hang the kaiser
On a sour apple tree——"*

Braddock Washington sat in inscrutable silence until the song was over. "You see," he remarked, when he could gain a modicum of attention. "I bear you no ill-will. I like to see you enjoying yourselves. That's why I didn't tell you the whole story at once. The man—what was his name? Critchtichiello?—was shot by some of my agents in fourteen different places."

Not guessing that the places referred to were cities, the tumult of rejoicing subsided immediately.

"Nevertheless," cried Washington with a touch of anger, "he tried to run away. Do you expect me to take chances with any of you after an experience like that?"

Again a series of ejaculations went up.

"Sure!"

"Would your daughter like to learn Chinese?"

"Hey, I can speak Italian! My mother was a wop."

"Maybe she'd like t'learna speak N'Yawk!"

"If she's the little one with the big blue eyes I can teach her a lot of things better than Italian."

"I know some Irish songs—and I could hammer brass once't."

Mr. Washington reached forward suddenly with his cane and pushed the button in the grass so that the picture below went out instantly, and there remained only that great dark mouth covered dismally with the black teeth of the grating.

"Hey!" called a single voice from below, "you ain't goin' away without givin' us your blessing?"

But Mr. Washington, followed by the two boys, was already strolling on toward the ninth hole of the golf course, as though the pit and its contents were no more than a hazard over which his facile iron had triumphed with ease.

· VII ·

JULY UNDER the lee of the diamond mountain was a month of blanket nights and of warm, glowing days. John and Kismine were in love. He did not know that the little gold football (inscribed with the legend *Pro deo et patria et St. Mida*) which he had given her rested on a platinum chain next to her bosom. But it did. And she for her part was not aware that a large sapphire which had dropped one day from her simple coiffure was stowed away tenderly in John's jewel box.

Late one afternoon when the ruby and ermine music room was quiet, they spent an hour there together. He held her hand and she gave him such a look that he whispered her name aloud. She bent toward him—then hesitated.

"Did you say 'Kismine'?" she asked softly, "or——"

She had wanted to be sure. She thought she might have misunderstood. Neither of them had ever kissed before, but in the course of an hour it seemed to make little difference.

The afternoon drifted away. That night when a last breath of music drifted down from the highest tower, they each lay awake, happily dreaming over the separate minutes of the day. They had decided to be married as soon as possible.

· VIII ·

EVERY DAY Mr. Washington and the two young men went hunting or fishing in the deep forests or played golf around the somnolent course—games which John diplomatically allowed his host to win—or swam in the mountain coolness of the lake. John found Mr. Washington a somewhat exacting personality—utterly uninterested in any ideas or opinions except his own. Mrs. Washington was aloof and reserved at all times. She was apparently indifferent to her two daughters, and entirely absorbed in her son Percy, with whom she held interminable conversations in rapid Spanish at dinner.

Jasmine, the elder daughter, resembled Kismine in appearance—except that she was somewhat bow-legged, and terminated in large hands and feet—but was utterly unlike her in temperament. Her favorite books had to do with poor girls who kept house for widowed fathers. John learned from Kismine that Jasmine had never recovered from the shock and disappointment caused her by the termination of the World War, just as she was about to start for Europe as a canteen expert. She had even pined away for a time, and Braddock Washington had taken steps to promote a new war in the Balkans—but she had seen a photograph of some wounded Serbian soldiers and lost interest in the whole proceedings. But Percy and Kismine seemed to have inherited the arrogant attitude in all its harsh magnificence from their father. A chaste and consistent selfishness ran like a pattern through their every idea.

John was enchanted by the wonders of the château and the valley. Braddock Washington, so Percy told him, had caused to be kidnapped a landscape gardener, an architect, a designer of state settings, and a French decadent poet left over from the last century. He had put his entire force of negroes at their disposal, guaranteed to supply them with any materials that the world could offer, and left them to work out some ideas of their own. But one by one they had shown their uselessness. The decadent poet had at once begun bewailing his separation from the boulevards in spring—he made some vague remarks about spices, apes, and ivories, but said nothing that was of any practical value. The stage designer on his part wanted to make the whole valley a series of tricks and sensational effects—a state of things that the Washingtons would soon have grown tired of. And as for the architect and the landscape gardener, they thought only in terms of convention. They must make this like this and that like that.

→ hired help.

But they had, at least, solved the problem of what was to be done with them—they all went mad early one morning after spending the night in a single room trying to agree upon the location of a fountain, and were now confined comfortably in an insane asylum at Westport, Connecticut.

"But," inquired John curiously, "who did plan all your wonderful reception rooms and halls, and approaches and bathrooms——?"

"Well," answered Percy, "I blush to tell you, but it was a moving-picture fella. He was the only man we found who was used to playing with an unlimited amount of money, though he did tuck his napkin in his collar and couldn't read or write."

As August drew to a close John began to regret that he must soon go back to school. He and Kismine had decided to elope the following June.

"It would be nicer to be married here," Kismine confessed, "but of course I could never get father's permission to marry you at all. Next to that I'd rather elope. It's terrible for wealthy people to be married in America at present—they always have to send out bulletins to the press saying that they're going to be married in remnants, when what they mean is just a peck of old second-hand pearls and some used lace worn once by the Empress Eugénie."

"I know," agreed John fervently. "When I was visiting the Schnlitzer-Murphys, the eldest daughter, Gwendolyn, married a man whose father owns half of West Virginia. She wrote home saying what a tough struggle she was carrying on on his salary as a bank clerk—and then she ended up by saying that 'Thank God, I have four good maids anyhow, and that helps a little.' "

spoiled rotten

"It's absurd," commented Kismine. "Think of the millions and millions of people in the world, laborers and all, who get along with only two maids."

One afternoon late in August a chance remark of Kismine's changed the face of the entire situation, and threw John into a state of terror.

They were in their favorite grove, and between kisses John was indulging in some romantic forebodings which he fancied added poignancy to their relations.

"Sometimes I think we'll never marry," he said sadly. "You're too wealthy, too magnificent. No one as rich as you are can be like other girls. I should marry the daughter of some well-to-do wholesale hardware man from Omaha or Sioux City, and be content with her half-million."

"I knew the daughter of a wholesale hardware man once," remarked Kismine. "I don't think you'd have been contented with her. She was a friend of my sister's. She visited here."

"Oh, then you've had other guests?" exclaimed John in surprise.

Kismine seemed to regret her words.

"Oh, yes," she said hurriedly, "we've had a few."

"But aren't you—wasn't your father afraid they'd talk outside?"

"Oh, to some extent, to some extent," she answered. "Let's talk about something pleasanter."

But John's curiosity was aroused.

"Something pleasanter!" he demanded. "What's unpleasant about that? Weren't they nice girls?"

To his great surprise Kismine began to weep.

"Yes—th—that's the—the whole t-trouble. I grew qu-quite attached to some of them. So did Jasmine, but she kept inv-viting them anyway. I couldn't under*stand* it."

A dark suspicion was born in John's heart.

"Do you mean that they *told,* and your father had them—removed?"

"Worse than that," she muttered brokenly. "Father took no chances—and Jasmine kept writing them to come, and they had *such* a good time!"

She was overcome by a paroxysm of grief.

Stunned with the horror of this revelation, John sat there open-mouthed, feeling the nerves of his body twitter like so many sparrows perched upon his spinal column.

"Now, I've told you, and I shouldn't have," she said, calming suddenly and drying her dark blue eyes.

"Do you mean to say that your father had them *murdered* before they left?"

She nodded.

"In August usually—or early in September. It's only natural for us to get all the pleasure out of them that we can first."

Jasmine's always causing the trouble

No more fantasy.

"How abominable! How—why, I must be going crazy! Did you really admit that——"

"I did," interrupted Kismine, shrugging her shoulders. "We can't very well imprison them like those aviators, where they'd be a continual reproach to us every day. And it's always been made easier for Jasmine and me, because father had it done sooner than we expected. In that way we avoided any farewell scene——"

"So you murdered them! Uh!" cried John.

"It was done very nicely. They were drugged while they were asleep—and their families were always told that they died of scarlet fever in Butte."

"But—I fail to understand why you kept on inviting them!"

"I didn't," burst out Kismine. "I never invited one. Jasmine did. And they always had a very good time. She'd give them the nicest presents toward the last. I shall probably have visitors too—I'll harden up to it. We can't let such an inevitable thing as death stand in the way of enjoying life while we have it. Think how lonesome it'd be out here if we never had *any* one. Why, father and mother have sacrificed some of their best friends just as we have."

what a tough life!

"And so," cried John accusingly, "and so you were letting me make love to you and pretending to return it, and talking about marriage, all the time knowing perfectly well that I'd never get out of here alive——"

"No," she protested passionately. "Not any more. I did at first. You were here. I couldn't help that, and I thought your last days might as well be pleasant for both of us. But then I fell in love with you, and—and I'm honestly sorry you're going to—going to be put away—though I'd rather you'd be put away than ever kiss another girl."

"Oh, you would, would you?" cried John ferociously.

"Much rather. Besides, I've always heard that a girl can have more fun with a man whom she knows she can never marry. Oh, why did I tell you? I've probably spoiled your whole good time now, and we were really enjoying things when you didn't know it. I knew it would make things sort of depressing for you."

"Oh, you did, did you?" John's voice trembled with anger. "I've heard about enough of this. If you haven't any more pride and decency than to have an affair with a fellow that you know isn't much better than a corpse, I don't want to have any more to do with you!"

"You're not a corpse!" she protested in horror. "You're not a corpse! I won't have you saying that I kissed a corpse!"

"I said nothing of the sort!"

"You did! You said I kissed a corpse!"

"I didn't!"

Their voices had risen, but upon a sudden interruption they both subsided into immediate silence. Footsteps were coming along the path in their direction, and a moment later the rose bushes were parted displaying Braddock Washington, whose intelligent eyes set in his good-looking vacuous face were peering in at them.

"Who kissed a corpse?" he demanded in obvious disapproval.

"Nobody," answered Kismine quickly. "We were just joking."

"What are you two doing here, anyhow?" he demanded gruffly. "Kismine, you ought to be—to be reading or playing golf with your sister. Go read! Go play golf! Don't let me find you here when I come back!"

Then he bowed at John and went up the path.

"See?" said Kismine crossly, when he was out of hearing. "You've spoiled it all. We can never meet any more. He won't let me meet you. He'd have you poisoned if he thought we were in love."

"We're not, any more!" cried John fiercely, "so he can set his mind at rest upon that. Moreover, don't fool yourself that I'm going to stay around here. Inside of six hours I'll be over those mountains, if I have to gnaw a passage through them, and on my way East."

They had both got to their feet, and at this remark Kismine came close and put her arm through his.

"I'm going, too."

"You must be crazy——"

"Of course I'm going," she interrupted impatiently.

"You most certainly are not. You——"

"Very well," she said quietly, "we'll catch up with father now and talk it over with him."

Defeated, John mustered a sickly smile.

"Very well, dearest," he agreed, with pale and unconvincing affection, "we'll go together."

His love for her returned and settled placidly on his heart. She was his— she would go with him to share his dangers. He put his arms about her and kissed her fervently. After all she loved him; she had saved him, in fact.

Discussing the matter, they walked slowly back toward the château. They decided that since Braddock Washington had seen them together they had best depart the next night. Nevertheless, John's lips were unusually dry at dinner, and he nervously emptied a great spoonful of peacock soup into his left lung. He had to be carried into the turquoise and sable card-room and pounded on the back by one of the under-butlers, which Percy considered a great joke.

· IX ·

LONG AFTER midnight John's body gave a nervous jerk, and he sat suddenly upright, staring into the veils of somnolence that draped the room. Through the squares of blue darkness that were his open windows, he had heard a faint far-away sound that died upon a bed of wind before identifying itself on his memory, clouded with uneasy dreams. But the sharp noise that had succeeded it was nearer, was just outside the room—the click of a turned knob, a footstep, a whisper, he could not tell; a hard lump gathered in the pit of his stomach, and his whole body ached in the moment that he strained agonizingly to hear. Then one of the veils seemed to dissolve, and he saw a vague figure standing by the door, a figure only faintly limned and blocked in upon the darkness, mingled so with the folds of the drapery as to seem distorted, like a reflection seen in a dirty pane of glass.

With a sudden movement of fright or resolution John pressed the button by his bedside, and the next moment he was sitting in the green sunken bath of the adjoining room, waked into alertness by the shock of the cold water which half filled it.

He sprang out, and, his wet pajamas scattering a heavy trickle of water behind him, ran for the aquamarine door which he knew led out onto the ivory landing of the second floor. The door opened noiselessly. A single crimson lamp burning in a great dome above lit the magnificent sweep of the carved stairways with a poignant beauty. For a moment John hesitated, appalled by the silent splendor massed about him, seeming to envelop in its gigantic folds and contours the solitary drenched little figure shivering upon the ivory landing. Then simultaneously two things happened. The door of his own sitting-room swung open, precipitating three naked negroes into the hall—and, as John swayed in wild terror toward the stairway, another door slid back in the wall on the other side of the corridor, and John saw Braddock Washington standing in the lighted lift, wearing a fur coat and a pair of riding boots which reached to his knees and displayed, above, the glow of his rose-colored pajamas.

On the instant the three negroes—John had never seen any of them before, and it flashed through his mind that they must be the professional executioners—paused in their movement toward John, and turned expectantly to the man in the lift, who burst out with an imperious command:

"Get in here! All three of you! Quick as hell!"

Then, within the instant, the three negroes darted into the cage, the oblong of light was blotted out as the lift door slid shut, and John was again alone in the hall. He slumped weakly down against an ivory stair.

It was apparent that something portentous had occurred, something which, for the moment at least, had postponed his own petty disaster. What was it? Had the negroes risen in revolt? Had the aviators forced aside the iron bars of the grating? Or had the men of Fish stumbled blindly through the hills and gazed with bleak, joyless eyes upon the gaudy valley? John did not know. He heard a faint whir of air as the lift whizzed up again, and then, a moment later, as it descended. It was probable that Percy was hurrying to his father's assistance, and it occurred to John that this was his opportunity to join Kismine and plan an immediate escape. He waited until the lift had been silent for several minutes; shivering a little with the night cool that whipped in through his wet pajamas, he returned to his room and dressed himself quickly. Then he mounted a long flight of stairs and turned down the corridor carpeted with Russian sable which led to Kismine's suite.

The door of her sitting-room was open and the lamps were lighted. Kismine, in an angora kimono, stood near the window of the room in a listening attitude, and as John entered noiselessly she turned toward him.

"Oh, it's you!" she whispered, crossing the room to him. "Did you hear them?"

"I heard your father's slaves in my——"

"No," she interrupted excitedly. "Aeroplanes!"

"Aeroplanes? Perhaps that was the sound that woke me."

"There're at least a dozen. I saw one a few moments ago dead against the moon. The guard back by the cliff fired his rifle and that's what roused father. We're going to open on them right away."

"Are they here on purpose?"

"Yes—it's that Italian who got away——"

Simultaneously with her last word, a succession of sharp cracks tumbled in through the open window. Kismine uttered a little cry, took a penny with fumbling fingers from a box on her dresser, and ran to one of the electric lights. In an instant the entire château was in darkness—she had blown out the fuse.

"Come on!" she cried to him. "We'll go up to the roof garden, and watch it from there!"

Drawing a cape about her, she took his hand, and they found their way out the door. It was only a step to the tower lift, and as she pressed the button that shot them upward he put his arms around her in the darkness and kissed her mouth. Romance had come to John Unger at last. A minute later they had stepped out upon the star-white platform. Above, under the misty moon, sliding in and out of the patches of cloud that eddied below it, floated a dozen dark-winged bodies in a constant circling course. From here and there in the valley flashes of fire leaped toward them, followed by

sharp detonations. Kismine clapped her hands with pleasure, which, a moment later, turned to dismay as the aeroplanes at some prearranged signal,
began to release their bombs and the whole of the valley became a panorama
of deep reverberate sound and lurid light.

Before long the aim of the attackers became concentrated upon the points
where the anti-aircraft guns were situated, and one of them was almost
immediately reduced to a giant cinder to lie smouldering in a park of rose
bushes.

"Kismine," begged John, "you'll be glad when I tell you that this attack
came on the eve of my murder. If I hadn't heard that guard shoot off his
gun back by the pass I should now be stone dead——"

"I can't hear you!" cried Kismine, intent on the scene before her. "You'll
have to talk louder!"

"I simply said," shouted John, "that we'd better get out before they begin
to shell the château!"

Suddenly the whole portico of the negro quarters cracked asunder, a geyser
of flame shot up from under the colonnades, and great fragments of jagged
marble were hurled as far as the borders of the lake.

"There go fifty thousand dollars' worth of slaves," cried Kismine, "at
prewar prices. So few Americans have any respect for property."

John renewed his efforts to compel her to leave. The aim of the aeroplanes
was becoming more precise minute by minute, and only two of the anti-
aircraft guns were still retaliating. It was obvious that the garrison, encircled
with fire, could not hold out much longer.

"Come on!" cried John, pulling Kismine's arm, "we've got to go. Do
you realize that those aviators will kill you without question if they find
you?"

She consented reluctantly.

"We'll have to wake Jasmine!" she said, as they hurried toward the lift.
Then she added in a sort of childish delight: "We'll be poor, won't we?
Like people in books. And I'll be an orphan and utterly free. Free and poor!
What fun!" She stopped and raised her lips to him in a delighted kiss.

"It's impossible to be both together," said John grimly. "People have
found that out. And I should choose to be free as preferable of the two. As
an extra caution you'd better dump the contents of your jewel box into your
pockets."

Ten minutes later the two girls met John in the dark corridor and they
descended to the main floor of the château. Passing for the last time through
the magnificence of the splendid halls, they stood for a moment out on the
terrace, watching the burning negro quarters and the flaming embers of two
planes which had fallen on the other side of the lake. A solitary gun was

still keeping up a sturdy popping, and the attackers seemed timorous about descending lower, but sent their thunderous fireworks in a circle around it, until any chance shot might annihilate its Ethiopian crew.

John and the two sisters passed down the marble steps, turned sharply to the left, and began to ascend a narrow path that wound like a garter about the diamond mountain. Kismine knew a heavily wooded spot half-way up, where they could lie concealed and yet be able to observe the wild night in the valley—finally to make an escape, when it should be necessary, along a secret path laid in a rocky gully. *safe to whom? secret to whom? John still has a death warrant*

· X ·

IT WAS THREE O'CLOCK when they attained their destination. The obliging and phlegmatic Jasmine fell off to sleep immediately, leaning against the trunk of a large tree, while John and Kismine sat, his arm around her, and watched the desperate ebb and flow of the dying battle among the ruins of a vista that had been a garden spot that morning. Shortly after four o'clock the last remaining gun gave out a clanging sound and went out of action in a swift tongue of red smoke. Though the moon was down, they saw that the flying bodies were circling closer to the earth. When the planes had made certain that the beleaguered possessed no further resources, they would land and the dark and glittering reign of the Washingtons would be over.

With the cessation of the firing the valley grew quiet. The embers of the two aeroplanes glowed like the eyes of some monster crouching in the grass. The château stood dark and silent, beautiful without light as it had been beautiful in the sun, while the woody rattles of Nemesis filled the air above with a growing and receding complaint. Then John perceived that Kismine, like her sister, had fallen sound asleep.

It was long after four when he became aware of footsteps along the path they had lately followed, and he waited in breathless silence until the persons to whom they belonged had passed the vantage-point he occupied. There was a faint stir in the air now that was not of human origin, and the dew was cold; he knew that the dawn would break soon. John waited until the steps had gone a safe distance up the mountain and were inaudible. Then he followed. About half-way to the steep summit the trees fell away and a hard saddle of rock spread itself over the diamond beneath. Just before he reached this point he slowed down his pace, warned by an animal sense that there was life just ahead of him. Coming to a high boulder, he lifted his head gradually above its edge. His curiosity was rewarded; this is what he saw:

Braddock Washington was standing there motionless, silhouetted against the gray sky without sound or sign of life. As the dawn came up out of the east, lending a cold green color to the earth, it brought the solitary figure into insignificant contrast with the new day.

While John watched, his host remained for a few moments absorbed in some inscrutable contemplation; then he signalled to the two negroes who crouched at his feet to lift the burden which lay between them. As they struggled upright, the first yellow beam of the sun struck through the innumerable prisms of an immense and exquisitely chiselled diamond—and a white radiance was kindled that glowed upon the air like a fragment of the morning star. The bearers staggered beneath its weight for a moment—then their rippling muscles caught and hardened under the wet shine of the skins and the three figures were again motionless in their defiant impotency before the heavens.

After a while the white man lifted his head and slowly raised his arms in a gesture of attention, as one who would call a great crowd to hear—but there was no crowd, only the vast silence of the mountain and the sky, broken by faint bird voices down among the trees. The figure on the saddle of rock began to speak ponderously and with an inextinguishable pride.

"You out there—" he cried in a trembling voice. "You—there—!" He paused, his arms still uplifted, his head held attentively as though he were expecting an answer. John strained his eyes to see whether there might be men coming down the mountain, but the mountain was bare of human life. There was only sky and a mocking flute of wind along the tree-tops. Could Washington be praying? For a moment John wondered. Then the illusion passed—there was something in the man's whole attitude antithetical to prayer.

"Oh, you above there!"

The voice was become strong and confident. This was no forlorn supplication. If anything, there was in it a quality of monstrous condescension.

"You there——"

Words, too quickly uttered to be understood, flowing one into the other. . . . John listened breathlessly, catching a phrase here and there, while the voice broke off, resumed, broke off again—now strong and argumentative, now colored with a slow, puzzled impatience. Then a conviction commenced to dawn on the single listener, and as realization crept over him a spray of quick blood rushed through his arteries. Braddock Washington was offering a bribe to God!

That was it—there was no doubt. The diamond in the arms of his slaves was some advance sample, a promise of more to follow.

. That, John perceived after a time, was the thread running through his sentences. Prometheus Enriched was calling to witness forgotten sacrifices, forgotten rituals, prayers obsolete before the birth of Christ. For a while his discourse took the form of reminding God of this gift or that which Divinity had deigned to accept from men—great churches if he would rescue cities from the plague, gifts of myrrh and gold, of human lives and beautiful women and captive armies, of children and queens, of beasts of the forest and field, sheep and goats, harvests and cities, whole conquered lands that had been offered up in lust or blood for His appeasal, buying a meed's worth of alleviation from the Divine wrath—and now he, Braddock Washington, Emperor of Diamonds, king and priest of the age of gold, arbiter of splendor and luxury, would offer up a treasure such as princes before him had never dreamed of, offer it up not in suppliance, but in pride.

He would give to God, he continued, getting down to specifications, the greatest diamond in the world. This diamond would be cut with many more thousand facets than there were leaves on a tree, and yet the whole diamond would be shaped with the perfection of a stone no bigger than a fly. Many men would work upon it for many years. It would be set in a great dome of beaten gold, wonderfully carved and equipped with gates of opal and crusted sapphire. In the middle would be hollowed out a chapel presided over by an altar of iridescent, decomposing, ever-changing radium which would burn out the eyes of any worshipper who lifted up his head from prayer—and on this altar there would be slain for the amusement of the Divine Benefactor any victim He should choose, even though it should be the greatest and most powerful man alive.

In return he asked only a simple thing, a thing that for God would be absurdly easy—only that matters should be as they were yesterday at this hour and that they should so remain. So very simple! Let but the heavens open, swallowing these men and their aeroplanes—and then close again. Let him have his slaves once more, restored to life and well.

There was no one else with whom he had ever needed to treat or bargain. He doubted only whether he had made his bribe big enough. God had His price, of course. God was made in man's image, so it had been said: He must have His price. And the price would be rare—no cathedral whose building consumed many years, no pyramid constructed by ten thousand workmen, would be like this cathedral, this pyramid.

He paused here. That was his proposition. Everything would be up to specifications and there was nothing vulgar in his assertion that it would be cheap at the price. He implied that Providence could take it or leave it.

As he approached the end his sentences became broken, became short and uncertain, and his body seemed tense, seemed strained to catch the slightest pressure or whisper of life in the spaces around him. His hair had turned gradually white as he talked, and now he lifted his head high to the heavens like a prophet of old—magnificently mad.

Then, as John stared in giddy fascination, it seemed to him that a curious phenomenon took place somewhere around him. It was as though the sky had darkened for an instant, as though there had been a sudden murmur in a gust of wind, a sound of far-away trumpets, a sighing like the rustle of a great silken robe—for a time the whole of nature round about partook of this darkness; the birds' song ceased; the trees were still, and far over the mountain there was a mutter of dull, menacing thunder.

That was all. The wind died along the tall grasses of the valley. The dawn and the day resumed their place in a time, and the risen sun sent hot waves of yellow mist that made its path bright before it. The leaves laughed in the sun, and their laughter shook the trees until each bough was like a girl's school in fairyland. God had refused to accept the bribe.

For another moment John watched the triumph of the day. Then, turning, he saw a flutter of brown down by the lake, then another flutter, then another, like the dance of golden angels alighting from the clouds. The aeroplanes had come to earth.

John slid off the boulder and ran down the side of the mountain to the clump of trees, where the two girls were awake and waiting for him. Kismine sprang to her feet, the jewels in her pockets jingling, a question on her parted lips, but instinct told John that there was no time for words. They must get off the mountain without losing a moment. He seized a hand of each, and in silence they threaded the tree-trunks, washed with light now and with the rising mist. Behind them from the valley came no sound at all, except the complaint of the peacocks far away and the pleasant undertone of morning.

When they had gone about half a mile, they avoided the park land and entered a narrow path that led over the next rise of ground. At the highest point of this they paused and turned around. Their eyes rested upon the mountainside they had just left—oppressed by some dark sense of tragic impendency.

Clear against the sky a broken, white-haired man was slowly descending the steep slope, followed by two gigantic and emotionless negroes, who carried a burden between them which still flashed and glittered in the sun. Half-way down two other figures joined them—John could see that they were Mrs. Washington and her son, upon whose arm she leaned. The aviators had clambered from their machines to the sweeping lawn in front of the château, and with rifles in hand were starting up the diamond mountain in skirmishing formation.

But the little group of five which had formed farther up and was engrossing all the watchers' attention had stopped upon a ledge of rock. The negroes stooped and pulled up what appeared to be a trap-door in the side of the mountain. Into this they all disappeared, the white-haired man first, then his wife and son, finally the two negroes, the glittering tips of whose jeweled head-dresses caught the sun for a moment before the trap-door descended and engulfed them all.

Kismine clutched John's arm.

"Oh," she cried wildly, "where are they going? What are they going to do?"

"It must be some underground way of escape——"

A little scream from the two girls interrupted his sentence.

"Don't you see?" sobbed Kismine hysterically. "The mountain is wired!"

Even as she spoke John put up his hands to shield his sight. Before their eyes the whole surface of the mountain had changed suddenly to a dazzling burning yellow, which showed up through the jacket of turf as light shows through a human hand. For a moment the intolerable glow continued, and then like an extinguished filament it disappeared, revealing a black waste from which blue smoke arose slowly, carrying off with it what remained of vegetation and of human flesh. Of the aviators there was left neither blood nor bone—they were consumed as completely as the five souls who had gone inside.

Simultaneously, and with an immense concussion, the château literally threw itself into the air, bursting into flaming fragments as it rose, and then tumbling back upon itself in a smoking pile that lay projecting half into the water of the lake. There was no fire—what smoke there was drifted off mingling with the sunshine, and for a few minutes longer a powdery dust of marble drifted from the great featureless pile that had once been the house of jewels. There was no more sound and the three people were alone in the valley.

· XI ·

At sunset John and his two companions reached the high cliff which had marked the boundaries of the Washingtons' dominion, and looking back found the valley tranquil and lovely in the dusk. They sat down to finish the food which Jasmine had brought with her in a basket.

"There!" she said, as she spread the table-cloth and put the sandwiches in a neat pile upon it. "Don't they look tempting? I always think that food tastes better outdoors."

"With that remark," remarked Kismine, "Jasmine enters the middle class."

"Now," said John eagerly, "turn out your pocket and let's see what jewels you brought along. If you made a good selection we three ought to live comfortably all the rest of our lives."

Obediently Kismine put her hand in her pocket and tossed two handfuls of glittering stones before him.

"Not so bad," cried John, enthusiastically. "They aren't very big, but— Hello!" His expression changed as he held one of them up to the declining sun. "Why, these aren't diamonds! There's something the matter!"

"By golly!" exclaimed Kismine, with a startled look. "What an idiot I am!"

"Why, these are rhinestones!" cried John.

"I know." She broke into a laugh. "I opened the wrong drawer. They belonged on the dress of a girl who visited Jasmine. I got her to give them to me in exchange for diamonds. I'd never seen anything but precious stones before."

"And this is what you brought?"

"I'm afraid so." She fingered the brilliants wistfully. "I think I like these better. I'm a little tired of diamonds."

"Very well," said John gloomily. "We'll have to live in Hades. And you will grow old telling incredulous women that you got the wrong drawer. Unfortunately your father's bank-books were consumed with him."

"Well, what's the matter with Hades?"

"If I come home with a wife at my age my father is just as liable as not to cut me off with a hot coal, as they say down there."

Jasmine spoke up.

"I love washing," she said quietly. "I have always washed my own hand-kerchiefs. I'll take in laundry and support you both."

"Do they have washwomen in Hades?" asked Kismine innocently.

"Of course," answered John. "It's just like anywhere else."

"I thought—perhaps it was too hot to wear any clothes."

John laughed.

"Just try it!" he suggested. "They'll run you out before you're half started."

"Will father be there?" she asked.

John turned to her in astonishment.

"Your father is dead," he replied somberly. "Why should he go to Hades? You have it confused with another place that was abolished long ago."

After supper they folded up the table-cloth and spread their blankets for the night.

"What a dream it was," Kismine sighed, gazing up at the stars. "How strange it seems to be here with one dress and a penniless fiancé!

"Under the stars," she repeated. "I never noticed the stars before. I always thought of them as great big diamonds that belonged to some one. Now they frighten me. They make me feel that it was all a dream, all my youth."

"It *was* a dream," said John quietly. "Everybody's youth is a dream, a form of chemical madness."

"How pleasant then to be insane!"

"So I'm told," said John gloomily. "I don't know any longer. At any rate, let us love for a while, for a year or so, you and me. That's a form of divine drunkenness that we can all try. There are only diamonds in the whole world, diamonds and perhaps the shabby gift of disillusion. Well, I have that last and I will make the usual nothing of it." He shivered. "Turn up your coat collar, little girl, the night's full of chill and you'll get pneumonia. His was a great sin who first invented consciousness. Let us lose it for a few hours."

So wrapping himself in his blanket he fell off to sleep.

WINTER DREAMS

◆

"Winter Dreams" first appeared in Metropolitan Magazine *(December 1922) and was collected in* All the Sad Young Men *(1926). Written while Fitzgerald was planning his third novel,* The Great Gatsby, *it is the strongest of the Gatsby-cluster stories. Like the novel, it examines a boy whose ambitions become identified with a selfish rich girl. Indeed, Fitzgerald removed Dexter Green's response to Judy Jones's home from the magazine text and wrote it into the novel as Jay Gatsby's response to Daisy Fay's home.*

The four closing paragraphs of this story are distinguished by Fitzgerald's complex explication of Dexter's sense of mutability: he grieves for the loss of his capacity to grieve.

◆

SOME OF THE CADDIES were poor as sin and lived in one-room houses with a neurasthenic cow in the front yard, but Dexter Green's father owned the second best grocery-store in Black Bear—the best one was "The Hub," patronized by the wealthy people from Sherry Island—and Dexter caddied only for pocket-money.

In the fall when the days became crisp and gray, and the long Minnesota winter shut down like the white lid of a box, Dexter's skis moved over the snow that hid the fairways of the golf course. At these times the country gave him a feeling of profound melancholy—it offended him that the links should lie in enforced fallowness, haunted by ragged sparrows for the long season. It was dreary, too, that on the tees where the gay colors fluttered in summer there were now only the desolate sand-boxes knee-deep in crusted ice. When he crossed the hills the wind blew cold as misery, and if the sun was out he tramped with his eyes squinted up against the hard dimensionless glare.

In April the winter ceased abruptly. The snow ran down into Black Bear Lake scarcely tarrying for the early golfers to brave the season with red and black balls. Without elation, without an interval of moist glory, the cold was gone.

Dexter knew that there was something dismal about this Northern spring, just as he knew there was something gorgeous about the fall. Fall made him clinch his hands and tremble and repeat idiotic sentences to himself, and make brisk abrupt gestures of command to imaginary audiences and armies. October filled him with hope which November raised to a sort of ecstatic triumph, and in this mood the fleeting brilliant impressions of the summer at Sherry Island were ready grist to his mill. He became a golf champion and defeated Mr. T. A. Hedrick in a marvellous match played a hundred times over the fairways of his imagination, a match each detail of which he changed about untiringly—sometimes he won with almost laughable ease, sometimes he came up magnificently from behind. Again, stepping from a Pierce-Arrow automobile, like Mr. Mortimer Jones, he strolled frigidly into the lounge of the Sherry Island Golf Club—or perhaps, surrounded by an admiring crowd, he gave an exhibition of fancy diving from the spring-board of the club raft. . . . Among those who watched him in open-mouthed wonder was Mr. Mortimer Jones. *her father!*

tears And one day it came to pass that Mr. Jones—himself and not his ghost—came up to Dexter with tears in his eyes and said that Dexter was the—— best caddy in the club, and wouldn't he decide not to quit if Mr. Jones made it worth his while, because every other——caddy in the club lost one ball a hole for him—regularly——

"No, sir," said Dexter decisively, "I don't want to caddy any more." Then, after a pause: "I'm too old."

ag "You're not more than fourteen. Why the devil did you decide just this morning that you wanted to quit? You promised that next week you'd go over to the State tournament with me."

"I decided I was too old."

Dexter handed in his "A Class" badge, collected what money was due him from the caddy master, and walked home to Black Bear Village.

Alc. "The best——caddy I ever saw," shouted Mr. Mortimer Jones over a drink that afternoon. "Never lost a ball! Willing! Intelligent! Quiet! Honest! Grateful!"

↗adj. caddy ↦ 3 year young
The little girl who had done this was eleven—beautifully ugly as little girls are apt to be who are destined after a few years to be inexpressibly lovely and bring no end of misery to a great number of men. The spark, however, was perceptible. There was a general ungodliness in the way her lips twisted down at the corners when she smiled, and in the—Heaven help *eyes* us!—in the almost passionate quality of her eyes. Vitality is born early in such women. It was utterly in evidence now, shining through her thin frame in a sort of glow.

She had come eagerly out on to the course at nine o'clock with a white

linen nurse and five small new golf-clubs in a white canvas bag which the
nurse was carrying. When Dexter first saw her she was standing by the
caddy house, rather ill at ease and trying to conceal the fact by engaging
her nurse in an obviously unnatural conversation graced by startling and
irrelevant grimaces from herself.

"Well, it's certainly a nice day, <u>Hilda</u>," Dexter heard her say. She drew *girl-*
down the corners of her mouth, smiled, and glanced furtively around, her *friend*
eyes in transit falling for an instant on Dexter.

Then to the nurse:

"Well, I guess there aren't very many people out here this morning, are
there?"

The smile again—radiant, blatantly artificial—convincing.

"I don't know what we're supposed to do now," said the nurse, looking
nowhere in particular.

"Oh, that's all right. I'll fix it up."

Dexter stood perfectly still, his mouth slightly ajar. He knew that if he
moved forward a step his stare would be in her <u>line of vision—if he moved</u> *vision*
backward he would <u>lose his full view of her face.</u> For a moment he had not
realized how young she was. Now he remembered having seen her several
times the year before—in <u>bloomers.</u> — *kid like, their young!*

Suddenly, involuntarily, he laughed, a short abrupt laugh—then, startled
by himself, he turned and began to walk quickly away.

"Boy!"

Dexter stopped.

"Boy——"

Beyond question he was addressed. Not only that, but he was treated to
that absurd smile, that preposterous smile—the memory of which at least
a dozen men were to carry into middle age. *already absorbed*

"Boy, do you know where the golf teacher is?"

"He's giving a lesson."

"Well, do you know where the caddy-master is?"

"He isn't here yet this morning."

"Oh." For a moment this baffled her. She stood alternately on her right
and left foot.

"We'd like to get a caddy," said the nurse. "Mrs. Mortimer Jones sent
us out to play golf, and we don't know how without we get a caddy."

Here she was stopped by an ominous glance from Miss Jones, followed
immediately by the smile.

"There aren't any caddies here except me," said Dexter to the nurse, "and
I got to stay here in charge until the caddy-master gets here."

"Oh." *calm diligent*

Values - Power - Rules - Worlds > Rich People [handwritten, top margin]

attention of high ranking person [handwritten]

POWER [handwritten, left margin]

Miss Jones and her retinue now withdrew, and at a proper distance from Dexter became involved in a heated conversation, which was concluded by Miss Jones taking one of the clubs and hitting it on the ground with violence. For further emphasis she raised it again and was about to bring it down smartly upon the nurse's bosom, when the nurse seized the club and twisted it from her hands.

"You damn little mean old *thing!*" cried Miss Jones wildly.

his own decision [handwritten, left margin]

followed [handwritten]

Another argument ensued. Realizing that the elements of the comedy were implied in the scene, Dexter several times began to laugh, but each time restrained the laugh before it reached audibility. He could not resist the monstrous conviction that the little girl was justified in beating the nurse.

unplanned [handwritten]

The situation was resolved by the fortuitous appearance of the caddy-master, who was appealed to immediately by the nurse.

"Miss Jones is to have a little caddy, and this one says he can't go."

"Mr. McKenna said I was to wait here till you came," said Dexter quickly.

"Well, he's here now." Miss Jones smiled cheerfully at the caddy-master. Then she dropped her bag and set off at a haughty mince toward the first tee.

"Well?" The caddy-master turned to Dexter. "What you standing there like a dummy for? Go pick up the young lady's clubs."

"I don't think I'll go out to-day," said Dexter.

"You don't——"

"I think I'll quit."

random decision #1 [handwritten, left margin]

The enormity of his decision frightened him. He was a favorite caddy, and the thirty dollars a month he earned through the summer were not to be made elsewhere around the lake. But he had received a strong emotional shock, and his perturbation required a violent and immediate outlet.

It is not so simple as that, either. As so frequently would be the case in the future, Dexter was unconsciously dictated to by his winter dreams.

dreams drive him, does not drive dream [handwritten]

II

→ what does the father do? irrelevant? [handwritten]

Now, OF COURSE, the quality and the seasonability of these winter dreams varied, but the stuff of them remained. They persuaded Dexter several years later to pass up a business course at the State university—his father, prospering now, would have paid his way—for the precarious advantage of attending an older and more famous university in the East, where he was bothered by his scanty funds. But do not get the impression, because his winter dreams happened to be concerned at first with musings on the rich, that there was anything merely snobbish in the boy. He wanted not

→ Not a snob, not a poor boy [handwritten]

[handwritten: Rich/Poor diff. plays role in the decision of boy - Dexter Green]

association with glittering things and glittering people—he wanted tering things themselves. Often he reached out for the best without knowing why he wanted it—and sometimes he ran up against the mysterious denials and prohibitions in which life indulges. It is with one of those denials and not with his career as a whole that this story deals. *[handwritten: STORY.]*

He made money. It was rather amazing. After college he went to the city from which Black Bear Lake draws its wealthy patrons. When he was only twenty-three and had been there not quite two years, there were already people who liked to say: "Now *there's* a boy—" All about him rich men's sons were peddling bonds precariously, or investing patrimonies precariously, or plodding through the two dozen volumes of the "George Washington Commercial Course," but Dexter borrowed a thousand dollars on his college degree and his confident mouth, and bought a partnership in a laundry.

It was a small laundry when he went into it but Dexter made a specialty of learning how the English washed fine woollen golf-stockings without shrinking them, and within a year he was catering to the trade that wore knickerbockers. Men were insisting that their Shetland hose and sweaters go to his laundry just as they had insisted on a caddy who could find golf-balls. A little later he was doing their wives' lingerie as well—and running five branches in different parts of the city. Before he was twenty-seven he *[handwritten: success!]* owned the largest string of laundries in his section of the country. It was then that he sold out and went to New York. But the part of his story that concerns us goes back to the days when he was making his first big success.

When he was twenty-three Mr. Hart—one of the gray-haired men who like to say "Now there's a boy"—gave him a guest card to the Sherry Island Golf Club for a week-end. So he signed his name one day on the register, and that afternoon played golf in a foursome with Mr. Hart and Mr. Sandwood and Mr. T. A. Hedrick. He did not consider it necessary to remark *[handwritten: change of his status]* that he had once carried Mr. Hart's bag over this same links, and that he knew every trap and gully with his eyes shut—but he found himself glancing at the four caddies who trailed them, trying to catch a gleam or gesture that would remind him of himself, that would lessen the gap which lay between his present and his past.

It was a curious day, slashed abruptly with fleeting, familiar impressions. One minute he had the sense of being a trespasser—in the next he was impressed by the tremendous superiority he felt toward Mr. T. A. Hedrick, who was a bore and not even a good golfer any more.

Then, because of a ball Mr. Hart lost near the fifteenth green, an enormous thing happened. While they were searching the stiff grasses of the rough there was a clear call of "Fore!" from behind a hill in their rear. And as

[handwritten: STATUS: Where does Dexter want to be?]

they all turned abruptly from their search a bright new ball sliced abruptly over the hill and caught Mr. T. A. Hedrick in the abdomen.

"By Gad!" cried Mr. T. A. Hedrick, "they ought to put some of these crazy women off the course. It's getting to be outrageous."

A head and a voice came up together over the hill:

"Do you mind if we go through?"

"You hit me in the stomach!" declared Mr. Hedrick wildly.

"Did I?" The girl approached the group of men. "I'm sorry. I yelled 'Fore!'"

Her glance fell casually on each of the men—then scanned the fairway for her ball.

"Did I bounce into the rough?"

It was impossible to determine whether this question was ingenuous or malicious. In a moment, however, she left no doubt, for as her partner came up over the hill she called cheerfully:

"Here I am! I'd have gone on the green except that I hit something."

As she took her stance for a short mashie shot, Dexter looked at her closely. She wore a blue gingham dress, rimmed at throat and shoulders with a white edging that accentuated her tan. The quality of exaggeration, of thinness, which had made her passionate eyes and down-turning mouth absurd at eleven, was gone now. She was arrestingly beautiful. The color in her cheeks was centered like the color in a picture—it was not a "high" color, but a sort of fluctuating and feverish warmth, so shaded that it seemed at any moment it would recede and disappear. This color and the mobility of her mouth gave a continual impression of flux, of intense life, of passionate vitality—balanced only partially by the sad luxury of her eyes.

She swung her mashie impatiently and without interest, pitching the ball into a sand-pit on the other side of the green. With a quick, insincere smile and a careless "Thank you!" she went on after it.

"That Judy Jones!" remarked Mr. Hedrick on the next tee, as they waited—some moments—for her to play on ahead. "All she needs is to be turned up and spanked for six months and then to be married off to an old-fashioned cavalry captain."

"My God, she's good-looking!" said Mr. Sandwood, who was just over thirty.

"Good-looking!" cried Mr. Hedrick contemptuously, "she always looks as if she wanted to be kissed! Turning those big cow-eyes on every calf in town!"

It was doubtful if Mr. Hedrick intended a reference to the maternal instinct.

"She'd play pretty good golf if she'd try," said Mr. Sandwood.

"She has no form," said Mr. Hedrick solemnly.

"She has a nice figure," said Mr. Sandwood.

"Better thank the Lord she doesn't drive a swifter ball," said Mr. Hart, winking at Dexter. ← *connection to him*

Later in the afternoon the sun went down with a riotous swirl of gold *color* and varying blues and scarlets, and left the dry, rustling night of Western summer. Dexter watched from the veranda of the Golf Club, watched the even overlap of the waters in the little wind, silver molasses under the *e* harvest-moon. Then the moon held a finger to her lips and the lake became a clear pool, pale and quiet. Dexter put on his bathing-suit and swam out to the farthest raft, where he stretched dripping on the wet canvas of the springboard.

dark/light

There was a fish jumping and a star shining and the lights around the lake were gleaming. Over on a dark peninsula a piano was playing the songs of last summer and of summers before that—songs from "Chin-Chin" and "The Count of Luxemburg" and "The Chocolate Soldier"—and because the sound of a piano over a stretch of water had always seemed beautiful to Dexter he lay perfectly quiet and listened.

The tune the piano was playing at that moment had been gay and new five years before when Dexter was a sophomore at college. They had played it at a prom once when he could not afford the luxury of proms, and he had stood outside the gymnasium and listened. The sound of the tune precipitated in him a sort of ecstasy and it was with that ecstasy he viewed what happened to him now. It was a mood of intense appreciation, a sense that, for once, he was magnificently attune to life and that everything about him was radiating a brightness and a glamour he might never know again.

A low, pale oblong detached itself suddenly from the darkness of the Island, spitting forth the reverberate sound of a racing motor-boat. Two white streamers of cleft water rolled themselves out behind it and almost immediately the boat was beside him, drowning out the hot tinkle of the piano in the drone of its spray. Dexter raising himself on his arms was aware of a figure standing at the wheel, of two dark eyes regarding him over the lengthening space of water—then the boat had gone by and was sweeping in an immense and purposeless circle of spray round and round in the middle of the lake. With equal eccentricity one of the circles flattened out and headed back toward the raft.

"Who's that?" she called, shutting off her motor. She was so near now that Dexter could see her bathing-suit, which consisted apparently of pink rompers. *her clothing, older now.*

The nose of the boat bumped the raft, and as the latter tilted rakishly he was precipitated toward her. With different degrees of interest they recognized each other.

"Aren't you one of those men we played through this afternoon?" she demanded.

He was.

"Well, do you know how to drive a motor-boat? Because if you do I wish you'd drive this one so I can ride on the surf-board behind. My name is Judy Jones"—she favored him with an absurd smirk—rather, what tried to be a smirk, for, twist her mouth as she might, it was not grotesque, it was merely beautiful—"and I live in a house over there on the Island, and in that house there is a man waiting for me. When he drove up at the door I drove out of the dock because he says I'm his ideal."

There was a fish jumping and a star shining and the lights around the lake were gleaming. Dexter sat beside Judy Jones and she explained how her boat was driven. Then she was in the water, swimming to the floating surf-board with a sinuous crawl. Watching her was without effort to the eye, watching a branch waving or a sea-gull flying. Her arms, burned to butternut, moved sinuously among the dull platinum ripples, elbow appearing first, casting the forearm back with a cadence of falling water, then reaching out and down, stabbing a path ahead.

They moved out into the lake; turning, Dexter saw that she was kneeling on the low rear of the now uptilted surf-board.

"Go faster," she called, "fast as it'll go."

Obediently he jammed the lever forward and the white spray mounted at the bow. When he looked around again the girl was standing up on the rushing board, her arms spread wide, her eyes lifted toward the moon.

"It's awful cold," she shouted. "What's your name?"

He told her.

"Well, why don't you come to dinner to-morrow night?"

His heart turned over like the fly-wheel of the boat, and, for the second time, her casual whim gave a new direction to his life.

· III ·

NEXT EVENING while he waited for her to come down-stairs, Dexter peopled the soft deep summer room and the sun-porch that opened from it with the men who had already loved Judy Jones. He knew the sort of men they were—the men who when he first went to college had entered from the great prep schools with graceful clothes and the deep tan of healthy summers. He had seen that, in one sense, he was better than these men. He *confidence —* was newer and stronger. Yet in acknowledging to himself that he wished his children to be like them he was admitting that he was but the rough, strong stuff from which they eternally sprang.

When the time had come for him to wear good clothes, he had known who were the best tailors in America, and the best tailors in America had made him the suit he wore this evening. He had acquired that particular *diff* reserve peculiar to his university, that set it off from other universities. He recognized the value to him of such a mannerism and he had adopted it; he knew that to be careless in dress and manner required more confidence than to be careful. But carelessness was for his children. His mother's name had been Krimslich. She was a Bohemian of the peasant class and she had talked *mut* broken English to the end of her days. Her son must keep to the set patterns.

At a little after seven Judy Jones came down-stairs. She wore a blue silk *again blue* afternoon dress, and he was disappointed at first that she had not put on something more elaborate. This feeling was accentuated when, after a brief greeting, she went to the door of a butler's pantry and pushing it open called: "You can serve dinner, Martha." He had rather expected that a butler would announce dinner, that there would be a cocktail. Then he put these thoughts behind him as they sat down side by side on a lounge and looked at each other. *Party not as extravagant*

"Father and mother won't be here," she said thoughtfully.

He remembered the last time he had seen her father, and he was glad the parents were not to be here to-night—they might wonder who he was. He had been born in Keeble, a Minnesota village fifty miles farther north, and he always gave Keeble as his home instead of Black Bear Village. Country towns were well enough to come from if they weren't inconveniently in sight and used as footstools by fashionable lakes. — *class/status*

They talked of his university, which she had visited frequently during the past two years, and of the near-by city which supplied Sherry Island with its patrons, and whither Dexter would return next day to his prospering laundries.

During dinner she slipped into a moody depression which gave Dexter a feeling of uneasiness. Whatever petulance she uttered in her throaty voice *unreasonably irritable* worried him. Whatever she smiled at—at him, at a chicken liver, at nothing—it disturbed him that her smile could have no root in mirth, or even in amusement. When the scarlet corners of her lips curved down, it was less a smile than an invitation to a kiss.

Then, after dinner, she led him out on the dark sun-porch and deliberately changed the atmosphere.

"Do you mind if I weep a little?" she said. *crying*

"I'm afraid I'm boring you," he responded quickly.

"You're not. I like you. But I've just had a terrible afternoon. There was a man I cared about, and this afternoon he told me out of a clear sky that he was poor as a church-mouse. He'd never even hinted it before. Does this sound horribly mundane?"

"Perhaps he was afraid to tell you."

"Suppose he was," she answered. "He didn't start right. You see, if I'd thought of him as poor—well, I've been mad about loads of poor men, and fully intended to marry them all. But in this case, I hadn't thought of him that way, and my interest in him wasn't strong enough to survive the shock. As if a girl calmly informed her fiancé that she was a widow. He might not object to widows, but——

"Let's start right," she interrupted herself suddenly. "Who are you, any-how?"

For a moment Dexter hesitated. Then:

"I'm nobody," he announced. "My career is largely a matter of futures."

"Are you poor?"

"No," he said frankly, "I'm probably making more money than any man my age in the Northwest. I know that's an obnoxious remark, but you advised me to start right."

There was a pause. Then she smiled and the corners of her mouth drooped and an almost imperceptible sway brought her closer to him, looking up into his eyes. A lump rose in Dexter's throat, and he waited breathless for the experiment, facing the unpredictable compound that would form mysteriously from the elements of their lips. Then he saw—she communicated her excitement to him, lavishly, deeply, with kisses that were not a promise but a fulfillment. They aroused in him not hunger demanding renewal but surfeit that would demand more surfeit . . . kisses that were like charity, creating want by holding back nothing at all.

It did not take him many hours to decide that he had wanted Judy Jones ever since he was a proud, desirous little boy.

· I V ·

IT BEGAN like that—and continued, with varying shades of intensity, on such a note right up to the dénouement. Dexter surrendered a part of himself to the most direct and unprincipled personality with which he had ever come in contact. Whatever Judy wanted, she went after with the full pressure of her charm. There was no divergence of method, no jockeying for position or premeditation of effects—there was a very little mental side to any of her affairs. She simply made men conscious to the highest degree of her physical loveliness. Dexter had no desire to change her. Her deficiencies were knit up with a passionate energy that transcended and justified them.

When, as Judy's head lay against his shoulder that first night, she whispered, "I don't know what's the matter with me. Last night I thought I was in love with a man and to-night I think I'm in love with you——"—it seemed to him a beautiful and romantic thing to say. It was the exquisite excitability that for the moment he controlled and owned. But a week later he was compelled to view this same quality in a different light. She took him in her roadster to a picnic supper, and after supper she disappeared, likewise in her roadster, with another man. Dexter became enormously upset and was scarcely able to be decently civil to the other people present. When she assured him that she had not kissed the other man, he knew she was lying—yet he was glad that she had taken the trouble to lie to him.

He was, as he found before the summer ended, one of a varying dozen who circulated about her. Each of them had at one time been favored above all others—about half of them still basked in the solace of occasional sentimental revivals. Whenever one showed signs of dropping out through long neglect, she granted him a brief honeyed hour, which encouraged him to tag along for a year or so longer. Judy made these forays upon the helpless and defeated without malice, indeed half unconscious that there was anything mischievous in what she did.

When a new man came to town every one dropped out—dates were automatically cancelled.

The helpless part of trying to do anything about it was that she did it all herself. She was not a girl who could be "won" in the kinetic sense—she was proof against cleverness, she was proof against charm; if any of these assailed her too strongly she would immediately resolve the affair to a physical basis, and under the magic of her physical splendor the strong as well as the brilliant played her game and not their own. She was entertained only by the gratification of her desires and by the direct exercise of her own charm. Perhaps from so much youthful love, so many youthful lovers, she had come, in self-defense, to nourish herself wholly from within.

Succeeding Dexter's first exhilaration came restlessness and dissatisfaction. The helpless ecstasy of losing himself in her was opiate rather than tonic. It was fortunate for his work during the winter that those moments of ecstasy came infrequently. Early in their acquaintance it had seemed for a while that there was a deep and spontaneous mutual attraction—that first August, for example—three days of long evenings on her dusky veranda, of strange wan kisses through the late afternoon, in shadowy alcoves or behind the protecting trellises of the garden arbors, of mornings when she was fresh as a dream and almost shy at meeting him in the clarity of the rising day. There was all the ecstasy of an engagement about it, sharpened by his realization that there was no engagement. It was during those three days that, for the first time, he had asked her to marry him. She said "maybe some day," she said "kiss me," she said "I'd like to marry you," she said "I love you"—she said—nothing.

The three days were interrupted by the arrival of a New York man who visited at her house for half September. To Dexter's agony, rumor engaged them. The man was the son of the president of a great trust company. But at the end of a month it was reported that Judy was yawning. At a dance one night she sat all evening in a motor-boat with a local beau, while the New Yorker searched the club for her frantically. She told the local beau that she was bored with her visitor, and two days later he left. She was seen with him at the station, and it was reported that he looked very mournful indeed.

On this note the summer ended. Dexter was twenty-four, and he found himself increasingly in a position to do as he wished. He joined two clubs in the city and lived at one of them. Though he was by no means an integral part of the stag-lines at these clubs, he managed to be on hand at dances where Judy Jones was likely to appear. He could have gone out socially as much as he liked—he was an eligible young man, now, and popular with down-town fathers. His confessed devotion to Judy Jones had rather solidified his position. But he had no social aspirations and rather despised the dancing men who were always on tap for the Thursday or Saturday parties and who filled in at dinners with the younger married set. Already he was playing with the idea of going East to New York. He wanted to take Judy Jones with him. No disillusion as to the world in which she had grown up could cure his illusion as to her desirability.

Remember that—for only in the light of it can what he did for her be understood.

Eighteen months after he first met Judy Jones he became engaged to another girl. Her name was Irene Scheerer, and her father was one of the men who had always believed in Dexter. Irene was light-haired and sweet and honorable, and a little stout, and she had two suitors whom she pleasantly relinquished when Dexter formally asked her to marry him.

Summer, fall, winter, spring, another summer, another fall—so much he had given of his active life to the incorrigible lips of Judy Jones. She had treated him with interest, with encouragement, with malice, with indifference, with contempt. She had inflicted on him the innumerable little slights and indignities possible in such a case—as if in revenge for having ever cared for him at all. She had beckoned him and yawned at him and beckoned him again and he had responded often with bitterness and narrowed eyes. She had brought him ecstatic happiness and intolerable agony of spirit. She had caused him untold inconvenience and not a little trouble. She had insulted him, and she had ridden over him, and she had played his interest in her against his interest in his work—for fun. She had done everything to him except to criticise him—this she had not done—it seemed to him only because it might have sullied the utter indifference she manifested and sincerely felt toward him.

When autumn had come and gone again it occurred to him that he could not have Judy Jones. He had to beat this into his mind but he convinced himself at last. He lay awake at night for a while and argued it over. He told himself the trouble and the pain she had caused him, he enumerated her glaring deficiencies as a wife. Then he said to himself that he loved her, and after a while he fell asleep. For a week, lest he imagine her husky voice over the telephone or her eyes opposite him at lunch, he worked hard and late, and at night he went to his office and plotted out his years.

At the end of a week he went to a dance and cut in on her once. For almost the first time since they had met he did not ask her to sit out with him or tell her that she was lovely. It hurt him that she did not miss these things—that was all. He was not jealous when he saw that there was a new man to-night. He had been hardened against jealousy long before.

He stayed late at the dance. He sat for an hour with Irene Scheerer and talked about books and about music. He knew very little about either. But he was beginning to be master of his own time now, and he had a rather priggish notion that he—the young and already fabulously successful Dexter Green—should know more about such things.

That was in October, when he was twenty-five. In January, Dexter and Irene became engaged. It was to be announced in June, and they were to be married three months later.

The Minnesota winter prolonged itself interminably, and it was almost May when the winds came soft and the snow ran down into Black Bear Lake at last. For the first time in over a year Dexter was enjoying a certain tranquility of spirit. Judy Jones had been in Florida, and afterward in Hot Springs, and somewhere she had been engaged, and somewhere she had broken it off. At first, when Dexter had definitely given her up, it had made him sad that people still linked them together and asked for news of her, but when he began to be placed at dinner next to Irene Scheerer people didn't ask him about her any more—they told him about her. He ceased to be an authority on her.

May at last. Dexter walked the streets at night when the darkness was damp as rain, wondering that so soon, with so little done, so much of ecstasy had gone from him. May one year back had been marked by Judy's poignant, unforgivable, yet forgiven turbulence—it had been one of those rare times when he fancied she had grown to care for him. That old penny's worth of happiness he had spent for this bushel of content. He knew that Irene would be no more than a curtain spread behind him, a hand moving among gleaming tea-cups, a voice calling to children . . . fire and loveliness were gone, the magic of nights and the wonder of the varying hours and seasons . . . slender lips, down-turning, dropping to his lips and bearing him up into a heaven of eyes. . . . The thing was deep in him. He was too strong and alive for it to die lightly.

In the middle of May when the weather balanced for a few days on the thin bridge that led to deep summer he turned in one night at Irene's house. Their engagement was to be announced in a week now—no one would be surprised at it. And to-night they would sit together on the lounge at the University Club and look on for an hour at the dancers. It gave him a sense of solidity to go with her—she was so sturdily popular, so intensely "great."

He mounted the steps of the brownstone house and stepped inside.

"Irene," he called.

Mrs. Scheerer came out of the living-room to meet him.

"Dexter," she said, "Irene's gone up-stairs with a splitting headache. She wanted to go with you but I made her go to bed."

"Nothing serious, I——"

"Oh, no. She's going to play golf with you in the morning. You can spare her for just one night, can't you, Dexter?"

Her smile was kind. She and Dexter liked each other. In the living-room he talked for a moment before he said good-night.

Returning to the University Club, where he had rooms, he stood in the doorway for a moment and watched the dancers. He leaned against the door-post, nodded at a man or two—yawned.

"Hello, darling."

The familiar voice at his elbow startled him. Judy Jones had left a man and crossed the room to him—Judy Jones, a slender enamelled doll in cloth of gold: gold in a band at her head, gold in two slipper points at her dress's hem. The fragile glow of her face seemed to blossom as she smiled at him. A breeze of warmth and light blew through the room. His hands in the pockets of his dinner-jacket tightened spasmodically. He was filled with a sudden excitement.

"When did you get back?" he asked casually.

"Come here and I'll tell you about it."

She turned and he followed her. She had been away—he could have wept at the wonder of her return. She had passed through enchanted streets, doing things that were like provocative music. All mysterious happenings, all fresh and quickening hopes, had gone away with her, come back with her now.

She turned in the doorway.

"Have you a car here? If you haven't, I have."

"I have a coupé."

In then, with a rustle of golden cloth. He slammed the door. Into so many cars she had stepped—like this—like that—her back against the leather, so—her elbow resting on the door—waiting. She would have been soiled long since had there been anything to soil her—except herself—but this was her own self outpouring.

With an effort he forced himself to start the car and back into the street. This was nothing, he must remember. She had done this before, and he had put her behind him, as he would have crossed a bad account from his books.

He drove slowly down-town and, affecting abstraction, traversed the deserted streets of the business section, peopled here and there where a movie was giving out its crowd or where consumptive or pugilistic youth lounged in front of pool halls. The clink of glasses and the slap of hands on the bars issued from saloons, cloisters of glazed glass and dirty yellow light.

She was watching him closely and the silence was embarrassing, yet in this crisis he could find no casual word with which to profane the hour. At a convenient turning he began to zigzag back toward the University Club.

"Have you missed me?" she asked suddenly.

"Everybody missed you."

He wondered if she knew of Irene Scheerer. She had been back only a day—her absence had been almost contemporaneous with his engagement.

"What a remark!" Judy laughed sadly—without sadness. She looked at him searchingly. He became absorbed in the dashboard.

"You're handsomer than you used to be," she said thoughtfully. "Dexter, you have the most rememberable eyes."

He could have laughed at this, but he did not laugh. It was the sort of thing that was said to sophomores. Yet it stabbed at him.

"I'm awfully tired of everything, darling." She called every one darling, endowing the endearment with careless, individual comraderie. "I wish you'd marry me."

The directness of this confused him. He should have told her now that he was going to marry another girl, but he could not tell her. He could as easily have sworn that he had never loved her.

"I think we'd get along," she continued, on the same note, "unless probably you've forgotten me and fallen in love with another girl."

Her confidence was obviously enormous. She had said, in effect, that she

author lets us know all, omniscient

found such a thing impossible to believe, that if it were true he had merely committed a childish indiscretion—and probably to show off. She would forgive him, because it was not a matter of any moment but rather something to be brushed aside lightly.

"Of course you could never love anybody but me," she continued. "I like the way you love me. Oh, Dexter, have you forgotten last year?"

LIE? "No, I haven't forgotten."

"Neither have I!"

Was she sincerely moved—or was she carried along by the wave of her own acting?

"I wish we could be like that again," she said, and he forced himself to answer:

"I don't think we can."

truth "I suppose not. . . . I hear you're giving Irene Scheerer a violent rush."

There was not the faintest emphasis on the name, yet Dexter was suddenly ashamed.

"Oh, take me home," cried Judy suddenly; "I don't want to go back to that idiotic dance—with those children."

CRY Then, as he turned up the street that led to the residence district, Judy began to cry quietly to herself. He had never seen her cry before. *yeah huh?*

The dark street lightened, the dwellings of the rich loomed up around them, he stopped his coupé in front of the great white bulk of the Mortimer Joneses house, somnolent, gorgeous, drenched with the splendor of the damp moonlight. Its solidity startled him. The strong walls, the steel of the girders, the breadth and beam and pomp of it were there only to bring out the contrast with the young beauty beside him. It was sturdy to accentuate *power* her slightness—as if to show what a breeze could be generated by a butterfly's wing. *she = butterfly — she moves, makes a roar*

He sat perfectly quiet, his nerves in wild clamor, afraid that if he moved he would find her irresistibly in his arms. Two tears had rolled down her wet face and trembled on her upper lip.

"I'm more beautiful than anybody else," she said brokenly, "why can't I be happy?" Her moist eyes tore at his stability—her mouth turned slowly downward with an exquisite sadness: "I'd like to marry you if you'll have me, Dexter. I suppose you think I'm not worth having, but I'll be so beautiful for you, Dexter."

A million phrases of anger, pride, passion, hatred, tenderness fought on his lips. Then a perfect wave of emotion washed over him, carrying off with it a sediment of wisdom, of convention, of doubt, of honor. This was his girl who was speaking, his own, his beautiful, his pride.

"Won't you come in?" He heard her draw in her breath sharply.

brief interlude of truth
Dexter made himself

Waiting.

"All right," his voice was trembling, "I'll come in." *he gives into her beauty*

· V ·

IT WAS STRANGE that neither when it was over nor a long time afterward
did he regret that night. Looking at it from the perspective of ten years, the
fact that Judy's flare for him endured just one month seemed of little importance. Nor did it matter that by his yielding he subjected himself to a *SEX*
deeper agony in the end and gave serious hurt to Irene Scheerer and to
Irene's parents, who had befriended him. There was nothing sufficiently
pictorial about Irene's grief to stamp itself on his mind.

Dexter was at bottom hard-minded. The attitude of the city on his action
was of no importance to him, not because he was going to leave the city,
but because any outside attitude on the situation seemed superficial. He was
completely indifferent to popular opinion. Nor, when he had seen that it
was no use, that he did not possess in himself the power to move fundamentally or to hold Judy Jones, did he bear any malice toward her. He
loved her, and he would love her until the day he was too old for loving—
but he could not have her. So he tasted the deep pain that is reserved only
for the strong, just as he had tasted for a little while the deep happiness.

Even the ultimate falsity of the grounds upon which Judy terminated the
engagement that she did not want to "take him away" from Irene—Judy,
who had wanted nothing else—did not revolt him. He was beyond any
revulsion or any amusement.

He went East in February with the intention of selling out his laundries
and settling in New York—but the war came to America in March and
changed his plans. He returned to the West, handed over the management
of the business to his partner, and went into the first officers' training-camp
in late April. He was one of those young thousands who greeted the war
with a certain amount of relief, welcoming the liberation from webs of
tangled emotion.

he escapes this mess of a life

· VI ·

THIS STORY is not his biography, remember, although things creep into
it which have nothing to do with those dreams he had when he was young.
We are almost done with them and with him now. There is only one more
incident to be related here, and it happens seven years farther on.

It took place in New York, where he had done well—so well that there were no barriers too high for him. He was thirty-two years old, and, except for one flying trip immediately after the war, he had not been West in seven years. A man named Devlin from Detroit came into his office to see him in a business way, and then and there this incident occurred, and closed out, so to speak, this particular side of his life.

"So you're from the Middle West," said the man Devlin with careless curiosity. "That's funny—I thought men like you were probably born and raised on Wall Street. You know—wife of one of my best friends in Detroit came from your city. I was an usher at the wedding."

Dexter waited with no apprehension of what was coming.

"Judy Simms," said Devlin with no particular interest; "Judy Jones she was once."

"Yes, I knew her." A dull impatience spread over him. He had heard, of course, that she was married—perhaps deliberately he had heard no more.

"Awfully nice girl," brooded Devlin meaninglessly, "I'm sort of sorry for her."

"Why?" Something in Dexter was alert, receptive, at once.

"Oh, Lud Simms has gone to pieces in a way. I don't mean he ill-uses her, but he drinks and runs around——"

"Doesn't she run around?"

"No. Stays at home with her kids."

"Oh."

"She's a little too old for him," said Devlin.

"Too old!" cried Dexter. "Why, man, she's only twenty-seven."

He was possessed with a wild notion of rushing out into the streets and taking a train to Detroit. He rose to his feet spasmodically.

"I guess you're busy," Devlin apologized quickly. "I didn't realize——"

"No, I'm not busy," said Dexter, steadying his voice. "I'm not busy at all. Not busy at all. Did you say she was—twenty-seven? No, I said she was twenty-seven."

"Yes, you did," agreed Devlin dryly.

"Go on, then. Go on."

"What do you mean?"

"About Judy Jones."

Devlin looked at him helplessly.

"Well, that's—I told you all there is to it. He treats her like the devil. Oh, they're not going to get divorced or anything. When he's particularly outrageous she forgives him. In fact, I'm inclined to think she loves him. She was a pretty girl when she first came to Detroit."

A pretty girl! The phrase struck Dexter as ludicrous.

"Isn't she—a pretty girl, any more?"

"Oh, she's all right."

"Look here," said Dexter, sitting down suddenly, "I don't understand. You say she was a 'pretty girl' and now you say she's 'all right.' I don't understand what you mean—Judy Jones wasn't a pretty girl, at all. She was a great beauty. Why, I knew her, I knew her. She was——"

Devlin laughed pleasantly.

"I'm not trying to start a row," he said. "I think Judy's a nice girl and I like her. I can't understand how a man like Lud Simms could fall madly in love with her, but he did." Then he added: "Most of the women like her."

Dexter looked closely at Devlin, thinking wildly that there must be a reason for this, some insensitivity in the man or some private malice.

"Lots of women fade just like *that*," Devlin snapped his fingers. "You must have seen it happen. Perhaps I've forgotten how pretty she was at her wedding. I've seen her so much since then, you see. She has nice eyes."

A sort of dulness settled down upon Dexter. For the first time in his life he felt like getting very drunk. He knew that he was laughing loudly at something Devlin had said, but he did not know what it was or why it was funny. When, in a few minutes, Devlin went he lay down on his lounge and looked out the window at the New York sky-line into which the sun was sinking in dull lovely shades of pink and gold.

He had thought that having nothing else to lose he was invulnerable at last—but he knew that he had just lost something more, as surely as if he had married Judy Jones and seen her fade away before his eyes.

The dream was gone. Something had been taken from him. In a sort of panic he pushed the palms of his hands into his eyes and tried to bring up a picture of the waters lapping on Sherry Island and the moonlit veranda, and gingham on the golf-links and the dry sun and the gold color of her neck's soft down. And her mouth damp to his kisses and her eyes plaintive with melancholy and her freshness like new fine linen in the morning. Why, these things were no longer in the world! They had existed and they existed no longer.

For the first time in years the tears were streaming down his face. But they were for himself now. He did not care about mouth and eyes and moving hands. He wanted to care, and he could not care. For he had gone away and he could never go back any more. The gates were closed, the sun was gone down, and there was no beauty but the gray beauty of steel that withstands all time. Even the grief he could have borne was left behind in the country of illusion, of youth, of the richness of life, where his winter dreams had flourished.

"Long ago," he said, "long ago, there was something in me, but now that thing is gone. Now that thing is gone, that thing is gone. I cannot cry. I cannot care. That thing will come back no more."

⤷ Does this have to do w/ the war —
This lovely girl married to wrong man?

Dreams Sustain Man,

Dexter Green is a Romantic —

Romancer / Romantic
⤷ goes after   ⤷ has a perfect picture, drives
the girls to   for that
success.   ⤷ idealist, still views the
                       world as perfect fairy land

gossamer — light + filmy

reality —

epiphany — sudden realization

Conrad, Joseph — Youth

DICE, BRASSKNUCKLES & GUITAR

♦

"Dice, Brassknuckles & Guitar" was published in Hearst's International *(May 1923) and was Fitzgerald's first story submitted under an option contract with the Hearst magazines. "Dice" is obviously one of the stories in which Fitzgerald tested ideas that would be more profoundly developed in* The Great Gatsby. *Here the theme of the hardness of the rich is treated humorously, but Amanthis's statement to the outsider—"You're better than all of them put together, Jim"—anticipates Nick Carraway's judgment that Gatsby is "worth the whole damn bunch put together." "Dice" also expresses, again comically, Fitzgerald's sense of the cultural and social differences between the South and the North.*

♦

PARTS OF New Jersey, as you know, are under water, and other parts are under continual surveillance by the authorities. But here and there lie patches of garden country dotted with old-fashioned frame mansions, which have wide shady porches and a red swing on the lawn. And perhaps, on the widest and shadiest of the porches there is even a hammock left over from the hammock days, stirring gently in a mid-Victorian wind.

When tourists come to such last-century landmarks they stop their cars and gaze for a while and then mutter: "Well, thank God this age is joined on to *some*thing" or else they say: "Well, of course, that house is mostly halls and has a thousand rats and one bathroom, but there's an atmosphere about it——"

The tourist doesn't stay long. He drives on to his Elizabethan villa of pressed cardboard or his early Norman meat-market or his medieval Italian pigeon-coop—because this is the twentieth century and Victorian houses are as unfashionable as the works of Mrs. Humphry Ward.

He can't see the hammock from the road—but sometimes there's a girl in the hammock. There was this afternoon. She was asleep in it and apparently unaware of the esthetic horrors which surrounded her, the stone statue of Diana, for instance, which grinned idiotically under the sunlight on the lawn.

There was something enormously yellow about the whole scene—there was this sunlight, for instance, that was yellow, and the hammock was of the particularly hideous yellow peculiar to hammocks, and the girl's yellow hair was spread out upon the hammock in a sort of invidious comparison.

She slept with her lips closed and her hands clasped behind her head, as it is proper for young girls to sleep. Her breast rose and fell slightly with no more emphasis than the sway of the hammock's fringe.

Her name, Amanthis, was as old-fashioned as the house she lived in. I regret to say that her mid-Victorian connections ceased abruptly at this point.

Now if this were a moving picture (as, of course, I hope it will some day be) I would take as many thousand feet of her as I was allowed—then I would move the camera up close and show the yellow down on the back of her neck where her hair stopped and the warm color of her cheeks and arms, because I like to think of her sleeping there, as you yourself might have slept, back in your young days. Then I would hire a man named Israel Glucose to write some idiotic line of transition, and switch thereby to another scene that was taking place at no particular spot far down the road.

In a moving automobile sat a southern gentleman accompanied by his body-servant. He was on his way, after a fashion, to New York but he was somewhat hampered by the fact that the upper and lower portions of his automobile were no longer in exact juxtaposition. In fact from time to time the two riders would dismount, shove the body on to the chassis, corner to corner, and then continue onward, vibrating slightly in involuntary unison with the motor.

Except that it had no door in back the car might have been built early in the mechanical age. It was covered with the mud of eight states and adorned in front by an enormous but defunct motometer and behind by a mangy pennant bearing the legend "Tarleton, Ga." In the dim past someone had begun to paint the hood yellow but unfortunately had been called away when but half through the task.

As the gentleman and his body-servant were passing the house where Amanthis lay beautifully asleep in the hammock, something happened—the body fell off the car. My only apology for stating this so suddenly is that it happened very suddenly indeed. When the noise had died down and the dust had drifted away master and man arose and inspected the two halves.

"Look-a-there," said the gentleman in disgust, "the doggone thing got all separated that time."

"She bust in two," agreed the body-servant.

"Hugo," said the gentleman, after some consideration, "we got to get a hammer an' nails an' *tack* it on."

They glanced up at the Victorian house. On all sides faintly irregular fields stretched away to a faintly irregular unpopulated horizon. There was no choice, so the black Hugo opened the gate and followed his master up a gravel walk, casting only the blasé glances of a confirmed traveler at the red swing and the stone statue of Diana which turned on them a storm-crazed stare.

At the exact moment when they reached the porch Amanthis awoke, sat up suddenly and looked them over.

The gentleman was young, perhaps twenty-four, and his name was Jim Powell. He was dressed in a tight and dusty readymade suit which was evidently expected to take flight at a moment's notice, for it was secured to his body by a line of six preposterous buttons.

There were supernumerary buttons upon the coat-sleeves also and Amanthis could not resist a glance to determine whether or not more buttons ran up the side of his trouser leg. But the trouser bottoms were distinguished only by their shape, which was that of a bell. His vest was cut low, barely restraining an amazing necktie from fluttering in the wind.

He bowed formally, dusting his knees with a thatched straw hat. Simultaneously he smiled, half shutting his faded blue eyes and displaying white and beautifully symmetrical teeth.

"Good evenin'," he said in abandoned Georgian. "My automobile has met with an accident out yonder by your gate. I wondered if it wouldn't be too much to ask you if I could have the use of a hammer and some tacks—nails, for a little while."

Amanthis laughed. For a moment she laughed uncontrollably. Mr. Jim Powell laughed, politely and appreciatively, with her. His body-servant, deep in the throes of colored adolescence, alone preserved a dignified gravity.

"I better introduce who I am, maybe," said the visitor. "My name's Powell. I'm a resident of Tarleton, Georgia. This here nigger's my boy Hugo."

"Your *son!*" The girl stared from one to the other in wild fascination.

"No, he's my body-servant, I guess you'd call it. We call a nigger a boy down yonder."

At this reference to the finer customs of his native soil the boy Hugo put his hands behind his back and looked darkly and superciliously down the lawn.

"Yas'm," he muttered, "I'm a body-servant."

"Where you going in your automobile," demanded Amanthis.

"Goin' north for the summer."

"Where to?"

The tourist waved his hand with a careless gesture as if to indicate the Adirondacks, the Thousand Islands, Newport—but he said:

"We're tryin' New York."

"Have you ever been there before?"

"Never have. But I been to Atlanta lots of times. An' we passed through all kinds of cities this trip. Man!"

He whistled to express the enormous spectacularity of his recent travels.

"Listen," said Amanthis intently, "you better have something to eat. Tell your—your body-servant to go 'round in back and ask the cook to send us out some sandwiches and lemonade. Or maybe you don't drink lemonade—very few people do any more."

Mr. Powell by a circular motion of his finger sped Hugo on the designated mission. Then he seated himself gingerly in a rocking-chair and began revolving his thatched straw hat rapidly in his hands.

"You cer'nly are mighty kind," he told her. "An' if I wanted anything stronger than lemonade I got a bottle of good old corn out in the car. I brought it along because I thought maybe I wouldn't be able to drink the whisky they got up here."

"Listen," she said, "my name's Powell too. Amanthis Powell."

"Say, is that right?" He laughed ecstatically. "Maybe we're kin to each other. I come from mighty good people," he went on. "Pore though. I got some money because my aunt she was using it to keep her in a sanitarium and she died." He paused, presumably out of respect to his late aunt. Then he concluded with brisk nonchalance, "I ain't touched the principal but I got a lot of the income all at once so I thought I'd come north for the summer."

At this point Hugo reappeared on the veranda steps and became audible.

"White lady back there she asked me don't I want eat some too. What I tell her?"

"You tell her yes mamm if she be so kind," directed his master. And as Hugo retired he confided to Amanthis: "That boy's got no sense at all. He don't want to do nothing without I tell him he can. I brought him up," he added, not without pride.

When the sandwiches arrived Mr. Powell stood up. He was unaccustomed to white servants and obviously expected an introduction.

"Are you a married lady?" he inquired of Amanthis, when the servant was gone.

"No," she answered, and added from the security of eighteen, "I'm an old maid."

Again he laughed politely.

"You mean you're a society girl."

She shook her head. Mr. Powell noted with embarrassed enthusiasm the particular yellowness of her yellow hair.

"Does this old place look like it?" she said cheerfully. "No, you perceive in me a daughter of the countryside. Color—one hundred percent spontaneous—in the daytime anyhow. Suitors—promising young barbers from the neighboring village with somebody's late hair still clinging to their coat-sleeves."

"Your daddy oughtn't to let you go with a country barber," said the tourist disapprovingly. He considered——"You ought to be a New York society girl."

"No." Amanthis shook her head sadly. "I'm too good-looking. To be a New York society girl you have to have a long nose and projecting teeth and dress like the actresses did three years ago."

Jim began to tap his foot rhythmically on the porch and in a moment Amanthis discovered that she was unconsciously doing the same thing.

"Stop!" she commanded, "Don't make me do that."

He looked down at his foot.

"Excuse me," he said humbly. "I don't know—it's just something I do."

This intense discussion was now interrupted by Hugo who appeared on the steps bearing a hammer and a handful of nails.

Mr. Powell arose unwillingly and looked at his watch.

"We got to go, daggone it," he said, frowning heavily. "See here. Wouldn't you *like* to be a New York society girl and go to those dances an' all, like you read about, where they throw gold pieces away?"

She looked at him with a curious expression.

"Don't your folks know some society people?" he went on.

"All I've got's my daddy—and, you see, he's a judge."

"That's too bad," he agreed.

She got herself by some means from the hammock and they went down toward the road, side by side.

"Well, I'll keep my eyes open for you and let you know," he persisted. "A pretty girl like you ought to go around in society. We may be kin to each other, you see, and us Powells ought to stick together."

"What are you going to do in New York?"

They were now almost at the gate and the tourist pointed to the two depressing sectors of his automobile.

"I'm goin' to drive a taxi. This one right here. Only it's got so it busts in two all the time."

"You're going to drive *that* in New York?"

Jim looked at her uncertainly. Such a pretty girl should certainly control the habit of shaking all over upon no provocation at all.

"Yes mamm," he said with dignity.

Amanthis watched while they placed the upper half of the car upon the lower half and nailed it severely into place. Then Mr. Powell took the wheel and his body-servant climbed in beside him.

"I'm cer'nly very much obliged to you indeed for your hospitality. Convey my respects to your father."

"I will," she assured him. "Come back and see me, if you don't mind barbers in the room."

He dismissed this unpleasant thought with a gesture.

"Your company would always be charming." He put the car into gear as though to drown out the temerity of his parting speech. "You're the prettiest girl I've seen up north—by far."

Then with a groan and a rattle Mr. Powell of southern Georgia with his own car and his own body-servant and his own ambitions and his own private cloud of dust continued on north for the summer.

She thought she would never see him again. She lay in her hammock, slim and beautiful, opened her left eye slightly to see June come in and then closed it and retired contentedly back into her dreams.

But one day when the midsummer vines had climbed the precarious sides of the red swing in the lawn, Mr. Jim Powell of Tarleton, Georgia, came vibrating back into her life. They sat on the wide porch as before.

"I've got a great scheme," he told her.

"Did you drive your taxi like you said?"

"Yes mamm, but the business was right bad. I waited around in front of all those hotels and theaters an' nobody ever got in."

"*Nobody?*"

"Well, one night there was some drunk fellas they got in, only just as I was gettin' started my automobile came apart. And another night it was rainin' and there wasn't no other taxis and a lady got in because she said she had to go a long ways. But before we got there she made me stop and she got out. She seemed kinda mad and she went walkin' off in the rain. Mighty proud lot of people they got up in New York."

"And so you're going home?" asked Amanthis sympathetically.

"No *mamm*. I got an idea." His blue eyes grew narrow. "Has that barber been around here—with hair on his sleeves?"

"No. He's—he's gone away."

"Well, then, first thing is I want to leave this car of mine here with you, if that's all right. It ain't the right color for a taxi. To pay for its keep I'd

like to have you drive it just as much as you want. 'Long as you got a
hammer an' nails with you there ain't much bad that can happen——"

"I'll take care of it," interrupted Amanthis, "but where are *you* going?"

"Southampton. It's about the most aristocratic watering trough—water-
ing-place there is around here, so that's where I'm going."

She sat up in amazement.

"What are you going to do there?"

"Listen." He leaned toward her confidentially. "Were you serious about
wanting to be a New York society girl?"

"Deadly serious."

"That's all I wanted to know," he said inscrutably. "You just wait here
on this porch a couple of weeks and—and sleep. And if any barbers come
to see you with hair on their sleeves you tell 'em you're too sleepy to see
'em."

"What then?"

"Then you'll hear from me. Just tell your old daddy he can do all the
judging he wants but you're goin' to do some *dancin'*. Mamm," he continued
decisively, "you talk about society! Before one month I'm goin' to have
you in more society than you ever saw."

Further than this he would say nothing. His manner conveyed that she
was going to be suspended over a perfect pool of gaiety and violently immersed, to an accompaniment of: "Is it gay enough for you, mamm? Shall
I let in a little more excitement, mamm?"

"Well," answered Amanthis, lazily considering, "there are few things for
which I'd forego the luxury of sleeping through July and August—but if
you'll write me a letter I'll—I'll run up to Southampton."

Jim snapped his fingers ecstatically.

"More society," he assured her with all the confidence at his command,
"than anybody ever saw."

Three days later a young man wearing a straw hat that might have been
cut from the thatched roof of an English cottage rang the doorbell of the
enormous and astounding Madison Harlan house at Southampton. He asked
the butler if there were any people in the house between the ages of sixteen
and twenty. He was informed that Miss Genevieve Harlan and Mr. Ronald
Harlan answered that description and thereupon he handed in a most peculiar
card and requested in fetching Georgian that it be brought to their attention.

As a result he was closeted for almost an hour with Mr. Ronald Harlan
(who was a student at the Hillkiss School) and Miss Genevieve Harlan (who
was not uncelebrated at Southampton dances). When he left he bore a short
note in Miss Harlan's handwriting which he presented together with his

peculiar card at the next large estate. It happened to be that of the Clifton Garneaus. Here, as if by magic, the same audience was granted him.

He went on—it was a hot day, and men who could not afford to do so were carrying their coats on the public highway, but Jim, a native of southernmost Georgia, was as fresh and cool at the last house as at the first. He visited ten houses that day. Anyone following him in his course might have taken him to be some curiously gifted book-agent with a much sought-after volume as his stock in trade.

There was something in his unexpected demand for the adolescent members of the family which made hardened butlers lose their critical acumen. As he left each house a close observer might have seen that fascinated eyes followed him to the door and excited voices whispered something which hinted at a future meeting.

The second day he visited twelve houses. Southampton has grown enormously—he might have kept on his round for a week and never seen the same butler twice—but it was only the palatial, the amazing houses which intrigued him.

On the third day he did a thing that many people have been told to do and few have done—he hired a hall. Perhaps the sixteen-to-twenty-year-old people in the enormous houses had told him to. The hall he hired had once been "Mr. Snorkey's Private Gymnasium for Gentlemen." It was situated over a garage on the south edge of Southampton and in the days of its prosperity had been, I regret to say, a place where gentlemen could, under Mr. Snorkey's direction, work off the effects of the night before. It was now abandoned—Mr. Snorkey had given up and gone away and died.

We will now skip three weeks during which time we may assume that the project which had to do with hiring a hall and visiting the two dozen largest houses in Southampton got under way.

The day to which we will skip was the July day on which Mr. James Powell sent a wire to Miss Amanthis Powell saying that if she still aspired to the gaiety of the highest society she should set out for Southampton by the earliest possible train. He himself would meet her at the station.

Jim was no longer a man of leisure, so when she failed to arrive at the time her wire had promised he grew restless. He supposed she was coming on a later train, turned to go back to his—his project—and met her entering the station from the street side.

"Why, how did you——"

"Well," said Amanthis, "I arrived this morning instead, and I didn't want to bother you so I found a respectable, not to say dull, boarding-house on the Ocean Road."

She was quite different from the indolent Amanthis of the porch hammock, he thought. She wore a suit of robins' egg blue and a rakish young hat with a curling feather—she was attired not unlike those young ladies between sixteen and twenty who of late were absorbing his attention. Yes, she would do very well.

He bowed her profoundly into a taxicab and got in beside her.

"Isn't it about time you told me your scheme?" she suggested.

"Well, it's about these society girls up here." He waved his hand airily. "I know 'em all."

"Where are they?"

"Right now they're with Hugo. You remember—that's my body-servant."

"With Hugo!" Her eyes widened. "Why? What's it all about?"

"Well, I got—I got sort of a school, I guess you'd call it."

"A school?"

"It's a sort of Academy. And I'm the head of it. I invented it."

He flipped a card from his case as though he were shaking down a thermometer.

"Look."

She took the card. In large lettering it bore the legend

JAMES POWELL; J. M.
"Dice, Brassknuckles and Guitar"

She stared in amazement.

"Dice, Brassknuckles and Guitar?" she repeated in awe.

"Yes mamm."

"What does it mean? What——do you *sell* 'em?"

"No mamm, I teach 'em. It's a profession."

"Dice, Brassknuckles and Guitar? What's the J. M.?"

"That stands for Jazz Master."

"But what *is* it? What's it about?"

"Well, you see, it's like this. One night when I was in New York I got talkin' to a young fella who was drunk. He was one of my fares. And he'd taken some society girl somewhere and lost her."

"*Lost* her?"

"Yes mamm. He forgot her, I guess. And he was right worried. Well, I got to thinkin' that these girls nowadays—these society girls—they lead a sort of dangerous life and my course of study offers a means of protection against these dangers."

"You teach 'em to use brassknuckles?"

"Yes mamm, if necessary. Look here, you take a girl and she goes into some cafe where she's got no business to go. Well then, her escort he gets a little too much to drink an' he goes to sleep an' then some other fella comes up and says 'Hello, sweet mamma' or whatever one of those mashers says up here. What does she do? She can't scream, on account of no real lady'll scream nowadays—no—She just reaches down in her pocket and slips her fingers into a pair of Powell's defensive brassknuckles, débutante's size, executes what I call the Society Hook, and *Wham!* that big fella's on his way to the cellar."

"Well—what—what's the guitar for?" whispered the awed Amanthis. "Do they have to knock somebody over with the guitar?"

"No, *mamm!*" exclaimed Jim in horror. "No mamm. In my course no lady would be taught to raise a guitar against anybody. I teach 'em to play. Shucks! you ought to hear 'em. Why, when I've given 'em two lessons you'd think some of 'em was colored."

"And the dice?"

"Dice? I'm related to a dice. My grandfather was a dice. I teach 'em how to make those dice perform. I protect pocketbook as well as person."

"Did you——Have you got any pupils?"

"Mamm I got all the really nice, rich people in the place. What I told you ain't all. I teach lots of things. I teach 'em the jellyroll—and the Mississippi Sunrise. Why, there was one girl she came to me and said she wanted to learn to snap her fingers. I mean *really* snap 'em—like they do. She said she never could snap her fingers since she was little. I gave her two lessons and now *Wham!* Her daddy says he's goin' to leave home."

"When do you have it?" demanded the weak and shaken Amanthis.

"Three times a week. We're goin' there right now."

"And where do I fit in?"

"Well, you'll just be one of the pupils. I got it fixed up that you come from very high-tone people down in New Jersey. I didn't tell 'em your daddy was a judge——I told 'em he was the man that had the patent on lump sugar."

She gasped.

"So all you got to do," he went on, "is to pretend you never saw no barber."

They were now at the south end of the village and Amanthis saw a row of cars parked in front of a two-story building. The cars were all low, long, rakish and of a brilliant hue. They were the sort of car that is manufactured to solve the millionaire's problem on his son's eighteenth birthday.

Then Amanthis was ascending a narrow stairs to the second story. Here, painted on a door from which came the sounds of music and laughter were the words:

JAMES POWELL; J. M.
"Dice, Brassknuckles and Guitar"
Mon.—Wed.—Fri.
Hours 3–5 P.M.

"Now if you'll just step this way——" said the Principal, pushing open the door.

Amanthis found herself in a long, bright room, populated with girls and men of about her own age. The scene presented itself to her at first as a sort of animated afternoon tea but after a moment she began to see, here and there, a motive and a pattern to the proceedings.

The students were scattered into groups, sitting, kneeling, standing, but all rapaciously intent on the subjects which engrossed them. From six young ladies gathered in a ring around some indistinguishable objects came a medley of cries and exclamations—plaintive, pleading, supplicating, exhorting, imploring and lamenting—their voices serving as tenor to an undertone of mysterious clatters.

Next to this group, four young men were surrounding an adolescent black, who proved to be none other than Mr. Powell's late body-servant. The young men were roaring at Hugo apparently unrelated phrases, expressing a wide gamut of emotion. Now their voices rose to a sort of clamor, now they spoke softly and gently, with mellow implication. Every little while Hugo would answer them with words of approbation, correction or disapproval.

"What are they doing?" whispered Amanthis to Jim.

"That there's a course in southern accent. Lot of young men up here want to learn southern accent—so we teach it—Georgia, Florida, Alabama, Eastern Shore, Ole Virginian. Some of 'em even want straight nigger—for song purposes."

They walked around among the groups. Some girls with metal knuckles were furiously insulting two punching bags on each of which was painted the leering, winking face of a "masher." A mixed group, led by a banjo tom-tom, were rolling harmonic syllables from their guitars. There were couples dancing flat-footed in the corner to a phonograph record made by Rastus Muldoon's Savannah Band; there were couples stalking a slow Chicago with a Memphis Sideswoop solemnly around the room.

"Are there any rules?" asked Amanthis.

Jim considered.

"Well," he answered finally, "they can't smoke unless they're over sixteen, and the boys have got to shoot square dice and I don't let 'em bring liquor into the Academy."

"I see."

"And now, Miss Powell, if you're ready I'll ask you to take off your hat and go over and join Miss Genevieve Harlan at that punching bag in the corner." He raised his voice. "Hugo," he called, "there's a new student here. Equip her with a pair of Powell's Defensive Brassknuckles—débutante size."

I regret to say that I never saw Jim Powell's famous Jazz School in action nor followed his personally conducted tours into the mysteries of Dice, Brassknuckles and Guitar. So I can give you only such details as were later reported to me by one of his admiring pupils. During all the discussion of it afterwards no one ever denied that it was an enormous success, and no pupil ever regretted having received its degree—Bachelor of Jazz.

The parents innocently assumed that it was a sort of musical and dancing academy, but its real curriculum was transmitted from Santa Barbara to Biddeford Pool by that underground associated press which links up the so-called younger generation. Invitations to visit Southampton were at a premium—and Southampton generally is almost as dull for young people as Newport.

The Academy branched out with a small but well-groomed Jazz Orchestra.

"If I could keep it dark," Jim confided to Amanthis, "I'd have up Rastus Muldoon's Band from Savannah. That's the band I've always wanted to lead."

He was making money. His charges were not exorbitant—as a rule his pupils were not particularly flush—but he moved from his boarding-house to the Casino Hotel where he took a suite and had Hugo serve him his breakfast in bed.

The establishing of Amanthis as a member of Southampton's younger set was easier than he had expected. Within a week she was known to everyone in the school by her first name. Miss Genevieve Harlan took such a fancy to her that she was invited to a sub-deb dance at the Harlan house—and evidently acquitted herself with tact, for thereafter she was invited to almost every such entertainment in Southampton.

Jim saw less of her than he would have liked. Not that her manner toward him changed—she walked with him often in the mornings, she was always willing to listen to his plans—but after she was taken up by the fashionable her evenings seemed to be monopolized. Several times Jim arrived at her boarding-house to find her out of breath, as if she had just come in at a run, presumably from some festivity in which he had no share.

So as the summer waned he found that one thing was lacking to complete the triumph of his enterprise. Despite the hospitality shown to Amanthis, the doors of Southampton were closed to him. Polite to, or rather, fascinated by him as his pupils were from three to five, after that hour they moved in another world.

His was the position of a golf professional who, though he may fraternize, and even command, on the links, loses his privileges with the sun-down. He may look in the club window but he cannot dance. And, likewise, it was not given to Jim to see his teachings put into effect. He could hear the gossip of the morning after—that was all.

But while the golf professional, being English, holds himself proudly below his patrons, Jim Powell, who "came from a right good family down there—pore though," lay awake many nights in his hotel bed and heard the music drifting into his window from the Katzbys' house or the Beach Club, and turned over restlessly and wondered what was the matter. In the early days of his success he had bought himself a dress-suit, thinking that he would soon have a chance to wear it—but it still lay untouched in the box in which it had come from the tailor's.

Perhaps, he thought, there was some real gap which separated him from the rest. It worried him. One boy in particular, Martin Van Vleck, son of Van Vleck the ash-can King, made him conscious of the gap. Van Vleck was twenty-one, a tutoring-school product who still hoped to enter Yale. Several times Jim had heard him make remarks not intended for Jim's ear —once in regard to the suit with multiple buttons, again in reference to Jim's long, pointed shoes. Jim had passed these over.

He knew that Van Vleck was attending the school chiefly to monopolize the time of little Martha Katzby, who was just sixteen and too young to have attention of a boy of twenty-one—especially the attention of Van Vleck, who was so spiritually exhausted by his educational failures that he drew on the rather exhaustible innocence of sixteen.

It was late in September, two days before the Harlan dance which was to be the last and biggest of the season for this younger crowd. Jim, as usual, was not invited. He had hoped that he would be. The two young Harlans, Ronald and Genevieve, had been his first patrons when he arrived at Southampton—and it was Genevieve who had taken such a fancy to Amanthis. To have been at their dance—the most magnificent dance of all—would have crowned and justified the success of the waning summer.

His class, gathering for the afternoon, was loudly anticipating the next day's revel with no more thought of him than if he had been the family butler. Hugo, standing beside Jim, chuckled suddenly and remarked:

"Look yonder that man Van Vleck. He paralyzed. He been havin' pow-erful lotta corn this evenin'."

Jim turned and stared at Van Vleck, who had linked arms with little

Martha Katzby and was saying something to her in a low voice. Jim saw her try to draw away.

He put his whistle to his mouth and blew it.

"All right," he cried, "Le's go! Group one tossin' the drumstick, high an' zig-zag, group two, test your mouth organs for the Riverfront Shuffle. Promise 'em sugar! Flatfoots this way! Orchestra—let's have the Florida Drag-Out played as a dirge."

There was an unaccustomed sharpness in his voice and the exercises began with a mutter of facetious protest.

With his smoldering grievance directing itself toward Van Vleck, Jim was walking here and there among the groups when Hugo tapped him suddenly on the arm. He looked around. Two participants had withdrawn from the mouth organ institute—one of them was Van Vleck and he was giving a drink out of his flask to fifteen-year-old Ronald Harlan.

Jim strode across the room. Van Vleck turned defiantly as he came up.

"All right," said Jim, trembling with anger, "you know the rules. You get out!"

The music died slowly away and there was a sudden drifting over in the direction of the trouble. Somebody snickered. An atmosphere of anticipation formed instantly. Despite the fact that they all liked Jim their sympathies were divided—Van Vleck was one of them.

"Get out!" repeated Jim, more quietly.

"Are you talking to me?" inquired Van Vleck coldly.

"Yes."

"Then you better say 'sir.' "

"I wouldn't say 'sir' to anybody that'd give a little boy whisky! You get out!"

"Look here!" said Van Vleck furiously. "You've butted in once too much. I've known Ronald since he was two years old. Ask *him* if he wants *you* to tell him what he can do!"

Ronald Harlan, his dignity offended, grew several years older and looked haughtily at Jim.

"Mind your own business!" he said defiantly, albeit a little guiltily.

"Hear that?" demanded Van Vleck. "My God, can't you see you're just a servant? Ronald here'd no more think of asking you to his party than he would his bootlegger."

"Youbettergetout!" cried Jim incoherently.

Van Vleck did not move. Reaching out suddenly, Jim caught his wrist and jerking it behind his back forced his arm upward until Van Vleck bent forward in agony. Jim leaned and picked the flask from the floor with his free hand. Then he signed Hugo to open the hall-door, uttered an abrupt

"You *step!*" and marched his helpless captive out into the hall where he literally *threw* him downstairs, head over heels bumping from wall to banister, and hurled his flask after him.

Then he reentered his academy, closed the door behind him and stood with his back against it.

"It—it happens to be a rule that nobody drinks while in this Academy." He paused, looking from face to face, finding there sympathy, awe, disapproval, conflicting emotions. They stirred uneasily. He caught Amanthis's eye, fancied he saw a faint nod of encouragement and, with almost an effort, went on:

"I just *had* to throw that fella out an' you-all know it." Then he concluded with a transparent affectation of dismissing an unimportant matter——"All right, let's go! Orchestra——!"

But no one felt exactly like going on. The spontaneity of the proceedings had been violently disturbed. Someone made a run or two on the sliding guitar and several of the girls began whamming at the leer on the punching bags, but Ronald Harlan, followed by two other boys, got their hats and went silently out the door.

Jim and Hugo moved among the groups as usual until a certain measure of routine activity was restored but the enthusiasm was unrecapturable and Jim, shaken and discouraged, considered discontinuing school for the day. But he dared not. If they went home in this mood they might not come back. The whole thing depended on a mood. He must recreate it, he thought frantically—now, at once!

But try as he might, there was little response. He himself was not happy —he could communicate no gaiety to them. They watched his efforts listlessly and, he thought, a little contemptuously.

Then the tension snapped when the door burst suddenly open, precipitating a brace of middle-aged and excited women into the room. No person over twenty-one had ever entered the Academy before—but Van Vleck had gone direct to headquarters. The women were Mrs. Clifton Garneau and Mrs. Poindexter Katzby, two of the most fashionable and, at present, two of the most flurried women in Southampton. They were in search of their daughters as, in these days, so many women continually are.

The business was over in about three minutes.

"And as for you!" cried Mrs. Clifton Garneau in an awful voice, "your idea is to run a bar and—and *opium* den for children! You ghastly, horrible, unspeakable man! I can smell morphin fumes! Don't tell me I can't smell morphin fumes. I can smell morphin fumes!"

"And," bellowed Mrs. Poindexter Katzby, "you have colored men around! You have colored girls hidden! I'm going to the police!"

Not content with herding their own daughters from the room, they insisted on the exodus of their friends' daughters. Jim was not a little touched when several of them—including even little Martha Katzby, before she was snatched fiercely away by her mother—came up and shook hands with him. But they were all going, haughtily, regretfully or with shame-faced mutters of apology.

"Good-by," he told them wistfully. "In the morning I'll send you the money that's due you."

And, after all, they were not sorry to go. Outside, the sound of their starting motors, the triumphant put-put of their cut-outs cutting the warm September air, was a jubilant sound—a sound of youth and hopes high as the sun. Down to the ocean, to roll in the waves and forget—forget him and their discomfort at his humiliation.

They were gone—he was alone with Hugo in the room. He sat down suddenly with his face in his hands.

"Hugo," he said huskily. "They don't want us up here."

"Don't you care," said a voice.

He looked up to see Amanthis standing beside him.

"You better go with them," he told her. "You better not be seen here with me."

"Why?"

"Because you're in society now and I'm no better to those people than a servant. You're in society—I fixed that up. You better go or they won't invite you to any of their dances."

"They won't anyhow, Jim," she said gently. "They didn't invite me to the one tomorrow night."

He looked up indignantly.

"They *did*n't?"

She shook her head.

"I'll *make* 'em!" he said wildly. "I'll tell 'em they got to. I'll—I'll——"

She came close to him with shining eyes.

"Don't you mind, Jim," she soothed him. "Don't you mind. They don't matter. We'll have a party of our own tomorrow—just you and I."

"I come from right good folks," he said, defiantly. "Pore though."

She laid her hand softly on his shoulder.

"I understand. You're better than all of them put together, Jim."

He got up and went to the window and stared out mournfully into the late afternoon.

"I reckon I should have let you sleep in that hammock."

She laughed.

"I'm awfully glad you didn't."

He turned and faced the room, and his face was dark.

"Sweep up and lock up, Hugo," he said, his voice trembling. "The summer's over and we're going down home."

Autumn had come early. Jim Powell woke next morning to find his room cool, and the phenomenon of frosted breath in September absorbed him for a moment to the exclusion of the day before. Then the lines of his face drooped with unhappiness as he remembered the humiliation which had washed the cheery glitter from the summer. There was nothing left for him except to go back where he was known, where under no provocation were such things said to white people as had been said to him here.

After breakfast a measure of his customary light-heartedness returned. He was a child of the South—brooding was alien to his nature. He could conjure up an injury only a certain number of times before it faded into the great vacancy of the past.

But when, from force of habit, he strolled over to his defunct establishment, already as obsolete as Snorkey's late sanitarium, melancholy again dwelt in his heart. Hugo was there, a specter of despair, deep in the lugubrious blues amidst his master's broken hopes.

Usually a few words from Jim were enough to raise him to an inarticulate ecstasy, but this morning there were no words to utter. For two months Hugo had lived on a pinnacle of which he had never dreamed. He had enjoyed his work simply and passionately, arriving before school hours and lingering long after Mr. Powell's pupils had gone.

The day dragged toward a not-too-promising night. Amanthis did not appear and Jim wondered forlornly if she had not changed her mind about dining with him that night. Perhaps it would be better if she were not seen with them. But then, he reflected dismally, no one would see them anyhow—everybody was going to the big dance at the Harlans' house.

When twilight threw unbearable shadows into the school hall he locked it up for the last time, took down the sign "James Powell; J. M., Dice, Brassknuckles and Guitar," and went back to his hotel. Looking over his scrawled accounts he saw that there was another month's rent to pay on his school and some bills for windows broken and new equipment that had hardly been used. Jim had lived in state, and he realized that financially he would have nothing to show for the summer after all.

When he had finished he took his new dress-suit out of its box and inspected it, running his hand over the satin of the lapels and lining. This, at least, he owned and perhaps in Tarleton somebody would ask him to a party where he could wear it.

"Shucks!" he said scoffingly. "It was just a no account old academy, anyhow. Some of those boys round the garage down home could beat it all hollow."

Whistling "Jeanne of Jelly-bean Town" to a not-dispirited rhythm Jim encased himself in his first dress-suit and walked downtown.

"Orchids," he said to the clerk. He surveyed his purchase with some pride. He knew that no girl at the Harlan dance would wear anything lovelier than these exotic blossoms that leaned languorously backward against green ferns.

In a taxi-cab, carefully selected to look like a private car, he drove to Amanthis's boarding-house. She came down wearing a rose-colored evening dress into which the orchids melted like colors into a sunset.

"I reckon we'll go to the Casino Hotel," he suggested, "unless you got some other place——"

At their table, looking out over the dark ocean, his mood became a contended sadness. The windows were shut against the cool but the orchestra played "Kalula" and "South Sea Moon" and for awhile, with her young loveliness opposite him, he felt himself to be a romantic participant in the life around him. They did not dance, and he was glad—it would have reminded him of that other brighter and more radiant dance to which they could not go.

After dinner they took a taxi and followed the sandy roads for an hour, glimpsing the now starry ocean through the casual trees.

"I want to thank you," she said, "for all you've done for me, Jim."

"That's all right—we Powells ought to stick together."

"What are you going to do?"

"I'm going to Tarleton tomorrow."

"I'm sorry," she said softly. "Are you going to drive down?"

"I got to. I got to get the car south because I couldn't get what she was worth by sellin' it. You don't suppose anybody's stole my car out of your barn?" he asked in sudden alarm.

She repressed a smile.

"No."

"I'm sorry about this—about you," he went on huskily, "and—and I would like to have gone to just one of their dances. You shouldn't of stayed with me yesterday. Maybe it kept 'em from asking you."

"Jim," she suggested eagerly, "let's go and stand outside and listen to their old music. We don't care."

"They'll be coming out," he objected.

"No, it's too cold. Besides there's nothing they could do to you any more than they *have* done."

She gave the chauffeur a direction and a few minutes later they stopped in front of the heavy Georgian beauty of the Madison Harlan house whence the windows cast their gaiety in bright patches on the lawn. There was laughter inside and the plaintive wind of fashionable horns, and now and again the slow, mysterious shuffle of dancing feet.

"Let's go up close," whispered Amanthis in an ecstatic trance, "I want to hear."

They walked toward the house, keeping in the shadow of the great trees. Jim proceeded with awe—suddenly he stopped and seized Amanthis's arm.

"Man!" he cried in an excited whisper. "Do you know what that is?"

"A night watchman?" Amanthis cast a startled look around.

"It's Rastus Muldoon's Band from Savannah! I heard 'em once, and I *know*. It's Rastus Muldoon's Band!"

They moved closer till they could see first pompadours, then slicked male heads, and high coiffures and finally even bobbed hair pressed under black ties. They could distinguish chatter below the ceaseless laughter. Two figures appeared on the porch, gulped something quickly from flasks and returned inside. But the music had bewitched Jim Powell. His eyes were fixed and he moved his feet like a blind man.

Pressed in close behind some dark bushes they listened. The number ended. A breeze from the ocean blew over them and Jim shivered slightly. Then, in a wistful whisper:

"I've always wanted to lead that band. Just once." His voice grew listless. "Come on. Let's go. I reckon I don't belong around here."

He held out his arm to her but instead of taking it she stepped suddenly out of the bushes and into a bright patch of light.

"Come on, Jim," she said startlingly. "Let's go inside."

"What——?"

She seized his arm and though he drew back in a sort of stupefied horror at her boldness she urged him persistently toward the great front door.

"Watch out!" he gasped. "Somebody's coming out of that house and see us."

"No, Jim," she said firmly. "Nobody's coming out of that house—but two people are going in."

"Why?" he demanded wildly, standing in full glare of the porte-cochère lamps. "Why?"

"Why?" she mocked him. "Why, just because this dance happens to be given for me."

He thought she was mad.

"Come home before they see us," he begged her.

The great doors swung open and a gentleman stepped out on the porch.

In horror Jim recognized Mr. Madison Harlan. He made a movement as though to break away and run. But the man walked down the steps holding out both hands to Amanthis.

"Hello at last," he cried. "Where on earth have you two been? Cousin Amanthis——" He kissed her, and turned cordially to Jim. "And for you, Mr. Powell," he went on, "to make up for being late you've got to promise that for just one number you're going to lead that band."

New Jersey was warm, all except the part that was under water, and that mattered only to the fishes. All the tourists who rode through the long green miles stopped their cars in front of a spreading old-fashioned country house and looked at the red swing on the lawn and the wide, shady porch, and sighed and drove on—swerving a little to avoid a jet-black body-servant in the road. The body-servant was applying a hammer and nails to a decayed flivver which flaunted from its rear the legend, "Tarleton, Ga."

A girl with yellow hair and a warm color to her face was lying in the hammock looking as though she could fall asleep any moment. Near her sat a gentleman in an extraordinarily tight suit. They had come down together the day before from the fashionable resort at Southampton.

"When you first appeared," she was explaining, "I never thought I'd see you again so I made that up about the barber and all. As a matter of fact, I've been around quite a bit—with or without brassknuckles. I'm coming out this autumn."

"I reckon I had a lot to learn," said Jim.

"And you see," went on Amanthis, looking at him rather anxiously, "I'd been invited up to Southampton to visit my cousins—and when you said you were going, I wanted to see what you'd do. I always slept at the Harlans' but I kept a room at the boarding-house so you wouldn't know. The reason I didn't get there on the right train was because I had to come early and warn a lot of people to pretend not to know me."

Jim got up, nodding his head in comprehension.

"I reckon I and Hugo had better be movin' along. We got to make Baltimore by night."

"That's a long way."

"I want to sleep south tonight," he said simply.

Together they walked down the path and past the idiotic statue of Diana on the lawn.

"You see," added Amanthis gently, "you don't have to be rich up here in order to—to go around, any more than you do in Georgia——" She broke off abruptly, "Won't you come back next year and start another Academy?"

"No mamm, not me. That Mr. Harlan told me I could go on with the one I had but I told him no."

"Haven't you——didn't you make money?"

"No mamm," he answered. "I got enough of my own income to just get me home. I didn't have my principal along. One time I was way ahead but I was livin' high and there was my rent an' apparatus and those musicians. Besides, there at the end I had to pay what they'd advanced me for their lessons."

"You shouldn't have done that!" cried Amanthis indignantly.

"They didn't want me to, but I told 'em they'd have to take it."

He didn't consider it necessary to mention that Mr. Harlan had tried to present him with a check.

They reached the automobile just as Hugo drove in his last nail. Jim opened a pocket of the door and took from it an unlabeled bottle containing a whitish-yellow liquid.

"I intended to get you a present," he told her awkwardly, "but my money got away before I could, so I thought I'd send you something from Georgia. This here's just a personal remembrance. It won't do for you to drink but maybe after you come out into society you might want to show some of those young fellas what good old corn tastes like."

She took the bottle.

"Thank you, Jim."

"That's all right." He turned to Hugo. "I reckon we'll go along now. Give the lady the hammer."

"Oh, you can have the hammer," said Amanthis tearfully. "Oh, won't you promise to come back?"

"Someday—maybe."

He looked for a moment at her yellow hair and her blue eyes misty with sleep and tears. Then he got into his car and as his foot found the clutch his whole manner underwent a change.

"I'll say good-by mamm," he announced with impressive dignity, "we're goin' south for the winter."

The gesture of his straw hat indicated Palm Beach, St. Augustine, Miami. His body-servant spun the crank, gained his seat and became part of the intense vibration into which the automobile was thrown.

"South for the winter," repeated Jim, and then he added softly, "You're the prettiest girl I ever knew. You go back up there and lie down in that hammock, and sleep—sle-eep——"

It was almost a lullaby, as he said it. He bowed to her, magnificently, profoundly, including the whole North in the splendor of his obeisance——

Then they were gone down the road in quite a preposterous cloud of dust. Just before they reached the first bend Amanthis saw them come to a full stop, dismount and shove the top part of the car on to the bottom part. They took their seats again without looking around. Then the bend —and they were out of sight, leaving only a faint brown mist to show that they had passed.

ABSOLUTION

♦

"Absolution" appeared in the June 1924 issue of H. L. Mencken's new magazine, The American Mercury, *and was collected in* All the Sad Young Men. *There has been reckless speculation about its relationship to* The Great Gatsby. *Written in June 1923, "Absolution" was part of a lost early draft of the novel; but it was not in the final manuscript version of* Gatsby. *Fitzgerald explained in June 1924 to Scribners editor Maxwell Perkins: "As you know it was to have been the prologue of the novel but it interfered with the neatness of the plan." Rudolph Miller is best regarded as a preliminary view of the character who developed into James Gatz—not as young Gatsby himself.*

♦

THERE WAS once a priest with cold, watery eyes, who, in the still of the night, wept cold tears. He wept because the afternoons were warm and long, and he was unable to attain a complete mystical union with our Lord. Sometimes, near four o'clock, there was a rustle of Swede girls along the path by his window, and in their shrill laughter he found a terrible dissonance that made him pray aloud for the twilight to come. At twilight the laughter and the voices were quieter, but several times he had walked past Romberg's Drug Store when it was dusk and the yellow lights shone inside and the nickel taps of the soda-fountain were gleaming, and he had found the scent of cheap toilet soap desperately sweet upon the air. He passed that way when he returned from hearing confessions on Saturday nights, and he grew careful to walk on the other side of the street so that the smell of the soap would float upward before it reached his nostrils as it drifted, rather like incense, toward the summer moon.

But there was no escape from the hot madness of four o'clock. From his window, as far as he could see, the Dakota wheat thronged the valley of the Red River. The wheat was terrible to look upon and the carpet pattern to which in agony he bent his eyes sent his thought brooding through grotesque labyrinths, open always to the unavoidable sun.

One afternoon when he had reached the point where the mind runs down like an old clock, his housekeeper brought into his study a beautiful, intense little boy of eleven named Rudolph Miller. The little boy sat down in a patch of sunshine, and the priest, at his walnut desk, pretended to be very busy. This was to conceal his relief that some one had come into his haunted room.

Presently he turned around and found himself staring into two enormous, staccato eyes, lit with gleaming points of cobalt light. For a moment their expression startled him—then he saw that his visitor was in a state of abject fear.

"Your mouth is trembling," said Father Schwartz, in a haggard voice.

The little boy covered his quivering mouth with his hand.

"Are you in trouble?" asked Father Schwartz, sharply. "Take your hand away from your mouth and tell me what's the matter."

The boy—Father Schwartz recognized him now as the son of a parishioner, Mr. Miller, the freight-agent—moved his hand reluctantly off his mouth and became articulate in a despairing whisper.

"Father Schwartz—I've committed a terrible sin."

"A sin against purity?"

"No, Father . . . worse."

Father Schwartz's body jerked sharply.

"Have you killed somebody?"

"No—but I'm afraid—" the voice rose to a shrill whimper.

"Do you want to go to confession?"

The little boy shook his head miserably. Father Schwartz cleared his throat so that he could make his voice soft and say some quiet, kind thing. In this moment he should forget his own agony, and try to act like God. He repeated to himself a devotional phrase, hoping that in return God would help him to act correctly.

"Tell me what you've done," said his new soft voice.

The little boy looked at him through his tears, and was reassured by the impression of moral resiliency which the distraught priest had created. Abandoning as much of himself as he was able to this man, Rudolph Miller began to tell his story.

"On Saturday, three days ago, my father he said I had to go to confession, because I hadn't been for a month, and the family they go every week, and I hadn't been. So I just as leave go, I didn't care. So I put it off till after supper because I was playing with a bunch of kids and father asked me if I went, and I said 'no,' and he took me by the neck and he said 'You go now,' so I said 'All right,' so I went over to church. And he yelled after me: 'Don't come back till you go.' . . ."

· I I ·

"On Saturday, Three Days Ago."

THE PLUSH curtain of the confessional rearranged its dismal creases, leaving exposed only the bottom of an old man's old shoe. Behind the curtain an immortal soul was alone with God and the Reverend Adolphus Schwartz, priest of the parish. Sound began, a labored whispering, sibilant and discreet, broken at intervals by the voice of the priest in audible question.

Rudolph Miller knelt in the pew beside the confessional and waited, straining nervously to hear, and yet not to hear what was being said within. The fact that the priest was audible alarmed him. His own turn came next, and the three or four others who waited might listen unscrupulously while he admitted his violations of the Sixth and Ninth Commandments.

Rudolph had never committed adultery, nor even coveted his neighbor's wife—but it was the confession of the associate sins that was particularly hard to contemplate. In comparison he relished the less shameful fallings away—they formed a grayish background which relieved the ebony mark of sexual offenses upon his soul.

He had been covering his ears with his hands, hoping that his refusal to hear would be noticed, and a like courtesy rendered to him in turn, when a sharp movement of the penitent in the confessional made him sink his face precipitately into the crook of his elbow. Fear assumed solid form, and pressed out a lodging between his heart and his lungs. He must try now with all his might to be sorry for his sins—not because he was afraid, but because he had offended God. He must convince God that he was sorry and to do so he must first convince himself. After a tense emotional struggle he achieved a tremulous self-pity, and decided that he was now ready. If, by allowing no other thought to enter his head, he could preserve this state of emotion unimpaired until he went into that large coffin set on end, he would have survived another crisis in his religious life.

For some time, however, a demoniac notion had partially possessed him. He could go home now, before his turn came, and tell his mother that he had arrived too late, and found the priest gone. This, unfortunately, involved the risk of being caught in a lie. As an alternative he could say that he *had* gone to confession, but this meant that he must avoid communion next day, for communion taken upon an uncleansed soul would turn to poison in his mouth, and he would crumple limp and damned from the altar-rail.

Again Father Schwartz's voice became audible.

"And for your——"

The words blurred to a husky mumble, and Rudolph got excitedly to his feet. He felt that it was impossible for him to go to confession this afternoon. He hesitated tensely. Then from the confessional came a tap, a creak, and a sustained rustle. The slide had fallen and the plush curtain trembled. Temptation had come to him too late. . . .

"Bless me, Father, for I have sinned. . . . I confess to Almighty God and to you, Father, that I have sinned. . . . Since my last confession it has been one month and three days. . . . I accuse myself of—taking the Name of the Lord in vain. . . ."

This was an easy sin. His curses had been but bravado—telling of them was little less than a brag.

". . . of being mean to an old lady."

The wan shadow moved a little on the latticed slat.

"How, my child?"

"Old lady Swenson," Rudolph's murmur soared jubilantly. "She got our baseball that we knocked in her window, and she wouldn't give it back, so we yelled 'Twenty-three, Skidoo,' at her all afternoon. Then about five o'clock she had a fit, and they had to have the doctor."

"Go on, my child."

"Of—of not believing I was the son of my parents."

"What?" The interrogation was distinctly startled.

"Of not believing that I was the son of my parents."

"Why not?"

"Oh, just pride," answered the penitent airily.

"You mean you thought you were too good to be the son of your parents?"

"Yes, Father." On a less jubilant note.

"Go on."

"Of being disobedient and calling my mother names. Of slandering people behind my back. Of smoking——"

Rudolph had now exhausted the minor offenses, and was approaching the sins it was agony to tell. He held his fingers against his face like bars as if to press out between them the shame in his heart.

"Of dirty words and immodest thoughts and desires," he whispered very low.

"How often?"

"I don't know."

"Once a week? Twice a week?"

"Twice a week."

"Did you yield to these desires?"

"No, Father."

"Were you alone when you had them?"

"No, Father. I was with two boys and a girl."

"Don't you know, my child, that you should avoid the occasions of sin as well as the sin itself? Evil companionship leads to evil desires and evil desires to evil actions. Where were you when this happened?"

"In a barn in back of——"

"I don't want to hear any names," interrupted the priest sharply.

"Well, it was up in the loft of this barn and this girl and—a fella, they were saying things—saying immodest things, and I stayed."

"You should have gone—you should have told the girl to go."

He should have gone! He could not tell Father Schwartz how his pulse had bumped in his wrist, how a strange, romantic excitement had possessed him when those curious things had been said. Perhaps in the houses of delinquency among the dull and hard-eyed incorrigible girls can be found those for whom has burned the whitest fire.

[margin handwritten: incapable of being corrected]
[margin handwritten: reminder]
[handwritten underline note: by hottest]

"Have you anything else to tell me?"

"I don't think so, Father."

Rudolph felt a great relief. Perspiration had broken out under his tight-pressed fingers.

"Have you told any lies?"

The question startled him. Like all those who habitually and instinctively lie, he had an enormous respect and awe for the truth. Something almost exterior to himself dictated a quick, hurt answer.

"Oh, no, Father, I never tell lies."

For a moment, like the commoner in the king's chair, he tasted the pride of the situation. Then as the priest began to murmur conventional admonitions he realized that in heroically denying he had told lies, he had committed a terrible sin—he had told a lie in confession.

[margin handwritten: worst]
[margin handwritten: * obligation]
[margin handwritten: reminder]
[margin handwritten: remorse for wrongdoing]

In automatic response to Father Schwartz's "Make an act of contrition," he began to repeat aloud meaninglessly:

"Oh, my God, I am heartily sorry for having offended Thee. . . ."

He must fix this now—it was a bad mistake—but as his teeth shut on the last words of his prayer there was a sharp sound, and the slat was closed.

A minute later when he emerged into the twilight the relief in coming from the muggy church into an open world of wheat and sky postponed the full realization of what he had done. Instead of worrying he took a deep breath of the crisp air and began to say over and over to himself the words "Blatchford Sarnemington, Blatchford Sarnemington!"

Blatchford Sarnemington was himself, and these words were in effect a lyric. When he became Blatchford Sarnemington a suave nobility flowed from him. Blatchford Sarnemington lived in great sweeping triumphs. When Rudolph half closed his eyes it meant that Blatchford had established dom-

[bottom margin handwritten: → Rudolph or Blatchford]

inance over him and, as he went by, there were envious mutters in the air: "Blatchford Sarnemington! There goes Blatchford Sarnemington."

He was Blatchford now for a while as he strutted homeward along the staggering road, but when the road braced itself in macadam in order to become the main street of Ludwig, Rudolph's exhilaration faded out and his mind cooled, and he felt the horror of his lie. God, of course, already knew of it—but Rudolph reserved a corner of his mind where he was safe from God, where he prepared the subterfuges with which he often tricked God. Hiding now in this corner he considered how he could best avoid the consequences of his misstatement.

At all costs he must avoid communion next day. The risk of angering God to such an extent was too great. He would have to drink water "by accident" in the morning, and thus, in accordance with a church law, render himself unfit to receive communion that day. In spite of its flimsiness this subterfuge was the most feasible that occurred to him. He accepted its risks and was concentrating on how best to put it into effect, as he turned the corner by Romberg's Drug Store and came in sight of his father's house.

III

RUDOLPH'S FATHER, the local freight-agent, had floated with the second wave of German and Irish stock to the Minnesota-Dakota country. Theoretically, great opportunities lay ahead of a young man of energy in that day and place, but Carl Miller had been incapable of establishing either with his superiors or his subordinates the reputation for approximate immutability which is essential to success in a hierarchic industry. Somewhat gross, he was, nevertheless, insufficiently hard-headed and unable to take fundamental relationships for granted, and this inability made him suspicious, unrestful, and continually dismayed.

His two bonds with the colorful life were his faith in the Roman Catholic Church and his mystical worship of the Empire Builder, James J. Hill. Hill was the apotheosis of that quality in which Miller himself was deficient— the sense of things, the feel of things, the hint of rain in the wind on the cheek. Miller's mind worked late on the old decisions of other men, and he had never in his life felt the balance of any single thing in his hands. His weary, sprightly, undersized body was growing old in Hill's gigantic shadow. For twenty years he had lived alone with Hill's name and God.

On Sunday morning Carl Miller awoke in the dustless quiet of six o'clock. Kneeling by the side of the bed he bent his yellow-gray hair and the full dapple bangs of his mustache into the pillow, and prayed for several minutes.

sound?

Then he drew off his night-shirt—like the rest of his generation he had never been able to endure pajamas—and clothed his thin, white, hairless body in woollen underwear.

He shaved. Silence in the other bedroom where his wife lay nervously asleep. Silence from the screened-off corner of the hall where his son's cot stood, and his son slept among his Alger books, his collection of cigar-bands, his mothy pennants—"Cornell," "Hamlin," and "Greetings from Pueblo, New Mexico"—and the other possessions of his private life. From outside Miller could hear the shrill birds and the whirring movement of the poultry, and, as an undertone, the low, swelling click-a-tick of the six-fifteen through-train for Montana and the green coast beyond. Then as the cold water dripped from the wash-rag in his hand he raised his head suddenly—he had heard a furtive sound from the kitchen below.

He dried his razor hastily, slipped his dangling suspenders to his shoulder, and listened. Some one was walking in the kitchen, and he knew by the light footfall that it was not his wife. With his mouth faintly ajar he ran quickly down the stairs and opened the kitchen door.

Standing by the sink, with one hand on the still dripping faucet and the other clutching a full glass of water, stood his son. The boy's eyes, still heavy with sleep, met his father's with a frightened, reproachful beauty. He was barefooted, and his pajamas were rolled up at the knees and sleeves.

For a moment they both remained motionless—Carl Miller's brow went down and his son's went up, as though they were striking a balance between the extremes of emotion which filled them. Then the bangs of the parent's moustache descended portentously until they obscured his mouth, and he gave a short glance around to see if anything had been disturbed.

The kitchen was garnished with sunlight which beat on the pans and made the smooth boards of the floor and table yellow and clean as wheat. It was the center of the house where the fire burned and the tins fitted into tins like toys, and the steam whistled all day on a thin pastel note. Nothing was moved, nothing touched—except the faucet where beads of water still formed and dripped with a white flash into the sink below.

"What are you doing?"

"I got awful thirsty, so I thought I'd just come down and get——"

"I thought you were going to communion."

A look of vehement astonishment spread over his son's face.

"I forgot all about it."

"Have you drunk any water?"

"No——"

As the word left his mouth Rudolph knew it was the wrong answer, but the faded indignant eyes facing him had signalled up the truth before the boy's will could act. He realized, too, that he should never have come down-stairs; some vague necessity for verisimilitude had made him want to leave a wet glass as evidence by the sink; the honesty of his imagination had betrayed him.

"Pour it out," commanded his father, "that water!"

Rudolph despairingly inverted the tumbler.

"What's the matter with you, anyways?" demanded Miller angrily.

"Nothing."

"Did you go to confession yesterday?"

"Yes."

"Then why were you going to drink water?"

"I don't know—I forgot."

"Maybe you care more about being a little bit thirsty than you do about your religion."

"I forgot." Rudolph could feel the tears straining in his eyes.

"That's no answer."

"Well, I did."

"You better look out!" His father held to a high, persistent, inquisitory note: "If you're so forgetful that you can't remember your religion something better be done about it."

Rudolph filled a sharp pause with:

"I can remember it all right."

"First you begin to neglect your religion," cried his father, fanning his own fierceness, "the next thing you'll begin to lie and steal, and the *next* thing is the *reform* school!"

Not even this familiar threat could deepen the abyss that Rudolph saw before him. He must either tell all now, offering his body for what he knew would be a ferocious beating, or else tempt the thunderbolts by receiving the Body and Blood of Christ with sacrilege upon his soul. And of the two the former seemed more terrible—it was not so much the beating he dreaded as the savage ferocity, outlet of the ineffectual man, which would lie be-hind it.

"Put down that glass and go up-stairs and dress!" his father ordered, "and when we get to church, before you go to communion, you better kneel down and ask God to forgive you for your carelessness."

Some accidental emphasis in the phrasing of this command acted like a catalytic agent on the confusion and terror of Rudolph's mind. A wild, proud anger rose in him, and he dashed the tumbler passionately into the sink.

His father uttered a strained, husky sound, and sprang for him. Rudolph dodged to the side, tipped over a chair, and tried to get beyond the kitchen table. He cried out sharply when a hand grasped his pajama shoulder, then he felt the dull impact of a fist against the side of his head, and glancing blows on the upper part of his body. As he slipped here and there in his father's grasp, dragged or lifted when he clung instinctively to an arm, aware of sharp smarts and strains, he made no sound except that he laughed hysterically several times. Then in less than a minute the blows abruptly ceased. After a lull during which Rudolph was tightly held, and during which they both trembled violently and uttered strange, truncated words, Carl Miller half dragged, half threatened his son up-stairs.

"Put on your clothes!"

Rudolph was now both hysterical and cold. His head hurt him, and there was a long, shallow scratch on his neck from his father's finger-nail, and he sobbed and trembled as he dressed. He was aware of his mother standing at the doorway in a wrapper, her wrinkled face compressing and squeezing and opening out into new series of wrinkles which floated and eddied from neck to brow. Despising her nervous ineffectuality and avoiding her rudely when she tried to touch his neck with witch-hazel, he made a hasty, choking toilet. Then he followed his father out of the house and along the road toward the Catholic church.

· I V ·

THEY WALKED without speaking except when Carl Miller acknowledged automatically the existence of passers-by. Rudolph's uneven breathing alone ruffled the hot Sunday silence.

His father stopped decisively at the door of the church.

"I've decided you'd better go to confession again. Go in and tell Father Schwartz what you did and ask God's pardon."

"You lost your temper, too!" said Rudolph quickly.

Carl Miller took a step toward his son, who moved cautiously backward.

"All right, I'll go."

"Are you going to do what I say?" cried his father in a hoarse whisper.

"All right."

Rudolph walked into the church, and for the second time in two days entered the confessional and knelt down. The slat went up almost at once.

"I accuse myself of missing my morning prayers."

"Is that all?"

"That's all."

A maudlin exultation filled him. Not easily ever again would he be able to put an abstraction before the necessities of his ease and pride. An invisible

line had been crossed, and he had become aware of his isolation—aware
that it applied not only to those moments when he was Blatchford Sarnemington but that it applied to all his inner life. Hitherto such phenomena
as "crazy" ambitions and petty shames and fears had been but private reservations, unacknowledged before the throne of his official soul. Now he
realized unconsciously that his private reservations were himself—and all
the rest a garnished front and a conventional flag. The pressure of his environment had driven him into the lonely secret road of adolescence.

He knelt in the pew beside his father. Mass began. Rudolph knelt up—
when he was alone he slumped his posterior back against the seat—and
tasted the consciousness of a sharp, subtle revenge. Beside him his father
prayed that God would forgive Rudolph, and asked also that his own outbreak of temper would be pardoned. He glanced sidewise at his son, and
was relieved to see that the strained, wild look had gone from his face and
that he had ceased sobbing. The Grace of God, inherent in the Sacrament,
would do the rest, and perhaps after Mass everything would be better. He
was proud of Rudolph in his heart, and beginning to be truly as well as
formally sorry for what he had done.

Usually, the passing of the collection box was a significant point for
Rudolph in the services. If, as was often the case, he had no money to drop
in he would be furiously ashamed and bow his head and pretend not to see
the box, lest Jeanne Brady in the pew behind should take notice and suspect
an acute family poverty. But to-day he glanced coldly into it as it skimmed
under his eyes, noting with casual interest the large number of pennies it
contained.

When the bell rang for communion, however, he quivered. There was no
reason why God should not stop his heart. During the past twelve hours
he had committed a series of mortal sins increasing in gravity, and he was
now to crown them all with a blasphemous sacrilege.

"*Domini, non sum dignus; ut interes sub tectum meum; sed tantum dic
verbo, et sanabitur anima mea. . . .*"

There was a rustle in the pews, and the communicants worked their ways
into the aisle with downcast eyes and joined hands. Those of larger piety
pressed together their finger-tips to form steeples. Among these latter was
Carl Miller. Rudolph followed him toward the altar-rail and knelt down,
automatically taking up the napkin under his chin. The bell rang sharply,
and the priest turned from the altar with the white Host held above the
chalice:

"*Corpus Domini nostri Jesu Christi custodiat animam meam in vitam
aeternam.*"

A cold sweat broke out on Rudolph's forehead as the communion began.

Along the line Father Schwartz moved, and with gathering nausea Rudolph felt his heart-valves weakening at the will of God. It seemed to him that the church was darker and that a great quiet had fallen, broken only by the inarticulate mumble which announced the approach of the Creator of Heaven and Earth. He dropped his head down between his shoulders and waited for the blow.

Then he felt a sharp nudge in his side. His father was poking him to sit up, not to slump against the rail; the priest was only two places away.

"*Corpus Domini nostri Jesu Christi custodiat animam meam in vitam aeternam.*"

Rudolph opened his mouth. He felt the sticky wax taste of the wafer on his tongue. He remained motionless for what seemed an interminable period of time, his head still raised, the wafer undissolved in his mouth. Then again he started at the pressure of his father's elbow, and saw that the people were falling away from the altar like leaves and turning with blind downcast eyes to their pews, alone with God.

Rudolph was alone with himself, drenched with perspiration and deep in mortal sin. As he walked back to his pew the sharp taps of his cloven hoofs were loud upon the floor, and he knew that it was a dark poison he carried in his heart.

· V ·

"Sagitta Volante in Dei"

THE BEAUTIFUL little boy with eyes like blue stones, and lashes that sprayed open from them like flower-petals had finished telling his sin to Father Schwartz—and the square of sunshine in which he sat had moved forward half an hour into the room. Rudolph had become less frightened now; once eased of the story a reaction had set in. He knew that as long as he was in the room with this priest God would not stop his heart, so he sighed and sat quietly, waiting for the priest to speak.

Father Schwartz's cold watery eyes were fixed upon the carpet pattern on which the sun had brought out the swastikas and the flat bloomless vines and the pale echoes of flowers. The hall-clock ticked insistently toward sunset, and from the ugly room and from the afternoon outside the window arose a stiff monotony, shattered now and then by the reverberate clapping of a far-away hammer on the dry air. The priest's nerves were strung thin and the beads of his rosary were crawling and squirming like snakes upon the green felt of his table top. He could not remember now what it was he should say.

Of all the things in this lost Swede town he was most aware of this little boy's eyes—the beautiful eyes, with lashes that left them reluctantly and curved back as though to meet them once more.

For a moment longer the silence persisted while Rudolph waited, and the priest struggled to remember something that was slipping farther and farther away from him, and the clock ticked in the broken house. Then Father Schwartz stared hard at the little boy and remarked in a peculiar voice:

"When a lot of people get together in the best places things go glimmering."

Rudolph started and looked quickly at Father Schwartz's face.

"I said—" began the priest, and paused, listening. "Do you hear the hammer and the clock ticking and the bees? Well, that's no good. The thing is to have a lot of people in the center of the world, wherever that happens to be. Then"—his watery eyes widened knowingly—"things go glimmering."

"Yes, Father," agreed Rudolph, feeling a little frightened.

"What are you going to be when you grow up?"

"Well, I was going to be a baseball-player for a while," answered Rudolph nervously, "but I don't think that's a very good ambition, so I think I'll be an actor or a Navy officer."

Again the priest stared at him.

"I see *exactly* what you mean," he said, with a fierce air.

Rudolph had not meant anything in particular, and at the implication that he had, he became more uneasy.

"This man is crazy," he thought, "and I'm scared of him. He wants me to help him out some way, and I don't want to."

"You look as if things went glimmering," cried Father Schwartz wildly. "Did you ever go to a party?"

"Yes, Father."

"And did you notice that everybody was properly dressed? That's what I mean. Just as you went into the party there was a moment when everybody was properly dressed. Maybe two little girls were standing by the door and some boys were leaning over the banisters, and there were bowls around full of flowers."

"I've been to a lot of parties," said Rudolph, rather relieved that the conversation had taken this turn.

"Of course," continued Father Schwartz triumphantly, "I knew you'd agree with me. But my theory is that when a whole lot of people get together in the best places things go glimmering all the time."

Rudolph found himself thinking of Blatchford Sarnemington.

[handwritten margin notes: "First weak priest?", "What is he getting at?", "Blatchford"]

[handwritten bottom note: glimmering—tempting to commit sin]

[handwritten top margin: "and not understandable to kid", "abandonment of one's religious faith"]

"Please listen to me!" commanded the priest impatiently. "Stop worrying about last Saturday. Apostasy implies an absolute damnation only on the supposition of a previous perfect faith. Does that fix it?"

[handwritten left margin: "assumption"]

Rudolph had not the faintest idea what Father Schwartz was talking about, but he nodded and the priest nodded back at him and returned to his mysterious preoccupation.

"Why," he cried, "they have lights now as big as stars—do you realize that? I heard of one light they had in Paris or somewhere that was as big as a star. A lot of people had it—a lot of gay people. They have all sorts of things now that you never dreamed of."

"Look here—" He came nearer to Rudolph, but the boy drew away, so Father Schwartz went back and sat down in his chair, his eyes dried out and hot. "Did you ever see an amusement park?"

"No, Father."

"Well, go and see an amusement park." The priest waved his hand vaguely. "It's a thing like a fair, only much more glittering. Go to one at night and stand a little way off from it in a dark place—under dark trees. You'll see a big wheel made of lights turning in the air, and a long slide shooting boats down into the water. A band playing somewhere, and a smell of peanuts —and everything will twinkle. But it won't remind you of anything, you see. It will all just hang out there in the night like a colored balloon—like a big yellow lantern on a pole."

Father Schwartz frowned as he suddenly thought of something.

"But don't get up close," he warned Rudolph, "because if you do you'll only feel the heat and the sweat and the life."

All this talking seemed particularly strange and awful to Rudolph, because this man was a priest. He sat there, half terrified, his beautiful eyes open wide and staring at Father Schwartz. But underneath his terror he felt that his own inner convictions were confirmed. There was something ineffably gorgeous somewhere that had nothing to do with God. He no longer thought that God was angry at him about the original lie, because He must have understood that Rudolph had done it to make things finer in the confessional, brightening up the dinginess of his admissions by saying a thing radiant and proud. At the moment when he had affirmed immaculate honor a silver pennon had flapped out into the breeze somewhere and there had been the crunch of leather and the shine of silver spurs and a troop of horsemen waiting for dawn on a low green hill. The sun had made stars of light on their breastplates like the picture at home of the German cuirassiers at Sedan. But now the priest was muttering inarticulate and heart-broken words, and the boy became wildly afraid. Horror entered suddenly in at the open

[handwritten left margin, top to bottom: "metaphor for the good things in life—the pulse"]

*[handwritten margin: "D/L *"]*

[handwritten left margin: "D/L"]

[handwritten left margin: "what he cannot have", "Rudolph Miller wants girls"]

[handwritten left margin: "sadness of priest (girls)"]

[handwritten right margin, top to bottom: "is this what the priest wishes?"]

[handwritten right margin: "self connection w/ priest"]

[handwritten right margin: "terror/emotion"]

[handwritten bottom margin: "connection + identification w/o knowing", " sex is better than prayer,", "a value judgement"]*

window, and the atmosphere of the room changed. Father Schwartz collapsed precipitously down on his knees, and let his body settle back against a chair.

"Oh, my God!" he cried out, in a strange voice, and wilted to the floor.

Then a human oppression rose from the priest's worn clothes, and mingled with the faint smell of old food in the corners. Rudolph gave a sharp cry and ran in a panic from the house—while the collapsed man lay there quite still, filling his room, filling it with voices and faces until it was crowded with echolalia, and rang loud with a steady, shrill note of laughter.

Outside the window the blue sirocco trembled over the wheat, and girls with yellow hair walked sensuously along roads that bounded the fields, calling innocent, exciting things to the young men who were working in the lines between the grain. Legs were shaped under starchless gingham, and rims of the necks of dresses were warm and damp. For five hours now hot fertile life had burned in the afternoon. It would be night in three hours, and all along the land there would be these blonde Northern girls and the tall young men from the farms lying out beside the wheat, under the moon.

[paralleling part one]

- denial of parents
- choice of sex over religion
- light—shadow of priest
- priest must always hide

RAGS MARTIN-JONES
AND THE PR-NCE OF W-LES

◆

"Rags Martin-Jones and the Pr-nce of W-les" was published in McCall's *(July 1924) and collected in* All the Sad Young Men. *Apart from its merit as a well-made story, it is instructive as a reprise of "The Offshore Pirate." Both stories entertainingly treat the key Fitzgerald theme of the capacity of imagination to transform reality.*

◆

THE *MAJESTIC* came gliding into New York harbor on an April morning. She sniffed at the tugboats and turtle-gaited ferries, winked at a gaudy young yacht, and ordered a cattle-boat out of her way with a snarling whistle of steam. Then she parked at her private dock with all the fuss of a stout lady sitting down, and announced complacently that she had just come from Cherbourg and Southampton with a cargo of the very best people in the world.

The very best people in the world stood on the deck and waved idiotically to their poor relations who were waiting on the dock for gloves from Paris. Before long a great toboggan had connected the *Majestic* with the North American continent, and the ship began to disgorge these very best people in the world—who turned out to be Gloria Swanson, two buyers from Lord & Taylor, the financial minister from Graustark with a proposal for funding the debt, and an African king who had been trying to land somewhere all winter and was feeling violently seasick.

The photographers worked passionately as the stream of passengers flowed on to the dock. There was a burst of cheering at the appearance of a pair of stretchers laden with two Middle-Westerners who had drunk themselves delirious on the last night out.

The deck gradually emptied, but when the last bottle of Benedictine had reached shore the photographers still remained at their posts. And the officer in charge of debarkation still stood at the foot of the gangway, glancing first at his watch and then at the deck as if some important part of the cargo was still on board. At last from the watchers on the pier there arose a long-drawn "Ah-h-h!" as a final entourage began to stream down from deck B.

First came two French maids, carrying small, purple dogs, and followed by a squad of porters, blind and invisible under innumerable bunches and bouquets of fresh flowers. Another maid followed, leading a sad-eyed orphan child of a French flavor, and close upon its heels walked the second officer pulling along three neurasthenic wolfhounds, much to their reluctance and his own.

A pause. Then the captain, Sir Howard George Witchcraft, appeared at the rail, with something that might have been a pile of gorgeous silver-fox fur standing by his side.

Rags Martin-Jones, after five years in the capitals of Europe, was returning to her native land!

Rags Martin-Jones was not a dog. She was half a girl and half a flower, and as she shook hands with Captain Sir Howard George Witchcraft she smiled as if some one had told her the newest, freshest joke in the world. All the people who had not already left the pier felt that smile trembling on the April air and turned around to see.

She came slowly down the gangway. Her hat, an expensive, inscrutable experiment, was crushed under her arm, so that her scant boy's hair, convict's hair, tried unsuccessfully to toss and flop a little in the harbor wind. Her face was like seven o'clock on a wedding morning save where she had slipped a preposterous monocle into an eye of clear childish blue. At every few steps her long lashes would tilt out the monocle, and she would laugh, a bored, happy laugh, and replace the supercilious spectacle in the other eye.

Tap! Her one hundred and five pounds reached the pier and it seemed to sway and bend from the shock of her beauty. A few porters fainted. A large, sentimental shark which had followed the ship across made a despairing leap to see her once more, and then dove, broken-hearted, back into the deep sea. Rags Martin-Jones had come home.

There was no member of her family there to meet her, for the simple reason that she was the only member of her family left alive. In 1913 her parents had gone down on the *Titanic* together rather than be separated in this world, and so the Martin-Jones fortune of seventy-five millions had been inherited by a very little girl on her tenth birthday. It was what the consumer always refers to as a "shame."

Rags Martin-Jones (everybody had forgotten her real name long ago) was now photographed from all sides. The monocle persistently fell out, and she kept laughing and yawning and replacing it, so no very clear picture of her was taken—except by the motion-picture camera. All the photographs, however, included a flustered, handsome young man, with an almost ferocious love-light burning in his eyes, who had met her on the dock. His name was John M. Chestnut, he had already written the story of his success for the *American Magazine,* and he had been hopelessly in love with Rags ever since the time when she, like the tides, had come under the influence of the summer moon.

When Rags became really aware of his presence they were walking down the pier, and she looked at him blankly as though she had never seen him before in this world.

"Rags," he began, "Rags——"

"John M. Chestnut?" she inquired, inspecting him with great interest.

"Of course!" he exclaimed angrily. "Are you trying to pretend you don't know me? That you didn't write me to meet you here?"

She laughed. A chauffeur appeared at her elbow, and she twisted out of her coat, revealing a dress made in great splashy checks of sea-blue and gray. She shook herself like a wet bird.

"I've got a lot of junk to declare," she remarked absently.

"So have I," said Chestnut anxiously, "and the first thing I want to declare is that I've loved you, Rags, every minute since you've been away."

She stopped him with a groan.

"Please! There were some young Americans on the boat. The subject has become a bore."

"My God!" cried Chestnut, "do you mean to say that you class *my* love with what was said to you on a *boat?*"

His voice had risen, and several people in the vicinity turned to hear.

"Sh!" she warned him, "I'm not giving a circus. If you want me to even see you while I'm here, you'll have to be less violent."

But John M. Chestnut seemed unable to control his voice.

"Do you mean to say"—it trembled to a carrying pitch—"that you've forgotten what you said on this very pier five years ago last Thursday?"

Half the passengers from the ship were now watching the scene on the dock, and another little eddy drifted out of the customs-house to see.

"John"—her displeasure was increasing—"if you raise your voice again I'll arrange it so you'll have plenty of chance to cool off. I'm going to the Ritz. Come and see me there this afternoon."

"But, Rags!" he protested hoarsely. "Listen to me. Five years ago——"

Then the watchers on the dock were treated to a curious sight. A beautiful lady in a checkered dress of sea-blue and gray took a brisk step forward so that her hands came into contact with an excited young man by her side.

The young man retreating instinctively reached back with his foot, but, finding nothing, relapsed gently off the thirty-foot dock and plopped, after a not ungraceful revolution, into the Hudson River.

A shout of alarm went up, and there was a rush to the edge just as his head appeared above water. He was swimming easily, and, perceiving this, the young lady who had apparently been the cause of the accident leaned over the pier and made a megaphone of her hands.

"I'll be in at half past four," she cried.

And with a cheerful wave of her hand, which the engulfed gentleman was unable to return, she adjusted her monocle, threw one haughty glance at the gathered crowd, and walked leisurely from the scene.

· II ·

THE FIVE DOGS, the three maids, and the French orphan were installed in the largest suite at the Ritz, and Rags tumbled lazily into a steaming bath, fragrant with herbs, where she dozed for the greater part of an hour. At the end of that time she received business calls from a masseuse, a manicure, and finally a Parisian hair-dresser, who restored her hair-cut to criminal's length. When John M. Chestnut arrived at four he found half a dozen lawyers and bankers, the administrators of the Martin-Jones trust fund, waiting in the hall. They had been there since half past one, and were now in a state of considerable agitation.

After one of the maids had subjected him to a severe scrutiny, possibly to be sure that he was thoroughly dry, John was conducted immediately into the presence of m'selle. M'selle was in her bedroom reclining on the chaise-longue among two dozen silk pillows that had accompanied her from the other side. John came into the room somewhat stiffly and greeted her with a formal bow.

"You look better," she said, raising herself from her pillows and staring at him appraisingly. "It gave you a color."

He thanked her coldly for the compliment.

"You ought to go in every morning." And then she added irrelevantly: "I'm going back to Paris tomorrow."

John Chestnut gasped.

"I wrote you that I didn't intend to stay more than a week anyhow," she added.

"But, Rags——"

"Why should I? There isn't an amusing man in New York."

"But listen, Rags, won't you give me a chance? Won't you stay for, say, ten days and get to know me a little?"

"Know you!" Her tone implied that he was already a far too open book. "I want a man who's capable of a gallant gesture."

"Do you mean you want me to express myself entirely in pantomime?" Rags uttered a disgusted sigh.

"I mean you haven't any imagination," she explained patiently. "No Americans have any imagination. Paris is the only large city where a civilized woman can breathe."

"Don't you care for me at all any more?"

"I wouldn't have crossed the Atlantic to see you if I didn't. But as soon as I looked over the Americans on the boat, I knew I couldn't marry one. I'd just hate you, John, and the only fun I'd have out of it would be the fun of breaking your heart."

She began to twist herself down among the cushions until she almost disappeared from view.

"I've lost my monocle," she explained.

After an unsuccessful search in the silken depths she discovered the illusive glass hanging down the back of her neck.

"I'd love to be in love," she went on, replacing the monocle in her childish eye. "Last spring in Sorrento I almost eloped with an Indian rajah, but he was half a shade too dark, and I took an intense dislike to one of his other wives."

"Don't talk that rubbish!" cried John, sinking his face into his hands.

"Well, I didn't marry him," she protested. "But in one way he had a lot to offer. He was the third richest subject of the British Empire. That's another thing—are you rich?"

"Not as rich as you."

"There you are. What have you to offer me?"

"Love."

"Love!" She disappeared again among the cushions. "Listen, John. Life to me is a series of glistening bazaars with a merchant in front of each one rubbing his hands together and saying 'Patronize this place here. Best bazaar in the world.' So I go in with my purse full of beauty and money and youth, all prepared to buy. 'What have you got for sale?' I ask him, and he rubs his hands together and says: 'Well, Mademoiselle, to-day we have some perfectly be-*oo*-tiful love.' Sometimes he hasn't even got that in stock, but he sends out for it when he finds I have so much money to spend. Oh, he always gives me love before I go—and for nothing. That's the one revenge I have."

John Chestnut rose despairingly to his feet and took a step toward the window.

"Don't throw yourself out," Rags exclaimed quickly.

"All right." He tossed his cigarette down into Madison Avenue.

"It isn't just you," she said in a softer voice. "Dull and uninspired as you are, I care for you more than I can say. But life's so endless here. Nothing ever comes off."

"Loads of things come off," he insisted. "Why, to-day there was an intellectual murder in Hoboken and a suicide by proxy in Maine. A bill to sterilize agnostics is before Congress——"

"I have no interest in humor," she objected, "but I have an almost archaic predilection for romance. Why, John, last month I sat at a dinner-table while two men flipped a coin for the kingdom of Schwartzberg-Rhine-minster. In Paris I knew a man named Blutchdak who really started the war, and has a new one planned for year after next."

"Well, just for a rest you come out with me tonight," he said doggedly.

"Where to?" demanded Rags with scorn. "Do you think I still thrill at a night-club and a bottle of sugary mousseaux? I prefer my own gaudy dreams."

"I'll take you to the most highly-strung place in the city."

"What'll happen? You've got to tell me what'll happen."

John Chestnut suddenly drew a long breath and looked cautiously around as if he were afraid of being overheard.

"Well, to tell you the truth," he said in a low, worried tone, "if everything was known, something pretty awful would be liable to happen to *me*."

She sat upright and the pillows tumbled about her like leaves.

"Do you mean to imply that there's anything shady in your life?" she cried, with laughter in her voice. "Do you expect me to believe that? No, John, you'll have your fun by plugging ahead on the beaten path—just plugging ahead."

Her mouth, a small insolent rose, dropped the words on him like thorns. John took his hat and coat from the chair and picked up his cane.

"For the last time—will you come along with me to-night and see what you will see?"

"See what? See who? Is there anything in this country worth seeing?"

"Well," he said, in a matter-of-fact tone, "for one thing you'll see the Prince of Wales."

"What?" She left the chaise-longue at a bound. "Is he back in New York?"

"He will be to-night. Would you care to see him?"

"Would I? I've never seen him. I've missed him everywhere. I'd give a year of my life to see him for an hour." Her voice trembled with excitement.

"He's been in Canada. He's down here incognito for the big prize-fight this afternoon. And I happen to know where he's going to be to-night."

Rags gave a sharp ecstatic cry:

"Dominic! Louise! Germaine!"

The three maids came running. The room filled suddenly with vibrations of wild, startled light.

"Dominic, the car!" cried Rags in French. "St. Raphael, my gold dress and the slippers with the real gold heels. The big pearls too—all the pearls, and the egg-diamond and the stockings with the sapphire clocks. Germaine—send for a beauty-parlor on the run. My bath again—ice cold and half full of almond cream. Dominic—Tiffany's, like lightning, before they close. Find me a brooch, a pendant, a tiara, anything—it doesn't matter—with the arms of the house of Windsor."

She was fumbling at the buttons of her dress—and as John turned quickly to go, it was already sliding from her shoulders.

"Orchids!" she called after him, "orchids, for the love of heaven! Four dozen, so I can choose four."

And then maids flew here and there about the room like frightened birds. "Perfume, St. Raphael, open the perfume trunk, and my rose-colored sables, and my diamond garters, and the sweet-oil for my hands! Here, take these things! This too—and this—ouch!—and this!"

With becoming modesty John Chestnut closed the outside door. The six trustees in various postures of fatigue, of ennui, of resignation, of despair, were still cluttering up the outer hall.

"Gentlemen," announced John Chestnut, "I fear that Miss Martin-Jones is much too weary from her trip to talk to you this afternoon."

· I I I ·

"THIS PLACE, for no particular reason, is called the Hole in the Sky."

Rags looked around her. They were on a roof-garden wide open to the April night. Overhead the true stars winked cold, and there was a lunar sliver of ice in the dark west. But where they stood it was warm as June, and the couples dining or dancing on the opaque glass floor were unconcerned with the forbidding sky.

"What makes it so warm?" she whispered as they moved toward a table.

"It's some new invention that keeps the warm air from rising. I don't know the principle of the thing, but I know that they can keep it open like this even in the middle of winter—"

"Where's the Prince of Wales?" she demanded tensely.

John looked around.

"He hasn't arrived yet. He won't be here for about half an hour."

She sighed profoundly.

"It's the first time I've been excited in four years."

Four years—one year less than he had loved her. He wondered if when she was sixteen, a wild lovely child, sitting up all night in restaurants with officers who were to leave for Brest next day, losing the glamour of life too soon in the old, sad, poignant days of the war, she had ever been so lovely as under these amber lights and this dark sky. From her excited eyes to her tiny slipper heels, which were striped with layers of real silver and gold, she was like one of those amazing ships that are carved complete in a bottle. She was finished with that delicacy, with that care; as though the long lifetime of some worker in fragility had been used to make her so. John Chestnut wanted to take her up in his hands, turn her this way and that, examine the tip of a slipper or the tip of an ear or squint closely at the fairy stuff from which her lashes were made.

"Who's that?" She pointed suddenly to a handsome Latin at a table over the way.

"That's Roderigo Minerlino, the movie and face-cream star. Perhaps he'll dance after a while."

Rags became suddenly aware of the sound of violins and drums, but the music seemed to come from far away, seemed to float over the crisp night and on to the floor with the added remoteness of a dream.

"The orchestra's on another roof," explained John. "It's a new idea— Look, the entertainment's beginning."

A negro girl, thin as a reed, emerged suddenly from a masked entrance into a circle of harsh barbaric light, startled the music to a wild minor, and commenced to sing a rhythmic, tragic song. The pipe of her body broke abruptly and she began a slow incessant step, without progress and without hope, like the failure of a savage insufficient dream. She had lost Papa Jack, she cried over and over with a hysterical monotony at once despairing and unreconciled. One by one the loud horns tried to force her from the steady beat of madness but she listened only to the mutter of the drums which were isolating her in some lost place in time, among many thousand forgotten years. After the failure of the piccolo, she made herself again into a thin brown line, wailed once with sharp and terrible intensity, then vanished into sudden darkness.

"If you lived in New York you wouldn't need to be told who she is," said John when the amber light flashed on. "The next fella is Sheik B. Smith, a comedian of the fatuous, garrulous sort——"

He broke off. Just as the lights went down for the second number Rags had given a long sigh, and leaned forward tensely in her chair. Her eyes were rigid like the eyes of a pointer dog, and John saw that they were fixed on a party that had come through a side entrance, and were arranging themselves around a table in the half-darkness.

The table was shielded with palms, and Rags at first made out only three dim forms. Then she distinguished a fourth who seemed to be placed well behind the other three—a pale oval of a face topped with a glimmer of dark-yellow hair.

"Hello!" ejaculated John. "There's his majesty now."

Her breath seemed to die murmurously in her throat. She was dimly aware that the comedian was now standing in a glow of white light on the dancing floor, that he had been talking for some moments, and that there was a constant ripple of laughter in the air. But her eyes remained motionless, enchanted. She saw one of the party bend and whisper to another, and after the low glitter of a match the bright button of a cigarette end gleamed in the background. How long it was before she moved she did not know. Then something seemed to happen to her eyes, something white, something terribly urgent, and she wrenched about sharply to find herself full in the center of a baby spot-light from above. She became aware that words were being said to her from somewhere, and that a quick trail of laughter was circling the roof, but the light blinded her, and instinctively she made a half-movement from her chair.

"Sit still!" John was whispering across the table. "He picks somebody out for this every night."

Then she realized—it was the comedian, Sheik B. Smith. He was talking to her, arguing with her—about something that seemed incredibly funny to every one else, but came to her ears only as a blur of muddled sound. Instinctively she had composed her face at the first shock of the light and now she smiled. It was a gesture of rare self-possession. Into this smile she insinuated a vast impersonality, as if she were unconscious of the light, unconscious of his attempt to play upon her loveliness—but amused at an infinitely removed *him*, whose darts might have been thrown just as successfully at the moon. She was no longer a "lady"—a lady would have been harsh or pitiful or absurd; Rags stripped her attitude to a sheer consciousness of her own impervious beauty, sat there glittering until the comedian began to feel alone as he had never felt alone before. At a signal from him the spot-light was switched suddenly out. The moment was over.

The moment was over, the comedian left the floor, and the far-away music began. John leaned toward her.

"I'm sorry. There really wasn't anything to do. You were wonderful."

She dismissed the incident with a casual laugh—then she started, there were now only two men sitting at the table across the floor.

"He's gone!" she exclaimed in quick distress.

"Don't worry—he'll be back. He's got to be awfully careful, you see, so he's probably waiting outside with one of his aides until it gets dark again."

"Why has he got to be careful?"

"Because he's not supposed to be in New York. He's even under one of his second-string names."

The lights dimmed again, and almost immediately a tall man appeared out of the darkness and approached their table.

"May I introduce myself?" he said rapidly to John in a supercilious British voice. "Lord Charles Este, of Baron Marchbanks' party." He glanced at John closely as if to be sure that he appreciated the significance of the name.

John nodded.

"That is between ourselves, you understand."

"Of course."

Rags groped on the table for her untouched champagne, and tipped the glassful down her throat.

"Baron Marchbanks requests that your companion will join his party during this number."

Both men looked at Rags. There was a moment's pause.

"Very well," she said, and glanced back again interrogatively at John. Again he nodded. She rose and with her heart beating wildly threaded the tables, making the half-circuit of the room; then melted, a slim figure in shimmering gold, into the table set in half-darkness.

· I V ·

THE NUMBER drew to a close, and John Chestnut sat alone at his table, stirring auxiliary bubbles in his glass of champagne. Just before the lights went on, there was a soft rasp of gold cloth, and Rags, flushed and breathing quickly, sank into her chair. Her eyes were shining with tears.

John looked at her moodily.

"Well, what did he say?"

"He was very quiet."

"Didn't he say a word?"

Her hand trembled as she took up her glass of champagne.

"He just looked at me while it was dark. And he said a few conventional things. He was like his pictures, only he looks very bored and tired. He didn't even ask my name."

"Is he leaving New York to-night?"

"In half an hour. He and his aides have a car outside, and they expect to be over the border before dawn."

"Did you find him—fascinating?"

She hesitated and then slowly nodded her head.

"That's what everybody says," admitted John glumly. "Do they expect you back there?"

"I don't know." She looked uncertainly across the floor but the celebrated personage had again withdrawn from his table to some retreat outside. As she turned back an utterly strange young man who had been standing for a moment in the main entrance came toward them hurriedly. He was a deathly pale person in a dishevelled and inappropriate business suit, and he had laid a trembling hand on John Chestnut's shoulder.

"Monte!" exclaimed John, starting up so suddenly that he upset his champagne. "What is it? What's the matter?"

"They've picked up the trail!" said the young man in a shaken whisper. He looked around. "I've got to speak to you alone."

John Chestnut jumped to his feet, and Rags noticed that his face too had become white as the napkin in his hand. He excused himself and they retreated to an unoccupied table a few feet away. Rags watched them curiously for a moment, then she resumed her scrutiny of the table across the floor. Would she be asked to come back? The prince had simply risen and bowed and gone outside. Perhaps she should have waited until he returned, but though she was still tense with excitement she had, to some extent, become Rags Martin-Jones again. Her curiosity was satisfied—any new urge must come from him. She wondered if she had really felt an intrinsic charm—she wondered especially if he had in any marked way responded to her beauty.

The pale person called Monte disappeared and John returned to the table. Rags was startled to find that a tremendous change had come over him. He lurched into his chair like a drunken man.

"John! What's the matter?"

Instead of answering, he reached for the champagne bottle, but his fingers were trembling so that the splattered wine made a wet yellow ring around his glass.

"Are you sick?"

"Rags," he said unsteadily, "I'm all through."

"What do you mean?"

"I'm all through, I tell you." He managed a sickly smile. "There's been a warrant out for me for over an hour."

"What have you done?" she demanded in a frightened voice. "What's the warrant for?"

The lights went out for the next number, and he collapsed suddenly over the table.

"What is it?" she insisted, with rising apprehension. She leaned forward—his answer was barely audible.

"Murder?" She could feel her body grow cold as ice.

He nodded. She took hold of both arms and tried to shake him upright, as one shakes a coat into place. His eyes were rolling in his head.

"Is it true? Have they got proof?"

Again he nodded drunkenly.

"Then you've got to get out of the country now! Do you understand, John? You've got to get out *now*, before they come looking for you here!"

He loosed a wild glance of terror toward the entrance.

"Oh, God!" cried Rags, "why don't you do something?" Her eyes strayed here and there in desperation, became suddenly fixed. She drew in her breath sharply, hesitated, and then whispered fiercely into his ear.

"If I arrange it, will you go to Canada tonight?"

"How?"

"I'll arrange it—if you'll pull yourself together a little. This is Rags talking to you, don't you understand, John? I want you to sit here and not move until I come back!"

A minute later she had crossed the room under cover of the darkness.

"Baron Marchbanks," she whispered softly, standing just behind his chair. He motioned her to sit down.

"Have you room in your car for two more passengers to-night?"

One of the aides turned around abruptly.

"His lordship's car is full," he said shortly.

"It's terribly urgent." Her voice was trembling.

"Well," said the prince hesitantly, "I don't know."

Lord Charles Este looked at the prince and shook his head.

"I don't think it's advisable. This is a ticklish business anyhow with contrary orders from home. You know we agreed there'd be no complications."

The prince frowned.

"This isn't a complication," he objected.

Este turned frankly to Rags.

"Why is it urgent?"

Rags hesitated.

"Why"—she flushed suddenly—"it's a runaway marriage."

The prince laughed.

"Good!" he exclaimed. "That settles it. Este is just being official. Bring him over right away. We're leaving shortly, what?"

Este looked at his watch.

"Right now!"

Rags rushed away. She wanted to move the whole party from the roof while the lights were still down.

"Hurry!" she cried in John's ear. "We're going over the border—with the Prince of Wales. You'll be safe by morning."

He looked up at her with dazed eyes. She hurriedly paid the check, and seizing his arm piloted him as inconspicuously as possible to the other table, where she introduced him with a word. The prince acknowledged his presence by shaking hands—the aides nodded, only faintly concealing their displeasure.

"We'd better start," said Este, looking impatiently at his watch.

They were on their feet when suddenly an exclamation broke from all of them—two policemen and a red-haired man in plain clothes had come in at the main door.

"Out we go," breathed Este, impelling the party toward the side entrance. "There's going to be some kind of riot here." He swore—two more bluecoats barred the exit there. They paused uncertainly. The plain-clothes man was beginning a careful inspection of the people at the tables.

Este looked sharply at Rags and then at John, who shrank back behind the palms.

"Is that one of your revenue fellas out there?" demanded Este.

"No," whispered Rags. "There's going to be trouble. Can't we get out this entrance?"

The prince with rising impatience sat down again in his chair.

"Let me know when you chaps are ready to go." He smiled at Rags. "Now just suppose we all get in trouble just for that jolly face of yours."

Then suddenly the lights went up. The plain-clothes man whirled around quickly and sprang to the middle of the cabaret floor.

"Nobody try to leave this room!" he shouted. "Sit down, that party behind the palms! Is John M. Chestnut in this room?"

Rags gave a short involuntary cry.

"Here!" cried the detective to the policeman behind him. "Take a look at that funny bunch across over there. Hands up, you men!"

"My God!" whispered Este, "we've got to get out of here!" He turned to the prince. "This won't do, Ted. You can't be seen here. I'll stall them off while you get down to the car."

He took a step toward the side entrance.

"Hands up, there!" shouted the plain-clothes man. "And when I say hands up I mean it! Which one of you's Chestnut?"

"You're mad!" cried Este. "We're British subjects. We're not involved in this affair in any way!"

A woman screamed somewhere, and there was a general movement toward the elevator, a movement which stopped short before the muzzles of two automatic pistols. A girl next to Rags collapsed in a dead faint to the floor, and at the same moment the music on the other roof began to play.

"Stop that music!" bellowed the plain-clothes man. "And get some ear-rings on that whole bunch—quick!"

Two policemen advanced toward the party, and simultaneously Este and the other aides drew their revolvers, and, shielding the prince as they best could, began to edge toward the side. A shot rang out and then another, followed by a crash of silver and china as half a dozen diners overturned their tables and dropped quickly behind.

The panic became general. There were three shots in quick succession, and then a fusillade. Rags saw Este firing coolly at the eight amber lights above, and a thick fume of gray smoke began to fill the air. As a strange undertone to the shouting and screaming came the incessant clamor of the distant jazz band.

Then in a moment it was all over. A shrill whistle rang out over the roof, and through the smoke Rags saw John Chestnut advancing toward the plain-clothes man, his hands held out in a gesture of surrender. There was a last nervous cry, a chill clatter as some one inadvertently stepped into a pile of dishes, and then a heavy silence fell on the roof—even the band seemed to have died away.

"It's all over!" John Chestnut's voice rang out wildly on the night air. "The party's over. Everybody who wants to can go home!"

Still there was silence—Rags knew it was the silence of awe—the strain of guilt had driven John Chestnut insane.

"It was a great performance," he was shouting. "I want to thank you one and all. If you can find any tables still standing, champagne will be served as long as you care to stay."

It seemed to Rags that the roof and the high stars suddenly began to swim round and round. She saw John take the detective's hand and shake it heartily, and she watched the detective grin and pocket his gun. The music had recommenced, and the girl who had fainted was suddenly dancing with Lord Charles Este in the corner. John was running here and there patting people on the back, and laughing and shaking hands. Then he was coming toward her, fresh and innocent as a child.

"Wasn't it wonderful?" he cried.

Rags felt a faintness stealing over her. She groped backward with her hand toward a chair.

"What was it?" she cried dazedly. "Am I dreaming?"

"Of course not! You're wide awake. I made it up, Rags, don't you see? I made up the whole thing for you. I had it invented! The only thing real about it was my name!"

She collapsed suddenly against his coat, clung to his lapels, and would have wilted to the floor if he had not caught her quickly in his arms.

"Some champagne—quick!" he called, and then he shouted at the Prince of Wales, who stood near by. "Order my car quick, you! Miss Martin-Jones has fainted from excitement."

· V ·

THE SKYSCRAPER rose bulkily through thirty tiers of windows before it attenuated itself to a graceful sugar-loaf of shining white. Then it darted up again another hundred feet, thinned to a mere oblong tower in its last fragile aspiration toward the sky. At the highest of its high windows Rags Martin-Jones stood full in the stiff breeze, gazing down at the city.

"Mr. Chestnut wants to know if you'll come right in to his private office."

Obediently her slim feet moved along the carpet into a high, cool chamber overlooking the harbor and the wide sea.

John Chestnut sat at his desk, waiting, and Rags walked to him and put her arms around his shoulder.

"Are you sure *you're* real?" she asked anxiously. "Are you absolutely *sure?*"

"You only wrote me a week before you came," he protested modestly, "or I could have arranged a revolution."

"Was the whole thing just *mine?*" she demanded. "Was it a perfectly useless, gorgeous thing, just for me?"

"Useless?" He considered. "Well, it started out to be. At the last minute I invited a big restaurant man to be there, and while you were at the other table I sold him the whole idea of the night-club."

He looked at his watch.

"I've got one more thing to do—and then we've got just time to be married before lunch." He picked up his telephone. "Jackson? . . . Send a triplicated cable to Paris, Berlin, and Budapest and have those two bogus dukes who tossed up for Schwartzberg-Rhineminster chased over the Polish border. If the Dutchy won't act, lower the rate of exchange to point triple zero naught two. Also, that idiot Blutchdak is in the Balkans again, trying to start a new war. Put him on the first boat for New York or else throw him in a Greek jail."

He rang off, turned to the startled cosmopolite with a laugh.

"The next stop is the City Hall. Then, if you like, we'll run over to Paris."

"John," she asked him intently, "who was the Prince of Wales?"

He waited till they were in the elevator, dropping twenty floors at a swoop. Then he leaned forward and tapped the lift-boy on the shoulder.

"Not so fast, Cedric. This lady isn't used to falls from high places."

The elevator-boy turned around, smiled. His face was pale, oval, framed in yellow hair. Rags blushed like fire.

"Cedric's from Wessex," explained John. "The resemblance is, to say the least, amazing. Princes are not particularly discreet, and I suspect Cedric of being a Guelph in some left-handed way."

Rags took the monocle from around her neck and threw the ribbon over Cedric's head.

"Thank you," she said simply, "for the second greatest thrill of my life."

John Chestnut began rubbing his hands together in a commercial gesture.

"Patronize this place, lady," he besought her. "Best bazaar in the city!"

"What have you got for sale?"

"Well, m'selle, to-day we have some perfectly bee-*oo*-tiful love."

"Wrap it up, Mr. Merchant," cried Rags Martin-Jones. "It looks like a bargain to me."

"THE SENSIBLE THING"

♦

" 'The Sensible Thing' " was published in Liberty for 15 July 1924 and collected in All the Sad Young Men. During 1923 and 1924 Harold Ober was offering Fitzgerald's stories to competing mass-circulation magazines in order to raise Fitzgerald's prices. This story brought $1,750. It is a highly effective Gatsby-cluster story, dealing with love and loss. George O'Kelly recaptures his beloved; but the story closes with his acceptance that love is unrepeatable—unlike Jay Gatsby's belief that he can repeat the past. (Fitzgerald's male characters are more faithful than the objects of their devotion.) Like many of Fitzgerald's stories—including "Winter Dreams"—" 'The Sensible Thing' " turns on a rapid change in fortune, reflecting Fitzgerald's experiences in 1919 and 1920 when he achieved early success and won back his girl.

♦

AT THE Great American Lunch Hour young George O'Kelly straightened his desk deliberately and with an assumed air of interest. No one in the office must know that he was in a hurry, for success is a matter of atmosphere, and it is not well to advertise the fact that your mind is separated from your work by a distance of seven hundred miles.

But once out of the building he set his teeth and began to run, glancing now and then at the gay noon of early spring which filled Times Square and loitered less than twenty feet over the heads of the crowd. The crowd all looked slightly upward and took deep March breaths, and the sun dazzled their eyes so that scarcely any one saw any one else but only their own reflection on the sky.

George O'Kelly, whose mind was over seven hundred miles away, thought that all outdoors was horrible. He rushed into the subway, and for ninety-five blocks bent a frenzied glance on a car-card which showed vividly how he had only one chance in five of keeping his teeth for ten years. At 137th Street he broke off his study of commercial art, left the subway, and began to run again, a tireless, anxious run that brought him this time to his home—one room in a high, horrible apartment-house in the middle of nowhere.

There it was on the bureau, the letter—in sacred ink, on blessed paper —all over the city, people, if they listened, could hear the beating of George O'Kelly's heart. He read the commas, the blots, and the thumb-smudge on the margin—then he threw himself hopelessly upon his bed.

He was in a mess, one of those terrific messes which are ordinary incidents in the life of the poor, which follow poverty like birds of prey. The poor go under or go up or go wrong or even go on, somehow, in a way the poor have—but George O'Kelly was so new to poverty that had any one denied the uniqueness of his case he would have been astounded.

Less than two years ago he had been graduated with honors from The Massachusetts Institute of Technology and had taken a position with a firm of construction engineers in southern Tennessee. All his life he had thought in terms of tunnels and skyscrapers and great squat dams and tall, three-towered bridges, that were like dancers holding hands in a row, with heads as tall as cities and skirts of cable strand. It had seemed romantic to George O'Kelly to change the sweep of rivers and the shape of mountains so that life could flourish in the old bad lands of the world where it had never taken root before. He loved steel, and there was always steel near him in his dreams, liquid steel, steel in bars, and blocks and beams and formless plastic masses, waiting for him, as paint and canvas to his hand. Steel inexhaustible, to be made lovely and austere in his imaginative fire . . .

At present he was an insurance clerk at forty dollars a week with his dream slipping fast behind him. The dark little girl who had made this mess, this terrible and intolerable mess, was waiting to be sent for in a town in Tennessee.

In fifteen minutes the woman from whom he sublet his room knocked and asked him with maddening kindness if, since he was home, he would have some lunch. He shook his head, but the interruption aroused him, and getting up from the bed he wrote a telegram.

"Letter depressed me have you lost your nerve you are foolish and just upset to think of breaking off why not marry me immediately sure we can make it all right——"

He hesitated for a wild minute, and then added in a hand that could scarcely be recognized as his own: "In any case I will arrive to-morrow at six o'clock."

When he finished he ran out of the apartment and down to the telegraph office near the subway stop. He possessed in this world not quite one hundred dollars, but the letter showed that she was "nervous" and this left him no choice. He knew what "nervous" meant—that she was emotionally depressed, that the prospect of marrying into a life of poverty and struggle was putting too much strain upon her love.

George O'Kelly reached the insurance company at his usual run, the run that had become almost second nature to him, that seemed best to express the tension under which he lived. He went straight to the manager's office.

"I want to see you, Mr. Chambers," he announced breathlessly.

"Well?" Two eyes, eyes like winter windows, glared at him with ruthless impersonality.

"I want to get four days' vacation."

"Why, you had a vacation just two weeks ago!" said Mr. Chambers in surprise.

"That's true," admitted the distraught young man, "but now I've got to have another."

"Where'd you go last time? To your home?"

"No, I went to—a place in Tennessee."

"Well, where do you want to go this time?"

"Well, this time I want to go to—a place in Tennessee."

"You're consistent, anyhow," said the manager dryly. "But I didn't realize you were employed here as a travelling salesman."

"I'm not," cried George desperately, "but I've got to go."

"All right," agreed Mr. Chambers, "but you don't have to come back. So don't!"

"I won't." And to his own astonishment as well as Mr. Chambers' George's face grew pink with pleasure. He felt happy, exultant—for the first time in six months he was absolutely free. Tears of gratitude stood in his eyes, and he seized Mr. Chambers warmly by the hand.

"I want to thank you," he said with a rush of emotion. "I don't want to come back. I think I'd have gone crazy if you'd said that I could come back. Only I couldn't quit myself, you see, and I want to thank you for—for quitting for me."

He waved his hand magnanimously, shouted aloud, "You owe me three days' salary but you can keep it!" and rushed from the office. Mr. Chambers rang for his stenographer to ask if O'Kelly had seemed queer lately. He had fired many men in the course of his career, and they had taken it in many different ways, but none of them had thanked him—ever before.

· II ·

Jonquil Cary was her name, and to George O'Kelly nothing had ever looked so fresh and pale as her face when she saw him and fled to him eagerly along the station platform. Her arms were raised to him, her mouth was half parted for his kiss, when she held him off suddenly and lightly and, with a touch of embarrassment, looked around. Two boys, somewhat younger than George, were standing in the background.

"This is Mr. Craddock and Mr. Holt," she announced cheerfully. "You met them when you were here before."

Disturbed by the transition of a kiss into an introduction and suspecting some hidden significance, George was more confused when he found that the automobile which was to carry them to Jonquil's house belonged to one of the two young men. It seemed to put him at a disadvantage. On the way Jonquil chattered between the front and back seats, and when he tried to slip his arm around her under cover of the twilight she compelled him with a quick movement to take her hand instead.

"Is this street on the way to your house?" he whispered. "I don't recognize it."

"It's the new boulevard. Jerry just got this car to-day, and he wants to show it to me before he takes us home."

When, after twenty minutes, they were deposited at Jonquil's house, George felt that the first happiness of the meeting, the joy he had recognized so surely in her eyes back in the station, had been dissipated by the intrusion of the ride. Something that he had looked forward to had been rather casually lost, and he was brooding on this as he said good night stiffly to the two young men. Then his ill-humor faded as Jonquil drew him into a familiar embrace under the dim light of the front hall and told him in a dozen ways, of which the best was without words, how she had missed him. Her emotion reassured him, promised his anxious heart that everything would be all right.

They sat together on the sofa, overcome by each other's presence, beyond all except fragmentary endearments. At the supper hour Jonquil's father and mother appeared and were glad to see George. They liked him, and had been interested in his engineering career when he had first come to Tennessee over a year before. They had been sorry when he had given it up and gone to New York to look for something more immediately profitable, but while they deplored the curtailment of his career they sympathized with him and were ready to recognize the engagement. During dinner they asked about his progress in New York.

"Everything's going fine," he told them with enthusiasm. "I've been promoted—better salary."

He was miserable as he said this—but they were all *so* glad.

"They must like you," said Mrs. Cary, "that's certain—or they wouldn't let you off twice in three weeks to come down here."

"I told them they had to," explained George hastily; "I told them if they didn't I wouldn't work for them any more."

"But you ought to save your money," Mrs. Cary reproached him gently. "Not spend it all on this expensive trip."

Dinner was over—he and Jonquil were alone and she came back into his arms.

"So glad you're here," she sighed. "Wish you never were going away again, darling."

"Do you miss me?"

"Oh, so much, so much."

"Do you—do other men come to see you often? Like those two kids?"

The question surprised her. The dark velvet eyes stared at him.

"Why, of course they do. All the time. Why—I've told you in letters that they did, dearest."

This was true—when he had first come to the city there had been already a dozen boys around her, responding to her picturesque fragility with adolescent worship, and a few of them perceiving that her beautiful eyes were also sane and kind.

"Do you expect me never to go anywhere"—Jonquil demanded, leaning back against the sofa-pillows until she seemed to look at him from many miles away—"and just fold my hands and sit still—forever?"

"What do you mean?" he blurted out in a panic. "Do you mean you think I'll never have enough money to marry you?"

"Oh, don't jump at conclusions so, George."

"I'm not jumping at conclusions. That's what you said."

George decided suddenly that he was on dangerous grounds. He had not intended to let anything spoil this night. He tried to take her again in his arms, but she resisted unexpectedly, saying:

"It's hot. I'm going to get the electric fan."

When the fan was adjusted they sat down again, but he was in a supersensitive mood and involuntarily he plunged into the specific world he had intended to avoid.

"When will you marry me?"

"Are you ready for me to marry you?"

All at once his nerves gave way, and he sprang to his feet.

"Let's shut off that damned fan," he cried, "it drives me wild. It's like a clock ticking away all the time I'll be with you. I came here to be happy and forget everything about New York and time——"

He sank down on the sofa as suddenly as he had risen. Jonquil turned off the fan, and drawing his head down into her lap began stroking his hair.

"Let's sit like this," she said softly, "just sit quiet like this, and I'll put you to sleep. You're all tired and nervous and your sweetheart'll take care of you."

"But I don't want to sit like this," he complained, jerking up suddenly, "I don't want to sit like this at all. I want you to kiss me. That's the only thing that makes me rest. And anyways I'm not nervous—it's you that's nervous. I'm not nervous at all."

To prove that he wasn't nervous he left the couch and plumped himself into a rocking-chair across the room.

"Just when I'm ready to marry you you write me the most nervous letters, as if you're going to back out, and I have to come rushing down here——"

"You don't have to come if you don't want to."

"But I *do* want to!" insisted George.

It seemed to him that he was being very cool and logical and that she was putting him deliberately in the wrong. With every word they were drawing farther and farther apart—and he was unable to stop himself or to keep worry and pain out of his voice.

But in a minute Jonquil began to cry sorrowfully and he came back to the sofa and put his arm around her. He was the comforter now, drawing her head close to his shoulder, murmuring old familiar things until she grew calmer and only trembled a little, spasmodically, in his arms. For over an hour they sat there, while the evening pianos thumped their last cadences into the street outside. George did not move, or think, or hope, lulled into numbness by the premonition of disaster. The clock would tick on, past eleven, past twelve, and then Mrs. Cary would call down gently over the banister—beyond that he saw only to-morrow and despair.

· III ·

IN THE HEAT OF the next day the breaking-point came. They had each guessed the truth about the other, but of the two she was the more ready to admit the situation.

"There's no use going on," she said miserably, "you know you hate the insurance business, and you'll never do well in it."

"That's not it," he insisted stubbornly; "I hate going on alone. If you'll marry me and come with me and take a chance with me, I can make good at anything, but not while I'm worrying about you down here."

She was silent a long time before she answered, not thinking—for she had seen the end—but only waiting, because she knew that every word would seem more cruel than the last. Finally she spoke:

"George, I love you with all my heart, and I don't see how I can ever love any one else but you. If you'd been ready for me two months ago I'd have married you—now I can't because it doesn't seem to be the sensible thing."

He made wild accusations—there was some one else—she was keeping something from him!

"No, there's no one else."

This was true. But reacting from the strain of this affair she had found relief in the company of young boys like Jerry Holt, who had the merit of meaning absolutely nothing in her life.

George didn't take the situation well, at all. He seized her in his arms and tried literally to kiss her into marrying him at once. When this failed, he broke into a long monologue of self-pity, and ceased only when he saw that he was making himself despicable in her sight. He threatened to leave when he had no intention of leaving, and refused to go when she told him that, after all, it was best that he should.

For a while she was sorry, then for another while she was merely kind.

"You'd better go now," she cried at last, so loud that Mrs. Cary came down-stairs in alarm.

"Is something the matter?"

"I'm going away, Mrs. Cary," said George brokenly. Jonquil had left the room.

"Don't feel so badly, George." Mrs. Cary blinked at him in helpless sympathy—sorry and, in the same breath, glad that the little tragedy was almost done. "If I were you I'd go home to your mother for a week or so. Perhaps after all this is the sensible thing——"

"Please don't talk," he cried. "Please don't say anything to me now!"

Jonquil came into the room again, her sorrow and her nervousness alike tucked under powder and rouge and hat.

"I've ordered a taxicab," she said impersonally. "We can drive around until your train leaves."

She walked out on the front porch. George put on his coat and hat and stood for a minute exhausted in the hall—he had eaten scarcely a bite since he had left New York. Mrs. Cary came over, drew his head down and kissed him on the cheek, and he felt very ridiculous and weak in his knowledge that the scene had been ridiculous and weak at the end. If he had only gone the night before—left her for the last time with a decent pride.

The taxi had come, and for an hour these two that had been lovers rode along the less-frequented streets. He held her hand and grew calmer in the sunshine, seeing too late that there had been nothing all along to do or say.

"I'll come back," he told her.

"I know you will," she answered, trying to put a cheery faith into her voice. "And we'll write each other—sometimes."

"No," he said, "we won't write. I couldn't stand that. Some day I'll come back."

"I'll never forget you, George."

They reached the station, and she went with him while he bought his ticket. . . .

"Why, George O'Kelly and Jonquil Cary!"

It was a man and a girl whom George had known when he had worked in town, and Jonquil seemed to greet their presence with relief. For an interminable five minutes they all stood there talking; then the train roared into the station, and with ill-concealed agony in his face George held out his arms toward Jonquil. She took an uncertain step toward him, faltered, and then pressed his hand quickly as if she were taking leave of a chance friend.

"Good-by, George," she was saying, "I hope you have a pleasant trip."

"Good-by, George. Come back and see us all again."

Dumb, almost blind with pain, he seized his suitcase, and in some dazed way got himself aboard the train.

Past clanging street-crossings, gathering speed through wide suburban spaces toward the sunset. Perhaps she too would see the sunset and pause for a moment, turning, remembering, before he faded with her sleep into the past. This night's dusk would cover up forever the sun and the trees and the flowers and laughter of his young world.

· I V ·

ON A DAMP afternoon in September of the following year a young man with his face burned to a deep copper glow got off a train at a city in Tennessee. He looked around anxiously, and seemed relieved when he found that there was no one in the station to meet him. He taxied to the best hotel in the city where he registered with some satisfaction as George O'Kelly, Cuzco, Peru.

Up in his room he sat for a few minutes at the window looking down into the familiar street below. Then with his hand trembling faintly he took off the telephone receiver and called a number.

"Is Miss Jonquil in?"

"This is she."

"Oh—" His voice after overcoming a faint tendency to waver went on with friendly formality.

"This is George Rollins. Did you get my letter?"

"Yes. I thought you'd be in to-day."

Her voice, cool and unmoved, disturbed him, but not as he had expected. This was the voice of a stranger, unexcited, pleasantly glad to see him—that was all. He wanted to put down the telephone and catch his breath.

"I haven't seen you for—a long time." He succeeded in making this sound offhand. "Over a year."

He knew how long it had been—to the day.

"It'll be awfully nice to talk to you again."

"I'll be there in about an hour."

He hung up. For four long seasons every minute of his leisure had been crowded with anticipation of this hour, and now this hour was here. He had thought of finding her married, engaged, in love—he had not thought she would be unstirred at his return.

There would never again in his life, he felt, be another ten months like these he had just gone through. He had made an admittedly remarkable showing for a young engineer—stumbled into two unusual opportunities, one in Peru, whence he had just returned, and another, consequent upon it, in New York, whither he was bound. In this short time he had risen from poverty into a position of unlimited opportunity.

He looked at himself in the dressing-table mirror. He was almost black with tan, but it was a romantic black, and in the last week, since he had had time to think about it, it had given him considerable pleasure. The hardiness of his frame, too, he appraised with a sort of fascination. He had lost part of an eyebrow somewhere, and he still wore an elastic bandage on his knee, but he was too young not to realize that on the steamer many women had looked at him with unusual tributary interest.

His clothes, of course, were frightful. They had been made for him by a Greek tailor in Lima—in two days. He was young enough, too, to have explained this sartorial deficiency to Jonquil in his otherwise laconic note. The only further detail it contained was a request that he should *not* be met at the station.

George O'Kelly, of Cuzco, Peru, waited an hour and a half in the hotel, until, to be exact, the sun had reached a midway position in the sky. Then, freshly shaven and talcum-powdered toward a somewhat more Caucasian hue, for vanity at the last minute had overcome romance, he engaged a taxicab and set out for the house he knew so well.

He was breathing hard—he noticed this but he told himself that it was excitement, not emotion. He was here; she was not married—that was enough. He was not even sure what he had to say to her. But this was the moment of his life that he felt he could least easily have dispensed with. There was no triumph, after all, without a girl concerned, and if he did not lay his spoils at her feet he could at least hold them for a passing moment before her eyes.

The house loomed up suddenly beside him, and his first thought was that it had assumed a strange unreality. There was nothing changed—only everything was changed. It was smaller and it seemed shabbier than before—there was no cloud of magic hovering over its roof and issuing from the windows of the upper floor. He rang the door-bell and an unfamiliar colored maid appeared. Miss Jonquil would be down in a moment. He wet his lips nervously and walked into the sitting-room—and the feeling of unreality increased. After all, he saw, this was only a room, and not the enchanted chamber where he had passed those poignant hours. He sat in a chair, amazed to find it a chair, realizing that his imagination had distorted and colored all these simple familiar things.

Then the door opened and Jonquil came into the room—and it was as though everything in it suddenly blurred before his eyes. He had not remembered how beautiful she was, and he felt his face grow pale and his voice diminish to a poor sigh in his throat.

She was dressed in pale green, and a gold ribbon bound back her dark, straight hair like a crown. The familiar velvet eyes caught his as she came through the door, and a spasm of fright went through him at her beauty's power of inflicting pain.

He said "Hello," and they each took a few steps forward and shook hands. Then they sat in chairs quite far apart and gazed at each other across the room.

"You've come back," she said, and he answered just as tritely: "I wanted to stop in and see you as I came through."

He tried to neutralize the tremor in his voice by looking anywhere but at her face. The obligation to speak was on him, but, unless he immediately began to boast, it seemed that there was nothing to say. There had never been anything casual in their previous relations—it didn't seem possible that people in this position would talk about the weather.

"This is ridiculous," he broke out in sudden embarrassment. "I don't know exactly what to do. Does my being here bother you?"

"No." The answer was both reticent and impersonally sad. It depressed him.

"Are you engaged?" he demanded.

"No."

"Are you in love with some one?"

She shook her head.

"Oh." He leaned back in his chair. Another subject seemed exhausted—the interview was not taking the course he had intended.

"Jonquil," he began, this time on a softer key, "after all that's happened between us, I wanted to come back and see you. Whatever I do in the future I'll never love another girl as I've loved you."

This was one of the speeches he had rehearsed. On the steamer it had seemed to have just the right note—a reference to the tenderness he would always feel for her combined with a non-committal attitude toward his present state of mind. Here with the past around him, beside him, growing minute by minute more heavy on the air, it seemed theatrical and stale.

She made no comment, sat without moving, her eyes fixed on him with an expression that might have meant everything or nothing.

"You don't love me any more, do you?" he asked her in a level voice.

"No."

When Mrs. Cary came in a minute later, and spoke to him about his success—there had been a half-column about him in the local paper—he was a mixture of emotions. He knew now that he still wanted this girl, and he knew that the past sometimes comes back—that was all. For the rest he must be strong and watchful and he would see.

"And now," Mrs. Cary was saying, "I want you two to go and see the lady who has the chrysanthemums. She particularly told me she wanted to see you because she'd read about you in the paper."

They went to see the lady with the chrysanthemums. They walked along the street, and he recognized with a sort of excitement just how her shorter footsteps always fell in between his own. The lady turned out to be nice, and the chrysanthemums were enormous and extraordinarily beautiful. The lady's gardens were full of them, white and pink and yellow, so that to be among them was a trip back into the heart of summer. There were two gardens full, and a gate between them; when they strolled toward the second garden the lady went first through the gate.

And then a curious thing happened. George stepped aside to let Jonquil pass, but instead of going through she stood still and stared at him for a minute. It was not so much the look, which was not a smile, as it was the moment of silence. They saw each other's eyes, and both took a short, faintly accelerated breath, and then they went on into the second garden. That was all.

The afternoon waned. They thanked the lady and walked home slowly, thoughtfully, side by side. Through dinner too they were silent. George told Mr. Cary something of what had happened in South America, and managed to let it be known that everything would be plain sailing for him in the future.

Then dinner was over, and he and Jonquil were alone in the room which had seen the beginning of their love affair and the end. It seemed to him long ago and inexpressibly sad. On that sofa he had felt agony and grief such as he would never feel again. He would never be so weak or so tired and miserable and poor. Yet he knew that that boy of fifteen months before had had something, a trust, a warmth that was gone forever. The sensible thing—they had done the sensible thing. He had traded his first youth for strength and carved success out of despair. But with his youth, life had carried away the freshness of his love.

"You won't marry me, will you?" he said quietly.

Jonquil shook her dark head.

"I'm never going to marry," she answered.

He nodded.

"I'm going on to Washington in the morning," he said.

"Oh——"

"I have to go. I've got to be in New York by the first, and meanwhile I want to stop off in Washington."

"Business!"

"No-o," he said as if reluctantly. "There's some one there I must see who was very kind to me when I was so—down and out."

This was invented. There was no one in Washington for him to see—but he was watching Jonquil narrowly, and he was sure that she winced a little, that her eyes closed and then opened wide again.

"But before I go I want to tell you the things that happened to me since I saw you, and, as maybe we won't meet again, I wonder if—if just this once you'd sit in my lap like you used to. I wouldn't ask except since there's no one else—yet—perhaps it doesn't matter."

She nodded, and in a moment was sitting in his lap as she had sat so often in that vanished spring. The feel of her head against his shoulder, of her familiar body, sent a shock of emotion over him. His arms holding her had a tendency to tighten around her, so he leaned back and began to talk thoughtfully into the air.

He told her of a despairing two weeks in New York which had terminated with an attractive if not very profitable job in a construction plant in Jersey City. When the Peru business had first presented itself it had not seemed an extraordinary opportunity. He was to be third assistant engineer on the expedition, but only ten of the American party, including eight rodmen and surveyors, had ever reached Cuzco. Ten days later the chief of the expedition was dead of yellow fever. That had been his chance, a chance for anybody but a fool, a marvellous chance——

"A chance for anybody but a fool?" she interrupted innocently.

"Even for a fool," he continued. "It was wonderful. Well, I wired New York——"

"And so," she interrupted again, "they wired that you ought to take a chance?"

"Ought to!" he exclaimed, still leaning back. "That I *had* to. There was no time to lose——"

"Not a minute?"

"Not a minute."

"Not even time for——" she paused.

"For what?"

"Look."

He bent his head forward suddenly, and she drew herself to him in the same moment, her lips half open like a flower.

"Yes," he whispered into her lips. "There's all the time in the world. . . ."

All the time in the world—his life and hers. But for an instant as he kissed her he knew that though he search through eternity he could never recapture those lost April hours. He might press her close now till the muscles knotted on his arms—she was something desirable and rare that he had fought for and made his own—but never again an intangible whisper in the dusk, or on the breeze of night. . . .

Well, let it pass, he thought; April is over, April is over. There are all kinds of love in the world, but never the same love twice.

LOVE IN THE NIGHT

◆

"Love in the Night" appeared in the Saturday Evening Post *(14 March 1925).
Written on the Riviera in November 1924 after he had sent* The Great Gatsby
*to Scribners, it was the first Fitzgerald story set abroad. "Love in the Night"
introduced a group of stories in which Fitzgerald contrasted America and
Europe. Some of the Riviera material in this story—for example, the evo-
cation of the pre-Revolution Russian colony—was salvaged for* Tender Is
the Night.

◆

THE WORDS thrilled Val. They had come into his mind sometime during
the fresh gold April afternoon and he kept repeating them to himself over
and over: "Love in the night; love in the night." He tried them in three
languages—Russian, French and English—and decided that they were best
in English. In each language they meant a different sort of love and a different
sort of night—the English night seemed the warmest and softest with a
thinnest and most crystalline sprinkling of stars. The English love seemed
the most fragile and romantic—a white dress and a dim face above it and
eyes that were pools of light. And when I add that it was a French night
he was thinking about, after all, I see I must go back and begin over.

Val was half Russian and half American. His mother was the daughter of
that Morris Hasylton who helped finance the Chicago World's Fair in 1892,
and his father was—see the Almanach de Gotha, issue of 1910—Prince Paul
Serge Boris Rostoff, son of Prince Vladimir Rostoff, grandson of a grand
duke—'Jimber-jawed Serge'—and third-cousin-once-removed to the czar.
It was all very impressive, you see, on that side—house in St. Petersburg,
shooting lodge near Riga, and swollen villa, more like a palace, overlooking
the Mediterranean. It was at this villa in Cannes that the Rostoffs passed
the winter—and it wasn't at all the thing to remind Princess Rostoff that
this Riviera villa, from the marble fountain—after Bernini—to the gold
cordial glasses—after dinner—was paid for with American gold.

The Russians, of course, were gay people on the Continent in the gala days before the war. Of the three races that used Southern France for a pleasure ground they were easily the most adept at the grand manner. The English were too practical, and the Americans, though they spent freely, had no tradition of romantic conduct. But the Russians—there was a people as gallant as the Latins, and rich besides! When the Rostoffs arrived at Cannes late in January the restaurateurs telegraphed north for the Prince's favorite labels to paste on their champagne, and the jewelers put incredibly gorgeous articles aside to show to him—but not to the princess—and the Russian Church was swept and garnished for the season that the Prince might beg orthodox forgiveness for his sins. Even the Mediterranean turned obligingly to a deep wine color in the spring evenings, and fishing boats with robin-breasted sails loitered exquisitely offshore.

In a vague way young Val realized that this was all for the benefit of him and his family. It was a privileged paradise, this white little city on the water, in which he was free to do what he liked because he was rich and young and the blood of Peter the Great ran indigo in his veins. He was only seventeen in 1914, when this history begins, but he had already fought a duel with a young man four years his senior, and he had a small hairless scar to show for it on top of his handsome head.

But the question of love in the night was the thing nearest his heart. It was a vague pleasant dream he had, something that was going to happen to him some day that would be unique and incomparable. He could have told no more about it than that there was a lovely unknown girl concerned in it, and that it ought to take place beneath the Riviera moon.

The odd thing about all this was not that he had this excited and yet almost spiritual hope of romance, for all boys of any imagination have just such hopes, but that it actually came true. And when it happened, it happened so unexpectedly; it was such a jumble of impressions and emotions, of curious phrases that sprang to his lips, of sights and sounds and moments that were here, were lost, were past, that he scarcely understood it at all. Perhaps its very vagueness preserved it in his heart and made him forever unable to forget.

There was an atmosphere of love all about him that spring—his father's loves, for instance, which were many and indiscreet, and which Val became aware of gradually from overhearing the gossip of servants, and definitely from coming on his American mother unexpectedly one afternoon, to find her storming hysterically at his father's picture on the salon wall. In the picture his father wore a white uniform with a furred dolman and looked back impassively at his wife as if to say "Were you under the impression, my dear, that you were marrying into a family of clergymen?"

Val tiptoed away, surprised, confused—and excited. It didn't shock him as it would have shocked an American boy of his age. He had known for years what life was among the Continental rich, and he condemned his father only for making his mother cry.

Love went on around him—reproachless love and illicit love alike. As he strolled along the seaside promenade at nine o'clock, when the stars were bright enough to compete with the bright lamps, he was aware of love on every side. From the open-air cafés, vivid with dresses just down from Paris, came a sweet pungent odor of flowers and chartreuse and fresh black coffee and cigarettes—and mingled with them all he caught another scent, the mysterious thrilling scent of love. Hands touched jewel-sparkling hands upon the white tables. Gay dresses and white shirt fronts swayed together, and matches were held, trembling a little, for slow-lighting cigarettes. On the other side of the boulevard lovers less fashionable, young Frenchmen who worked in the stores of Cannes, sauntered with their fiancées under the dim trees, but Val's young eyes seldom turned that way. The luxury of music and bright colors and low voices—they were all part of his dream. They were the essential trappings of Love in the night.

But assume as he might the rather fierce expression that was expected from a young Russian gentleman who walked the streets alone, Val was beginning to be unhappy. April twilight had succeeded March twilight, the season was almost over, and he had found no use to make of the warm spring evenings. The girls of sixteen and seventeen whom he knew, were chaperoned with care between dusk and bedtime—this, remember, was before the war—and the others who might gladly have walked beside him were an affront to his romantic desire. So April passed by—one week, two weeks, three weeks——

He had played tennis until seven and loitered at the courts for another hour, so it was half-past eight when a tired cab horse accomplished the hill on which gleamed the façade of the Rostoff villa. The lights of his mother's limousine were yellow in the drive, and the princess, buttoning her gloves, was just coming out the glowing door. Val tossed two francs to the cabman and went to kiss her on the cheek.

"Don't touch me," she said quickly. "You've been handling money."

"But not in my mouth, mother," he protested humorously.

The princess looked at him impatiently.

"I'm angry," she said. "Why must you be so late tonight? We're dining on a yacht and you were to have come along too."

"What yacht?"

"Americans." There was always a faint irony in her voice when she mentioned the land of her nativity. Her America was the Chicago of the nineties which she still thought of as the vast upstairs to a butcher shop. Even the irregularities of Prince Paul were not too high a price to have paid for her escape.

"Two yachts," she continued; "in fact we don't know which one. The note was very indefinite. Very careless indeed."

Americans. Val's mother had taught him to look down on Americans, but she hadn't succeeded in making him dislike them. American men noticed you, even if you were seventeen. He liked Americans. Although he was thoroughly Russian he wasn't immaculately so—the exact proportion, like that of a celebrated soap, was about ninety-nine and three-quarters per cent.

"I want to come," he said, "I'll hurry up, mother. I'll——"

"We're late now." The princess turned as her husband appeared in the door. "Now Val says he wants to come."

"He can't," said Prince Paul shortly. "He's too outrageously late."

Val nodded. Russian aristocrats, however indulgent about themselves, were always admirably Spartan with their children. There were no arguments.

"I'm sorry," he said.

Prince Paul grunted. The footman, in red and silver livery, opened the limousine door. But the grunt decided the matter for Val, because Princess Rostoff at that day and hour had certain grievances against her husband which gave her command of the domestic situation.

"On second thought you'd better come, Val," she announced coolly. "It's too late now, but come after dinner. The yacht is either the Minnehaha or the Privateer." She got into the limousine. "The one to come to will be the gayer one, I suppose—the Jacksons' yacht——"

"Find got sense," muttered the Prince cryptically, conveying that Val would find it if he had any sense. "Have my man take a look at you 'fore you start. Wear tie of mine 'stead of that outrageous string you affected in Vienna. Grow up. High time."

As the limousine crawled crackling down the pebbled drive Val's face was burning.

· II ·

IT WAS DARK in Cannes harbor, rather it seemed dark after the brightness of the promenade that Val had just left behind. Three frail dock lights glittered dimly upon innumerable fishing boats heaped like shells along the beach. Farther out in the water there were other lights where a fleet of slender yachts rode the tide with slow dignity, and farther still a full ripe moon made the water bosom into a polished dancing floor. Occasionally there was a swish! creak! drip! as a rowboat moved about in the shallows, and its blurred shape threaded the labyrinth of hobbled fishing skiffs and launches. Val, descending the velvet slope of sand, stumbled over a sleeping boatman and caught the rank savor of garlic and plain wine. Taking the man by the shoulders he shook open his startled eyes.

"Do you know where the Minnehaha is anchored, and the Privateer?"

As they slid out into the bay he lay back in the stern and stared with vague discontent at the Riviera moon. That was the right moon, all right. Frequently, five nights out of seven, there was the right moon. And here was the soft air, aching with enchantment, and here was the music, many strains of music from many orchestras, drifting out from the shore. Eastward lay the dark Cape of Antibes, and then Nice, and beyond that Monte Carlo, where the night rang chinking full of gold. Some day he would enjoy all that, too, know its every pleasure and success—when he was too old and wise to care.

But tonight—tonight, that stream of silver that waved like a wide strand of curly hair toward the moon; those soft romantic lights of Cannes behind him, the irresistible ineffable love in this air—that was to be wasted forever.

"Which one?" asked the boatman suddenly.

"Which what?" demanded Val, sitting up.

"Which boat?"

He pointed. Val turned; above hovered the gray, sword-like prow of a yacht. During the sustained longing of his wish they had covered half a mile.

He read the brass letters over his head. It was the Privateer, but there were only dim lights on board, and no music and no voices, only a murmurous k-plash at intervals as the small waves leaped at the sides.

"The other one," said Val; "the Minnehaha."

"Don't go yet."

Val started. The voice, low and soft, had dropped down from the darkness overhead.

"What's the hurry?" said the soft voice. "Thought maybe somebody was coming to see me, and have suffered terrible disappointment."

The boatman lifted his oars and looked hesitatingly at Val. But Val was silent, so the man let the blades fall into the water and swept the boat out into the moonlight.

"Wait a minute!" cried Val sharply.

"Good-by," said the voice. "Come again when you can stay longer."

"But I am going to stay now," he answered breathlessly.

He gave the necessary order and the rowboat swung back to the foot of the small companionway. Someone young, someone in a misty white dress, someone with a lovely low voice, had actually called to him out of the velvet dark. "If she has eyes!" Val murmured to himself. He liked the romantic sound of it and repeated it under his breath—"If she has eyes."

"What are you?" She was directly above him now; she was looking down and he was looking up as he climbed the ladder, and as their eyes met they both began to laugh.

She was very young, slim, almost frail, with a dress that accentuated her youth by its blanched simplicity. Two wan dark spots on her cheeks marked where the color was by day.

"What are you?" she repeated, moving back and laughing again as his head appeared on the level of the deck. "I'm frightened now and I want to know."

"I am a gentleman," said Val, bowing.

"What sort of a gentleman? There are all sorts of gentlemen. There was a—there was a colored gentleman at the table next to ours in Paris, and so——" She broke off. "You're not American, are you?"

"I'm Russian," he said, as he might have announced himself to be an archangel. He thought quickly and then added, "And I am the most fortunate of Russians. All this day, all this spring I have dreamed of falling in love on such a night, and now I see that heaven has sent me to you."

"Just one moment!" she said, with a little gasp. "I'm sure now that this visit is a mistake. I don't go in for anything like that. Please!"

"I beg your pardon." He looked at her in bewilderment, unaware that he had taken too much for granted. Then he drew himself up formally.

"I have made an error. If you will excuse me I will say good night."

He turned away. His hand was on the rail.

"Don't go," she said, pushing a strand of indefinite hair out of her eyes. "On second thoughts you can talk any nonsense you like if you'll only not go. I'm miserable and I don't want to be left alone."

Val hesitated; there was some element in this that he failed to understand. He had taken it for granted that a girl who called to a strange man at night, even from the deck of a yacht, was certainly in a mood for romance. And he wanted intensely to stay. Then he remembered that this was one of the two yachts he had been seeking.

"I imagine that the dinner's on the other boat," he said.

"The dinner? Oh, yes, it's on the Minnehaha. Were you going there?"

"I was going there—a long time ago."

"What's your name?"

He was on the point of telling her when something made him ask a question instead.

"And you? Why are you not at the party?"

"Because I preferred to stay here. Mrs. Jackson said there would be some

Russians there—I suppose that's you." She looked at him with interest. "You're a very young man, aren't you?"

"I am much older than I look," said Val stiffly. "People always comment on it. It's considered rather a remarkable thing."

"How old are you?"

"Twenty-one," he lied.

She laughed.

"What nonsense! You're not more than nineteen."

His annoyance was so perceptible that she hastened to reassure him. "Cheer up! I'm only seventeen myself. I might have gone to the party if I'd thought there'd be anyone under fifty there."

He welcomed the change of subject.

"You preferred to sit and dream here beneath the moon."

"I've been thinking of mistakes." They sat down side by side in two canvas deck chairs. "It's a most engrossing subject—the subject of mistakes. Women very seldom brood about mistakes—they're much more willing to forget than men are. But when they do brood——"

"You have made a mistake?" inquired Val.

She nodded.

"Is it something that cannot be repaired?"

"I think so," she answered. "I can't be sure. That's what I was considering when you came along."

"Perhaps I can help in some way," said Val. "Perhaps your mistake is not irreparable, after all."

"You can't," she said unhappily. "So let's not think about it. I'm very tired of my mistake and I'd much rather you'd tell me about all the gay, cheerful things that are going on in Cannes tonight."

They glanced shoreward at the line of mysterious and alluring lights, the big toy banks with candles inside that were really the great fashionable hotels, the lighted clock in the old town, the blurred glow of the Café de Paris, the pricked-out points of villa windows rising on slow hills toward the dark sky.

"What is everyone doing there?" she whispered. "It looks as though something gorgeous was going on, but what it is I can't quite tell."

"Everyone there is making love," said Val quietly.

"Is that it?" She looked for a long time, with a strange expression in her eyes. "Then I want to go home to America," she said. "There is too much love here. I want to go home tomorrow."

"You are afraid of being in love then?"

She shook her head.

"It isn't that. It's just because—there is no love here for me."

"Or for me either," added Val quietly. "It is sad that we two should be at such a lovely place on such a lovely night and have—nothing."

He was leaning toward her intently, with a sort of inspired and chaste romance in his eyes—and she drew back.

"Tell me more about yourself," she inquired quickly. "If you are Russian where did you learn to speak such excellent English?"

"My mother was American," he admitted. "My grandfather was American also, so she had no choice in the matter."

"Then you're American too!"

"I am Russian," said Val with dignity.

She looked at him closely, smiled and decided not to argue. "Well then," she said diplomatically, "I suppose you must have a Russian name."

But he had no intention now of telling her his name. A name, even the Rostoff name, would be a desecration of the night. They were their own low voices, their two white faces—and that was enough. He was sure, without any reason for being sure but with a sort of instinct that sang triumphantly through his mind, that in a little while, a minute or an hour, he was going to undergo an initiation into the life of romance. His name had no reality beside what was stirring in his heart.

"You are beautiful," he said suddenly.

"How do you know?"

"Because for women moonlight is the hardest light of all."

"Am I nice in the moonlight?"

"You are the loveliest thing that I have ever known."

"Oh." She thought this over. "Of course I had no business to let you come on board. I might have known what we'd talk about—in this moon. But I can't sit here and look at the shore—forever. I'm too young for that. Don't you think I'm too young for that?"

"Much too young," he agreed solemnly.

Suddenly they both became aware of new music that was close at hand, music that seemed to come out of the water not a hundred yards away.

"Listen!" she cried. "It's from the Minnehaha. They've finished dinner."

For a moment they listened in silence.

"Thank you," said Val suddenly.

"For what?"

He hardly knew he had spoken. He was thanking the deep low horns for singing in the breeze, the sea for its warm murmurous complaint against the bow, the milk of the stars for washing over them until he felt buoyed up in a substance more taut than air.

"So lovely," she whispered.

"What are we going to do about it?"

"Do we have to do something about it? I thought we could just sit and enjoy——"

"You didn't think that," he interrupted quietly. "You know that we must do something about it. I am going to make love to you—and you are going to be glad."

"I can't," she said very low. She wanted to laugh now, to make some light cool remark that would bring the situation back into the safe waters of a casual flirtation. But it was too late now. Val knew that the music had completed what the moon had begun.

"I will tell you the truth," he said. "You are my first love. I am seventeen—the same age as you, no more."

There was something utterly disarming about the fact that they were the same age. It made her helpless before the fate that had thrown them together. The deck chairs creaked and he was conscious of a faint illusive perfume as they swayed suddenly and childishly together.

· I I I ·

WHETHER HE kissed her once or several times he could not afterward remember, though it must have been an hour that they sat there close together and he held her hand. What surprised him most about making love was that it seemed to have no element of wild passion—regret, desire, despair—but a delirious promise of such happiness in the world, in living, as he had never known. First love—this was only first love! What must love itself in its fullness, its perfection be. He did not know that what he was experiencing then, that unreal, undesirous medley of ecstasy and peace, would be unrecapturable forever.

The music had ceased for some time when presently the murmurous silence was broken by the sound of a rowboat disturbing the quiet waves. She sprang suddenly to her feet and her eyes strained out over the bay.

"Listen!" she said quickly. "I want you to tell me your name."

"No."

"Please," she begged him. "I'm going away tomorrow."

He didn't answer.

"I don't want you to forget me," she said. "My name is——"

"I won't forget you. I will promise to remember you always. Whoever I may love I will always compare her to you, my first love. So long as I live you will always have that much freshness in my heart."

"I want you to remember," she murmured brokenly. "Oh, this has meant more to me than it has to you—much more."

She was standing so close to him that he felt her warm young breath on his face. Once again they swayed together. He pressed her hands and wrists between his as it seemed right to do, and kissed her lips. It was the right kiss, he thought, the romantic kiss—not too little or too much. Yet there was a sort of promise in it of other kisses he might have had, and it was with a slight sinking of his heart that he heard the rowboat close to the yacht and realized that her family had returned. The evening was over.

"And this is only the beginning," he told himself. "All my life will be like this night."

She was saying something in a low quick voice and he was listening tensely.

"You must know one thing—I am married. Three months ago. That was the mistake that I was thinking about when the moon brought you out here. In a moment you will understand."

She broke off as the boat swung against the companionway and a man's voice floated up out of the darkness.

"Is that you, my dear?"

"Yes."

"What is this other rowboat waiting?"

"One of Mrs. Jackson's guests came here by mistake and I made him stay and amuse me for an hour."

A moment later the thin white hair and weary face of a man of sixty appeared above the level of the deck. And then Val saw and realized too late how much he cared.

· I V ·

WHEN THE RIVIERA season ended in May the Rostoffs and all the other Russians closed their villas and went north for the summer. The Russian Orthodox Church was locked up and so were the bins of rarer wine, and the fashionable spring moonlight was put away, so to speak, to wait for their return.

"We'll be back next season," they said as a matter of course.

But this was premature, for they were never coming back any more. Those few who straggled south again after five tragic years were glad to get work as chambermaids or *valets de chambre* in the great hotels where they had once dined. Many of them, of course, were killed in the war or in the revolution; many of them faded out as spongers and small cheats in the big capitals, and not a few ended their lives in a sort of stupefied despair. When the Kerensky government collapsed in 1917, Val was a lieutenant on the eastern front, trying desperately to enforce authority in his company long after any vestige of it remained. He was still trying when Prince Paul Rostoff and his wife gave up their lives one rainy morning to atone for the blunders of the Romanoffs—and the enviable career of Morris Hasylton's daughter ended in a city that bore even more resemblance to a butcher shop than had Chicago in 1892.

After that Val fought with Denikin's army for a while until he realized that he was participating in a hollow farce and the glory of Imperial Russia was over. Then he went to France and was suddenly confronted with the astounding problem of keeping his body and soul together.

It was, of course, natural that he should think of going to America. Two vague aunts with whom his mother had quarreled many years ago still lived there in comparative affluence. But the idea was repugnant to the prejudices his mother had implanted in him, and besides he hadn't sufficient money left to pay for his passage over. Until a possible counter-revolution should restore to him the Rostoff properties in Russia he must somehow keep alive in France.

So he went to the little city he knew best of all. He went to Cannes. His last two hundred francs bought him a third-class ticket and when he arrived he gave his dress suit to an obliging party who dealt in such things and received in return money for food and bed. He was sorry afterward that he had sold the dress suit, because it might have helped him to a position as a waiter. But he obtained work as a taxi driver instead and was quite as happy, or rather quite as miserable, at that.

Sometimes he carried Americans to look at villas for rent, and when the front glass of the automobile was up, curious fragments of conversation drifted out to him from within.

"——heard this fellow was a Russian prince." . . . "Sh!" . . . "No, this one right here." . . ."Be quiet, Esther!"—followed by subdued laughter.

When the car stopped, his passengers would edge around to have a look at him. At first he was desperately unhappy when girls did this; after a while he didn't mind any more. Once a cheerfully intoxicated American asked him if it were true and invited him to lunch, and another time an elderly woman seized his hand as she got out of the taxi, shook it violently and then pressed a hundred-franc note into his hand.

"Well, Florence, now I can tell 'em back home I shook hands with a Russian prince."

The inebriated American who had invited him to lunch thought at first that Val was a son of the czar, and it had to be explained to him that a prince in Russia was simply the equivalent of a British courtesy lord. But he was puzzled that a man of Val's personality didn't go out and make some real money.

"This is Europe," said Val gravely. "Here money is not made. It is inherited or else it is slowly saved over a period of many years and maybe in three generations a family moves up into a higher class."

"Think of something people want—like we do."

"That is because there is more money to want with in America. Everything that people want here has been thought of long ago."

But after a year and with the help of a young Englishman he had played tennis with before the war, Val managed to get into the Cannes branch of an English bank. He forwarded mail and bought railroad tickets and arranged tours for impatient sight-seers. Sometimes a familiar face came to his window; if Val was recognized he shook hands; if not he kept silence. After two years he was no longer pointed out as a former prince, for the Russians were an old story now—the splendor of the Rostoffs and their friends was forgotten.

He mixed with people very little. In the evenings he walked for a while on the promenade, took a slow glass of beer in a café, and went early to bed. He was seldom invited anywhere because people thought that his sad, intent face was depressing—and he never accepted anyhow. He wore cheap French clothes now instead of the rich tweeds and flannels that had been ordered with his father's from England. As for women, he knew none at all. Of the many things he had been certain about at seventeen, he had been most certain about this—that his life would be full of romance. Now after eight years he knew that it was not to be. Somehow he had never had time for love—the war, the revolution and now his poverty had conspired against his expectant heart. The springs of his emotion which had first poured forth one April night had dried up immediately and only a faint trickle remained.

His happy youth had ended almost before it began. He saw himself growing older and more shabby, and living always more and more in the memories of his gorgeous boyhood. Eventually he would become absurd, pulling out an old heirloom of a watch and showing it to amused young fellow clerks who would listen with winks to his tales of the Rostoff name.

He was thinking these gloomy thoughts one April evening in 1922 as he walked beside the sea and watched the never-changing magic of the awakening lights. It was no longer for his benefit, that magic, but it went on, and he was somehow glad. Tomorrow he was going away on his vacation, to a cheap hotel farther down the shore where he could bathe and rest and read; then he would come back and work some more. Every year for three years he had taken his vacation during the last two weeks in April, perhaps because it was then that he felt the most need for remembering. It was in April that what was destined to be the best part of his life had come to a culmination under a romantic moonlight. It was sacred to him—for what he had thought of as an initiation and a beginning had turned out to be the end.

He paused now in front of the Café des Étrangers and after a moment crossed the street on impulse and sauntered down to the shore. A dozen yachts, already turned to a beautiful silver color, rode at anchor in the bay. He had seen them that afternoon, and read the names painted on their bows—but only from habit. He had done it for three years now, and it was almost a natural function of his eye.

"*Un beau soir,*" remarked a French voice at his elbow. It was a boatman who had often seen Val here before. "Monsieur finds the sea beautiful?"

"Very beautiful."

"I too. But a bad living except in the season. Next week, though, I earn something special. I am paid well for simply waiting here and doing nothing more from eight o'clock until midnight."

"That's very nice," said Val politely.

"A widowed lady, very beautiful, from America, whose yacht always anchors in the harbor for the last two weeks in April. If the Privateer comes tomorrow it will make three years."

· V ·

ALL NIGHT Val didn't sleep—not because there was any question in his mind as to what he should do, but because his long stupefied emotions were suddenly awake and alive. Of course he must not see her—not he, a poor failure with a name that was now only a shadow—but it would make him a little happier always to know that she remembered. It gave his own memory another dimension, raised it like those stereopticon glasses that bring out a picture from the flat paper. It made him sure that he had not deceived himself—he had been charming once upon a time to a lovely woman, and she did not forget.

An hour before train time next day he was at the railway station with his grip, so as to avoid any chance encounter in the street. He found himself a place in a third-class carriage of the waiting train.

Somehow as he sat there he felt differently about life—a sort of hope, faint and illusory, that he hadn't felt twenty-four hours before. Perhaps there was some way in these next few years in which he could make it possible to meet her once again—if he worked hard, threw himself passionately into whatever was at hand. He knew of at least two Russians in

Cannes who had started over again with nothing except good manners and
ingenuity and were now doing surprisingly well. The blood of Morris Hasylton began to throb a little in Val's temples and made him remember
something he had never before cared to remember—that Morris Hasylton,
who had built his daughter a palace in St. Petersburg, had also started from
nothing at all.

Simultaneously another emotion possessed him, less strange, less dynamic
but equally American—the emotion of curiosity. In case he did—well, in
case life should ever make it possible for him to seek her out, he should at
least know her name.

He jumped to his feet, fumbled excitedly at the carriage handle and jumped
from the train. Tossing his valise into the check room he started at a run
for the American consulate.

"A yacht came in this morning," he said hurriedly to a clerk, "an American
yacht—the Privateer. I want to know who owns it."

"Just a minute," said the clerk, looking at him oddly. "I'll try to find
out."

After what seemed to Val an interminable time he returned.

"Why, just a minute," he repeated hesitantly. "We're—it seems we're
finding out."

"Did the yacht come?"

"Oh, yes—it's here all right. At least I think so. If you'll just wait in
that chair."

After another ten minutes Val looked impatiently at his watch. If they
didn't hurry he'd probably miss his train. He made a nervous movement as
if to get up from his chair.

"Please sit still," said the clerk, glancing at him quickly from his desk.
"I ask you. Just sit down in that chair."

Val stared at him. How could it possibly matter to the clerk whether or
not he waited?

"I'll miss my train," he said impatiently. "I'm sorry to have given you
all this bother——"

"Please sit still! We're glad to get it off our hands. You see, we've been
waiting for your inquiry for—ah—three years."

Val jumped to his feet and jammed his hat on his head.

"Why didn't you tell me that?" he demanded angrily.

"Because we had to get word to our—our client. Please don't go! It's—
ah, it's too late."

Val turned. Someone slim and radiant with dark frightened eyes was
standing behind him, framed against the sunshine of the doorway.

"Why——"

Val's lips parted, but no words came through. She took a step toward him.

"I——" She looked at him helplessly, her eyes filling with tears. "I just wanted to say hello," she murmured. "I've come back for three years just because I wanted to say hello."

Still Val was silent.

"You might answer," she said impatiently. "You might answer when I'd—when I'd just about begun to think you'd been killed in the war." She turned to the clerk. "Please introduce us!" she cried. "You see, I can't say hello to him when we don't even know each other's names."

It's the thing to distrust these international marriages, of course. It's an American tradition that they always turn out badly, and we are accustomed to such headlines as: "Would Trade Coronet for True American Love, Says Duchess," and "Claims Count Mendicant Tortured Toledo Wife." The other sort of headlines are never printed, for who would want to read: "Castle is Love Nest, Asserts Former Georgia Belle," or "Duke and Packer's Daughter Celebrate Golden Honeymoon."

So far there have been no headlines at all about the young Rostoffs. Prince Val is much too absorbed in that string of moonlight-blue taxicabs which he manipulates with such unusual efficiency, to give out interviews. He and his wife only leave New York once a year—but there is still a boatman who rejoices when the Privateer steams into Cannes harbor on a mid-April night.

THE RICH BOY

•

"The Rich Boy" is Fitzgerald's most important novelette and includes his most promiscuously misquoted sentence: "They are different from you and me." He wrote it on Capri as a three-part story while awaiting publication of The Great Gatsby, *and revised it in Paris as a two-parter for* Red Book *(January and February 1926).*

Anson Hunter was based on Fitzgerald's school friend Ludlow Fowler:

> *I have written a fifteen thousand word story about you called* The Rich Boy—*it is so disguised that no one except you and me and maybe two of the girls concerned would recognize, unless you give it away, but it is in a large measure the story of your life, toned down here and there and symplified. Also many gaps had to come out of my imagination. It is frank, unsparing but sympathetic and I think you will like it—it is one of the best things I have ever one.*

At Fowler's request two anecdotes about Hunter were cut from the magazine version when it was collected in All the Sad Young Men. *These passages have been restored in brackets here.*

His friend Ring Lardner's statement that "The Rich Boy" should have been enlarged into a novel troubled Fitzgerald; and he explained to Maxwell Perkins that "it would have been absolutely impossible for me to have stretched 'The Rich Boy' into anything bigger than a novelette."

•

—deviating from the normal/expected or strange—
ECCENTRIC

BEGIN WITH AN individual, and before you know it you find that you have created a type; begin with a type, and you find that you have created—nothing. That is because we are all <u>queer</u> fish, queerer behind our faces and voices than we want any one to know or than we know ourselves. When I hear a man proclaiming himself an "average, honest, open fellow," I feel pretty sure that he has some definite and perhaps terrible abnormality which he has agreed to conceal—and his protestation

completely
agree w/ him

of being average and honest and open is his way of reminding himself of his misprision.

There are no types, no plurals. There is a rich boy, and this is his and not his brothers' story. All my life I have lived among his brothers but this one has been my friend. Besides, if I wrote about his brothers I should have to begin by attacking all the lies that the poor have told about the rich and the rich have told about themselves—such a wild structure they have erected that when we pick up a book about the rich, some instinct prepares us for unreality. Even the intelligent and impassioned reporters of life have made the country of the rich as unreal as fairy-land.

Let me tell you about the very rich. They are different from you and me. They possess and enjoy early, and it does something to them, makes them soft where we are hard, and cynical where we are trustful, in a way that, unless you were born rich, it is very difficult to understand. They think, deep in their hearts, that they are better than we are because we had to discover the compensations and refuges of life for ourselves. Even when they enter deep into our world or sink below us, they still think that they are better than we are. They are different. The only way I can describe young Anson Hunter is to approach him as if he were a foreigner and cling stubbornly to my point of view. If I accept his for a moment I am lost—I have nothing to show but a preposterous movie.

[handwritten left margin: land of rich = land of lies]

[handwritten left margin: always think they are better]

[handwritten: They are lost, in lies?]

· II ·

ANSON WAS the eldest of six children who would some day divide a fortune of fifteen million dollars, and he reached the age of reason—is it seven?—at the beginning of the century when daring young women were already gliding along Fifth Avenue in electric "mobiles." In those days he and his brother had an English governess who spoke the language very clearly and crisply and well, so that the two boys grew to speak as she did—their words and sentences were all crisp and clear and not run together as ours are. They didn't talk exactly like English children but acquired an accent that is peculiar to fashionable people in the city of New York.

In the summer the six children were moved from the house on 71st Street to a big estate in northern Connecticut. It was not a fashionable locality—Anson's father wanted to delay as long as possible his children's knowledge of that side of life. He was a man somewhat superior to his class, which composed New York society, and to his period, which was the snobbish and formalized vulgarity of the Gilded Age, and he wanted his sons to learn

[handwritten left margin: what is this side of life]

[handwritten: thinly gold covered]

habits of concentration and have sound constitutions and grow up into right-living and successful men. He and his wife kept an eye on them as well as they were able until the two older boys went away to school, but in huge establishments this is difficult—it was much simpler in the series of small and medium-sized houses in which my own youth was spent—I was never far out of the reach of my mother's voice, of the sense of her presence, her approval or disapproval.

Anson's first sense of his superiority came to him when he realized the half-grudging American deference that was paid to him in the Connecticut village. The parents of the boys he played with always inquired after his father and mother, and were vaguely excited when their own children were asked to the Hunters' house. He accepted this as the natural state of things, and a sort of impatience with all groups of which he was not the center—in money, in position, in authority—remained with him for the rest of his life. He disdained to struggle with other boys for precedence—he expected it to be given him freely, and when it wasn't he withdrew into his family. His family was sufficient, for in the East money is still a somewhat feudal thing, a clan-forming thing. In the snobbish West, money separates families to form "sets."

At eighteen, when he went to New Haven, Anson was tall and thick-set, with a clear complexion and a healthy color from the ordered life he had led in school. His hair was yellow and grew in a funny way on his head, his nose was beaked—these two things kept him from being handsome—but he had a confident charm and a certain brusque style, and the upper-class men who passed him on the street knew without being told that he was a rich boy and had gone to one of the best schools. Nevertheless, his very superiority kept him from being a success in college—the independence was mistaken for egotism, and the refusal to accept Yale standards with the proper awe seemed to belittle all those who had. So, long before he graduated, he began to shift the center of his life to New York.

He was at home in New York—there was his own house with "the kind of servants you can't get any more"—and his own family, of which, because of his good humor and a certain ability to make things go, he was rapidly becoming the center, and the débutante parties, and the correct manly world of the men's clubs, and the occasional wild spree with the gallant girls whom New Haven only knew from the fifth row. His aspirations were conventional enough—they included even the irreproachable shadow he would some day marry, but they differed from the aspirations of the majority of young men in that there was no mist over them, none of that quality which is variously known as "idealism" or "illusion." Anson accepted without reservation the world of high finance and high extravagance, of divorce and dissipation, of snobbery and of privilege. Most of our lives end as a compromise—it was as a compromise that his life began.

He and I first met in the late summer of 1917 when he was just out of Yale, and, like the rest of us, was swept up into the systematized hysteria of the war. In the blue-green uniform of the naval aviation he came down to Pensacola, where the hotel orchestras played "I'm sorry, dear," and we young officers danced with the girls. Every one liked him, and though he ran with the drinkers and wasn't an especially good pilot, even the instructors treated him with a certain respect. He was always having long talks with them in his confident, logical voice—talks which ended by his getting himself, or, more frequently, another officer, out of some impending trouble. He was convivial, bawdy, robustly avid for pleasure, and we were all surprised when he fell in love with a conservative and rather proper girl.

Her name was Paula Legendre, a dark, serious beauty from somewhere in California. Her family kept a winter residence just outside of town, and in spite of her primness she was enormously popular; there is a large class of men whose egotism can't endure humor in a woman. But Anson wasn't that sort, and I couldn't understand the attraction of her "sincerity"—that was the thing to say about her—for his keen and somewhat sardonic mind.

Nevertheless, they fell in love—and on her terms. He no longer joined the twilight gathering at the De Sota bar, and whenever they were seen together they were engaged in a long, serious dialogue, which must have gone on several weeks. Long afterward he told me that it was not about anything in particular but was composed on both sides of immature and even meaningless statements—the emotional content that gradually came to fill it grew up not out of the words but out of its enormous seriousness. It was a sort of hypnosis. Often it was interrupted, giving way to that emasculated humor we call fun; when they were alone it was resumed again, solemn, low-keyed, and pitched so as to give each other a sense of unity in feeling and thought. They came to resent any interruptions of it, to be unresponsive to facetiousness about life, even to the mild cynicism of their contemporaries. They were only happy when the dialogue was going on, and its seriousness bathed them like the amber glow of an open fire. Toward the end there came an interruption they did not resent—it began to be interrupted by passion.

Oddly enough, Anson was as engrossed in the dialogue as she was and as profoundly affected by it, yet at the same time aware that on his side much was insincere, and on hers much was merely simple. At first, too, he despised her emotional simplicity as well, but with his love her nature deepened and blossomed, and he could despise it no longer. He felt that if he could enter into Paula's warm safe life he would be happy. The long preparation of the dialogue removed any constraint—he taught her some of what he had learned from more adventurous women, and she responded with a rapt holy intensity. One evening after a dance they agreed to marry, and he wrote a long letter about her to his mother. The next day Paula told him that she was rich, that she had a personal fortune of nearly a million dollars.

Right tool, Move pretty fast

· I I I ·

IT WAS EXACTLY as if they could say "Neither of us has anything: we shall be poor together"—just as delightful that they should be rich instead. It gave them the same communion of adventure. Yet when Anson got leave in April, and Paula and her mother accompanied him North, she was impressed with the standing of his family in New York and with the scale on which they lived. Alone with Anson for the first time in the rooms where he had played as a boy, she was filled with a comfortable emotion, as though she were pre-eminently safe and taken care of. The pictures of Anson in a skull cap at his first school, of Anson on horseback with the sweetheart of a mysterious forgotten summer, of Anson in a gay group of ushers and bridesmaids at a wedding, made her jealous of his life apart from her in the past, and so completely did his authoritative person seem to sum up and typify these possessions of his that she was inspired with the idea of being married immediately and returning to Pensacola as his wife.

But an immediate marriage wasn't discussed—even the engagement was to be secret until after the war. When she realized that only two days of his leave remained, her dissatisfaction crystallized in the intention of making him as unwilling to wait as she was. They were driving to the country for dinner and she determined to force the issue that night.

Now a cousin of Paula's was staying with them at the Ritz, a severe, bitter girl who loved Paula but was somewhat jealous of her impressive engagement, and as Paula was late in dressing, the cousin, who wasn't going to the party, received Anson in the parlor of the suite.

Anson had met friends at five o'clock and drunk freely and indiscreetly with them for an hour. He left the Yale Club at a proper time, and his mother's chauffeur drove him to the Ritz, but his usual capacity was not in evidence, and the impact of the steam-heated sitting-room made him suddenly dizzy. He knew it, and he was both amused and sorry.

Paula's cousin was twenty-five, but she was exceptionally naïve, and at first failed to realize what was up. She had never met Anson before, and she was surprised when he mumbled strange information and nearly fell off his chair, but until Paula appeared it didn't occur to her that what she had taken for the odor of a dry-cleaned uniform was really whiskey. But Paula understood as soon as she appeared; her only thought was to get Anson away before her mother saw him, and at the look in her eyes the cousin understood too.

When Paula and Anson descended to the limousine they found two men inside, both asleep; they were the men with whom he had been drinking at the Yale Club, and they were also going to the party. He had entirely forgotten their presence in the car. On the way to Hempstead they awoke and sang. Some of the songs were rough, and though Paula tried to reconcile herself to the fact that Anson had few verbal inhibitions, her lips tightened with shame and distaste.

Back at the hotel the cousin, confused and agitated, considered the incident, and then walked into Mrs. Legendre's bedroom, saying: "Isn't he funny?"

"Who is funny?"

"Why—Mr. Hunter. He seemed so funny."

Mrs. Legendre looked at her sharply.

"How is he funny?"

"Why, he said he was French. I didn't know he was French."

"That's absurd. You must have misunderstood." She smiled: "It was a joke."

The cousin shook her head stubbornly.

"No. He said he was brought up in France. He said he couldn't speak any English, and that's why he couldn't talk to me. And he couldn't!"

Mrs. Legendre looked away with impatience just as the cousin added thoughtfully, "Perhaps it was because he was so drunk," and walked out of the room.

This curious report was true. Anson, finding his voice thick and uncontrollable, had taken the unusual refuge of announcing that he spoke no English. Years afterward he used to tell that part of the story, and he invariably communicated the uproarious laughter which the memory aroused in him.

Five times in the next hour Mrs. Legendre tried to get Hempstead on the phone. When she succeeded, there was a ten-minute delay before she heard Paula's voice on the wire.

"Cousin Jo told me Anson was intoxicated."

"Oh, no. . . ."

"Oh, yes. Cousin Jo says he was intoxicated. He told her he was French, and fell off his chair and behaved as if he was very intoxicated. I don't want you to come home with him."

"Mother, he's all right! Please don't worry about——"

"But I do worry. I think it's dreadful. I want you to promise me not to come home with him."

"I'll take care of it, mother. . . ."

this cousin is retarded

"I don't want you to come home with him."

"All right, mother. Good-by."

"Be sure now, Paula. Ask some one to bring you."

Deliberately Paula took the receiver from her ear and hung it up. Her face was flushed with helpless annoyance. Anson was stretched asleep out in a bedroom up-stairs, while the dinner-party below was proceeding lamely toward conclusion.

The hour's drive had sobered him somewhat—his arrival was merely hilarious—and Paula hoped that the evening was not spoiled, after all, but two imprudent cocktails before dinner completed the disaster. He talked boisterously and somewhat offensively to the party at large for fifteen minutes, and then slid silently under the table; like a man in an old print—but, unlike an old print, it was rather horrible without being at all quaint. None of the young girls present remarked upon the incident—it seemed to merit only silence. His uncle and two other men carried him up-stairs, and it was just after this that Paula was called to the phone.

An hour later Anson awoke in a fog of nervous agony, through which he perceived after a moment the figure of his uncle Robert standing by the door.

". . . I said are you better?"

"What?"

"Do you feel better, old man?"

"Terrible," said Anson.

"I'm going to try you on another bromo-seltzer. If you can hold it down, it'll do you good to sleep."

With an effort Anson slid his legs from the bed and stood up.

"I'm all right," he said dully.

"Take it easy."

"I thin' if you gave me a glassbrandy I could go down-stairs."

"Oh, no——"

"Yes, that's the only thin'. I'm all right now. . . . I suppose I'm in Dutch dow' there."

"They know you're a little under the weather," said his uncle deprecatingly. "But don't worry about it. Schuyler didn't even get here. He passed away in the locker-room over at the Links."

still better than the rest.

Indifferent to any opinion, except Paula's, Anson was nevertheless determined to save the débris of the evening, but when after a cold bath he made his appearance most of the party had already left. Paula got up immediately to go home.

In the limousine the old serious dialogue began. She had known that he drank, she admitted, but she had never expected anything like this—it seemed to her that perhaps they were not suited to each other, after all. Their ideas about life were too different, and so forth. When she finished speaking, Anson spoke in turn, very soberly. Then Paula said she'd have to think it over; she wouldn't decide to-night; she was not angry but she was terribly sorry. Nor would she let him come into the hotel with her, but just before she got out of the car she leaned and kissed him unhappily on the cheek.

The next afternoon Anson had a long talk with Mrs. Legendre while Paula sat listening in silence. It was agreed that Paula was to brood over the incident for a proper period and then, if mother and daughter thought it best, they would follow Anson to Pensacola. On his part he apologized with sincerity and dignity—that was all; with every card in her hand Mrs. Legendre was unable to establish any advantage over him. He made no promises, showed no humility, only delivered a few serious comments on life which brought him off with rather a moral superiority at the end. When they came South three weeks later, neither Anson in his satisfaction nor Paula in her relief at the reunion realized that the psychological moment had passed forever.

IV.

HE DOMINATED and attracted her, and at the same time filled her with anxiety. Confused by his mixture of solidity and self-indulgence, of sentiment and cynicism—incongruities which her gentle mind was unable to resolve—Paula grew to think of him as two alternating personalities. When she saw him alone, or at a formal party, or with his casual inferiors, she felt a tremendous pride in his strong, attractive presence, the paternal, understanding stature of his mind. In other company she became uneasy when what had been a fine imperviousness to mere gentility showed its other face. The other face was gross, humorous, reckless of everything but pleasure. It startled her mind temporarily away from him, even led her into a short covert experiment with an old beau, but it was no use—after four months of Anson's enveloping vitality there was an anæmic pallor in all other men.

In July he was ordered abroad, and their tenderness and desire reached a crescendo. Paula considered a last-minute marriage—decided against it

only because there were always cocktails on his breath now, but the parting itself made her physically ill with grief. After his departure she wrote him long letters of regret for the days of love they had missed by waiting. In August Anson's plane slipped down into the North Sea. He was pulled onto a destroyer after a night in the water and sent to hospital with pneumonia; the armistice *true* was signed before he was finally sent home.

Then, with every opportunity given back to them, with no material obstacle to overcome, the secret weavings of their temperaments came between them, drying up their kisses and their tears, making their voices less loud to one another, muffling the intimate chatter of their hearts until the old communication was only possible by letters, from far away. One afternoon *crazy* a society reporter waited for two hours in the Hunters' house for a confirmation of their engagement. Anson denied it; nevertheless an early issue carried the report as a leading paragraph—they were "constantly seen together at Southampton, Hot Springs, and Tuxedo Park." But the serious dialogue had turned a corner into a long-sustained quarrel, and the affair was almost played out. Anson got drunk flagrantly and missed an engagement with her, whereupon Paula made certain behavioristic demands. His *over.* despair was helpless before his pride and his knowledge of himself: the engagement was definitely broken.

"Dearest," said their letters now, "Dearest, Dearest, when I wake up in the middle of the night and realize that after all it was not to be, I feel that I want to die. I can't go on living any more. Perhaps when we meet this summer we may talk things over and decide differently—we were so excited and sad that day, and I don't feel that I can live all my life without you. You speak of other people. Don't you know there are no other people for me, but only you. . . ."

But as Paula drifted here and there around the East she would sometimes *she plays* mention her gaieties to make him wonder. Anson was too acute to wonder. *him* When he saw a man's name in her letters he felt more sure of her and a little disdainful—he was always superior to such things. But he still hoped that they would some day marry.

Meanwhile he plunged vigorously into all the movement and glitter of post-bellum New York, entering a brokerage house, joining half a dozen clubs, dancing late, and moving in three worlds—his own world, the world *he didn't grad.* of young Yale graduates, and that section of the half-world which rests one end on Broadway. But there was always a thorough and infractible eight hours devoted to his work in Wall Street, where the combination of his influential family connection, his sharp intelligence, and his abundance of sheer physical energy brought him almost immediately forward. He had one of those invaluable minds with partitions in it; sometimes he appeared *incredibly brilliant* at his office refreshed by less than an hour's sleep, but such occurrences were rare. So early as 1920 his income in salary and commissions exceeded twelve thousand dollars.

As the Yale tradition slipped into the past he became more and more of a popular figure among his classmates in New York, more popular than he had ever been in college. He lived in a great house, and had the means of introducing young men into other great houses. Moreover, his life already seemed secure, while theirs, for the most part, had arrived again at precarious beginnings. They commenced to turn to him for amusement and escape, and Anson responded readily, taking pleasure in helping people and arranging their affairs.

There were no men in Paula's letters now, but a note of tenderness ran through them that had not been there before. From several sources he heard that she had "a heavy beau," Lowell Thayer, a Bostonian of wealth and position, and though he was sure she still loved him, it made him uneasy to think that he might lose her, after all. Save for one unsatisfactory day she had not been in New York for almost five months, and as the rumors multiplied he became increasingly anxious to see her. In February he took his vacation and went down to Florida.

Palm Beach sprawled plump and opulent between the sparkling sapphire of Lake Worth, flawed here and there by house-boats at anchor, and the great turquoise bar of the Atlantic Ocean. The huge bulks of the Breakers and the Royal Poinciana rose as twin paunches from the bright level of the sand, and around them clustered the Dancing Glade, Bradley's House of Chance, and a dozen modistes and milliners with goods at triple prices from New York. Upon the trellissed veranda of the Breakers two hundred women stepped right, stepped left, wheeled, and slid in that then celebrated calisthenic known as the double-shuffle, while in half-time to the music two thousand bracelets clicked up and down on two hundred arms.

At the Everglades Club after dark Paula and Lowell Thayer and Anson and a casual fourth played bridge with hot cards. It seemed to Anson that her kind, serious face was wan and tired—she had been around now for four, five, years. He had known her for three.

"Two spades."

"Cigarette? . . . Oh, I beg your pardon. By me."

"By."

"I'll double three spades."

There were a dozen tables of bridge in the room, which was filling up with smoke. Anson's eyes met Paula's, held them persistently even when Thayer's glance fell between them. . . .

"What was bid?" he asked abstractedly.

"Rose of Washington Square" ← Paula?

sang the young people in the corners:

> *"I'm withering there
> In basement air——"*
>   ↳ Anson?

The smoke banked like fog, and the opening of a door filled the room with blown swirls of ectoplasm. Little Bright Eyes streaked past the tables seeking Mr. Conan Doyle among the Englishmen who were posing as Englishmen about the lobby.

"You could cut it with a knife."

". . . cut it with a knife."

". . . a knife."

At the end of the rubber Paula suddenly got up and spoke to Anson in a tense, low voice. With scarcely a glance at Lowell Thayer, they walked out the door and descended a long flight of stone steps—in a moment they were walking hand in hand along the moonlit beach.   *say? what?*

"Darling, darling. . . ." They embraced recklessly, passionately, in a shadow. . . . Then Paula drew back her face to let his lips say what she wanted to hear—she could feel the words forming as they kissed again. . . . Again she broke away, listening, but as he pulled her close once more she realized that he had said nothing—only *"Darling! Darling!"* in that deep, sad whisper that always made her cry. Humbly, obediently, her emotions yielded to him and the tears streamed down her face, but her heart kept on crying: "Ask me—oh, Anson, dearest, ask me!"

"Paula. . . . *Paula!*"

The words wrung her heart like hands, and Anson, feeling her tremble, knew that emotion was enough. He need say no more, commit their destinies to no practical enigma. Why should he, when he might hold her so, biding his own time, for another year—forever? He was considering them both, her more than himself. For a moment, when she said suddenly that she must go back to her hotel, he hesitated, thinking, first, "This is the moment, after all," and then: "No, let it wait—she is mine. . . ."   *wrong*

that's a first.

He had forgotten that Paula too was worn away inside with the strain of three years. Her mood passed forever in the night.   *too much strain?*

He went back to New York next morning filled with a certain restless dissatisfaction. [There was a pretty débutante he knew in his car, and for two days they took their meals together. At first he told her a little about Paula and invented an esoteric incompatibility that was keeping them apart. The girl was of a wild, impulsive nature, and she was flattered by Anson's

#1 b/c he didn't ask her

confidences. Like Kipling's soldier, he might have possessed himself of most
of her before he reached New York, but luckily he was sober and kept
control.] Late in April, without warning, he received a telegram from Bar
Harbor in which Paula told him that she was engaged to Lowell Thayer,
and that they would be married immediately in Boston. What he never really
believed could happen had happened at last.

Anson filled himself with whiskey that morning, and going to the office,
carried on his work without a break—rather with a fear of what would
happen if he stopped. In the evening he went out as usual, saying nothing
of what had occurred; he was cordial, humorous, unabstracted. But one
thing he could not help—for three days, in any place, in any company, he
would suddenly bend his head into his hands and cry like a child.

· V ·

IN 1922 WHEN ANSON went abroad with the junior partner to investigate
some London loans, the journey intimated that he was to be taken into the
firm. He was twenty-seven now, a little heavy without being definitely stout,
and with a manner older than his years. Old people and young people liked
him and trusted him, and mothers felt safe when their daughters were in
his charge, for he had a way, when he came into a room, of putting himself
on a footing with the oldest and most conservative people there. "You and
I," he seemed to say, "we're solid. We understand."

He had an instinctive and rather charitable knowledge of the weaknesses
of men and women, and, like a priest, it made him the more concerned for
the maintenance of outward forms. It was typical of him that every Sunday
morning he taught in a fashionable Episcopal Sunday-school—even though
a cold shower and a quick change into a cutaway coat were all that separated
him from the wild night before. [Once, by some mutual instinct, several
children got up from the front row and moved to the last. He told this story
frequently, and it was usually greeted with hilarious laughter.]

After his father's death he was the practical head of his family, and, in
effect, guided the destinies of the younger children. Through a complication
his authority did not extend to his father's estate, which was administrated
by his Uncle Robert, who was the horsey member of the family, a good-
natured, hard-drinking member of that set which centers about Wheatley
Hills.

Uncle Robert and his wife, Edna, had been great friends of Anson's youth,
and the former was disappointed when his nephew's superiority failed to
take a horsey form. He backed him for a city club which was the most

difficult in America to enter—one could only join if one's family had "helped to build up New York" (or, in other words, were rich before 1880)—and when Anson, after his election, neglected it for the Yale Club, Uncle Robert gave him a little talk on the subject. But when on top of that Anson declined to enter Robert Hunter's own conservative and somewhat neglected brokerage house, his manner grew cooler. Like a primary teacher who has taught all he knew, he slipped out of Anson's life.

There were so many friends in Anson's life—scarcely one for whom he had not done some unusual kindness and scarcely one whom he did not occasionally embarrass by his bursts of rough conversation or his habit of getting drunk whenever and however he liked. It annoyed him when any one else blundered in that regard—about his own lapses he was always humorous. Odd things happened to him and he told them with infectious laughter.

I was working in New York that spring, and I used to lunch with him at the Yale Club, which my university was sharing until the completion of our own. I had read of Paula's marriage, and one afternoon, when I asked him about her, something moved him to tell me the story. After that he frequently invited me to family dinners at his house and behaved as though there was a special relation between us, as though with his confidence a little of that consuming memory had passed into me.

I found that despite the trusting mothers, his attitude toward girls was not indiscriminately protective. It was up to the girl—if she showed an inclination toward looseness, she must take care of herself, even with him. "Life," he would explain sometimes, "has made a cynic of me."

By life he meant Paula. Sometimes, especially when he was drinking, it became a little twisted in his mind, and he thought that she had callously thrown him over.

This "cynicism," or rather his realization that naturally fast girls were not worth sparing, led to his affair with Dolly Karger. It wasn't his only affair in those years, but it came nearest to touching him deeply, and it had a profound effect upon his attitude toward life.

Dolly was the daughter of a notorious "publicist" who had married into society. She herself grew up into the Junior League, came out at the Plaza, and went to the Assembly; and only a few old families like the Hunters could question whether or not she "belonged," for her picture was often in the papers, and she had more enviable attention than many girls who undoubtedly did. She was dark-haired, with carmine lips and a high, lovely color, which she concealed under pinkish-gray powder all through the first year out, because high color was unfashionable—Victorian-pale was the thing to be. She wore black, severe suits and stood with her hands in her pockets leaning a little forward, with a humorous restraint on her face. She danced exquisitely—better than anything she liked to dance—better than anything except making love. Since she was ten she had always been in love, and, usually, with some boy who didn't respond to her. Those who did—and there were many—bored her after a brief encounter, but for her failures she reserved the warmest spot in her heart. When she met them she would always try once more—sometimes she succeeded, more often she failed.

It never occurred to this gypsy of the unattainable that there was a certain resemblance in those who refused to love her—they shared a hard intuition that saw through to her weakness, not a weakness of emotion but a weakness of rudder. Anson perceived this when he first met her, less than a month after Paula's marriage. He was drinking rather heavily, and he pretended for a week that he was falling in love with her. Then he dropped her abruptly and forgot—immediately he took up the commanding position in her heart.

Like so many girls of that day Dolly was slackly and indiscreetly wild. The unconventionality of a slightly older generation had been simply one facet of a post-war movement to discredit obsolete manners—Dolly's was both older and shabbier, and she saw in Anson the two extremes which the emotionally shiftless woman seeks, an abandon to indulgence alternating with a protective strength. In his character she felt both the sybarite and the solid rock, and these two satisfied every need of her nature.

She felt that it was going to be difficult, but she mistook the reason—she thought that Anson and his family expected a more spectacular marriage, but she guessed immediately that her advantage lay in his tendency to drink.

They met at the large débutante dances, but as her infatuation increased they managed to be more and more together. Like most mothers, Mrs. Karger believed that Anson was exceptionally reliable, so she allowed Dolly to go with him to distant country clubs and suburban houses without inquiring closely into their activities or questioning her explanations when they came in late. At first these explanations might have been accurate, but Dolly's worldly ideas of capturing Anson were soon engulfed in the rising sweep of her emotion. Kisses in the back of taxis and motor-cars were no longer enough; they did a curious thing:

They dropped out of their world for a while and made another world just beneath it where Anson's tippling and Dolly's irregular hours would be less noticed and commented on. It was composed, this world, of varying elements—several of Anson's Yale friends and their wives, two or three young brokers and bond salesmen and a handful of unattached men, fresh from college, with money and a propensity to dissipation. What this world lacked in spaciousness and scale it made up for by allowing them a liberty that it scarcely permitted itself. Moreover, it centered around them and permitted Dolly the pleasure of a faint condescension—a pleasure which Anson, whose whole life was a condescension from the certitudes of his childhood, was unable to share.

He was not in love with her, and in the long feverish winter of their affair he frequently told her so. In the spring he was weary—he wanted to renew his life at some other source—moreover, he saw that either he must break with her now or accept the responsibility of a definite seduction. Her family's encouraging attitude precipitated his decision—one evening when Mr. Karger knocked discreetly at the library door to announce that he had left a bottle of old brandy in the dining-room, Anson felt that life was hemming him in. That night he wrote her a short letter in which he told her that he was going on his vacation, and that in view of all the circumstances they had better meet no more.

It was June. His family had closed up the house and gone to the country, so he was living temporarily at the Yale Club. I had heard about his affair with Dolly as it developed—accounts salted with humor, for he despised unstable women, and granted them no place in the social edifice in which he believed—and when he told me that night that he was definitely breaking with her I was glad. I had seen Dolly here and there, and each time with a feeling of pity at the hopelessness of her struggle, and of shame at knowing so much about her that I had no right to know. She was what is known as "a pretty little thing," but there was a certain recklessness which rather fascinated me. Her dedication to the goddess of waste would have been less obvious had she been less spirited—she would most certainly throw herself away, but I was glad when I heard that the sacrifice would not be consummated in my sight.

Anson was going to leave the letter of farewell at her house next morning. It was one of the few houses left open in the Fifth Avenue district, and he knew that the Kargers, acting upon erroneous information from Dolly, had foregone a trip abroad to give their daughter her chance. As he stepped out the door of the Yale Club into Madison Avenue the postman passed him, and he followed back inside. The first letter that caught his eye was in Dolly's hand.

He knew what it would be—a lonely and tragic monologue, full of the reproaches he knew, the invoked memories, the "I wonder if's"—all the immemorial intimacies that he had communicated to Paula Legendre in what seemed another age. Thumbing over some bills, he brought it on top again and opened it. To his surprise it was a short, somewhat formal note, which said that Dolly would be unable to go to the country with him for the weekend, because Perry Hull from Chicago had unexpectedly come to town. It added that Anson had brought this on himself: "—if I felt that you loved me as I love you I would go with you at any time, any place, but Perry is so nice, and he so much wants me to marry him——"

Anson smiled contemptuously—he had had experience with such decoy epistles. Moreover, he knew how Dolly had labored over this plan, probably sent for the faithful Perry and calculated the time of his arrival—even labored over the note so that it would make him jealous without driving him away. Like most compromises, it had neither force nor vitality but only a timorous despair.

Suddenly he was angry. He sat down in the lobby and read it again. Then he went to the phone, called Dolly and told her in his clear, compelling voice that he had received her note and would call for her at five o'clock as they had previously planned. Scarcely waiting for the pretended uncertainty of her "Perhaps I can see you for an hour," he hung up the receiver and went down to his office. On the way he tore his own letter into bits and dropped it in the street.

He was not jealous—she meant nothing to him—but at her pathetic ruse everything stubborn and self-indulgent in him came to the surface. It was a presumption from a mental inferior and it could not be overlooked. If she wanted to know to whom she belonged she would see.

He was on the door-step at quarter past five. Dolly was dressed for the street, and he listened in silence to the paragraph of "I can only see you for an hour," which she had begun on the phone.

"Put on your hat, Dolly," he said, "we'll take a walk."

They strolled up Madison Avenue and over to Fifth while Anson's shirt dampened upon his portly body in the deep heat. He talked little, scolding her, making no love to her, but before they had walked six blocks she was his again, apologizing for the note, offering not to see Perry at all as an atonement, offering anything. She thought that he had come because he was beginning to love her.

"I'm hot," he said when they reached 71st Street. "This is a winter suit. If I stop by the house and change, would you mind waiting for me downstairs? I'll only be a minute."

She was happy; the intimacy of his being hot, of any physical fact about him, thrilled her. When they came to the iron-grated door and Anson took out his key she experienced a sort of delight.

Down-stairs it was dark, and after he ascended in the lift Dolly raised a curtain and looked out through opaque lace at the houses over the way. She heard the lift machinery stop, and with the notion of teasing him pressed the button that brought it down. Then on what was more than an impulse she got into it and sent it up to what she guessed was his floor.

"Anson," she called, laughing a little.

"Just a minute," he answered from his bedroom . . . then after a brief delay: "Now you can come in."

He had changed and was buttoning his vest. "This is my room," he said lightly. "How do you like it?"

She caught sight of Paula's picture on the wall and stared at it in fascination, just as Paula had stared at the pictures of Anson's childish sweethearts five years before. She knew something about Paula—sometimes she tortured herself with fragments of the story.

Suddenly she came close to Anson, raising her arms. They embraced. Outside the area window a soft artificial twilight already hovered, though the sun was still bright on a back roof across the way. In half an hour the room would be quite dark. The uncalculated opportunity overwhelmed them, made them both breathless, and they clung more closely. It was eminent, inevitable. Still holding one another, they raised their heads—their eyes fell together upon Paula's picture, staring down at them from the wall.

Suddenly Anson dropped his arms, and sitting down at his desk tried the drawer with a bunch of keys.

"Like a drink?" he asked in a gruff voice.

"No, Anson."

He poured himself half a tumbler of whiskey, swallowed it, and then opened the door into the hall.

"Come on," he said.

Dolly hesitated.

"Anson—I'm going to the country with you tonight, after all. You understand that, don't you?"

"Of course," he answered brusquely.

In Dolly's car they rode on to Long Island, closer in their emotions than they had ever been before. They knew what would happen—not with Paula's SEX face to remind them that something was lacking, but when they were alone in the still, hot Long Island night they did not care.

The estate in Port Washington where they were to spend the week-end belonged to a cousin of Anson's who had married a Montana copper operator. An interminable drive began at the lodge and twisted under imported poplar saplings toward a huge, pink, Spanish house. Anson had often visited there before.

After dinner they danced at the Linx Club. About midnight Anson assured himself that his cousins would not leave before two—then he explained that Dolly was tired; he would take her home and return to the dance later. Trembling a little with excitement, they got into a borrowed car together and drove to Port Washington. As they reached the lodge he stopped and spoke to the night-watchman.

"When are you making a round, Carl?"

"Right away."

"Then you'll be here till everybody's in?"

"Yes, sir."

"All right. Listen: if any automobile, no matter whose it is, turns in at this gate, I want you to phone the house immediately." He put a five-dollar bill into Carl's hand. "Is that clear?"

"Yes, Mr. Anson." Being of the Old World, he neither winked nor smiled. Yet Dolly sat with her face turned slightly away.

Anson had a key. Once inside he poured a drink for both of them— Dolly left hers untouched—then he ascertained definitely the location of the phone, and found that it was within easy hearing distance of their rooms, both of which were on the first floor.

Five minutes later he knocked at the door of Dolly's room.

"Anson?" He went in, closing the door behind him. She was in bed, leaning up anxiously with elbows on the pillow; sitting beside her he took her in his arms.

"Anson, darling."

He didn't answer.

"Anson. . . . Anson! I love you. . . . Say you love me. Say it now— can't you say it now? Even if you don't mean it?"

He did not listen. Over her head he perceived that the picture of Paula was hanging here upon this wall.

He got up and went close to it. The frame gleamed faintly with thrice-reflected moonlight—within was a blurred shadow of a face that he saw he did not know. Almost sobbing, he turned around and stared with abomination at the little figure on the bed.

"This is all foolishness," he said thickly. "I don't know what I was thinking about. I don't love you and you'd better wait for somebody that loves you. I don't love you a bit, can't you understand?"

His voice broke, and he went hurriedly out. Back in the salon he was pouring himself a drink with uneasy fingers, when the front door opened suddenly, and his cousin came in.

"Why, Anson, I hear Dolly's sick," she began solicitously. "I hear she's sick. . . ."

"It was nothing," he interrupted, raising his voice so that it would carry into Dolly's room. "She was a little tired. She went to bed."

For a long time afterward Anson believed that a protective God sometimes interfered in human affairs. But Dolly Karger, lying awake and staring at the ceiling, never again believed in anything at all.

· VI ·

WHEN DOLLY married during the following autumn, Anson was in London on business. Like Paula's marriage, it was sudden, but it affected him in a different way. At first he felt that it was funny, and had an inclination to laugh when he thought of it. Later it depressed him—it made him feel old.

There was something repetitive about it—why, Paula and Dolly had belonged to different generations. He had a foretaste of the sensation of a man of forty who hears that the daughter of an old flame has married. He wired congratulations and, as was not the case with Paula, they were sincere—he had never really hoped that Paula would be happy.

When he returned to New York, he was made a partner in the firm, and, as his responsibilities increased, he had less time on his hands. The refusal of a life-insurance company to issue him a policy made such an impression on him that he stopped drinking for a year, and claimed that he felt better physically, though I think he missed the convivial recounting of those Celliniesque adventures which, in his early twenties, had played such a part of his life. But he never abandoned the Yale Club. He was a figure there, a personality, and the tendency of his class, who were now seven years out of college, to drift away to more sober haunts was checked by his presence.

His day was never too full nor his mind too weary to give any sort of aid to any one who asked it. What had been done at first through pride and superiority had become a habit and a passion. And there was always something—a younger brother in trouble at New Haven, a quarrel to be patched up between a friend and his wife, a position to be found for this man, an investment for that. But his specialty was the solving of problems for young married people. Young married people fascinated him and their apartments were almost sacred to him—he knew the story of their love-affair, advised them where to live and how, and remembered their babies' names. Toward young wives his attitude was circumspect: he never abused the trust which their husbands—strangely enough in view of his unconcealed irregularities—invariably reposed in him.

He came to take a vicarious pleasure in happy marriages, and to be inspired to an almost equally pleasant melancholy by those that went astray. Not a season passed that he did not witness the collapse of an affair that perhaps he himself had fathered. When Paula was divorced and almost immediately remarried to another Bostonian, he talked about her to me all one afternoon. He would never love any one as he had loved Paula, but he insisted that he no longer cared.

"I'll never marry," he came to say; "I've seen too much of it, and I know a happy marriage is a very rare thing. Besides, I'm too old."

But he did believe in marriage. Like all men who spring from a happy and successful marriage, he believed in it passionately—nothing he had seen would change his belief, his cynicism dissolved upon it like air. But he did really believe he was too old. At twenty-eight he began to accept with equanimity the prospect of marrying without romantic love; he resolutely chose a New York girl of his own class, pretty, intelligent, congenial, above reproach—and set about falling in love with her. The things he had said to Paula with sincerity, to other girls with grace, he could no longer say at all without smiling, or with the force necessary to convince.

"When I'm forty," he told his friends, "I'll be ripe. I'll fall for some chorus girl like the rest."

Nevertheless, he persisted in his attempt. His mother wanted to see him married, and he could now well afford it—he had a seat on the Stock Exchange, and his earned income came to twenty-five thousand a year. The idea was agreeable: when his friends—he spent most of his time with the set he and Dolly had evolved—closed themselves in behind domestic doors at night, he no longer rejoiced in his freedom. He even wondered if he should have married Dolly. Not even Paula had loved him more, and he was learning the rarity, in a single life, of encountering true emotion.

Just as this mood began to creep over him a disquieting story reached his ear. His aunt Edna, a woman just this side of forty, was carrying on an open intrigue with a dissolute, hard-drinking young man named Cary Sloane. Every one knew of it except Anson's Uncle Robert, who for fifteen years had talked long in clubs and taken his wife for granted.

Anson heard the story again and again with increasing annoyance. Something of his old feeling for his uncle came back to him, a feeling that was more than personal, a reversion toward that family solidarity on which he had based his pride. His intuition singled out the essential point of the affair, which was that his uncle shouldn't be hurt. It was his first experiment in unsolicited meddling, but with his knowledge of Edna's character he felt that he could handle the matter better than a district judge or his uncle.

His uncle was in Hot Springs. Anson traced down the sources of the scandal so that there should be no possibility of mistake and then he called Edna and asked her to lunch with him at the Plaza next day. Something in his tone must have frightened her, for she was reluctant, but he insisted, putting off the date until she had no excuse for refusing.

She met him at the appointed time in the Plaza lobby, a lovely, faded, gray-eyed blonde in a coat of Russian sable. Five great rings, cold with

diamonds and emeralds, sparkled on her slender hands. It occurred to
Anson that it was his father's intelligence and not his uncle's that had
earned the fur and the stones, the rich brilliance that buoyed up her passing
beauty.

Though Edna scented his hostility, she was unprepared for the directness
of his approach.

"Edna, I'm astonished at the way you've been acting," he said in a strong,
frank voice. "At first I couldn't believe it."

"Believe what?" she demanded sharply.

"You needn't pretend with me, Edna. I'm talking about Cary Sloane.
Aside from any other consideration, I didn't think you could treat Uncle
Robert——"

"Now look here, Anson—" she began angrily, but his peremptory voice
broke through hers:

"—and your children in such a way. You've been married eighteen years,
and you're old enough to know better."

"You can't talk to me like that! You——"

"Yes, I can. Uncle Robert has always been my best friend." He was
tremendously moved. He felt a real distress about his uncle, about his three
young cousins.

Edna stood up, leaving her crab-flake cocktail untasted.

"This is the silliest thing——"

"Very well, if you won't listen to me I'll go to Uncle Robert and tell him
the whole story—he's bound to hear it sooner or later. And afterward I'll
go to old Moses Sloane."

Edna faltered back into her chair.

"Don't talk so loud," she begged him. Her eyes blurred with tears. "You
have no idea how your voice carries. You might have chosen a less public
place to make all these crazy accusations."

He didn't answer.

"Oh, you never liked me, I know," she went on. "You're just taking
advantage of some silly gossip to try and break up the only interesting
friendship I've ever had. What did I ever do to make you hate me so?"

Still Anson waited. There would be the appeal to his chivalry, then to his
pity, finally to his superior sophistication—when he had shouldered his way
through all these there would be admissions, and he could come to grips
with her. By being silent, by being impervious, by returning constantly to
his main weapon, which was his own true emotion, he bullied her into
frantic despair as the luncheon hour slipped away. At two o'clock she took
out a mirror and a handkerchief, shined away the marks of her tears and

powdered the slight hollows where they had lain. She had agreed to meet him at her own house at five.

When he arrived she was stretched on a chaise-longue which was covered with cretonne for the summer, and the tears he had called up at luncheon seemed still to be standing in her eyes. Then he was aware of Cary Sloane's dark anxious presence upon the cold hearth.

"What's this idea of yours?" broke out Sloane immediately. "I understand you invited Edna to lunch and then threatened her on the basis of some cheap scandal."

Anson sat down.

"I have no reason to think it's only scandal."

"I hear you're going to take it to Robert Hunter, and to my father."

Anson nodded.

"Either you break it off—or I will," he said.

"What God damned business is it of yours, Hunter?"

"Don't lose your temper, Cary," said Edna nervously. "It's only a question of showing him how absurd——"

"For one thing, it's my name that's being handed around," interrupted Anson. "That's all that concerns you, Cary."

"Edna isn't a member of your family."

"She most certainly is!" His anger mounted. "Why—she owes this house and the rings on her fingers to my father's brains. When Uncle Robert married her she didn't have a penny."

They all looked at the rings as if they had a significant bearing on the situation. Edna made a gesture to take them from her hand.

"I guess they're not the only rings in the world," said Sloane.

"Oh, this is absurd," cried Edna. "Anson, will you listen to me? I've found out how the silly story started. It was a maid I discharged who went right to the Chilicheffs—all these Russians pump things out of their servants and then put a false meaning on them." She brought down her fist angrily on the table: "And after Tom lent them the limousine for a whole month when we were South last winter——"

"Do you see?" demanded Sloane eagerly. "This maid got hold of the wrong end of the thing. She knew that Edna and I were friends, and she carried it to the Chilicheffs. In Russia they assume that if a man and a woman——"

He enlarged the theme to a disquisition upon social relations in the Caucasus.

"If that's the case it better be explained to Uncle Robert," said Anson dryly, "so that when the rumors do reach him he'll know they're not true."

Adopting the method he had followed with Edna at luncheon he let them explain it all away. He knew that they were guilty and that presently they would cross the line from explanation into justification and convict themselves more definitely than he could ever do. By seven they had taken the desperate step of telling him the truth—Robert Hunter's neglect, Edna's empty life, the casual dalliance that had flamed up into passion—but like so many true stories it had the misfortune of being old, and its enfeebled body beat helplessly against the armor of Anson's will. The threat to go to Sloane's father sealed their helplessness, for the latter, a retired cotton broker out of Alabama, was a notorious fundamentalist who controlled his son by a rigid allowance and the promise that at his next vagary the allowance would stop forever.

They dined at a small French restaurant, and the discussion continued— at one time Sloane resorted to physical threats, a little later they were both imploring him to give them time. But Anson was obdurate. He saw that Edna was breaking up, and that her spirit must not be refreshed by any renewal of their passion.

At two o'clock in a small night-club on 53d Street, Edna's nerves suddenly collapsed, and she cried to go home. Sloane had been drinking heavily all evening, and he was faintly maudlin, leaning on the table and weeping a little with his face in his hands. Quickly Anson gave them his terms. Sloane was to leave town for six months, and he must be gone within forty-eight hours. When he returned there was to be no resumption of the affair, but at the end of a year Edna might, if she wished, tell Robert Hunter that she wanted a divorce and go about it in the usual way.

He paused, gaining confidence from their faces for his final word.

"Or there's another thing you can do," he said slowly, "if Edna wants to leave her children, there's nothing I can do to prevent your running off together."

"I want to go home!" cried Edna again. "Oh, haven't you done enough to us for one day?"

Outside it was dark, save for a blurred glow from Sixth Avenue down the street. In that light those two who had been lovers looked for the last time into each other's tragic faces, realizing that between them there was not enough youth and strength to avert their eternal parting. Sloane walked suddenly off down the street and Anson tapped a dozing taxi-driver on the arm.

It was almost four; there was a patient flow of cleaning water along the ghostly pavement of Fifth Avenue, and the shadows of two night women flitted over the dark façade of St. Thomas's church. Then the desolate shrubbery of Central Park where Anson had often played as a child, and the mounting numbers, significant as names, of the marching streets. This was his city, he thought, where his name had flourished through five generations. No change could alter the permanence of its place here, for change itself was the essential substratum by which he and those of his name identified themselves with the spirit of New York. Resourcefulness and a powerful will—for his threats in weaker hands would have been less than nothing—had beaten the gathering dust from his uncle's name, from the name of his family, from even this shivering figure that sat beside him in the car.

Cary Sloane's body was found next morning on the lower shelf of a pillar of Queensboro Bridge. In the darkness and in his excitement he had thought that it was the water flowing black beneath him, but in less than a second it made no possible difference—unless he had planned to think one last thought of Edna, and call out her name as he struggled feebly in the water.

· VII ·

ANSON NEVER blamed himself for his part in this affair—the situation which brought it about had not been of his making. But the just suffer with the unjust, and he found that his oldest and somehow his most precious friendship was over. He never knew what distorted story Edna told, but he was welcome in his uncle's house no longer.

Just before Christmas Mrs. Hunter retired to a select Episcopal heaven, and Anson became the responsible head of his family. An unmarried aunt who had lived with them for years ran the house, and attempted with helpless inefficiency to chaperone the younger girls. All the children were less self-reliant than Anson, more conventional both in their virtues and in their shortcomings. Mrs. Hunter's death had postponed the début of one daughter and the wedding of another. Also it had taken something deeply material from all of them, for with her passing the quiet, expensive superiority of the Hunters came to an end.

For one thing, the estate, considerably diminished by two inheritance taxes and soon to be divided among six children, was not a notable fortune any more. Anson saw a tendency in his youngest sisters to speak rather respectfully of families that hadn't "existed" twenty years ago. His own feeling of precedence was not echoed in them—sometimes they were conventionally snobbish, that was all. For another thing, this was the last summer they would spend on the Connecticut estate; the clamor against it was too loud: "Who wants to waste the best months of the year shut up in that dead old town?" Reluctantly he yielded—the house would go into the market in the fall, and next summer they would rent a smaller place in Westchester County. It was a step down from the expensive simplicity of his father's idea, and, while he sympathized with the revolt, it also annoyed him; during his mother's lifetime he had gone up there at least every other week-end—even in the gayest summers.

Yet he himself was part of this change, and his strong instinct for life had turned him in his twenties from the hollow obsequies of that abortive leisure class. He did not see this clearly—he still felt that there was a norm, a standard of society. But there was no norm, it was doubtful if there had ever been a true norm in New York. The few who still paid and fought to enter a particular set succeeded only to find that as a society it scarcely functioned—or, what was more alarming, that the Bohemia from which they fled sat above them at table.

At twenty-nine Anson's chief concern was his own growing loneliness. He was sure now that he would never marry. The number of weddings at which he had officiated as best man or usher was past all counting—there was a drawer at home that bulged with the official neckties of this or that wedding-party, neckties standing for romances that had not endured a year, for couples who had passed completely from his life. Scarf-pins, gold pencils, cuff-buttons, presents from a generation of grooms had passed through his jewel-box and been lost—and with every ceremony he was less and less able to imagine himself in the groom's place. Under his hearty good-will toward all those marriages there was despair about his own.

And as he neared thirty he became not a little depressed at the inroads that marriage, especially lately, had made upon his friendships. Groups of people had a disconcerting tendency to dissolve and disappear. The men from his own college—and it was upon them he had expended the most time and affection—were the most elusive of all. Most of them were drawn deep into domesticity, two were dead, one lived abroad, one was in Hollywood writing continuities for pictures that Anson went faithfully to see.

Most of them, however, were permanent commuters with an intricate family life centering around some suburban country club, and it was from these that he felt his estrangement most keenly.

In the early days of their married life they had all needed him; he gave them advice about their slim finances, he exorcised their doubts about the advisability of bringing a baby into two rooms and a bath, especially he stood for the great world outside. But now their financial troubles were in the past and the fearfully expected child had evolved into an absorbing family. They were always glad to see old Anson, but they dressed up for him and tried to impress him with their present importance, and kept their troubles to themselves. They needed him no longer.

A few weeks before his thirtieth birthday the last of his early and intimate friends was married. Anson acted in his usual rôle of best man, gave his usual silver tea-service, and went down to the usual *Homeric* to say good-by. It was a hot Friday afternoon in May, and as he walked from the pier he realized that Saturday closing had begun and he was free until Monday morning.

"Go where?" he asked himself.

The Yale Club, of course; bridge until dinner, then four or five raw cocktails in somebody's room and a pleasant confused evening. He regretted that this afternoon's groom wouldn't be along—they had always been able to cram so much into such nights: they knew how to attach women and how to get rid of them, how much consideration any girl deserved from their intelligent hedonism. A party was an adjusted thing—you took certain girls to certain places and spent just so much on their amusement; you drank a little, not much, more than you ought to drink, and at a certain time in the morning you stood up and said you were going home. You avoided college boys, sponges, future engagements, fights, sentiment, and indiscretions. That was the way it was done. All the rest was dissipation.

In the morning you were never violently sorry—you made no resolutions, but if you had overdone it and your heart was slightly out of order, you went on the wagon for a few days without saying anything about it, and waited until an accumulation of nervous boredom projected you into another party.

The lobby of the Yale Club was unpopulated. In the bar three very young alumni looked up at him, momentarily and without curiosity.

"Hello there, Oscar," he said to the bartender. "Mr. Cahill been around this afternoon?"

"Mr. Cahill's gone to New Haven."

"Oh . . . that so?"

"Gone to the ball game. Lot of men gone up."

Anson looked once again into the lobby, considered for a moment, and then walked out and over to Fifth Avenue. From the broad window of one of his clubs—one that he had scarcely visited in five years—a gray man with watery eyes stared down at him. Anson looked quickly away—that figure sitting in vacant resignation, in supercilious solitude, depressed him. He stopped and, retracing his steps, started over 47th Street toward Teak Warden's apartment. Teak and his wife had once been his most familiar friends—it was a household where he and Dolly Karger had been used to go in the days of their affair. But Teak had taken to drink, and his wife had remarked publicly that Anson was a bad influence on him. The remark reached Anson in an exaggerated form—when it was finally cleared up, the delicate spell of intimacy was broken, never to be renewed.

"Is Mr. Warden at home?" he inquired.

"They've gone to the country."

The fact unexpectedly cut at him. They were gone to the country and he hadn't known. Two years before he would have known the date, the hour, come up at the last moment for a final drink, and planned his first visit to them. Now they had gone without a word.

Anson looked at his watch and considered a week-end with his family, but the only train was a local that would jolt through the aggressive heat for three hours. And to-morrow in the country, and Sunday—he was in no mood for porch-bridge with polite undergraduates, and dancing after dinner at a rural roadhouse, a diminutive of gaiety which his father had estimated too well.

"Oh, no," he said to himself. . . . "No."

He was a dignified, impressive young man, rather stout now, but otherwise unmarked by dissipation. He could have been cast for a pillar of something—at times you were sure it was not society, at others nothing else—for the law, for the church. He stood for a few minutes motionless on the sidewalk in front of a 47th Street apartment-house; for almost the first time in his life he had nothing whatever to do.

Then he began to walk briskly up Fifth Avenue, as if he had just been reminded of an important engagement there. The necessity of dissimulation is one of the few characteristics that we share with dogs, and I think of Anson on that day as some well-bred specimen who had been disappointed at a familiar back door. He was going to see Nick, once a fashionable bartender in demand at all private dances, and now employed in cooling non-alcoholic champagne among the labyrinthine cellars of the Plaza Hotel.

"Nick," he said, "what's happened to everything?"

"Dead," Nick said.

"Make me a whiskey sour." Anson handed a pint bottle over the counter. "Nick, the girls are different; I had a little girl in Brooklyn and she got married last week without letting me know."

"That a fact? Ha-ha-ha," responded Nick diplomatically. "Slipped it over on you."

"Absolutely," said Anson. "And I was out with her the night before."

"Ha-ha-ha," said Nick, "ha-ha-ha!"

"Do you remember the wedding, Nick, in Hot Springs where I had the waiters and the musicians singing 'God save the King'?"

"Now where was that, Mr. Hunter?" Nick concentrated doubtfully. "Seems to me that was——"

"Next time they were back for more, and I began to wonder how much I'd paid them," continued Anson.

"—seems to me that was at Mr. Trenholm's wedding."

"Don't know him," said Anson decisively. He was offended that a strange name should intrude upon his reminiscences; Nick perceived this.

"Naw—aw—" he admitted, "I ought to know that. It was one of *your* crowd—Brakins. . . . Baker——"

"Bicker Baker," said Anson responsively. "They put me in a hearse after it was over and covered me up with flowers and drove me away."

"Ha-ha-ha," said Nick. "Ha-ha-ha."

Nick's simulation of the old family servant paled presently and Anson went up-stairs to the lobby. He looked around—his eyes met the glance of an unfamiliar clerk at the desk, then fell upon a flower from the morning's marriage hesitating in the mouth of a brass cuspidor. He went out and walked slowly toward the blood-red sun over Columbus Circle. Suddenly he turned around and, retracing his steps to the Plaza, immured himself in a telephone-booth.

Later he said that he tried to get me three times that afternoon, that he tried every one who might be in New York—men and girls he had not seen for years, an artist's model of his college days whose faded number was still in his address book—Central told him that even the exchange existed no longer. At length his quest roved into the country, and he held brief disappointing conversations with emphatic butlers and maids. So-and-so was out, riding, swimming, playing golf, sailed to Europe last week. Who shall I say phoned?

It was intolerable that he should pass the evening alone—the private reckonings which one plans for a moment of leisure lose every charm when the solitude is enforced. There were always women of a sort, but the ones he knew had temporarily vanished, and to pass a New York evening in the hired company of a stranger never occurred to him—he would have considered that that was something shameful and secret, the diversion of a travelling salesman in a strange town.

Anson paid the telephone bill—the girl tried unsuccessfully to joke with him about its size—and for the second time that afternoon started to leave the Plaza and go he knew not where. Near the revolving door the figure of a woman, obviously with child, stood sideways to the light—a sheer beige cape fluttered at her shoulders when the door turned and, each time, she looked impatiently toward it as if she were weary of waiting. At the first sight of her a strong nervous thrill of familiarity went over him, but not until he was within five feet of her did he realize that it was Paula.

"Why, Anson Hunter!"

His heart turned over.

"Why, Paula——"

"Why, this is wonderful. I can't believe it, *Anson!*"

She took both his hands, and he saw in the freedom of the gesture that the memory of him had lost poignancy to her. But not to him—he felt that old mood that she evoked in him stealing over his brain, that gentleness with which he had always met her optimism as if afraid to mar its surface.

"We're at Rye for the summer. Pete had to come East on business—you know of course I'm Mrs. Peter Hagerty now—so we brought the children and took a house. You've got to come out and see us."

"Can I?" he asked directly. "When?"

"When you like. Here's Pete." The revolving door functioned, giving up a fine tall man of thirty with a tanned face and a trim mustache. His immaculate fitness made a sharp contrast with Anson's increasing bulk, which was obvious under the faintly tight cut-away coat.

"You oughtn't to be standing," said Hagerty to his wife. "Let's sit down here." He indicated lobby chairs, but Paula hesitated.

"I've got to go right home," she said. "Anson, why don't you—why don't you come out and have dinner with us to-night? We're just getting settled, but if you can stand that——"

Hagerty confirmed the invitation cordially.

"Come out for the night."

Their car waited in front of the hotel, and Paula with a tired gesture sank back against silk cushions in the corner.

"There's so much I want to talk to you about," she said, "it seems hopeless."

"I want to hear about you."

"Well"—she smiled at Hagerty—"that would take a long time too. I have three children—by my first marriage. The oldest is five, then four, then three." She smiled again. "I didn't waste much time having them, did I?"

"Boys?"

"A boy and two girls. Then—oh, a lot of things happened, and I got a divorce in Paris a year ago and married Pete. That's all—except that I'm awfully happy."

In Rye they drove up to a large house near the Beach Club, from which there issued presently three dark, slim children who broke from an English governess and approached them with an esoteric cry. Abstractedly and with difficulty Paula took each one into her arms, a caress which they accepted stiffly, as they had evidently been told not to bump into Mummy. Even against their fresh faces Paula's skin showed scarcely any weariness—for all her physical languor she seemed younger than when he had last seen her at Palm Beach seven years ago.

At dinner she was preoccupied, and afterward, during the homage to the radio, she lay with closed eyes on the sofa, until Anson wondered if his presence at this time were not an intrusion. But at nine o'clock, when Hagerty rose and said pleasantly that he was going to leave them by themselves for a while, she began to talk slowly about herself and the past.

"My first baby," she said—"the one we call Darling, the biggest little girl—I wanted to die when I knew I was going to have her, because Lowell was like a stranger to me. It didn't seem as though she could be my own. I wrote you a letter and tore it up. Oh, you were *so* bad to me, Anson."

It was the dialogue again, rising and falling. Anson felt a sudden quickening of memory.

"Weren't you engaged once?" she asked—"a girl named Dolly something?"

"I wasn't ever engaged. I tried to be engaged, but I never loved anybody but you, Paula."

"Oh," she said. Then after a moment: "This baby is the first one I ever really wanted. You see, I'm in love now—at last."

He didn't answer, shocked at the treachery of her remembrance. She must have seen that the "at last" bruised him, for she continued:

"I was infatuated with you, Anson—you could make me do anything you liked. But we wouldn't have been happy. I'm not smart enough for you. I don't like things to be complicated like you do." She paused. "You'll never settle down," she said.

The phrase struck at him from behind—it was an accusation that of all accusations he had never merited.

"I could settle down if women were different," he said. "If I didn't understand so much about them, if women didn't spoil you for other women, if they had only a little pride. If I could go to sleep for a while and wake up into a home that was really mine—why, that's what I'm made for, Paula, that's what women have seen in me and liked in me. It's only that I can't get through the preliminaries any more."

Hagerty came in a little before eleven; after a whiskey Paula stood up and announced that she was going to bed. She went over and stood by her husband.

"Where did you go, dearest?" she demanded.

"I had a drink with Ed Saunders."

"I was worried. I thought maybe you'd run away."

She rested her head against his coat.

"He's sweet, isn't he, Anson?" she demanded.

"Absolutely," said Anson, laughing.

She raised her face to her husband.

"Well, I'm ready," she said. She turned to Anson: "Do you want to see our family gymnastic stunt?"

"Yes," he said in an interested voice.

"All right. Here we go!"

Hagerty picked her up easily in his arms.

"This is called the family acrobatic stunt," said Paula. "He carries me up-stairs. Isn't it sweet of him?"

"Yes," said Anson.

Hagerty bent his head slightly until his face touched Paula's.

"And I love him," she said. "I've just been telling you, haven't I, Anson?"

"Yes," he said.

"He's the dearest thing that ever lived in this world; aren't you, darling? . . . Well, good night. Here we go. Isn't he strong?"

"Yes," Anson said.

"You'll find a pair of Pete's pajamas laid out for you. Sweet dreams— see you at breakfast."

"Yes," Anson said.

· VIII ·

THE OLDER MEMBERS of the firm insisted that Anson should go abroad for the summer. He had scarcely had a vacation in seven years, they said. He was stale and needed a change. Anson resisted.

"If I go," he declared, "I won't come back any more."

"That's absurd, old man. You'll be back in three months with all this depression gone. Fit as ever."

"No." He shook his head stubbornly. "If I stop, I won't go back to work. If I stop, that means I've given up—I'm through."

"We'll take a chance on that. Stay six months if you like—we're not afraid you'll leave us. Why, you'd be miserable if you didn't work."

They arranged his passage for him. They liked Anson—every one liked Anson—and the change that had been coming over him cast a sort of pall over the office. The enthusiasm that had invariably signalled up business, the consideration toward his equals and his inferiors, the lift of his vital presence—within the past four months his intense nervousness had melted down these qualities into the fussy pessimism of a man of forty. On every transaction in which he was involved he acted as a drag and a strain.

"If I go I'll never come back," he said.

Three days before he sailed Paula Legendre Hagerty died in childbirth. I was with him a great deal then, for we were crossing together, but for the first time in our friendship he told me not a word of how he felt, nor did I see the slightest sign of emotion. His chief preoccupation was with the fact that he was thirty years old—he would turn the conversation to the point where he could remind you of it and then fall silent, as if he assumed that the statement would start a chain of thought sufficient to itself. Like his partners, I was amazed at the change in him, and I was glad when the *Paris* moved off into the wet space between the worlds, leaving his principality behind.

"How about a drink?" he suggested.

We walked into the bar with that defiant feeling that characterizes the day of departure and ordered four Martinis. After one cocktail a change came over him—he suddenly reached across and slapped my knee with the first joviality I had seen him exhibit for months.

"Did you see that girl in the red tam?" he demanded, "the one with the high color who had the two police dogs down to bid her good-by."

"She's pretty," I agreed.

"I looked her up in the purser's office and found out that she's alone. I'm going down to see the steward in a few minutes. We'll have dinner with her to-night."

After a while he left me, and within an hour he was walking up and down the deck with her, talking to her in his strong, clear voice. Her red tam was a bright spot of color against the steel-green sea, and from time to time she looked up with a flashing bob of her head, and smiled with amusement and interest, and anticipation. At dinner we had champagne, and were very joyous—afterward Anson ran the pool with infectious gusto, and several people who had seen me with him asked me his name. He and the girl were talking and laughing together on a lounge in the bar when I went to bed.

I saw less of him on the trip than I had hoped. He wanted to arrange a foursome, but there was no one available, so I saw him only at meals. Sometimes, though, he would have a cocktail in the bar, and he told me about the girl in the red tam, and his adventures with her, making them all bizarre and amusing, as he had a way of doing, and I was glad that he was himself again, or at least the self that I knew, and with which I felt at home. I don't think he was ever happy unless some one was in love with him, responding to him like filings to a magnet, helping him to explain himself, promising him something. What it was I do not know. Perhaps they promised that there would always be women in the world who would spend their brightest, freshest, rarest hours to nurse and protect that superiority he cherished in his heart.

JACOB'S LADDER

◆

"Jacob's Ladder" was published in the Saturday Evening Post *for 20 August 1927 and elicited editorial praise as well as a raise to $3,000. The story is closely connected with* Tender Is the Night, *for the Jacob/Jenny and Dick/ Rosemary relationships were both based on Fitzgerald's interest in Lois Moran, the young movie actress he met in 1927. Material from "Jacob's Ladder" was incorporated into* Tender.

◆

It was a particularly sordid and degraded murder trial, and Jacob Booth, writhing quietly on a spectators' bench, felt that he had childishly gobbled something without being hungry, simply because it was there. The newspapers had humanized the case, made a cheap, neat problem play out of an affair of the jungle, so passes that actually admitted one to the court room were hard to get. Such a pass had been tendered him the evening before.

Jacob looked around at the doors, where a hundred people, inhaling and exhaling with difficulty, generated excitement by their eagerness, their breathless escape from their own private lives. The day was hot and there was sweat upon the crowd—obvious sweat in large dewy beads that would shake off on Jacob if he fought his way through to the doors. Someone behind him guessed that the jury wouldn't be out half an hour.

With the inevitability of a compass needle, his head swung toward the prisoner's table and he stared once more at the murderess' huge blank face garnished with red button eyes. She was Mrs. Choynski, *née* Delehanty, and fate had ordained that she should one day seize a meat ax and divide her sailor lover. The puffy hands that had swung the weapon turned an ink bottle about endlessly; several times she glanced at the crowd with a nervous smile.

Jacob frowned and looked around quickly; he had found a pretty face and lost it again. The face had edged sideways into his consciousness when he was absorbed in a mental picture of Mrs. Choynski in action; now it was faded back into the anonymity of the crowd. It was the face of a dark saint with tender, luminous eyes and a skin pale and fair. Twice he searched the room, then he forgot and sat stiffly and uncomfortably, waiting.

The jury brought in a verdict of murder in the first degree; Mrs. Choynski squeaked, "Oh, my God!" The sentence was postponed until next day. With a slow rhythmic roll, the crowd pushed out into the August afternoon.

Jacob saw the face again, realizing why he hadn't seen it before. It belonged to a young girl beside the prisoner's table and it had been hidden by the full moon of Mrs. Choynski's head. Now the clear, luminous eyes were bright with tears, and an impatient young man with a squashed nose was trying to attract the attention of the shoulder.

"Oh, get out!" said the girl, shaking the hand off impatiently. "Le' me alone, will you? Le' me alone. Geeze!"

The man sighed profoundly and stepped back. The girl embraced the dazed Mrs. Choynski and another lingerer remarked to Jacob that they were sisters. Then Mrs. Choynski was taken off the scene—her expression absurdly implied an important appointment—and the girl sat down at the desk and began to powder her face. Jacob waited; so did the young man with the squashed nose. The sergeant came up brusquely and Jacob gave him five dollars.

"Geeze!" cried the girl to the young man. "Can't you le' me alone?" She stood up. Her presence, the obscure vibrations of her impatience, filled the court room. "Every day itsa same!"

Jacob moved nearer. The other man spoke to her rapidly:

"Miss Delehanty, we've been more than liberal with you and your sister and I'm only asking you to carry out your share of the contract. Our paper goes to press at——"

Miss Delehanty turned despairingly to Jacob. "Can you beat it?" she demanded. "Now he wants a pitcher of my sister when she was a baby, and it's got my mother in it too."

"We'll take your mother out."

"I want my mother though. It's the only one I got of her."

"I'll promise to give you the picture back tomorrow."

"Oh, I'm sicka the whole thing." Again she was speaking to Jacob, but without seeing him except as some element of the vague, omnipresent public. "It gives me a pain in the eye." She made a clicking sound in her teeth that comprised the essence of all human scorn.

"I have a car outside, Miss Delehanty," said Jacob suddenly. "Don't you want me to run you home?"

"All right," she answered indifferently.

The newspaper man assumed a previous acquaintance between them; he began to argue in a low voice as the three moved toward the door.

"Every day it's like this," said Miss Delehanty bitterly. "These newspaper guys!" Outside, Jacob signaled for his car and as it drove up, large, open and bright, and the chauffeur jumped out and opened the door, the reporter, on the verge of tears, saw the picture slipping away and launched into a peroration of pleading.

"Go jump in the river!" said Miss Delehanty, sitting in Jacob's car. "Go—jump—in—the—river!"

The extraordinary force of her advice was such that Jacob regretted the limitations of her vocabulary. Not only did it evoke an image of the unhappy journalist hurling himself into the Hudson but it convinced Jacob that it was the only fitting and adequate way of disposing of the man. Leaving him to face his watery destiny, the car moved off down the street.

"You dealt with him pretty well," Jacob said.

"Sure," she admitted. "I get sore after a while and then I can deal with anybody no matter who. How old would you think I was?"

"How old are you?"

"Sixteen."

She looked at him gravely, inviting him to wonder. Her face, the face of a saint, an intense little Madonna, was lifted fragilely out of the mortal dust of the afternoon. On the pure parting of her lips no breath hovered; he had never seen a texture pale and immaculate as her skin, lustrous and garish as her eyes. His own well-ordered person seemed for the first time in his life gross and well worn to him as he knelt suddenly at the heart of freshness.

"Where do you live?" he asked. The Bronx, perhaps Yonkers, Albany —Baffin's Bay. They could curve over the top of the world, drive on forever.

Then she spoke, and as the toad words vibrated with life in her voice, the moment passed: "Eas' Hun'erd thuyty-thuyd. Stayin' with a girl friend there."

They were waiting for a traffic light to change and she exchanged a haughty glance with a flushed man peering from a flanking taxi. The man took off his hat hilariously. "Somebody's stenog," he cried. "And oh, what a stenog!"

An arm and hand appeared in the taxi window and pulled him back into the darkness of the cab.

Miss Delehanty turned to Jacob, a frown, the shadow of a hair in breadth, appearing between her eyes. "A lot of 'em know me," she said. "We got a lot of publicity and pictures in the paper."

"I'm sorry it turned out badly."

She remembered the event of the afternoon, apparently for the first time in half an hour. "She had it comin' to her, mister. She never had a chance. But they'll never send no woman to the chair in New York State."

"No; that's sure."

"She'll get life." Surely it was not she who had spoken. The tranquillity
of her face made her words separate themselves from her as soon as they
were uttered and take on a corporate existence of their own.

"Did you use to live with her?"

"Me? Say, read the papers! I didn't even know she was my sister till they
come and told me. I hadn't seen her since I was a baby." She pointed
suddenly at one of the world's largest department stores. "There's where I
work. Back to the old pick and shovel day after tomorrow."

"It's going to be a hot night," said Jacob. "Why don't we ride out into
the country and have dinner?"

She looked at him. His eyes were polite and kind. "All right," she said.

Jacob was thirty-three. Once he had possessed a tenor voice with destiny
in it, but laryngitis had despoiled him of it in one feverish week ten years
before. In despair that concealed not a little relief, he bought a plantation
in Florida and spent five years turning it into a golf course. When the land
boom came in 1924 he sold his real estate for eight hundred thousand dollars.

Like so many Americans, he valued things rather than cared about them.
His apathy was neither fear of life nor was it an affectation; it was the racial
violence grown tired. It was a humorous apathy. With no need for money,
he had tried—tried hard—for a year and a half to marry one of the richest
women in America. If he had loved her, or pretended to, he could have had
her; but he had never been able to work himself up to more than the formal
lie.

In person, he was short, trim and handsome. Except when he was overcome by a desperate attack of apathy, he was unusually charming; he went
with a crowd of men who were sure that they were the best of New York
and had by far the best time. During a desperate attack of apathy he was
like a gruff white bird, ruffled and annoyed, and disliking mankind with all
his heart.

He liked mankind that night under the summer moonshine of the Borghese
Gardens. The moon was a radiant egg, smooth and bright as Jenny Delehanty's face across the table; a salt wind blew in over the big estates collecting
flower scents from their gardens and bearing them to the road-house lawn.
The waiters hopped here and there like pixies through the hot night, their
black backs disappearing into the gloom, their white shirt fronts gleaming
startlingly out of an unfamiliar patch of darkness.

They drank a bottle of champagne and he told Jenny Delehanty a story.
"You are the most beautiful thing I have ever seen," he said, "but as it
happens you are not my type and I have no designs on you at all. Nevertheless, you can't go back to that store. Tomorrow I'm going to arrange a

meeting between you and Billy Farrelly, who's directing a picture on Long Island. Whether he'll see how beautiful you are I don't know, because I've never introduced anybody to him before."

There was no shadow, no ripple of a change in her expression, but there was irony in her eyes. Things like that had been said to her before, but the movie director was never available next day. Or else she had been tactful enough not to remind men of what they had promised last night.

"Not only are you beautiful," continued Jacob, "but you are somehow on the grand scale. Everything you do—yes, like reaching for that glass, or pretending to be self-conscious, or pretending to despair of me—gets across. If somebody's smart enough to see it, you might be something of an actress."

"I like Norma Shearer the best. Do you?"

Driving homeward through the soft night, she put up her face quietly to be kissed. Holding her in the hollow of his arm, Jacob rubbed his cheek against her cheek's softness and then looked down at her for a long moment.

"Such a lovely child," he said gravely.

She smiled back at him; her hands played conventionally with the lapels of his coat. "I had a wonderful time," she whispered. "Geeze! I hope I never have to go to court again."

"I hope you don't."

"Aren't you going to kiss me good night?"

"This is Great Neck," he said, "that we're passing through. A lot of moving-picture stars live here."

"You're a card, handsome."

"Why?"

She shook her head from side to side and smiled. "You're a card."

She saw then that he was a type with which she was not acquainted. He was surprised, not flattered, that she thought him droll. She saw that whatever his eventual purpose he wanted nothing of her now. Jenny Delehanty learned quickly; she let herself become grave and sweet and quiet as the night, and as they rolled over Queensboro Bridge into the city she was half asleep against his shoulder.

· II ·

HE CALLED UP Billy Farrelly next day. "I want to see you," he said. "I found a girl I wish you'd take a look at."

"My gosh!" said Farrelly. "You're the third today."

"Not the third of this kind."

"All right. If she's white, she can have the lead in a picture I'm starting Friday."

"Joking aside, will you give her a test?"

"I'm not joking. She can have the lead, I tell you. I'm sick of these lousy actresses. I'm going out to the Coast next month. I'd rather be Constance Talmadge's water boy than own most of these young——" His voice was bitter with Irish disgust. "Sure, bring her over, Jake. I'll take a look at her."

Four days later, when Mrs. Choynski, accompanied by two deputy sheriffs, had gone to Auburn to pass the remainder of her life, Jacob drove Jenny over the bridge to Astoria, Long Island.

"You've got to have a new name," he said; "and remember you never had a sister."

"I thought of that," she answered. "I thought of a name too—Tootsie Defoe."

"That's rotten," he laughed; "just rotten."

"Well, you think of one if you're so smart."

"How about Jenny—Jenny—oh, anything—Jenny Prince?"

"All right, handsome."

Jenny Prince walked up the steps of the motion-picture studio, and Billy Farrelly, in a bitter Irish humor, in contempt for himself and his profession, engaged her for one of the three leads in his picture.

"They're all the same," he said to Jacob. "Shucks! Pick 'em up out of the gutter today and they want gold plates tomorrow. I'd rather be Constance Talmadge's water boy than own a harem full of them."

"Do you like this girl?"

"She's all right. She's got a good side face. But they're all the same."

Jacob bought Jenny Prince an evening dress for a hundred and eighty dollars and took her to the Lido that night. He was pleased with himself, and excited. They both laughed a lot and were happy.

"Can you believe you're in the movies?" he demanded.

"They'll probably kick me out tomorrow. It was too easy."

"No, it wasn't. It was very good—psychologically. Billy Farrelly was in just the one mood——"

"I liked him."

"He's fine," agreed Jacob. But he was reminded that already another man was helping to open doors for her success. "He's a wild Irishman, look out for him."

"I know. You can tell when a guy wants to make you."

"What?"

"I don't mean he wanted to make me, handsome. But he's got that look about him, if you know what I mean." She distorted her lovely face with a wise smile. "He likes 'em; you could tell that this afternoon."

They drank a bottle of charged and very alcoholic grape juice.

Presently the head waiter came over to their table.

"This is Miss Jenny Prince," said Jacob. "You'll see a lot of her, Lorenzo, because she's just signed a big contract with the pictures. Always treat her with the greatest possible respect."

When Lorenzo had withdrawn, Jenny said, "You got the nicest eyes I ever seen." It was her effort, the best she could do. Her face was serious and sad. "Honest," she repeated herself, "the nicest eyes I ever seen. Any girl would be glad to have eyes like yours."

He laughed, but he was touched. His hand covered her arm lightly. "Be good," he said. "Work hard and I'll be so proud of you—and we'll have some good times together."

"I always have a good time with you." Her eyes were full on his, in his, held there like hands. Her voice was clear and dry. "Honest, I'm not kidding about your eyes. You always think I'm kidding. I want to thank you for all you've done for me."

"I haven't done anything, you lunatic. I saw your face and I was—I was beholden to it—everybody ought to be beholden to it."

Entertainers appeared and her eyes wandered hungrily away from him.

She was so young—Jacob had never been so conscious of youth before. He had always considered himself on the young side until tonight.

Afterward, in the dark cave of the taxicab, fragrant with the perfume he had bought for her that day, Jenny came close to him, clung to him. He kissed her, without enjoying it. There was no shadow of passion in her eyes or on her mouth; there was a faint spray of champagne on her breath. She clung nearer, desperately. He took her hands and put them in her lap.

She leaned away from him resentfully.

"What's the matter? Don't you like me?"

"I shouldn't have let you have so much champagne."

"Why not? I've had a drink before. I was tight once."

"Well, you ought to be ashamed of yourself. And if I hear of your taking any more drinks, you'll hear from me."

"You sure have got your nerve, haven't you?"

"What do you do? Let all the corner soda jerkers maul you around whenever they want?"

"Oh, shut up!"

For a moment they rode in silence. Then her hand crept across to his. "I like you better than any guy I ever met, and I can't help that, can I?"

"Dear little Jenny." He put his arm around her again.

Hesitating tentatively, he kissed her and again he was chilled by the innocence of her kiss, the eyes that at the moment of contact looked beyond him out into the darkness of the night, the darkness of the world. She did not know yet that splendor was something in the heart; at the moment when she should realize that and melt into the passion of the universe he could take her without question or regret.

"I like you enormously," he said; "better than almost anyone I know. I mean that about drinking though. You mustn't drink."

"I'll do anything you want," she said; and she repeated, looking at him directly, "Anything."

The car drew up in front of her flat and he kissed her good night.

He rode away in a mood of exultation, living more deeply in her youth and future than he had lived in himself for years. Thus, leaning forward a little on his cane, rich, young and happy, he was borne along dark streets and light toward a future of his own which he could not foretell.

· III ·

A MONTH LATER, climbing into a taxicab with Farrelly one night, he gave the latter's address to the driver. "So you're in love with this baby," said Farrelly pleasantly. "Very well, I'll get out of your way."

Jacob experienced a vast displeasure. "I'm not in love with her," he said slowly. "Billy, I want you to leave her alone."

"Sure! I'll leave her alone," agreed Farrelly readily. "I didn't know you were interested—she told me she couldn't make you."

"The point is you're not interested either," said Jacob. "If I thought that you two really cared about each other, do you think I'd be fool enough to try to stand in the way? But you don't give a darn about her, and she's impressed and a little fascinated."

"Sure," agreed Farrelly, bored. "I wouldn't touch her for anything."

Jacob laughed. "Yes, you would. Just for something to do. That's what I object to—anything—anything casual happening to her."

"I see what you mean. I'll let her alone."

Jacob was forced to be content with that. He had no faith in Billy Farrelly, but he guessed that Farrelly liked him and wouldn't offend him unless stronger feelings were involved. But the holding hands under the table to-night had annoyed him. Jenny lied about it when he reproached her; she offered to let him take her home immediately, offered not to speak to Farrelly again all evening. Then he had seemed silly and pointless to himself. It would have been easier, when Farrelly said "So you're in love with this baby," to have been able to answer simply, "I am."

But he wasn't. He valued her now more than he had ever thought possible. He watched in her the awakening of a sharply individual temperament. She liked quiet and simple things. She was developing the capacity to discriminate and shut the trivial and the unessential out of her life. He tried giving her books; then wisely he gave up that and brought her into contact with a variety of men. He made situations and then explained them to her, and he was pleased, as appreciation and politeness began to blossom before his eyes. He valued, too, her utter trust in him and the fact that she used him as a standard for judgments on other men.

Before the Farrelly picture was released, she was offered a two-year contract on the strength of her work in it—four hundred a week for six months and an increase on a sliding scale. But she would have to go to the Coast.

"Wouldn't you rather have me wait?" she said, as they drove in from the country one afternoon. "Wouldn't you rather have me stay here in New York—near you?"

"You've got to go where your work takes you. You ought to be able to look out for yourself. You're seventeen."

Seventeen—she was as old as he; she was ageless. Her dark eyes under a yellow straw hat were as full of destiny as though she had not just offered to toss destiny away.

"I wonder if you hadn't come along, someone else would of," she said —"to make me do things, I mean."

"You'd have done them yourself. Get it out of your head that you're dependent on me."

"I am. Everything is, thanks to you."

"It isn't, though," he said emphatically, but he brought no reasons; he liked her to think that.

"I don't know what I'll do without you. You're my only friend"—and she added—"that I care about. You see? You understand what I mean?"

He laughed at her, enjoying the birth of her egotism implied in her right to be understood. She was lovelier that afternoon than he had ever seen her, delicate, resonant and, for him, undesirable. But sometimes he wondered if that sexlessness wasn't for him alone, wasn't a side that, perhaps purposely, she turned toward him. She was happiest of all with younger men, though she pretended to despise them. Billy Farrelly, obligingly and somewhat to her mild chagrin, had left her alone.

"When will you come out to Hollywood?"

"Soon," he promised. "And you'll be coming back to New York."

She began to cry. "Oh, I'll miss you so much! I'll miss you so much!" Large tears of distress ran down her warm ivory cheeks. "Oh, geeze!" she cried softly. "You been good to me! Where's your hand? Where's your hand? You been the best friend anybody ever had. Where am I ever going to find a friend like you?"

She was acting now, but a lump arose in his throat and for a moment a wild idea ran back and forth in his mind, like a blind man, knocking over its solid furniture—to marry her. He had only to make the suggestion, he knew, and she would become close to him and know no one else, because he would understand her forever.

Next day, in the station, she was pleased with her flowers, her compartment, with the prospect of a longer trip than she had ever taken before. When she kissed him good-by her deep eyes came close to his again and she pressed against him as if in protest against the separation. Again she cried, but he knew that behind her tears lay the happiness of adventure in new fields. As he walked out of the station, New York was curiously empty. Through her eyes he had seen old colors once more; now they had faded back into the gray tapestry of the past. The next day he went to an office high in a building on Park Avenue and talked to a famous specialist he had not visited for a decade.

"I want you to examine the larynx again," he said. "There's not much hope, but something might have changed the situation."

He swallowed a complicated system of mirrors. He breathed in and out, made high and low sounds, coughed at a word of command. The specialist fussed and touched. Then he sat back and took out his eyeglass. "There's no change," he said. "The cords are not diseased—they're simply worn out. It isn't anything that can be treated."

"I thought so," said Jacob, humbly, as if he had been guilty of an impertinence. "That's practically what you told me before. I wasn't sure how permanent it was."

He had lost something when he came out of the building on Park Avenue—a half hope, the love child of a wish, that some day——

"New York desolate," he wired her. "The night clubs all closed. Black wreaths on the Statue of Civic Virtue. Please work hard and be remarkably happy."

"Dear Jacob," she wired back, "miss you so. You are the nicest man that ever lived and I mean it, dear. Please don't forget me. Love from Jenny."

Winter came. The picture Jenny had made in the East was released, together with preliminary interviews and articles in the fan magazines. Jacob sat in his apartment, playing the Kreutzer Sonata over and over on his new phonograph, and read her meager and stilted but affectionate letters and the articles which said she was a discovery of Billy Farrelly's. In February he became engaged to an old friend, now a widow.

They went to Florida and were suddenly snarling at each other in hotel corridors and over bridge games, so they decided not to go through with it after all. In the spring he took a stateroom on the Paris, but three days before sailing he disposed of it and went to California.

· IV ·

JENNY MET HIM at the station, kissed him and clung to his arm in the car all the way to the Ambassador Hotel. "Well, the man came," she cried. "I never thought I'd get him to come. I never did."

Her accent betrayed an effort at control. The emphatic "Geeze!" with all the wonder, horror, disgust or admiration she could put in it was gone, but there was no mild substitute, no "swell" or "grand." If her mood required expletives outside her repertoire, she kept silent.

But at seventeen, months are years and Jacob perceived a change in her; in no sense was she a child any longer. There were fixed things in her mind—not distractions, for she was instinctively too polite for that, but simply things there. No longer was the studio a lark and a wonder and a divine accident; no longer "for a nickel I wouldn't turn up tomorrow." It was part of her life. Circumstances were stiffening into a career which went on independently of her casual hours.

"If this picture is as good as the other—I mean if I make a personal hit again, Hecksher'll break the contract. Everybody that's seen the rushes says it's the first one I've had sex appeal in."

"What are the rushes?"

"When they run off what they took the day before. They say it's the first time I've had sex appeal."

"I don't notice it," he teased her.

"You wouldn't. But I have."

"I know you have," he said, and, moved by an ill-considered impulse, he took her hand.

She glanced quickly at him. He smiled—half a second too late. Then she smiled and her glowing warmth veiled his mistake.

"Jake," she cried, "I could bawl, I'm so glad you're here! I got you a room at the Ambassador. They were full, but they kicked out somebody because I said I had to have a room. I'll send my car back for you in half an hour. It's good you came on Sunday, because I got all day free."

They had luncheon in the furnished apartment she had leased for the winter. It was 1920 Moorish, taken over complete from a favorite of yesterday. Someone had told her it was horrible, for she joked about it; but when he pursued the matter he found that she didn't know why.

"I wish they had more nice men out here," she said once during luncheon. "Of course there's a lot of nice ones, but I mean——Oh, you know, like in New York—men that know even more than a girl does, like you."

After luncheon he learned that they were going to tea. "Not today," he objected. "I want to see you alone."

"All right," she agreed doubtfully. "I suppose I could telephone. I thought——It's a lady that writes for a lot of newspapers and I've never been asked there before. Still, if you don't want to——"

Her face had fallen a little and Jacob assured her that he couldn't be more willing. Gradually he found that they were going not to one party but to three.

"In my position, it's sort of the thing to do," she explained. "Otherwise you don't see anybody except the people on your own lot, and that's narrow." He smiled. "Well, anyhow," she finished—"anyhow, you smart Aleck, that's what everybody does on Sunday afternoon."

At the first tea, Jacob noticed that there was an enormous preponderance of women over men, and of supernumeraries—lady journalists, cameramen's daughters, cutters' wives—over people of importance. A young Latin named Raffino appeared for a brief moment, spoke to Jenny and departed; several stars passed through, asking about children's health with a domesticity that was somewhat overpowering. Another group of celebrities posed immobile, statue-like, in a corner. There was a somewhat inebriated and very much excited author apparently trying to make engagements with one girl after another. As the afternoon waned, more people were suddenly a little tight; the communal voice was higher in pitch and greater in volume as Jacob and Jenny went out the door.

At the second tea, young Raffino—he was an actor, one of innumerable hopeful Valentinos—appeared again for a minute, talked to Jenny a little longer, a little more attentively this time, and went out. Jacob gathered that this party was not considered to have quite the swagger of the other. There was a bigger crowd around the cocktail table. There was more sitting down.

Jenny, he saw, drank only lemonade. He was surprised and pleased at her distinction and good manners. She talked to one person, never to everyone within hearing; then she listened, without finding it necessary to shift her eyes about. Deliberate or not on her part, he noticed that at both teas she was sooner or later talking to the guest of most consequence. Her seriousness, her air of saying "This is my opportunity of learning something," beckoned their egotism imperatively near.

When they left to drive to the last party, a buffet supper, it was dark and the electric legends of hopeful real-estate brokers were gleaming to some vague purpose on Beverly Hills. Outside Grauman's Theater a crowd was already gathered in the thin, warm rain.

"Look! Look!" she cried. It was the picture she had finished a month before.

They slid out of the thin Rialto of Hollywood Boulevard and into the deep gloom of a side street; he put his arm about her and kissed her.

"Dear Jake." She smiled up at him.

"Jenny, you're so lovely; I didn't know you were so lovely."

She looked straight ahead, her face mild and quiet. A wave of annoyance passed over him and he pulled her toward him urgently, just as the car stopped at a lighted door.

They went into a bungalow crowded with people and smoke. The impetus of the formality which had begun the afternoon was long exhausted; everything had become at once vague and strident.

"This is Hollywood," explained an alert talkative lady who had been in his vicinity all day. "No airs on Sunday afternoon." She indicated the hostess. "Just a plain, simple, sweet girl." She raised her voice: "Isn't that so, darling—just a plain, simple, sweet girl?"

The hostess said, "Yeah. Who is?" And Jacob's informant lowered her voice again: "But that little girl of yours is the wisest one of the lot."

The totality of the cocktails Jacob had swallowed was affecting him pleasantly, but try as he might, the plot of the party—the key on which he could find ease and tranquillity—eluded him. There was something tense in the air—something competitive and insecure. Conversations with the men had a way of becoming empty and overjovial or else melting off into a sort of suspicion. The women were nicer. At eleven o'clock, in the pantry, he suddenly realized that he hadn't seen Jenny for an hour. Returning to the living room, he saw her come in, evidently from outside, for she tossed a raincoat from her shoulders. She was with Raffino. When she came up, Jacob saw that she was out of breath and her eyes were very bright. Raffino smiled at Jacob pleasantly and negligently; a few moments later, as he turned to go, he bent and whispered in Jenny's ear and she looked at him without smiling as she said good night.

"I got to be on the lot at eight o'clock," she told Jacob presently. "I'll look like an old umbrella unless I go home. Do you mind, dear?"

"Heavens, no!"

Their car drove over one of the interminable distances of the thin, stretched city.

"Jenny," he said, "you've never looked like you were tonight. Put your head on my shoulder."

"I'd like to. I'm tired."

"I can't tell you how radiant you've got to be."

"I'm just the same."

"No, you're not." His voice suddenly became a whisper, trembling with emotion. "Jenny, I'm in love with you."

"Jacob, don't be silly."

"I'm in love with you. Isn't it strange, Jenny? It happened just like that."

"You're not in love with me."

"You mean the fact doesn't interest you." He was conscious of a faint twinge of fear.

She sat up out of the circle of his arm. "Of course it interests me; you know I care more about you than anything in the world."

"More than about Mr. Raffino?"

"Oh—my—gosh!" she protested scornfully. "Raffino's nothing but a baby."

"I love you, Jenny."

"No, you don't."

He tightened his arm. Was it his imagination or was there a small instinctive resistance in her body? But she came close to him and he kissed her.

"You know that's crazy about Raffino."

"I suppose I'm jealous." Feeling insistent and unattractive, he released her. But the twinge of fear had become an ache. Though he knew that she was tired and that she felt strange at this new mood in him, he was unable to let the matter alone. "I didn't realize how much a part of my life you were. I didn't know what it was I missed—but I know now. I wanted you near."

"Well, here I am."

He took her words as an invitation, but this time she relaxed wearily in his arms. He held her thus for the rest of the way, her eyes closed, her short hair falling straight back, like a girl drowned.

"The car'll take you to the hotel," she said when they reached the apartment. "Remember, you're having lunch with me at the studio tomorrow."

Suddenly they were in a discussion that was almost an argument, as to whether it was too late for him to come in. Neither could yet appreciate the change that his declaration had made in the other. Abruptly they had become like different people, as Jacob tried desperately to turn back the clock to that night in New York six months before, and Jenny watched this mood, which was more than jealousy and less than love, snow under, one

by one, the qualities of consideration and understanding which she knew
in him and with which she felt at home.

"But I don't love you like that," she cried. "How can you come to me
all at once and ask me to love you like that?"

"You love Raffino like that!"

"I swear I don't! I never even kissed him—not really!"

"H'm!" He was a gruff white bird now. He could scarcely credit his own
unpleasantness, but something illogical as love itself urged him on. "An
actor!"

"Oh, Jake," she cried, "please lemme go. I never felt so terrible and
mixed up in my life."

"I'll go," he said suddenly. "I don't know what's the matter, except that
I'm so mad about you that I don't know what I'm saying. I love you and
you don't love me. Once you did, or thought you did, but that's evidently
over."

"But I do love you." She thought for a moment; the red-and-green glow
of a filling station on the corner lit up the struggle in her face. "If you love
me that much, I'll marry you tomorrow."

"Marry me!" he exclaimed. She was so absorbed in what she had just said
that she did not notice.

"I'll marry you tomorrow," she repeated. "I like you better than anybody
in the world and I guess I'll get to love you the way you want me to." She
uttered a single half-broken sob. "But—I didn't know this was going to
happen. Please let me alone tonight."

Jacob didn't sleep. There was music from the Ambassador grill till late
and a fringe of working girls hung about the carriage entrance waiting for
their favorites to come out. Then a long-protracted quarrel between a man
and a woman began in the hall outside, moved into the next room and
continued as a low two-toned mumble through the intervening door. He
went to the window sometime toward three o'clock and stared out into the
clear splendor of the California night. Her beauty rested outside on the
grass, on the damp, gleaming roofs of the bungalows, all around him, borne
up like music on the night. It was in the room, on the white pillow, it
rustled ghostlike in the curtains. His desire recreated her until she lost all
vestiges of the old Jenny, even of the girl who had met him at the train that
morning. Silently, as the night hours went by, he molded her over into an
image of love—an image that would endure as long as love itself, or even
longer—not to perish till he could say, "I never really loved her." Slowly
he created it with this and that illusion from his youth, this and that sad
old yearning, until she stood before him identical with her old self only by
name.

Later, when he drifted off into a few hours' sleep, the image he had made stood near him, lingering in the room, joined in mystic marriage to his heart.

· V ·

"I won't marry you unless you love me," he said, driving back from the studio. She waited, her hands folded tranquilly in her lap. "Do you think I'd want you if you were unhappy and unresponsive, Jenny—knowing all the time you didn't love me?"

"I do love you. But not that way."

"What's 'that way'?"

She hesitated, her eyes were far off. "You don't—thrill me, Jake. I don't know—there have been some men that sort of thrilled me when they touched me, dancing or anything. I know it's crazy, but——"

"Does Raffino thrill you?"

"Sort of, but not so much."

"And I don't at all?"

"I just feel comfortable and happy with you."

He should have urged her that that was best, but he couldn't say it, whether it was an old truth or an old lie.

"Anyhow, I told you I'll marry you; perhaps you might thrill me later."

He laughed, stopped suddenly. "If I didn't thrill you, as you call it, why did you seem to care so much last summer?"

"I don't know. I guess I was young. You never know how you once felt, do you?"

She had become elusive to him, with that elusiveness that gives a hidden significance to the least significant remarks. And with the clumsy tools of jealousy and desire, he was trying to create the spell that is ethereal and delicate as the dust on a moth's wing.

"Listen, Jake," she said suddenly. "That lawyer my sister had—that Scharnhorst—called up the studio this afternoon."

"Your sister's all right," he said absently, and he added: "So a lot of men thrill you."

"Well, if I've felt it with a lot of men, it couldn't have anything to do with real love, could it?" she said hopefully.

"But your theory is that love couldn't come without it."

"I haven't got any theories or anything. I just told you how I felt. You know more than me."

"I don't know anything at all."

There was a man waiting in the lower hall of the apartment house. Jenny went up and spoke to him; then, turning back to Jake, said in a low voice: "It's Scharnhorst. Would you mind waiting downstairs while he talks to me? He says it won't take half an hour."

He waited, smoking innumerable cigarettes. Ten minutes passed. Then the telephone operator beckoned him.

"Quick!" she said. "Miss Prince wants you on the telephone."

Jenny's voice was tense and frightened. "Don't let Scharnhorst get out," she said. "He's on the stairs, maybe in the elevator. Make him come back here."

Jacob put down the receiver just as the elevator clicked. He stood in front of the elevator door, barring the man inside. "Mr. Scharnhorst?"

"Yeah." The face was keen and suspicious.

"Will you come up to Miss Prince's apartment again? There's something she forgot to say."

"I can see her later." He attempted to push past Jacob. Seizing him by the shoulders, Jacob shoved him back into the cage, slammed the door and pressed the button for the eighth floor.

"I'll have you arrested for this!" Scharnhorst remarked. "Put into jail for assault!"

Jacob held him firmly by the arms. Upstairs, Jenny, with panic in her eyes, was holding open her door. After a slight struggle, the lawyer went inside.

"What is it?" demanded Jacob.

"Tell him, you," she said. "Oh, Jake, he wants twenty thousand dollars!"

"What for?"

"To get my sister a new trial."

"But she hasn't a chance!" exclaimed Jacob. He turned to Scharnhorst. "You ought to know she hasn't a chance."

"There are some technicalities," said the lawyer uneasily—"things that nobody but an attorney would understand. She's very unhappy there, and her sister so rich and successful. Mrs. Choynski thought she ought to get another chance."

"You've been up there working on her, heh?"

"She sent for me."

"But the blackmail idea was your own. I suppose if Miss Prince doesn't feel like supplying twenty thousand to retain your firm, it'll come out that she's the sister of the notorious murderess."

Jenny nodded. "That's what he said."

"Just a minute!" Jacob walked to the phone. "Western Union, please. Western Union? Please take a telegram." He gave the name and address of a man high in the political world of New York. "Here's the message:

The convict Choynski threatening her sister, who is a picture actress, with exposure of relationship stop Can you arrange it with warden that she be cut off from visitors until I can get East and explain the situation stop Also wire me if two witnesses to an attempted blackmailing scene are enough to disbar a lawyer in New York if charges proceed from such a quarter as Read, Van Tyne, Biggs & Company, or my uncle the surrogate stop Answer Ambassador Hotel, Los Angeles.

> *Jacob C. K. Booth*"

He waited until the clerk had repeated the message. "Now, Mr. Scharnhorst," he said, "the pursuit of art should not be interrupted by such alarms and excursions. Miss Prince, as you see, is considerably upset. It will show in her work tomorrow and a million people will be just a little disappointed. So we won't ask her for any decisions. In fact you and I will leave Los Angeles on the same train tonight."

· V I ·

THE SUMMER passed. Jacob went about his useless life, sustained by the knowledge that Jenny was coming East in the fall. By fall there would have been many Raffinos, he supposed, and she would find that the thrill of their hands and eyes—and lips—was much the same. They were the equivalent, in a different world, of the affairs at a college house party, the undergraduates of a casual summer. And if it was still true that her feeling for him was less than romantic, then he would take her anyway, letting romance come after marriage as—so he had always heard—it had come to many wives before.

Her letters fascinated and baffled him. Through the ineptitude of expression he caught gleams of emotion—an ever-present gratitude, a longing to talk to him, and a quick, almost frightened reaction toward him, from—he could only imagine—some other man. In August she went on location; there were only post cards from some lost desert in Arizona, then for a while nothing at all. He was glad of the break. He had thought over all the things that might have repelled her—of his portentousness, his jealousy, his manifest misery. This time it would be different. He would keep control of the situation. She would at least admire him again, see in him the incomparably dignified and well adjusted life.

Two nights before her arrival Jacob went to see her latest picture in a huge nightbound vault on Broadway. It was a college story. She walked into it with her hair knotted on the crown of her head—a familiar symbol for dowdiness—inspired the hero to a feat of athletic success and faded out of it, always subsidiary to him, in the shadow of the cheering stands. But there was something new in her performance; for the first time the arresting quality he had noticed in her voice a year before had begun to get over on the screen. Every move she made, every gesture, was poignant and important. Others in the audience saw it too. He fancied he could tell this by some change in the quality of their breathing, by a reflection of her clear, precise expression in their casual and indifferent faces. Reviewers, too, were aware of it, though most of them were incapable of any precise definition of a personality.

But his first real consciousness of her public existence came from the attitude of her fellow passengers disembarking from the train. Busy as they were with friends or baggage, they found time to stare at her, to call their friends' attention, to repeat her name.

She was radiant. A communicative joy flowed from her and around her, as though her perfumer had managed to imprison ecstasy in a bottle. Once again there was a mystical transfusion, and blood began to course again through the hard veins of New York—there was the pleasure of Jacob's chauffeur when she remembered him, the respectful frisking of the bell boys at the Plaza, the nervous collapse of the head waiter at the restaurant where they dined. As for Jacob, he had control of himself now. He was gentle, considerate and polite, as it was natural for him to be—but as, in this case, he had found it necessary to plan. His manner promised and outlined an ability to take care of her, a will to be leaned on.

After dinner, their corner of the restaurant cleared gradually of the theater crowd and the sense of being alone settled over them. Their faces became grave, their voices very quiet.

"It's been five months since I saw you." He looked down at his hands thoughtfully. "Nothing has changed with me, Jenny. I love you with all my heart. I love your face and your faults and your mind and everything about you. The one thing I want in this world is to make you happy."

"I know," she whispered. "Gosh, I know!"

"Whether there's still only affection in your feeling toward me, I don't know. If you'll marry me, I think you'll find that the other things will come, will be there before you know it—and what you called a thrill will seem a joke to you, because life isn't for boys and girls, Jenny, but for men and women."

"Jacob," she whispered, "you don't have to tell me. I know."

He raised his eyes for the first time. "What do you mean—you know?"

"I get what you mean. Oh, this is terrible! Jacob, listen! I want to tell you. Listen, dear, don't say anything. Don't look at me. Listen, Jacob, I fell in love with a man."

"What?" he asked blankly.

"I fell in love with somebody. That's what I mean about understanding about a silly thrill."

"You mean you're in love with me?"

"No."

The appalling monosyllable floated between them, danced and vibrated over the table: "No—no—no—no—no!"

"Oh, this is awful!" she cried. "I fell in love with a man I met on location this summer. I didn't mean to—I tried not to, but first thing I knew there I was in love and all the wishing in the world couldn't help it. I wrote you and asked you to come, but I didn't send the letter, and there I was, crazy about this man and not daring to speak to him, and bawling myself to sleep every night."

"An actor?" he heard himself saying in a dead voice. "Raffino?"

"Oh, no, no, no! Wait a minute, let me tell you. It went on for three weeks and I honestly wanted to kill myself, Jake. Life wasn't worth while unless I could have him. And one night we got in a car by accident alone and he just caught me and made me tell him I loved him. He knew—he couldn't help knowing."

"It just—swept over you," said Jacob steadily. "I see."

"Oh, I knew you'd understand, Jake! You understand everything. You're the best person in the world, Jake, and don't I know it?"

"You're going to marry him?"

Slowly she nodded her head. "I said I'd have to come East first and see you." As her fear lessened, the extent of his grief became more apparent to her and her eyes filled with tears. "It only comes once, Jake, like that. That's what kept in my mind all those weeks I didn't hardly speak to him—if you lose it once, it'll never come like that again and then what do you want to live for? He was directing the picture—he was the same about me."

"I see."

As once before, her eyes held his like hands. "Oh, Ja-a-ake!" In that sudden croon of compassion, all-comprehending and deep as a song, the first force of the shock passed off. Jacob's teeth came together again and he struggled to conceal his misery. Mustering his features into an expression of irony, he called for the check. It seemed an hour later they were in a taxi going toward the Plaza Hotel.

She clung to him. "Oh, Jake, say it's all right! Say you understand! Darling Jake, my best friend, my only friend, say you understand!"

"Of course I do, Jenny." His hand patted her back automatically.

"Oh-h-h, Jake, you feel just awful, don't you?"

"I'll survive."

"Oh-h-h, Jake!"

They reached the hotel. Before they got out Jenny glanced at her face in her vanity mirror and turned up the collar of her fur cape. In the lobby, Jacob ran into several people and said, "Oh, I'm so sorry," in a strained, unconvincing voice. The elevator waited. Jenny, her face distraught and tearful, stepped in and held out her hand toward him with the fist clenched helplessly.

"Jake," she said once more.

"Good night, Jenny."

She turned her face to the wire wall of the cage. The gate clanged.

"Hold on!" he almost said. "Do you realize what you're doing, starting that car like that?"

He turned and went out the door blindly. "I've lost her," he whispered to himself, awed and frightened. "I've lost her!"

He walked over Fifty-ninth Street to Columbus Circle and then down Broadway. There were no cigarettes in his pocket—he had left them at the restaurant—so he went into a tobacco store. There was some confusion about the change and someone in the store laughed.

When he came out he stood for a moment puzzled. Then the heavy tide of realization swept over him and beyond him, leaving him stunned and exhausted. It swept back upon him and over him again. As one rereads a tragic story with the defiant hope that it will end differently, so he went back to the morning, to the beginning, to the previous year. But the tide came thundering back with the certainty that she was cut off from him forever in a high room at the Plaza Hotel.

He walked down Broadway. In great block letters over the porte-cochère of the Capitol Theater five words glittered out into the night: "Carl Barbour and Jenny Prince."

The name startled him, as if a passer-by had spoken it. He stopped and stared. Other eyes rose to that sign, people hurried by him and turned in. Jenny Prince.

Now that she no longer belonged to him, the name assumed a significance entirely its own.

It hung there, cool and impervious, in the night, a challenge, a defiance. Jenny Prince.

"Come and rest upon my loveliness," it said. "Fulfill your secret dreams in wedding me for an hour."

Jenny Prince.

It was untrue—she was back at the Plaza Hotel, in love with somebody. But the name, with its bright insistence, rode high upon the night.

"I love my dear public. They are all so sweet to me."

The wave appeared far off, sent up whitecaps, rolled toward him with the might of pain, washed over him. "Never any more. Never any more." The wave beat upon him, drove him down, pounding with hammers of agony on his ears. Proud and impervious, the name on high challenged the night.

Jenny Prince.

She was there! All of her, the best of her—the effort, the power, the triumph, the beauty.

Jacob moved forward with a group and bought a ticket at the window.

Confused, he stared around the great lobby. Then he saw an entrance and walking in, found himself a place in the fast-throbbing darkness.

A SHORT TRIP HOME

◆

"A Short Trip Home" appeared in the Saturday Evening Post *for 17 December 1927 and was collected in* Taps at Reveille *(1935). Fitzgerald described it as "the first real ghost story I ever wrote"—as distinguished from fantasy. The* Post *was troubled by the material; "but the story is so well done that we have not been able to resist it." This neglected story is one of Fitzgerald's most effective treatments of the theme of sexual corruption—here linking it with death.*

◆

I WAS NEAR HER, for I had lingered behind in order to get the short walk with her from the living room to the front door. That was a lot, for she had flowered suddenly and I, being a man and only a year older, hadn't flowered at all, had scarcely dared to come near her in the week we'd been home. Nor was I going to say anything in that walk of ten feet, or touch her; but I had a vague hope she'd do something, give a gay little performance of some sort, personal only in so far as we were alone together.

She had bewitchment suddenly in the twinkle of short hairs on her neck, in the sure, clear confidence that at about eighteen begins to deepen and sing in attractive American girls. The lamp light shopped in the yellow strands of her hair.

Already she was sliding into another world—the world of Joe Jelke and Jim Cathcart waiting for us now in the car. In another year she would pass beyond me forever.

As I waited, feeling the others outside in the snowy night, feeling the excitement of Christmas week and the excitement of Ellen here, blooming

Author's Note: In a moment of hasty misjudgment a whole paragraph of description was lifted out of this tale where it originated, and properly belongs, and applied to quite a different character in a novel of mine. I have ventured nonetheless to leave it here, even at the risk of seeming to serve warmed-over fare.

Editor's Note: Fitzgerald's note above refers to the paragraph on p. 374 beginning "Vaguely," which was used in Tender Is the Night (Book I, Chapter 21).

away, filling the room with "sex appeal"—a wretched phrase to express a quality that isn't like that at all—a maid came in from the dining room, spoke to Ellen quietly and handed her a note. Ellen read it and her eyes faded down, as when the current grows weak on rural circuits, and smouldered off into space. Then she gave me an odd look—in which I probably didn't show—and without a word, followed the maid into the dining room and beyond. I sat turning over the pages of a magazine for a quarter of an hour.

Joe Jelke came in, red-faced from the cold, his white silk muffler gleaming at the neck of his fur coat. He was a senior at New Haven, I was a sophomore. He was prominent, a member of Scroll and Keys, and, in my eyes, very distinguished and handsome.

"Isn't Ellen coming?"

"I don't know," I answered discreetly. "She was all ready."

"Ellen!" he called. "Ellen!"

He had left the front door open behind him and a great cloud of frosty air rolled in from outside. He went halfway up the stairs—he was a familiar in the house—and called again, till Mrs. Baker came to the banister and said that Ellen was below. Then the maid, a little excited, appeared in the dining-room door.

"Mr. Jelke," she called in a low voice.

Joe's face fell as he turned toward her, sensing bad news.

"Miss Ellen says for you to go on to the party. She'll come later."

"What's the matter?"

"She can't come now. She'll come later."

He hesitated, confused. It was the last big dance of vacation, and he was mad about Ellen. He had tried to give her a ring for Christmas, and failing that, got her to accept a gold mesh bag that must have cost two hundred dollars. He wasn't the only one—there were three or four in the same wild condition, and all in the ten days she'd been home—but his chance came first, for he was rich and gracious and at that moment the "desirable" boy of St. Paul. To me it seemed impossible that she could prefer another, but the rumor was she'd described Joe as much too perfect. I suppose he lacked mystery for her, and when a man is up against that with a young girl who isn't thinking of the practical side of marriage yet—well——.

"She's in the kitchen," Joe said angrily.

"No, she's not." The maid was defiant and a little scared.

"She is."

"She went out the back way, Mr. Jelke."

"I'm going to see."

I followed him. The Swedish servants washing dishes looked up sideways at our approach and an interested crashing of pans marked our passage through. The storm door, unbolted, was flapping in the wind and as we walked out into the snowy yard we saw the tail light of a car turn the corner at the end of the back alley.

"I'm going after her," Joe said slowly. "I don't understand this at all."

I was too awed by the calamity to argue. We hurried to his car and drove in a fruitless, despairing zigzag all over the residence section, peering into every machine on the streets. It was half an hour before the futility of the affair began to dawn upon him—St. Paul is a city of almost three hundred thousand people—and Jim Cathcart reminded him that we had another girl to stop for. Like a wounded animal he sank into a melancholy mass of fur in the corner, from which position he jerked upright every few minutes and waved himself backward and forward a little in protest and despair.

Jim's girl was ready and impatient, but after what had happened her impatience didn't seem important. She looked lovely though. That's one thing about Christmas vacation—the excitement of growth and change and adventure in foreign parts transforming the people you've known all your life. Joe Jelke was polite to her in a daze—he indulged in one burst of short, loud, harsh laughter by way of conversation—and we drove to the hotel.

The chauffeur approached it on the wrong side—the side on which the line of cars was not putting forth guests—and because of that we came suddenly upon Ellen Baker just getting out of a small coupé. Even before we came to a stop, Joe Jelke had jumped excitedly from the car.

Ellen turned toward us, a faintly distracted look—perhaps of surprise, but certainly not of alarm—in her face; in fact, she didn't seem very aware of us. Joe approached her with a stern, dignified, injured and, I thought, just exactly correct reproof in his expression. I followed.

Seated in the coupé—he had not dismounted to help Ellen out—was a hard thin-faced man of about thirty-five with an air of being scarred, and a slight sinister smile. His eyes were a sort of taunt to the whole human family—they were the eyes of an animal, sleepy and quiescent in the presence of another species. They were helpless yet brutal, unhopeful yet confident. It was as if they felt themselves powerless to originate activity, but infinitely capable of profiting by a single gesture of weakness in another.

Vaguely I placed him as one of the sort of men whom I had been conscious of from my earliest youth as "hanging around"—leaning with one elbow on the counters of tobacco stores, watching, through heaven knows what small chink of the mind, the people who hurried in and out. Intimate to garages, where he had vague business conducted in undertones, to barber shops and to the lobbies of theatres—in such places, anyhow, I placed the type, if type it was, that he reminded me of. Sometimes his face bobbed up in one of Tad's more savage cartoons, and I had always from earliest boyhood thrown a nervous glance toward the dim borderland where he stood, and seen him watching me and despising me. Once, in a dream, he had taken a few steps toward me, jerking his head back and muttering: "Say, kid" in what was intended to be a reassuring voice, and I had broken for the door in terror. This was that sort of man.

Joe and Ellen faced each other silently; she seemed, as I have said, to be in a daze. It was cold, but she didn't notice that her coat had blown open; Joe reached out and pulled it together, and automatically she clutched it with her hand.

Suddenly the man in the coupé, who had been watching them silently, laughed. It was a bare laugh, done with the breath—just a noisy jerk of the head—but it was an insult if I had ever heard one; definite and not to be passed over. I wasn't surprised when Joe, who was quick tempered, turned to him angrily and said:

"What's your trouble?"

The man waited a moment, his eyes shifting and yet staring, and always seeing. Then he laughed again in the same way. Ellen stirred uneasily.

"Who is this—this—" Joe's voice trembled with annoyance.

"Look out now," said the man slowly.

Joe turned to me.

"Eddie, take Ellen and Catherine in, will you?" he said quickly. . . . "Ellen, go with Eddie."

"Look out now," the man repeated.

Ellen made a little sound with her tongue and teeth, but she didn't resist when I took her arm and moved her toward the side door of the hotel. It struck me as odd that she should be so helpless, even to the point of acquiescing by her silence in this imminent trouble.

"Let it go, Joe!" I called back over my shoulder. "Come inside!"

Ellen, pulling against my arm, hurried us on. As we were caught up into the swinging doors I had the impression that the man was getting out of his coupé.

Ten minutes later, as I waited for the girls outside the women's dressing-room, Joe Jelke and Jim Cathcart stepped out of the elevator. Joe was very white, his eyes were heavy and glazed, there was a trickle of dark blood on his forehead and on his white muffler. Jim had both their hats in his hand.

"He hit Joe with brass knuckles," Jim said in a low voice. "Joe was out cold for a minute or so. I wish you'd send a bell boy for some witch-hazel and court-plaster."

It was late and the hall was deserted; brassy fragments of the dance below reached us as if heavy curtains were being blown aside and dropping back into place. When Ellen came out I took her directly downstairs. We avoided the receiving line and went into a dim room set with scraggly hotel palms where couples sometimes sat out during the dance; there I told her what had happened.

"It was Joe's own fault," she said, surprisingly. "I told him not to interfere."

This wasn't true. She had said nothing, only uttered one curious little click of impatience.

"You ran out the back door and disappeared for almost an hour," I protested. "Then you turned up with a hard-looking customer who laughed in Joe's face."

"A hard-looking customer," she repeated, as if tasting the sound of the words.

"Well, wasn't he? Where on earth did you get hold of him, Ellen?"

"On the train," she answered. Immediately she seemed to regret this admission. "You'd better stay out of things that aren't your business, Eddie. You see what happened to Joe."

Literally I gasped. To watch her, seated beside me, immaculately glowing, her body giving off wave after wave of freshness and delicacy—and to hear her talk like that.

"But that man's a thug!" I cried. "No girl could be safe with him. He used brass knuckles on Joe—brass knuckles!"

"Is that pretty bad?"

She asked this as she might have asked such a question a few years ago. She looked at me at last and really wanted an answer; for a moment it was as if she were trying to recapture an attitude that had almost departed; then she hardened again. I say "hardened," for I began to notice that when she was concerned with this man her eyelids fell a little, shutting other things —everything else—out of view.

That was a moment I might have said something, I suppose, but in spite of everything, I couldn't light into her. I was too much under the spell of her beauty and its success. I even began to find excuses for her—perhaps that man wasn't what he appeared to be; or perhaps—more romantically— she was involved with him against her will to shield some one else. At this point people began to drift into the room and come up to speak to us. We couldn't talk any more, so we went in and bowed to the chaperones. Then I gave her up to the bright restless sea of the dance, where she moved in an eddy of her own among the pleasant islands of colored favors set out on tables and the south winds from the brasses moaning across the hall. After a while I saw Joe Jelke sitting in a corner with a strip of court-plaster on his forehead watching Ellen as if she herself had struck him down, but I didn't go up to him. I felt queer myself—like I feel when I wake up after sleeping through an afternoon, strange and portentous, as if something had gone on in the interval that changed the values of everything and that I didn't see.

The night slipped on through successive phases of cardboard horns, amateur tableaux and flashlights for the morning papers. Then was the grand march and supper, and about two o'clock some of the committee dressed up as revenue agents pinched the party, and a facetious newspaper was distributed, burlesquing the events of the evening. And all the time out of the corner of my eye I watched the shining orchid on Ellen's shoulder as it moved like Stuart's plume about the room. I watched it with a definite foreboding until the last sleepy groups had crowded into the elevators, and then, bundled to the eyes in great shapeless fur coats, drifted out into the clear dry Minnesota night.

· II ·

THERE IS A sloping mid-section of our city which lies between the residence quarter on the hill and the business district on the level of the river. It is a vague part of town, broken by its climb into triangles and odd shapes— there are names like Seven Corners—and I don't believe a dozen people could draw an accurate map of it, though every one traversed it by trolley, auto or shoe leather twice a day. And though it was a busy section, it would be hard for me to name the business that comprised its activity. There were always long lines of trolley cars waiting to start somewhere; there was a big movie theatre and many small ones with posters of Hoot Gibson and Wonder Dogs and Wonder Horses outside; there were small stores with "Old King Brady" and "The Liberty Boys of '76" in the windows, and marbles, cigarettes and candy inside; and—one definite place at least—a fancy costumer whom we all visited at least once a year. Some time during boyhood I became aware that one side of a certain obscure street there were bawdy houses, and all through the district were pawnshops, cheap jewellers, small athletic clubs and gymnasiums and somewhat too blatantly run-down saloons.

The morning after the Cotillion Club party, I woke up late and lazy, with the happy feeling that for a day or two more there was no chapel, no classes—nothing to do but wait for another party tonight. It was crisp and bright—one of those days when you forget how cold it is until your cheek freezes—and the events of the evening before seemed dim and far away. After luncheon I started downtown on foot through a light, pleasant snow of small flakes that would probably fall all afternoon, and I was about half through that halfway section of town—so far as I know, there's no inclusive name for it—when suddenly whatever idle thought was in my head blew away like a hat and I began thinking hard of Ellen Baker. I began worrying about her as I'd never worried about anything outside myself before. I began to loiter, with an instinct to go up on the hill again and find her and talk to her; then I remembered that she was at a tea, and I went on again, but still thinking of her, and harder than ever. Right then the affair opened up again.

It was snowing, I said, and it was four o'clock on a December afternoon, when there is a promise of darkness in the air and the street lamps are just going on. I passed a combination pool parlor and restaurant, with a stove loaded with hot-dogs in the window, and a few loungers hanging around the door. The lights were on inside—not bright lights but just a few pale yellow high up on the ceiling—and the glow they threw out into the frosty dusk wasn't bright enough to tempt you to stare inside. As I went past, thinking hard of Ellen all this time, I took in the quartet of loafers out of the corner of my eye. I hadn't gone half a dozen steps down the street when one of them called to me, not by name but in a way clearly intended for my ear. I thought it was a tribute to my raccoon coat and paid no attention, but a moment later whoever it was called to me again in a peremptory voice. I was annoyed and turned around. There, standing in the group not ten feet away and looking at me with the half-sneer on his face with which he'd looked at Joe Jelke, was the scarred, thin-faced man of the night before.

He had on a black fancy-cut coat, buttoned up to his neck as if he were cold. His hands were deep in his pockets and he wore a derby and high button shoes. I was startled, and for a moment I hesitated, but I was most of all angry, and knowing that I was quicker with my hands than Joe Jelke, I took a tentative step back toward him. The other men weren't looking at me—I don't think they saw me at all—but I knew that this one recognized me; there was nothing casual about his look, no mistake.

"Here I am. What are you going to do about it?" his eyes seemed to say.

I took another step toward him and he laughed soundlessly, but with active contempt, and drew back into the group. I followed. I was going to speak to him—I wasn't sure what I was going to say—but when I came up he had either changed his mind and backed off, or else he wanted me to follow him inside, for he had slipped off and the three men watched my intent approach without curiosity. They were the same kind—sporty, but, unlike him, smooth rather than truculent; I didn't find any personal malice in their collective glance.

"Did he go inside?" I asked.

They looked at one another in that cagy way; a wink passed between them, and after a perceptible pause, one said:

"Who go inside?"

"I don't know his name."

There was another wink. Annoyed and determined, I walked past them and into the pool room. There were a few people at a lunch counter along one side and a few more playing billiards, but he was not among them.

Again I hesitated. If his idea was to lead me into any blind part of the establishment—there were some half-open doors farther back—I wanted more support. I went up to the man at the desk.

"What became of the fellow who just walked in here?"

Was he on his guard immediately, or was that my imagination?

"What fellow?"

"Thin face—derby hat."

"How long ago?"

"Oh—a minute."

He shook his head again. "Didn't see him," he said.

I waited. The three men from outside had come in and were lined up beside me at the counter. I felt that all of them were looking at me in a peculiar way. Feeling helpless and increasingly uneasy, I turned suddenly and went out. A little way down the street I turned again and took a good look at the place, so I'd know it and could find it again. On the next corner I broke impulsively into a run, found a taxicab in front of the hotel and drove back up the hill.

Ellen wasn't home. Mrs. Baker came downstairs and talked to me. She seemed entirely cheerful and proud of Ellen's beauty, and ignorant of anything being amiss or of anything unusual having taken place the night before. She was glad that vacation was almost over—it was a strain and Ellen wasn't very strong. Then she said something that relieved my mind enormously. She was glad that I had come in, for of course Ellen would want to see me, and the time was so short. She was going back at half-past eight tonight.

"Tonight!" I exclaimed. "I thought it was the day after tomorrow."

"She's going to visit the Brokaws in Chicago," Mrs. Baker said. "They want her for some party. We just decided it today. She's leaving with the Ingersoll girls tonight."

I was so glad I could barely restrain myself from shaking her hand. Ellen was safe. It had been nothing all along but a moment of the most casual adventure. I felt like an idiot, but I realized how much I cared about Ellen and how little I could endure anything terrible happening to her.

"She'll be in soon?"

"Any minute now. She just phoned from the University Club."

I said I'd be over later—I lived almost next door and I wanted to be alone. Outside I remembered I didn't have a key, so I started up the Bakers' driveway to take the old cut we used in childhood through the intervening yard. It was still snowing, but the flakes were bigger now against the darkness, and trying to locate the buried walk I noticed that the Bakers' back door was ajar.

I scarcely know why I turned and walked into that kitchen. There was a time when I would have known the Bakers' servants by name. That wasn't true now, but they knew me, and I was aware of a sudden suspension as I came in—not only a suspension of talk but of some mood or expectation that had filled them. They began to go to work too quickly; they made unnecessary movements and clamor—those three. The parlor maid looked at me in a frightened way and I suddenly guessed she was waiting to deliver another message. I beckoned her into the pantry.

"I know all about this," I said. "It's a very serious business. Shall I go to Mrs. Baker now, or will you shut and lock that back door?"

"Don't tell Mrs. Baker, Mr. Stinson!"

"Then I don't want Miss Ellen disturbed. If she is—and if she is I'll know of it—" I delivered some outrageous threat about going to all the employment agencies and seeing she never got another job in the city. She was thoroughly intimidated when I went out; it wasn't a minute before the back door was locked and bolted behind me.

Simultaneously I heard a big car drive up in front, chains crunching on the soft snow; it was bringing Ellen home, and I went in to say good-by.

Joe Jelke and two other boys were along, and none of the three could manage to take their eyes off her, even to say hello to me. She had one of those exquisite rose skins frequent in our part of the country, and beautiful until the little veins begin to break at about forty; now, flushed with the cold, it was a riot of lovely delicate pinks like many carnations. She and Joe had reached some sort of reconciliation, or at least he was too far gone in love to remember last night; but I saw that though she laughed a lot she wasn't really paying any attention to him or any of them. She wanted them to go, so that there'd be a message from the kitchen, but I knew that the message wasn't coming—that she was safe. There was talk of the Pump and Slipper dance at New Haven and of the Princeton Prom, and then, in various moods, we four left and separated quickly outside. I walked home with a certain depression of spirit and lay for an hour in a hot bath thinking that vacation was all over for me now that she was gone; feeling, even more deeply than I had yesterday, that she was out of my life.

And something eluded me, some one more thing to do, something that

I had lost amid the events of the afternoon, promising myself to go back and pick it up, only to find that it had escaped me. I associated it vaguely with Mrs. Baker, and now I seemed to recall that it had poked up its head somewhere in the stream of conversation with her. In my relief about Ellen I had forgotten to ask her a question regarding something she had said.

The Brokaws—that was it—where Ellen was to visit. I knew Bill Brokaw well; he was in my class at Yale. Then I remembered and sat bolt upright in the tub—the Brokaws weren't in Chicago this Christmas; they were at Palm Beach!

Dripping I sprang out of the tub, threw an insufficient union suit around my shoulders and sprang for the phone in my room. I got the connection quick, but Miss Ellen had already started for the train.

Luckily our car was in, and while I squirmed, still damp, into my clothes, the chauffeur brought it around to the door. The night was cold and dry, and we made good time to the station through the hard, crusty snow. I felt queer and insecure starting out this way, but somehow more confident as the station loomed up bright and new against the dark, cold air. For fifty years my family had owned the land on which it was built and that made my temerity seem all right somehow. There was always a possibility that I was rushing in where angels feared to tread, but that sense of having a solid foothold in the past made me willing to make a fool of myself. This business was all wrong—terribly wrong. Any idea I had entertained that it was harmless dropped away now; between Ellen and some vague overwhelming catastrophe there stood me, or else the police and a scandal. I'm no moralist—there was another element here, dark and frightening, and I didn't want Ellen to go through it alone.

There are three competing trains from St. Paul to Chicago that all leave within a few minutes of half-past eight. Hers was the Burlington, and as I ran across the station I saw the grating being pulled over and the light above it go out. I knew, though, that she had a drawing-room with the Ingersoll girls, because her mother had mentioned buying the ticket, so she was, literally speaking, tucked in until tomorrow.

The C., M. & St. P. gate was down at the other end and I raced for it and made it. I had forgotten one thing, though, and that was enough to keep me awake and worried half the night. This train got into Chicago ten minutes after the other. Ellen had that much time to disappear into one of the largest cities in the world.

I gave the porter a wire to my family to send from Milwaukee, and at eight o'clock next morning I pushed violently by a whole line of passengers, clamoring over their bags parked in the vestibule, and shot out of the door with a sort of scramble over the porter's back. For a moment the confusion of a great station, the voluminous sounds and echoes and cross-currents of bells and smoke struck me helpless. Then I dashed for the exit and toward the only chance I knew of finding her.

I had guessed right. She was standing at the telegraph counter, sending off heaven knows what black lie to her mother, and her expression when she saw me had a sort of terror mixed up with its surprise. There was cunning in it too. She was thinking quickly—she would have liked to walk away from me as if I weren't there, and go about her own business, but she couldn't. I was too matter-of-fact a thing in her life. So we stood silently watching each other and each thinking hard.

"The Brokaws are in Florida," I said after a minute.

"It was nice of you to take such a long trip to tell me that."

"Since you've found it out, don't you think you'd better go on to school?"

"Please let me alone, Eddie," she said.

"I'll go as far as New York with you. I've decided to go back early myself."

"You'd better let me alone." Her lovely eyes narrowed and her face took on a look of dumb-animal-like resistance. She made a visible effort, the cunning flickered back into it, then both were gone, and in their stead was a cheerful reassuring smile that all but convinced me.

"Eddie, you silly child, don't you think I'm old enough to take care of myself?" I didn't answer. "I'm going to meet a man, you understand. I just want to see him today. I've got my ticket East on the five o'clock train. If you don't believe it, here it is in my bag."

"I believe you."

"The man isn't anybody that you know and—frankly, I think you're being awfully fresh and impossible."

"I know who the man is."

Again she lost control of her face. That terrible expression came back into it and she spoke with almost a snarl:

"You'd better let me alone."

I took the blank out of her hand and wrote out an explanatory telegram to her mother. Then I turned to Ellen and said a little roughly:

"We'll take the five o'clock train East together. Meanwhile you're going to spend the day with me."

The mere sound of my own voice saying this so emphatically encouraged me, and I think it impressed her too; at any rate, she submitted—at least temporarily—and came along without protest while I bought my ticket.

When I start to piece together the fragments of that day a sort of confusion begins, as if my memory didn't want to yield up any of it, or my consciousness let any of it pass through. There was a bright, fierce morning during which we rode about in a taxicab and went to a department store where Ellen said she wanted to buy something and then tried to slip away from me by a back way. I had the feeling, for an hour, that someone was following us along Lake Shore Drive in a taxicab, and I would try to catch them by turning quickly or looking suddenly into the chauffeur's mirror; but I could find no one, and when I turned back I could see that Ellen's face was contorted with mirthless, unnatural laughter.

All morning there was a raw, bleak wind off the lake, but when we went to the Blackstone for lunch a light snow came down past the windows and we talked almost naturally about our friends, and about casual things. Suddenly her tone changed; she grew serious and looked me in the eye, straight and sincere.

"Eddie, you're the oldest friend I have," she said, "and you oughtn't to find it too hard to trust me. If I promise you faithfully on my word of honor to catch that five o'clock train, will you let me alone a few hours this afternoon?"

"Why?"

"Well"—she hesitated and hung her head a little—"I guess everybody has a right to say—good-by."

"You want to say good-by to that——"

"Yes, yes," she said hastily; "just a few hours, Eddie, and I promise faithfully that I'll be on that train."

"Well, I suppose no great harm could be done in two hours. If you really want to say good-by——"

I looked up suddenly, and surprised a look of such tense cunning in her face that I winced before it. Her lip was curled up and her eyes were slits again; there wasn't the faintest touch of fairness and sincerity in her whole face.

We argued. The argument was vague on her part and somewhat hard and reticent on mine. I wasn't going to be cajoled again into any weakness or be infected with any—and there was a contagion of evil in the air. She kept trying to imply, without any convincing evidence to bring forward, that everything was all right. Yet she was too full of the thing itself— whatever it was—to build up a real story, and she wanted to catch at any credulous and acquiescent train of thought that might start in my head, and work that for all it was worth. After every reassuring suggestion she threw out, she stared at me eagerly, as if she hoped I'd launch into a comfortable moral lecture with the customary sweet at the end—which in this case would be her liberty. But I was wearing her away a little. Two or three times it needed just a touch of pressure to bring her to the point of tears— which, of course, was what I wanted—but I couldn't seem to manage it.

Almost I had her—almost possessed her interior attention—then she would slip away.

I bullied her remorselessly into a taxi about four o'clock and started for the station. The wind was raw again, with a sting of snow in it, and the people in the streets, waiting for busses and street cars too small to take them all in, looked cold and disturbed and unhappy. I tried to think how lucky we were to be comfortably off and taken care of, but all the warm, respectable world I had been part of yesterday had dropped away from me. There was something we carried with us now that was the enemy and the opposite of all that; it was in the cabs beside us, the streets we passed through. With a touch of panic, I wondered if I wasn't slipping almost imperceptibly into Ellen's attitude of mind. The column of passengers waiting to go aboard the train were as remote from me as people from another world, but it was I that was drifting away and leaving them behind.

My lower was in the same car with her compartment. It was an old-fashioned car, its lights somewhat dim, its carpets and upholstery full of the dust of another generation. There were half a dozen other travellers, but they made no special impression on me, except that they shared the unreality that I was beginning to feel everywhere around me. We went into Ellen's compartment, shut the door and sat down.

Suddenly I put my arms around her and drew her over to me, just as tenderly as I knew how—as if she were a little girl—as she was. She resisted a little, but after a moment she submitted and lay tense and rigid in my arms.

"Ellen," I said helplessly, "you asked me to trust you. You have much more reason to trust me. Wouldn't it help to get rid of all this, if you told me a little?"

"I can't," she said, very low—"I mean, there's nothing to tell."

"You met this man on the train coming home and you fell in love with him, isn't that true?"

"I don't know."

"Tell me, Ellen. You fell in love with him?"

"I don't know. Please let me alone."

"Call it anything you want," I went on, "he has some sort of hold over you. He's trying to use you; he's trying to get something from you. He's not in love with you."

"What does that matter?" she said in a weak voice.

"It does matter. Instead of trying to fight this—this thing—you're trying to fight me. And I love you, Ellen. Do you hear? I'm telling you all of a sudden, but it isn't new with me. I love you."

She looked at me with a sneer on her gentle face; it was an expression I had seen on men who were tight and didn't want to be taken home. But it was human. I was reaching her, faintly and from far away, but more than before.

"Ellen, I want you to answer me one question. Is he going to be on this train?"

She hesitated; then, an instant too late, she shook her head.

"Be careful, Ellen. Now I'm going to ask you one thing more, and I wish you'd try very hard to answer. Coming West, when did this man get on the train?"

"I don't know," she said with an effort.

Just at that moment I became aware, with the unquestionable knowledge reserved for facts, that he was just outside the door. She knew it, too; the blood left her face and that expression of low-animal perspicacity came creeping back. I lowered my face into my hands and tried to think.

We must have sat there, with scarcely a word, for well over an hour. I was conscious that the lights of Chicago, then of Englewood and of endless suburbs, were moving by, and then there were no more lights and we were out on the dark flatness of Illinois. The train seemed to draw in upon itself; it took on an air of being alone. The porter knocked at the door and asked if he could make up the berth, but I said no and he went away.

After a while I convinced myself that the struggle inevitably coming wasn't beyond what remained of my sanity, my faith in the essential all-rightness of things and people. That this person's purpose was what we call "criminal," I took for granted, but there was no need of ascribing to him an intelligence that belonged to a higher plane of human, or inhuman, endeavor. It was still as a man that I considered him, and tried to get at his essence, his self-interest—what took the place in him of a comprehensible heart—but I suppose I more than half knew what I would find when I opened the door.

When I stood up Ellen didn't seem to see me at all. She was hunched into the corner staring straight ahead with a sort of film over her eyes, as if she were in a state of suspended animation of body and mind. I lifted her and put two pillows under her head and threw my fur coat over her knees. Then I knelt beside her and kissed her two hands, opened the door and went out into the hall.

I closed the door behind me and stood with my back against it for a minute. The car was dark save for the corridor lights at each end. There was no sound except the groaning of the couplers, the even click-a-click of the rails and someone's loud sleeping breath farther down the car. I became aware after a moment that the figure of a man was standing by the water cooler just outside the men's smoking room, his derby hat on his head, his coat collar turned up around his neck as if he were cold, his hands in his coat pockets. When I saw him, he turned and went into the smoking room, and I followed. He was sitting in the far corner of the long leather bench; I took the single armchair beside the door.

As I went in I nodded to him and he acknowledged my presence with one of those terrible soundless laughs of his. But this time it was prolonged, it seemed to go on forever, and mostly to cut it short, I asked: "Where are you from?" in a voice I tried to make casual.

He stopped laughing and looked at me narrowly, wondering what my game was. When he decided to answer, his voice was muffled as though he were speaking through a silk scarf, and it seemed to come from a long way off.

"I'm from St. Paul, Jack."

"Been making a trip home?"

He nodded. Then he took a long breath and spoke in a hard, menacing voice:

"You better get off at Fort Wayne, Jack."

He was dead. He was dead as hell—he had been dead all along, but what force had flowed through him, like blood in his veins, out to St. Paul and back, was leaving him now. A new outline—the outline of him dead—was coming through the palpable figure that had knocked down Joe Jelke.

He spoke again, with a sort of jerking effort:

"You get off at Fort Wayne, Jack, or I'm going to wipe you out." He moved his hand in his coat pocket and showed me the outline of a revolver.

I shook my head. "You can't touch me," I answered. "You see, I know." His terrible eyes shifted over me quickly, trying to determine whether or not I did know. Then he gave a snarl and made as though he were going to jump to his feet.

"You climb off here or else I'm going to get you, Jack!" he cried hoarsely. The train was slowing up for Fort Wayne and his voice rang loud in the comparative quiet, but he didn't move from his chair—he was too weak, I think—and we sat staring at each other while workmen passed up and down outside the window banging the brakes and wheels, and the engine gave out loud mournful pants up ahead. No one got into our car. After a while the porter closed the vestibule door and passed back along the corridor, and we slid out of the murky yellow station light and into the long darkness.

What I remember next must have extended over a space of five or six hours, though it comes back to me as something without any existence in time—something that might have taken five minutes or a year. There began a slow, calculated assault on me, wordless and terrible. I felt what I can only call a strangeness stealing over me—akin to the strangeness I had felt all afternoon, but deeper and more intensified. It was like nothing so much as the sensation of drifting away, and I gripped the arms of the chair convulsively, as if to hang onto a piece in the living world. Sometimes I felt myself going out with a rush. There would be almost a warm relief about it, a sense of not caring; then, with a violent wrench of the will, I'd pull myself back into the room.

Suddenly I realized that from a while back I had stopped hating him, stopped feeling violently alien to him, and with the realization, I went cold and sweat broke out all over my head. He was getting around my abhorrence, as he had got around Ellen coming West on the train; and it was just that strength he drew from preying on people that had brought him up to the point of concrete violence in St. Paul, and that, fading and flickering out, still kept him fighting now.

He must have seen that faltering in my heart, for he spoke at once, in a low, even, almost gentle voice: "You better go now."

"Oh, I'm not going," I forced myself to say.

"Suit yourself, Jack."

He was my friend, he implied. He knew how it was with me and he wanted to help. He pitied me. I'd better go away before it was too late. The rhythm of his attack was soothing as a song: I'd better go away—*and let him get at Ellen.* With a little cry I sat bolt upright.

"What do you want of this girl?" I said, my voice shaking. "To make a sort of walking hell of her."

His glance held a quality of dumb surprise, as if I were punishing an animal for a fault of which he was not conscious. For an instant I faltered; then I went on blindly:

"You've lost her; she's put her trust in me."

His countenance went suddenly black with evil, and he cried: "You're a liar!" in a voice that was like cold hands.

"She trusts me," I said. "You can't touch her. She's safe!"

He controlled himself. His face grew bland, and I felt that curious weakness and indifference begin again inside me. What was the use of all this? What was the use?

"You haven't got much time left," I forced myself to say, and then, in a flash of intuition, I jumped at the truth. "You died, or you were killed, not far from here!"—Then I saw what I had not seen before—that his forehead was drilled with a small round hole like a larger picture nail leaves when it's pulled from a plaster wall. "And now you're sinking. You've only got a few hours. The trip home is over!"

His face contorted, lost all semblance of humanity, living or dead. Simultaneously the room was full of cold air and with a noise that was something between a paroxysm of coughing and a burst of horrible laughter, he was on his feet, reeking of shame and blasphemy.

"Come and look!" he cried. "I'll show you——"

He took a step toward me, then another and it was exactly as if a door stood open behind him, a door yawning out to an inconceivable abyss of darkness and corruption. There was a scream of mortal agony, from him or from somewhere behind, and abruptly the strength went out of him in a long husky sigh and he wilted to the floor. . . .

How long I sat there, dazed with terror and exhaustion, I don't know. The next thing I remember is the sleepy porter shining shoes across the room from me, and outside the window the steel fires of Pittsburgh breaking the flat perspective also—something too faint for a man, too heavy for a shadow, of the night. There was something extended on the bench. Even as I perceived it it faded off and away.

Some minutes later I opened the door of Ellen's compartment. She was asleep where I had left her. Her lovely cheeks were white and wan, but she lay naturally—her hands relaxed and her breathing regular and clear. What had possessed her had gone out of her, leaving her exhausted but her own dear self again.

I made her a little more comfortable, tucked a blanket around her, extinguished the light and went out.

· I I I ·

WHEN I CAME home for Easter vacation, almost my first act was to go down to the billiard parlor near Seven Corners. The man at the cash register quite naturally didn't remember my hurried visit of three months before.

"I'm trying to locate a certain party who, I think, came here a lot some time ago."

I described the man rather accurately, and when I had finished, the cashier called to a little jockeylike fellow who was sitting near with an air of having something very important to do that he couldn't quite remember.

"Hey, Shorty, talk to this guy, will you? I think he's looking for Joe Varland."

The little man gave me a tribal look of suspicion. I went and sat near him.

"Joe Varland's dead, fella," he said grudgingly. "He died last winter."

I described him again—his overcoat, his laugh, the habitual expression of his eyes.

"That's Joe Varland you're looking for all right, but he's dead."

"I want to find out something about him."

"What you want to find out?"

"What did he do, for instance?"

"How should I know?"

"Look here! I'm not a policeman. I just want some kind of information about his habits. He's dead now and it can't hurt him. And it won't go beyond me."

"Well"—he hesitated, looking me over—"he was a great one for travelling. He got in a row in the station in Pittsburgh and a dick got him."

I nodded. Broken pieces of the puzzle began to assemble in my head.

"Why was he a lot on trains?"

"How should I know, fella?"

"If you can use ten dollars, I'd like to know anything you may have heard on the subject."

"Well," said Shorty reluctantly, "all I know is they used to say he worked the trains."

"Worked the trains?"

"He had some racket of his own he'd never loosen up about. He used to work the girls travelling alone on the trains. Nobody ever knew much about it—he was a pretty smooth guy—but sometimes he'd turn up here with a lot of dough and he let 'em know it was the janes he got it off of."

I thanked him and gave him the ten dollars and went out, very thoughtful, without mentioning that part of Joe Varland had made a last trip home.

Ellen wasn't West for Easter, and even if she had been I wouldn't have gone to her with the information, either—at least I've seen her almost every day this summer and we've managed to talk about everything else. Sometimes, though, she gets silent about nothing and wants to be very close to me, and I know what's in her mind.

Of course she's coming out this fall, and I have two more years at New Haven; still, things don't look so impossible as they did a few months ago. She belongs to me in a way—even if I lose her she belongs to me. Who knows? Anyhow, I'll always be there.

THE BOWL

◆

"The Bowl" (Saturday Evening Post, 21 January 1928) started as a "two-part sophisticated football story," which Fitzgerald tried to complete in time for publication during the 1927 football season. This story was difficult to write, and he interrupted it for "A Short Trip Home." When Post fiction editor Thomas Costain read "The Bowl" he told Harold Ober that Fitzgerald had "got the real spirit of the game as it has perhaps never been done before." Although Fitzgerald felt lifelong disappointment at his inability to play football for Princeton, "The Bowl" is his only commercially published football story, except for parts of the Basil series.

◆

THERE WAS A MAN in my class at Princeton who never went to football games. He spent his Saturday afternoons delving for minutiae about Greek athletics and the somewhat fixed battles between Christians and wild beasts under the Antonines. Lately—several years out of college—he has discovered football players and is making etchings of them in the manner of the late George Bellows. But he was once unresponsive to the very spectacle at his door, and I suspect the originality of his judgments on what is beautiful, what is remarkable and what is fun.

I reveled in football, as audience, amateur statistician and foiled participant—for I had played in prep school, and once there was a headline in the school newspaper: "Deering and Mullins Star Against Taft in Stiff Game Saturday." When I came in to lunch after the battle the school stood up and clapped and the visiting coach shook hands with me and prophesied—incorrectly—that I was going to be heard from. The episode is laid away in the most pleasant lavender of my past. That year I grew very tall and thin, and when at Princeton the following fall I looked anxiously over the freshman candidates and saw the polite disregard with which they looked back at me, I realized that that particular dream was over. Keene said he might make me into a very fair pole vaulter—and he did—but it was a poor substitute; and my terrible disappointment that I wasn't going to be a great football player was probably the foundation of my friendship with Dolly Harlan. I want to begin this story about Dolly with a little rehashing of the Yale game up at New Haven, sophomore year.

Dolly was started at halfback; this was his first big game. I roomed with him and I had scented something peculiar about his state of mind, so I didn't let him out of the corner of my eye during the whole first half. With field glasses I could see the expression on his face; it was strained and incredulous, as it had been the day of his father's death, and it remained so, long after any nervousness had had time to wear off. I thought he was sick and wondered why Keene didn't see and take him out; it wasn't until later that I learned what was the matter.

It was the Yale Bowl. The size of it or the enclosed shape of it or the height of the sides had begun to get on Dolly's nerves when the team practiced there the day before. In that practice he dropped one or two punts, for almost the first time in his life, and he began thinking it was because of the Bowl.

There is a new disease called agoraphobia—afraid of crowds—and another called siderodromophobia—afraid of railroad traveling—and my friend Doctor Glock, the psychoanalyst, would probably account easily for Dolly's state of mind. But here's what Dolly told me afterward:

"Yale would punt and I'd look up. The minute I looked up, the sides of that damn pan would seem to go shooting up too. Then when the ball started to come down, the sides began leaning forward and bending over me until I could see all the people on the top seats screaming at me and shaking their fists. At the last minute I couldn't see the ball at all, but only the Bowl; every time it was just luck that I was under it and every time I juggled it in my hands."

To go back to the game. I was in the cheering section with a good seat on the forty-yard line—good, that is, except when a very vague graduate, who had lost his friends and his hat, stood up in front of me at intervals and faltered, "Stob Ted Coy!" under the impression that we were watching a game played a dozen years before. When he realized finally that he was funny he began performing for the gallery and aroused a chorus of whistles and boos until he was dragged unwillingly under the stand.

It was a good game—what is known in college publications as a historic game. A picture of the team that played it now hangs in every barber shop in Princeton, with Captain Gottlieb in the middle wearing a white sweater, to show that they won a championship. Yale had had a poor season, but they had the breaks in the first quarter, which ended 3 to 0 in their favor.

Between quarters I watched Dolly. He walked around panting and sucking a water bottle and still wearing that strained stunned expression. Afterward he told me he was saying over and over to himself: "I'll speak to Roper. I'll tell him between halves. I'll tell him I can't go through this any more." Several times already he had felt an almost irresistible impulse to shrug his shoulders and trot off the field, for it was not only this unexpected complex about the Bowl; the truth was that Dolly fiercely and bitterly hated the game.

He hated the long, dull period of training, the element of personal conflict, the demand on his time, the monotony of the routine and the nervous apprehension of disaster just before the end. Sometimes he imagined that all the others detested it as much as he did, and fought down their aversion as he did and carried it around inside them like a cancer that they were afraid to recognize. Sometimes he imagined that a man here and there was about to tear off the mask and say, "Dolly, do you hate this lousy business as much as I do?"

His feeling had begun back at St. Regis' School and he had come up to Princeton with the idea that he was through with football forever. But upper classmen from St. Regis kept stopping him on the campus and asking him how much he weighed, and he was nominated for vice president of our class on the strength of his athletic reputation—and it was autumn, with achievement in the air. He wandered down to freshman practice one afternoon, feeling oddly lost and dissatisfied, and smelled the turf and smelled the thrilling season. In half an hour he was lacing on a pair of borrowed shoes and two weeks later he was captain of the freshman team.

Once committed, he saw that he had made a mistake; he even considered leaving college. For, with his decision to play, Dolly assumed a moral responsibility, personal to him, besides. To lose or to let down, or to be let down, was simply intolerable to him. It offended his Scotch sense of waste. Why sweat blood for an hour with only defeat at the end?

Perhaps the worst of it was that he wasn't really a star player. No team in the country could have spared using him, but he could do no spectacular thing superlatively well, neither run, pass nor kick. He was five-feet-eleven and weighed a little more than a hundred and sixty; he was a first-rate defensive man, sure in interference, a fair line plunger and a fair punter. He never fumbled and he was never inadequate; his presence, his constant cold sure aggression, had a strong effect on other men. Morally, he captained any team he played on and that was why Roper had spent so much time trying to get length in his kicks all season—he wanted him in the game.

In the second quarter Yale began to crack. It was a mediocre team composed of flashy material, but uncoordinated because of injuries and impending changes in the Yale coaching system. The quarterback, Josh Logan, had been a wonder at Exeter—I could testify to that—where games can be won by the sheer confidence and spirit of a single man. But college teams are too highly organized to respond so simply and boyishly, and they recover less easily from fumbles and errors of judgment behind the line.

So, with nothing to spare, with much grunting and straining, Princeton moved steadily down the field. On the Yale twenty-yard line things suddenly happened. A Princeton pass was intercepted; the Yale man, excited by his own opportunity, dropped the ball and it bobbed leisurely in the general direction of the Yale goal. Jack Devlin and Dolly Harlan of Princeton and somebody—I forget who—from Yale were all about the same distance from it. What Dolly did in that split second was all instinct; it presented no problem to him. He was a natural athlete and in a crisis his nervous system thought for him. He might have raced the two others for the ball; instead, he took out the Yale man with savage precision while Devlin scooped up the ball and ran ten yards for a touchdown.

This was when the sports writers still saw games through the eyes of Ralph Henry Barbour. The press box was right behind me, and as Princeton lined up to kick goal I heard the radio man ask:

"Who's Number 22?"

"Harlan."

"Harlan is going to kick goal. Devlin, who made the touchdown, comes from Lawrenceville School. He is twenty years old. The ball went true between the bars."

Between the halves, as Dolly sat shaking with fatigue in the locker room, Little, the back-field coach, came and sat beside him.

"When the ends are right on you, don't be afraid to make a fair catch," Little said. "That big Havemeyer is liable to jar the ball right out of your hands."

Now was the time to say it: "I wish you'd tell Bill——" But the words twisted themselves into a trivial question about the wind. His feeling would have to be explained, gone into, and there wasn't time. His own self seemed less important in this room, redolent with the tired breath, the ultimate effort, the exhaustion of ten other men. He was shamed by a harsh sudden quarrel that broke out between an end and tackle; he resented the former players in the room—especially the graduate captain of two years before, who was a little tight and over-vehement about the referee's favoritism. It seemed terrible to add one more jot to all this strain and annoyance. But he might have come out with it all the same if Little hadn't kept saying in a low voice: "What a take-out, Dolly! What a beautiful take-out!" and if Little's hand hadn't rested there, patting his shoulder.

· I I ·

IN THE THIRD QUARTER Joe Dougherty kicked an easy field goal from the twenty-yard line and we felt safe, until toward twilight a series of desperate forward passes brought Yale close to a score. But Josh Logan had exhausted his personality in sheer bravado and he was outguessed by the defense at the last. As the substitutes came running in, Princeton began a last march down the field. Then abruptly it was over and the crowd poured from the stands, and Gottlieb, grabbing the ball, leaped up in the air. For a while everything was confused and crazy and happy; I saw some freshmen try to carry Dolly, but they were shy and he got away.

We all felt a great personal elation. We hadn't beaten Yale for three years and now everything was going to be all right. It meant a good winter at college, something pleasant and slick to think back upon in the damp cold days after Christmas, when a bleak futility settles over a university town. Down on the field, an improvised and uproarious team ran through plays with a derby, until the snake dance rolled over them and blotted them out. Outside the Bowl, I saw two abysmally gloomy and disgusted Yale men get into a waiting taxi and in a tone of final abnegation tell the driver "New York." You couldn't find Yale men; in the manner of the vanquished, they had absolutely melted away.

I begin Dolly's story with my memories of this game because that evening the girl walked into it. She was a friend of Josephine Pickman's and the four of us were going to drive up to the Midnight Frolic in New York. When I suggested to him that he'd be too tired he laughed dryly—he'd have gone anywhere that night to get the feel and rhythm of football out of his head. He walked into the hall of Josephine's house at half-past six, looking as if he'd spent the day in the barber shop save for a small and fetching strip of court plaster over one eye. He was one of the handsomest men I ever knew, anyhow; he appeared tall and slender in street clothes, his hair was dark, his eyes big and sensitive and dark, his nose aquiline and, like all his features, somehow romantic. It didn't occur to me then, but I suppose he was pretty vain—not conceited, but vain—for he always dressed in brown or soft light gray, with black ties, and people don't match themselves so successfully by accident.

He was smiling a little to himself as he came in. He shook my hand buoyantly and said, "Why, what a surprise to meet you here, Mr. Deering," in a kidding way. Then he saw the two girls through the long hall, one dark and shining, like himself, and one with gold hair that was foaming and frothing in the firelight, and said in the happiest voice I've ever heard, "Which one is mine?"

"Either you want, I guess."

"Seriously, which is Pickman?"

"She's light."

"Then the other one belongs to me. Isn't that the idea?"

"I think I'd better warn them about the state you're in."

Miss Thorne, small, flushed and lovely, stood beside the fire. Dolly went right up to her.

"You're mine," he said; "you belong to me."

She looked at him coolly, making up her mind; suddenly she liked him and smiled. But Dolly wasn't satisfied. He wanted to do something incredibly silly or startling to express his untold jubilation that he was free.

"I love you," he said. He took her hand, his brown velvet eyes regarding her tenderly, unseeingly, convincingly. "I love you."

For a moment the corners of her lips fell as if in dismay that she had met someone stronger, more confident, more challenging than herself. Then, as she drew herself together visibly, he dropped her hand and the little scene in which he had expended the tension of the afternoon was over.

It was a bright cold November night and the rush of air past the open car brought a vague excitement, a sense that we were hurrying at top speed toward a brilliant destiny. The roads were packed with cars that came to long inexplicable halts while police, blinded by the lights, walked up and down the line giving obscure commands. Before we had been gone an hour New York began to be a distant hazy glow against the sky.

Miss Thorne, Josephine told me, was from Washington, and had just come down from a visit in Boston.

"For the game?" I said.

"No; she didn't go to the game."

"That's too bad. If you'd let me know I could have picked up a seat——"

"She wouldn't have gone. Vienna never goes to games."

I remembered now that she hadn't even murmured the conventional congratulations to Dolly.

"She hates football. Her brother was killed in a prep-school game last year. I wouldn't have brought her tonight, but when we got home from the game I saw she'd been sitting there holding a book open at the same page all afternoon. You see, he was this wonderful kid and her family saw it happen and naturally never got over it."

"But does she mind being with Dolly?"

"Of course not. She just ignores football. If anyone mentions it she simply changes the subject."

I was glad that it was Dolly and not, say, Jack Devlin who was sitting back there with her. And I felt rather sorry for Dolly. However strongly he felt about the game, he must have waited for some acknowledgment that his effort had existed.

He was probably giving her credit for a subtle consideration, yet, as the images of the afternoon flashed into his mind he might have welcomed a compliment to which he could respond "What nonsense!" Neglected entirely, the images would become insistent and obtrusive.

I turned around and was somewhat startled to find that Miss Thorne was in Dolly's arms; I turned quickly back and decided to let them take care of themselves.

As we waited for a traffic light on upper Broadway, I saw a sporting extra headlined with the score of the game. The green sheet was more real than the afternoon itself—succinct, condensed and clear:

PRINCETON CONQUERS YALE 10–3
SEVENTY THOUSAND WATCH TIGER TRIM
BULLDOG

DEVLIN SCORES ON YALE FUMBLE

There it was—not like the afternoon, muddled, uncertain, patchy and scrappy to the end, but nicely mounted now in the setting of the past:

PRINCETON, 10; YALE, 3

Achievement was a curious thing, I thought. Dolly was largely responsible for that. I wondered if all things that screamed in the headlines were simply arbitrary accents. As if people should ask, "What does it look like?"

"It looks most like a cat."

"Well, then, let's call it a cat."

My mind, brightened by the lights and the cheerful tumult, suddenly grasped the fact that all achievement was a placing of emphasis—a molding of the confusion of life into form.

Josephine stopped in front of the New Amsterdam Theater, where her chauffeur met us and took the car. We were early, but a small buzz of excitement went up from the undergraduates waiting in the lobby—"There's Dolly Harlan"—and as we moved toward the elevator several acquaintances came up to shake his hand. Apparently oblivious to these ceremonies, Miss Thorne caught my eye and smiled. I looked at her with curiosity; Josephine had imparted the rather surprising information that she was just sixteen years old. I suppose my return smile was rather patronizing, but instantly I realized that the fact could not be imposed on. In spite of all the warmth and delicacy of her face, the figure that somehow reminded me of an exquisite, romanticized little ballerina, there was a quality in her that was as hard as steel. She had been brought up in Rome, Vienna and Madrid, with flashes of Washington; her father was one of those charming American diplomats who, with fine obstinacy, try to re-create the Old World in their children by making their education rather more royal than that of princes. Miss Thorne was sophisticated. In spite of all the abandon of American young people, sophistication is still a Continental monopoly.

We walked in upon a number in which a dozen chorus girls in orange and black were racing wooden horses against another dozen dressed in Yale blue. When the lights went on, Dolly was recognized and some Princeton students set up a clatter of approval with the little wooden hammers given out for applause; he moved his chair unostentatiously into a shadow.

Almost immediately a flushed and very miserable young man appeared beside our table. In better form he would have been extremely prepossessing; indeed, he flashed a charming and dazzling smile at Dolly, as if requesting his permission to speak to Miss Thorne.

Then he said, "I thought you weren't coming to New York tonight."

"Hello, Carl." She looked up at him coolly.

"Hello, Vienna. That's just it; 'Hello Vienna—Hello Carl.' But why? I thought you weren't coming to New York tonight."

Miss Thorne made no move to introduce the man, but we were conscious of his somewhat raised voice.

"I thought you promised me you weren't coming."

"I didn't expect to, child. I just left Boston this morning."

"And who did you meet in Boston—the fascinating Tunti?" he demanded.

"I didn't meet anyone, child."

"Oh, yes, you did! You met the fascinating Tunti and you discussed living on the Riviera." She didn't answer. "Why are you so dishonest, Vienna?" he went on. "Why did you tell me on the phone——"

"I am not going to be lectured," she said, her tone changing suddenly. "I told you if you took another drink I was through with you. I'm a person of my word and I'd be enormously happy if you went away."

"Vienna!" he cried in a sinking, trembling voice.

At this point I got up and danced with Josephine. When we came back there were people at the table—the men to whom we were to hand over Josephine and Miss Thorne, for I had allowed for Dolly being tired, and several others. One of them was Al Ratoni, the composer, who, it appeared, had been entertained at the embassy in Madrid. Dolly Harlan had drawn his chair aside and was watching the dancers. Just as the lights went down for a new number a man came up out of the darkness and leaning over Miss Thorne whispered in her ear. She started and made a motion to rise, but he put his hand on her shoulder and forced her down. They began to talk together in low excited voices.

The tables were packed close at the old Frolic. There was a man rejoining the party next to us and I couldn't help hearing what he said:

"A young fellow just tried to kill himself down in the wash room. He shot himself through the shoulder, but they got the pistol away before——" A minute later his voice again: "Carl Sanderson, they said."

When the number was over I looked around. Vienna Thorne was staring very rigidly at Miss Lillian Lorraine, who was rising toward the ceiling as an enormous telephone doll. The man who had leaned over Vienna was gone and the others were obliviously unaware that anything had happened. I turned to Dolly and suggested that he and I had better go, and after a glance at Vienna in which reluctance, weariness and then resignation were mingled, he consented. On the way to the hotel I told Dolly what had happened.

"Just some souse," he remarked after a moment's fatigued consideration. "He probably tried to miss himself and get a little sympathy. I suppose those are the sort of things a really attractive girl is up against all the time."

This wasn't my attitude. I could see that mussed white shirt front with very young blood pumping over it, but I didn't argue, and after a while Dolly said, "I suppose that sounds brutal, but it seems a little soft and weak, doesn't it? Perhaps that's just the way I feel tonight."

When Dolly undressed I saw that he was a mass of bruises, but he assured me that none of them would keep him awake. Then I told him why Miss Thorne hadn't mentioned the game and he woke up suddenly; the familiar glitter came back into his eyes.

"So that was it! I wondered. I thought maybe you'd told her not to say anything about it."

Later, when the lights had been out half an hour, he suddenly said "I see" in a loud clear voice. I don't know whether he was awake or asleep.

· III ·

I'VE PUT DOWN as well as I can everything I can remember about the first meeting between Dolly and Miss Vienna Thorne. Reading it over, it sounds casual and insignificant, but the evening lay in the shadow of the game and all that happened seemed like that. Vienna went back to Europe almost immediately and for fifteen months passed out of Dolly's life.

It was a good year—it still rings true in my memory as a good year. Sophomore year is the most dramatic at Princeton, just as junior year is at Yale. It's not only the elections to the upperclass clubs but also everyone's destiny begins to work itself out. You can tell pretty well who's going to

come through, not only by their immediate success but by the way they
survive failure. Life was very full for me. I made the board of the Princetonian, and our house burned down out in Dayton, and I had a silly half-
hour fist fight in the gymnasium with a man who later became one of my
closest friends, and in March Dolly and I joined the upperclass club we'd
always wanted to be in. I fell in love, too, but it would be an irrelevancy
to tell about that here.

April came and the first real Princeton weather, the lazy green-and-gold
afternoons and the bright thrilling nights haunted with the hour of senior
singing. I was happy, and Dolly would have been happy except for the
approach of another football season. He was playing baseball, which excused
him from spring practice, but the bands were beginning to play faintly in
the distance. They rose to concert pitch during the summer, when he had
to answer the question, "Are you going back early for football?" a dozen
times a day. On the fifteenth of September he was down in the dust and
heat of late-summer Princeton, crawling over the ground on all fours, trot-
ting through the old routine and turning himself into just the sort of specimen
that I'd have given ten years of my life to be.

From first to last, he hated it, and never let down for a minute. He went
into the Yale game that fall weighing a hundred and fifty-three pounds,
though that wasn't the weight printed in the paper, and he and Joe McDonald
were the only men who played all through that disastrous game. He could
have been captain by lifting his finger—but that involves some stuff that I
know confidentially and can't tell. His only horror was that by some chance
he'd have to accept it. Two seasons! He didn't even talk about it now. He
left the room or the club when the conversation veered around to football.
He stopped announcing to me that he "wasn't going through that business
any more." This time it took the Christmas holidays to drive that unhappy
look from his eyes.

Then at the New Year Miss Vienna Thorne came home from Madrid and
in February a man named Case brought her down to the Senior Prom.

· I V ·

S H E W A S even prettier than she had been before, softer, externally at least,
and a tremendous success. People passing her on the street jerked their heads
quickly to look at her—a frightened look, as if they realized that they had
almost missed something. She was temporarily tired of European men, she
told me, letting me gather that there had been some sort of unfortunate love
affair. She was coming out in Washington next fall.

Vienna and Dolly. She disappeared with him for two hours the night of the club dances, and Harold Case was in despair. When they walked in again at midnight I thought they were the handsomest pair I saw. They were both shining with that peculiar luminosity that dark people sometimes have. Harold Case took one look at them and went proudly home.

Vienna came back a week later, solely to see Dolly. Late that evening I had occasion to go up to the deserted club for a book and they called me from the rear terrace, which opens out to the ghostly stadium and to an unpeopled sweep of night. It was an hour of thaw, with spring voices in the warm wind, and wherever there was light enough you could see drops glistening and falling. You could feel the cold melting out of the stars and the bare trees and shrubbery toward Stony Brook turning lush in the darkness.

They were sitting together on a wicker bench, full of themselves and romantic and happy.

"We had to tell someone about it," they said.

"Now can I go?"

"No, Jeff," they insisted; "stay here and envy us. We're in the stage where we want someone to envy us. Do you think we're a good match?"

What could I say?

"Dolly's going to finish at Princeton next year," Vienna went on, "but we're going to announce it after the season in Washington in the autumn."

I was vaguely relieved to find that it was going to be a long engagement.

"I approve of you, Jeff," Vienna said.

"I want Dolly to have more friends like you. You're stimulating for him—you have ideas. I told Dolly he could probably find others like you if he looked around his class."

Dolly and I both felt a little uncomfortable.

"She doesn't want me to be a Babbitt," he said lightly.

"Dolly's perfect," asserted Vienna. "He's the most beautiful thing that ever lived, and you'll find I'm very good for him, Jeff. Already I've helped him make up his mind about one important thing." I guessed what was coming. "He's going to speak a little piece if they bother him about playing football next autumn, aren't you, child?"

"Oh, they won't bother me," said Dolly uncomfortably. "It isn't like that——"

"Well, they'll try to bully you into it, morally."

"Oh, no," he objected. "It isn't like that. Don't let's talk about it now, Vienna. It's such a swell night."

Such a swell night! When I think of my own love passages at Princeton, I always summon up that night of Dolly's, as if it had been I and not he who sat there with youth and hope and beauty in his arms.

Dolly's mother took a place on Ram's Point, Long Island, for the summer, and late in August I went East to visit him. Vienna had been there a week when I arrived, and my impressions were: first, that he was very much in love; and, second, that it was Vienna's party. All sorts of curious people used to drop in to see Vienna. I wouldn't mind them now—I'm more sophisticated—but then they seemed rather a blot on the summer. They were all slightly famous in one way or another, and it was up to you to find out how. There was a lot of talk, and especially there was much discussion of Vienna's personality. Whenever I was alone with any of the other guests we discussed Vienna's sparkling personality. They thought I was dull, and most of them thought Dolly was dull. He was better in his line than any of them were in theirs, but his was the only specialty that wasn't mentioned. Still, I felt vaguely that I was being improved and I boasted about knowing most of those people in the ensuing year, and was annoyed when people failed to recognize their names.

The day before I left, Dolly turned his ankle playing tennis, and afterward he joked about it to me rather somberly.

"If I'd only broken it things would be so much easier. Just a quarter of an inch more bend and one of the bones would have snapped. By the way, look here."

He tossed me a letter. It was a request that he report at Princeton for practice on September fifteenth and that meanwhile he begin getting himself in good condition.

"You're not going to play this fall?"

He shook his head.

"No. I'm not a child any more. I've played for two years and I want this year free. If I went through it again it'd be a piece of moral cowardice."

"I'm not arguing, but—would you have taken this stand if it hadn't been for Vienna?"

"Of course I would. If I let myself be bullied into it I'd never be able to look myself in the face again."

Two weeks later I got the following letter:

DEAR JEFF:

When you read this you'll be somewhat surprised. I have, actually, this time, broken my ankle playing tennis. I can't even walk with crutches at present; it's on a chair in front of me swollen up and wrapped up as big as a house as I write. No one, not even Vienna, knows about our conversation on the same subject last summer and so let us both absolutely forget it. One thing, though —an ankle is a darn hard thing to break, though I never knew it before.

I feel happier than I have for years—no early-season practice, no sweat and suffer, a little discomfort and inconvenience, but free. I feel as if I've outwitted a whole lot of people, and it's nobody's business but that of your

Machiavellian (sic) friend,

DOLLY.

P.S. You might as well tear up this letter.

It didn't sound like Dolly at all.

· V ·

ONCE DOWN AT Princeton I asked Frank Kane—who sells sporting goods on Nassau Street and can tell you offhand the name of the scrub quarterback in 1901—what was the matter with Bob Tatnall's team senior year.

"Injuries and tough luck," he said. "They wouldn't sweat after the hard games. Take Joe McDonald, for instance, All-American tackle the year before; he was slow and stale, and he knew it and didn't care. It's a wonder Bill got that outfit through the season at all."

I sat in the stands with Dolly and watched them beat Lehigh 3-0 and tie Bucknell by a fluke. The next week we were trimmed 14-0 by Notre Dame. On the day of the Notre Dame game Dolly was in Washington with Vienna, but he was awfully curious about it when he came back next day. He had all the sporting pages of all the papers and he sat reading them and shaking his head. Then he stuffed them suddenly into the wastepaper basket.

"This college is football crazy," he announced. "Do you know that English teams don't even train for sports?"

I didn't enjoy Dolly so much in those days. It was curious to see him with nothing to do. For the first time in his life he hung around—around the room, around the club, around casual groups—he who had always been going somewhere with dynamic indolence. His passage along a walk had once created groups—groups of classmates who wanted to walk with him, of underclassmen who followed with their eyes a moving shrine. He became democratic, he mixed around, and it was somehow not appropriate. He explained that he wanted to know more men in his class.

But people want their idols a little above them, and Dolly had been a sort of private and special idol. He began to hate to be alone, and that, of course, was most apparent to me. If I got up to go out and he didn't happen to be writing a letter to Vienna, he'd ask "Where are you going?" in a rather alarmed way and make an excuse to limp along with me.

"Are you glad you did it, Dolly?" I asked him suddenly one day.

He looked at me with reproach behind the defiance in his eyes.

"Of course I'm glad."

"I wish you were in that back field, all the same."

"It wouldn't matter a bit. This year's game's in the Bowl. I'd probably be dropping kicks for them."

The week of the Navy game he suddenly began going to all the practices. He worried; that terrible sense of responsibility was at work. Once he had hated the mention of football; now he thought and talked of nothing else. The night before the Navy game I woke up several times to find the lights burning brightly in his room.

We lost 7 to 3 on Navy's last-minute forward pass over Devlin's head. After the first half Dolly left the stands and sat down with the players on the field. When he joined me afterward his face was smudgy and dirty as if he had been crying.

The game was in Baltimore that year. Dolly and I were going to spend the night in Washington with Vienna, who was giving a dance. We rode over there in an atmosphere of sullen gloom and it was all I could do to keep him from snapping out at two naval officers who were holding an exultant post mortem in the seat behind.

The dance was what Vienna called her second coming-out party. She was having only the people she liked this time, and these turned out to be chiefly importations from New York. The musicians, the playwrights, the vague supernumeraries of the arts, who had dropped in at Dolly's house on Ram's Point, were here in force. But Dolly, relieved of his obligations as host, made no clumsy attempt to talk their language that night. He stood moodily against the wall with some of that old air of superiority that had first made me want to know him. Afterward, on my way to bed, I passed Vienna's sitting room and she called me to come in. She and Dolly, both a little white, were sitting across the room from each other and there was tensity in the air.

"Sit down, Jeff," said Vienna wearily. "I want you to witness the collapse of a man into a schoolboy." I sat down reluctantly. "Dolly's changed his mind," she said. "He prefers football to me."

"That's not it," said Dolly stubbornly.

"I don't see the point," I objected. "Dolly can't possibly play."

"But he thinks he can. Jeff, just in case you imagine I'm being pig-headed

about it, I want to tell you a story. Three years ago, when we first came
back to the United States, father put my young brother in school. One
afternoon we all went out to see him play football. Just after the game
started he was hurt, but father said, 'It's all right. He'll be up in a minute.
It happens all the time.' But, Jeff, he never got up. He lay there, and finally
they carried him off the field and put a blanket over him. Just as we got to
him he died."

She looked from one to the other of us and began to sob convulsively.
Dolly went over, frowning, and put his arm around her shoulder.

"Oh, Dolly," she cried, "won't you do this for me—just this one little
thing for me?"

He shook his head miserably. "I tried, but I can't," he said.

"It's my stuff, don't you understand, Vienna? People have got to do their
stuff."

Vienna had risen and was powdering her tears at a mirror; now she flashed
around angrily.

"Then I've been laboring under a misapprehension when I supposed you
felt about it much as I did."

"Let's not go over all that. I'm tired of talking, Vienna; I'm tired of my
own voice. It seems to me that no one I know does anything but talk any
more."

"Thanks. I suppose that's meant for me."

"It seems to me your friends talk a great deal. I've never heard so much
jabber as I've listened to tonight. Is the idea of actually doing anything
repulsive to you, Vienna?"

"It depends upon whether it's worth doing."

"Well, this is worth doing—to me."

"I know your trouble, Dolly," she said bitterly. "You're weak and you
want to be admired. This year you haven't had a lot of little boys following
you around as if you were Jack Dempsey, and it almost breaks your heart.
You want to get out in front of them all and make a show of yourself and
hear the applause."

He laughed shortly. "If that's your idea of how a football player
feels——"

"Have you made up your mind to play?" she interrupted.

"If I'm any use to them—yes."

"Then I think we're both wasting our time."

Her expression was ruthless, but Dolly refused to see that she was in
earnest. When I got away he was still trying to make her "be rational," and
next day on the train he said that Vienna had been "a little nervous." He
was deeply in love with her, and he didn't dare think of losing her; but he

was still in the grip of the sudden emotion that had decided him to play, and his confusion and exhaustion of mind made him believe vainly that everything was going to be all right. But I had seen that look on Vienna's face the night she talked with Mr. Carl Sanderson at the Frolic two years before.

Dolly didn't get off the train at Princeton Junction, but continued on to New York. He went to two orthopedic specialists and one of them arranged a bandage braced with a whole little fence of whalebones that he was to wear day and night. The probabilities were that it would snap at the first brisk encounter, but he could run on it and stand on it when he kicked. He was out on University Field in uniform the following afternoon.

His appearance was a small sensation. I was sitting in the stands watching practice with Harold Case and young Daisy Cary. She was just beginning to be famous then, and I don't know whether she or Dolly attracted the most attention. In those times it was still rather daring to bring down a moving-picture actress; if that same young lady went to Princeton today she would probably be met at the station with a band.

Dolly limped around and everyone said, "He's limping!" He got under a punt and everyone said, "He did that pretty well!" The first team were laid off after the hard Navy game and everyone watched Dolly all afternoon. After practice I caught his eye and he came over and shook hands. Daisy asked him if he'd like to be in a football picture she was going to make. It was only conversation, but he looked at me with a dry smile.

When he came back to the room his ankle was swollen up as big as a stove pipe, and next day he and Keene fixed up an arrangement by which the bandage would be loosened and tightened to fit its varying size. We called it the balloon. The bone was nearly healed, but the little bruised sinews were stretched out of place again every day. He watched the Swarthmore game from the sidelines and the following Monday he was in scrimmage with the second team against the scrubs.

In the afternoons sometimes he wrote to Vienna. His theory was that they were still engaged, but he tried not to worry about it, and I think the very pain that kept him awake at night was good for that. When the season was over he would go and see.

We played Harvard and lost 7 to 3. Jack Devlin's collar bone was broken and he was out for the season, which made it almost sure that Dolly would play. Amid the rumors and fears of mid-November the news aroused a spark of hope in an otherwise morbid undergraduate body—hope all out of proportion to Dolly's condition. He came back to the room the Thursday before the game with his face drawn and tired.

"They're going to start me," he said, "and I'm going to be back for punts. If they only knew——"

"Couldn't you tell Bill how you feel about that?"

He shook his head and I had a sudden suspicion that he was punishing himself for his "accident" last August. He lay silently on the couch while I packed his suitcase for the team train.

The actual day of the game was, as usual, like a dream—unreal with its crowds of friends and relatives and the inessential trappings of a gigantic show. The eleven little men who ran out on the field at last were like bewitched figures in another world, strange and infinitely romantic, blurred by a throbbing mist of people and sound. One aches with them intolerably, trembles with their excitement, but they have no traffic with us now, they are beyond help, consecrated and unreachable—vaguely holy.

The field is rich and green, the preliminaries are over and the teams trickle out into position. Head guards are put on; each man claps his hands and breaks into a lonely little dance. People are still talking around you, arranging themselves, but you have fallen silent and your eye wanders from man to man. There's Jack Whitehead, a senior, at end; Joe McDonald, large and reassuring, at tackle; Toole, a sophomore, at guard; Red Hopman, center; someone you can't identify at the other guard—Bunker probably—he turns and you see his number—Bunker; Bean Gile, looking unnaturally dignified and significant at the other tackle; Poore, another sophomore at end. Back of them is Wash Sampson at quarter—imagine how he feels! But he runs here and there on light feet, speaking to this man and that, trying to communicate his alertness and his confidence of success. Dolly Harlan stands motionless, his hands on his hips, watching the Yale kicker tee up the ball; near him is Captain Bob Tatnall——

There's the whistle! The line of the Yale team sways ponderously forward from its balance and a split second afterward comes the sound of the ball. The field streams with running figures and the whole Bowl strains forward as if thrown by the current of an electric chair.

Suppose we fumbled right away.

Tatnall catches it, goes back ten yards, is surrounded and blotted out of sight. Spears goes through center for three. A short pass, Sampson to Tatnall, is completed, but for no gain. Harlan punts to Devereaux, who is downed in his tracks on the Yale forty-yard line.

Now we'll see what they've got.

It developed immediately that they had a great deal. Using an effective crisscross and a short pass over center, they carried the ball fifty-four yards to the Princeton six-yard line, where they lost it on a fumble, recovered by

Red Hopman. After a trade of punts, they began another push, this time
to the fifteen-yard line, where, after four hair-raising forward passes, two
of them batted down by Dolly, we got the ball on downs. But Yale was
still fresh and strong, and with a third onslaught the weaker Princeton line
began to give way. Just after the second quarter began Devereaux took the
ball over for a touchdown and the half ended with Yale in possession of the
ball on our ten-yard line. Score, Yale, 7; Princeton, 0.

We hadn't a chance. The team was playing above itself, better than it had
played all year, but it wasn't enough. Save that it was the Yale game, when
anything could happen, anything *had* happened, the atmosphere of gloom
would have been deeper than it was, and in the cheering section you could
cut it with a knife.

Early in the game Dolly Harlan had fumbled Devereaux's high punt, but
recovered without gain; toward the end of the half another kick slipped
through his fingers, but he scooped it up, and slipping past the end, went
back twelve yards. Between halves he told Roper he couldn't seem to get
under the ball, but they kept him there. His own kicks were carrying well
and he was essential in the only back-field combination that could hope to
score.

After the first play of the game he limped slightly, moving around as little
as possible to conceal the fact. But I knew enough about football to see that
he was in every play, starting at that rather slow pace of his and finishing
with a quick side lunge that almost always took out his man. Not a single
Yale forward pass was finished in his territory, but toward the end of the
third quarter he dropped another kick—backed around in a confused little
circle under it, lost it and recovered on the five-yard line just in time to
avert a certain score. That made the third time, and I saw Ed Kimball throw
off his blanket and begin to warm up on the sidelines.

Just at that point our luck began to change. From a kick formation, with
Dolly set to punt from behind our goal, Howard Bement, who had gone
in for Wash Sampson at quarter, took the ball through the center of the
line, got by the secondary defense and ran twenty-six yards before he was
pulled down. Captain Tasker, of Yale, had gone out with a twisted knee,
and Princeton began to pile plays through his substitute, between Bean Gile
and Hopman, with George Spears and sometimes Bob Tatnall carrying the
ball. We went up to the Yale forty-yard line, lost the ball on a fumble and
recovered it on another as the third quarter ended. A wild ripple of enthusiasm ran through the Princeton stands. For the first time we had the ball
in their territory with first down and the possibility of tying the score. You
could hear the tenseness growing all around you in the intermission; it was

reflected in the excited movements of the cheer leaders and the uncontrollable patches of sound that leaped out of the crowd, catching up voices here and there and swelling to an undisciplined roar.

I saw Kimball dash out on the field and report to the referee and I thought Dolly was through at last, and was glad, but it was Bob Tatnall who came out, sobbing, and brought the Princeton side cheering to its feet.

With the first play pandemonium broke loose and continued to the end of the game. At intervals it would swoon away to a plaintive humming; then it would rise to the intensity of wind and rain and thunder, and beat across the twilight from one side of the Bowl to the other like the agony of lost souls swinging across a gap in space.

The teams lined up on Yale's forty-one yard line and Spears immediately dashed off tackle for six yards. Again he carried the ball—he was a wild unpopular Southerner with inspired moments—going through the same hole for five more and a first down. Dolly made two on a cross buck and Spears was held at center. It was third down, with the ball on Yale's twenty-nine-yard line and eight to go.

There was some confusion immediately behind me, some pushing and some voices; a man was sick or had fainted—I never discovered which. Then my view was blocked out for a minute by rising bodies and then everything went definitely crazy. Substitutes were jumping around down on the field, waving their blankets, the air was full of hats, cushions, coats and a deafening roar. Dolly Harlan, who had scarcely carried the ball a dozen times in his Princeton career, had picked a long pass from Kimball out of the air and, dragging a tackler, struggled five yards to the Yale goal.

· VI ·

SOME TIME later the game was over. There was a bad moment when Yale began another attack, but there was no scoring and Bob Tatnall's eleven had redeemed a mediocre season by tying a better Yale team. For us there was the feel of victory about it, the exaltation if not the jubilance, and the Yale faces issuing from out the Bowl wore the look of defeat. It would be a good year, after all—a good fight at the last, a tradition for next year's team. Our class—those of us who cared—would go out from Princeton without the taste of final defeat. The symbol stood—such as it was; the banners blew proudly in the wind. All that is childish? Find us something to fill the niche of victory.

I waited for Dolly outside the dressing rooms until almost everyone had come out; then, as he still lingered, I went in. Someone had given him a little brandy, and since he never drank much, it was swimming in his head.

"Have a chair, Jeff." He smiled, broadly and happily. "Rubber! Tony! Get the distinguished guest a chair. He's an intellectual and he wants to interview one of the bone-headed athletes. Tony, this is Mr. Deering. They've got everything in this funny Bowl but armchairs. I love this Bowl. I'm going to build here."

He fell silent, thinking about all things happily. He was content. I persuaded him to dress—there were people waiting for us. Then he insisted on walking out upon the field, dark now, and feeling the crumbled turf with his shoe.

He picked up a divot from a cleat and let it drop, laughed, looked distracted for a minute, and turned away.

With Tad Davis, Daisy Cary and another girl, we drove to New York. He sat beside Daisy and was silly, charming and attractive. For the first time since I'd known him he talked about the game naturally, even with a touch of vanity.

"For two years I was pretty good and I was always mentioned at the bottom of the column as being among those who played. This year I dropped three punts and slowed up every play till Bob Tatnall kept yelling at me, 'I don't see why they won't take you out!' But a pass not even aimed at me fell in my arms and I'll be in the headlines tomorrow."

He laughed. Somebody touched his foot; he winced and turned white.

"How did you hurt it?" Daisy asked. "In football?"

"I hurt it last summer," he said shortly.

"It must have been terrible to play on it."

"It was."

"I suppose you had to."

"That's the way sometimes."

They understood each other. They were both workers; sick or well, there were things that Daisy also had to do. She spoke of how, with a vile cold, she had had to fall into an open-air lagoon out in Hollywood the winter before.

"Six times—with a fever of a hundred and two. But the production was costing ten thousand dollars a day."

"Couldn't they use a double?"

"They did whenever they could—I only fell in when it had to be done."

She was eighteen and I compared her background of courage and independence and achievement, of politeness based upon the realities of cooperation, with that of most society girls I had known. There was no way in which she wasn't inestimably their superior—if she had looked for a moment my way—but it was Dolly's shining velvet eyes that signaled to her own.

"Can't you go out with me tonight?" I heard her ask him.

He was sorry, but he had to refuse. Vienna was in New York; she was going to see him. I didn't know, and Dolly didn't know, whether there was to be a reconciliation or a good-by.

When she dropped Dolly and me at the Ritz there was real regret, that lingering form of it, in both their eyes.

"There's a marvelous girl," Dolly said. I agreed. "I'm going up to see Vienna. Will you get a room for us at the Madison?"

So I left him. What happened between him and Vienna I don't know; he has never spoken about it to this day. But what happened later in the evening was brought to my attention by several surprised and even indignant witnesses to the event.

Dolly walked into the Ambassador Hotel about ten o'clock and went to the desk to ask for Miss Cary's room. There was a crowd around the desk, among them some Yale or Princeton undergraduates from the game. Several of them had been celebrating and evidently one of them knew Daisy and had tried to get her room by phone. Dolly was abstracted and he must have made his way through them in a somewhat brusque way and asked to be connected with Miss Cary.

One young man stepped back, looked at him unpleasantly and said, "You seem to be in an awful hurry. Just who are you?"

There was one of those slight silent pauses and the people near the desk all turned to look. Something happened inside Dolly; he felt as if life had arranged his role to make possible this particular question—a question that now he had no choice but to answer. Still, there was silence. The small crowd waited.

"Why, I'm Dolly Harlan," he said deliberately. "What do you think of that?"

It was quite outrageous. There was a pause and then a sudden little flurry and chorus: "Dolly Harlan! What? What did he say?"

The clerk had heard the name; he gave it as the phone was answered from Miss Cary's room.

"Mr. Harlan's to go right up, please."

Dolly turned away, alone with his achievement, taking it for once to his breast. He found suddenly that he would not have it long so intimately; the memory would outlive the triumph and even the triumph would outlive the glow in his heart that was best of all. Tall and straight, an image of victory and pride, he moved across the lobby, oblivious alike to the fate ahead of him or the small chatter behind.

THE CAPTURED SHADOW

♦

The Basil Duke Lee stories were Fitzgerald's most successful series and brought him $31,500. The eight stories published in the Saturday Evening Post *during 1928 and 1929 take Basil from boyhood in the Midwest through eastern prep school to Yale. "The Captured Shadow," the fifth in the series, was published in the 29 December 1928 issue. These stories differ from most of the then-popular fiction about boys and adolescents in that Fitzgerald treats Basil seriously—not as a comic figure. Basil is obviously an autobiographical character, and the events in the stories were based on Fitzgerald's experiences. In 1912, when he was fifteen, he wrote and produced his play entitled* The Captured Shadow *in St. Paul.*

Fitzgerald rejected the plan of bringing out the Basil stories as a book, telling his agent, Harold Ober, in 1930: "These Post stories in the Post *are at least not any spot on me—they're honest and if their form is stereotyped people know what to expect when they pick up the* Post. *The novel is another thing—if, after four years I published the Basil stories as a book I might as well get tickets for Hollywood immediately." However, in 1934 he considered a volume of the Basil stories and the Josephine stories (see "First Blood" and "Emotional Bankruptcy") with new stories that would bring the characters together; this project was abandoned.*

♦

BASIL DUKE LEE shut the front door behind him and turned on the dining-room light. His mother's voice drifted sleepily downstairs:

"Basil, is that you?"

"No, mother, it's a burglar."

"It seems to me twelve o'clock is pretty late for a fifteen-year-old boy."

"We went to Smith's and had a soda."

Whenever a new responsibility devolved upon Basil he was "a boy almost sixteen," but when a privilege was in question, he was "a fifteen-year-old boy."

There were footsteps above, and Mrs. Lee, in kimono, descended to the first landing.

"Did you and Riply enjoy the play?"

"Yes, very much."

"What was it about?"

"Oh, it was just about this man. Just an ordinary play."

"Didn't it have a name?"

" 'Are You a Mason?' "

"Oh." She hesitated, covetously watching his alert and eager face, holding him there. "Aren't you coming to bed?"

"I'm going to get something to eat."

"Something more?"

For a moment he didn't answer. He stood in front of a glassed-in bookcase in the living room, examining its contents with an equally glazed eye.

"We're going to get up a play," he said suddenly. "I'm going to write it."

"Well—that'll be very nice. Please come to bed soon. You were up late last night, too, and you've got dark circles under your eyes."

From the bookcase Basil presently extracted "Van Bibber and Others," from which he read while he ate a large plate of straw softened with half a pint of cream. Back in the living room he sat for a few minutes at the piano, digesting, and meanwhile staring at the colored cover of a song from "The Midnight Sons." It showed three men in evening clothes and opera hats sauntering jovially along Broadway against the blazing background of Times Square.

Basil would have denied incredulously the suggestion that that was currently his favorite work of art. But it was.

He went upstairs. From a drawer of his desk he took out a composition book and opened it.

BASIL DUKE LEE
St. Regis School
Eastchester, Conn.
Fifth Form French

and on the next page, under Irregular Verbs:

PRESENT
je connais   nous con
tu connais
il connaît

He turned over another page.

MR. WASHINGTON SQUARE
A Musical Comedy by
BASIL DUKE LEE
Music by Victor Herbert

ACT I

[*The porch of the Millionaires' Club, near New York. Opening Chorus,*
LEILIA *and* DEBUTANTES:

> We sing not soft, we sing not loud
>   For no one ever heard an opening chorus.
> We are a very merry crowd
>   But no one ever heard an opening chorus.
> We're just a crowd of debutantes
>   As merry as can be
>   And nothing that there is could ever bore us
> We're the wittiest ones, the prettiest ones.
>   In all society
>   But no one ever heard an opening chorus.

LEILIA (*stepping forward*): Well, girls, has Mr. Washington Square been
around here today?

Basil turned over a page. There was no answer to Leilia's question. Instead
in capitals was a brand-new heading:

HIC! HIC! HIC!

A Hilarious Farce in One Act

by

BASIL DUKE LEE

SCENE

[*A fashionable apartment near Broadway, New York City. It is almost midnight. As the curtain goes up there is a knocking at the door and a few
minutes later it opens to admit a handsome man in a full evening dress
and a companion. He has evidently been imbibing, for his words are thick,*

*his nose is red, and he can hardly stand up. He turns up the light and
comes down center.*

STUYVESANT: Hic! Hic! Hic!
O'HARA (*his companion*): Begorra, you been sayin' nothing else all this
evening.

Basil turned over a page and then another, reading hurriedly, but not
without interest.

PROFESSOR PUMPKIN: Now, if you are an educated man, as you claim,
perhaps you can tell me the Latin word for "this."
STUYVESANT: Hic! Hic! Hic!
PROFESSOR PUMPKIN: Correct. Very good indeed. I——

At this point Hic! Hic! Hic! came to an end in midsentence. On the
following page, in just as determined a hand as if the last two works had
not faltered by the way, was the heavily underlined beginning of another:

THE CAPTURED SHADOW

A Melodramatic Farce in Three Acts

by
BASIL DUKE LEE

SCENE

[*All three acts take place in the library of the* VAN BAKERS' *house in New
York. It is well furnished with a red lamp on one side and some crossed
spears and helmets and so on and a divan and a general air of an oriental
den.*

When the curtain rises MISS SAUNDERS, LEILIA VAN BAKER *and* ESTELLA
CARRAGE *are sitting at a table.* MISS SAUNDERS *is an old maid about forty
very kittenish.* LEILIA *is pretty with dark hair.* ESTELLA *has light hair.
They are a striking combination.*

"The Captured Shadow" filled the rest of the book and ran over into
several loose sheets at the end. When it broke off Basil sat for a while in
thought. This had been a season of "crook comedies" in New York, and
the feel, the swing, the exact and vivid image of the two he had seen, were
in the foreground of his mind. At the time they had been enormously

suggestive, opening out into a world much larger and more brilliant than themselves that existed outside their windows and beyond their doors, and it was this suggested world rather than any conscious desire to imitate "Officer 666," that had inspired the effort before him. Presently he printed ACT II at the head of a new tablet and began to write.

An hour passed. Several times he had recourse to a collection of joke books and to an old Treasury of Wit and Humor which embalmed the faded Victorian cracks of Bishop Wilberforce and Sydney Smith. At the moment when, in his story, a door moved slowly open, he heard a heavy creak upon the stairs. He jumped to his feet, aghast and trembling, but nothing stirred; only a white moth bounced against the screen, a clock struck the half-hour far across the city, a bird whacked its wings in a tree outside.

Voyaging to the bathroom at half-past four, he saw with a shock that morning was already blue at the window. He had stayed up all night. He remembered that people who stayed up all night went crazy, and transfixed in the hall, he tried agonizingly to listen to himself, to feel whether or not he was going crazy. The things around him seemed preternaturally unreal, and rushing frantically back into his bedroom, he began tearing off his clothes, racing after the vanishing night. Undressed, he threw a final regretful glance at his pile of manuscript—he had the whole next scene in his head. As a compromise with incipient madness he got into bed and wrote for an hour more.

Late next morning he was startled awake by one of the ruthless Scandinavian sisters who, in theory, were the Lees' servants. "Eleven o'clock!" she shouted. "Five after!"

"Let me alone," Basil mumbled. "What do you come and wake me up for?"

"Somebody downstairs." He opened his eyes. "You ate all the cream last night," Hilda continued. "Your mother didn't have any for her coffee."

"All the cream!" he cried. "Why, I saw some more."

"It was sour."

"That's terrible," he exclaimed, sitting up. "Terrible!"

For a moment she enjoyed his dismay. Then she said, "Riply Buckner's downstairs," and went out, closing the door.

"Send him up!" he called after her. "Hilda, why don't you ever listen for a minute? Did I get any mail?"

There was no answer. A moment later Riply came in.

"My gosh, are you still in bed?"

"I wrote on the play all night. I almost finished Act Two." He pointed to his desk.

"That's what I want to talk to you about," said Riply. "Mother thinks we ought to get Miss Halliburton."

"What for?"

"Just to sort of be there."

Though Miss Halliburton was a pleasant person who combined the occupations of French teacher and bridge teacher, unofficial chaperon and children's friend, Basil felt that her superintendence would give the project an unprofessional ring.

"She wouldn't interfere," went on Riply, obviously quoting his mother. "I'll be the business manager and you'll direct the play, just like we said, but it would be good to have her there for prompter and to keep order at rehearsals. The girls' mothers'll like it."

"All right," Basil agreed reluctantly. "Now look, let's see who we'll have in the cast. First, there's the leading man—this gentleman burglar that's called The Shadow. Only it turns out at the end that he's really a young man about town doing it on a bet, and not really a burglar at all."

"That's you."

"No, that's you."

"Come on! You're the best actor," protested Riply.

"No, I'm going to take a smaller part, so I can coach."

"Well, haven't I got to be business manager?"

Selecting the actresses, presumably all eager, proved to be a difficult matter. They settled finally on Imogene Bissel for leading lady; Margaret Torrence for her friend, and Connie Davies for "Miss Saunders, an old maid very kittenish."

On Riply's suggestion that several other girls wouldn't be pleased at being left out, Basil introduced a maid and a cook, "who could just sort of look in from the kitchen." He rejected firmly Riply's further proposal that there should be two or three maids, "a sort of sewing woman," and a trained nurse. In a house so clogged with femininity even the most umbrageous of gentleman burglars would have difficulty in moving about.

"I'll tell you two people we won't have," Basil said meditatively—"that's Joe Gorman and Hubert Blair."

"I wouldn't be in it if we had Hubert Blair," asserted Riply.

"Neither would I."

Hubert Blair's almost miraculous successes with girls had caused Basil and Riply much jealous pain.

They began calling up the prospective cast and immediately the enterprise received its first blow. Imogene Bissel was going to Rochester, Minnesota, to have her appendix removed, and wouldn't be back for three weeks.

They considered.

"How about Margaret Torrence?"

Basil shook his head. He had vision of Leilia Van Baker as someone rarer and more spirited than Margaret Torrence. Not that Leilia had much being, even to Basil—less than the Harrison Fisher girls pinned around his wall at school. But she was not Margaret Torrence. She was no one you could inevitably see by calling up half an hour before on the phone.

He discarded candidate after candidate. Finally a face began to flash before his eyes, as if in another connection, but so insistently that at length he spoke the name.

"Evelyn Beebe."

"Who?"

Though Evelyn Beebe was only sixteen, her precocious charms had elevated her to an older crowd and to Basil she seemed of the very generation of his heroine, Leilia Van Baker. It was a little like asking Sarah Bernhardt for her services, but once her name had occurred to him, other possibilities seemed pale.

At noon they rang the Beebes' door-bell, stricken by a paralysis of embarrassment when Evelyn opened the door herself and, with politeness that concealed a certain surprise, asked them in.

Suddenly, through the portière of the living room, Basil saw and recognized a young man in golf knickerbockers.

"I guess we better not come in," he said quickly.

"We'll come some other time," Riply added.

Together they started precipitately for the door, but she barred their way.

"Don't be silly," she insisted. "It's just Andy Lockheart."

Just Andy Lockheart—winner of the Western Golf Championship at eighteen, captain of his freshman baseball team, handsome, successful at everything he tried, a living symbol of the splendid, glamorous world of Yale. For a year Basil had walked like him and tried unsuccessfully to play the piano by ear as Andy Lockheart was able to do.

Through sheer ineptitude at escaping, they were edged into the room. Their plan suddenly seemed presumptuous and absurd.

Perceiving their condition Evelyn tried to soothe them with pleasant banter.

"Well it's about time you came to see me," she told Basil. "Here I've been sitting at home every night waiting for you—ever since the Davies dance. Why haven't you been here before?"

He stared at her blankly, unable even to smile, and muttered: "Yes, you have."

"I have though. Sit down and tell me why you've been neglecting me! I suppose you've both been rushing the beautiful Imogene Bissel."

"Why, I understand——" said Basil. "Why, I heard from somewhere that she's gone up to have some kind of an appendicitis—that is——" He ran down to a pitch of inaudibility as Andy Lockheart at the piano began playing a succession of thoughtful chords, which resolved itself into the maxixe, an eccentric stepchild of the tango. Kicking back a rug and lifting her skirts a little, Evelyn fluently tapped out a circle with her heels around the floor.

They sat inanimate as cushions on the sofa watching her. She was almost beautiful, with rather large features and bright fresh color behind which her heart seemed to be trembling a little with laughter. Her voice and her lithe body were always mimicking, ceaselessly caricaturing every sound and movement near by, until even those who disliked her admitted that "Evelyn could always make you laugh." She finished her dance now with a false stumble and an awed expression as she clutched at the piano, and Basil and Riply chuckled. Seeing their embarrassment lighten, she came and sat down beside them, and they laughed again when she said: "Excuse my lack of self-control."

"Do you want to be the leading lady in a play we're going to give?" demanded Basil with sudden desperation. "We're going to have it at the Martindale School, for the benefit of the Baby Welfare."

"Basil, this is so sudden."

Andy Lockheart turned around from the piano.

"What're you going to give—a minstrel show?"

"No, it's a crook play named The Captured Shadow. Miss Halliburton is going to coach it." He suddenly realized the convenience of that name to shelter himself behind.

"Why don't you give something like 'The Private Secretary'?" interrupted Andy. "There's a good play for you. We gave it my last year at school."

"Oh, no, it's all settled," said Basil quickly. "We're going to put on this play that I wrote."

"You wrote it yourself?" exclaimed Evelyn.

"Yes."

"My-y gosh!" said Andy. He began to play again.

"Look, Evelyn," said Basil. "It's only for three weeks, and you'd be the leading lady."

She laughed. "Oh, no. I couldn't. Why don't you get Imogene?"

"She's sick, I tell you. Listen——"

"Or Margaret Torrence?"

"I don't want anybody but you."

The directness of this appeal touched her and momentarily she hesitated. But the hero of the Western Golf Championship turned around from the piano with a teasing smile and she shook her head.

"I can't do it, Basil. I may have to go East with the family."

Reluctantly Basil and Riply got up.

"Gosh, I wish you'd be in it, Evelyn."

"I wish I could."

Basil lingered, thinking fast, wanting her more than ever; indeed, without her, it scarcely seemed worth while to go on with the play. Suddenly a desperate expedient took shape on his lips:

"You certainly would be wonderful. You see, the leading man is going to be Hubert Blair."

Breathlessly he watched her, saw her hesitate.

"Good-by," he said.

She came with them to the door and then out on the veranda, frowning a little.

"How long did you say the rehearsals would take?" she asked thoughtfully.

· II ·

ON AN AUGUST evening three days later Basil read the play to the cast on Miss Halliburton's porch. He was nervous and at first there were interruptions of "Louder" and "Not so fast." Just as his audience was beginning to be amused by the repartee of the two comic crooks—repartee that had seen service with Weber and Fields—he was interrupted by the late arrival of Hubert Blair.

Hubert was fifteen, a somewhat shallow boy save for two or three felicities which he possessed to an extraordinary degree. But one excellence suggests the presence of others, and young ladies never failed to respond to his most casual fancy, enduring his fickleness of heart and never convinced that his fundamental indifference might not be overcome. They were dazzled by his flashing self-confidence, by his cherubic ingenuousness, which concealed a shrewd talent for getting around people, and by his extraordinary physical grace. Long-legged, beautifully proportioned, he had that tumbler's balance usually characteristic only of men "built near the ground." He was in constant motion that was a delight to watch, and Evelyn Beebe was not the only older girl who had found in him a mysterious promise and watched him for a long time with something more than curiosity.

He stood in the doorway now with an expression of bogus reverence on his round pert face.

"Excuse me," he said. "Is this the First Methodist Episcopal Church?" Everybody laughed—even Basil. "I didn't know. I thought maybe I was in the right church, but in the wrong pew."

They laughed again, somewhat discouraged. Basil waited until Hubert had seated himself beside Evelyn Beebe. Then he began to read once more, while the others, fascinated, watched Hubert's efforts to balance a chair on its hind legs. This squeaky experiment continued as an undertone to the reading. Not until Basil's desperate "Now, here's where you come in, Hube," did attention swing back to the play.

Basil read for more than an hour. When, at the end, he closed the composition book and looked up shyly, there was a burst of spontaneous applause. He had followed his models closely, and for all its grotesqueries, the result was actually interesting—it was a play. Afterward he lingered, talking to Miss Halliburton, and he walked home glowing with excitement and rehearsing a little by himself into the August night.

The first week of rehearsal was a matter of Basil climbing back and forth from auditorium to stage, crying, "No! Look here, Connie; you come in more like this." Then things began to happen. Mrs. Van Schellinger came to rehearsal one day, and lingering afterward, announced that she couldn't let Gladys be in "a play about criminals." Her theory was that this element could be removed; for instance, the two comic crooks could be changed to "two funny farmers."

Basil listened with horror. When she had gone he assured Miss Halliburton that he would change nothing. Luckily Gladys played the cook, an interpolated part that could be summarily struck out, but her absence was felt in another way. She was tranquil and tractable, "the most carefully brought-up girl in town," and at her withdrawal rowdiness appeared during rehearsals. Those who had only such lines as "I'll ask Mrs. Van Baker, sir," in Act I and "No, ma'am," in Act III showed a certain tendency to grow restless in between. So now it was:

"Please keep that dog quiet or else send him home!" or:

"Where's that maid? Wake up, Margaret, for heaven's sake!" or:

"What is there to laugh at that's so darn funny?"

More and more the chief problem was the tactful management of Hubert Blair. Apart from his unwillingness to learn his lines, he was a satisfactory hero, but off the stage he became a nuisance. He gave an endless private performance for Evelyn Beebe, which took such forms as chasing her amorously around the hall or of flipping peanuts over his shoulder to land mysteriously on the stage. Called to order, he would mutter, "Aw, shut up yourself," just loud enough for Basil to guess, but not to hear.

But Evelyn Beebe was all that Basil had expected. Once on the stage, she compelled a breathless attention, and Basil recognized this by adding to her part. He envied the half-sentimental fun that she and Hubert derived from their scenes together and he felt a vague, impersonal jealousy that almost every night after rehearsal they drove around together in Hubert's car.

One afternoon when matters had progressed a fortnight, Hubert came in an hour late, loafed through the first act and then informed Miss Halliburton that he was going home.

"What for?" Basil demanded.

"I've got some things I got to do."

"Are they important?"

"What business is that of yours?"

"Of course it's my business," said Basil heatedly, whereupon Miss Halliburton interfered.

"There's no use of anybody getting angry. What Basil means, Hubert, is that if it's just some small thing—why, we're all giving up our pleasures to make this play a success."

Hubert listened with obvious boredom.

"I've got to drive downtown and get father."

He looked coolly at Basil, as if challenging him to deny the adequacy of this explanation.

"Then why did you come an hour late?" demanded Basil.

"Because I had to do something for mother."

A group had gathered and he glanced around triumphantly. It was one of those sacred excuses, and only Basil saw that it was disingenuous.

"Oh, tripe!" he said.

"Maybe you think so—Bossy."

Basil took a step toward him, his eyes blazing.

"What'd you say?"

"I said 'Bossy.' Isn't that what they call you at school?"

It was true. It had followed him home. Even as he went white with rage a vast impotence surged over him at the realization that the past was always lurking near. The faces of school were around him, sneering and watching. Hubert laughed.

"Get out!" said Basil in a strained voice. "Go on! Get right out!"

Hubert laughed again, but as Basil took a step toward him he retreated.

"I don't want to be in your play anyhow. I never did."

"Then go on out of this hall."

"Now, Basil!" Miss Halliburton hovered breathlessly beside them. Hubert laughed again and looked about for his cap.

"I wouldn't be in your crazy old show," he said. He turned slowly and jauntily, and sauntered out the door.

Riply Buckner read Hubert's part that afternoon, but there was a cloud upon the rehearsal. Miss Beebe's performance lacked its customary verve and the others clustered and whispered, falling silent when Basil came near. After the rehearsal, Miss Halliburton, Riply and Basil held a conference. Upon Basil flatly refusing to take the leading part, it was decided to enlist a certain Mayall De Bec, known slightly to Riply, who had made a name for himself in theatricals at the Central High School.

But next day a blow fell that was irreparable. Evelyn, flushed and uncomfortable, told Basil and Miss Halliburton that her family's plans had changed—they were going East next week and she couldn't be in the play after all. Basil understood. Only Hubert had held her this long.

"Good-by," he said gloomily.

His manifest despair shamed her and she tried to justify herself.

"Really, I can't help it. Oh, Basil, I'm so sorry!"

"Couldn't you stay over a week with me after your family goes?" Miss Halliburton asked innocently.

"Not possibly. Father wants us all to go together. That's the only reason. If it wasn't for that I'd stay."

"All right," Basil said. "Good-by."

"Basil, you're not mad, are you?" A gust of repentance swept over her. "I'll do anything to help. I'll come to rehearsals this week until you get someone else, and then I'll try to help her all I can. But father says we've got to go."

In vain Riply tried to raise Basil's morale after the rehearsal that afternoon, making suggestions which he waved contemptuously away. Margaret Torrence? Connie Davies? They could hardly play the parts they had. It seemed to Basil as if the undertaking was falling to pieces before his eyes.

It was still early when he got home. He sat dispiritedly by his bedroom window, watching the little Barnfield boy playing a lonesome game by himself in the yard next door.

His mother came in at five, and immediately sensed his depression.

"Teddy Barnfield has the mumps," she said, in an effort to distract him. "That's why he's playing there all alone."

"Has he?" he responded listlessly.

"It isn't at all dangerous, but it's very contagious. You had it when you were seven."

"H'm."

She hesitated.

"Are you worrying about your play? Has anything gone wrong?"

"No, mother. I just want to be alone."

After a while he got up and started after a malted milk at the soda fountain around the corner. It was half in his mind to see Mr. Beebe and ask him if he couldn't postpone his trip East. If he could only be sure that that was Evelyn's real reason.

The sight of Evelyn's nine-year-old brother coming along the street broke in on his thoughts.

"Hello, Ham. I hear you're going away."

Ham nodded.

"Going next week. To the seashore."

Basil looked at him speculatively, as if, through his proximity to Evelyn, he held the key to the power of moving her.

"Where are you going now?" he asked.

"I'm going to play with Teddy Barnfield."

"What!" Basil exclaimed. "Why, didn't you know—" He stopped. A wild, criminal idea broke over him; his mother's words floated through his mind: "It isn't at all dangerous, but it's very contagious." If little Ham Beebe got the mumps, and Evelyn *couldn't* go away—

He came to a decision quickly and coolly.

"Teddy's playing in his back yard," he said. "If you want to see him without going through his house, why don't you go down this street and turn up the alley?"

"All right. Thanks," said Ham trustingly.

Basil stood for a minute looking after him until he turned the corner into the alley, fully aware that it was the worst thing he had ever done in his life.

· III ·

A WEEK LATER Mrs. Lee had an early supper—all Basil's favorite things: chipped beef, french-fried potatoes, sliced peaches and cream, and devil's food.

Every few minutes Basil said, "Gosh! I wonder what time it is," and went out in the hall to look at the clock. "Does that clock work right?" he demanded with sudden suspicion. It was the first time the matter had ever interested him.

"Perfectly all right. If you eat so fast you'll have indigestion and then you won't be able to act well."

"What do you think of the program?" he asked for the third time. "Riply Buckner, Jr., presents Basil Duke Lee's comedy, 'The Captured Shadow.'"

"I think it's very nice."

"He doesn't really present it."

"It sounds very well though."

"I wonder what time it is?" he inquired.

"You just said it was ten minutes after six."

"Well, I guess I better be starting."

"Eat your peaches, Basil. If you don't eat you won't be able to act."

"I don't have to act," he said patiently. "All I am is a small part, and it wouldn't matter—" It was too much trouble to explain.

"Please don't smile at me when I come on, mother," he requested. "Just act as if I was anybody else."

"Can't I even say how-do-you-do?"

"What?" Humor was lost on him. He said good-by. Trying very hard to digest not his food but his heart, which had somehow slipped down into his stomach, he started off for the Martindale School.

As its yellow windows loomed out of the night his excitement became insupportable; it bore no resemblance to the building he had been entering so casually for three weeks. His footsteps echoed symbolically and portentously in its deserted hall; upstairs there was only the janitor setting out the chairs in rows, and Basil wandered about the vacant stage until someone came in.

It was Mayall De Bec, the tall, clever, not very likeable youth they had imported from Lower Crest Avenue to be the leading man. Mayall, far from being nervous, tried to engage Basil in casual conversation. He wanted to know if Basil thought Evelyn Beebe would mind if he went to see her sometime when the show was over. Basil supposed not. Mayall said he had a friend whose father owned a brewery who owned a twelve-cylinder car.

Basil said, "Gee!"

At quarter to seven the participants arrived in groups—Riply Buckner with the six boys he had gathered to serve as ticket takers and ushers; Miss Halliburton, trying to seem very calm and reliable; Evelyn Beebe, who came in as if she were yielding herself up to something and whose glance at Basil seemed to say: "Well, it looks as if I'm really going through with it after all."

Mayall De Bec was to make up the boys and Miss Halliburton the girls. Basil soon came to the conclusion that Miss Halliburton knew nothing about make-up, but he judged it diplomatic, in that lady's overwrought condition, to say nothing, but to take each girl to Mayall for corrections when Miss Halliburton had done.

An exclamation from Bill Kampf, standing at a crack in the curtain, brought Basil to his side. A tall bald-headed man in spectacles had come in and was shown to a seat in the middle of the house, where he examined the program. He was the public. Behind those waiting eyes, suddenly so mysterious and incalculable, was the secret of the play's failure or success. He finished the program, took off his glasses and looked around. Two old ladies and two little boys came in, followed immediately by a dozen more.

"Hey, Riply," Basil called softly. "Tell them to put the children down in front."

Riply, struggling into his policeman's uniform, looked up, and the long black mustache on his upper lip quivered indignantly.

"I thought of that long ago."

The hall, filling rapidly, was now alive with the buzz of conversation. The children in front were jumping up and down in their seats, and everyone was talking and calling back and forth save the several dozen cooks and housemaids who sat in stiff and quiet pairs about the room.

Then, suddenly, everything was ready. It was incredible. "Stop! Stop!" Basil wanted to say. "It can't be ready. There must be something—there always has been something," but the darkened auditorium and the piano and violin from Geyer's Orchestra playing "Meet Me in the Shadows" belied his words. Miss Saunders, Leilia Van Baker and Leilia's friend, Estella Carrage, were already seated on the stage, and Miss Halliburton stood in the wings with the prompt book. Suddenly the music ended and the chatter in front died away.

"Oh, gosh!" Basil thought. "Oh, my gosh!"

The curtain rose. A clear voice floated up from somewhere. Could it be from that unfamiliar group on the stage?

I will, Miss Saunders. I tell you I will!

But, Miss Leilia, I don't consider the newspapers proper for young ladies nowadays.

I don't care. I want to read about this wonderful gentleman burglar they call The Shadow.

It was actually going on. Almost before he realized it, a ripple of laughter passed over the audience as Evelyn gave her imitation of Miss Saunders behind her back.

"Get ready, Basil," breathed Miss Halliburton.

Basil and Bill Kampf, the crooks, each took an elbow of Victor Van Baker, the dissolute son of the house, and made ready to aid him through the front door.

It was strangely natural to be out on the stage with all those eyes looking up encouragingly. His mother's face floated past him, other faces that he recognized and remembered.

Bill Kampf stumbled on a line and Basil picked him up quickly and went on.

> MISS SAUNDERS: So you are alderman from the Sixth Ward?
> RABBIT SIMMONS: Yes, ma'am.
> MISS SAUNDERS (*shaking her head kittenishly*): Just what is an alderman?
> CHINAMAN RUDD: An alderman is halfway between a politician and a pirate.

This was one of Basil's lines that he was particularly proud of—but there was not a sound from the audience, not a smile. A moment later Bill Kampf absent-mindedly wiped his forehead with his handkerchief and then stared at it, startled by the red stains of make-up on it—and the audience roared. The theater was like that.

> MISS SAUNDERS: Then you believe in spirits, Mr. Rudd.
> CHINAMAN RUDD: Yes, ma'am, I certainly do believe in spirits. Have you got any?

The first big scene came. On the darkened stage a window rose slowly and Mayall De Bec, "in a full evening dress," climbed over the sill. He was tiptoeing cautiously from one side of the stage to the other, when Leilia Van Baker came in. For a moment she was frightened, but he assured her that he was a friend of her brother Victor. They talked. She told him naïvely yet feelingly of her admiration for The Shadow, of whose exploits she had read. She hoped, though, that The Shadow would not come here tonight, as the family jewels were all in that safe at the right.

The stranger was hungry. He had been late for his dinner and so had not been able to get any that night. Would he have some crackers and milk? That would be fine. Scarcely had she left the room when he was on his knees by the safe, fumbling at the catch, undeterred by the unpromising word "Cake" stencilled on the safe's front. It swung open, but he heard footsteps outside and closed it just as Leilia came back with the crackers and milk.

They lingered, obviously attracted to each other. Miss Saunders came in, very kittenish, and was introduced. Again Evelyn mimicked her behind her back and the audience roared. Other members of the household appeared and were introduced to the stranger.

What's this? A banging at the door, and Mulligan, a policeman, rushes in.

We have just received word from the Central Office that the notorious Shadow has been seen climbing in the window! No one can leave this house tonight!

The curtain fell. The first rows of the audience—the younger brothers and sisters of the cast—were extravagant in their enthusiasm. The actors took a bow.

A moment later Basil found himself alone with Evelyn Beebe on the stage. A weary doll in her make-up she was leaning against a table.

"Heigh-ho, Basil," she said.

She had not quite forgiven him for holding her to her promise after her little brother's mumps had postponed their trip East, and Basil had tactfully avoided her, but now they met in the genial glow of excitement and success.

"You were wonderful," he said—"Wonderful!"

He lingered a moment. He could never please her, for she wanted someone like herself, someone who could reach her through her senses, like Hubert Blair. Her intuition told her that Basil was of a certain vague consequence; beyond that his incessant attempts to make people think and feel, bothered and wearied her. But suddenly, in the glow of the evening, they leaned forward and kissed peacefully, and from that moment, because they had no common ground even to quarrel on, they were friends for life.

When the curtain rose upon the second act Basil slipped down a flight of stairs and up to another to the back of the hall, where he stood watching in the darkness. He laughed silently when the audience laughed, enjoying it as if it were a play he had never seen before.

There was a second and a third act scene that were very similar. In each of them The Shadow, alone on the stage, was interrupted by Miss Saunders. Mayall De Bec, having had but ten days of rehearsal, was inclined to confuse the two, but Basil was totally unprepared for what happened. Upon Connie's entrance Mayall spoke his third-act line and involuntarily Connie answered in kind.

Others coming on the stage were swept up in the nervousness and confusion, and suddenly they were playing the third act in the middle of the second. It happened so quickly that for a moment Basil had only a vague sense that something was wrong. Then he dashed down one stairs and up another and into the wings, crying:

"Let down the curtain! Let down the curtain!"

The boys who stood there aghast sprang to the rope. In a minute Basil, breathless, was facing the audience.

"Ladies and gentlemen," he said, "there's been changes in the cast and what just happened was a mistake. If you'll excuse us we'd like to do that scene over."

He stepped back in the wings to a flutter of laughter and applause.

"All right, Mayall!" he called excitedly. "On the stage alone. Your line is: 'I just want to see that the jewels are all right,' and Connie's is: 'Go ahead, don't mind me.' All right! Curtain up!"

In a moment things righted themselves. Someone brought water for Miss Halliburton, who was in a state of collapse, and as the act ended they all took a curtain call once more. Twenty minutes later it was over. The hero clasped Leilia Van Baker to his breast, confessing that he was The Shadow, "and a captured Shadow at that"; the curtain went up and down, up and down; Miss Halliburton was dragged unwillingly on the stage and the ushers came up the aisles laden with flowers. Then everything became informal and the actors mingled happily with the audience, laughing and important, congratulated from all sides. An old man whom Basil didn't know came up to him and shook his hand, saying, "You're a young man that's going to be heard from some day," and a reporter from the paper asked him if he was really only fifteen. It might all have been very bad and demoralizing for Basil, but it was already behind him. Even as the crowd melted away and the last few people spoke to him and went out, he felt a great vacancy come into his heart. It was over, it was done and gone—all that work, and interest and absorption. It was a hollowness like fear.

"Good night, Miss Halliburton. Good night, Evelyn."

"Good night, Basil. Congratulations, Basil. Good night."

"Where's my coat? Good night, Basil."

"Leave your costumes on the stage, please. They've got to go back tomorrow."

He was almost the last to leave, mounting to the stage for a moment and looking around the deserted hall. His mother was waiting and they strolled home together through the first cool night of the year.

"Well, I thought it went very well indeed. Were you satisfied?" He didn't answer for a moment. "Weren't you satisfied with the way it went?"

"Yes." He turned his head away.

"What's the matter?"

"Nothing," and then, "Nobody really cares, do they?"

"About what?"

"About anything."

"Everybody cares about different things. I care about you, for instance."

Instinctively he ducked away from a hand extended caressingly toward him: "Oh, don't. I don't mean like that."

"You're just overwrought, dear."

"I am not overwrought. I just feel sort of sad."

"You shouldn't feel sad. Why, people told me after the play—"

"Oh, that's all over. Don't talk about that—don't ever talk to me about that any more."

"Then what are you sad about?"

"Oh, about a little boy."

"What little boy?"

"Oh, little Ham—you wouldn't understand."

"When we get home I want you to take a real hot bath and quiet your nerves."

"All right."

But when he got home he fell immediately into deep sleep on the sofa. She hesitated. Then covering him with a blanket and a comforter, she pushed a pillow under his protesting head and went upstairs.

She knelt for a long time beside her bed.

"God, help him! help him," she prayed, "because he needs help that I can't give him any more."

BASIL AND CLEOPATRA

◆

*"Basil and Cleopatra" (Saturday Evening Post, 27 April 1929) was the final
story in the Basil Duke Lee series. Fitzgerald did not include it in Taps at
Reveille although it is one of the strongest of the Basils. Perhaps he felt that
it wraps up Basil's youth too neatly; at the end of the story Basil, unlike
Mark Antony, chooses discipline over love.*

◆

WHEREVER SHE WAS, became a beautiful and enchanted place to Basil,
but he did not think of it that way. He thought the fascination was inherent
in the locality, and long afterward a commonplace street or the mere name
of a city would exude a peculiar glow, a sustained sound, that struck his
soul alert with delight. In her presence he was too absorbed to notice his
surroundings; so that her absence never made them empty, but, rather, sent
him seeking for her through haunted rooms and gardens that he had never
really seen before.

This time, as usual, he saw only the expression of her face, the mouth
that gave an attractive interpretation of any emotion she felt or pretended
to feel—oh, invaluable mouth—and the rest of her, new as a peach and old
as sixteen. He was almost unconscious that they stood in a railroad station
and entirely unconscious that she had just glanced over his shoulder and
fallen in love with another young man. Turning to walk with the rest to the
car, she was already acting for the stranger; no less so because her voice
was pitched for Basil and she clung to him, squeezing his arm.

Had Basil noticed this other young man that the train discharged he
would merely have been sorry for him—as he had been sorry for the
wretched people in the villages along the railroad and for his fellow
travelers—they were not entering Yale in a fortnight nor were they about
to spend three days in the same town with Miss Erminie Gilberte Labouisse
Bibble. There was something dense, hopeless and a little contemptible about
them all.

Basil had come to visit here because Erminie Bibble was visiting here.

On the sad eve of her departure from his native Western city a month before, she had said, with all the promise one could ask in her urgent voice:

"If you know a boy in Mobile, why don't you make him invite you down when I'll be there?"

He had followed this suggestion. And now with the soft, unfamiliar Southern city actually flowing around him, his excitement led him to believe that Fat Gaspar's car floated off immediately they entered it. A voice from the curb came as a surprise:

"Hi, Bessie Belle. Hi, William. How you all?"

The newcomer was tall and lean and a year or so older than Basil. He wore a white linen suit and a panama hat, under which burned fierce, undefeated Southern eyes.

"Why, Littleboy Le Moyne!" exclaimed Miss Cheever. "When did you get home?"

"Jus' now, Bessie Belle. Saw you lookin' so fine and pretty, had to come and see closer."

He was introduced to Minnie and Basil.

"Drop you somewhere, Littleboy?" asked Fat—on his native heath, William.

"Why—" Le Moyne hesitated. "You're very kind, but the man ought to be here with the car."

"Jump in."

Le Moyne swung his bag on top of Basil's and with courteous formality got in the back seat beside them. Basil caught Minnie's eye and she smiled quickly back, as if to say, "This is too bad, but it'll soon be over."

"Do you happen to come from New Orleans, Miss Bibble?" asked Le Moyne.

"Sure do."

" 'Cause I just came from there and they told me one of their mos' celebrated heartbreakers was visiting up here, and meanwhile her suitors were shooting themselves all over the city. That's the truth. I used to help pick 'em up myself sometimes when they got littering the streets."

"This must be Mobile Bay on the left," Basil thought; "Down Mobile," and the Dixie moonlight and darky stevedores singing. The houses on either side of the street were gently faded behind proud, protecting vines; there had been crinolines on these balconies, and guitars by night in these broken gardens.

It was so warm; the voices were so sure they had time to say everything —even Minnie's voice, answering the banter of the youth with the odd nickname, seemed slower and lazier—he had scarcely ever thought of her as a Southern girl before. They stopped at a large gate where flickers of a yellow house showed through luscious trees. Le Moyne got out.

"I certainly hope you both enjoy your visit here. If you'll permit me I'll call around and see if there's anything I can do to add to your pleasure." He swooped his panama. "I bid you good day."

As they started off, Bessie Belle turned around and smiled at Minnie. "Didn't I tell you?" she demanded.

"I guessed it in the station, before he came up to the car," said Minnie. "Something told me that was him."

"Did you think he was good-looking?"

"He was divine," Minnie said.

"Of course he's always gone with an older crowd."

To Basil, this prolonged discussion seemed a little out of place. After all, the young man was simply a local Southerner who lived here; add to that, that he went with an older crowd, and it seemed that his existence was being unnecessarily insisted upon.

But now Minnie turned to him, said, "Basil," wriggled invitingly and folded her hands in a humble, expectant way that invariably caused disturbances in his heart.

"I loved your letters," she said.

"You might have answered them."

"I haven't had a minute, Basil. I visited in Chicago and then in Nashville. I haven't even been home." She lowered her voice. "Father and mother are getting a divorce, Basil. Isn't that awful?"

He was startled; then, after a moment, he adjusted the idea to her and she became doubly poignant; because of its romantic connection with her, the thought of divorce would never shock him again.

"That's why I didn't write. But I've thought of you so much. You're the best friend I have, Basil. You always understand."

This was decidedly not the note upon which they had parted in St. Paul. A dreadful rumor that he hadn't intended to mention rose to his lips.

"Who is this fellow Bailey you met at Lake Forest?" he inquired lightly.

"Buzz Bailey!" Her big eyes opened in surprise. "He's very attractive and a divine dancer, but we're just friends." She frowned. "I bet Connie Davies has been telling tales in St. Paul. Honestly, I'm so sick of girls that, just out of jealousy or nothing better to do, sit around and criticize you if you have a good time."

He was convinced now that something had occurred in Lake Forest, but he concealed the momentary pang from Minnie.

"Anyhow, you're a fine one to talk." She smiled suddenly. "I guess everybody knows how fickle you are, Mr. Basil Duke Lee."

Generally such an implication is considered flattering, but the lightness, almost the indifference, with which she spoke increased his alarm—and then suddenly the bomb exploded.

"You needn't worry about Buzz Bailey. At present I'm absolutely heart-whole and fancy free."

Before he could even comprehend the enormity of what she had said, they stopped at Bessie Belle Cheever's door and the two girls ran up the steps, calling back, "We'll see you this afternoon."

Mechanically Basil climbed into the front seat beside his host.

"Going out for freshman football, Basil?" William asked.

"What? Oh, sure. If I can get off my two conditions." There was no if in his heart; it was the greatest ambition of his life.

"You'll probably make the freshman team easy. That fellow Littleboy Le Moyne you just met is going to Princeton this fall. He played end at V. M. I."

"Where'd he get that crazy name?"

"Why, his family always called him that and everybody picked it up." After a moment he added, "He asked them to the country-club dance with him tonight."

"When did he?" Basil demanded in surprise.

"Right then. That's what they were talking about. I meant to ask them and I was just leading up to it gradually, but he stepped in before I could get a chance." He sighed, blaming himself. "Well, anyhow, we'll see them there."

"Sure; it doesn't matter," said Basil. But was it Fat's mistake? Couldn't Minnie have said right out: "But Basil came all this way to see me and I ought to go with him on his first night here."

What had happened? One month ago, in the dim, thunderous Union Station at St. Paul, they had gone behind a baggage truck and he had kissed her, and her eyes had said: "Again." Up to the very end, when she disappeared in a swirl of vapor at the car window, she had been his—those weren't things you thought; they were things you knew. He was bewildered. It wasn't like Minnie, who, for all her glittering popularity, was invariably kind. He tried to think of something in his letters that might have offended her, and searched himself for new shortcomings. Perhaps she didn't like him the way he was in the morning. The joyous mood in which he had arrived was vanishing into air.

She was her familiar self when they played tennis that afternoon; she admired his strokes and once, when they were close at the net, she suddenly patted his hand. But later, as they drank lemonade on the Cheevers' wide, shady porch, he couldn't seem to be alone with her even for a minute. Was it by accident that, coming back from the courts, she had sat in front with

Fat? Last summer she had made opportunities to be alone with him—made them out of nothing. It was in a state that seemed to border on some terrible realization that he dressed for the country-club dance.

The club lay in a little valley, almost roofed over by willows, and down through their black silhouettes, in irregular blobs and patches, dripped the light of a huge harvest moon. As they parked the car, Basil's tune of tunes, Chinatown, drifted from the windows and dissolved into its notes which thronged like elves through the glade. His heart quickened, suffocating him; the throbbing tropical darkness held a promise of such romance as he had dreamed of; but faced with it, he felt himself too small and impotent to seize the felicity he desired. When he danced with Minnie he was ashamed of inflicting his merely mortal presence on her in this fairyland whose un-familiar figures reached towering proportions of magnificence and beauty. To make him king here, she would have to reach forth and draw him close to her with soft words; but she only said, "Isn't it wonderful, Basil? Did you ever have a better time?"

Talking for a moment with Le Moyne in the stag line, Basil was hesitantly jealous and oddly shy. He resented the tall form that stooped down so fiercely over Minnie as they danced, but he found it impossible to dislike him or not to be amused by the line of sober-faced banter he kept up with passing girls. He and William Gasper were the youngest boys here, as Bessie Belle and Minnie were the youngest girls, and for the first time in his life he wanted passionately to be older, less impressionable, less impressed. Quivering at every scent, sight or tune, he wanted to be blasé and calm. Wretchedly he felt the whole world of beauty pour down upon him like moonlight, pressing on him, making his breath now sighing, now short, as he wallowed helplessly in a superabundance of youth for which a hundred adults present would have given years of life.

Next day, meeting her in a world that had shrunk back to reality, things were more natural, but something was gone and he could not bring himself to be amusing and gay. It would be like being brave after the battle. He should have been all that the night before. They went downtown in an unpaired foursome and called at a photographer's for some pictures of Minnie. Basil liked one proof that no one else liked—somehow, it re-minded him of her as she had been in St. Paul—so he ordered two—one for her to keep and one to send after him to Yale. All afternoon she was distracted and vaguely singing, but back at the Cheevers' she sprang up the steps at the sound of the phone inside. Ten minutes later she appeared, sulky and lowering, and Basil heard a quick exchange between the two girls:

"He can't get out of it."

"—a pity."

"—back Friday."

It could only be Le Moyne who had gone away, and to Minnie it mattered. Presently, unable to endure her disappointment, he got up wretchedly and suggested to William that they go home. To his surprise, Minnie's hand on his arm arrested him.

"Don't go, Basil. It doesn't seem as if I've seen you a minute since you've been here."

He laughed unhappily.

"As if it mattered to you."

"Basil, don't be silly." She bit her lip as if she were hurt. "Let's go out to the swing."

He was suddenly radiant with hope and happiness. Her tender smile, which seemed to come from the heart of freshness, soothed him and he drank down her lies in grateful gulps like cool water. The last sunshine touched her cheeks with the unearthly radiance he had seen there before, as she told him how she hadn't wanted to accept Le Moyne's invitation, and how surprised and hurt she had been when he hadn't come near her last night.

"Then do one thing, Minnie," he pleaded: "Won't you let me kiss you just once?"

"But not here," she exclaimed, "you silly!"

"Let's go in the summerhouse, for just a minute."

"Basil, I can't. Bessie Belle and William are on the porch. Maybe some other time."

He looked at her distraught, unable to believe or disbelieve in her, and she changed the subject quickly:

"I'm going to Miss Beecher's school, Basil. It's only a few hours from New Haven. You can come up and see me this fall. The only thing is, they say you have to sit in glass parlors. Isn't that terrible?"

"Awful," he agreed fervently.

William and Bessie Belle had left the veranda and were out in front, talking to some people in a car.

"Minnie, come into the summerhouse now—for just a minute. They're so far away."

Her face set unwillingly.

"I can't, Basil. Don't you see I can't?"

"Why not? I've got to leave tomorrow."

"Oh, no."

"I have to. I only have four days to get ready for my exams. Minnie—"

He took her hand. It rested calmly enough in his, but when he tried to pull her to her feet she plucked it sharply away. The swing moved with the little struggle and Basil put out his foot and made it stop. It was terrible to swing when one was at a disadvantage.

She laid the recovered hand on his knee.

"I've stopped kissing people, Basil. Really. I'm too old; I'll be seventeen next May."

"I'll bet you kissed Le Moyne," he said bitterly.

"Well, you're pretty fresh—"

Basil got out of the swing.

"I think I'll go."

Looking up, she judged him dispassionately, as she never had before—his sturdy graceful figure; the high, warm color through his tanned skin; his black, shining hair that she had once thought so romantic. She felt, too—as even those who disliked him felt—that there was something else in his face—a mark, a hint of destiny, a persistence that was more than will, that was rather a necessity of pressing its own pattern on the world, of having its way. That he would most probably succeed at Yale, that it would be nice to go there this year as his girl, meant nothing to her. She had never needed to be calculating. Hesitating, she alternatingly drew him toward her in her mind and let him go. There were so many men and they wanted her so much. If Le Moyne had been here at hand she wouldn't have hesitated, for nothing must interfere with the mysterious opening glory of that affair; but he was gone for three days and she couldn't decide quite yet to let Basil go.

"Stay over till Wednesday and I'll—I'll do what you want," she said.

"But I can't. I've got these exams to study for. I ought to have left this afternoon."

"Study on the train."

She wriggled, dropped her hands in her lap and smiled at him. Taking her hand suddenly, he pulled her to her feet and toward the summerhouse and the cool darkness behind its vines.

· II ·

THE FOLLOWING FRIDAY Basil arrived in New Haven and set about crowding five days' work into two. He had done no studying on the train; instead he sat in a trance and concentrated upon Minnie, wondering what was happening now that Le Moyne was there. She had kept her promise to him, but only literally—kissed him once in the playhouse, once, grudgingly, the second evening; but the day of his departure there had been a telegram from Le Moyne, and in front of Bessie Belle she had not even dared to kiss him good-by. As a sort of amend she had given him permission to call on the first day permitted by Miss Beecher's school.

The opening of college found him rooming with Brick Wales and George Dorsey in a suite of two bedrooms and a study in Wright Hall. Until the result of his trigonometry examination was published he was ineligible to play football, but watching the freshmen practice on Yale field, he saw that the quarterback position lay between Cullum, last year's Andover captain, and a man named Danziger from a New Bedford high school. There was a rumor that Cullum would be moved to halfback. The other quarterbacks did not appear formidable and Basil felt a great impatience to be out there with a team in his hands to move over the springy turf. He was sure he could at least get in some of the games.

Behind everything, as a light showing through, was the image of Minnie; he would see her in a week, three days, tomorrow. On the eve of the occasion he ran into Fat Gaspar, who was in Sheff, in the oval by Haughton Hall. In the first busy weeks they had scarcely met; now they walked along for a little way together.

"We all came North together," Fat said. "You ought to have been along. We had some excitement. Minnie got in a jam with Littleboy Le Moyne."

Basil's blood ran cold.

"It was funny afterward, but she was pretty scared for a while," continued Fat. "She had a compartment with Bessie Belle, but she and Littleboy wanted to be alone; so in the afternoon Bessie Belle came and played cards in ours. Well, after about two hours Bessie Belle and I went back, and there were Minnie and Littleboy standing in the vestibule arguing with the conductor; Minnie white as a sheet. Seems they locked the door and pulled down the blinds, and I guess there was a little petting going on. When he came along after the tickets and knocked on the door, they thought it was us kidding them, and wouldn't let him in at first, and when they did, he was pretty upset. He asked Littleboy if that was his compartment, and whether he and Minnie were married that they locked the door, and Littleboy lost his temper trying to explain that there was nothing wrong. He said the conductor had insulted Minnie and he wanted him to fight. But that conductor could have made trouble, and believe me, I had an awful time smoothing it all over."

With every detail imagined, with every refinement of jealousy beating in his mind, including even envy for their community of misfortune as they stood together in the vestibule, Basil went up to Miss Beecher's next day. Radiant and glowing, more mysteriously desirable than ever, wearing her very sins like stars, she came down to him in her plain white uniform dress, and his heart turned over at the kindness of her eyes.

"You were wonderful to come up, Basil. I'm so excited having a beau so soon. Everybody's jealous of me."

The glass doors hinged like French windows, shutting them in on all sides. It was hot. Down through three more compartments he could see another couple—a girl and her brother, Minnie said—and from time to time they moved and gestured soundlessly, as unreal in these tiny human conservatories as the vase of paper flowers on the table. Basil walked up and down nervously.

"Minnie, I want to be a great man some day and I want to do everything for you. I understand you're tired of me now. I don't know how it happened, but somebody else came along—it doesn't matter. There isn't any hurry. But I just want you to—oh, remember me in some different way—try to think of me as you used to, not as if I was just another one you threw over. Maybe you'd better not see me for a while—I mean at the dance this fall. Wait till I've accomplished some big scene or deed, you know, and I can show it to you and say I did that all for you."

It was very futile and young and sad. Once, carried away by the tragedy of it all, he was on the verge of tears, but he controlled himself to that extent. There was sweat on his forehead. He sat across the room from her, and Minnie sat on the couch, looking at the floor, and said several times: "Can't we be friends, Basil? I always think of you as one of my best friends."

Toward the end she rose patiently.

"Don't you want to see the chapel?"

They walked upstairs and he glanced dismally into a small dark space, with her living, sweet-smelling presence half a yard from his shoulder. He was almost glad when the funereal business was over and he walked out of the school into the fresh autumn air.

Back in New Haven he found two pieces of mail on his desk. One was a notice from the registrar telling him that he had failed his trigonometry examination and would be ineligible for football. The second was a photograph of Minnie—the picture that he had liked and ordered two of in Mobile. At first the inscription puzzled him: "L. L. from E. G. L. B. Trains are bad for the heart." Then suddenly he realized what had happened, and threw himself on his bed, shaken with wild laughter.

· I I I ·

THREE WEEKS LATER, having requested and passed a special examination in trigonometry, Basil began to look around him gloomily to see if there was anything left in life. Not since his miserable first year at school had he passed through such a period of misery; only now did he begin for the first time to be aware of Yale. The quality of romantic speculation reawoke, and, listlessly at first, then with growing determination, he set about merging himself into this spirit which had fed his dreams so long.

"I want to be chairman of the News or the Record," thought his old self one October morning, "and I want to get my letter in football, and I want to be in Skull and Bones."

Whenever the vision of Minnie and Le Moyne on the train occurred to him, he repeated this phrase like an incantation. Already he thought with shame of having stayed over in Mobile, and there began to be long strings of hours when he scarcely brooded about her at all.

He had missed half of the freshman football season, and it was with scant hope that he joined the squad on Yale field. Dressed in his black and white St. Regis jersey, amid the motley of forty schools, he looked enviously at the proud two dozen in Yale blue. At the end of four days he was reconciling himself to obscurity for the rest of the season when the voice of Carson, assistant coach, singled him suddenly out of a crowd of scrub backs.

"Who was throwing those passes just now?"

"I was, sir."

"I haven't seen you before, have I?"

"I just got eligible."

"Know the signals?"

"Yes, sir."

"Well, you take this team down the field—ends, Krutch and Bispam; tackles—"

A moment later he heard his own voice snapping out on the crisp air: "Thirty-two, sixty-five, sixty-seven, twenty-two—"

There was a ripple of laughter.

"Wait a minute! Where'd you learn to call signals like that?" said Carson.

"Why, we had a Harvard coach, sir."

"Well, just drop the Haughton emphasis. You'll get everybody too excited."

After a few minutes they were called in and told to put on headgears.

"Where's Waite?" Carson asked. "Test, eh? Well, you then—what's your name?—in the black and white sweater?"

"Lee."

"You call signals. And let's see you get some life into this outfit. Some of you guards and tackles are big enough for the varsity. Keep them on their toes, you—what's your name?"

"Lee."

They lined up with possession of the ball on the freshmen's twenty-yard line. They were allowed unlimited downs, but when, after a dozen plays, they were in approximately that same place, the ball was given to the first team.

"That's that!" thought Basil. "That finishes me."

But an hour later, as they got out of the bus, Carson spoke to him:

"Did you weigh this afternoon?"

"Yes. Hundred and fifty-eight."

"Let me give you a tip—you're still playing prep-school football. You're still satisfied with stopping them. The idea here is that if you lay them down hard enough you wear them out. Can you kick?"

"No, sir."

"Well, it's too bad you didn't get out sooner."

A week later his name was read out as one of those to go to Andover. Two quarterbacks ranked ahead of him, Danziger and a little hard rubber ball of a man, named Appleton, and Basil watched the game from the sidelines, but when, the following Tuesday, Danziger splintered his arm in practice, Basil was ordered to report to training table.

On the eve of the game with the Princeton freshmen, the egress of the student body to Princeton for the Varsity encounter left the campus almost deserted. Deep autumn had set in, with a crackling wind from the west, and walking back to his room after final skull practice, Basil felt the old lust for glory sweep over him. Le Moyne was playing end on the Princeton freshman and it was probable that Minnie would be in the stands, but now, as he ran along the springy grass in front of Osborne, swaying to elude imaginary tacklers, the fact seemed of less importance than the game. Like most Americans, he was seldom able really to grasp the moment, to say: "This, for me, is the great equation by which everything else will be measured; this is the golden time," but for once the present was sufficient. He was going to spend two hours in a country where life ran at the pace he demanded of it.

The day was fair and cool; an unimpassioned crowd, mostly townsmen, was scattered through the stands. The Princeton freshmen looked sturdy and solid in their diagonal stripes, and Basil picked out Le Moyne, noting coldly that he was exceptionally fast, and bigger than he had seemed in his clothes. On an impulse Basil turned and searched for Minnie in the crowd, but he could not find her. A minute later the whistle blew; sitting at the coach's side, he concentrated all his faculties on the play.

The first half was played between the thirty-yard lines. The main principles of Yale's offense seemed to Basil too simple; less effective than the fragments of the Haughton system he had learned at school, while the Princeton tactics, still evolved in Sam White's long shadow, were built around a punter and the hope of a break. When the break came, it was Yale's. At the start of the second half Princeton fumbled and Appleton sent over a drop kick from the thirty-yard line.

It was his last act of the day. He was hurt on the next kick-off and, to a burst of freshmen cheering, assisted from the game.

With his heart in a riot, Basil sprinted out on the field. He felt an overpowering strangeness, and it was someone else in his skin who called the first signals and sent an unsuccessful play through the line. As he forced his eyes to take in the field slowly, they met Le Moyne's, and Le Moyne grinned at him. Basil called for a short pass over the line, throwing it himself for a gain of seven yards. He sent Cullum off tackle for three more and a first down. At the forty, with more latitude, his mind began to function smoothly and surely. His short passes worried the Princeton fullback, and, in consequence, the running gains through the line were averaging four yards instead of two.

At the Princeton forty he dropped back to kick formation and tried Le Moyne's end, but Le Moyne went under the interfering halfback and caught Basil by a foot. Savagely Basil tugged himself free, but too late—the halfback bowled him over. Again Le Moyne's face grinned at him, and Basil hated it. He called the same end and, with Cullum carrying the ball, they rolled over Le Moyne six yards, to Princeton's thirty-two. He was slowing down, was he? Then run him ragged! System counseled a pass, but he heard himself calling the end again. He ran parallel to the line, saw his interference melt away and Le Moyne, his jaw set, coming for him. Instead of cutting in, Basil turned full about and tried to reverse his field. When he was trapped he had lost fifteen yards.

A few minutes later the ball changed hands and he ran back to the safety position thinking: "They'd yank me if they had anybody to put in my place."

The Princeton team suddenly woke up. A long pass gained thirty yards. A fast new back dazzled his way through the line for another first down. Yale was on the defensive, but even before they had realized the fact, the disaster had happened. Basil was drawn on an apparently developed play; too late he saw the ball shoot out of scrimmage to a loose end; saw, as he was neatly blocked, that the Princeton substitutes were jumping around wildly, waving their blankets. They had scored.

He got up with his heart black, but his brain cool. Blunders could be atoned for—if they only wouldn't take him out. The whistle blew for the quarter, and squatting on the turf with the exhausted team, he made himself believe that he hadn't lost their confidence, kept his face intent and rigid, refusing no man's eye. He had made his errors for today.

On the kick-off he ran the ball back to the thirty-five, and a steady rolling progress began. The short passes, a weak spot inside tackle, Le Moyne's end. Le Moyne was tired now. His face was drawn and dogged as he smashed blindly into the interference; the ball carrier eluded him—Basil or another.

Thirty more to go—twenty—over Le Moyne again. Disentangling himself from the pile, Basil met the Southerner's weary glance and insulted him in a crisp voice:

"You've quit, Littleboy. They better take you out."

He started the next play at him and, as Le Moyne charged in furiously, tossed a pass over his head for the score. Yale 10, Princeton 7. Up and down the field again, with Basil fresher every minute and another score in sight, and suddenly the game was over.

Trudging off the field, Basil's eye ranged over the stands, but he could not see her.

"I wonder if she knows I was pretty bad," he thought, and then bitterly: "If I don't, he'll tell her."

He could hear him telling her in that soft Southern voice—the voice that had wooed her so persuasively that afternoon on the train. As he emerged from the dressing room an hour later he ran into Le Moyne coming out of the visitors' quarters next door. He looked at Basil with an expression at once uncertain and angry.

"Hello, Lee." After a momentary hesitation he added: "Good work."

"Hello, Le Moyne," said Basil, clipping his words.

Le Moyne turned away, turned back again.

"What's the matter?" he demanded. "Do you want to carry this any further?"

Basil didn't answer. The bruised face and the bandaged hand assuaged his hatred a little, but he couldn't bring himself to speak. The game was over, and now Le Moyne would meet Minnie somewhere, make the defeat negligible in the victory of the night.

"If it's about Minnie, you're wasting your time being sore," Le Moyne exploded suddenly. "I asked her to the game, but she didn't come."

"Didn't she?" Basil was startled.

"That was it, eh? I wasn't sure. I thought you were just trying to get my goat in there." His eyes narrowed. "The young lady kicked me about a month ago."

"Kicked you?"

"Threw me over. Got a little weary of me. She runs through things quickly."

Basil perceived that his face was miserable.

"Who is it now?" he asked in more civil tone.

"It seems to be a classmate of yours named Jubal—and a mighty sad bird, if you ask me. She met him in New York the day before her school opened, and I hear it's pretty heavy. She'll be at the Lawn Club Dance tonight."

· I V ·

BASIL HAD DINNER at the Taft with Jobena Dorsey and her brother George. The Varsity had won at Princeton and the college was jubilant and enthusiastic; as they came in, a table of freshmen by the door gave Basil a hand.

"You're getting very important," Jobena said.

A year ago Basil had thought for a few weeks that he was in love with Jobena; when they next met he knew immediately that he was not.

"And why was that?" he asked her now, as they danced. "Why did it all go so quick?"

"Do you really want to know?"

"Yes."

"Because I let it go."

"You let it go?" he repeated. "I like that!"

"I decided you were too young."

"Didn't I have anything to do with it?"

She shook her head.

"That's what Bernard Shaw says," Basil admitted thoughtfully. "But I thought it was just about older people. So you go after the men."

"Well, I should say not!" Her body stiffened indignantly in his arms. "The men are usually there, and the girl blinks at them or something. It's just instinct."

"Can't a man make a girl fall for him?"

"Some men can—the ones who really don't care."

He pondered this awful fact for a moment and stowed it away for future examination. On the way to the Lawn Club he brought forth more questions.

If a girl who had been "crazy about a boy" became suddenly infatuated with another, what ought the first boy to do?

"Let her go," said Jobena.

"Supposing he wasn't willing to do that. What ought he to do?"

"There isn't anything to do."

"Well, what's the best thing?"

Laughing, Jobena laid her head on his shoulder.

"Poor Basil," she said, "I'll be Laura Jean Libbey and you tell me the whole story."

He summarized the affair. "You see," he concluded, "if she was just anybody I could get over it, no matter how much I loved her. But she isn't—she's the most popular, most beautiful girl I've ever seen. I mean she's like Messalina and Cleopatra and Salome and all that."

"Louder," requested George from the front seat.

"She's sort of an immortal woman," continued Basil in a lower voice. "You know, like Madame du Barry and all that sort of thing. She's not just—"

"Not just like me."

"No. That is, you're sort of like her—all the girls I've cared about are sort of the same. Oh, Jobena, you know what I mean."

As the lights of the New Haven Lawn Club loomed up she became obligingly serious:

"There's nothing to do. I can see that. She's more sophisticated than you. She staged the whole thing from the beginning, even when you thought it was you. I don't know why she got tired, but evidently she is, and she couldn't create it again, even if she wanted to, and you couldn't because you're—"

"Go on. What?"

"You're too much in love. All that's left for you to do is to show her you don't care. Any girl hates to lose an old beau; so she may even smile at you—but don't go back. It's all over."

In the dressing room Basil stood thoughtfully brushing his hair. It was all over. Jobena's words had taken away his last faint hope, and after the strain of the afternoon the realization brought tears to his eyes. Hurriedly filling the bowl, he washed his face. Someone came in and slapped him on the back.

"You played a nice game, Lee."

"Thanks, but I was rotten."

"You were great. That last quarter—"

He went into the dance. Immediately he saw her, and in the same breath he was dizzy and confused with excitement. A little dribble of stags pursued her wherever she went, and she looked up at each one of them with the bright-eyed, passionate smile he knew so well. Presently he located her escort and indignantly discovered it was a flip, blatant boy from Hill School he had already noticed and set down as impossible. What quality lurked behind those watery eyes that drew her? How could that raw temperament appreciate that she was one of the immortal sirens of the world?

Having examined Mr. Jubal desperately and in vain for the answers to these questions, he cut in and danced all of twenty feet with her, smiling with cynical melancholy when she said:

"I'm so proud to know you, Basil. Everybody says you were wonderful this afternoon."

But the phrase was precious to him and he stood against the wall repeating it over to himself, separating it into its component parts and trying to suck out any lurking meaning. If enough people praised him it might influence her. "I'm proud to know you, Basil. Everybody says you were wonderful this afternoon."

There was a commotion near the door and someone said, "By golly, they got in after all!"

"Who?" another asked.

"Some Princeton freshmen. Their football season's over and three or four of them broke training at the Hofbrau."

And now suddenly the curious specter of a young man burst out of the commotion, as a back breaks through a line, and neatly straight-arming a member of the dance committee, rushed unsteadily onto the floor. He wore no collar with his dinner coat, his shirt front had long expelled its studs, his hair and eyes were wild. For a moment he glanced around as if blinded by the lights; then his glance fell on Minnie Bibble and an unmistakable love light came into his face. Even before he reached her he began to call her name aloud in a strained, poignant Southern voice.

Basil sprang forward, but others were before him, and Littleboy Le Moyne, fighting hard, disappeared into the coatroom in a flurry of legs and arms, many of which were not his own. Standing in the doorway. Basil found his disgust tempered with a monstrous sympathy; for Le Moyne, each time his head emerged from under the faucet, spoke desperately of his rejected love.

But when Basil danced with Minnie again, he found her frightened and angry; so much so that she seemed to appeal to Basil for support, made him sit down.

"Wasn't he a fool?" she cried feelingly. "That sort of thing gives a girl a terrible reputation. They ought to have put him in jail."

"He didn't know what he was doing. He played a hard game and he's all in, that's all."

But her eyes filled with tears.

"Oh, Basil," she pleaded, "am I just perfectly terrible? I never want to be mean to anybody; things just happen."

He wanted to put his arm around her and tell her she was the most romantic person in the world, but he saw in her eyes that she scarcely perceived him; he was a lay figure—she might have been talking to another girl. He remembered what Jobena had said—there was nothing left except to escape with his pride.

"You've got more sense." Her soft voice flowed around him like an enchanted river. "You know that when two people aren't—aren't crazy about each other any more, the thing is to be sensible."

"Of course," he said, and forced himself to add lightly: "When a thing's over, it's over."

"Oh, Basil, you're so satisfactory. You always understand." And now suddenly, for the first time in months, she was actually thinking of him. He would be an invaluable person in any girl's life, she thought, if that brain of his, which was so annoying sometimes, was really used "to sort of understand."

He was watching Jobena dance, and Minnie followed his eyes.

"You brought a girl, didn't you? She's awfully pretty."

"Not as pretty as you."

"Basil."

Resolutely he refused to look at her, guessing that she had wriggled slightly and folded her hands in her lap. And as he held on to himself an extraordinary thing happened—the world around, outside of her, brightened a little. Presently more freshmen would approach him to congratulate him on the game, and he would like it—the words and the tribute in their eyes. There was a good chance he would start against Harvard next week.

"Basil!"

His heart made a dizzy tour of his chest. Around the corner of his eyes he felt her eyes waiting. Was she really sorry? Should he seize the opportunity to turn to her and say: "Minnie, tell this crazy nut to go jump in the river, and come back to me." He wavered, but a thought that had helped him this afternoon returned: He had made all his mistakes for this time. Deep inside of him the plea expired slowly.

Jubal the impossible came up with an air of possession, and Basil's heart went bobbing off around the ballroom in a pink silk dress. Lost again in a fog of indecision, he walked out on the veranda. There was a flurry of premature snow in the air and the stars looked cold. Staring up at them he saw that they were his stars as always—symbols of ambition, struggle and glory. The wind blew through them, trumpeting that high white note for which he always listened, and the thin-blown clouds, stripped for battle, passed in review. The scene was of an unparalleled brightness and magnificence, and only the practiced eye of the commander saw that one star was no longer there.

THE LAST OF THE BELLES

♦

"The Last of the Belles" (Saturday Evening Post, 2 *March 1929) was, appropriately, Fitzgerald's last treatment of the figure he had introduced in "The Ice Palace" (1920). As the title indicates, "The Last of the Belles" belongs with the retrospective and reassessing stories Fitzgerald wrote at the end of the Twenties: as though, like Andy, he was "looking for my youth in a clapboard or a strip of roofing or a rusty tomato can." Fitzgerald selected "The Last of the Belles" for* Taps at Reveille, *and it has become one of his most frequently anthologized stories.*

♦

AFTER ATLANTA'S ELABORATE and theatrical rendition of Southern charm, we all underestimated Tarleton. It was a little hotter than anywhere we'd been—a dozen rookies collapsed the first day in that Georgia sun— and when you saw herds of cows drifting through the business streets, hi-yaed by colored drovers, a trance stole down over you out of the hot light; you wanted to move a hand or foot to be sure you were alive.

So I stayed out at camp and let Lieutenant Warren tell me about the girls. This was fifteen years ago, and I've forgotten how I felt, except that the days went along, one after another, better than they do now, and I was empty-hearted, because up North she whose legend I had loved for three years was getting married. I saw the clippings and newspaper photographs. It was "a romantic wartime wedding," all very rich and sad. I felt vividly the dark radiance of the sky under which it took place, and as a young snob, was more envious than sorry.

A day came when I went into Tarleton for a haircut and ran into a nice fellow named Bill Knowles, who was in my time at Harvard. He'd been in the National Guard division that preceded us in camp; at the last moment he had transferred to aviation and been left behind.

"I'm glad I met you, Andy," he said with undue seriousness. "I'll hand you on all my information before I start for Texas. You see, there're really only three girls here——"

I was interested; there was something mystical about there being three girls.

"——and here's one of them now."

We were in front of a drug store and he marched me in and introduced me to a lady I promptly detested.

"The other two are Ailie Calhoun and Sally Carrol Happer."

I guessed from the way he pronounced her name, that he was interested in Ailie Calhoun. It was on his mind what she would be doing while he was gone; he wanted her to have a quiet, uninteresting time.

At my age I don't even hesitate to confess that entirely unchivalrous images of Ailie Calhoun—that lovely name—rushed into my mind. At twenty-three there is no such thing as a preëmpted beauty; though, had Bill asked me, I would doubtless have sworn in all sincerity to care for her like a sister. He didn't; he was just fretting out loud at having to go. Three days later he telephoned me that he was leaving next morning and he'd take me to her house that night.

We met at the hotel and walked uptown through the flowery, hot twilight. The four white pillars of the Calhoun house faced the street, and behind them the veranda was dark as a cave with hanging, weaving, climbing vines.

When we came up the walk a girl in a white dress tumbled out of the front door, crying, "I'm so sorry I'm late!" and seeing us, added: "Why, I thought I heard you come ten minutes——"

She broke off as a chair creaked and another man, an aviator from Camp Harry Lee, emerged from the obscurity of the veranda.

"Why, Canby!" she cried. "How are you?"

He and Bill Knowles waited with the tenseness of open litigants.

"Canby, I want to whisper to you, honey," she said, after just a second. "You'll excuse us, Bill."

They went aside. Presently Lieutenant Canby, immensely displeased, said in a grim voice, "Then we'll make it Thursday, but that means sure." Scarcely nodding to us, he went down the walk, the spurs with which he presumably urged on his aeroplane gleaming in the lamplight.

"Come in—I don't just know your name——"

There she was—the Southern type in all its purity. I would have recognized Ailie Calhoun if I'd never heard Ruth Draper or read Marse Chan. She had the adroitness sugar-coated with sweet, voluble simplicity, the suggested background of devoted fathers, brothers and admirers stretching back into the South's heroic age, the unfailing coolness acquired in the endless struggle with the heat. There were notes in her voice that ordered slaves around, that withered up Yankee captains, and then soft, wheedling notes that mingled in unfamiliar loveliness with the night.

I could scarcely see her in the darkness, but when I rose to go—it was plain that I was not to linger—she stood in the orange light from the doorway. She was small and very blond; there was too much fever-colored rouge on her face, accentuated by a nose dabbed clownish white, but she shone through that like a star.

"After Bill goes I'll be sitting here all alone night after night. Maybe you'll take me to the country-club dances." The pathetic prophecy brought a laugh from Bill. "Wait a minute," Ailie murmured. "Your guns are all crooked."

She straightened my collar pin, looking up at me for a second with something more than curiosity. It was a seeking look, as if she asked, "Could it be you?" Like Lieutenant Canby, I marched off unwillingly into the suddenly insufficient night.

Two weeks later I sat with her on the same veranda, or rather she half lay in my arms and yet scarcely touched me—how she managed that I don't remember. I was trying unsuccessfully to kiss her, and had been trying for the best part of an hour. We had a sort of joke about my not being sincere. My theory was that if she'd let me kiss her I'd fall in love with her. Her argument was that I was obviously insincere.

In a lull between two of these struggles she told me about her brother who had died in his senior year at Yale. She showed me his picture—it was a handsome, earnest face with a Leyendecker forelock—and told me that when she met someone who measured up to him she'd marry. I found this family idealism discouraging; even my brash confidence couldn't compete with the dead.

The evening and other evenings passed like that, and ended with my going back to camp with the remembered smell of magnolia flowers and a mood of vague dissatisfaction. I never kissed her. We went to the vaudeville and to the country club on Saturday nights, where she seldom took ten consecutive steps with one man, and she took me to barbecues and rowdy watermelon parties, and never thought it was worth while to change what I felt for her into love. I see now that it wouldn't have been hard, but she was a wise nineteen and she must have seen that we were emotionally incompatible. So I became her confidant instead.

We talked about Bill Knowles. She was considering Bill; for, though she wouldn't admit it, a winter at school in New York and a prom at Yale had turned her eyes North. She said she didn't think she'd marry a Southern man. And by degrees I saw that she was consciously and voluntarily different from these other girls who sang nigger songs and shot craps in the country-club bar. That's why Bill and I and others were drawn to her. We recognized her.

June and July, while the rumors reached us faintly, ineffectually, of battle and terror overseas, Ailie's eyes roved here and there about the country-club floor, seeking for something among the tall young officers. She attached several, choosing them with unfailing perspicacity—save in the case of Lieutenant Canby, whom she claimed to despise, but, nevertheless, gave dates to "because he was so sincere"—and we apportioned her evenings among us all summer.

One day she broke all her dates—Bill Knowles had leave and was coming. We talked of the event with scientific impersonality—would he move her to a decision? Lieutenant Canby, on the contrary, wasn't impersonal at all; made a nuisance of himself. He told her that if she married Knowles he was going to climb up six thousand feet in his aeroplane, shut off the motor and let go. He frightened her—I had to yield him my last date before Bill came.

On Saturday night she and Bill Knowles came to the country club. They were very handsome together and once more I felt envious and sad. As they danced out on the floor the three-piece orchestra was playing After You've Gone, in a poignant incomplete way that I can hear yet, as if each bar were trickling off a precious minute of that time. I knew then that I had grown to love Tarleton, and I glanced about half in panic to see if some face wouldn't come in for me out of that warm, singing, outer darkness that yielded up couple after couple in organdie and olive drab. It was a time of youth and war, and there was never so much love around.

When I danced with Ailie she suddenly suggested that we go outside to a car. She wanted to know why didn't people cut in on her tonight? Did they think she was already married?

"Are you going to be?"

"I don't know, Andy. Sometimes, when he treats me as if I were sacred, it thrills me." Her voice was hushed and far away. "And then——"

She laughed. Her body, so frail and tender, was touching mine, her face was turned up to me, and there, suddenly, with Bill Knowles ten yards off, I could have kissed her at last. Our lips just touched experimentally; then an aviation officer turned a corner of the veranda near us, peered into our darkness and hesitated.

"Ailie."

"Yes."

"You heard about this afternoon?"

"What?" She leaned forward, tenseness already in her voice.

"Horace Canby crashed. He was instantly killed."

She got up slowly and stepped out of the car.

"You mean he was killed?" she said.

"Yes. They don't know what the trouble was. His motor——"

"Oh-h-h!" Her rasping whisper came through the hands suddenly cov-

ering her face. We watched her helplessly as she put her head on the side
of the car, gagging dry tears. After a minute I went for Bill, who was standing
in the stag line, searching anxiously about for her, and told him she wanted
to go home.

I sat on the steps outside. I had disliked Canby, but his terrible, pointless
death was more real to me then than the day's toll of thousands in France.
In a few minutes Ailie and Bill came out. Ailie was whimpering a little, but
when she saw me her eyes flexed and she came over swiftly.

"Andy"—she spoke in a quick, low voice—"of course you must never
tell anybody what I told you about Canby yesterday. What he said, I mean."

"Of course not."

She looked at me a second longer as if to be quite sure. Finally she was
sure. Then she sighed in such a quaint little way that I could hardly believe
my ears, and her brow went up in what can only be described as mock
despair.

"An-dy!"

I looked uncomfortably at the ground, aware that she was calling my
attention to her involuntarily disastrous effect on men.

"Good night, Andy!" called Bill as they got into a taxi.

"Good night," I said, and almost added: "You poor fool."

· II ·

OF COURSE I should have made one of those fine moral decisions that
people make in books, and despised her. On the contrary, I don't doubt
that she could still have had me by raising her hand.

A few days later she made it all right by saying wistfully, "I know you
think it was terrible of me to think of myself at a time like that, but it was
such a shocking coincidence."

At twenty-three I was entirely unconvinced about anything, except that
some people were strong and attractive and could do what they wanted,
and others were caught and disgraced. I hoped I was of the former. I was
sure Ailie was.

I had to revise other ideas about her. In the course of a long discussion
with some girl about kissing—in those days people still talked about kissing
more than they kissed—I mentioned the fact that Ailie had only kissed two
or three men, and only when she thought she was in love. To my considerable
disconcertion the girl figuratively just lay on the floor and howled.

"But it's true," I assured her, suddenly knowing it wasn't. "She told me
herself."

"Ailie Calhoun! Oh, my heavens! Why, last year at the Tech spring house party——"

This was in September. We were going over-seas any week now, and to bring us up to full strength a last batch of officers from the fourth training camp arrived. The fourth camp wasn't like the first three—the candidates were from the ranks; even from the drafted divisions. They had queer names without vowels in them, and save for a few young militiamen, you couldn't take it for granted that they came out of any background at all. The addition to our company was Lieutenant Earl Schoen from New Bedford, Massachusetts; as fine a physical specimen as I have ever seen. He was six-foot-three, with black hair, high color and glossy dark-brown eyes. He wasn't very smart and he was definitely illiterate, yet he was a good officer, high-tempered and commanding, and with that becoming touch of vanity that sits well on the military. I had an idea that New Bedford was a country town, and set down his bumptious qualities to that.

We were doubled up in living quarters and he came into my hut. Inside of a week there was a cabinet photograph of some Tarleton girl nailed brutally to the shack wall.

"She's no jane or anything like that. She's a society girl; goes with all the best people here."

The following Sunday afternoon I met the lady at a semiprivate swimming pool in the country. When Ailie and I arrived, there was Schoen's muscular body rippling out of a bathing suit at the far end of the pool.

"Hey, lieutenant!"

When I waved back at him he grinned and winked, jerking his head toward the girl at his side. Then, digging her in the ribs, he jerked his head at me. It was a form of introduction.

"Who's that with Kitty Preston?" Ailie asked, and when I told her she said he looked like a street-car conductor, and pretended to look for her transfer.

A moment later he crawled powerfully and gracefully down the pool and pulled himself up at our side. I introduced him to Ailie.

"How do you like my girl, lieutenant?" he demanded. "I told you she was all right, didn't I?" He jerked his head toward Ailie; this time to indicate that his girl and Ailie moved in the same circles. "How about us all having dinner together down at the hotel some night?"

I left them in a moment, amused as I saw Ailie visibly making up her mind that here, anyhow, was not the ideal. But Lieutenant Earl Schoen was not to be dismissed so lightly. He ran his eyes cheerfully and inoffensively over her cute, slight figure, and decided that she would do even better than the other. Then minutes later I saw them in the water together, Ailie swimming away with a grim little stroke she had, and Schoen wallowing riotously around her and ahead of her, sometimes pausing and staring at her, fascinated, as a boy might look at a nautical doll.

While the afternoon passed he remained at her side. Finally Ailie came over to me and whispered, with a laugh: "He's following me around. He thinks I haven't paid my carfare."

She turned quickly. Miss Kitty Preston, her face curiously flustered, stood facing us.

"Ailie Calhoun, I didn't think it of you to go out and delib'ately try to take a man away from another girl."—An expression of distress at the impending scene flitted over Ailie's face.—"I thought you considered yourself above anything like that."

Miss Preston's voice was low, but it held that tensity that can be felt farther than it can be heard, and I saw Ailie's clear lovely eyes glance about in panic. Luckily, Earl himself was ambling cheerfully and innocently toward us.

"If you care for him you certainly oughtn't to belittle yourself in front of him," said Ailie in a flash, her head high.

It was her acquaintance with the traditional way of behaving against Kitty Preston's naïve and fierce possessiveness, or if you prefer it, Ailie's "breeding" against the other's "commonness." She turned away.

"Wait a minute, kid!" cried Earl Schoen. "How about your address? Maybe I'd like to give you a ring on the phone."

She looked at him in a way that should have indicated to Kitty her entire lack of interest.

"I'm very busy at the Red Cross this month," she said, her voice as cool as her slicked-back blond hair. "Good-by."

On the way home she laughed. Her air of having been unwittingly involved in a contemptible business vanished.

"She'll never hold that young man," she said. "He wants somebody new."

"Apparently he wants Ailie Calhoun."

The idea amused her.

"He could give me his ticket punch to wear, like a fraternity pin. What fun! If mother ever saw anybody like that come in the house, she'd just lie down and die."

And to give Ailie credit, it was fully a fortnight before he did come in her house, although he rushed her until she pretended to be annoyed at the next country-club dance.

"He's the biggest tough, Andy," she whispered to me. "But he's so sincere."

She used the word "tough" without the conviction it would have carried had he been a Southern boy. She only knew it with her mind; her ear couldn't distinguish between one Yankee voice and another. And somehow Mrs. Calhoun didn't expire at his appearance on the threshold. The supposedly ineradicable prejudices of Ailie's parents were a convenient phenomenon that disappeared at her wish. It was her friends who were astonished. Ailie, always a little above Tarleton, whose beaux had been very carefully the "nicest" men of the camp—Ailie and Lieutenant Schoen! I grew tired of assuring people that she was merely distracting herself—and indeed every week or so there was someone new—an ensign from Pensacola, an old friend from New Orleans—but always, in between times, there was Earl Schoen.

Orders arrived for an advance party of officers and sergeants to proceed to the port of embarkation and take ship to France. My name was on the list. I had been on the range for a week and when I got back to camp, Earl Schoen buttonholed me immediately.

"We're giving a little farewell party in the mess. Just you and I and Captain Craker and three girls."

Earl and I were to call for the girls. We picked up Sally Carrol Happer and Nancy Lamar, and went on to Ailie's house; to be met at the door by the butler with the announcement that she wasn't home.

"Isn't home?" Earl repeated blankly. "Where is she?"

"Didn't leave no information about that; just said she wasn't home."

"But this is a darn funny thing!" he exclaimed. He walked around the familiar dusky veranda while the butler waited at the door. Something occurred to him. "Say," he informed me—"say, I think she's sore."

I waited. He said sternly to the butler, "You tell her I've got to speak to her a minute."

"How'm I goin' tell her that when she ain't home?"

Again Earl walked musingly around the porch. Then he nodded several times and said:

"She's sore at something that happened downtown."

In a few words he sketched out the matter to me.

"Look here; you wait in the car," I said. "Maybe I can fix this." And when he reluctantly retreated: "Oliver, you tell Miss Ailie I want to see her alone."

After some argument he bore this message and in a moment returned with a reply:

"Miss Ailie say she don't want to see that other gentleman about nothing never. She say come in if you like."

She was in the library. I had expected to see a picture of cool, outraged dignity, but her face was distraught, tumultuous, despairing. Her eyes were red-rimmed, as though she had been crying slowly and painfully, for hours.

"Oh, hello, Andy," she said brokenly. "I haven't seen you for so long. Has he gone?"

"Now, Ailie——"

"Now, Ailie!" she cried. "Now, Ailie! He spoke to me, you see. He lifted his hat. He stood there ten feet from me with that horrible—that horrible woman—holding her arm and talking to her, and then when he saw me he raised his hat. Andy, I didn't know what to do. I had to go in the drug store and ask for a glass of water, and I was so afraid he'd follow in after me that I asked Mr. Rich to let me go out the back way. I never want to see him or hear of him again."

I talked. I said what one says in such cases. I said it for half an hour. I could not move her. Several times she answered by murmuring something about his not being "sincere," and for the fourth time I wondered what the word meant to her. Certainly not constancy; it was, I half suspected, some special way she wanted to be regarded.

I got up to go. And then, unbelievably, the automobile horn sounded three times impatiently outside. It was stupefying. It said as plainly as if Earl were in the room, "All right; go to the devil then! I'm not going to wait here all night."

Ailie looked at me aghast. And suddenly a peculiar look came into her face, spread, flickered, broke into a teary, hysterical smile.

"Isn't he awful?" she cried in helpless despair. "Isn't he terrible?"

"Hurry up," I said quickly. "Get your cape. This is our last night."

And I can still feel that last night vividly, the candlelight that flickered over the rough boards of the mess shack, over the frayed paper decorations left from the supply company's party, the sad mandolin down a company street that kept picking My Indiana Home out of the universal nostalgia of the departing summer. The three girls lost in this mysterious men's city felt something, too—a bewitched impermanence as though they were on a magic carpet that had lighted on the Southern countryside, and any moment the wind would lift it and waft it away. We toasted ourselves and the South. Then we left our napkins and empty glasses and a little of the past on the table, and hand in hand went out into the moonlight itself. Taps had been played; there was no sound but the far-away whinny of a horse, and a loud persistent snore at which we laughed, and the leathery snap of a sentry coming to port over by the guardhouse. Craker was on duty; we others got into a waiting car, motored into Tarleton and left Craker's girl.

Then Ailie and Earl, Sally and I, two and two in the wide back seat, each couple turned from the other, absorbed and whispering, drove away into the wide, flat darkness.

We drove through pine woods heavy with lichen and Spanish moss, and between the fallow cotton fields along a road white as the rim of the world. We parked under the broken shadow of a mill where there was the sound of running water and restive squawky birds and over everything a brightness that tried to filter in anywhere—into the lost nigger cabins, the automobile, the fastnesses of the heart. The South sang to us—I wonder if they remember. I remember—the cool pale faces, the somnolent amorous eyes and the voices:

"Are you comfortable?"

"Yes; are you?"

"Are you sure you are?"

"Yes."

Suddenly we knew it was late and there was nothing more. We turned home.

Our detachment started for Camp Mills next day, but I didn't go to France after all. We passed a cold month on Long Island, marched aboard a transport with steel helmets slung at our sides and then marched off again. There wasn't any more war. I had missed the war. When I came back to Tarleton I tried to get out of the Army, but I had a regular commission and it took most of the winter. But Earl Schoen was one of the first to be demobilized. He wanted to find a good job "while the picking was good." Ailie was noncommittal, but there was an understanding between them that he'd be back.

By January the camps, which for two years had dominated the little city, were already fading. There was only the persistent incinerator smell to remind one of all that activity and bustle. What life remained centered bitterly about divisional headquarters building, with the disgruntled regular officers who had also missed the war.

And now the young men of Tarleton began drifting back from the ends of the earth—some with Canadian uniforms, some with crutches or empty sleeves. A returned battalion of the National Guard paraded through the streets with open ranks for their dead, and then stepped down out of romance forever and sold you things over the counters of local stores. Only a few uniforms mingled with the dinner coats at the country-club dance.

Just before Christmas, Bill Knowles arrived unexpectedly one day and left the next—either he gave Ailie an ultimatum or she had made up her mind at last. I saw her sometimes when she wasn't busy with returned heroes from Savannah and Augusta, but I felt like an outmoded survival—and I was. She was waiting for Earl Schoen with such a vast uncertainty that she didn't like to talk about it. Three days before I got my final discharge he came.

I first happened upon them walking down Market Street together, and I don't think I've ever been so sorry for a couple in my life; though I suppose the same situation was repeating itself in every city where there had been camps. Exteriorly Earl had about everything wrong with him that could be imagined. His hat was green, with a radical feather; his suit was slashed and braided in a grotesque fashion that national advertising and the movies have put an end to. Evidently he had been to his old barber, for his hair bloused neatly on his pink, shaved neck. It wasn't as though he had been shiny and poor, but the background of mill-town dance halls and outing clubs flamed out at you—or rather flamed out at Ailie. For she had never quite imagined the reality; in these clothes even the natural grace of that magnificent body had departed. At first he boasted of his fine job; it would get them along all right until he could "see some easy money." But from the moment he came back into her world on its own terms he must have known it was hopeless. I don't know what Ailie said or how much her grief weighed against her stupefaction. She acted quickly—three days after his arrival, Earl and I went North together on the train.

"Well, that's the end of that," he said moodily. "She's a wonderful girl, but too much of a highbrow for me. I guess she's got to marry some rich guy that'll give her a great social position. I can't see that stuck-up sort of thing." And then, later: "She said to come back and see her in a year, but I'll never go back. This aristocrat stuff is all right if you got the money for it, but——"

"But it wasn't real," he meant to finish. The provincial society in which he had moved with so much satisfaction for six months already appeared to him as affected, "dudish" and artificial.

"Say, did you see what I saw getting on the train?" he asked me after a while. "Two wonderful janes, all alone. What do you say we mosey into the next car and ask them to lunch? I'll take the one in blue." Halfway down the car he turned around suddenly. "Say, Andy," he demanded, frowning; "one thing—how do you suppose she knew I used to command a street car? I never told her that."

"Search me."

· III ·

THIS NARRATIVE ARRIVES now at one of the big gaps that stared me in the face when I began. For six years, while I finished at Harvard Law and built commercial aeroplanes and backed a pavement block that went gritty under trucks, Ailie Calhoun was scarcely more than a name on a Christmas card; something that blew a little in my mind on warm nights when I remembered the magnolia flowers. Occasionally an acquaintance of Army days would ask me, "What became of that blond girl who was so popular?" but I didn't know. I ran into Nancy Lamar at the Montmartre in New York one evening and learned that Ailie had become engaged to a man in Cincinnati, had gone North to visit his family and then broken it off. She was lovely as ever and there was always a heavy beau or two. But neither Bill Knowles nor Earl Schoen had ever come back.

And somewhere about that time I heard that Bill Knowles had married a girl he met on a boat. There you are—not much of a patch to mend six years with.

Oddly enough, a girl seen at twilight in a small Indiana station started me thinking about going South. The girl, in stiff pink organdie, threw her arms about a man who got off our train and hurried him to a waiting car, and I felt a sort of pang. It seemed to me that she was bearing him off into the lost midsummer world of my early twenties, where time had stood still and charming girls, dimly seen like the past itself, still loitered along the dusky streets. I suppose that poetry is a Northern man's dream of the South. But it was months later that I sent off a wire to Ailie, and immediately followed it to Tarleton.

It was July. The Jefferson Hotel seemed strangely shabby and stuffy—a boosters' club burst into intermittent song in the dining room that my memory had long dedicated to officers and girls. I recognized the taxi driver who took me up to Ailie's house, but his "Sure, I do, lieutenant," was unconvincing. I was only one of twenty thousand.

It was a curious three days. I suppose some of Ailie's first young lustre must have gone the way of such mortal shining, but I can't bear witness to it. She was still so physically appealing that you wanted to touch the personality that trembled on her lips. No—the change was more profound than that.

At once I saw she had a different line. The modulations of pride, the vocal hints that she knew the secrets of a brighter, finer ante-bellum day, were gone from her voice; there was no time for them now as it rambled on in the half-laughing, half-desperate banter of the newer South. And everything was swept into this banter in order to make it go on and leave no time for thinking—the present, the future, herself, me. We went to a rowdy party at the house of some young married people, and she was the nervous, glowing center of it. After all, she wasn't eighteen, and she was as attractive in her rôle of reckless clown as she had ever been in her life.

"Have you heard anything from Earl Schoen?" I asked her the second night, on our way to the country-club dance.

"No." She was serious for a moment. "I often think of him. He was the——" She hesitated.

"Go on."

"I was going to say the man I loved most, but that wouldn't be true. I never exactly loved him, or I'd have married him any old how, wouldn't I?" She looked at me questioningly. "At least I wouldn't have treated him like that."

"It was impossible."

"Of course," she agreed uncertainly. Her mood changed; she became flippant: "How the Yankees did deceive us poor little Southern girls. Ah, me!"

When we reached the country club she melted like a chameleon into the—to me—unfamiliar crowd. There was a new generation upon the floor, with less dignity than the ones I had known, but none of them were more a part of its lazy, feverish essence than Ailie. Possibly she had perceived that in her initial longing to escape from Tarleton's provincialism she had been walking alone, following a generation which was doomed to have no successors. Just where she lost the battle, waged behind the white pillars of her veranda, I don't know. But she had guessed wrong, missed out somewhere. Her wild animation, which even now called enough men around her to rival the entourage of the youngest and freshest, was an admission of defeat.

I left her house, as I had so often left it that vanished June, in a mood of vague dissatisfaction. It was hours later, tossing about my bed in the hotel, that I realized what was the matter, what had always been the matter—I was deeply and incurably in love with her. In spite of every incompatibility, she was still, she would always be to me, the most attractive girl I had ever known. I told her so next afternoon. It was one of those hot days I knew so well, and Ailie sat beside me on a couch in the darkened library.

"Oh, no, I couldn't marry you," she said, almost frightened; "I don't love you that way at all. . . . I never did. And you don't love me. I didn't mean to tell you now, but next month I'm going to marry another man. We're not even announcing it, because I've done that twice before." Suddenly it occurred to her that I might be hurt: "Andy, you just had a silly idea, didn't you? You know I couldn't ever marry a Northern man."

"Who is he?" I demanded.

"A man from Savannah."

"Are you in love with him?"

"Of course I am." We both smiled. "Of course I am! What are you trying to make me say?"

There were no doubts, as there had been with other men. She couldn't afford to let herself have doubts. I knew this because she had long ago stopped making any pretensions with me. This very naturalness, I realized, was because she didn't consider me as a suitor. Beneath her mask of an instinctive thoroughbred she had always been on to herself, and she couldn't believe that anyone not taken in to the point of uncritical worship could really love her. That was what she called being "sincere"; she felt most security with men like Canby and Earl Schoen, who were incapable of passing judgments on the ostensibly aristocratic heart.

"All right," I said, as if she had asked my permission to marry. "Now, would you do something for me?"

"Anything."

"Ride out to camp."

"But there's nothing left there, honey."

"I don't care."

We walked downtown. The taxi driver in front of the hotel repeated her objection: "Nothing there now, cap."

"Never mind. Go there anyhow."

Twenty minutes later he stopped on a wide unfamiliar plain powdered with new cotton fields and marked with isolated clumps of pine.

"Like to drive over yonder where you see the smoke?" asked the driver. "That's the new state prison."

"No. Just drive along this road. I want to find where I used to live."

An old race course, inconspicuous in the camp's day of glory, had reared its dilapidated grandstand in the desolation. I tried in vain to orient myself.

"Go along this road past that clump of trees, and then turn right—no, turn left."

He obeyed, with professional disgust.

"You won't find a single thing, darling," said Ailie. "The contractors took it all down."

We rode slowly along the margin of the fields. It might have been here—

"All right. I want to get out," I said suddenly.

I left Ailie sitting in the car, looking very beautiful with the warm breeze stirring her long, curly bob.

It might have been here. That would make the company streets down there and the mess shack, where we dined that night, just over the way.

The taxi driver regarded me indulgently while I stumbled here and there in the knee-deep underbrush, looking for my youth in a clapboard or a strip of roofing or a rusty tomato can. I tried to sight on a vaguely familiar clump of trees, but it was growing darker now and I couldn't be quite sure they were the right trees.

"They're going to fix up the old race course," Ailie called from the car. "Tarleton's getting quite doggy in its old age."

No. Upon consideration they didn't look like the right trees. All I could be sure of was this place that had once been so full of life and effort was gone, as if it had never existed, and that in another month Ailie would be gone, and the South would be empty for me forever.

MAJESTY

◆

"Majesty" was published in the 13 July 1929 issue of the Saturday Evening Post. *Harold Ober and* Post *editor Thomas Costain praised it, and Fitzgerald selected it for* Taps at Reveille. *Although the plot is far-fetched, this story is redeemed by Fitzgerald's development of one of his favorite characters: the courageous young American woman determined to fulfill the possibilities of life.*

◆

THE EXTRAORDINARY THING is not that people in a lifetime turn out worse or better than we had prophesied; particularly in America that is to be expected. The extraordinary thing is how people keep their levels, fulfill their promises, seem actually buoyed up by an inevitable destiny.

One of my conceits is that no one has ever disappointed me since I turned eighteen and could tell a real quality from a gift for sleight of hand, and even many of the merely showy people in my past seem to go on being blatantly and successfully showy to the end.

Emily Castleton was born in Harrisburg in a medium-sized house, moved to New York at sixteen to a big house, went to the Briarly School, moved to an enormous house, moved to a mansion at Tuxedo Park, moved abroad, where she did various fashionable things and was in all the papers. Back in her débutante year one of those French artists who are so dogmatic about American beauties, included her with eleven other public and semipublic celebrities as one of America's perfect types. At the time numerous men agreed with him.

She was just faintly tall, with fine, rather large features, eyes with such an expanse of blue in them that you were really aware of it whenever you looked at her, and a good deal of thick blond hair—arresting and bright. Her mother and father did not know very much about the new world they had commandeered so Emily had to learn everything for herself, and she became involved in various situations and some of the first bloom wore off. However, there was bloom to spare. There were engagements and semi-engagements, short passionate attractions, and then a big affair at twenty-two that embittered her and sent her wandering the continents looking for happiness. She became "artistic" as most wealthy unmarried girls do at that age, because artistic people seem to have some secret, some inner refuge, some escape. But most of her friends were married now, and her life was a great disappointment to her father; so, at twenty-four, with marriage in her head if not in her heart, Emily came home.

This was a low point in her career and Emily was aware of it. She had not done well. She was one of the most popular, most beautiful girls of her generation with charm, money and a sort of fame, but her generation was moving into new fields. At the first note of condescension from a former schoolmate, now a young "matron," she went to Newport and was won by William Brevoort Blair. Immediately she was again the incomparable Emily Castleton. The ghost of the French artist walked once more in the newspapers; the most-talked-of leisure-class event of October was her wedding day.

> Splendor to mark society nuptials. . . . Harold Castleton sets out a series of five-thousand-dollar pavilions arranged like the interconnecting tents of a circus, in which the reception, the wedding supper and the ball will be held. . . . Nearly a thousand guests, many of them leaders in business, will mingle with those who dominate the social world. . . . The wedding gifts are estimated to be worth a quarter of a million dollars. . . .

An hour before the ceremony, which was to be solemnized at St. Bartholomew's, Emily sat before a dressing-table and gazed at her face in the glass. She was a little tired of her face at that moment and the depressing thought suddenly assailed her that it would require more and more looking after in the next fifty years.

"I ought to be happy," she said aloud, "but every thought that comes into my head is sad."

Her cousin, Olive Mercy, sitting on the side of the bed, nodded. "All brides are sad."

"It's such a waste," Emily said.

Olive frowned impatiently.

"Waste of what? Women are incomplete unless they're married and have children."

For a moment Emily didn't answer. Then she said slowly, "Yes, but whose children?"

For the first time in her life, Olive, who worshipped Emily, almost hated her. Not a girl in the wedding party but would have been glad of Brevoort Blair—Olive among the others.

"You're lucky," she said. "You're so lucky you don't even know it. You ought to be paddled for talking like that."

"I shall learn to love him," announced Emily facetiously. "Love will come with marriage. Now, isn't that a hell of a prospect?"

"Why so deliberately unromantic?"

"On the contrary, I'm the most romantic person I've ever met in my life. Do you know what I think when he puts his arms around me? I think that if I look up I'll see Garland Kane's eyes."

"But why, then——"

"Getting into his plane the other day I could only remember Captain Marchbanks and the little two-seater we flew over the Channel in, just breaking our hearts for each other and never saying a word about it because of his wife. I don't regret those men; I just regret the part of me that went into caring. There's only the sweepings to hand to Brevoort in a pink waste-basket. There should have been something more; I thought even when I was most carried away that I was saving something for the one. But apparently I wasn't." She broke off and then added: "And yet I wonder."

The situation was no less provoking to Olive for being comprehensible, and save for her position as a poor relation, she would have spoken her mind. Emily was well spoiled—eight years of men had assured her they were not good enough for her and she had accepted the fact as probably true.

"You're nervous." Olive tried to keep the annoyance out of her voice. "Why not lie down for an hour?"

"Yes," answered Emily absently.

Olive went out and downstairs. In the lower hall she ran into Brevoort Blair, attired in a nuptial cutaway even to the white carnation, and in a state of considerable agitation.

"Oh, excuse me," he blurted out. "I wanted to see Emily. It's about the rings—which ring, you know. I've got four rings and she never decided and I can't just hold them out in the church and have her take her pick."

"I happen to know she wants the plain platinum band. If you want to see her anyhow——"

"Oh, thanks very much. I don't want to disturb her."

They were standing close together, and even at this moment when he was gone, definitely preëmpted, Olive couldn't help thinking how alike she and Brevoort were. Hair, coloring, features—they might have been brother and sister—and they shared the same shy serious temperaments, the same simple straightforwardness. All this flashed through her mind in an instant, with the added thought that the blond, tempestuous Emily, with her vitality and amplitude of scale, was, after all, better for him in every way; and then, beyond this, a perfect wave of tenderness, of pure physical pity and yearning swept over her and it seemed that she must step forward only half a foot to find his arms wide to receive her.

She stepped backward instead, relinquishing him as though she still touched him with the tip of her fingers and then drew the tips away. Perhaps some vibration of her emotion fought its way into his consciousness, for he said suddenly:

"We're going to be good friends, aren't we? Please don't think I'm taking Emily away. I know I can't own her—nobody could—and I don't want to."

Silently, as he talked, she said good-by to him, the only man she had ever wanted in her life.

She loved the absorbed hesitancy with which he found his coat and hat and felt hopefully for the knob on the wrong side of the door.

When he had gone she went into the drawing-room, gorgeous and portentous; with its painted bacchanals and massive chandeliers and the eighteenth-century portraits that might have been Emily's ancestors, but weren't, and by that very fact belonged the more to her. There she rested, as always, in Emily's shadow.

Through the door that led out to the small, priceless patch of grass on Sixtieth Street now inclosed by the pavilions, came her uncle, Mr. Harold Castleton. He had been sampling his own champagne.

"Olive so sweet and fair." He cried emotionally, "Olive, baby, she's done it. She was all right inside, like I knew all the time. The good ones come through, don't they—the real thoroughbreds? I began to think that the Lord and me, between us, had given her too much, that she'd never be satisfied, but now she's come down to earth just like a"—he searched unsuccessfully for a metaphor—"like a thoroughbred, and she'll find it not such a bad place after all." He came closer. "You've been crying, little Olive."

"Not much."

"It doesn't matter," he said magnanimously. "If I wasn't so happy I'd cry too."

Later, as she embarked with two other bridesmaids for the church, the solemn throbbing of a big wedding seemed to begin with the vibration of the car. At the door the organ took it up, and later it would palpitate in the cellos and base viols of the dance, to fade off finally with the sound of the car that bore bride and groom away.

The crowd was thick around the church, and ten feet out of it the air was heavy with perfume and faint clean humanity and the fabric smell of new clean clothes. Beyond the massed hats in the van of the church the two families sat in front rows on either side. The Blairs—they were assured a family resemblance by their expression of faint condescension, shared by their in-laws as well as by true Blairs—were represented by the Gardiner Blairs, senior and junior; Lady Mary Bowes Howard, née Blair; Mrs. Potter Blair; Mrs. Princess Potowki Parr Blair, née Inchbit; Miss Gloria Blair, Master Gardiner Blair III, and the kindred branches, rich and poor, of Smythe, Bickle, Diffendorfer and Hamn. Across the aisle the Castletons made a less impressive showing—Mr. Harold Castleton, Mr. and Mrs. Theodore Castleton and children, Harold Castleton Junior, and, from Harrisburg, Mr. Carl Mercy, and two little old aunts named O'Keefe hidden off in a corner. Somewhat to their surprise the two aunts had been bundled off in a limousine and dressed from head to foot by a fashionable couturière that morning.

In the vestry, where the bridesmaids fluttered about like birds in their big floppy hats, there was a last lip rouging and adjustment of pins before Emily should arrive. They represented several stages of Emily's life—a schoolmate at Briarly, a last unmarried friend of débutante year, a travelling companion of Europe, and the girl she had visited in Newport when she met Brevoort Blair.

"They've got Wakeman," this last one said, standing by the door listening to the music. "He played for my sister, but I shall never have Wakeman."

"Why not?"

"Why, he's playing the same thing over and over—'At Dawning.' He's played it half a dozen times."

At this moment another door opened and the solicitous head of a young man appeared around it. "Almost ready?" he demanded of the nearest bridesmaid. "Brevoort's having a quiet little fit. He just stands there wilting collar after collar——"

"Be calm," answered the young lady. "The bride is always a few minutes late."

"A few minutes!" protested the best man. "I don't call it a few minutes. They're beginning to rustle and wriggle like a circus crowd out there, and the organist has been playing the same tune for half an hour. I'm going to get him to fill in with a little jazz."

"What time is it?" Olive demanded.

"Quarter of five—ten minutes of five."

"Maybe there's been a traffic tie-up." Olive paused as Mr. Harold Castleton, followed by an anxious curate, shouldered his way in, demanding a phone.

And now there began a curious dribbling back from the front of the church, one by one, then two by two, until the vestry was crowded with relatives and confusion.

"What's happened?"

"What on earth's the matter?"

A chauffeur came in and reported excitedly. Harold Castleton swore and, his face blazing, fought his way roughly toward the door. There was an attempt to clear the vestry, and then, as if to balance the dribbling, a ripple of conversation commenced at the rear of the church and began to drift up toward the altar, growing louder and faster and more excited, mounting always, bringing people to their feet, rising to a sort of subdued roar. The announcement from the altar that the marriage had been postponed was scarcely heard, for by that time everyone knew that they were participating in a front-page scandal, that Brevoort Blair had been left waiting at the altar and Emily Castleton had run away.

· II ·

THERE WERE a dozen reporters outside the Castleton house on Sixtieth Street when Olive arrived, but in her absorption she failed even to hear their questions; she wanted desperately to go and comfort a certain man whom she must not approach, and as a sort of substitute she sought her Uncle Harold. She entered through the interconnecting five-thousand-dollar pavilions, where caterers and servants still stood about in a respectful funereal half-light, waiting for something to happen, amid trays of caviar and turkey's breast and pyramided wedding cake. Upstairs, Olive found her uncle sitting on a stool before Emily's dressing-table. The articles of make-up spread before him, the repertoire of feminine preparation in evidence about, made his singularly inappropriate presence a symbol of the mad catastrophe.

"Oh, it's you." His voice was listless; he had aged in two hours. Olive put her arm about his bowed shoulder.

"I'm so terribly sorry, Uncle Harold."

Suddenly a stream of profanity broke from him, died away, and a single large tear welled slowly from one eye.

"I want to get my massage man," he said. "Tell McGregor to get him." He drew a long broken sigh, like a child's breath after crying, and Olive saw that his sleeves were covered with a dust of powder from the dressing-table, as if he had been leaning forward on it, weeping, in the reaction from his proud champagne.

"There was a telegram," he muttered.

"It's somewhere."

And he added slowly,

"From now on *you*'re my daughter."

"Oh, no, you mustn't say that!"

Unrolling the telegram, she read:

I can't make the grade I would feel like a fool either way but this
will be over sooner so damn sorry for you

EMILY

When Olive had summoned the masseur and posted a servant outside her
uncle's door, she went to the library, where a confused secretary was trying
to say nothing over an inquisitive and persistent telephone.

"I'm so upset, Miss Mercy," he cried in a despairing treble. "I do declare
I'm so upset I have a frightful headache. I've thought for half an hour I
heard dance music from down below."

Then it occurred to Olive that she, too, was becoming hysterical; in the
breaks of the street traffic a melody was drifting up, distinct and clear:

> "—Is she fair
> Is she sweet
> I don't care—cause
> I can't compete—
> Who's the——"

She ran quickly downstairs and through the drawing-room, the tune growing louder in her ears. At the entrance of the first pavilion she stopped in
stupefaction.

To the music of a small but undoubtedly professional orchestra a dozen
young couples were moving about the canvas floor. At the bar in the corner
stood additional young men, and half a dozen of the caterer's assistants were
busily shaking cocktails and opening champagne.

"Harold!" she called imperatively to one of the dancers. "Harold!"

A tall young man of eighteen handed his partner to another and came
toward her.

"Hello, Olive. How did father take it?"

"Harold, what in the name of——"

"Emily's crazy," he said consolingly. "I always told you Emily was crazy.
Crazy as a loon. Always was."

"What's the idea of this?"

"This?" He looked around innocently. "Oh, these are just some fellows
that came down from Cambridge with me."

"But—*dancing!*"

"Well, nobody's dead, are they? I thought we might as well use up some of this——"

"Tell them to go home," said Olive.

"Why? What on earth's the harm? These fellows came all the way down from Cambridge——"

"It simply isn't dignified."

"But they don't care, Olive. One fellow's sister did the same thing—only she did it the day after instead of the day before. Lots of people do it nowadays."

"Send the music home, Harold," said Olive firmly, "or I'll go to your father."

Obviously he felt that no family could be disgraced by an episode on such a magnificent scale, but he reluctantly yielded. The abysmally depressed butler saw to the removal of the champagne, and the young people, somewhat insulted, moved nonchalantly out into the more tolerant night. Alone with the shadow—Emily's shadow—that hung over the house, Olive sat down in the drawing-room to think. Simultaneously the butler appeared in the doorway.

"It's Mr. Blair, Miss Olive."

She jumped tensely to her feet.

"Who does he want to see?"

"He didn't say. He just walked in."

"Tell him I'm in here."

He entered with an air of abstraction rather than depression, nodded to Olive and sat down on a piano stool. She wanted to say, "Come here. Lay your head here, poor man. Never mind." But she wanted to cry, too, and so she said nothing.

"In three hours," he remarked quietly, "we'll be able to get the morning papers. There's a shop on Fifty-ninth Street."

"That's foolish——" she began.

"I am not a superficial man"—he interrupted her—"nevertheless, my chief feeling now is for the morning papers. Later there will be a politely silent gauntlet of relatives, friends and business acquaintances. About the actual affair I surprise myself by not caring at all."

"I shouldn't care about any of it."

"I'm rather grateful that she did it in time."

"Why don't you go away?" Olive leaned forward earnestly. "Go to Europe until it all blows over."

"Blows over." He laughed. "Things like this don't ever blow over. A little snicker is going to follow me around the rest of my life." He groaned.

"Uncle Hamilton started right for Park Row to make the rounds of the newspaper offices. He's a Virginian and he was unwise enough to use the old-fashioned word 'horsewhip' to one editor. I can hardly wait to see *that* paper." He broke off. "How is Mr. Castleton?"

"He'll appreciate your coming to inquire."

"I didn't come about that." He hesitated. "I came to ask you a question. I want to know if you'll marry me in Greenwich tomorrow morning."

For a minute Olive fell precipitately through space; she made a strange little sound; her mouth dropped ajar.

"I know you like me," he went on quickly. "In fact, I once imagined you loved me a little bit, if you'll excuse the presumption. Anyhow, you're very like a girl that once did love me, so maybe you would—" His face was pink with embarrassment, but he struggled grimly on; "anyhow, I like you enormously and whatever feeling I may have had for Emily has, I might say, flown."

The clangor and alarm inside her was so loud that it seemed he must hear it.

"The favor you'll be doing me will be very great," he continued. "My heavens, I know it sounds a little crazy, but what could be crazier than the whole afternoon? You see, if you married me the papers would carry quite a different story; they'd think that Emily went off to get out of our way, and the joke would be on her after all."

Tears of indignation came to Olive's eyes.

"I suppose I ought to allow for your wounded egotism, but do you realize you're making me an insulting proposition?"

His face fell.

"I'm sorry," he said after a moment. "I guess I was an awful fool even to think of it, but a man hates to lose the whole dignity of his life for a girl's whim. I see it would be impossible. I'm sorry."

He got up and picked up his cane.

Now he was moving toward the door, and Olive's heart came into her throat and a great, irresistible wave of self-preservation swept over her—swept over all her scruples and her pride. His steps sounded in the hall.

"Brevoort!" she called. She jumped to her feet and ran to the door. He turned. "Brevoort, what was the name of that paper—the one your uncle went to?"

"Why?"

"Because it's not too late for them to change their story if I telephone now! I'll say we were married tonight!"

· III ·

THERE IS A SOCIETY in Paris which is merely a heterogeneous prolongation of American society. People moving in are connected by a hundred threads to the motherland, and their entertainments, eccentricities and ups and downs are an open book to friends and relatives at Southampton, Lake Forest or Back Bay. So during her previous European sojourn Emily's whereabouts, as she followed the shifting Continental seasons, were publicly advertised; but from the day, one month after the unsolemnized wedding, when she sailed from New York, she dropped completely from sight. There was an occasional letter for her father, an occasional rumor that she was in Cairo, Constantinople or the less frequented Riviera—that was all.

Once, after a year, Mr. Castleton saw her in Paris, but, as he told Olive, the meeting only served to make him uncomfortable.

"There was something about her," he said vaguely, "as if—well, as if she had a lot of things in the back of her mind I couldn't reach. She was nice enough, but it was all automatic and formal.—She asked about you."

Despite her solid background of a three-month-old baby and a beautiful apartment on Park Avenue, Olive felt her heart falter uncertainly.

"What did she say?"

"She was delighted about you and Brevoort." And he added to himself, with a disappointment he could not conceal: "Even though you picked up the best match in New York when she threw it away." . . .

. . . It was more than a year after this that his secretary's voice on the telephone asked Olive if Mr. Castleton could see them that night. They found the old man walking his library in a state of agitation.

"Well, it's come," he declared vehemently. "People won't stand still; nobody stands still. You go up or down in this world. Emily chose to go down. She seems to be somewhere near the bottom. Did you ever hear of a man described to me as a"—he referred to a letter in his hand—"dissipated ne'er-do-well named Petrocobesco? He calls himself Prince Gabriel Petrocobesco, apparently from—from nowhere. This letter is from Hallam, my European man, and it incloses a clipping from the Paris *Matin*. It seems that this gentleman was invited by the police to leave Paris, and among the small entourage who left with him was an American girl, Miss Castleton, 'rumored to be the daughter of a millionaire.' The party was escorted to the station by gendarmes." He handed clipping and letter to Brevoort Blair with trembling fingers. "What do you make of it? Emily come to that!"

"It's not so good," said Brevoort, frowning.

"It's the end. I thought her drafts were big recently, but I never suspected that she was supporting——"

"It may be a mistake," Olive suggested. "Perhaps it's another Miss Castleton."

"It's Emily all right. Hallam looked up the matter. It's Emily, who was afraid ever to dive into the nice clean stream of life and ends up now by swimming around in the sewers."

Shocked, Olive had a sudden sharp taste of fate in its ultimate diversity. She with a mansion building in Westbury Hills, and Emily was mixed up with a deported adventurer in disgraceful scandal.

"I've got no right to ask you this," continued Mr. Castleton. "Certainly no right to ask Brevoort anything in connection with Emily. But I'm seventy-two and Fraser says if I put off the cure another fortnight he won't be responsible, and then Emily will be alone for good. I want you to set your trip abroad forward by two months and go over and bring her back."

"But do you think we'd have the necessary influence?" Brevoort asked. "I've no reason for thinking that she'd listen to me."

"There's no one else. If you can't go I'll have to."

"Oh, no," said Brevoort quickly. "We'll do what we can, won't we, Olive?"

"Of course."

"Bring her back—it doesn't matter how—but bring her back. Go before a court if necessary and swear she's crazy."

"Very well. We'll do what we can."

Just ten days after this interview the Brevoort Blairs called on Mr. Castleton's agent in Paris to glean what details were available. They were plentiful but unsatisfactory. Hallam had seen Petrocobesco in various restaurants—a fat little fellow with an attractive leer and a quenchless thirst. He was of some obscure nationality and had been moved around Europe for several years, living heaven knew how—probably on Americans, though Hallam understood that of late even the most outlying circles of international society were closed to him. About Emily, Hallam knew very little. They had been reported last week in Berlin and yesterday in Budapest. It was probably that such an undesirable as Petrocobesco was required to register with the police everywhere, and this was the line he recommended the Blairs to follow.

Forty-eight hours later, accompanied by the American vice consul, they called upon the prefect of police in Budapest. The officer talked in rapid Hungarian to the vice consul, who presently announced the gist of his remarks—the Blairs were too late.

"Where have they gone?"

"He doesn't know. He received orders to move them on and they left last night."

Suddenly the prefect wrote something on a piece of paper and handed it, with a terse remark, to the vice consul.

"He says try there."

Brevoort looked at the paper.

"Sturmdorp—where's that?"

Another rapid conversation in Hungarian.

"Five hours from here on a local train that leaves Tuesdays and Fridays. This is Saturday."

"We'll get a car at the hotel," said Brevoort.

They set out after dinner. It was a rough journey through the night across the still Hungarian plain. Olive awoke once from a worried doze to find Brevoort and the chauffeur changing a tire; then again as they stopped at a muddy little river, beyond which glowed the scattered lights of a town. Two soldiers in an unfamiliar uniform glanced into the car; they crossed a bridge and followed a narrow, warped main street to Sturmdorp's single inn; the roosters were already crowing as they tumbled down on the mean beds.

Olive awoke with a sudden sure feeling that they had caught up with Emily; and with it came that old sense of helplessness in the face of Emily's moods; for a moment the long past and Emily dominant in it, swept back over her, and it seemed almost a presumption to be here. But Brevoort's singleness of purpose reassured her and confidence had returned when they went downstairs, to find a landlord who spoke fluent American, acquired in Chicago before the war.

"You are not in Hungary now," he explained. "You have crossed the border into Czjeck-Hansa. But it is only a little country with two towns, this one and the capital. We don't ask the visa from Americans."

"That's probably why they came here," Olive thought.

"Perhaps you could give us some information about strangers?" asked Brevoort. "We're looking for an American lady—" He described Emily, without mentioning her probable companion; as he proceeded a curious change came over the innkeeper's face.

"Let me see your passports," he said; then: "And why you want to see her?"

"This lady is her cousin."

The innkeeper hesitated momentarily.

"I think perhaps I be able to find her for you," he said.

He called the porter; there were rapid instructions in an unintelligible patois. Then:

"Follow this boy—he take you there."

They were conducted through filthy streets to a tumble-down house on the edge of town. A man with a hunting rifle, lounging outside, straightened up and spoke sharply to the porter, but after an exchange of phrases they passed, mounted the stairs and knocked at a door. When it opened a head peered around the corner; the porter spoke again and they went in.

They were in a large dirty room which might have belonged to a poor boarding house in any quarter of the Western world—faded walls, split upholstery, a shapeless bed and an air, despite its bareness, of being over-crowded by the ghostly furniture, indicated by dust rings and worn spots, of the last decade. In the middle of the room stood a small stout man with hammock eyes and a peering nose over a sweet, spoiled little mouth, who stared intently at them as they opened the door, and then with a single disgusted "Chut!" turned impatiently away. There were several other people in the room, but Brevoort and Olive saw only Emily, who reclined in a chaise longue with half-closed eyes.

At the sight of them the eyes opened in mild astonishment; she made a move as though to jump up, but instead held out her hand, smiled and spoke their names in a clear polite voice, less as a greeting than as a sort of explanation to the others of their presence here. At their names a grudging amenity replaced the sullenness on the little man's face.

The girls kissed.

"Tutu!" said Emily, as if calling him to attention—"Prince Petrocobesco, let me present my cousin Mrs. Blair, and Mr. Blair."

"*Plaisir*," said Petrocobesco. He and Emily exchanged a quick glance, whereupon he said, "Won't you sit down?" and immediately seated himself in the only available chair, as if they were playing Going to Jerusalem.

"Plaisir," he repeated. Olive sat down on the foot of Emily's chaise longue and Brevoort took a stool from against the wall, meanwhile noting the other occupants of the room. There was a very fierce young man in a cape who stood, with arms folded and teeth gleaming, by the door, and two ragged, bearded men, one holding a revolver, the other with his head sunk dejectedly on his chest, who sat side by side in the corner.

"You come here long?" the prince asked.

"Just arrived this morning."

For a moment Olive could not resist comparing the two, the tall fair-featured American and the unprepossessing South European, scarcely a likely candidate for Ellis Island. Then she looked at Emily—the same thick bright hair with sunshine in it, the eyes with the hint of vivid seas. Her face was faintly drawn, there were slight new lines around her mouth, but she was the Emily of old—dominant, shining, large of scale. It seemed shameful for all that beauty and personality to have arrived in a cheap boarding house at the world's end.

The man in the cape answered a knock at the door and handed a note to Petrocobesco, who read it, cried *"Chut!"* and passed it to Emily.

"You see, there are no carriages," he said tragically in French. "The carriages were destroyed—all except one, which is in a museum. Anyhow, I prefer a horse."

"No," said Emily.

"Yes, yes, yes!" he cried. "Whose business is it how I go?"

"Don't let's have a scene, Tutu."

"Scene!" He fumed. "Scene!"

Emily turned to Olive: "You came by automobile?"

"Yes."

"A big de luxe car? With a back that opens?"

"Yes."

"There," said Emily to the prince. "We can have the arms painted on the side of that."

"Hold on," said Brevoort. "This car belongs to a hotel in Budapest."

Apparently Emily didn't hear.

"Janierka could do it," she continued thoughtfully.

At this point there was another interruption. The dejected man in the corner suddenly sprang to his feet and made as though to run to the door, whereupon the other man raised his revolver and brought the butt down on his head. The man faltered and would have collapsed had not his assailant hauled him back to the chair, where he sat comatose, a slow stream of blood trickling over his forehead.

"Dirty townsman! Filthy, dirty spy!" shouted Petrocobesco between clenched teeth.

"Now that's just the kind of remark you're not to make!" said Emily sharply.

"Then why we don't hear?" he cried. "Are we going to sit here in this pigsty forever?"

Disregarding him, Emily turned to Olive and began to question her conventionally about New York. Was prohibition any more successful? What were the new plays? Olive tried to answer and simultaneously to catch Brevoort's eye. The sooner their purpose was broached, the sooner they could get Emily away.

"Can we see you alone, Emily?" demanded Brevoort abruptly.

"Why, for the moment we haven't got another room."

Petrocobesco had engaged the man with the cape in agitated conversation, and taking advantage of this, Brevoort spoke hurriedly to Emily in a lowered voice:

"Emily, your father's getting old; he needs you at home. He wants you to give up this crazy life and come back to America. He sent us because he couldn't come himself and no one else knew you well enough——"

She laughed. "You mean, knew the enormities I was capable of."

"No," put in Olive quickly. "Cared for you as we do. I can't tell you how awful it is to see you wandering over the face of the earth."

"But we're not wandering now," explained Emily. "This is Tutu's native country."

"Where's your pride, Emily?" said Olive impatiently. "Do you know that affair in Paris was in the papers? What do you suppose people think back home?"

"That affair in Paris was an outrage." Emily's blue eyes flashed around her. "Someone will pay for that affair in Paris."

"It'll be the same everywhere. Just sinking lower and lower, dragged in the mire, and one day deserted——"

"Stop, please!" Emily's voice was cold as ice. "I don't think you quite understand——"

Emily broke off as Petrocobesco came back, threw himself into his chair and buried his face in his hands.

"I can't stand it," he whispered. "Would you mind taking my pulse? I think it's bad. Have you got the thermometer in your purse?"

She held his wrist in silence for a moment.

"It's all right, Tutu." Her voice was soft now, almost crooning. "Sit up. Be a man."

"All right."

He crossed his legs as if nothing had happened and turned abruptly to Breevort:

"How are financial conditions in New York?" he demanded.

But Brevoort was in no humor to prolong the absurd scene. The memory of a certain terrible hour three years before swept over him. He was no man to be made a fool of twice, and his jaw set as he rose to his feet.

"Emily, get your things together," he said tersely. "We're going home."

Emily did not move; an expression of astonishment, melting to amusement, spread over her face. Olive put her arm around her shoulder.

"Come, dear. Let's get out of this nightmare." Then:

"We're waiting," Brevoort said.

Petrocobesco spoke suddenly to the man in the cape, who approached and seized Brevoort's arm. Brevoort shook him off angrily, whereupon the man stepped back, his hand searching his belt.

"No!" cried Emily imperatively.

Once again there was an interruption. The door opened without a knock and two stout men in frock coats and silk hats rushed in and up to Petrocobesco. They grinned and patted him on the back chattering in a strange language, and presently he grinned and patted them on the back and they kissed all around; then, turning to Emily, Petrocobesco spoke to her in French.

"It's all right," he said excitedly. "They did not even argue the matter. I am to have the title of king."

With a long sigh Emily sank back in her chair and her lips parted in a relaxed, tranquil smile.

"Very well, Tutu. We'll get married."

"Oh, heavens, how happy!" He clasped his hands and gazed up ecstatically at the faded ceiling. "How extremely happy!" He fell on his knees beside her and kissed her inside arm.

"What's all this about kings?" Brevoort demanded. "Is this—is he a king?"

"He's a king. Aren't you, Tutu?" Emily's hand gently stroked his oiled hair and Olive saw that her eyes were unusually bright.

"I am your husband," cried Tutu weepily. "The most happy man alive."

"His uncle was Prince of Czjeck-Hansa before the war," explained Emily, her voice singing her content. "Since then there's been a republic, but the peasant party wanted a change and Tutu was next in line. Only I wouldn't marry him unless he insisted on being king instead of prince."

Brevoort passed his hand over his wet forehead.

"Do you mean that this is actually a fact?"

Emily nodded. "The assembly voted it this morning. And if you'll lend us this de luxe limousine of yours we'll make our official entrance into the capital this afternoon."

· I V ·

OVER TWO YEARS later Mr. and Mrs. Brevoort Blair and their two children stood upon a balcony of the Carlton Hotel in London, a situation recommended by the management for watching royal processions pass. This one began with a fanfare of trumpets down by the Strand, and presently a scarlet line of horse guards came into sight.

"But, mummy," the little boy demanded, "is Aunt Emily Queen of England?"

"No, dear; she's queen of a little tiny country, but when she visits here she rides in the queen's carriage."

"Oh."

"Thanks to the magnesium deposits," said Brevoort dryly.

"Was she a princess before she got to be queen?" the little girl asked.

"No, dear; she was an American girl and then she got to be a queen."

"Why?"

"Because nothing else was good enough for her," said her father. "Just think, one time she could have married me. Which would you rather do, baby—marry me or be a queen?"

The little girl hesitated.

"Marry you," she said politely, but without conviction.

"That'll do, Brevoort," said her mother. "Here they come."

"I see them!" the little boy cried.

The cavalcade swept down the crowded street. There were more horse guards, a company of dragoons, outriders, then Olive found herself holding her breath and squeezing the balcony rail as, between a double line of beefeaters, a pair of great gilt-and-crimson coaches rolled past. In the first were the royal sovereigns, their uniforms gleaming with ribbons, crosses and stars, and in the second their two royal consorts, one old, the other young. There was about the scene the glamour shed always by the old empire of half the world, by her ships and ceremonies, her pomps and symbols; and the crowd felt it, and a slow murmur rolled along before the carriage, rising to a strong steady cheer. The two ladies bowed to left and right, and though few knew who the second queen was, she was cheered too. In a moment the gorgeous panoply had rolled below the balcony and on out of sight.

When Olive turned away from the window there were tears in her eyes.

"I wonder if she likes it, Brevoort. I wonder if she's really happy with that terrible little man."

"Well, she got what she wanted, didn't she? And that's something."

Olive drew a long breath.

"Oh, she's so wonderful," she cried—"so wonderful! She could always move me like that, even when I was angriest at her."

"It's all so silly," Brevoort said.

"I suppose so," answered Olive's lips. But her heart, winged with helpless adoration, was following her cousin through the palace gates half a mile away.

AT YOUR AGE

◆

"At Your Age" appeared in the Saturday Evening Post *for 17 August 1929. Harold Ober's enthusiasm for "the finest story you have ever written—and the finest I have ever read" enabled Fitzgerald to obtain a raise to $4,000 —his top story price. This praise is hyperbolic; nevertheless, "At Your Age" shows how Fitzgerald could rescue a stale plot through sheer good writing. Fitzgerald did not share his agent's judgment of "At Your Age" and did not reprint it.*

◆

TOM SQUIRES CAME into the drug store to buy a toothbrush, a can of talcum, a gargle, Castile soap, Epsom salts and a box of cigars. Having lived alone for many years, he was methodical, and while waiting to be served he held the list in his hand. It was Christmas week and Minneapolis was under two feet of exhilarating, constantly refreshed snow; with his cane Tom knocked two clean crusts of it from his overshoes. Then, looking up, he saw the blonde girl.

She was a rare blonde, even in that Promised Land of Scandinavians, where pretty blondes are not rare. There was warm color in her cheeks, lips and pink little hands that folded powders into papers; her hair, in long braids twisted about her head, was shining and alive. She seemed to Tom suddenly the cleanest person he knew of, and he caught his breath as he stepped forward and looked into her gray eyes.

"A can of talcum."

"What kind?"

"Any kind. . . . That's fine."

She looked back at him apparently without self-consciousness, and, as the list melted away, his heart raced with it wildly.

"I am not old," he wanted to say. "At fifty I'm younger than most men of forty. Don't I interest you at all?"

But she only said "What kind of gargle?"

And he answered, "What can you recommend? . . . That's fine."

Almost painfully he took his eyes from her, went out and got into his coupé.

"If that young idiot only knew what an old imbecile like me could do for her," he thought humorously—"what worlds I could open out to her!"

As he drove away into the winter twilight he followed this train of thought to a totally unprecedented conclusion. Perhaps the time of day was the responsible stimulant, for the shop windows glowing into the cold, the tinkling bells of a delivery sleigh, the white gloss left by shovels on the sidewalks, the enormous distance of the stars, brought back the feel of other nights thirty years ago. For an instant the girls he had known then slipped like phantoms out of their dull matronly selves of today and fluttered past him with frosty, seductive laughter, until a pleasant shiver crawled up his spine.

"Youth! Youth! Youth!" he apostrophized with conscious lack of originality, and, as a somewhat ruthless and domineering man of no morals whatsoever, he considered going back to the drug store to seek the blonde girl's address. It was not his sort of thing, so the half-formed intention passed; the idea remained.

"Youth, by heaven—youth!" he repeated under his breath. "I want it near me, all around me, just once more before I'm too old to care."

He was tall, lean and handsome, with the ruddy, bronzed face of a sportsman and a just faintly graying mustache. Once he had been among the city's best beaus, organizer of cotillions and charity balls, popular with men and women, and with several generations of them. After the war he had suddenly felt poor, gone into business, and in ten years accumulated nearly a million dollars. Tom Squires was not introspective, but he perceived now that the wheel of his life had revolved again, bringing up forgotten, yet familiar, dreams and yearnings. Entering his house, he turned suddenly to a pile of disregarded invitations to see whether or not he had been bidden to a dance tonight.

Throughout his dinner, which he ate alone at the Downtown Club, his eyes were half closed and on his face was a faint smile. He was practicing so that he would be able to laugh at himself painlessly, if necessary.

"I don't even know what they talk about," he admitted. "They pet— prominent broker goes to petting party with débutante. What is a petting party? Do they serve refreshments? Will I have to learn to play a saxophone?"

These matters, lately as remote as China in a news reel, came alive to him. They were serious questions. At ten o'clock he walked up the steps of the College Club to a private dance with the same sense of entering a new world as when he had gone into a training camp back in '17. He spoke to a hostess of his generation and to her daughter, overwhelmingly of another, and sat down in a corner to acclimate himself.

He was not alone long. A silly young man named Leland Jaques, who lived across the street from Tom, remarked him kindly and came over to brighten his life. He was such an exceedingly fatuous young man that, for a moment, Tom was annoyed, but he perceived craftily that he might be of service.

"Hello, Mr. Squires. How are you, sir?"

"Fine, thanks, Leland. Quite a dance."

As one man of the world with another, Mr. Jaques sat, or lay, down on the couch and lit—or so it seemed to Tom—three or four cigarettes at once.

"You should of been here last night, Mr. Squires. Oh, boy, that was a party and a half! The Caulkins. Hap-past five!"

"Who's that girl who changes partners every minute?" Tom asked. . . . "No, the one in white passing the door."

"That's Annie Lorry."

"Arthur Lorry's daughter?"

"Yes."

"She seems popular."

"About the most popular girl in town—anyway, at a dance."

"Not popular except at dances?"

"Oh, sure, but she hangs around with Randy Cambell all the time."

"What Cambell?"

"D. B."

There were new names in town in the last decade.

"It's a boy-and-girl affair." Pleased with this phrase, Jaques tried to repeat it: "One of those boy-and-girls affair—boys-and-girl affairs——" He gave it up and lit several more cigarettes, crushing out the first series on Tom's lap.

"Does she drink?"

"Not especially. At least I never saw her passed out. . . . That's Randy Cambell just cut in on her now."

They were a nice couple. Her beauty sparkled bright against his strong, tall form, and they floated hoveringly, delicately, like two people in a nice, amusing dream. They came near and Tom admired the faint dust of powder over her freshness, the guarded sweetness of her smile, the fragility of her body calculated by Nature to a millimeter to suggest a bud, yet guarantee a flower. Her innocent, passionate eyes were brown, perhaps; but almost violet in the silver light.

"Is she out this year?"

"Who?"

"Miss Lorry."

"Yes."

Although the girl's loveliness interested Tom, he was unable to picture himself as one of the attentive, grateful queue that pursued her around the room. Better meet her when the holidays were over and most of these young men were back in college "where they belonged." Tom Squires was old enough to wait.

He waited a fortnight while the city sank into the endless northern midwinter, where gray skies were friendlier than metallic blue skies, and dusk, whose lights were a reassuring glimpse into the continuity of human cheer, was warmer than the afternoons of bloodless sunshine. The coat of snow lost its press and became soiled and shabby, and ruts froze in the street; some of the big houses on Crest Avenue began to close as their occupants went South. In those cold days Tom asked Annie and her parents to go as his guests to the last Bachelors' Ball.

The Lorrys were an old family in Minneapolis, grown a little harassed and poor since the war. Mrs. Lorry, a contemporary of Tom's, was not surprised that he should send mother and daughter orchids and dine them luxuriously in his apartment on fresh caviar, quail and champagne. Annie saw him only dimly—he lacked vividness, as the old do for the young— but she perceived his interest in her and performed for him the traditional ritual of young beauty—smiles, polite, wide-eyed attention, a profile held obligingly in this light or in that. At the ball he danced with her twice, and, though she was teased about it, she was flattered that such a man of the world—he had become that instead of a mere old man—had singled her out. She accepted his invitation to the symphony the following week, with the idea that it would be uncouth to refuse.

There were several "nice invitations" like that. Sitting beside him, she dozed in the warm shadow of Brahms and thought of Randy Cambell and other romantic nebulosities who might appear tomorrow. Feeling casually mellow one afternoon, she deliberately provoked Tom to kiss her on the way home, but she wanted to laugh when he took her hands and told her fervently he was falling in love.

"But how could you?" she protested. "Really, you musn't say such crazy things. I won't go out with you any more, and then you'll be sorry."

A few days later her mother spoke to her as Tom waited outside in his car:

"Who's that, Annie?"

"Mr. Squires."

"Shut the door a minute. You're seeing him quite a bit."

"Why not?"

"Well, dear, he's fifty years old."

"But, mother, there's hardly anybody else in town."

"But you musn't get any silly ideas about him."

"Don't worry. Actually, he bores me to extinction most of the time."
She came to a sudden decision: "I'm not going to see him any more. I just
couldn't get out of going with him this afternoon."

And that night, as she stood by her door in the circle of Randy Cambell's
arm, Tom and his single kiss had no existence for her.

"Oh, I do love you so," Randy whispered. "Kiss me once more."

Their cool cheeks and warm lips met in the crisp darkness, and, watching
the icy moon over his shoulder, Annie knew that she was his surely and,
pulling his face down, kissed him again, trembling with emotion.

"When'll you marry me then?" he whispered.

"When can you—we afford it?"

"Couldn't you announce our engagement? If you knew the misery of
having you out with somebody else and then making love to you."

"Oh, Randy, you ask so much."

"It's so awful to say good night. Can't I come in for a minute?"

"Yes."

Sitting close together in a trance before the flickering, lessening fire, they
were oblivious that their common fate was being coolly weighed by a man
of fifty who lay in a hot bath some blocks away.

· II ·

TOM SQUIRES HAD GUESSED from Annie's extremely kind and detached
manner of the afternoon that he had failed to interest her. He had promised
himself that in such an eventuality he would drop the matter, but now he
found himself in no such humor. He did not want to marry her; he simply
wanted to see her and be with her a little; and up to the moment of her
sweetly casual, half passionate, yet wholly unemotional kiss, giving her up
would have been easy, for he was past the romantic age; but since that kiss
the thought of her made his heart move up a few inches in his chest and
beat there steady and fast.

"But this is the time to get out," he said to himself. "My age; no possible
right to force myself into her life."

He rubbed himself dry, brushed his hair before the mirror, and, as he laid down the comb, said decisively: "That is that." And after reading for an hour he turned out the lamp with a snap and repeated aloud: "That is that."

In other words, that was not that at all, and the click of material things did not finish off Annie Lorry as a business decision might be settled by the tap of a pencil on the table.

"I'm going to carry this matter a little further," he said to himself about half-past four; on that acknowledgment he turned over and found sleep.

In the morning she had receded somewhat, but by four o'clock in the afternoon she was all around him—the phone was for calling her, a woman's footfalls passing his office were her footfalls, the snow outside the window was blowing, perhaps, against her rosy face.

"There is always the little plan I thought of last night," he said to himself. "In ten years I'll be sixty, and then no youth, no beauty for me ever any more."

In a sort of panic he took a sheet of note paper and composed a carefully phrased letter to Annie's mother, asking permission to pay court to her daughter. He took it himself into the hall, but before the letter slide he tore it up and dropped the pieces in a cuspidor.

"I couldn't do such an underhand trick," he told himself, "at my age." But this self-congratulation was premature, for he rewrote the letter and mailed it before he left his office that night.

Next day the reply he had counted on arrived—he could have guessed its very words in advance. It was a curt and indignant refusal.

It ended:

> I think it best that you and my daughter meet no more.
> Very Sincerely Yours,
> MABEL TOLLMAN LORRY.

"And now," Tom thought coolly, "we'll see what the girl says to that."

He wrote a note to Annie. Her mother's letter had surprised him, it said, but perhaps it was best that they should meet no more, in view of her mother's attitude.

By return post came Annie's defiant answer to her mother's fiat: "This isn't the Dark Ages. I'll see you whenever I like." She named a rendezvous for the following afternoon. Her mother's short-sightedness brought about what he had failed to achieve directly; for where Annie had been on the point of dropping him, she was now determined to do nothing of the sort. And the secrecy engendered by disapproval at home simply contributed the missing excitement. As February hardened into deep, solemn, interminable winter, she met him frequently and on a new basis. Sometimes they drove over to St. Paul to see a picture or to have dinner; sometimes they parked far out on a boulevard in his coupé, while the bitter sleet glazed the windshield to opacity and furred his lamps with ermine. Often he brought along something special to drink—enough to make her gay, but, carefully, never more; for mingled with his other emotions about her was something paternally concerned.

Laying his cards on the table, he told her that it was her mother who had unwittingly pushed her toward him, but Annie only laughed at his duplicity.

She was having a better time with him than with anyone else she had ever known. In place of the selfish exigency of a younger man, he showed her a never-failing consideration. What if his eyes were tired, his cheeks a little leathery and veined, if his will was masculine and strong. Moreover, his experience was a window looking out upon a wider, richer world; and with Randy Cambell next day she would feel less taken care of, less valued, less rare.

It was Tom now who was vaguely discontented. He had what he wanted—her youth at his side—and he felt that anything further would be a mistake. His liberty was precious to him and he could offer her only a dozen years before he would be old, but she had become something precious to him and he perceived that drifting wasn't fair. Then one day late in February the matter was decided out of hand.

They had ridden home from St. Paul and dropped into the College Club for tea, breaking together through the drifts that masked the walk and rimmed the door. It was a revolving door; a young man came around in it, and stepping into his space, they smelt onions and whisky. The door revolved again after them, and he was back within, facing them. It was Randy Cambell; his face was flushed, his eyes dull and hard.

"Hello, beautiful," he said, approaching Annie.

"Don't come so close," she protested lightly. "You smell of onions."

"You're particular all of a sudden."

"Always. I'm always particular." Annie made a slight movement back toward Tom.

"Not always," said Randy unpleasantly. Then, with increased emphasis and a fractional glance at Tom: "Not always." With his remark he seemed to join the hostile world outside. "And I'll just give you a tip," he continued: "Your mother's inside."

The jealous ill-temper of another generation reached Tom only faintly, like the protest of a child, but at this impertinent warning he bristled with annoyance.

"Come on, Annie," he said brusquely. "We'll go in."

With her glance uneasily averted from Randy, Annie followed Tom into the big room.

It was sparsely populated; three middle-aged women sat near the fire. Momentarily Annie drew back, then she walked toward them.

"Hello, mother . . . Mrs. Trumble . . . Aunt Caroline."

The two latter responded; Mrs. Trumble even nodded faintly at Tom. But Annie's mother got to her feet without a word, her eyes frozen, her mouth drawn. For a moment she stood staring at her daughter; then she turned abruptly and left the room.

Tom and Annie found a table across the room.

"Wasn't she terrible?" said Annie, breathing aloud. He didn't answer.

"For three days she hasn't spoken to me." Suddenly she broke out: "Oh, people can be so small! I was going to sing the leading part in the Junior League show, and yesterday Cousin Mary Betts, the president, came to me and said I couldn't."

"Why not?"

"Because a representative Junior League girl mustn't defy her mother. As if I were a naughty child!"

Tom stared on at a row of cups on the mantelpiece—two or three of them bore his name. "Perhaps she was right," he said suddenly. "When I begin to do harm to you it's time to stop."

"What do you mean?"

At her shocked voice his heart poured a warm liquid forth into his body, but he answered quietly: "You remember I told you I was going South? Well, I'm going tomorrow."

There was an argument, but he had made up his mind. At the station next evening she wept and clung to him.

"Thank you for the happiest month I've had in years," he said.

"But you'll come back, Tom."

"I'll be two months in Mexico; then I'm going East for a few weeks."

He tried to sound fortunate, but the frozen city he was leaving seemed to be in blossom. Her frozen breath was a flower on the air, and his heart sank as he realized that some young man was waiting outside to take her home in a car hung with blooms.

"Good-by, Annie. Good-by, sweet!"

Two days later he spent the morning in Houston with Hal Meigs, a classmate at Yale.

"You're in luck for such an old fella," said Meigs at luncheon, "because I'm going to introduce you to the cutest little traveling companion you ever saw, who's going all the way to Mexico City."

The lady in question was frankly pleased to learn at the station that she was not returning alone. She and Tom dined together on the train and later played rummy for an hour; but when, at ten o'clock, standing in the door of the stateroom, she turned back to him suddenly with a certain look, frank and unmistakable, and stood there holding that look for a long moment, Tom Squires was suddenly in the grip of an emotion that was not the one in question. He wanted desperately to see Annie, call her for a second on the phone, and then fall asleep, knowing she was young and pure as a star, and safe in bed.

"Good night," he said, trying to keep any repulsion out of his voice.

"Oh! Good night."

Arriving in El Paso next day, he drove over the border to Juarez. It was bright and hot, and after leaving his bags at the station he went into a bar for an iced drink; as he sipped it a girl's voice addressed him thickly from the table behind:

"You'n American?"

He had noticed her slumped forward on her elbows as he came in; now, turning, he faced a young girl of about seventeen, obviously drunk, yet with gentility in her unsteady, sprawling voice. The American bartender leaned confidentially forward.

"I don't know what to do about her," he said. "She come in about three o'clock with two young fellows—one of them her sweetie. They had a fight and the men went off, and this one's been here ever since."

A spasm of distaste passed over Tom—the rules of his generation were outraged and defied. That an American girl should be drunk and deserted in a tough foreign town—that such things happened, might happen to Annie. He looked at his watch, hesitated.

"Has she got a bill?" he asked.

"She owes for five gins. But suppose her boy friends come back?"

"Tell them she's at the Roosevelt Hotel in El Paso."

Approaching, he put his hand on her shoulder. She looked up.

"You look like Santa Claus," she said vaguely. "You couldn't possibly be Santa Claus, could you?"

"I'm going to take you to El Paso."

"Well," she considered, "you look perfectly safe to me."

She was so young—a drenched little rose. He could have wept for her wretched unconsciousness of the old facts, the old penalties of life. Jousting at nothing in an empty tilt yard with a shaking spear. The taxi moved too slowly through the suddenly poisonous night.

Having explained things to a reluctant night clerk, he went out and found a telegraph office.

"Have given up Mexican trip," he wired. "Leaving here tonight. Please meet train in the St. Paul station at three o'clock and ride with me to Minneapolis, as I can't spare you for another minute. All my love."

He could at least keep an eye on her, advise her, see what she did with her life. That silly mother of hers!

On the train, as the baked tropical lands and green fields fell away and the North swept near again with patches of snow, then fields of it, fierce winds in the vestibule and bleak, hibernating farms, he paced the corridors with intolerable restlessness. When they drew into the St. Paul station he swung himself off like a young man and searched the platform eagerly, but his eyes failed to find her. He had counted on those few minutes between the cities; they had become a symbol of her fidelity to their friendship, and as the train started again he searched it desperately from smoker to observation car. But he could not find her, and now he knew that he was mad for her; at the thought that she had taken his advice and plunged into affairs with other men, he grew weak with fear.

Drawing into Minneapolis, his hands fumbled so that he must call the porter to fasten his baggage. Then there was an interminable wait in the corridor while the baggage was taken off and he was pressed up against a girl in a squirrel-trimmed coat.

"Tom!"

"Well, I'll be——"

Her arms went up around his neck. "But, Tom," she cried, "I've been right here in this car since St. Paul!"

His cane fell in the corridor, he drew her very tenderly close and their lips met like starved hearts.

· I I I ·

THE NEW INTIMACY of their definite engagement brought Tom a feeling of young happiness. He awoke on winter mornings with the sense of undeserved joy hovering in the room; meeting young men, he found himself matching the vigor of his mind and body against theirs. Suddenly his life had a purpose and a background; he felt rounded and complete. On gray March afternoons when she wandered familiarly in his apartment the warm sureties of his youth flooded back—ecstasy and poignancy, the mortal and the eternal posed in their immemorially tragic juxtaposition and, a little astounded, he found himself relishing the very terminology of young romance. But he was more thoughtful than a younger lover; and to Annie he seemed to "know everything," to stand holding open the gates for her passage into the truly golden world.

"We'll go to Europe first," he said.

"Oh, we'll go there a lot, won't we? Let's spend our winters in Italy and the spring in Paris."

"But, little Annie, there's business."

"Well, we'll stay away as much as we can anyhow. I hate Minneapolis."

"Oh, no." He was a little shocked. "Minneapolis is all right."

"When you're here it's all right."

Mrs. Lorry yielded at length to the inevitable. With ill grace she acknowledged the engagement, asking only that the marriage should not take place until fall.

"Such a long time," Annie sighed.

"After all, I'm your mother. It's so little to ask."

It was a long winter, even in a land of long winters. March was full of billowy drifts, and when it seemed at last as though the cold must be defeated, there was a series of blizzards, desperate as last stands. The people waited; their first energy to resist was spent, and man, like weather, simply hung on. There was less to do now and the general restlessness was expressed by surliness in daily contacts. Then, early in April, with a long sigh the ice cracked, the snow ran into the ground and the green, eager spring broke up through.

One day, riding along a slushy road in a fresh, damp breeze with a little starved, smothered grass in it, Annie began to cry. Sometimes she cried for nothing, but this time Tom suddenly stopped the car and put his arm around her.

"Why do you cry like that? Are you unhappy?"

"Oh, no, no!" she protested.

"But you cried yesterday the same way. And you wouldn't tell me why. You must always tell me."

"Nothing, except the spring. It smells so good, and it always has so many sad thoughts and memories in it."

"It's our spring, my sweetheart," he said. "Annie, don't let's wait. Let's be married in June."

"I promised mother, but if you like we can announce our engagement in June."

The spring came fast now. The sidewalks were damp, then dry, and the children roller-skated on them and boys played baseball in the soft, vacant lots. Tom got up elaborate picnics of Annie's contemporaries and encouraged her to play golf and tennis with them. Abruptly, with a final, triumphant lurch of Nature, it was full summer.

On a lovely May evening Tom came up the Lorrys' walk and sat down beside Annie's mother on the porch.

"It's so pleasant," he said, "I thought Annie and I would walk instead of driving this evening. I want to show her the funny old house I was born in."

"On Chambers Street, wasn't it? Annie'll be home in a few minutes. She went riding with some young people after dinner."

"Yes, on Chambers Street."

He looked at his watch presently, hoping Annie would come while it was still light enough to see. Quarter of nine. He frowned. She had kept him waiting the night before, kept him waiting an hour yesterday afternoon.

"If I was twenty-one," he said to himself, "I'd make scenes and we'd both be miserable."

He and Mrs. Lorry talked; the warmth of the night precipitated the vague evening lassitude of the fifties and softened them both, and for the first time since his attentions to Annie began, there was no unfriendliness between them. By and by long silences fell, broken only by the scratch of a match or the creak of her swinging settee. When Mr. Lorry came home Tom threw away his second cigar in surprise and looked at his watch; it was after ten.

"Annie's late," Mrs. Lorry said.

"I hope there's nothing wrong," said Tom anxiously. "Who is she with?"

"There were four when they started out. Randy Cambell and another couple—I didn't notice who. They were only going for a soda."

"I hope there hasn't been any trouble. Perhaps——Do you think I ought to go and see?"

"Ten isn't late nowadays. You'll find——" Remembering that Tom Squires was marrying Annie, not adopting her, she kept herself from adding: "You'll get used to it."

Her husband excused himself and went up to bed, and the conversation became more forced and desultory. When the church clock over the way struck eleven they both broke off and listened to the beats. Twenty minutes later just as Tom impatiently crushed out his last cigar, an automobile drifted down the street and came to rest in front of the door.

For a minute no one moved on the porch or in the auto. Then Annie, with a hat in her hand, got out and came quickly up the walk. Defying the tranquil night, the car snorted away.

"Oh, hello!" she cried. "I'm so sorry! What time is it? Am I terribly late?"

Tom didn't answer. The street lamp threw wine color upon her face and expressed with a shadow the heightened flush of her cheek. Her dress was crushed, her hair was in brief, expressive disarray. But it was the strange little break in her voice that made him afraid to speak, made him turn his eyes aside.

"What happened?" Mrs. Lorry asked casually.

"Oh, a blow-out and something wrong with the engine—and we lost our way. Is it terribly late?"

And then, as she stood before them, her hat still in her hand, her breast rising and falling a little, her eyes wide and bright, Tom realized with a shock that he and her mother were people of the same age looking at a person of another. Try as he might, he could not separate himself from Mrs. Lorry. When she excused herself he suppressed a frantic tendency to say, "But why should you go now? After sitting here all evening?"

They were alone. Annie came up to him and pressed his hand. He had never been so conscious of her beauty; her damp hands were touched with dew.

"You were out with young Cambell," he said.

"Yes. Oh, don't be mad. I feel—I feel so upset tonight."

"Upset?"

She sat down, whimpering a little.

"I couldn't help it. Please don't be mad. He wanted so for me to take a ride with him and it was such a wonderful night, so I went just for an hour. And we began talking and I didn't realize the time. I felt so sorry for him."

"How do you think I felt?" He scorned himself, but it was said now.

"Don't, Tom. I told you I was terribly upset. I want to go to bed."

"I understand. Good night, Annie."

"Oh, please don't act that way, Tom. Can't you understand?"

But he could, and that was just the trouble. With the courteous bow of another generation, he walked down the steps and off into the obliterating moonlight. In a moment he was just a shadow passing the street lamps and then a faint footfall up the street.

· IV ·

ALL THROUGH THAT summer he often walked abroad in the evenings. He liked to stand for a minute in front of the house where he was born, and then in front of another house where he had been a little boy. On his customary routes there were other sharp landmarks of the 90's, converted habitats of gayeties that no longer existed—the shell of Jansen's Livery Stables and the old Nushka Rink, where every winter his father had curled on the well-kept ice.

"And it's a darn pity," he would mutter. "A darn pity."

He had a tendency, too, to walk past the lights of a certain drug store, because it seemed to him that it had contained the seed of another and nearer branch of the past. Once he went in, and inquiring casually about the blonde clerk, found that she had married and departed several months before. He obtained her name and on an impulse sent her a wedding present "from a dumb admirer," for he felt he owed something to her for his happiness and pain. He had lost the battle against youth and spring, and with his grief paid the penalty for age's unforgivable sin—refusing to die. But he could not have walked down wasted into the darkness without being used up a little; what he had wanted, after all, was only to break his strong old heart. Conflict itself has a value beyond victory and defeat, and those three months—he had them forever.

THE SWIMMERS

♦

"The Swimmers" appeared in the Saturday Evening Post *issue of 19 October 1929—just before the Wall Street Crash. Fitzgerald described it to Harold Ober as "the hardest story I ever wrote, too big for its space + not even now satisfactory. I've had a terrible 10 days finishing it, when I thought I had only an hour.... However, its done + its not bad...." Fitzgerald did not reprint it, but Ober praised it as "the ablest and most thoughtful story you have ever done." "The Swimmers" is one of a significant group of stories in which Fitzgerald contrasts America with Europe, as in the eloquent concluding analysis of American idealism.*

♦

IN THE PLACE BENOÎT, a suspended mass of gasoline exhaust cooked slowly by the June sun. It was a terrible thing, for, unlike pure heat, it held no promise of rural escape, but suggested only roads choked with the same foul asthma. In the offices of The Promissory Trust Company, Paris Branch, facing the square, an American man of thirty-five inhaled it, and it became the odor of the thing he must presently do. A black horror suddenly descended upon him, and he went up to the washroom, where he stood, trembling a little, just inside the door.

Through the washroom window his eyes fell upon a sign—1000 Chemises. The shirts in question filled the shop window, piled, cravated and stuffed, or else draped with shoddy grace on the show-case floor. 1000 Chemises —Count them! To the left he read Papeterie, Pâtisserie, Solde, Réclame, and Constance Talmadge in Déjeuner de Soleil; and his eye, escaping to the right, met yet more somber announcements: Vêtements Ecclésiastiques, Déclaration de Décès, and Pompes Funèbres. Life and Death.

Henry Marston's trembling became a shaking; it would be pleasant if this were the end and nothing more need be done, he thought, and with a certain hope he sat down on a stool. But it is seldom really the end, and after a while, as he became too exhausted to care, the shaking stopped and he was better. Going downstairs, looking as alert and self-possessed as any other officer of the bank, he spoke to two clients he knew, and set his face grimly toward noon.

"Well, Henry Clay Marston!" A handsome old man shook hands with him and took the chair beside his desk.

"Henry, I want to see you in regard to what we talked about the other night. How about lunch? In that green little place with all the trees."

"Not lunch, Judge Waterbury; I've got an engagement."

"I'll talk now, then; because I'm leaving this afternoon. What do these plutocrats give you for looking important around here?"

Henry Marston knew what was coming.

"Ten thousand and certain expense money," he answered.

"How would you like to come back to Richmond at about double that? You've been over here eight years and you don't know the opportunities you're missing. Why both my boys——"

Henry listened appreciatively, but this morning he couldn't concentrate on the matter. He spoke vaguely about being able to live more comfortably in Paris and restrained himself from stating his frank opinion upon existence at home.

Judge Waterbury beckoned to a tall, pale man who stood at the mail desk. "This is Mr. Wiese," he said. "Mr. Wiese's from downstate; he's a halfway partner of mine."

"Glad to meet you, suh." Mr. Wiese's voice was rather too deliberately Southern. "Understand the judge is makin' you a proposition."

"Yes," Henry answered briefly. He recognized and detested the type—the prosperous sweater, presumably evolved from a cross between carpet-bagger and poor white. When Wiese moved away, the judge said almost apologetically:

"He's one of the richest men in the South, Henry." Then, after a pause: "Come home, boy."

"I'll think it over, judge." For a moment the gray and ruddy head seemed so kind; then it faded back into something one-dimensional, machine-fin-ished, blandly and bleakly un-European. Henry Marston respected that open kindness—in the bank he touched it with daily appreciation, as a curator in a museum might touch a precious object removed in time and space; but there was no help in it for him; the questions which Henry Marston's life propounded could be answered only in France. His seven generations of Virginia ancestors were definitely behind him every day at noon when he turned home.

Home was a fine high-ceiling apartment hewn from the palace of a Re-naissance cardinal in the Rue Monsieur—the sort of thing Henry could not have afforded in America. Choupette, with something more than the rigid traditionalism of a French bourgeois taste, had made it beautiful, and moved through gracefully with their children. She was a frail Latin blonde with fine large features and vividly sad French eyes that had first fascinated Henry in a Grenoble *pension* in 1918. The two boys took their looks from Henry, voted the handsomest man at the University of Virginia a few years before the war.

Climbing the two broad flights of stairs, Henry stood panting a moment in the outside hall. It was quiet and cool here, and yet it was vaguely like the terrible thing that was going to happen. He heard a clock inside his apartment strike one, and inserted his key in the door.

The maid who had been in Choupette's family for thirty years stood before him, her mouth open in the utterance of a truncated sigh.

"*Bonjour,* Louise."

"Monsieur!" He threw his hat on a chair. "But, monsieur—but I thought monsieur said on the phone he was going to Tours for the children!"

"I changed my mind, Louise."

He had taken a step forward, his last doubt melting away at the constricted terror in the woman's face.

"Is madame home?"

Simultaneously he perceived a man's hat and stick on the hall table and for the first time in his life he heard silence—a loud, singing silence, oppressive as heavy guns or thunder. Then, as the endless moment was broken by the maid's terrified little cry, he pushed through the portières into the next room.

An hour later Doctor Derocco, *de la Faculté de Médecine,* rang the apartment bell. Choupette Marston, her face a little drawn and rigid, answered the door. For a moment they went through French forms; then:

"My husband has been feeling unwell for some weeks," she said concisely. "Nevertheless, he did not complain in a way to make me uneasy. He has suddenly collapsed; he cannot articulate or move his limbs. All this, I must say, might have been precipitated by a certain indiscretion of mine—in all events, there was a violent scene, a discussion, and sometimes when he is agitated, my husband cannot comprehend well in French."

"I will see him," said the doctor; thinking: "Some things are comprehended instantly in all languages."

During the next four weeks several people listened to strange speeches about one thousand chemises, and heard how all the population of Paris was becoming etherized by cheap gasoline—there was a consulting psychiatrist, not inclined to believe in any underlying mental trouble; there was a nurse from the American Hospital, and there was Choupette, frightened, defiant and, after her fashion, deeply sorry. A month later, when Henry awoke to his familiar room, lit with a dimmed lamp, he found her sitting beside his bed and reached out for her hand.

"I still love you," he said—"that's the odd thing."

"Sleep, male cabbage."

"At all costs," he continued with a certain feeble irony, "you can count on me to adopt the Continental attitude."

"Please! You tear at my heart."

When he was sitting up in bed they were ostensibly close together again—closer than they had been for months.

"Now you're going to have another holiday," said Henry to the two boys, back from the country. "Papa has got to go to the seashore and get really well."

"Will we swim?"

"And get drowned, my darlings?" Choupette cried. "But fancy, at your age. Not at all!"

So, at St. Jean de Luz they sat on the shore instead, and watched the English and Americans and a few hardy French pioneers of *le sport* voyage between raft and diving tower, motorboat and sand. There were passing ships, and bright islands to look at, and mountains reaching into cold zones, and red and yellow villas, called Fleur des Bois, Mon Nid, or Sans-Souci; and farther back, tired French villages of baked cement and gray stone.

Choupette sat at Henry's side, holding a parasol to shelter her peach-bloom skin from the sun.

"Look!" she would say, at the sight of tanned American girls. "Is that lovely? Skin that will be leather at thirty—a sort of brown veil to hide all blemishes, so that everyone will look alike. And women of a hundred kilos in such bathing suits! Weren't clothes intended to hide Nature's mistakes?"

Henry Clay Marston was a Virginian of the kind who are prouder of being Virginians than of being Americans. That mighty word printed across a continent was less to him than the memory of his grandfather, who freed his slaves in '58, fought from Manassas to Appomattox, knew Huxley and Spencer as light reading, and believed in caste only when it expressed the best of race.

To Choupette all this was vague. Her more specific criticisms of his compatriots were directed against the women.

"How would you place them?" she exclaimed. "Great ladies, bourgeoises, adventuresses—they are all the same. Look! Where would I be if I tried to act like your friend, Madame de Richepin? My father was a professor in a provincial university, and I have certain things I wouldn't do because they wouldn't please my class, my family. Madame de Richepin has other things she wouldn't do because of her class, her family." Suddenly she pointed to an American girl going into the water: "But that young lady may be a stenographer and yet be compelled to warp herself, dressing and acting as if she had all the money in the world."

"Perhaps she will have, some day."

"That's the story they are told; it happens to one, not to the ninety-nine. That's why all their faces over thirty are discontented and unhappy."

Though Henry was in general agreement, he could not help being amused at Choupette's choice of target this afternoon. The girl—she was perhaps eighteen—was obviously acting like nothing but herself—she was what his father would have called a thoroughbred. A deep, thoughtful face that was pretty only because of the irrepressible determination of the perfect features to be recognized, a face that could have done without them and not yielded up its poise and distinction.

In her grace, at once exquisite and hardy, she was that perfect type of American girl that makes one wonder if the male is not being sacrificed to it, much as, in the last century, the lower strata in England were sacrificed to produce the governing class.

The two young men, coming out of the water as she went in, had large shoulders and empty faces. She had a smile for them that was no more than they deserved—that must do until she chose one to be the father of her children and gave herself up to destiny. Until then—Henry Marston was glad about her as her arms, like flying fish, clipped the water in a crawl, as her body spread in a swan dive or doubled in a jackknife from the spring-board and her head appeared from the depth, jauntily flipping the damp hair away.

The two young men passed near.

"They push water," Choupette said, "then they go elsewhere and push other water. They pass months in France and they couldn't tell you the name of the President. They are parasites such as Europe has not known in a hundred years."

But Henry had stood up abruptly, and now all the people on the beach were suddenly standing up. Something had happened out there in the fifty yards between the deserted raft and the shore. The bright head showed upon the surface; it did not flip water now, but called: "*Au secours!* Help!" in a feeble and frightened voice.

"Henry!" Choupette cried. "Stop! Henry!"

The beach was almost deserted at noon, but Henry and several others were sprinting toward the sea; the two young Americans heard, turned and sprinted after them. There was a frantic little time with half a dozen bobbing heads in the water. Choupette, still clinging to her parasol, but managing to wring her hands at the same time, ran up and down the beach crying: "Henry! Henry!"

Now there were more helping hands, and then two swelling groups around prostrate figures on the shore. The young fellow who pulled in the girl brought her around in a minute or so, but they had more trouble getting the water out of Henry, who had never learned to swim.

· II ·

"THIS IS THE MAN who didn't know whether he could swim, because he'd never tried."

Henry got up from his sun chair, grinning. It was next morning, and the saved girl had just appeared on the beach with her brother. She smiled back at Henry, brightly casual, appreciative rather than grateful.

"At the very least, I owe it to you to teach you how," she said.

"I'd like it. I decided that in the water yesterday, just before I went down the tenth time."

"You can trust me. I'll never again eat chocolate ice cream before going in."

As she went on into the water, Choupette asked: "How long do you think we'll stay here? After all, this life wearies one."

"We'll stay till I can swim. And the boys too."

"Very well. I saw a nice bathing suit in two shades of blue for fifty francs that I will buy you this afternoon."

Feeling a little paunchy and unhealthily white, Henry, holding his sons by the hand, took his body into the water. The breakers leaped at him, staggering him, while the boys yelled with ecstasy; the returning water curled threateningly around his feet as it hurried back to sea. Farther out, he stood waist deep with other intimidated souls, watching the people dive from the raft tower, hoping the girl would come to fulfill her promise, and somewhat embarrassed when she did.

"I'll start with your eldest. You watch and then try it by yourself."

He floundered in the water. It went into his nose and started a raw stinging; it blinded him; it lingered afterward in his ears, rattling back and forth like pebbles for hours. The sun discovered him, too, peeling long strips of parchment from his shoulders, blistering his back so that he lay in a feverish agony for several nights. After a week he swam, painfully, pantingly, and not very far. The girl taught him a sort of crawl, for he saw that the breast stroke was an obsolete device that lingered on with the inept and the old. Choupette caught him regarding his tanned face in the mirror with a sort of fascination, and the youngest boy contracted some sort of mild skin infection in the sand that retired him from competition. But one day Henry battled his way desperately to the float and drew himself up on it with his last breath.

"That being settled," he told the girl, when he could speak, "I can leave St. Jean tomorrow."

"I'm sorry."

"What will you do now?"

"My brother and I are going to Antibes; there's swimming there all through October. Then Florida."

"And swim?" he asked with some amusement.

"Why, yes. We'll swim."

"Why do you swim?"

"To get clean," she answered surprisingly.

"Clean from what?"

She frowned. "I don't know why I said that. But it feels clean in the sea."

"Americans are too particular about that," he commented.

"How could anyone be?"

"I mean we've got too fastidious even to clean up our messes."

"I don't know."

"But tell me why you——" He stopped himself in surprise. He had been about to ask her to explain a lot of other things—to say what was clean and unclean, what was worth knowing and what was only words—to open up a new gate to life. Looking for a last time into her eyes, full of cool secrets, he realized how much he was going to miss these mornings, without knowing whether it was the girl who interested him or what she represented of his ever-new, ever-changing country.

"All right," he told Choupette that night. "We'll leave tomorrow."

"For Paris?"

"For America."

"You mean I'm to go too? And the children?"

"Yes."

"But that's absurd," she protested. "Last time it cost more than we spend in six months here. And then there were only three of us. Now that we've managed to get ahead at last——"

"That's just it. I'm tired of getting ahead on your skimping and saving and going without dresses. I've got to make more money. American men are incomplete without money."

"You mean we'll stay?"

"It's very possible."

They looked at each other, and against her will, Choupette understood. For eight years, by a process of ceaseless adaptation, he had lived her life, substituting for the moral confusion of his own country, the tradition, the wisdom, the sophistication of France. After that matter in Paris, it had seemed the bigger part to understand and to forgive, to cling to the home as something apart from the vagaries of love. Only now, glowing with a good health that he had not experienced for years, did he discover his true reaction. It had released him. For all his sense of loss, he possessed again the masculine self he had handed over to the keeping of a wise little Provençal girl eight years ago.

She struggled on for a moment.

"You've got a good position and we really have plenty of money. You know we can live cheaper here."

"The boys are growing up now, and I'm not sure I want to educate them in France."

"But that's all decided," she wailed. "You admit yourself that education in America is superficial and full of silly fads. Do you want them to be like those two dummies on the beach?"

"Perhaps I was thinking more of myself, Choupette. Men just out of college who brought their letters of credit into the bank eight years ago, travel about with ten-thousand-dollar cars now. I didn't use to care. I used to tell myself that I had a better place to escape to, just because, we knew that lobster armoricaine was really lobster américaine.* Perhaps I haven't that feeling any more."

She stiffened. "If that's it——"

"It's up to you. We'll make a new start."

Choupette thought for a moment. "Of course my sister can take over the apartment."

"Of course." He waxed enthusiastic. "And there are sure to be things that'll tickle you—we'll have a nice car, for instance, and one of those electric ice boxes, and all sorts of funny machines to take the place of servants. It won't be bad. You'll learn to play golf and talk about children all day. Then there are the movies."

Choupette groaned.

"It's going to be pretty awful at first," he admitted, "but there are still a few good nigger cooks, and we'll probably have two bathrooms."

"I am unable to use more than one at a time."

---

* The *Post* printed this as "lobster American was really lobster American"—which has no point. Lobster with "sauce à l'américaine" was invented in 1867 by chef Noel Peters, but some French restaurateurs balked at the name and called it "sauce à l'armoricaine" from the old name for Brittany, l'Armorique.

"You'll learn."

A month afterward, when the beautiful white island floated toward them in the Narrows, Henry's throat grew constricted with the rest and he wanted to cry out to Choupette and all foreigners, "Now, you see!"

· III ·

ALMOST THREE YEARS LATER, Henry Marston walked out of his office in the Calumet Tobacco Company and along the hall to Judge Waterbury's suite. His face was older, with a suspicion of grimness, and a slight irrepressible heaviness of body was not concealed by his white linen suit.

"Busy, judge?"

"Come in, Henry."

"I'm going to the shore tomorrow to swim off this weight. I wanted to talk to you before I go."

"Children going too?"

"Oh, sure."

"Choupette'll go abroad, I suppose."

"Not this year. I think she's coming with me, if she doesn't stay here in Richmond."

The judge thought: "There isn't a doubt but what he knows everything." He waited.

"I wanted to tell you, judge, that I'm resigning the end of September."

The judge's chair creaked backward as he brought his feet to the floor.

"You're quitting, Henry?"

"Not exactly. Walter Ross wants to come home; let me take his place in France."

"Boy, do you know what we pay Walter Ross?"

"Seven thousand."

"And you're getting twenty-five."

"You've probably heard I've made something in the market," said Henry deprecatingly.

"I've heard everything between a hundred thousand and half a million."

"Somewhere in between."

"Then why a seven-thousand-dollar job? Is Choupette homesick?"

"No, I think Choupette likes it over here. She's adapted herself amazingly."

"He knows," the judge thought. "He wants to get away."

After Henry had gone, he looked up at the portrait of his grandfather on the wall. In those days the matter would have been simpler. Dueling pistols in the old Wharton meadow at dawn. It would be to Henry's advantage if things were like that today.

Henry's chauffeur dropped him in front of a Georgian house in a new suburban section. Leaving his hat in the hall, he went directly out on the side veranda.

From the swaying canvas swing Choupette looked up with a polite smile. Save for a certain alertness of feature and a certain indefinable knack of putting things on, she might have passed for an American. Southernisms overlay her French accent with a quaint charm; there were still college boys who rushed her like a débutante at the Christmas dances.

Henry nodded at Mr. Charles Wiese, who occupied a wicker chair, with a gin fizz at his elbow.

"I want to talk to you," he said, sitting down.

Wiese's glance and Choupette's crossed quickly before coming to rest on him.

"You're free, Wiese," Henry said. "Why don't you and Choupette get married?"

Choupette sat up, her eyes flashing.

"Now wait." Henry turned back to Wiese. "I've been letting this thing drift for about a year now, while I got my financial affairs in shape. But this last brilliant idea of yours makes me feel a little uncomfortable, a little sordid, and I don't want to feel that way."

"Just what do you mean?" Wiese inquired.

"On my last trip to New York you had me shadowed. I presume it was with the intention of getting divorce evidence against me. It wasn't a success."

"I don't know where you got such an idea in your head, Marston; you——"

"Don't lie!"

"Suh——" Wiese began, but Henry interrupted impatiently:

"Now don't 'Suh' me, and don't try to whip yourself up into a temper. You're not talking to a scared picker full of hookworm. I don't want a scene; my emotions aren't sufficiently involved. I want to arrange a divorce."

"Why do you bring it up like this?" Choupette cried, breaking into French. "Couldn't we talk of it alone, if you think you have so much against me?"

"Wait a minute; this might as well be settled now," Wiese said. "Choupette does want a divorce. Her life with you is unsatisfactory, and the only reason she has kept on is because she's an idealist. You don't seem to appreciate that fact, but it's true; she couldn't bring herself to break up her home."

"Very touching." Henry looked at Choupette with bitter amusement.

"But let's come down to facts. I'd like to close up this matter before I go back to France."

Again Wiese and Choupette exchanged a look.

"It ought to be simple," Wiese said. "Choupette doesn't want a cent of your money."

"I know. What she wants is the children. The answer is, You can't have the children."

"How perfectly outrageous!" Choupette cried. "Do you imagine for a minute I'm going to give up my children?"

"What's your idea, Marston?" demanded Wiese. "To take them back to France and make them expatriates like yourself?"

"Hardly that. They're entered for St. Regis School and then for Yale. And I haven't any idea of not letting them see their mother whenever she so desires—judging from the past two years, it won't be often. But I intend to have their entire legal custody."

"Why?" they demanded together.

"Because of the home."

"What the devil do you mean?"

"I'd rather apprentice them to a trade than have them brought up in the sort of home yours and Choupette's is going to be."

There was a moment's silence. Suddenly Choupette picked up her glass, dashed the contents at Henry and collapsed on the settee, passionately sobbing.

Henry dabbed his face with his handkerchief and stood up.

"I was afraid of that," he said, "but I think I've made my position clear."

He went up to his room and lay down on the bed. In a thousand wakeful hours during the past year he had fought over in his mind the problem of keeping his boys without taking those legal measures against Choupette that he could not bring himself to take. He knew that she wanted the children only because without them she would be suspect, even *déclassée*, to her family in France; but with that quality of detachment peculiar to old stock, Henry recognized this as a perfectly legitimate motive. Furthermore, no public scandal must touch the mother of his sons—it was this that had rendered his challenge so ineffectual this afternoon.

When difficulties became insurmountable, inevitable, Henry sought surcease in exercise. For three years, swimming had been a sort of refuge, and he turned to it as one man to music or another to drink. There was a point when he would resolutely stop thinking and go to the Virginia coast for a week to wash his mind in the water. Far out past the breakers he could survey the green-and-brown line of the Old Dominion with the pleasant impersonality of a porpoise. The burden of his wretched marriage fell away with the buoyant tumble of his body among the swells, and he would begin to move in a child's dream of space. Sometimes remembered playmates of his youth swam with him; sometimes, with his two sons beside him, he seemed to be setting off along the bright pathway to the moon. Americans, he liked to say, should be born with fins, and perhaps they were—perhaps money was a form of fin. In England property begot a strong place sense, but Americans, restless and with shallow roots, needed fins and wings. There was even a recurrent idea in America about an education that would leave out history and the past, that should be a sort of equipment for aerial adventure, weighed down by none of the stowaways of inheritance or tradition.

Thinking of this in the water the next afternoon brought Henry's mind to the children; he turned and at a slow trudgen started back toward shore. Out of condition, he rested, panting, at the raft, and glancing up, he saw familiar eyes. In a moment he was talking with the girl he had tried to rescue four years ago.

He was overjoyed. He had not realized how vividly he remembered her. She was a Virginian—he might have guessed it abroad—the laziness, the apparent casualness that masked an unfailing courtesy and attention; a good form devoid of forms was based on kindness and consideration. Hearing her name for the first time, he recognized it—an Eastern Shore name, "good" as his own.

Lying in the sun, they talked like old friends, not about races and manners and the things that Henry brooded over Choupette, but rather as if they naturally agreed about those things; they talked about what they liked themselves and about what was fun. She showed him a sitting-down, standing-up dive from the high springboard, and he emulated her inexpertly—that was fun. They talked about eating soft-shelled crabs, and she told him how, because of the curious acoustics of the water, one could lie here and be diverted by conversations on the hotel porch. They tried it and heard two ladies over their tea say:

"Now, at the Lido——"

"Now, at Asbury Park——"

"Oh, my dear, he just scratched and scratched all night; he just scratched and scratched——"

"My dear, at Deauville——"

"——scratched and scratched all night."

After a while the sea got to be that very blue color of four o'clock, and the girl told him how, at nineteen, she had been divorced from a Spaniard who locked her in the hotel suite when he went out at night.

"It was one of those things," she said lightly. "But speaking more cheerfully, how's your beautiful wife? And the boys—did they learn to float? Why can't you all dine with me tonight?"

"I'm afraid I won't be able to," he said, after a moment's hesitation. He must do nothing, however trivial, to furnish Choupette weapons, and with a feeling of disgust, it occurred to him that he was possibly being watched this afternoon. Nevertheless, he was glad of his caution when she unexpectedly arrived at the hotel for dinner that night.

After the boys had gone to bed, they faced each other over coffee on the hotel veranda.

"Will you kindly explain why I'm not entitled to a half share in my own children?" Choupette began. "It is not like you to be vindictive, Henry."

It was hard for Henry to explain. He told her again that she could have the children when she wanted them, but that he must exercise entire control over them because of certain old-fashioned convictions—watching her face grow harder, minute by minute, he saw there was no use, and broke off. She made a scornful sound.

"I wanted to give you a chance to be reasonable before Charles arrives."

Henry sat up. "Is he coming here this evening?"

"Happily. And I think perhaps your selfishness is going to have a jolt, Henry. You're not dealing with a woman now."

When Wiese walked out on the porch an hour later, Henry saw that his pale lips were like chalk; there was a deep flush on his forehead and hard confidence in his eyes. He was cleared for action and he wasted no time. "We've got something to say to each other, suh, and since I've got a motorboat here, perhaps that'd be the quietest place to say it."

Henry nodded coolly; five minutes later the three of them were headed out into Hampton Roads on the wide fairway of the moonlight. It was a tranquil evening, and half a mile from shore Wiese cut down the engine to a mild throbbing, so that they seemed to drift without will or direction through the bright water. His voice broke the stillness abruptly:

"Marston, I'm going to talk to you straight from the shoulder. I love Choupette and I'm not apologizing for it. These things have happened before in this world. I guess you understand that. The only difficulty is this matter of the custody of Choupette's children. You seem determined to try and take them away from the mother that bore them and raised them"—Wiese's words became more clearly articulated, as if they came from a wider mouth—"but you left one thing out of your calculations, and that's me. Do you happen to realize that at this moment I'm one of the richest men in Virginia?"

"I've heard as much."

"Well, money is power, Marston. I repeat, suh, money is power."

"I've heard that too. In fact, you're a bore, Wiese." Even by the moon Henry could see the crimson deepen on his brow.

"You'll hear it again, suh. Yesterday you took us by surprise and I was unprepared for your brutality to Choupette. But this morning I received a letter from Paris that puts the matter in a new light. It is a statement by a specialist in mental diseases, declaring you to be of unsound mind, and unfit to have the custody of children. The specialist is the one who attended you in your nervous breakdown four years ago."

Henry laughed incredulously, and looked at Choupette, half expecting her to laugh, too, but she had turned her face away, breathing quickly through parted lips. Suddenly he realized that Wiese was telling the truth —that by some extraordinary bribe he had obtained such a document and fully intended to use it.

For a moment Henry reeled as if from a material blow. He listened to his own voice saying, "That's the most ridiculous thing I ever heard," and to Wiese's answer: "They don't always tell people when they have mental troubles."

Suddenly Henry wanted to laugh, and the terrible instant when he had wondered if there could be some shred of truth in the allegation passed. He turned to Choupette, but again she avoided his eyes.

"How could you, Choupette?"

"I want my children," she began, but Wiese broke in quickly:

"If you'd been halfway fair, Marston, we wouldn't have resorted to this step."

"Are you trying to pretend you arranged this scurvy trick since yesterday afternoon?"

"I believe in being prepared, but if you had been reasonable; in fact, if you will be reasonable, this opinion needn't be used." His voice became suddenly almost paternal, almost kind: "Be wise, Marston. On your side there's an obstinate prejudice; on mine there are forty million dollars. Don't fool yourself. Let me repeat, Marston, that money is power. You were abroad so long that perhaps you're inclined to forget that fact. Money made this country, built its great and glorious cities, created its industries, covered it with an iron network of railroads. It's money that harnesses the forces of Nature, creates the machine and makes it go when money says go, and stop when money says stop."

As though interpreting this as a command, the engine gave forth a sudden hoarse sound and came to rest.

"What is it?" demanded Choupette.

"It's nothing." Wiese pressed the self-starter with his foot. "I repeat,

Marston, that money——The battery is dry. One minute while I spin the wheel."

He spun it for the best part of fifteen minutes while the boat meandered about in a placid little circle.

"Choupette, open that drawer behind you and see if there isn't a rocket."

A touch of panic had crept into her voice when she answered that there was no rocket. Wiese eyed the shore tentatively.

"There's no use in yelling; we must be half a mile out. We'll just have to wait here until someone comes along."

"We won't wait here," Henry remarked.

"Why not?"

"We're moving toward the bay. Can't you tell? We're moving out with the tide."

"That's impossible!" said Choupette sharply.

"Look at those two lights on shore—one passing the other now. Do you see?"

"Do something!" she wailed, and then, in a burst of French: *"Ah, c'est épouvantable! N'est-ce pas qu'il y a quelque chose qu'on peut faire?"*

The tide was running fast now, and the boat was drifting down the Roads with it toward the sea. The vague blots of two ships passed them, but at a distance, and there was no answer to their hail. Against the western sky a lighthouse blinked, but it was impossible to guess how near to it they would pass.

"It looks as if all our difficulties would be solved for us," Henry said.

"What difficulties?" Choupette demanded. "Do you mean there's nothing to be done? Can you sit there and just float away like this?"

"It may be easier on the children, after all." He winced as Choupette began to sob bitterly, but he said nothing. A ghostly idea was taking shape in his mind.

"Look here, Marston. Can you swim?" demanded Wiese, frowning.

"Yes, but Choupette can't."

"I can't either—I didn't mean that. If you could swim in and get to a telephone, the coast-guard people would send for us."

Henry surveyed the dark, receding shore.

"It's too far," he said.

"You can try!" said Choupette.

Henry shook his head.

"Too risky. Besides, there's an outside chance that we'll be picked up."

The lighthouse passed them, far to the left and out of earshot. Another one, the last, loomed up half a mile away.

"We might drift to France like that man Gerbault," Henry remarked. "But then, of course, we'd be expatriates—and Wiese wouldn't like that, would you, Wiese?"

Wiese, fussing frantically with the engine, looked up.

"See what you can do with this," he said.

"I don't know anything about mechanics," Henry answered. "Besides, this solution of our difficulties grows on me. Just suppose you were dirty dog enough to use that statement and got the children because of it—in that case I wouldn't have much impetus to go on living. We're all failures—I as head of my household, Choupette as a wife and a mother, and you, Wiese, as a human being. It's just as well that we go out of life together."

"This is no time for a speech, Marston."

"Oh, yes, it's a fine time. How about a little more house-organ oratory about money being power?"

Choupette sat rigid in the bow; Wiese stood over the engine, biting nervously at his lips.

"We're not going to pass that lighthouse very close." An idea suddenly occurred to him. "Couldn't you swim to that, Marston?"

"Of course he could!" Choupette cried.

Henry looked at it tentatively.

"I might. But I won't."

"You've got to!"

Again he flinched at Choupette's weeping; simultaneously he saw the time had come.

"Everything depends on one small point," he said rapidly. "Wiese, have you got a fountain pen?"

"Yes. What for?"

"If you'll write and sign about two hundred words at my dictation, I'll swim to the lighthouse and get help. Otherwise, so help me God, we'll drift out to sea! And you better decide in about one minute."

"Oh, anything!" Choupette broke out frantically. "Do what he says, Charles; he means it. He always means what he says. Oh, please don't wait!"

"I'll do what you want"—Wiese's voice was shaking—"only, for God's sake, go on. What is it you want—an agreement about the children? I'll give you my personal word of honor——"

"There's no time for humor," said Henry savagely. "Take this piece of paper and write."

The two pages that Wiese wrote at Henry's dictation relinquished all lien on the children thence and forever for himself and Choupette. When they had affixed trembling signatures Wiese cried:

"Now go, for God's sake, before it's too late!"

"Just one thing more: The certificate from the doctor."

"I haven't it here."

"You lie."

Wiese took it from his pocket.

"Write across the bottom that you paid so much for it, and sign your name to that."

A minute later, stripped to his underwear, and with the papers in an oiled-silk tobacco pouch suspended from his neck, Henry dived from the side of the boat and struck out toward the light.

The waters leaped up at him for an instant, but after the first shock it was all warm and friendly, and the small murmur of the waves was an encouragement. It was the longest swim he had ever tried, and he was straight from the city, but the happiness in his heart buoyed him up. Safe now, and free. Each stroke was stronger for knowing that his two sons, sleeping back in the hotel, were safe from what he dreaded. Divorced from her own country, Choupette had picked the things out of American life that pandered best to her own self-indulgence. That, backed by a court decree, she should be permitted to hand on this preposterous moral farrago to his sons was unendurable. He would have lost them forever.

Turning on his back, he saw that already the motorboat was far away, the blinding light was nearer. He was very tired. If one let go—and, in the relaxation from strain, he felt an alarming impulse to let go—one died very quickly and painlessly, and all these problems of hate and bitterness disappeared. But he felt the fate of his sons in the oiled-silk pouch about his neck, and with a convulsive effort he turned over again and concentrated all his energies on his goal.

Twenty minutes later he stood shivering and dripping in the signal room while it was broadcast out to the coast patrol that a launch was drifting in the bay.

"There's not much danger without a storm," the keeper said. "By now they've probably struck a cross current from the river and drifted into Peyton Harbor."

"Yes," said Henry, who had come to this coast for three summers. "I knew that too."

· I V ·

IN OCTOBER, Henry left his sons in school and embarked on the Majestic for Europe. He had come home as to a generous mother and had been profusely given more than he asked—money, release from an intolerable situation, and the fresh strength to fight for his own. Watching the fading city, the fading shore, from the deck of the Majestic, he had a sense of overwhelming gratitude and of gladness that America was there, that under the ugly débris of industry the rich land still pushed up, incorrigibly lavish and fertile, and that in the heart of the leaderless people the old generosities and devotions fought on, breaking out sometimes in fanaticism and excess, but indomitable and undefeated. There was a lost generation in the saddle at the moment, but it seemed to him that the men coming on, the men of the war, were better; and all his old feeling that America was a bizarre accident, a sort of historical sport, had gone forever. The best of America was the best of the world.

Going down to the purser's office, he waited until a fellow passenger was through at the window. When she turned, they both started, and he saw it was the girl.

"Oh, hello!" she cried. "I'm glad you're going! I was just asking when the pool opened. The great thing about this ship is that you can always get a swim."

"Why do you like to swim?" he demanded.

"You always ask me that." She laughed.

"Perhaps you'd tell me if we had dinner together tonight."

But when, in a moment, he left her he knew that she could never tell him—she or another. France was a land, England was a people, but America, having about it still that quality of the idea, was harder to utter—it was the graves at Shiloh and the tired, drawn, nervous faces of its great men, and the country boys dying in the Argonne for a phrase that was empty before their bodies withered. It was a willingness of the heart.

TWO WRONGS

◆

"Two Wrongs" (Saturday Evening Post, *18 January 1930) is one of the stories dealing with marital strife that Fitzgerald wrote during 1929 and 1930 reflecting his own problems—here, his alcoholism and Zelda Fitzgerald's unsuccessful attempt to become a professional ballet dancer. He was concerned that it might be "too heavy" for the* Post, *but his agent, Harold Ober, assured him that it "is one of the best things you have ever done." Fitzgerald selected "Two Wrongs" for* Taps at Reveille.

◆

"LOOK AT THOSE SHOES," said Bill—"twenty-eight dollars."

Mr. Brancusi looked. "Purty."

"Made to order."

"I knew you were a great swell. You didn't get me up here to show me those shoes, did you?"

"I am not a great swell. Who said I was a great swell?" demanded Bill. "Just because I've got more education than most people in show business."

"And then, you know, you're a handsome young fellow," said Brancusi dryly.

"Sure I am—compared to you anyhow. The girls think I must be an actor, till they find out. . . . Got a cigarette? What's more, I look like a man—which is more than most of these pretty boys round Times Square do."

"Good-looking. Gentleman. Good shoes. Shot with luck."

"You're wrong there," objected Bill. "Brains. Three years—nine shows —four big hits—only one flop. Where do you see any luck in that?"

A little bored, Brancusi just gazed. What he would have seen—had he not made his eyes opaque and taken to thinking about something else—was a fresh-faced young Irishman exuding aggressiveness and self-confidence until the air of his office was thick with it. Presently, Brancusi knew, Bill would hear the sound of his own voice and be ashamed and retire into his other humor—the quietly superior, sensitive one, the patron of the arts, modelled on the intellectuals of the Theatre Guild. Bill McChesney had not quite decided between the two, such blends are seldom complete before thirty.

"Take Ames, take Hopkins, take Harris—take any of them," Bill insisted. "What have they got on me? What's the matter? Do you want a drink?"— seeing Brancusi's glance wander toward the cabinet on the opposite wall.

"I never drink in the morning. I just wondered who was it keeps on knocking. You ought to make it stop it. I get a nervous fidgets, kind of half crazy, with that kind of thing."

Bill went quickly to the door and threw it open.

"Nobody," he said . . . "Hello! What do you want?"

"Oh, I'm so sorry," a voice answered; "I'm terribly sorry. I got so excited and I didn't realize I had this pencil in my hand."

"What is it you want?"

"I want to see you, and the clerk said you were busy. I have a letter for you from Alan Rogers, the playwright—and I wanted to give it to you personally."

"I'm busy," said Bill. "See Mr. Cadorna."

"I did, but he wasn't very encouraging, and Mr. Rogers said——"

Brancusi, edging over restlessly, took a quick look at her. She was very young, with beautiful red hair, and more character in her face than her chatter would indicate; it did not occur to Mr. Brancusi that this was due to her origin in Delaney, South Carolina.

"What shall I do?" she inquired, quietly laying her future in Bill's hands. "I had a letter to Mr. Rogers, and he just gave me this one to you."

"Well, what do you want me to do—marry you?" exploded Bill.

"I'd like to get a part in one of your plays."

"Then sit down and wait. I'm busy. . . . Where's Miss Cohalan?" He rang a bell, looked once more, crossly, at the girl and closed the door of his office. But during the interruption his other mood had come over him, and he resumed his conversation with Brancusi in the key of one who was hand in glove with Reinhardt for the artistic future of the theater.

By 12:30 he had forgotten everything except that he was going to be the greatest producer in the world and that he had an engagement to tell Sol Lincoln about it at lunch. Emerging from his office, he looked expectantly at Miss Cohalan.

"Mr. Lincoln won't be able to meet you," she said. "He jus 'is minute called."

"Just this minute," repeated Bill, shocked. "All right. Just cross him off that list for Thursday night."

Miss Cohalan drew a line on a sheet of paper before her.

"Mr. McChesney, now you haven't forgotten me, have you?"

He turned to the red-headed girl.

"No," he said vaguely, and then to Miss Cohalan: "That's all right; ask him for Thursday anyhow. To hell with him."

He did not want to lunch alone. He did not like to do anything alone now, because contacts were too much fun when one had prominence and power.

"If you would just let me talk to you two minutes——" she began.

"Afraid I can't now." Suddenly he realized that she was the most beautiful person he had ever seen in his life.

He stared at her.

"Mr. Rogers told me——"

"Come and have a spot of lunch with me," he said, and then, with an air of great hurry, he gave Miss Cohalan some quick and contradictory instructions and held open the door.

They stood on Forty-second Street and he breathed his pre-empted air —there is only enough air there for a few people at a time. It was November and the first exhilarating rush of the season was over, but he could look east and see the electric sign of one of his plays, and west and see another. Around the corner was the one he had put on with Brancusi—the last time he would produce anything except alone.

They went to the Bedford, where there was a to-do of waiters and captains as he came in.

"This is ver tractive restaurant," she said, impressed and on company behavior.

"This is hams' paradise." He nodded to several people. "Hello, Jimmy —Bill. . . . Hello there, Jack. . . . That's Jack Dempsey. . . . I don't eat here much. I usually eat up at the Harvard Club."

"Oh, did you go to Harvard? I used to know——"

"Yes." He hesitated; there were two versions about Harvard, and he decided suddenly on the true one. "Yes, and they had me down for a hick there, but not any more. About a week ago I was out on Long Island at the Gouverneer Haights—very fashionable people—and a couple of Gold Coast boys that never knew I was alive up in Cambridge began pulling this 'Hello, Bill, old boy' on me."

He hesitated and suddenly decided to leave the story there.

"What do you want—a job?" he demanded. He remembered suddenly that she had holes in her stockings. Holes in stockings always moved him, softened him.

"Yes, or else I've got to go home," she said. "I want to be a dancer— you know, Russian ballet. But the lessons cost so much, so I've got to get a job. I thought it'd give me stage presence anyhow."

"Hoofer, eh?"

"Oh, no, serious."

"Well, Pavlova's a hoofer, isn't she?"

"Oh, no." She was shocked at this profanity, but after a moment she continued: "I took with Miss Campbell—Georgia Berriman Campbell— back home—maybe you know her. She took from Ned Wayburn, and she's really wonderful. She——"

"Yeah?" he said abstractedly. "Well, it's a tough business—casting agencies bursting with people that can all do anything, till I give them a try. How old are you?"

"Eighteen."

"I'm twenty-six. Came here four years ago without a cent."

"My!"

"I could quit now and be comfortable the rest of my life."

"My!"

"Going to take a year off next year—get married. . . . Ever hear of Irene Rikker?"

"I should say! She's about my favorite of all."

"We're engaged."

"My!"

When they went out into Times Square after a while he said carelessly, "What are you doing now?"

"Why, I'm trying to get a job."

"I mean right this minute."

"Why, nothing."

"Do you want to come up to my apartment on Forty-sixth Street and have some coffee?"

Their eyes met, and Emmy Pinkard made up her mind she could take care of herself.

It was a great bright studio apartment with a ten-foot divan, and after she had coffee and he a highball, his arm dropped round her shoulder.

"Why should I kiss you?" she demanded. "I hardly know you, and besides, you're engaged to somebody else."

"Oh, that! She doesn't care."

"No, really!"

"You're a good girl."

"Well, I'm certainly not an idiot."

"All right, go on being a good girl."

She stood up, but lingered a minute, very fresh and cool, and not upset at all.

"I suppose this means you won't give me a job?" she asked pleasantly.

He was already thinking about something else—about an interview and a rehearsal—but now he looked at her again and saw that she still had holes in her stockings. He telephoned:

"Joe, this is the Fresh Boy. . . . You didn't think I knew you called me that, did you? . . . It's all right. . . . Say, have you got those three girls for the party scene? Well, listen; save one for a Southern kid I'm sending around today."

He looked at her jauntily, conscious of being such a good fellow.

"Well, I don't know how to thank you. And Mr. Rogers," she added audaciously. "Good-by, Mr. McChesney."

He disdained to answer.

· I I ·

DURING REHEARSAL he used to come around a great deal and stand watching with a wise expression, as if he knew everything in people's minds; but actually he was in a haze about his own good fortune and didn't see much and didn't for the moment care. He spent most of his week-ends on Long Island with the fashionable people who had "taken him up." When Brancusi referred to him as the "big social butterfly," he would answer, "Well, what about it? Didn't I go to Harvard? You think they found me in a Grand Street apple cart, like you?" He was well liked among his new friends for his good looks and good nature, as well as his success.

His engagement to Irene Rikker was the most unsatisfactory thing in his life; they were tired of each other but unwilling to put an end to it. Just as, often, the two richest young people in a town are drawn together by the fact, so Bill McChesney and Irene Rikker, borne side by side on waves of triumph, could not spare each other's nice appreciation of what was due such success. Nevertheless, they indulged in fiercer and more frequent quarrels, and the end was approaching. It was embodied in one Frank Llewellen, a big, fine-looking actor playing opposite Irene. Seeing the situation at once, Bill became bitterly humorous about it; from the second week of rehearsals there was tension in the air.

Meanwhile Emmy Pinkard, with enough money for crackers and milk, and a friend who took her out to dinner, was being happy. Her friend, Easton Hughes from Delaney, was studying at Columbia to be a dentist. He sometimes brought along other lonesome young men studying to be dentists, and at the price, if it can be called that, of a few casual kisses in taxicabs, Emmy dined when hungry. One afternoon she introduced Easton to Bill McChesney at the stage door, and afterward Bill made his facetious jealousy the basis of their relationship.

"I see that dental number has been slipping it over on me again. Well, don't let him give you any laughing gas is my advice."

Though their encounters were few, they always looked at each other. When Bill looked at her he stared for an instant as if he had not seen her before, and then remembered suddenly that she was to be teased. When she looked at him she saw many things—a bright day outside, with great crowds of people hurrying through the streets; a very good new limousine that waited at the curb for two people with very good new clothes, who got in and went somewhere that was just like New York, only away, and more fun there. Many times she had wished she had kissed him, but just as many times she was glad she hadn't; since, as the weeks passed, he grew less romantic, tied up, like the rest of them, to the play's laborious evolution.

They were opening in Atlantic City. A sudden moodiness apparent to everyone, came over Bill. He was short with the director and sarcastic with the actors. This, it was rumored, was because Irene Rikker had come down with Frank Llewellen on a different train. Sitting beside the author on the night of the dress rehearsal, he was an almost sinister figure in the twilight of the auditorium; but he said nothing until the end of the second act, when, with Llewellen and Irene Rikker on the stage alone, he suddenly called:

"We'll go over that again—and cut out the mush!"

Llewellen came down to the footlights.

"What do you mean—cut out the mush?" he inquired. "Those are the lines, aren't they?"

"You know what I mean—stick to business."

"I don't know what you mean."

Bill stood up. "I mean all that damn whispering."

"There wasn't any whispering. I simply asked——"

"That'll do—take it over."

Llewellen turned away furiously and was about to proceed, when Bill added audibly: "Even a ham has got to do his stuff."

Llewellen whipped about. "I don't have to stand that kind of talk, Mr. McChesney."

"Why not? You're a ham, aren't you? When did you get ashamed of being a ham? I'm putting on this play and I want you to stick to your stuff." Bill got up and walked down the aisle. "And when you don't do it, I'm going to call you just like anybody else."

"Well, you watch out for your tone of voice——"

"What'll you do about it?"

Llewellen jumped down into the orchestra pit.

"I'm not taking anything from you!" he shouted.

Irene Rikker called to them from the stage, "For heaven's sake, are you two crazy?" And then Llewellen swung at him, one short, mighty blow. Bill pitched back across a row of seats, fell through one, splintering it, and lay wedged there. There was a moment's wild confusion, then people holding Llewellen, then the author, with a white face, pulling Bill up, and the stage manager crying: "Shall I kill him, chief? Shall I break his fat face?" and Llewellen panting and Irene Rikker frightened.

"Get back there!" Bill cried, holding a handkerchief to his face and teetering in the author's supporting arms. "Everybody get back! Take that scene again, and no talk! Get back, Llewellen!"

Before they realized it they were all back on the stage, Irene pulling Llewellen's arm and talking to him fast. Someone put on the auditorium lights full and then dimmed them again hurriedly. When Emmy came out presently for her scene, she saw in a quick glance that Bill was sitting with a whole mask of handkerchiefs over his bleeding face. She hated Llewellen and was afraid that presently they would break up and go back to New York. But Bill had saved the show from his own folly, since for Llewellen to take the further initiative of quitting would hurt his professional standing. The act ended and the next one began without an interval. When it was over, Bill was gone.

Next night, during the performance, he sat on a chair in the wings in view of everyone coming on or off. His face was swollen and bruised, but he neglected to seem conscious of the fact and there were no comments. Once he went around in front, and when he returned, word leaked out that two of the New York agencies were making big buys. He had a hit—they all had a hit.

At the sight of him to whom Emmy felt they all owed so much, a great wave of gratitude swept over her. She went up and thanked him.

"I'm a good picker, red-head," he agreed grimly.

"Thank you for picking me."

And suddenly Emmy was moved to a rash remark.

"You've hurt your face so badly!" she exclaimed. "Oh, I think it was so brave of you not to let everything go to pieces last night."

He looked at her hard for a moment and then an ironic smile tried unsuccessfully to settle on his swollen face.

"Do you admire me, baby?"

"Yes."

"Even when I fell in the seats, did you admire me?"

"You got control of everything so quick."

"That's loyalty for you. You found something to admire in that fool mess."

And her happiness bubbled up into, "Anyhow, you behaved just wonderfully." She looked so fresh and young that Bill, who had had a wretched day, wanted to rest his swollen cheek against her cheek.

He took both the bruise and the desire with him to New York next morning; the bruise faded, but the desire remained. And when they opened in the city, no sooner did he see other men begin to crowd around her beauty than she became this play for him, this success, the thing that he came to see when he came to the theater. After a good run it closed just as he was drinking too much and needed someone on the gray days of reaction. They were married suddenly in Connecticut, early in June.

· III ·

TWO MEN SAT in the Savoy Grill in London, waiting for the Fourth of July. It was already late in May.

"Is he a nice guy?" asked Hubbel.

"Very nice," answered Brancusi; "very nice, very handsome, very popular." After a moment, he added: "I want to get him to come home."

"That's what I don't get about him," said Hubbel. "Show business over here is nothing compared to home. What does he want to stay here for?"

"He goes around with a lot of dukes and ladies."

"Oh?"

"Last week when I met him he was with three ladies—Lady this, Lady that, Lady the other thing."

"I thought he was married."

"Married three years," said Brancusi, "got a fine child, going to have another."

He broke off as McChesney came in, his very American face staring about boldly over the collar of a box-shouldered topcoat.

"Hello, Mac; meet my friend Mr. Hubbel."

"J'doo," said Bill. He sat down, continuing to stare around the bar to see who was present. After a few minutes Hubbel left, and Bill asked:

"Who's that bird?"

"He's only been here a month. He ain't got a title yet. You been here six months, remember."

Bill grinned.

"You think I'm high-hat, don't you? Well, I'm not kidding myself anyhow. I like it; it gets me. I'd like to be the Marquis of McChesney."

"Maybe you can drink yourself into it," suggested Brancusi.

"Shut your trap. Who said I was drinking? Is that what they say now? Look here; if you can tell me any American manager in the history of the theater who's had the success that I've had in London in less than eight months, I'll go back to America with you tomorrow. If you'll just tell me——"

"It was with your old shows. You had two flops in New York."

Bill stood up, his face hardening.

"Who do you think you are?" he demanded. "Did you come over here to talk to me like that?"

"Don't get sore now, Bill. I just want you to come back. I'd say anything for that. Put over three seasons like you had in '22 and '23, and you're fixed for life."

"New York makes me sick," said Bill moodily. "One minute you're a king; then you have two flops, they go around saying you're on the toboggan."

Brancusi shook his head.

"That wasn't why they said it. It was because you had that quarrel with Aronstael, your best friend."

"Friend hell!"

"Your best friend in business anyhow. Then——"

"I don't want to talk about it." He looked at his watch. "Look here; Emmy's feeling bad so I'm afraid I can't have dinner with you tonight. Come around to the office before you sail."

Five minutes later, standing by the cigar counter, Brancusi saw Bill enter the Savoy again and descend the steps that led to the tea room.

"Grown to be a great diplomat," thought Brancusi; "he used to just say when he had a date. Going with these dukes and ladies is polishing him up even more."

Perhaps he was a little hurt, though it was not typical of him to be hurt. At any rate he made a decision, then and there, that McChesney was on the down grade; it was quite typical of him that at that point he erased him from his mind forever.

There was no outward indication that Bill was on the down grade; a hit at the New Strand, a hit at the Prince of Wales, and the weekly grosses pouring in almost as well as they had two or three years before in New York. Certainly a man of action was justified in changing his base. And the man who, an hour later, turned into his Hyde Park house for dinner had all the vitality of the late twenties. Emmy, very tired and clumsy, lay on a couch in the upstairs sitting room. He held her for a moment in his arms.

"Almost over now," he said. "You're beautiful."

"Don't be ridiculous."

"It's true. You're always beautiful. I don't know why. Perhaps because you've got character, and that's always in your face, even when you're like this."

She was pleased; she ran her hand through his hair.

"Character is the greatest thing in the world," he declared, "and you've got more than anybody I know."

"Did you see Brancusi?"

"I did, the little louse! I decided not to bring him home to dinner."

"What was the matter?"

"Oh, just snooty—talking about my row with Aronstael, as if it was my fault."

She hesitated, closed her mouth tight, and then said quietly, "You got into that fight with Aronstael because you were drinking."

He rose impatiently.

"Are you going to start——"

"No, Bill, but you're drinking too much now. You know you are."

Aware that she was right, he evaded the matter and they went in to dinner. On the glow of a bottle of claret he decided he would go on the wagon tomorrow till after the baby was born.

"I always stop when I want, don't I? I always do what I say. You never saw me quit yet."

"Never yet."

They had coffee together, and afterward he got up.

"Come back early," said Emmy.

"Oh, sure. . . . What's the matter, baby?"

"I'm just crying. Don't mind me. Oh, go on; don't just stand there like a big idiot."

"But I'm worried, naturally. I don't like to see you cry."

"Oh, I don't know where you go in the evenings; I don't know who you're with. And that Lady Sybil Combrinck who kept phoning. It's all right, I suppose, but I wake up in the night and I feel so alone, Bill. Because we've always been together, haven't we, until recently?"

"But we're together still. . . . What's happened to you, Emmy?"

"I know—I'm just crazy. We'd never let each other down, would we? We never have——"

"Of course not."

"Come back early, or when you can."

He looked in for a minute at the Prince of Wales Theatre; then he went into the hotel next door and called a number.

"I'd like to speak to her Ladyship. Mr. McChesney calling."

It was some time before Lady Sybil answered:

"This is rather a surprise. It's been several weeks since I've been lucky enough to hear from you."

Her voice was flip as a whip and cold as automatic refrigeration, in the mode grown familiar since British ladies took to piecing themselves together out of literature. It had fascinated Bill for a while, but just for a while. He had kept his head.

"I haven't had a minute," he explained easily. "You're not sore, are you?"

"I should scarcely say 'sore.'"

"I was afraid you might be; you didn't send me an invitation to your party tonight. My idea was that after we talked it all over we agreed——"

"You talked a great deal," she said; "possibly a little too much."

Suddenly, to Bill's astonishment, she hung up.

"Going British on me," he thought. "A little skit entitled The Daughter of a Thousand Earls."

The snub roused him, the indifference revived his waning interest. Usually women forgave his changes of heart because of his obvious devotion to Emmy, and he was remembered by various ladies with a not unpleasant sigh. But he had detected no such sigh upon the phone.

"I'd like to clear up this mess," he thought. Had he been wearing evening clothes, he might have dropped in at the dance and talked it over with her, still he didn't want to go home. Upon consideration it seemed important that the misunderstanding should be fixed up at once, and presently he began to entertain the idea of going as he was; Americans were excused unconventionalities of dress. In any case, it was not nearly time, and, in the company of several highballs, he considered the matter for an hour.

At midnight he walked up the steps of her Mayfair house. The coat-room attendants scrutinized his tweeds disapprovingly and a footman peered in vain for his name on the list of guests. Fortunately his friend Sir Humphrey Dunn arrived at the same time and convinced the footman it must be a mistake.

Inside, Bill immediately looked about for his hostess.

She was a very tall young woman, half American and all the more intensely English. In a sense, she had discovered Bill McChesney, vouched for his savage charms; his retirement was one of her most humiliating experiences since she had begun being bad.

She stood with her husband at the head of the receiving line—Bill had never seen them together before. He decided to choose a less formal moment for presenting himself.

As the receiving went on interminably, he became increasingly uncomfortable. He saw a few people he knew, but not many, and he was conscious that his clothes were attracting a certain attention; he was aware also that Lady Sybil saw him and could have relieved his embarrassment with a wave of her hand, but she made no sign. He was sorry he had come, but to withdraw now would be absurd, and going to a buffet table, he took a glass of champagne.

When he turned around she was alone at last, and he was about to approach her when the butler spoke to him:

"Pardon me, sir. Have you a card?"

"I'm a friend of Lady Sybil's," said Bill impatiently. He turned away, but the butler followed.

"I'm sorry, sir, but I'll have to ask you to step aside with me and straighten this up."

"There's no need. I'm just about to speak to Lady Sybil now."

"My orders are different, sir," said the butler firmly.

Then, before Bill realized what was happening, his arms were pressed quietly to his sides and he was propelled into a little anteroom back of the buffet.

There he faced a man in a pince-nez in whom he recognized the Combrincks' private secretary.

The secretary nodded to the butler, saying, "This is the man"; whereupon Bill was released.

"Mr. McChesney," said the secretary, "you have seen fit to force your way here without a card, and His Lordship requests that you leave his house at once. Will you kindly give me the check for your coat?"

Then Bill understood, and the single word that he found applicable to Lady Sybil sprang to his lips; whereupon the secretary gave a sign to two footmen, and in a furious struggle Bill was carried through a pantry where busy bus boys stared at the scene, down a long hall, and pushed out a door into the night. The door closed; a moment later it was opened again to let his coat billow forth and his cane clatter down the steps.

As he stood there, overwhelmed, stricken aghast, a taxicab stopped beside him and the driver called:

"Feeling ill, gov'nor?"

"What?"

"I know where you can get a good pick-me-up, gov'nor. Never too late." The door of the taxi opened on a nightmare. There was a cabaret that broke the closing hours; there was being with strangers he had picked up somewhere; then there were arguments, and trying to cash a check, and suddenly proclaiming over and over that he was William McChesney, the producer, and convincing no one of the fact, not even himself. It seemed important to see Lady Sybil right away and call her to account; but presently nothing was important at all. He was in a taxicab whose driver had just shaken him awake in front of his own home.

The telephone was ringing as he went in, but he walked stonily past the maid and only heard her voice when his foot was on the stair.

"Mr. McChesney, it's the hospital calling again. Mrs. McChesney's there and they've been phoning every hour."

Still in a daze, he held the receiver up to his ear.

"We're calling from the Midland Hospital, for your wife. She was delivered of a still-born child at nine this morning."

"Wait a minute." His voice was dry and cracking. "I don't understand."

After a while he understood that Emmy's child was dead and she wanted him. His knees sagged groggily as he walked down the street, looking for a taxi.

The room was dark; Emmy looked up and saw him from a rumpled bed. "It's you!" she cried. "I thought you were dead! Where did you go?"

He threw himself down on his knees beside the bed, but she turned away. "Oh, you smell awful," she said. "It makes me sick."

But she kept her hand in his hair, and he knelt there motionless for a long time.

"I'm done with you," she muttered, "but it was awful when I thought you were dead. Everybody's dead. I wish I was dead."

A curtain parted with the wind, and as he rose to arrange it, she saw him in the full morning light, pale and terrible, with rumpled clothes and bruises on his face. This time she hated him instead of those who had hurt him. She could feel him slipping out of her heart, feel the space he left, and all at once he was gone, and she could even forgive him and be sorry for him. All this in a minute.

She had fallen down at the door of the hospital, trying to get out of the taxicab alone.

· I V ·

WHEN EMMY WAS WELL, physically and mentally, her incessant idea was to learn to dance; the old dream inculcated by Miss Georgia Berriman Campbell of South Carolina persisted as a bright avenue leading back to first youth and days of hope in New York. To her, dancing meant that elaborate blend of tortuous attitudes and formal pirouettes that evolved out of Italy several hundred years ago and reached its apogee in Russia at the beginning of this century. She wanted to use herself on something she could believe in, and it seemed to her that the dance was woman's interpretation of music; instead of strong fingers, one had limbs with which to render Tschaikowsky and Stravinksi; and feet could be as eloquent in Chopiniana as voices in "The Ring." At the bottom, it was something sandwiched in between the acrobats and the trained seals; at the top it was Pavlova and art.

Once they were settled in an apartment back in New York, she plunged into her work like a girl of sixteen—four hours a day at bar exercises, attitudes, *sauts*, arabesques and pirouettes. It became the realest part of her life, and her only worry was whether or not she was too old. At twenty-six she had ten years to make up, but she was a natural dancer with a fine body—and that lovely face.

Bill encouraged it; when she was ready he was going to build the first real American ballet around her. There were even times when he envied her her absorption; for affairs in his own line were more difficult since they had come home. For one thing, he had made many enemies in those early days of self-confidence; there were exaggerated stories of his drinking and of his being hard on actors and difficult to work with.

It was against him that he had always been unable to save money and must beg a backing for each play. Then, too, in a curious way, he was intelligent, as he was brave enough to prove in several uncommercial ventures, but he had no Theatre Guild behind him, and what money he lost was charged against him.

There were successes, too, but he worked harder for them, or it seemed so, for he had begun to pay a price for his irregular life. He always intended to take a rest or give up his incessant cigarettes, but there was so much competition now—new men coming up, with new reputations for infallibility—and besides, he wasn't used to regularity. He liked to do his work in those great spurts, inspired by black coffee, that seem so inevitable in show business, but which took so much out of a man after thirty. He had come to lean, in a way, on Emmy's fine health and vitality. They were always together, and if he felt a vague dissatisfaction that he had grown to need her more than she needed him, there was always the hope that things would break better for him next month, next season.

Coming home from ballet school one November evening, Emmy swung her little gray bag, pulled her hat far down over her still damp hair, and gave herself up to pleasant speculation. For a month she had been aware of people who had come to the studio especially to watch her—she was ready to dance. Once she had worked just as hard and for as long a time on something else—her relations with Bill—only to reach a climax of misery and despair, but here there was nothing to fail her except herself. Yet even now she felt a little rash in thinking: "Now it's come. I'm going to be happy."

She hurried, for something had come up today that she must talk over with Bill.

Finding him in the living room, she called him to come back while she dressed. She began to talk without looking around:

"Listen what happened!" Her voice was loud, to compete with the water running in the tub. "Paul Makova wants me to dance with him at the Metropolitan this season; only it's not sure, so it's a secret—even I'm not supposed to know."

"That's great."

"The only thing is whether it wouldn't be better for me to make a début abroad? Anyhow Donilof says I'm ready to appear. What do you think?"

"I don't know."

"You don't sound very enthusiastic."

"I've got something on my mind. I'll tell you about it later. Go on."

"That's all, dear. If you still feel like going to Germany for a month, like you said, Donilof would arrange a début for me in Berlin, but I'd rather open here and dance with Paul Makova. Just imagine—" She broke off, feeling suddenly through the thick skin of her elation how abstracted he was. "Tell me what you've got on your mind."

"I went to Doctor Kearns this afternoon."

"What did he say?" Her mind was still singing with her own happiness. Bill's intermittent attacks of hypochondria had long ceased to worry her.

"I told him about that blood this morning, and he said what he said last year—it was probably a little broken vein in my throat. But since I'd been coughing and was worried, perhaps it was safer to take an X-ray and clear the matter up. Well, we cleared it up all right. My left lung is practically gone."

"Bill!"

"Luckily there are no spots on the other."

She waited, horribly afraid.

"It's come at a bad time for me," he went on steadily, "but it's got to be faced. He thinks I ought to go to the Adirondacks or to Denver for the winter, and his idea is Denver. That way it'll probably clear up in five or six months."

"Of course we'll have to—" she stopped suddenly.

"I wouldn't expect you to go—especially if you have this opportunity."

"Of course I'll go," she said quickly. "Your health comes first. We've always gone everywhere together."

"Oh, no."

"Why, of course." She made her voice strong and decisive. "We've always been together. I couldn't stay here without you. When do you have to go?"

"As soon as possible. I went in to see Brancusi to find out if he wanted to take over the Richmond piece, but he didn't seem enthusiastic." His face hardened. "Of course there won't be anything else for the present, but I'll have enough, with what's owing——"

"Oh, if I was only making some money!" Emmy cried. "You work so hard, and here I've been spending two hundred dollars a week for just my dancing lessons alone—more than I'll be able to earn for years."

"Of course in six months I'll be as well as ever—he says."

"Sure, dearest; we'll get you well. We'll start as soon as we can."

She put an arm around him and kissed his cheek.

"I'm just an old parasite," she said. "I should have known my darling wasn't well."

He reached automatically for a cigarette, and then stopped.

"I forgot—I've got to start cutting down smoking." He rose to the occasion suddenly: "No, baby, I've decided to go alone. You'd go crazy with boredom out there, and I'd just be thinking I was keeping you away from your dancing."

"Don't think about that. The thing is to get you well."

They discussed the matter hour after hour for the next week, each of them saying everything except the truth—that he wanted her to go with him and that she wanted passionately to stay in New York. She talked it over guardedly with Donilof, her ballet master, and found that he thought any postponement would be a terrible mistake. Seeing other girls in the ballet school making plans for the winter, she wanted to die rather than go, and Bill saw all the involuntary indications of her misery. For a while they talked of compromising on the Adirondacks, whither she would commute by aeroplane for the week-ends, but he was running a little fever now and he was definitely ordered West.

Bill settled it all one gloomy Sunday night, with that rough, generous justice that had first made her admire him, that made him rather tragic in his adversity, as he had always been bearable in his overweening success:

"It's just up to me, baby. I got into this mess because I didn't have any self-control—you seem to have all of that in this family—and now it's only me that can get me out. You've worked hard at your stuff for three years and you deserve your chance—and if you came out there now you'd have it on me the rest of my life." He grinned. "And I couldn't stand that. Besides, it wouldn't be good for the kid."

Eventually she gave in, ashamed of herself, miserable—and glad. For the world of her work, where she existed without Bill, was bigger to her now than the world in which they existed together. There was more room to be glad in one than to be sorry in the other.

Two days later, with his ticket bought for that afternoon at five, they passed the last hours together, talking of everything hopeful. She protested still, and sincerely; had he weakened for a moment she would have gone. But the shock had done something to him, and he showed more character under it than he had for years. Perhaps it would be good for him to work it out alone.

"In the spring!" they said.

Then in the station with little Billy, and Bill saying: "I hate these grave-side partings. You leave me here. I've got to make a phone call from the train before it goes."

They had never spent more than a night apart in six years, save when Emmy was in the hospital; save for the time in England they had a good record of faithfulness and of tenderness toward each other, even though she had been alarmed and often unhappy at this insecure bravado from the first. After he went through the gate alone, Emmy was glad he had a phone call to make and tried to picture him making it.

She was a good woman; she had loved him with all her heart. When she went out into Thirty-third Street, it was just as dead as dead for a while, and the apartment he paid for would be empty of him, and she was here, about to do something that would make her happy.

She stopped after a few blocks, thinking: "Why, this is terrible—what I'm doing! I'm letting him down like the worst person I ever heard of. I'm leaving him flat and going off to dinner with Donilof and Paul Makova, whom I like for being beautiful and for having the same color eyes and hair. Bill's on the train alone."

She swung little Billy around suddenly as if to go back to the station. She could see him sitting in the train, with his face so pale and tired, and no Emmy.

"I can't let him down," she cried to herself as wave after wave of sentiment washed over her. But only sentiment—hadn't he let her down—hadn't he done what he wanted in London?

"Oh, poor Bill!"

She stood irresolute, realizing for one last honest moment how quickly she would forget this and find excuses for what she was doing. She had to think hard of London, and her conscience cleared. But with Bill all alone in the train it seemed terrible to think that way. Even now she could turn and go back to the station and tell him that she was coming, but still she waited, with life very strong in her, fighting for her. The sidewalk was narrow where she stood; presently a great wave of people, pouring out of the theater, came flooding along it, and she and little Billy were swept along with the crowd.

In the train, Bill telephoned up to the last minute, postponed going back to his stateroom, because he knew it was almost certain that he would not find her there. After the train started he went back and, of course, there was nothing but his bags in the rack and some magazines on the seat.

He knew then that he had lost her. He saw the set-up without any illusions—this Paul Makova, and months of proximity, and loneliness— afterward nothing would ever be the same. When he had thought about it all a long time, reading *Variety* and *Zit's* in between, it began to seem, each time he came back to it, as if Emmy somehow were dead.

"She was a fine girl—one of the best. She had character." He realized perfectly that he had brought all this on himself and that there was some law of compensation involved. He saw, too, that by going away he had again become as good as she was; it was all evened up at last.

He felt beyond everything, even beyond his grief, an almost comfortable sensation of being in the hands of something bigger than himself; and grown a little tired and unconfident—two qualities he could never for a moment tolerate—it did not seem so terrible if he were going West for a definite finish. He was sure that Emmy would come at the end, no matter what she was doing or how good an engagement she had.

FIRST BLOOD

The favorable response to the Basil stories prompted Fitzgerald to undertake a companion series about Josephine Perry. The five stories published in 1930 and 1931 were loosely based on Ginevra King, the Chicago girl Fitzgerald fell in love with when he was at Princeton. The Josephine stories are harsher than the Basil stories, probably because they were written during a time of personal and professional anxiety.

"First Blood" (Saturday Evening Post, 5 April 1930) was the first story in the series and was reprinted in Taps at Reveille.

♦

"I REMEMBER YOUR coming to me in despair when Josephine was about three!" cried Mrs. Bray. "George was furious because he couldn't decide what to go to work at, so he used to spank little Josephine."

"I remember," said Josephine's mother.

"And so this is Josephine."

This was, indeed, Josephine. She looked at Mrs. Bray and smiled, and Mrs. Bray's eyes hardened imperceptibly. Josephine kept on smiling.

"How old are you, Josephine?"

"Just sixteen."

"Oh-h. I would have said you were older."

At the first opportunity Josephine asked Mrs. Perry, "Can I go to the movies with Lillian this afternoon?"

"No, dear; you have to study." She turned to Mrs. Bray as if the matter were dismissed—but: "You darn fool," muttered Josephine audibly.

Mrs. Bray said some words quickly to cover the situation, but, of course, Mrs. Perry could not let it pass unreproved.

"What did you call mother, Josephine?"

"I don't see why I can't go to the movies with Lillian."

Her mother was content to let it go at this.

"Because you've got to study. You go somewhere every day, and your father wants it to stop."

"How crazy!" said Josephine, and she added vehemently, "How utterly insane! Father's got to be a maniac I think. Next thing he'll start tearing his hair and think he's Napoleon or something."

"No," interposed Mrs. Bray jovially as Mrs. Perry grew rosy. "Perhaps she's right. Maybe George *is* crazy—I'm sure my husband's crazy. It's this war."

But she was not really amused; she thought Josephine ought to be beaten with sticks.

They were talking about Anthony Harker, a contemporary of Josephine's older sister.

"He's divine," Josephine interposed—not rudely, for, despite the foregoing, she was not rude; it was seldom even that she appeared to talk too much, though she lost her temper, and swore sometimes when people were unreasonable. "He's perfectly——"

"He's very popular. Personally, I don't see very much to him. He seems rather superficial."

"Oh, no, mother," said Josephine. "He's far from it. Everybody says he has a great deal of personality—which is more than you can say of most of these jakes. Any girl would be glad to get their hands on him. I'd marry him in a minute."

She had never thought of this before; in fact, the phrase had been invented to express her feeling for Travis de Coppet. When, presently, tea was served, she excused herself and went to her room.

It was a new house, but the Perrys were far from being new people. They were Chicago Society, and almost very rich, and not uncultured as things went thereabouts in 1914. But Josephine was an unconscious pioneer of the generation that was destined to "get out of hand."

In her room she dressed herself for going to Lillian's house, thinking meanwhile of Travis de Coppet and of riding home from the Davidsons' dance last night. Over his tuxedo, Travis had worn a loose blue cape inherited from an old-fashioned uncle. He was tall and thin, an exquisite dancer, and his eyes had often been described by female contemporaries as "very dark"—to an adult it appeared that he had two black eyes in the collisional sense, and that probably they were justifiably renewed every night; the area surrounding them was so purple, or brown, or crimson, that they were the first thing you noticed about his face, and, save for his white teeth, the last. Like Josephine, he was also something new. There were a lot of new things in Chicago then, but lest the interest of this narrative be divided, it should be remarked that Josephine was the newest thing of all.

Dressed, she went down the stairs and through a softly opening side door, out into the street. It was October and a harsh breeze blew her along under trees without leaves, past houses with cold corners, past caves of the wind that were the mouths of residential streets. From that time until April, Chicago is an indoor city, where entering by a door is like going into another world, for the cold of the lake is unfriendly and not like real northern cold—it serves only to accentuate the things that go on inside. There is no music outdoors, or love-making, and even in prosperous times the wealth that rolls by in limousines is less glamorous than embittering to those on the sidewalk. But in the houses there is a deep, warm quiet, or else an excited, singing noise, as if those within were inventing things like new dances. That is part of what people mean when they say they love Chicago.

Josephine was going to meet her friend Lillian Hammel, but their plan did not include attending the movies. In comparison to it, their mothers would have preferred the most objectionable, the most lurid movie. It was no less than to go for a long auto ride with Travis de Coppet and Howard Page, in the course of which they would kiss not once but a lot. The four of them had been planning this since the previous Saturday, when unkind circumstances had combined to prevent its fulfillment.

Travis and Howard were already there—not sitting down, but still in their overcoats, like symbols of action, hurrying the girls breathlessly into the future. Travis wore a fur collar on his overcoat and carried a gold-headed cane; he kissed Josephine's hand facetiously yet seriously, and she said, "Hello, Travis!" with the warm affection of a politician greeting a prospective vote. But for a minute the two girls exchanged news aside.

"I saw him," Lillian whispered, "just now."

"Did you?"

Their eyes blazed and fused together.

"Isn't he divine?" said Josephine.

They were referring to Mr. Anthony Harker, who was twenty-two, and unconscious of their existence, save that in the Perry house he occasionally recognized Josephine as Constance's younger sister.

"He has the most beautiful nose," cried Lillian, suddenly laughing. "It's—" She drew it on the air with her finger and they both became hilarious. But Josephine's face composed itself as Travis' black eyes, conspicuous as if they had been freshly made the previous night, peered in from the hall.

"Well!" he said tensely.

The four young people went out, passed through fifty bitter feet of wind and entered Page's car. They were all very confident and knew exactly what they wanted. Both girls were expressly disobeying their parents, but they had no more sense of guilt about it than a soldier escaping from an enemy prison camp. In the back seat, Josephine and Travis looked at each other; she waited as he burned darkly.

"Look," he said to his hand; it was trembling. "Up till five this morning. Girls from the Follies."

"Oh, Travis!" she cried automatically, but for the first time a communication such as this failed to thrill her. She took his hand, wondering what the matter was inside herself.

It was quite dark, and he bent over her suddenly, but as suddenly she turned her face away. Annoyed, he made cynical nods with his head and lay back in the corner of the car. He became engaged in cherishing his dark secret—the secret that always made her yearn toward him. She could see it come into his eyes and fill them, down to the cheek bones and up to the brows, but she could not concentrate on him. The romantic mystery of the world had moved into another man.

Travis waited ten minutes for her capitulation; then he tried again, and with this second approach she saw him plain for the first time. It was enough. Josephine's imagination and her desires were easily exploited up to a certain point, but after that her very impulsiveness protected her. Now, suddenly, she found something real against Travis, and her voice was modulated with lowly sorrow.

"I heard what you did last night. I heard very well."

"What's the matter?"

"You told Ed Bement you were in for a big time because you were going to take me home in your car."

"Who told you that?" he demanded, guilty but belittling.

"Ed Bement did, and he told me he almost hit you in the face when you said it. He could hardly keep restraining himself."

Once more Travis retired to his corner of the seat. He accepted this as the reason for her coolness, as in a measure it was. In view of Doctor Jung's theory that innumerable male voices argue in the subconscious of a woman, and even speak through her lips, then the absent Ed Bement was probably speaking through Josephine at that moment.

"I've decided not to kiss any more boys, because I won't have anything left to give the man I really love."

"Bull!" replied Travis.

"It's true. There's been too much talk around Chicago about me. A man certainly doesn't respect a girl he can kiss whenever he wants to, and I want to be respected by the man I'm going to marry some day."

Ed Bement would have been overwhelmed had he realized the extent of his dominance over her that afternoon.

Walking from the corner, where the youths discreetly left her, to her house, Josephine felt that agreeable lightness which comes with the end of a piece of work. She would be a good girl now forever, see less of boys, as her parents wished, try to be what Miss Benbower's school denominated An Ideal Benbower Girl. Then next year, at Breerly, she could be an Ideal Breerly Girl. But the first stars were out over Lake Shore Drive, and all about her she could feel Chicago swinging around its circle at a hundred miles an hour, and Josephine knew that she only wanted to want such wants for her soul's sake. Actually, she had no desire for achievement. Her grandfather had had that, her parents had had the consciousness of it, but Josephine accepted the proud world into which she was born. This was easy in Chicago, which, unlike New York, was a city state, where the old families formed a caste—intellect was represented by the university professors, and there were no ramifications, save that even the Perrys had to be nice to half a dozen families even richer and more important than themselves. Josephine loved to dance, but the field of feminine glory, the ballroom floor, was something you slipped away from with a man.

As Josephine came to the iron gate of her house, she saw her sister shivering on the top steps with a departing young man; then the front door closed and the man came down the walk. She knew who he was.

He was abstracted, but he recognized her for just a moment in passing. "Oh, hello," he said.

She turned all the way round so that he could see her face by the street lamp; she lifted her face full out of her fur collar and toward him, and then smiled.

"Hello," she said modestly.

They passed. She drew in her head like a turtle.

"Well, now he knows what I look like, anyhow," she told herself excitedly as she went on into the house.

· I I ·

SEVERAL DAYS LATER Constance Perry spoke to her mother in a serious tone:

"Josephine is so conceited that I really think she's a little crazy."

"She's very conceited," admitted Mrs. Perry. "Father and I were talking and we decided that after the first of the year she should go East to school. But you don't say a word about it until we know more definitely."

"Heavens, mother, it's none too soon! She and that terrible Travis de Coppet running around with his cloak, as if they were about a thousand years old. They came into the Blackstone last week and my *spine* crawled. They looked just like two maniacs—Travis slinking along, and Josephine twisting her mouth around as if she had St. Vitus dance. *Honestly*——"

"What did you begin to say about Anthony Harker?" interrupted Mrs. Perry.

"That she's got a crush on him, and he's about old enough to be her grandfather."

"Not quite."

"Mother, he's twenty-two and she's sixteen. Every time Jo and Lillian go by him, they giggle and stare——"

"Come here, Josephine," said Mrs. Perry.

Josephine came into the room slowly and leaned her backbone against the edge of the opened door, teetering upon it calmly.

"What, mother?"

"Dear, you don't want to be laughed at, do you?"

Josephine turned sulkily to her sister. "Who laughs at me? You do, I guess. You're the only one that does."

"You're so conceited that you don't see it. When you and Travis de Coppet came into the Blackstone that afternoon, my *spine* crawled. Everybody at our table and most of the other tables laughed—the ones that weren't shocked."

"I guess they were more shocked," guessed Josephine complacently.

"You'll have a fine reputation by the time you come out."

"Oh, shut your mouth!" said Josephine.

There was a moment's silence. Then Mrs. Perry whispered solemnly, "I'll have to tell your father about this as soon as he comes home."

"Go on, tell him." Suddenly Josephine began to cry. "Oh, why can't anybody ever leave me alone? I wish I was dead."

Her mother stood with her arm around her, saying, "Josephine—now, Josephine"; but Josephine went on with deep, broken sobs that seemed to come from the bottom of her heart.

"Just a lot—of—of ugly and jealous girls who get mad when anybody looks at m-me, and make up all sorts of stories that are absolutely untrue, just because I can get anybody I want. I suppose that Constance is mad about it because I went in and sat for *five* minutes with Anthony Harker while he was waiting last night."

"Yes, I was *ter*ribly jealous! I sat up and cried all night about it. Especially because he comes to talk to me about Marice Whaley. Why!—you got him so crazy about you in that five minutes that he couldn't stop laughing all the way to the Warrens."

Josephine drew in her breath in one last gasp, and stopped crying. "If you want to know, I've decided to give him up."

"Ha-ha!" Constance exploded. "Listen to *that*, mother! She's going to give him up—as if he ever looked at her or knew she was al*ive*! Of all the conceited——"

But Mrs. Perry could stand no more. She put her arm around Josephine and hurried her to her room down the hall.

"All your sister meant was that she didn't like to see you laughed at," she explained.

"Well, I've given him up," said Josephine gloomily.

She had given him up, renouncing a thousand kisses she had never had, a hundred long, thrilling dances in his arms, a hundred evenings not to be recaptured. She did not mention the letter she had written him last night—and had not sent, and now would never send.

"You musn't think about such things at your age," said Mrs. Perry. "You're just a child."

Josephine got up and went to the mirror.

"I promised Lillian to come over to her house. I'm late now."

Back in her room, Mrs. Perry thought: "Two months to February." She was a pretty woman who wanted to be loved by everyone around her; there was no power of governing in her. She tied up her mind like a neat package and put it in the post office, with Josephine inside it safely addressed to the Breerly School.

An hour later, in the tea room at the Blackstone Hotel, Anthony Harker and another young man lingered at table. Anthony was a happy fellow, lazy, rich enough, pleased with his current popularity. After a brief career in an Eastern university, he had gone to a famous college in Virginia and in its less exigent shadow completed his education; at least, he had absorbed certain courtesies and mannerisms that Chicago girls found charming.

"There's that guy Travis de Coppet," his companion had just remarked. "What's he think he is, anyhow?"

Anthony looked remotely at the young people across the room, recognizing the little Perry girl and other young females whom he seemed to have encountered frequently in the street of late. Although obviously much at home, they seemed silly and loud; presently his eyes left them and searched the room for the party he was due to join for dancing, but he was still sitting there when the room—it had a twilight quality, in spite of the lights within and the full dark outside—woke up to confident and exciting music. A thickening parade drifted past him. The men in sack suits, as though they had just come from portentous affairs, and the women in hats that seemed about to take flight, gave a special impermanence to the scene. This implication that this gathering, a little more than uncalculated, a little less than clandestine, would shortly be broken into formal series, made him anxious to seize its last minutes, and he looked more and more intently into the crowd for the face of anyone he knew.

One face emerged suddenly around a man's upper arm not five feet away, and for a moment Anthony was the object of the saddest and most tragic regard that had ever been directed upon him. It was a smile and not a smile—two big gray eyes with bright triangles of color underneath, and a mouth twisted into a universal sympathy that seemed to include both him and herself—yet withal, the expression not of a victim, but rather of the very *de*mon of tender melancholy—and for the first time Anthony really saw Josephine.

His immediate instinct was to see with whom she was dancing. It was a young man he knew, and with this assurance he was on his feet giving a quick tug to his coat, and then out upon the floor.

"May I cut in, please?"

Josephine came close to him as they started, looked up into his eyes for an instant, and then down and away. She said nothing. Realizing that she could not possibly be more than sixteen, Anthony hoped that the party he was to join would not arrive in the middle of the dance.

When that was over, she raised eyes to him again; a sense of having been mistaken, of her being older than he had thought, possessed him. Just before he left her at her table, he was moved to say:

"Couldn't I have another later?"

"Oh, sure."

She united her eyes with his, every glint a spike—perhaps from the railroads on which their family fortunes were founded, and upon which they depended. Anthony was disconcerted as he went back to his table.

One hour later, they left the Blackstone together in her car.

This had simply happened—Josephine's statement, at the end of their second dance, that she must leave, then her request, and his own extreme self-consciousness as he walked beside her across the empty floor. It was a favor to her sister to take her home—but he had that unmistakable feeling of expectation.

Nevertheless, once outside and shocked into reconsideration by the bitter cold, he tried again to allocate his responsibilities in the matter. This was hard going with Josephine's insistent dark and ivory youth pressed up against him. As they got in the car he tried to dominate the situation with a masculine stare, but her eyes, shining as if with fever, melted down his bogus austerity in a whittled second.

Idly he patted her hand—then suddenly he was inside the radius of her perfume and kissing her breathlessly. . . .

"So that's that," she whispered after a moment. Startled, he wondered if he had forgotten something—something he had said to her before.

"What a cruel remark," he said, "just when I was getting interested."

"I only meant that any minute with you may be the last one," she said miserably. "The family are going to send me away to school—they think I haven't found that out yet."

"Too bad."

"—and today they got together—and tried to tell me that you didn't know I was al*ive!*"

After a long pause, Anthony contributed feebly. "I hope you didn't let them convince you."

She laughed shortly. "I just laughed and came down here."

Her hand burrowed its way into his; when he pressed it, her eyes, bright now, not dark, rose until they were as high as his, and came toward him. A minute later he thought to himself: "This is a rotten trick I'm doing."

He was sure he was doing it.

"You're so sweet," she said.

"You're a dear child."

"I hate jealousy worse than anything in the world," Josephine broke forth, "and *I* have to suffer from it. And my own sister worse than all the rest."

"Oh, no," he protested.

"I couldn't help it if I fell in love with you. I tried to help it. I used to go out of the house when I knew you were coming."

The force of her lies came from her sincerity and from her simple and superb confidence that whomsoever she loved must love her in return. Josephine was never either ashamed or plaintive. She was in the world of being alone with a male, a world through which she had moved surely since she was eight years old. She did not plan; she merely let herself go, and the overwhelming life in her did the rest. It is only when youth is gone and experience has given us a sort of cheap courage that most of us realize how simple such things are.

"But you couldn't be in love with me," Anthony wanted to say, and couldn't. He fought with a desire to kiss her again, even tenderly, and began to tell her that she was being unwise, but before he got really started at this handsome project, she was in his arms again, and whispering something that he had to accept, since it was wrapped up in a kiss. Then he was alone, driving away from her door.

What had he agreed to? All they had said rang and beat in his ear like an unexpected temperature—tomorrow at four o'clock on that corner.

"Good God!" he thought uneasily. "All that stuff about giving me up. She's a crazy kid, she'll get into trouble if somebody looking for trouble comes along. *Big* chance of my meeting her tomorrow!"

But neither at dinner nor the dance that he went to that night could Anthony get the episode out of his mind; he kept looking around the ball-room regretfully, as if he missed someone who should be there.

· I I I ·

TWO WEEKS LATER, waiting for Marice Whaley in a meager, indefinable down-stairs "sitting room," Anthony reached in his pocket for some half-forgotten mail. Three letters he replaced; the other—after a moment of listening—he opened quickly and read with his back to the door. It was the third of a series—for one had followed each of his meetings with Josephine—and it was exactly like the others—the letter of a child. Whatever maturity of emotion could accumulate in her expression, when once she set pen to paper was snowed under by ineptitude. There was much about "your feeling for me" and "my feeling for you," and sentences began, "Yes, I know I am sentimental," or more gawkily, "I have always been sort of pash, and I can't help that," and inevitably much quoting of lines from current popular songs, as if they expressed the writer's state of mind more fully than verbal struggles of her own.

The letter disturbed Anthony. As he reached the postscript, which coolly made a rendezvous for five o'clock this afternoon, he heard Marice coming down-stairs, and put it back in his pocket.

Marice hummed and moved about the room. Anthony smoked.

"I saw you Tuesday afternoon," she said suddenly. "You seemed to be having a fine time."

"Tuesday," he repeated, as if thinking. "Oh, yeah. I ran into some kids and we went to a tea dance. It was amusing."

"You were *al*most alone when I saw you."

"What are you getting at?"

Marice hummed again. "Let's go out. Let's go to a matinée."

On the way Anthony explained how he had happened to be with Connie's little sister; the necessity of the explanation somehow angered him. When he had done, Marice said crisply:

"If you wanted to rob the cradle, why did you have to pick out that little devil? Her reputation's so bad already that Mrs. McRae didn't want to invite her to dancing class this year—she only did it on account of Constance."

"Why is she so awful?" asked Anthony, disturbed.

"I'd rather not discuss it."

His five-o'clock engagement was on his mind throughout the matinée. Though Marice's remarks served only to make him dangerously sorry for Josephine, he was nevertheless determined that this meeting should be the last. It was embarrassing to have been remarked in her company, even though he had tried honestly to avoid it. The matter could very easily develop into a rather dangerous little mess, with no benefit either to Josephine or to himself. About Marice's indignation he did not care; she had been his for the asking all autumn, but Anthony did not want to get married; did not want to get involved with anybody at all.

It was dark when he was free at 5:30, and turned his car toward the new Philanthrophilogical Building in the maze of reconstruction in Grant Park. The bleakness of place and time depressed him, gave a further painfulness to the affair. Getting out of his car, he walked past a young man in a waiting roadster—a young man whom he seemed to recognize—and found Josephine in the half darkness of the little chamber that the storm doors formed.

With an indefinable sound of greeting, she walked determinedly into his arms, putting up her face.

"I can only stay for a sec" she protested, just as if he had begged her to come. "I'm supposed to go to a wedding with sister, but I had to see you."

When Anthony spoke, his voice froze into a white mist, obvious in the darkness. He said things he had said to her before but this time firmly and finally. It was easier, because he could scarcely see her face and because somewhere in the middle she irritated him by starting to cry.

"I knew you were supposed to be fickle," she whispered, "but I didn't expect this. Anyhow, I've got enough pride not to bother you any further." She hesitated. "But I wish we could meet just once more to try and arrive at a more different settlement."

"No."

"Some jealous girl has been talking to you about me."

"No." Then, in despair, he struck at her heart. "I'm *not* fickle. I've never loved you and I *never* told you I did."

Guessing at the forlorn expression that would come into her face, Anthony turned away and took a purposeless step; when he wheeled nervously about, the storm door had just shut—she was gone.

"Josephine!" he shouted in helpless pity, but there was no answer. He waited, heart in his boots, until presently he heard a car drive away.

At home, Josephine thanked Ed Bement, whom she had used, with a tartlet of hope, went in by a side door and up to her room. The window was open and, as she dressed hurriedly for the wedding she stood close to it so that she would catch cold and die.

Seeing her face in the bathroom mirror, she broke down and sat on the edge of the tub, making a small choking sound like a struggle with a cough, and cleaning her finger nails. Later she could cry all night in bed when every one else was asleep, but now it was still afternoon.

The two sisters and their mother stood side by side at the wedding of Mary Jackson and Jackson Dillon. It was a sad and sentimental wedding—an end to the fine, glamorous youth of a girl who was universally admired and loved. Perhaps to no onlooker were its details symbolical of the end of a period, yet from the vantage point of a decade, certain things that happened are already powdered with yesterday's ridiculousness, and even tinted with the lavender of the day before. The bride raised her veil, smiling that grave sweet smile that made her "adored," but with tears pouring down her cheeks, and faced dozens of friends hands outheld as if embracing all of them for the last time. Then she turned to a husband as serious and immaculate as herself, and looked at him as if to say, "That's done. All this that I am is yours forever and ever."

In her pew, Constance, who had been at school with Mary Jackson, was frankly weeping, from a heart that was a ringing vault. But the face of Josephine beside her was a more intricate study; it watched intently. Once or twice, though her eyes lost none of their level straight intensity, an isolated tear escaped, and, as if startled by the feel of it, the face hardened slightly and the mouth remained in defiant immobility, like a child well warned against making a disturbance. Only once did she move; hearing a voice behind her say: "That's the little Perry girl. Isn't she lovely looking?" she turned presently and gazed at a stained-glass window lest her unknown admirers miss the sight of the side face.

Josephine's family went on to the reception, so she dined alone—or rather with her little brother and his nurse, which was the same thing.

She felt all empty. Tonight Anthony Harker, "so deeply lovable—so sweetly lovable—so deeply, sweetly lovable" was making love to someone new, kissing her ugly, jealous face; soon he would have disappeared forever, together with all the men of his generation, into a loveless matrimony, leaving only a world of Travis de Coppets and Ed Bements—people so easy as to scarcely be worth the effort of a smile.

Up in her room, she was excited again by the sight of herself in the bathroom mirror. Oh, what if she should die in her sleep tonight?

"Oh, what a shame," she whispered.

She opened the window, and holding her only souvenir of Anthony, a big initialed linen handkerchief, crept desolately into bed. While the sheets were still cold, there was a knock at the door.

"Special-delivery letter," said the maid.

Putting on the light, Josephine opened it, turned to the signature, then back again, her breast rising and falling quickly under her nightgown.

DARLING LITTLE JOSEPHINE: It's no use, I can't help it, I can't lie about it. I'm desperately, terribly in love with you. When you went away this afternoon, it all rushed over me, and I knew I couldn't give you up. I drove home, and I couldn't eat or sit still, but only walk up and down thinking of your darling face and your darling tears, there in that vestibule. And now I sit writing this letter—

It was four pages long. Somewhere it disposed of their disparate ages as unimportant, and the last words were:

I know how miserable you must be, and I would give ten years of my life to be there to kiss your sweet lips good night.

When she had read it through, Josephine sat motionless for some minutes; grief was suddenly gone, and for a moment she was so overwhelmed that she supposed joy had come in its stead. On her face was a twinkling frown.

"Gosh!" she said to herself. She read over the letter once more.

Her first instinct was to call up Lillian, but she thought better of it. The image of the bride at the wedding popped out at her—the reproachless bride, unsullied, beloved and holy with a sweet glow. An adolescence of uprightness, a host of friends, then the appearance of the perfect lover, the Ideal. With an effort, she recalled her drifting mind to the present occasion. Certainly Mary Jackson would never have kept such a letter. Getting out of bed, Josephine tore it into little pieces and, with some difficulty, caused by an unexpected amount of smoke, burned it on a glass-topped table. No well-brought-up girl would have answered such a letter; the proper thing was to simply ignore it.

She wiped up the table top with the man's linen handkerchief she held in her hand, threw it absently into a laundry basket and crept into bed. She suddenly was very sleepy.

· I V ·

FOR WHAT ENSUED, no one, not even Constance, blamed Josephine. If a man of twenty-two should so debase himself as to pay frantic court to a girl of sixteen against the wishes of her parents and herself, there was only one answer—he was a person who shouldn't be received by decent people. When Travis de Coppet made a controversial remark on the affair at a dance, Ed Bement beat him into what was described as "a pulp," down in the washroom, and Josephine's reputation rose to normal and stayed there. Accounts of how Anthony had called time and time again at the house, each time denied admittance, how he had threatened Mr. Perry, how he had tried to bribe a maid to deliver letters, how he had attempted to waylay Josephine on her way back from school—these things pointed to the fact that he was a little mad. It was Anthony Harker's own family who insisted that he should go West.

All this was a trying time for Josephine. She saw how close she had come to disaster, and by constant consideration and implicit obedience, tried to make up to her parents for the trouble she had unwittingly caused. At first she decided she didn't want to go to any Christmas dances, but she was persuaded by her mother, who hoped she would be distracted by boys and girls home from school for the holidays. Mrs. Perry was taking her East to the Breerly School early in January, and in the buying of clothes and uniforms, mother and daughter were much together, and Mrs. Perry was delighted at Josephine's new feeling of responsibility and maturity.

As a matter of fact, it was sincere, and only once did Josephine do anything that she could not have told the world. The day after New Year's she put on her new travelling suit and her new fur coat and went out by her familiar egress, the side door, and walked down the block to the waiting car of Ed Bement. Downtown she left Ed waiting at a corner and entered a drug store opposite the old Union Station on LaSalle Street. A man with an unhappy mouth and desperate, baffled eyes was waiting for her there.

"Thank you for coming," he said miserably.

She didn't answer. Her face was grave and polite.

"Here's what I want—just one thing," he said quickly: "Why did you change? What did I do that made you change so suddenly? Was it something that happened, something I did? Was it what I said in the vestibule that night?"

Still looking at him, she tried to think, but she could only think how unattractive and rather terrible she found him now, and try not to let him see it. There would have been no use saying the simple truth—that she could not help what she had done, that great beauty has a need, almost an obligation, of trying itself, that her ample cup of emotion had spilled over on its own accord, and it was an accident that it had destroyed him and not her. The eyes of pity might follow Anthony Harker in his journey West, but most certainly the eyes of destiny followed Josephine as she crossed the street through the falling snow to Ed Bement's car.

She sat quiet for a minute as they drove away, relieved and yet full of awe. Anthony Harker was twenty-two, handsome, popular and sought after—and how he had loved her—so much that he had to go away. She was as impressed as if they had been two other people.

Taking her silence for depression, Ed Bement said:

"Well, it did one thing anyhow—it stopped that other story they had around about you."

She turned to him quickly. "What story?"

"Oh, just some crazy story."

"What was it?" she demanded.

"Oh, nothing much," he said hesitantly, "but there was a story around last August that you and Travis de Coppet were married."

"Why, how perfectly terrible!" she exclaimed. "Why, I never heard of such a lie. It—" She stopped herself short of saying the truth—that though she and Travis had adventurously driven twenty miles to New Ulm, they had been unable to find a minister willing to marry them. It all seemed ages behind her, childish, forgotten.

"Oh, how perfectly terrible!" she repeated. "That's the kind of story that gets started by jealous girls."

"I know," agreed Ed. "I'd just like to hear any boy try to repeat it to me. Nobody believed it anyhow."

It was the work of ugly and jealous girls. Ed Bement, aware of her body next to him, and of her face shining like fire through the half darkness, knew that nobody so beautiful could ever do anything really wrong.

Editor's Note: On page 542, lines 21 and 25, the *Saturday Evening Post* readings have been restored: "herself, and looked at" for "herself, at"; and "study; it watched" for "study watched."

EMOTIONAL BANKRUPTCY

◆

"Emotional Bankruptcy" (Saturday Evening Post, 15 August 1931) was the last of the Josephine Perry stories and closes the series with a strong judgment: she has ruined herself. The title refers to Fitzgerald's conviction that people have a fixed amount of emotional capital, and that reckless expenditure of it leaves an individual incapable of generating new emotions. It is, of course, significant that he expressed a theory of behavior in terms of a financial metaphor. Although "Emotional Bankruptcy" is ranked as the best of the Josephine stories, Fitzgerald did not collect it in Taps at Reveille—*possibly because he felt that he had squandered an idea that he wanted to develop more profoundly elsewhere.*

◆

"THERE'S THAT NUT with the spyglass again," remarked Josephine. Lillian Hammel unhooked a lace sofa cushion from her waist and came to the window. "He's standing back so we can't see him. He's looking at the room above."

The peeper was working from a house on the other side of narrow Sixty-eighth Street, all unconscious that his activities were a matter of knowledge and, lately, of indifference to the pupils of Miss Truby's finishing school. They had even identified him as the undistinguished but quite proper young man who issued from the house with a brief case at eight every morning, apparently oblivious of the school across the street.

"What a horrible person," said Lillian.

"They're all the same," Josephine said. "I'll bet almost every man we know would do the same thing, if he had a telescope and nothing to do in the afternoon. I'll bet Louie Randall would, anyhow."

"Josephine, is he actually following you to Princeton?" Lillian asked.

"Yes, dearie."

"Doesn't he think he's got his nerve?"

"He'll get away with it," Josephine assured her.

"Won't Paul be wild?"

"I can't worry about that. I only know half a dozen boys at Princeton, and with Louie I know I'll have at least one good dancer to depend on. Paul's too short for me, and he's a bum dancer anyhow."

Not that Josephine was very tall; she was an exquisite size for seventeen and of a beauty that was flowering marvelously day by day into something richer and warmer. People gasped nowadays, whereas a year ago they would merely have stared, and scarcely glanced at her a year before that. She was manifestly to be the spectacular débutante of Chicago next year, in spite of the fact that she was an egotist who played not for popularity but for individual men. While Josephine always recovered, the men frequently didn't—her mail from Chicago, from New Haven, from the Yale Battery on the border, averaged a dozen letters a day.

This was in the fall of 1916, with the thunder of far-off guns already growing louder on the air. When the two girls started for the Princeton prom two days later, they carried with them the Poems of Alan Seeger, supplemented by copies of Smart Set and Snappy Stories, bought surreptitiously at the station news stand. When compared to a seventeen-year-old girl of today, Lillian Hammel was an innocent; Josephine Perry, however, belonged to the ages.

They read nothing en route save a few love epigrams beginning: "A woman of thirty is——" The train was crowded and a sustained, excited chatter flowed along the aisles of the coaches. There were very young girls in a gallantly concealed state of terror; there were privately bored girls who would never see twenty-five again; there were unattractive girls, blandly unconscious of what was in store; and there were little, confident parties who felt as though they were going home.

"They say it's not like Yale," said Josephine. "They don't do things so elaborately here. They don't rush you from place to place, from one tea to another, like they do at New Haven."

"Will you ever forget that divine time last spring?" exclaimed Lillian.

They both sighed.

"At least there'll be Louie Randall," said Josephine.

There would indeed be Louie Randall, whom Josephine had seen fit to invite herself, without the formality of telling her Princeton escort that he was coming. The escort, at that moment pacing up and down at the station platform with many other young men, was probably under the impression that it was his party. But he was wrong; it was Josephine's party; even Lillian was coming with another Princeton man, named Martin Munn, whom Josephine had thoughtfully provided. "Please ask her," she had written. "We'll manage to see a lot of each other, if you do, because the man I'm coming with isn't really very keen about me, so he won't mind."

But Paul Dempster cared a lot; so much so that when the train came puffing up from the Junction he gulped a full pint of air, which is a mild form of swooning. He had been devoted to Josephine for a year—long after her own interest had waned—he had long lost any power of judging her objectively; she was become simply a projection of his own dreams, a radiant, nebulous mass of light.

But Josephine saw Paul clearly enough as they stepped off the train. She gave herself up to him immediately, as if to get it over with, to clear the decks for more vital action.

"So thrilled—so thrilled! So darling to ask me!" Immemorial words, still doing service after fifteen years.

She took his arm snugly, settling it in hers with a series of little read-justments, as if she wanted it right because it was going to be there forever.

"I bet you're not glad to see me at all," she whispered. "I'll bet you've forgotten me. I know you."

Rudimentary stuff, but it sent Paul Dempster into a confused and happy trance. He had the adequate surface of nineteen, but, within, all was still in a ferment of adolescence.

He could only answer gruffly: "Big chance." And then: "Martin had a chemistry lab. He'll meet us at the club."

Slowly the crowd of youth swirled up the steps and beneath Blair arch, floating in an autumn dream and scattering the yellow leaves with their feet. Slowly they moved between stretches of greensward under the elms and cloisters, with breath misty upon the crisp evening, following the hope that lay just ahead, the goal of happiness almost reached.

They sat before a big fire in the Witherspoon Club, the largest of those undergraduate mansions for which Princeton is famous. Martin Munn, Lillian's escort, was a quiet, handsome boy whom Josephine had met several times, but whose sentimental nature she had not explored. Now, with the phonograph playing Down Among the Sheltering Palms, with the soft orange light of the great room glowing upon the scattered groups, who seemed to have brought in the atmosphere of infinite promise from outside, Josephine looked at him appraisingly. A familiar current of curiosity coursed through her; already her replies to Paul had grown abstracted. But still in the warm enchantment of the walk from the station, Paul did not notice. He was far from guessing that he had already been served his ration; of special attention he would get no more. He was now cast for another rôle.

At the exact moment when it was suggested that they dress for dinner the party became aware of an individual who had just entered the club and was standing by the entrance looking not exactly at home, for he blinked about unfamiliarly, but not in the least ill at ease. He was tall, with long, dancing legs, and his face was that of an old, experienced weasel to whom no henhouse was impregnable.

"Why, Louie Randall!" exclaimed Josephine in a tone of astonishment.

She talked to him for a moment as if unwillingly, and then introduced him all around, meanwhile whispering to Paul: "He's a boy from New Haven. I never dreamed he'd follow me down here."

Randall within a few minutes was somehow one of the party. He had a light and witty way about him; no dark suspicions had penetrated Paul's mind.

"Oh, by the way," said Louie Randall, "I wonder if I can find a place to change my clothes. I've got a suitcase outside."

There was a pause. Josephine was apparently uninterested. The pause grew difficult, and Paul heard himself saying: "You can change in my room if you want to."

"I don't want to put you out."

"Not at all."

Josephine raised her eyebrows at Paul, disclaiming responsibility for the man's presumption; a moment later, Randall said: "Do you live near here?"

"Pretty near."

"Because I have a taxi and I could take you there if you're going to change, and you could show me where it is. I don't want to put you out."

The repetition of this ambiguous statement suggested that otherwise Paul might find his belongings in the street. He rose unwillingly; he did not hear Josephine whisper to Martin Munn: "Please don't you go yet." But Lillian did, and without minding at all. Her love affairs never conflicted with Josephine's, which is why they had been intimate friends so long. When Louie Randall and his involuntary host had departed, she excused herself and went to dress upstairs.

"I'd like to see all over the clubhouse," suggested Josephine. She felt the old excitement mounting in her pulse, felt her cheeks begin to glow like an electric heater.

"These are the private dining rooms," Martin explained as they walked around. . . . "The billiard room. . . . The squash courts. . . . This library is modeled on something in a Cercersion monastery in—in India or somewhere. . . . This"—he opened a door and peered in—"this is the president's room, but I don't know where the light is."

Josephine walked in with a little laugh. "It's very nice in here," she said. "You can't see anything at all. Oh, what have I run into? Come and save me!"

When they emerged a few minutes later, Martin smoothed back his hair hurriedly.

"You darling!" he said.

Josephine made a funny little clicking sound.

"What is it?" he demanded. "Why have you got such a funny look on your face?"

Josephine didn't answer.

"Have I done something? Are you angry? You look as if you'd seen a ghost," he said.

"You haven't done anything," she answered, and added, with an effort: "You were—sweet." She shuddered. "Show me my room, will you?"

"How strange," she was thinking. "He's so attractive, but I didn't enjoy kissing him at all. For the first time in my life—even when it was a man I didn't especially care for—I had no feeling about him at all. I've often been bored afterward, but at the time it's always meant something."

The experience depressed her more than she could account for. This was only her second prom, but neither before nor after did she ever enjoy one so little. She had never been more enthusiastically rushed, but through it all she seemed to float in a detached dream. The men were not individuals tonight, but dummies; men from Princeton, men from New Haven, new men, old beaus—were all as unreal as sticks. She wondered if her face wore that bovine expression she had often noted on the faces of stupid and apathetic girls.

"It's a mood," she told herself. "I'm just tired."

But next day, at a bright and active luncheon, she seemed to herself to have less vivacity than the dozen girls who boasted wanly that they hadn't gone to bed at all. After the football game she walked with Paul Dempster to the station, trying contritely to give him the last end of the week-end, as she had given him the beginning.

"Then why won't you go to the theater with us tonight?" he was pleading. "That was the understanding in my letter. We were to come to New York with you and all go to the theater."

"Because," she explained patiently, "Lillian and I have to be back to school by eight. That's the only condition on which we were allowed to come."

"Oh, hell," he said. "I'll bet you're doing something tonight with that Randall."

She denied this scornfully, but Paul was suddenly realizing that Randall had dined with them, Randall had slept upon his couch, and Randall, though at the game he had sat on the Yale side of the field, was somehow with them now.

His was the last face that Paul saw as the train pulled out for the Junction.

He had thanked Paul very graciously and asked him to stay with him if he was ever in New Haven.

Nevertheless, if the miserable Princetonian had witnessed a scene in the Pennsylvania Station an hour later, his pain would have been moderated, for now Louie Randall was arguing bitterly:

"But why not take a chance? The chaperon doesn't know what time you have to be in."

"We do."

When finally he had accepted the inevitable and departed, Josephine sighed and turned to Lillian.

"Where are we going to meet Wallie and Joe? At the Ritz?"

"Yes, and we'd better hurry," said Lillian. "The Follies begin at nine."

· II ·

IT HAD BEEN LIKE that for almost a year—a game played with technical mastery, but with the fire and enthusiasm gone—and Josephine was still a month short of eighteen. One evening during Thanksgiving vacation, as they waited for dinner in the library of Christine Dicer's house on Gramercy Park, Josephine said to Lillian:

"I keep thinking how excited I'd have been a year ago. A new place, a new dress, meeting new men."

"You've been around too much, dearie; you're blasé."

Josephine bridled impatiently: "I hate that word, and it's not true. I don't care about anything in the world except men, and you know it. But they're not like they used to be. . . . What are you laughing at?"

"When you were six years old they were different?"

"They were. They used to have more spirit when we played drop-the-handkerchief—even the little Ikeys that used to come in the back gate. The boys at dancing school were so exciting; they were all so sweet. I used to wonder what it would be like to kiss every one of them, and sometimes it was wonderful. And then came Travis and Tony Harker and Ridge Saunders and Ralph and John Bailey, and finally I began to realize that I was doing it all. They were nothing, most of them—not heroes or men of the world or anything I thought. They were just easy. That sounds conceited, but it's true."

She paused for a moment.

"Last night in bed I was thinking of the sort of man I really could love, but he'd be different from anybody I've ever met. He'd have to have certain things. He wouldn't necessarily be very handsome, but pleasant looking; and with a good figure, and strong. Then he'd have to have some kind of position in the world, or else not care whether he had one or not; if you see what I mean. He'd have to be a leader, not just like everybody else. And dignified, but very pash, and with lots of experience, so I'd believe everything he said or thought was right. And every time I looked at him I'd have to get that thrill I sometimes get out of a new man; only with him I'd have to get it over and over every time I looked at him, all my life."

"And you'd want him to be very much in love with you. That's what I'd want first of all."

"Of course," said Josephine abstractedly, "but principally I'd want to be always sure of loving him. It's much more fun to love someone than to be loved by someone."

There were footsteps in the hall outside and a man walked into the room. He was an officer in the uniform of the French aviation—a glove-fitting tunic of horizon blue, and boots and belt that shone like mirrors in the lamplight. He was young, with gray eyes that seemed to be looking off into the distance, and a red-brown military mustache. Across his left breast was a line of colored ribbons, and there were gold-embroidered stripes on his arms and wings on his collar.

"Good evening," he said courteously. "I was directed in here. I hope I'm not breaking into something."

Josephine did not move; from head to foot she saw him, and as she watched he seemed to come nearer, filling her whole vision. She heard Lillian's voice, and then the officer's voice, saying:

"My name's Dicer; I'm Christine's cousin. Do you mind if I smoke a cigarette?"

He didn't sit down. He moved about the room and turned over a magazine, not oblivious to their presence, but as if respecting their conversation. But when he saw that silence had fallen, he sat against a table near them with his arms folded and smiled at them.

"You're in the French army," Lillian ventured.

"Yes, I've just got back, and very glad to be here."

He didn't look glad, Josephine noticed. He looked as if he wanted to get out now, but had no place to go to.

For the first time in her life she felt no confidence. She had absolutely nothing to say. She hoped the emptiness that she had felt ever since her soul poured suddenly out toward his beautiful image didn't show in her face. She made her lips into a smile, and kept thinking how once, long ago, Travis de Coppet had worn his uncle's opera cloak to dancing school and suddenly seemed like a man out of the great world. So, now, the war overseas had gone on so long, touched us so little, save for confining us to our own shores, that it had a legendary quality about it, and the figure before her seemed to have stepped out of a gigantic red fairy tale.

She was glad when the other dinner guests came and the room filled with people, strangers she could talk to or laugh with or yawn at, according to their deserts. She despised the girls fluttering around Captain Dicer, but she admired him for not showing by a flicker of his eye that he either enjoyed it or hated it. Especially she disliked a tall, possessive blonde who once passed, her hand on his arm; he should have flicked away with a handkerchief the contamination of his immaculateness.

They went in to dinner; he was far away from her, and she was glad. All she could see of him was his blue cuff farther up the table when he reached for a glass, but she felt that they were alone together, none the less because he did not know.

The man next to her gave her the superfluous information that he was a hero:

"He's Christine's cousin, brought up in France, and joined at the beginning of the war. He was shot down behind the German lines and escaped by jumping off a train. There was a lot about it in the papers. I think he's over here on some kind of propaganda work. . . . Great horseman too. Everybody likes him."

After dinner she sat quietly while two men talked over her, sat persistently willing him to come to her. Ah, but she would be so nice, avoiding any curiosity or sentimentality about his experiences, avoiding any of the things that must have bored and embarrassed him since he had been home. She heard the voices around him:

"Captain Dicer. . . . Germans crucify all the Canadian soldiers they capture. . . . How much longer do you think the war . . . to be behind the enemy lines. . . . Were you frightened?" And then a heavy, male voice telling him about it, between puffs of a cigar: "The way I see it, Captain Dicer, neither side is getting anywhere. It strikes me they're afraid of each other."

It seemed a long time later that he came over to her, but at just the right moment, when there was a vacant seat beside her and he could slip into it.

"I wanted to talk to the prettiest girl for a while. I've wanted to all evening; it's been pretty heavy going."

Josephine wanted to lean against the shining leather of his belt, and more, she wanted to take his head in her lap. All her life had pointed toward this moment. She knew what he wanted, and gave it to him; not words, but a smile of warmth and delight—a smile that said, "I'm yours for the asking; I'm won." It was not a smile that undervalued herself, because through its beauty it spoke for both of them, expressed all the potential joy that existed between them.

"Who are you?" he asked.

"I'm a girl."

"I thought you were a flower. I wondered why they put you on a chair."

"*Vive la France,*" answered Josephine demurely. She dropped her eyes to his chest. "Do you collect stamps, too, or only coins?"

He laughed. "It's good to meet an American girl again. I hoped they'd at least put me across from you at table, so I could rest my eyes on you."

"I could see your cuff."

"I could see your arm. At least—yes, I thought it was your green bracelet."

Later he suggested: "Why couldn't you come out with me one of these evenings?"

"It's not done. I'm still in school."

"Well, some afternoon then. I'd like to go to a tea-dance place and hear some new tunes. The newest thing I know is Waiting for the Robert E. Lee."

"My nurse used to sing me to sleep with it."

"When could you?"

"I'm afraid you'll have to make up a party. Your aunt, Mrs. Dicer, is very strict."

"I keep forgetting," he agreed. "How old are you?"

"Eighteen," she said, anticipating by a month.

That was the point at which they were interrupted and the evening ended for her. The other young men in dinner coats looked like people in mourning beside the banner of his uniform. Some of them were persistent about Josephine, but she was in a reverie of horizon blue and she wanted to be alone.

"This is it at last," something whispered inside her.

Later that night and next day, she still moved in a trance. Another day more and she would see him—forty-eight hours, forty, thirty. The very word "blasé" made her laugh; she had never known such excitement, such expectation. The blessed day itself was a haze of magic music and softly lit winter rooms, of automobiles where her knee trembled against the top lacing of his boot. She was proud of the eyes that followed them when they danced; she was proud of him even when he was dancing with another girl.

"He may think I'm too young," she thought anxiously. "That's why he won't say anything. If he did, I'd leave school; I'd run away with him tonight."

School opened next day and Josephine wrote home:

DEAR MOTHER: I wonder if I can't spend part of the vacation in New York. Christine Dicer wants me to stay a week with her, which would still leave me a full ten days in Chicago. One reason is that the Metropolitan is putting on Wagner's Der Ring des Nibelungen and if I come home right away I can only see the Rheingold. Also there are two evening dresses that aren't finished——

The answer came by return post:

. . . because, in the first place, your eighteenth birthday falls then, and your father would feel very badly, because it would be the first birthday you hadn't passed with us; and, in the second place, I've never met the Dicers; and, thirdly, I've planned a little dance for you and I need your help; and, lastly, I can't believe that the reasons you give are your real ones. During Christmas week the Chicago Grand Opera Company is giving——

Meanwhile Capt. Edward Dicer had sent flowers and several formal little notes that sounded to her like translations from the French. She was self-conscious, answering them; so she did it in slang. His French education and his years in the war while America was whirling toward the Jazz Age had made him, though he was only twenty-three, seem of a more formal, more courteous generation than her own. She wondered what he would think of such limp exotics as Travis de Coppet, or Book Chaffee, or Louie Randall. Two days before vacation he wrote asking when her train left for the West. That was something, and for seventy-two hours she lived on it, unable to turn her attention to the masses of Christmas invitations and unheeded letters that she had meant to answer before leaving. But on the day itself, Lillian brought her a marked copy of Town Tattle that, from its ragged appearance, had already been passed around the school.

It is rumored that a certain Tuxedo papa who was somewhat irrasticable about the marital choice of a previous offspring views with equanimity the fact that his remaining daughter is so often in company with a young man fresh from his exploits in the French army.

Captain Dicer did not come to the train. He sent no flowers. Lillian, who loved Josephine like part of herself, wept in their compartment.
Josephine comforted her, saying: "But listen, darling; it's all the same to

me. I didn't have a chance, being in school like we were. It's all right." But she was awake hours and hours after Lillian was asleep.

· III ·

EIGHTEEN—it was to have meant so many things: When I'm eighteen I can——Until a girl's eighteen——You'll see things differently when you're eighteen.

That, at least, was true. Josephine saw her vacation invitations as so many overdue bills. Abstractedly she counted them as she always had before— twenty-eight dances, nineteen dinner and theater parties, fifteen tea dances and receptions, a dozen luncheons, a few miscellaneous bids, ranging from early breakfast for the Yale Glee Club to a bob party at Lake Forest— seventy-eight in all, and with the small dance she was giving herself, seventy-nine. Seventy-nine promises of gayety, seventy-nine offers to share fun with her. Patiently she sat down, choosing and weighing, referring doubtful cases to her mother.

"You seem a little white and tired," her mother said.

"I'm wasting away. I've been jilted."

"That won't worry you very long. I know my Josephine. Tonight at the Junior League german you'll meet the most marvelous men."

"No, I won't, mother. The only hope for me is to get married. I'll learn to love him and have his children and scratch his back——"

"Josephine!"

"I know two girls who married for love who told me they were supposed to scratch their husbands' backs and send out the laundry. But I'll go through with it, and the sooner the better."

"Every girl feels like that sometimes," said her mother cheerfully. "Before I was married I had three or four beaus, and I honestly liked each one of them as well as the others. Each one had certain qualities I liked, and I worried about it so long that it didn't seem worth while; I might as well have counted eenie, meenie, mynie, mo. Then one day when I was feeling lonely your father came to take me driving, and from that day I never had a single doubt. Love isn't like it is in books."

"But it is," said Josephine gloomily. "At least for me it always has been."

For the first time it seemed to her more peaceful to be with a crowd than to be alone with a man. The beginning of a line wearied her; how many lines had she listened to in three years? New men were pointed out as exciting, were introduced, and she took pleasure in freezing them to unhappiness with languid answers and wandering glances. Ancient admirers looked favorably upon the metamorphosis, grateful for a little overdue time at last. Josephine was glad when the holiday drew to a close. Returning from a luncheon one gray afternoon, the day after New Year's, she thought that for once it was nice to think she had nothing to do until dinner. Kicking off her overshoes in the hall, she found herself staring at something on the table that at first seemed a projection of her own imagination. It was a card fresh from a case—MR. EDWARD DICER.

Instantly the world jerked into life, spun around dizzily and came to rest on a new world. The hall where he must have stood throbbed with life; she pictured his straight figure against the open door, and thought how he must have stood with his hat and cane in hand. Outside the house, Chicago, permeated with his presence, pulsed with the old delight. She heard the phone ring in the downstairs lounge and, still in her fur coat, ran for it.

"Hello!"

"Miss Josephine, please."

"Oh, hello!"

"Oh. This is Edward Dicer."

"I saw your card."

"I must have just missed you."

What did the words matter when every word was winged and breathless?

"I'm only here for the day. Unfortunately, I'm tied up for dinner tonight with the people I'm visiting."

"Can you come over now?"

"If you like."

"Come right away."

She rushed upstairs to change her dress, singing for the first time in weeks. She sang:

> "Where's my shoes?
>   Where's my new gray shoes, shoes, shoes?
> I think I put them here,
>   But I guess—oh, where the deuce——"

Dressed, she was at the head of the stairs when the bell rang.

"Never mind," she called to the maid; "I'll answer."

She opened upon Mr. and Mrs. Warren Dillon. They were old friends and she hadn't seen them before, this Christmas.

"Josephine! We came to meet Constance here, but we hoped we'd have a glimpse of you; but you're rushing around so."

Aghast, she led the way into the library. "What time is sister meeting you?" she asked when she could.

"Oh, in half an hour, if she isn't delayed."

She tried to be especially polite, to atone in advance for what impoliteness might be necessary later. In five minutes the bell rang again; there was the romantic figure on the porch, cut sharp and clear against the bleak sky; and up the steps behind him came Travis de Coppet and Ed Bement.

"Stay!" she whispered quickly. "These people will all go."

"I've two hours," he said. "Of course, I'll wait if you want me to."

She wanted to throw her arms around him then, but she controlled herself, even her hands. She introduced everyone, she sent for tea. The men asked Edward Dicer questions about the war and he parried them politely but restlessly.

After half an hour he asked Josephine: "Have you the time? I must keep track of my train."

They might have noticed the watch on his own wrist and taken the hint, but he fascinated them all, as though they had isolated a rare specimen and were determined to find out all about it. Even had they realized Josephine's state of mind, it would have seemed to them that she was selfish to want something of such general interest for her own.

The arrival of Constance, her married sister, did not help matters; again Dicer was caught up into the phenomenon of human curiosity. As the clock in the hall struck six, he shot a desperate glance at Josephine. With a belated appreciation of the situation, the group broke itself up. Constance took the Dillons upstairs to the other sitting room, the two young men went home.

Silence, save for the voices fading off on the stairs, the automobile crunching away on the snow outside. Before a word was said, Josephine rang for the maid, and instructing her that she was not at home, closed the door into the hall. Then she went and sat down on the couch next to him and clasped her hands and waited.

"Thank God," he said. "I thought if they stayed another minute——"

"Wasn't it terrible?"

"I came out here because of you. The night you left New York I was ten minutes late getting to the train because I was detained at the French propaganda office. I'm not much good at letters. Since then I've thought of nothing but getting out here to see you."

"I felt sad." But not now; now she was thinking that in a moment she would be in his arms, feeling the buttons of his tunic press bruisingly against her, feeling his diagonal belt as something that bound them both and made her part of him. There were no doubts, no reservations, he was everything she wanted.

"I'm over here for six months more—perhaps a year. Then, if this damned war goes on, I'll have to go back. I suppose I haven't really got the right——"

"Wait—wait!" she cried. She wanted a moment longer to taste, to feel fully her happiness. "Wait," she repeated, putting her hand on his. She felt every object in the room vividly; she saw the seconds passing, each one carrying a load of loveliness toward the future. "All right; now tell me."

"Just that I love you," he whispered. She was in his arms, her hair against his cheek. "We haven't known each other long, and you're only eighteen, but I've learned to be afraid of waiting."

Now she leaned her head back until she was looking up at him, supported by his arm. Her neck curved gracefully, full and soft, and she leaned in toward his shoulder, as she knew how, so that her lips were every minute closer to him. "Now," she thought. He gave a funny little sigh and pulled her face up to his.

After a minute she leaned away from him and twisted herself upright.

"Darling—darling—darling," he said.

She looked at him, stared at him. Gently he pulled her over again and kissed her. This time, when she sat up, she rose and went across the room, where she opened a dish of almonds and dropped some in her mouth. Then she came back and sat beside him, looking straight ahead, then darting a sudden glance at him.

"What are you thinking, darling, darling Josephine?" She didn't answer; he put both hands over hers. "What are you feeling, then?"

As he breathed, she could hear the faint sound of his leather belt moving on his shoulder; she could feel his strong, kind handsome eyes looking at her; she could feel his proud self feeding on glory as others feed on security; she heard the jingle of spurs ring in his strong, rich, compelling voice.

"I feel nothing at all," she said.

"What do you mean?" He was startled.

"Oh, help me!" she cried. "Help me!"

"I don't understand what you mean."

"Kiss me again."

He kissed her. This time he held on to her and looked down into her face.

"What do you mean?" he demanded. "You mean you don't love me?"

"I don't feel anything."

"But you did love me."

"I don't know."

He let her go. She went across the room and sat down.

"I don't understand," he said after a minute.

"I think you're perfect," she said, her lips quivering.

"But I'm not—thrilling to you?"

"Oh, yes, very thrilling. I was thrilled all afternoon."

"Then what is it, darling?"

"I don't know. When you kissed me I wanted to laugh." It made her sick to say this, but a desperate, interior honesty drove her on. She saw his eyes change, saw him withdrawing a little from her. "Help me," she repeated.

"Help you how? You'll have to be more definite. I love you; I thought perhaps you loved me. That's all. If I don't please you——"

"But you do. You're everything—you're everything I've always wanted." Her voice continued inside herself: "But I've had everything."

"But you simply don't love me."

"I've got nothing to give you. I don't feel anything at all."

He got up abruptly. He felt her vast, tragic apathy pervading the room, and it set up an indifference in him now, too—a lot of things suddenly melted out of him.

"Good-by."

"You won't help me," she murmured abstractedly.

"How in the devil can I help you?" he answered impatiently. "You feel indifferent to me. You can't change that, but neither can I. Good-by."

"Good-by."

She was very tired and lay face downward on the couch with that awful, awful realization that all the old things are true. One cannot both spend and have. The love of her life had come by, and looking in her empty basket, she had found not a flower left for him—not one. After a while she wept.

"Oh, what have I done to myself?" she wailed. "What have I done? What have I done?"

THE BRIDAL PARTY

◆

"The Bridal Party" (Saturday Evening Post, *9 August 1930*) *was based on the May 1930 Paris wedding of Powell Fowler, the brother of Ludlow Fowler. (See "The Rich Boy.") An examination of the influence of money on character, it is the first Fitzgerald story that deals with the stock-market crash. "The Bridal Party" celebrates the end of the period when Paris was colonized by wealthy Americans.*

◆

THERE WAS THE usual insincere little note saying: "I wanted you to be the first to know." It was a double shock to Michael, announcing, as it did, both the engagement and the imminent marriage; which, moreover, was to be held, not in New York, decently and far away, but here in Paris under his very nose, if that could be said to extend over the Protestant Episcopal Church of the Holy Trinity, Avenue George-Cinq. The date was two weeks off, early in June.

At first Michael was afraid and his stomach felt hollow. When he left the hotel that morning, the *femme de chambre*, who was in love with his fine, sharp profile and his pleasant buoyancy, scented the hard abstraction that had settled over him. He walked in a daze to his bank, he bought a detective story at Smith's on the Rue de Rivoli, he sympathetically stared for a while at a faded panorama of the battlefields in a tourist-office window and cursed a Greek tout who followed him with a half-displayed packet of innocuous post cards warranted to be very dirty indeed.

But the fear stayed with him, and after a while he recognized it as the fear that now he would never be happy. He had met Caroline Dandy when she was seventeen, possessed her young heart all through her first season in New York, and then lost her, slowly, tragically, uselessly, because he had no money and could make no money; because, with all the energy and good will in the world, he could not find himself; because, loving him still, Caroline had lost faith and begun to see him as something pathetic, futile and shabby, outside the great, shining stream of life toward which she was inevitably drawn.

Since his only support was that she loved him, he leaned weakly on that; the support broke, but still he held on to it and was carried out to sea and washed up on the French coast with its broken pieces still in his hands. He carried them around with him in the form of photographs and packets of correspondence and a liking for a maudlin popular song called "Among My Souvenirs." He kept clear of other girls, as if Caroline would somehow know it and reciprocate with a faithful heart. Her note informed him that he had lost her forever.

It was a fine morning. In front of the shops in the Rue de Castiglione, proprietors and patrons were on the sidewalk gazing upward, for the Graf Zeppelin, shining and glorious, symbol of escape and destruction—of escape, if necessary, through destruction—glided in the Paris sky. He heard a woman say in French that it would not her astonish if that commenced to let fall the bombs. Then he heard another voice, full of husky laughter, and the void in his stomach froze. Jerking about, he was face to face with Caroline Dandy and her fiancé.

"Why, Michael! Why, we were wondering where you were. I asked at the Guaranty Trust, and Morgan and Company, and finally sent a note to the National City——"

Why didn't they back away? Why didn't they back right up, walking backward down the Rue de Castiglione, across the Rue de Rivoli, through the Tuileries Gardens, still walking backward as fast as they could till they grew vague and faded out across the river?

"This is Hamilton Rutherford, my fiancé."

"We've met before."

"At Pat's, wasn't it?"

"And last spring in the Ritz Bar."

"Michael, where have you been keeping yourself?"

"Around here." This agony. Previews of Hamilton Rutherford flashed before his eyes—a quick series of pictures, sentences. He remembered hearing that he had bought a seat in 1920 for a hundred and twenty-five thousand of borrowed money, and just before the break sold it for more than half a million. Not handsome like Michael, but vitally attractive, confident, authoritative, just the right height over Caroline there—Michael had always been too short for Caroline when they danced.

Rutherford was saying: "No, I'd like it very much if you'd come to the bachelor dinner. I'm taking the Ritz Bar from nine o'clock on. Then right after the wedding there'll be a reception and breakfast at the Hotel George-Cinq."

"And, Michael, George Packman is giving a party day after tomorrow at Chez Victor, and I want you to be sure and come. And also to tea Friday at Jebby West's; she'd want to have you if she knew where you were. What's your hotel, so we can send you an invitation? You see, the reason we decided to have it over here is because mother has been sick in a nursing home here and the whole clan is in Paris. Then Hamilton's mother's being here too——"

The entire clan; they had always hated him, except her mother; always discouraged his courtship. What a little counter he was in this game of families and money! Under his hat his brow sweated with the humiliation of the fact that for all his misery he was worth just exactly so many invitations. Frantically he began to mumble something about going away.

Then it happened—Caroline saw deep into him, and Michael knew that she saw. She saw through to his profound woundedness, and something quivered inside her, died out along the curve of her mouth and in her eyes. He had moved her. All the unforgettable impulses of first love had surged up once more; their hearts had in some way touched across two feet of Paris sunlight. She took her fiancé's arm suddenly, as if to steady herself with the feel of it.

They parted. Michael walked quickly for a minute; then he stopped, pretending to look in a window, and saw them farther up the street, walking fast into the Place Vendôme, people with much to do.

He had things to do also—he had to get his laundry.

"Nothing will ever be the same again," he said to himself. "She will never be happy in her marriage and I will never be happy at all any more."

The two vivid years of his love for Caroline moved back around him like years in Einstein's physics. Intolerable memories arose—of rides in the Long Island moonlight; of a happy time at Lake Placid with her cheeks so cold there, but warm just underneath the surface; of a despairing afternoon in a little café on Forty-eighth Street in the last sad months when their marriage had come to seem impossible.

"Come in," he said aloud.

The concierge with a telegram; brusque because Mr. Curly's clothes were a little shabby. Mr. Curly gave few tips; Mr. Curly was obviously a *petit client*.

Michael read the telegram.

"An answer?" the concierge asked.

"No," said Michael, and then, on an impulse: "Look."

"Too bad—too bad," said the concierge. "Your grandfather is dead."

"Not too bad," said Michael. "It means that I come into a quarter of a million dollars."

Too late by a single month; after the first flush of the news his misery was deeper than ever. Lying awake in bed that night, he listened endlessly to the long caravan of a circus moving through the street from one Paris fair to another.

When the last van had rumbled out of hearing and the corners of the furniture were pastel blue with the dawn, he was still thinking of the look in Caroline's eyes that morning—the look that seemed to say: "Oh, why couldn't you have done something about it? Why couldn't you have been stronger, made me marry you? Don't you see how sad I am?"

Michael's fists clenched.

"Well, I won't give up till the last moment," he whispered. "I've had all the bad luck so far, and maybe it's turned at last. One takes what one can get, up to the limit of one's strength, and if I can't have her, at least she'll go into this marriage with some of me in her heart."

· I I ·

ACCORDINGLY HE went to the party at Chez Victor two days later, upstairs and into the little salon off the bar where the party was to assemble for cocktails. He was early; the only other occupant was a tall lean man of fifty. They spoke.

"You waiting for George Packman's party?"

"Yes. My name's Michael Curly."

"My name's——"

Michael failed to catch the name. They ordered a drink, and Michael supposed that the bride and groom were having a gay time.

"Too much so," the other agreed, frowning. "I don't see how they stand it. We all crossed on the boat together; five days of that crazy life and then two weeks of Paris. You"—he hesitated, smiling faintly—"you'll excuse me for saying that your generation drinks too much."

"Not Caroline."

"No, not Caroline. She seems to take only a cocktail and a glass of champagne, and then she's had enough, thank God. But Hamilton drinks too much and all this crowd of young people drink too much. Do you live in Paris?"

"For the moment," said Michael.

"I don't like Paris. My wife—that is to say, my ex-wife, Hamilton's mother—lives in Paris."

"You're Hamilton Rutherford's father?"

"I have that honor. And I'm not denying that I'm proud of what he's done; it was just a general comment."

"Of course."

Michael glanced up nervously as four people came in. He felt suddenly that his dinner coat was old and shiny; he had ordered a new one that morning. The people who had come in were rich and at home in their richness with one another—a dark, lovely girl with a hysterical little laugh whom he had met before; two confident men whose jokes referred invariably to last night's scandal and tonight's potentialities, as if they had important rôles in a play that extended indefinitely into the past and the future. When Caroline arrived, Michael had scarcely a moment of her, but it was enough to note that, like all the others, she was strained and tired. She was pale beneath her rouge; there were shadows under her eyes. With a mixture of relief and wounded vanity, he found himself placed far from her and at another table; he needed a moment to adjust himself to his surroundings. This was not like the immature set in which he and Caroline had moved; the men were more than thirty and had an air of sharing the best of this world's good. Next to him was Jebby West, whom he knew; and, on the other side, a jovial man who immediately began to talk to Michael about a stunt for the bachelor dinner: They were going to hire a French girl to appear with an actual baby in her arms, crying: "Hamilton, you can't desert me now!" The idea seemed stale and unamusing to Michael, but its originator shook with anticipatory laughter.

Farther up the table there was talk of the market—another drop today, the most appreciable since the crash; people were kidding Rutherford about it: "Too bad, old man. You better not get married, after all."

Michael asked the man on his left, "Has he lost a lot?"

"Nobody knows. He's heavily involved, but he's one of the smartest young men in Wall Street. Anyhow, nobody ever tells you the truth."

It was a champagne dinner from the start, and toward the end it reached a pleasant level of conviviality, but Michael saw that all these people were too weary to be exhilarated by any ordinary stimulant; for weeks they had drunk cocktails before meals like Americans, wines and brandies like Frenchmen, beer like Germans, whisky-and-soda like the English, and as they were no longer in the twenties, this preposterous *mélange,* that was like some gigantic cocktail in a nightmare, served only to make them temporarily less conscious of the mistakes of the night before. Which is to say that it was not really a gay party; what gayety existed was displayed in the few who drank nothing at all.

But Michael was not tired, and the champagne stimulated him and made his misery less acute. He had been away from New York for more than eight months and most of the dance music was unfamiliar to him, but at the first bars of the "Painted Doll," to which he and Caroline had moved through so much happiness and despair the previous summer, he crossed to Caroline's table and asked her to dance.

She was lovely in a dress of thin ethereal blue, and the proximity of her crackly yellow hair, of her cool and tender gray eyes, turned his body clumsy and rigid; he stumbled with their first step on the floor. For a moment it seemed that there was nothing to say; he wanted to tell her about his inheritance, but the idea seemed abrupt, unprepared for.

"Michael, it's so nice to be dancing with you again."

He smiled grimly.

"I'm so happy you came," she continued. "I was afraid maybe you'd be silly and stay away. Now we can be just good friends and natural together. Michael, I want you and Hamilton to like each other."

The engagement was making her stupid; he had never heard her make such a series of obvious remarks before.

"I could kill him without a qualm," he said pleasantly, "but he looks like a good man. He's fine. What I want to know is, what happens to people like me who aren't able to forget?"

As he said this he could not prevent his mouth from dropping suddenly, and glancing up, Caroline saw, and her heart quivered violently, as it had the other morning.

"Do you mind so much, Michael?"

"Yes."

For a second as he said this, in a voice that seemed to have come up from his shoes, they were not dancing; they were simply clinging together. Then she leaned away from him and twisted her mouth into a lovely smile.

"I didn't know what to do at first, Michael. I told Hamilton about you —that I'd cared for you an awful lot—but it didn't worry him, and he was right. Because I'm over you now—yes, I am. And you'll wake up some sunny morning and be over me just like that."

He shook his head stubbornly.

"Oh, yes. We weren't for each other. I'm pretty flighty, and I need somebody like Hamilton to decide things. It was that more than the question of—of——"

"Of money." Again he was on the point of telling her what had happened, but again something told him it was not the time.

"Then how do you account for what happened when we met the other day," he demanded helplessly—"what happened just now? When we just pour toward each other like we used to—as if we were one person, as if the same blood was flowing through both of us?"

"Oh, don't," she begged him. "You mustn't talk like that; everything's decided now. I love Hamilton with all my heart. It's just that I remember certain things in the past and I feel sorry for you—for us—for the way we were."

Over her shoulder, Michael saw a man come toward them to cut in. In a panic he danced her away, but inevitably the man came on.

"I've got to see you alone, if only for a minute," Michael said quickly. "When can I?"

"I'll be at Jebby West's tea tomorrow," she whispered as a hand fell politely upon Michael's shoulder.

But he did not talk to her at Jebby West's tea. Rutherford stood next to her, and each brought the other into all conversations. They left early. The next morning the wedding cards arrived in the first mail.

Then Michael, grown desperate with pacing up and down his room, determined on a bold stroke; he wrote to Hamilton Rutherford, asking him for a rendezvous the following afternoon. In a short telephone communication Rutherford agreed, but for a day later than Michael had asked. And the wedding was only six days away.

They were to meet in the bar of the Hotel Jena. Michael knew what he would say: "See here, Rutherford, do you realize the responsibility you're taking in going through with this marriage? Do you realize the harvest of trouble and regret you're sowing in persuading a girl into something contrary to the instincts of her heart?" He would explain that the barrier between Caroline and himself had been an artificial one and was now removed, and demand that the matter be put up to Caroline frankly before it was too late.

Rutherford would be angry, conceivably there would be a scene, but Michael felt that he was fighting for his life now.

He found Rutherford in conversation with an older man, whom Michael had met at several of the wedding parties.

"I saw what happened to most of my friends," Rutherford was saying, "and I decided it wasn't going to happen to me. It isn't so difficult; if you take a girl with common sense, and tell her what's what, and do your stuff damn well, and play decently square with her, it's a marriage. If you stand for any nonsense at the beginning, it's one of these arrangements—within five years the man gets out, or else the girl gobbles him up and you have the usual mess."

"Right!" agreed his companion enthusiastically. "Hamilton, boy, you're right."

Michael's blood boiled slowly.

"Doesn't it strike you," he inquired coldly, "that your attitude went out of fashion about a hundred years ago?"

"No, it didn't," said Rutherford pleasantly, but impatiently. "I'm as modern as anybody. I'd get married in an aeroplane next Saturday if it'd please my girl."

"I don't mean that way of being modern. You can't take a sensitive woman——"

"Sensitive? Women aren't so darn sensitive. It's fellows like you who are sensitive; it's fellows like you they exploit—all your devotion and kindness and all that. They read a couple of books and see a few pictures because they haven't got anything else to do, and then they say they're finer in grain than you are, and to prove it they take the bit in their teeth and tear off for a fare-you-well—just about as sensitive as a fire horse."

"Caroline happens to be sensitive," said Michael in a clipped voice.

At this point the other man got up to go; when the dispute about the check had been settled and they were alone, Rutherford leaned back to Michael as if a question had been asked him.

"Caroline's more than sensitive," he said. "She's got sense."

His combative eyes, meeting Michael's, flickered with a gray light. "This all sounds pretty crude to you, Mr. Curly, but it seems to me that the average man nowadays just asks to be made a monkey of by some woman who doesn't even get any fun out of reducing him to that level. There are darn few men who possess their wives any more, but I am going to be one of them."

To Michael it seemed time to bring the talk back to the actual situation: "Do you realize the responsibility you're taking?"

"I certainly do," interrupted Rutherford. "I'm not afraid of responsibility. I'll make the decisions—fairly, I hope, but anyhow they'll be final."

"What if you didn't start right?" said Michael impetuously. "What if your marriage isn't founded on mutual love?"

"I think I see what you mean," Rutherford said, still pleasant. "And since you've brought it up, let me say that if you and Caroline had married, it wouldn't have lasted three years. Do you know what your affair was founded on? On sorrow. You got sorry for each other. Sorrow's a lot of fun for most women and for some men, but it seems to me that a marriage ought to be based on hope." He looked at his watch and stood up.

"I've got to meet Caroline. Remember, you're coming to the bachelor dinner day after tomorrow."

Michael felt the moment slipping away. "Then Caroline's personal feelings don't count with you?" he demanded fiercely.

"Caroline's tired and upset. But she has what she wants, and that's the main thing."

"Are you referring to yourself?" demanded Michael incredulously.

"Yes."

"May I ask how long she's wanted you?"

"About two years." Before Michael could answer, he was gone.

During the next two days Michael floated in an abyss of helplessness. The idea haunted him that he had left something undone that would sever this knot drawn tighter under his eyes. He phoned Caroline, but she insisted that it was physically impossible for her to see him until the day before the wedding, for which day she granted him a tentative rendezvous. Then he went to the bachelor dinner, partly in fear of an evening alone at his hotel, partly from a feeling that by his presence at that function he was somehow nearer to Caroline, keeping her in sight.

The Ritz Bar had been prepared for the occasion by French and American banners and by a great canvas covering one wall, against which the guests were invited to concentrate their proclivities in breaking glasses.

At the first cocktail, taken at the bar, there were many slight spillings from many trembling hands, but later, with the champagne, there was a rising tide of laughter and occasional bursts of song.

Michael was surprised to find what a difference his new dinner coat, his new silk hat, his new, proud linen made in his estimate of himself; he felt less resentment toward all these people for being so rich and assured. For the first time since he had left college he felt rich and assured himself; he felt that he was part of all this, and even entered into the scheme of Johnson, the practical joker, for the appearance of the woman betrayed, now waiting tranquilly in the room across the hall.

"We don't want to go too heavy," Johnson said, "because I imagine Ham's had a pretty anxious day already. Did you see Fullman Oil's sixteen points off this morning?"

"Will that matter to him?" Michael asked, trying to keep the interest out of his voice.

"Naturally. He's in heavily; he's always in everything heavily. So far he's had luck; anyhow, up to a month ago."

The glasses were filled and emptied faster now, and men were shouting at one another across the narrow table. Against the bar a group of ushers was being photographed, and the flash light surged through the room in a stifling cloud.

"Now's the time," Johnson said. "You're to stand by the door, remember, and we're both to try and keep her from coming in—just till we get everybody's attention."

He went on out into the corridor, and Michael waited obediently by the door. Several minutes passed. Then Johnson reappeared with a curious expression on his face.

"There's something funny about this."

"Isn't the girl there?"

"She's there all right, but there's another woman there, too; and it's nobody we engaged either. She wants to see Hamilton Rutherford, and she looks as if she had something on her mind."

They went out into the hall. Planted firmly in a chair near the door sat an American girl a little the worse for liquor, but with a determined expression on her face. She looked up at them with a jerk of her head.

"Well, j'tell him?" she demanded. "The name is Marjorie Collins, and he'll know it. I've come a long way, and I want to see him now and quick, or there's going to be more trouble than you ever saw." She rose unsteadily to her feet.

"You go in and tell Ham," whispered Johnson to Michael. "Maybe he'd better get out. I'll keep her here."

Back at the table, Michael leaned close to Rutherford's ear and, with a certain grimness, whispered:

"A girl outside named Marjorie Collins says she wants to see you. She looks as if she wanted to make trouble."

Hamilton Rutherford blinked and his mouth fell ajar; then slowly the lips came together in a straight line and he said in a crisp voice:

"Please keep her there. And send the head barman to me right away."

Michael spoke to the barman, and then, without returning to the table, asked quietly for his coat and hat. Out in the hall again, he passed Johnson and the girl without speaking and went out into the Rue Cambon. Calling a cab, he gave the address of Caroline's hotel.

His place was beside her now. Not to bring bad news, but simply to be with her when her house of cards came falling around her head.

Rutherford had implied that he was soft—well, he was hard enough not to give up the girl he loved without taking advantage of every chance within the pale of honor. Should she turn away from Rutherford, she would find him there.

She was in; she was surprised when he called, but she was still dressed and would be down immediately. Presently she appeared in a dinner gown, holding two blue telegrams in her hand. They sat down in armchairs in the deserted lobby.

"But, Michael, is the dinner over?"

"I wanted to see you, so I came away."

"I'm glad." Her voice was friendly, but matter-of-fact. "Because I'd just phoned your hotel that I had fittings and rehearsals all day tomorrow. Now we can have our talk after all."

"You're tired," he guessed. "Perhaps I shouldn't have come."

"No. I was waiting up for Hamilton. Telegrams that may be important. He said he might go on somewhere, and that may mean any hour, so I'm glad I have someone to talk to."

Michael winced at the impersonality in the last phrase.

"Don't you care when he gets home?"

"Naturally," she said, laughing, "but I haven't got much say about it, have I?"

"Why not?"

"I couldn't start by telling him what he could and couldn't do."

"Why not?"

"He wouldn't stand for it."

"He seems to want merely a housekeeper," said Michael ironically.

"Tell me about your plans, Michael," she asked quickly.

"My plans? I can't see any future after the day after tomorrow. The only real plan I ever had was to love you."

Their eyes brushed past each other's, and the look he knew so well was staring out at him from hers. Words flowed quickly from his heart:

"Let me tell you just once more how well I've loved you, never wavering for a moment, never thinking of another girl. And now when I think of all the years ahead without you, without any hope, I don't want to live, Caroline darling. I used to dream about our home, our children, about holding you in my arms and touching your face and hands and hair that used to belong to me, and now I just can't wake up."

Caroline was crying softly. "Poor Michael—poor Michael." Her hand reached out and her fingers brushed the lapel of his dinner coat. "I was so sorry for you the other night. You looked so thin, and as if you needed a new suit and somebody to take care of you." She sniffled and looked more closely at his coat. "Why, you've got a new suit! And a new silk hat! Why, Michael, how swell!" She laughed, suddenly cheerful through her tears. "You must have come into money, Michael; I never saw you so well turned out."

For a moment, at her reaction, he hated his new clothes.

"I have come into money," he said. "My grandfather left me about a quarter of a million dollars."

"Why, Michael," she cried, "how perfectly swell! I can't tell you how glad I am. I've always thought you were the sort of person who ought to have money."

"Yes, just too late to make a difference."

The revolving door from the street groaned around and Hamilton Rutherford came into the lobby. His face was flushed, his eyes were restless and impatient.

"Hello, darling; hello, Mr. Curly." He bent and kissed Caroline. "I broke away for a minute to find out if I had any telegrams. I see you've got them there." Taking them from her, he remarked to Curly, "That was an odd business there in the bar, wasn't it? Especially as I understand some of you had a joke fixed up in the same line." He opened one of the telegrams, closed it and turned to Caroline with the divided expression of a man carrying two things in his head at once.

"A girl I haven't seen for two years turned up," he said. "It seemed to be some clumsy form of blackmail, for I haven't and never have had any sort of obligation toward her whatever."

"What happened?"

"The head barman had a Sûreté Générale man there in ten minutes and it was settled in the hall. The French blackmail laws make ours look like a sweet wish, and I gather they threw a scare into her that she'll remember. But it seems wiser to tell you."

"Are you implying that I mentioned the matter?" said Michael stiffly.

"No," Rutherford said slowly. "No, you were just going to be on hand. And since you're here, I'll tell you some news that will interest you even more."

He handed Michael one telegram and opened the other.

"This is in code," Michael said.

"So is this. But I've got to know all the words pretty well this last week. The two of them together mean that I'm due to start life all over."

Michael saw Caroline's face grow a shade paler, but she sat quiet as a mouse.

"It was a mistake and I stuck to it too long," continued Rutherford. "So you see I don't have all the luck, Mr. Curly. By the way, they tell me you've come into money."

"Yes," said Michael.

"There we are, then." Rutherford turned to Caroline. "You understand, darling, that I'm not joking or exaggerating. I've lost almost every cent I had and I'm starting life over."

Two pairs of eyes were regarding her—Rutherford's noncommittal and unrequiring, Michael's hungry, tragic, pleading. In a minute she had raised herself from the chair and with a little cry thrown herself into Hamilton Rutherford's arms.

"Oh, darling," she cried, "what does it matter! It's better; I like it better,

honestly I do! I want to start that way; I want to! Oh, please don't worry
or be sad even for a minute!"

"All right, baby," said Rutherford. His hand stroked her hair gently for
a moment; then he took his arm from around her.

"I promised to join the party for an hour," he said. "So I'll say good
night, and I want you to go to bed soon and get a good sleep. Good night,
Mr. Curly. I'm sorry to have let you in for all these financial matters."

But Michael had already picked up his hat and cane. "I'll go along with
you," he said.

· III ·

IT WAS SUCH a fine morning. Michael's cutaway hadn't been delivered, so
he felt rather uncomfortable passing before the cameras and moving-picture
machines in front of the little church on the Avenue George-Cinq.

It was such a clean, new church that it seemed unforgivable not to be
dressed properly, and Michael, white and shaky after a sleepless night,
decided to stand in the rear. From there he looked at the back of Hamilton
Rutherford, and the lacy, filmy back of Caroline, and the fat back of George
Packman, which looked unsteady, as if it wanted to lean against the bride
and groom.

The ceremony went on for a long time under the gay flags and pennons
overhead, under the thick beams of June sunlight slanting down through
the tall windows upon the well-dressed people.

As the procession, headed by the bride and groom, started down the aisle,
Michael realized with alarm he was just where everyone would dispense
with their parade stiffness, become informal and speak to him.

So it turned out. Rutherford and Caroline spoke first to him; Rutherford
grim with the strain of being married, and Caroline lovelier than he had ever
seen her, floating all softly down through the friends and relatives of her
youth, down through the past and forward to the future by the sunlit door.

Michael managed to murmur, "Beautiful, simply beautiful," and then
other people passed and spoke to him—old Mrs. Dandy, straight from her
sickbed and looking remarkably well, or carrying it off like the very fine
old lady she was; and Rutherford's father and mother, ten years divorced,
but walking side by side and looking made for each other and proud. Then
all Caroline's sisters and their husbands and her little nephews in Eton suits,
and then a long parade, all speaking to Michael because he was still standing
paralyzed just at that point where the procession broke.

He wondered what would happen now. Cards had been issued for a reception at the George-Cinq; an expensive enough place, heaven knew. Would Rutherford try to go through with that on top of those disastrous telegrams? Evidently, for the procession outside was streaming up there through the June morning, three by three and four by four. On the corner the long dresses of girls, five abreast, fluttered many-colored in the wind. Girls had become gossamer again, perambulatory flora; such lovely fluttering dresses in the bright noon wind.

Michael needed a drink; he couldn't face that reception line without a drink. Diving into a side doorway of the hotel, he asked for the bar, whither a *chasseur* led him through half a kilometer of new American-looking passages.

But—how did it happen?—the bar was full. There were ten—fifteen men and two—four girls, all from the wedding, all needing a drink. There were cocktails and champagne in the bar; Rutherford's cocktails and champagne, as it turned out, for he had engaged the whole bar and the ballroom and the two great reception rooms and all the stairways leading up and down, and windows looking out over the whole square block of Paris. By and by Michael went and joined the long, slow drift of the receiving line. Through a flowery mist of "Such a lovely wedding," "My dear, you were simply lovely," "You're a lucky man, Rutherford" he passed down the line. When Michael came to Caroline, she took a single step forward and kissed him on the lips, but he felt no contact in the kiss; it was unreal and he floated on away from it. Old Mrs. Dandy, who had always liked him, held his hand for a minute and thanked him for the flowers he had sent when he heard she was ill.

"I'm so sorry not to have written; you know, we old ladies are grateful for——" The flowers, the fact that she had not written, the wedding— Michael saw that they all had the same relative importance to her now; she had married off five other children and seen two of the marriages go to pieces, and this scene, so poignant, so confusing to Michael, appeared to her simply a familiar charade in which she had played her part before.

A buffet luncheon with champagne was already being served at small tables and there was an orchestra playing in the empty ballroom. Michael sat down with Jebby West; he was still a little embarrassed at not wearing a morning coat, but he perceived now that he was not alone in the omission and felt better. "Wasn't Caroline divine?" Jebby West said. "So entirely self-possessed. I asked her this morning if she wasn't a little nervous at stepping off like this. And she said, 'Why should I be? I've been after him for two years, and now I'm just happy, that's all.' "

"It must be true," said Michael gloomily.

"What?"

"What you just said."

He had been stabbed, but, rather to his distress, he did not feel the wound.

He asked Jebby to dance. Out on the floor, Rutherford's father and mother were dancing together.

"It makes me a little sad, that," she said. "Those two hadn't met for years; both of them were married again and she divorced again. She went to the station to meet him when he came over for Caroline's wedding, and invited him to stay at her house in the Avenue du Bois with a whole lot of other people, perfectly proper, but he was afraid his wife would hear about it and not like it, so he went to a hotel. Don't you think that's sort of sad?"

An hour or so later Michael realized suddenly that it was afternoon. In one corner of the ballroom an arrangement of screens like a moving-picture stage had been set up and photographers were taking official pictures of the bridal party. The bridal party, still as death and pale as wax under the bright lights, appeared, to the dancers circling the modulated semidarkness of the ballroom, like those jovial or sinister groups that one comes upon in The Old Mill at an amusement park.

After the bridal party had been photographed, there was a group of the ushers; then the bridesmaids, the families, the children. Later, Caroline, active and excited, having long since abandoned the repose implicit in her flowing dress and great bouquet, came and plucked Michael off the floor.

"Now we'll have them take one of just old friends." Her voice implied that this was best, most intimate of all. "Come here, Jebby, George—not you, Hamilton; this is just my friends—Sally——"

A little after that, what remained of formality disappeared and the hours flowed easily down the profuse stream of champagne. In the modern fashion, Hamilton Rutherford sat at the table with his arm about an old girl of his and assured his guests, which included not a few bewildered but enthusiastic Europeans, that the party was not nearly at an end; it was to reassemble at Zelli's after midnight. Michael saw Mrs. Dandy, not quite over her illness, rise to go and become caught in polite group after group, and he spoke of it to one of her daughters, who thereupon forcibly abducted her mother and called her car. Michael felt very considerate and proud of himself after having done this, and drank much more champagne.

"It's amazing," George Packman was telling him enthusiastically. "This show will cost Ham about five thousand dollars, and I understand they'll be just about his last. But did he countermand a bottle of champagne or a flower? Not he! He happens to have it—that young man. Do you know that T. G. Vance offered him a salary of fifty thousand dollars a year ten minutes before the wedding this morning? In another year he'll be back with the millionaires."

The conversation was interrupted by a plan to carry Rutherford out on communal shoulders—a plan which six of them put into effect, and then stood in the four-o'clock sunshine waving good-by to the bride and groom. But there must have been a mistake somewhere, for five minutes later Michael saw both bride and groom descending the stairway to the reception, each with a glass of champagne held defiantly on high.

"This is our way of doing things," he thought. "Generous and fresh and free; a sort of Virginia-plantation hospitality, but at a different pace now, nervous as a ticker tape."

Standing unself-consciously in the middle of the room to see which was the American ambassador, he realized with a start that he hadn't really thought of Caroline for hours. He looked about him with a sort of alarm, and then he saw her across the room, very bright and young, and radiantly happy. He saw Rutherford near her, looking at her as if he could never look long enough, and as Michael watched them they seemed to recede as he had wished them to do that day in the Rue de Castiglione—recede and fade off into joys and griefs of their own, into the years that would take the toll of Rutherford's fine pride and Caroline's young, moving beauty; fade far away, so that now he could scarcely see them, as if they were shrouded in something as misty as her white, billowing dress.

Michael was cured. The ceremonial function, with its pomp and its revelry, had stood for a sort of initiation into a life where even his regret could not follow them. All the bitterness melted out of him suddenly and the world reconstituted itself out of the youth and happiness that was all around him, profligate as the spring sunshine. He was trying to remember which one of the bridesmaids he had made a date to dine with tonight as he walked forward to bid Hamilton and Caroline Rutherford good-by.

ONE TRIP ABROAD

♦

"One Trip Abroad" first appeared in the Saturday Evening Post *(11 October 1930). Fitzgerald did not collect this brilliant story because he drew heavily on it in* Tender Is the Night. *"One Trip Abroad" is one of the stories in which he assessed the expatriate experience—as in "The Swimmers" and "Babylon Revisited." In contradiction to the fashionable Twenties view that life was richer abroad, Fitzgerald's Americans are damaged by Europe: "Switzerland is a country where very few things begin, but many things end." This story was written during Zelda Fitzgerald's hospitalization in Switzerland following her mental collapse. It belongs with a group of self-judging, retrospective stories written during the Thirties in response to Fitzgerald's marital, health, and career problems. "One Trip Abroad" has been particularly admired for Fitzgerald's effective adaptation of the Doppelgänger device (the other couple who double for the Kellys).*

♦

IN THE AFTERNOON the air became black with locusts, and some of the women shrieked, sinking to the floor of the motorbus and covering their hair with traveling rugs. The locusts were coming north, eating everything in their path, which was not so much in that part of the world; they were flying silently and in straight lines, flakes of black snow. But none struck the windshield or tumbled into the car, and presently humorists began holding out their hands, trying to catch some. After ten minutes the cloud thinned out, passed, and the women emerged from the blankets, disheveled and feeling silly. And everyone talked together.

Everyone talked; it would have been absurd not to talk after having been through a swarm of locusts on the edge of the Sahara. The Smyrna-American talked to the British widow going down to Biskra to have one last fling with an as-yet-unencountered sheik. The member of the San Francisco Stock Exchange talked shyly to the author. "Aren't you an author?" he said. The father and daughter from Wilmington talked to the cockney airman who was going to fly to Timbuctoo. Even the French chauffeur turned about and explained in a loud, clear voice: "Bumblebees," which sent the trained nurse from New York into shriek after shriek of hysterical laughter.

Amongst the unsubtle rushing together of the travelers there was one interchange more carefully considered. Mr. and Mrs. Liddell Miles, turning as one person, smiled and spoke to the young American couple in the seat behind:

"Didn't catch any in your hair?"

The young couple smiled back politely.

"No. We survived that plague."

They were in their twenties, and there was still a pleasant touch of bride and groom upon them. A handsome couple; the man rather intense and sensitive, the girl arrestingly light of hue in eyes and hair, her face without shadows, its living freshness modulated by a lovely confident calm. Mr. and Mrs. Miles did not fail to notice their air of good breeding, of a specifically "swell" background, expressed both by their unsophistication and by their ingrained reticence that was not stiffness. If they held aloof, it was because they were sufficient to each other, while Mr. and Mrs. Miles' aloofness toward the other passengers was a conscious mask, a social attitude, quite as public an affair in its essence as the ubiquitous advances of the Smyrna-American, who was snubbed by all.

The Mileses had, in fact, decided that the young couple were "possible" and, bored with themselves, were frankly approaching them.

"Have you been to Africa before? It's been so utterly fascinating! Are you going on to Tunis?"

The Mileses, if somewhat worn away inside by fifteen years of a particular set in Paris, had undeniable style, even charm, and before the evening arrival at the little oasis town of Bou Saada they had all four become companionable. They uncovered mutual friends in New York and, meeting for a cocktail in the bar of the Hotel Transatlantique, decided to have dinner together.

As the young Kellys came downstairs later, Nicole was conscious of a certain regret that they had accepted, realizing that now they were probably committed to seeing a certain amount of their new acquaintances as far as Constantine, where their routes diverged.

In the eight months of their marriage she had been so very happy that it seemed like spoiling something. On the Italian liner that had brought them to Gibraltar they had not joined the groups that leaned desperately on one another in the bar; instead, they seriously studied French, and Nelson worked on business contingent on his recent inheritance of half a million dollars. Also he painted a picture of a smokestack. When one member of the gay crowd in the bar disappeared permanently into the Atlantic just this side of the Azores, the young Kellys were almost glad, for it justified their aloof attitude.

But there was another reason Nicole was sorry they had committed themselves. She spoke to Nelson about it: "I passed that couple in the hall just now."

"Who—the Mileses?"

"No, that young couple—about our age—the ones that were on the other motorbus, that we thought looked so nice, in Bir Rabalou after lunch, in the camel market."

"They did look nice."

"Charming," she said emphatically; "the girl and man, both. I'm almost sure I've met the girl somewhere before."

The couple referred to were sitting across the room at dinner, and Nicole found her eyes drawn irresistibly toward them. They, too, now had companions, and again Nicole, who had not talked to a girl of her own age for two months, felt a faint regret. The Mileses, being formally sophisticated and frankly snobbish, were a different matter. They had been to an alarming number of places and seemed to know all the flashing phantoms of the newspapers.

They dined on the hotel veranda under a sky that was low and full of the presence of a strange and watchful God; around the corners of the hotel the night already stirred with the sounds of which they had so often read but that were even so hysterically unfamiliar—drums from Senegal, a native flute, the selfish, effeminate whine of a camel, the Arabs pattering past in shoes made of old automobile tires, the wail of Magian prayer.

At the desk in the hotel, a fellow passenger was arguing monotonously with the clerk about the rate of exchange, and the inappropriateness added to the detachment which had increased steadily as they went south.

Mrs. Miles was the first to break the lingering silence; with a sort of impatience she pulled them with her, in from the night and up to the table.

"We really should have dressed. Dinner's more amusing if people dress, because they feel differently in formal clothes. The English know that."

"Dress here?" her husband objected. "I'd feel like that man in the ragged dress suit we passed today, driving the flock of sheep."

"I always feel like a tourist if I'm not dressed."

"Well, we are, aren't we?" asked Nelson.

"I don't consider myself a tourist. A tourist is somebody who gets up early and goes to cathedrals and talks about scenery."

Nicole and Nelson, having seen all the official sights from Fez to Algiers, and taken reels of moving pictures and felt improved, confessed themselves, but decided that their experiences on the trip would not interest Mrs. Miles.

"Every place is the same," Mrs. Miles continued. "The only thing that matters is who's there. New scenery is fine for half an hour, but after that you want your own kind to see. That's why some places have a certain vogue, and then the vogue changes and the people move on somewhere else. The place itself really never matters."

"But doesn't somebody first decide that the place is nice?" objected Nelson. "The first ones go there because they like the place."

"Where were you going this spring?" Mrs. Miles asked.

"We thought of San Remo, or maybe Sorrento. We've never been to Europe before."

"My children, I know both Sorrento and San Remo, and you won't stand either of them for a week. They're full of the most awful English, reading the Daily Mail and waiting for letters and talking about the most incredibly dull things. You might as well go to Brighton or Bournemouth and buy a white poodle and a sunshade and walk on the pier. How long are you staying in Europe?"

"We don't know; perhaps several years." Nicole hesitated. "Nelson came into a little money, and we wanted a change. When I was young, my father had asthma and I had to live in the most depressing health resorts with him for years; and Nelson was in the fur business in Alaska and he loathed it; so when we were free we came abroad. Nelson's going to paint and I'm going to study singing." She looked triumphantly at her husband. "So far, it's been absolutely gorgeous."

Mrs. Miles decided, from the evidence of the younger woman's clothes, that it was quite a bit of money, and their enthusiasm was infectious.

"You really must go to Biarritz," she advised them. "Or else come to Monte Carlo."

"They tell me there's a great show here," said Miles, ordering champagne. "The Ouled Naïls. The concierge says they're some kind of tribe of girls who come down from the mountains and learn to be dancers, and what not, till they've collected enough gold to go back to their mountains and marry. Well, they give a performance tonight."

Walking over to the Café of the Ouled Naïls afterward, Nicole regretted that she and Nelson were not strolling alone through the ever-lower, ever-softer, ever-brighter night. Nelson had reciprocated the bottle of champagne at dinner, and neither of them was accustomed to so much. As they drew near the sad flute she didn't want to go inside, but rather to climb to the top of a low hill where a white mosque shone clear as a planet through the night. Life was better than any show; closing in toward Nelson, she pressed his hand.

The little cave of a café was filled with the passengers from the two busses.

The girls—light-brown, flat-nosed Berbers with fine, deep-shaded eyes—were already doing each one her solo on the platform. They wore cotton dresses, faintly reminiscent of Southern mammies; under these their bodies writhed in a slow nautch, culminating in a stomach dance, with silver belts bobbing wildly and their strings of real gold coins tinkling on their necks and arms. The flute player was also a comedian; he danced, burlesquing the girls. The drummer, swathed in goatskins like a witch doctor, was a true black from the Sudan.

Through the smoke of cigarettes each girl went in turn through the finger movement, like piano playing in the air—outwardly facile, yet, after a few moments, so obviously exacting—and then through the very simply languid yet equally precise steps of the feet—these were but preparation to the wild sensuality of the culminated dance.

Afterward there was a lull. Though the performance seemed not quite over, most of the audience gradually got up to go, but there was a whispering in the air.

"What is it?" Nicole asked her husband.

"Why, I believe—it appears that for a consideration the Ouled Naïls dance in more or less—ah—Oriental style—in very little except jewelry."

"Oh."

"We're all staying," Mr. Miles assured her jovially. "After all, we're here to see the real customs and manners of the country; a little prudishness shouldn't stand in our way."

Most of the men remained, and several of the women. Nicole stood up suddenly.

"I'll wait outside," she said.

"Why not stay, Nicole? After all, Mrs. Miles is staying."

The flute player was making preliminary flourishes. Upon the raised dais two pale brown children of perhaps fourteen were taking off their cotton dresses. For an instant Nicole hesitated, torn between repulsion and the desire not to appear to be a prig. Then she saw another young American woman get up quickly and start for the door. Recognizing the attractive young wife from the other bus, her own decision came quickly and she followed.

Nelson hurried after her. "I'm going if you go," he said, but with evident reluctance.

"Please don't bother. I'll wait with the guide outside."

"Well—" The drum was starting. He compromised: "I'll only stay a minute. I want to see what it's like."

Waiting in the fresh night, she found that the incident had hurt her—Nelson's not coming with her at once, giving as an argument the fact that

Mrs. Miles was staying. From being hurt, she grew angry and made signs to the guide that she wanted to return to the hotel.

Twenty minutes later, Nelson appeared, angry with the anxiety at finding her gone, as well as to hide his guilt at having left her. Incredulous with themselves, they were suddenly in a quarrel.

Much later, when there were no sounds at all in Bou Saada and the nomads in the market place were only motionless bundles rolled up in their burnouses, she was asleep upon his shoulder. Life is progressive, no matter what our intentions, but something was harmed, some precedent of possible nonagreement was set. It was a love match, though, and it could stand a great deal. She and Nelson had passed lonely youths, and now they wanted the taste and smell of the living world; for the present they were finding it in each other.

A month later they were in Sorrento, where Nicole took singing lessons and Nelson tried to paint something new into the Bay of Naples. It was the existence they had planned and often read about. But they found, as so many have found, that the charm of idyllic interludes depends upon one person's "giving the party"—which is to say, furnishing the background, the experience, the patience, against which the other seems to enjoy again the spells of pastoral tranquillity recollected from childhood. Nicole and Nelson were at once too old and too young, and too American, to fall into immediate soft agreement with a strange land. Their vitality made them restless, for as yet his painting had no direction and her singing no immediate prospect of becoming serious. They said they were not "getting anywhere"—the evenings were long, so they began to drink a lot of *vin de Capri* at dinner.

The English owned the hotel. They were aged, come South for good weather and tranquillity; Nelson and Nicole resented the mild tenor of their days. Could people be content to talk eternally about the weather, promenade the same walks, face the same variant of macaroni at dinner month after month? They grew bored, and Americans bored are already in sight of excitement. Things came to head all in one night.

Over a flask of wine at dinner they decided to go to Paris, settle in an apartment and work seriously. Paris promised metropolitan diversion, friends of their own age, a general intensity that Italy lacked. Eager with new hopes, they strolled into the salon after dinner, when, for the tenth time, Nelson noticed an ancient and enormous mechanical piano and was moved to try it.

Across the salon sat the only English people with whom they had had any connection—Gen. Sir Evelyne Fragelle and Lady Fragelle. The connection had been brief and unpleasant—seeing them walking out of the hotel in peignoirs to swim, she had announced, over quite a few yards of floor space, that it was disgusting and shouldn't be allowed.

But that was nothing compared with her response to the first terrific bursts of sound from the electric piano. As the dust of years trembled off the keyboard at the vibration, she shot galvanically forward with the sort of jerk associated with the electric chair. Somewhat stunned himself by the sudden din of Waiting for the Robert E. Lee, Nelson had scarcely sat down when she projected herself across the room, her train quivering behind her, and, without glancing at the Kellys, turned off the instrument.

It was one of those gestures that are either plainly justified, or else outrageous. For a moment Nelson hesitated uncertainly; then, remembering Lady Fragelle's arrogant remark about his bathing suit, he returned to the instrument in her still-billowing wake and turned it on again.

The incident had become international. The eyes of the entire salon fell eagerly upon the protagonists, watching for the next move. Nicole hurried after Nelson, urging him to let the matter pass, but it was too late. From the outraged English table there arose, joint by joint, Gen. Sir Evelyne Fragelle, faced with perhaps his most crucial situation since the relief of Ladysmith.

" 'T'lee outrageous!—'t'lee outrageous!"

"I beg your pardon," said Nelson.

"Here for fifteen years!" screamed Sir Evelyne to himself. "Never heard of anyone doing such a thing before!"

"I gathered that this was put here for the amusement of the guests."

Scorning to answer, Sir Evelyne knelt, reached for the catch, pushed it the wrong way, whereupon the speed and volume of the instrument tripled until they stood in a wild pandemonium of sound; Sir Evelyne livid with military emotions, Nelson on the point of maniacal laughter.

In a moment the firm hand of the hotel manager settled the matter; the instrument gulped and stopped, trembling a little from its unaccustomed outburst, leaving behind it a great silence in which Sir Evelyne turned to the manager.

"Most outrageous affair ever heard of in my life. My wife turned it off once, and he"—this was his first acknowledgment of Nelson's identity as distinct from the instrument—"he put it on again!"

"This is a public room in a hotel," Nelson protested. "The instrument is apparently here to be used."

"Don't get in an argument," Nicole whispered. "They're old."

But Nelson said, "If there's any apology, it's certainly due to me."

Sir Evelyne's eye was fixed menacingly upon the manager, waiting for him to do his duty. The latter thought of Sir Evelyne's fifteen years of residence, and cringed.

"It is not the habitude to play the instrument in the evening. The clients are each one quiet on his or her table."

"American cheek!" snapped Sir Evelyne.

"Very well," Nelson said; "we'll relieve the hotel of our presence to-morrow."

As a reaction from this incident, as a sort of protest against Sir Evelyne Fragelle, they went not to Paris but to Monte Carlo after all. They were through with being alone.

· II ·

A LITTLE MORE than two years after the Kellys' first visit to Monte Carlo, Nicole woke up one morning into what, though it bore the same name, had become to her a different place altogether.

In spite of hurried months in Paris or Biarritz, it was now home to them. They had a villa, they had a large acquaintance among the spring and summer crowd—a crowd which, naturally, did not include people on charted trips or the shore parties from Mediterranean cruises; these latter had become for them "tourists."

They loved the Riviera in full summer with many friends there and the nights open and full of music. Before the maid drew the curtains this morning to shut out the glare, Nicole saw from her window the yacht of T. F. Golding, placid among the swells of the Monacan Bay, as if constantly bound on a romantic voyage not dependent upon actual motion.

The yacht had taken the slow tempo of the coast; it had gone no farther than to Cannes and back all summer, though it might have toured the world. The Kellys were dining on board that night.

Nicole spoke excellent French; she had five new evening dresses and four others that would do; she had her husband; she had two men in love with her, and she felt sad for one of them. She had her pretty face. At 10:30 she was meeting a third man, who was just beginning to be in love with her "in a harmless way." At one she was having a dozen charming people to luncheon. All that.

"I'm happy," she brooded toward the bright blinds. "I'm young and good-looking, and my name is often in the paper as having been here and there, but really I don't care about chi-chi. I think it's all awfully silly, but if you do want to see people, you might as well see the chic, amusing ones;

and if people call you a snob, it's envy, and they know it and everybody knows it."

She repeated the substance of this to Oscar Dane on the Mont Agel golf course two hours later, and he cursed her quietly.

"Not at all," he said. "You're just getting to be an old snob. Do you call that crowd of drunks you run with amusing people? Why, they're not even very swell. They're so hard that they've shifted down through Europe like nails in a sack of wheat, till they stick out of it a little into the Mediterranean Sea."

Annoyed, Nicole fired a name at him, but he answered: "Class C. A good solid article for beginners."

"The Colbys—anyway, her."

"Third flight."

"Marquis and Marquise de Kalb."

"If she didn't happen to take dope and he didn't have other peculiarities."

"Well, then, where are the amusing people?" she demanded impatiently.

"Off by themselves somewhere. They don't hunt in herds, except occasionally."

"How about you? You'd snap up an invitation from every person I named. I've heard stories about you wilder than any you can make up. There's not a man that's known you six months that would take your check for ten dollars. You're a sponge and a parasite and everything—"

"Shut up for a minute," he interrupted. "I don't want to spoil this drive. . . . I just don't like to see you kid yourself," he continued. "What passes with you for international society is just about as hard to enter nowadays as the public rooms at the Casino; and if I can make my living by sponging off it, I'm still giving twenty times more than I get. We dead beats are about the only people in it with any stuff, and we stay with it because we have to."

She laughed, liking him immensely, wondering how angry Nelson would be when he found that Oscar had walked off with his nail scissors and his copy of the New York Herald this morning.

"Anyhow," she thought afterward, as she drove home toward luncheon, "we're getting out of it all soon, and we'll be serious and have a baby. After this last summer."

Stopping for a moment at a florist's, she saw a young woman coming out with an armful of flowers. The young woman glanced at her over the heap of color, and Nicole perceived that she was extremely smart, and then that her face was familiar. It was someone she had known once, but only slightly; the name had escaped her, so she did not nod, and forgot the incident until that afternoon.

They were twelve for luncheon: The Goldings' party from the yacht, Liddell and Cardine Miles, Mr. Dane—seven different nationalities she counted; among them an exquisite young French-woman, Madame Delauney, whom Nicole referred to lightly as "Nelson's girl." Noel Delauney was perhaps her closest friend; when they made up foursomes for golf or for trips, she paired off with Nelson; but today, as Nicole introduced her to someone as "Nelson's girl," the bantering phrase filled Nicole with distaste.

She said aloud at luncheon: "Nelson and I are going to get away from it all."

Everybody agreed that they, too, were going to get away from it all.

"It's all right for the English," someone said, "because they're doing a sort of dance of death—you know, gayety in the doomed fort, with the Sepoys at the gate. You can see it by their faces when they dance—the intensity. They know it and they want it, and they don't see any future. But you Americans, you're having a rotten time. If you want to wear the green hat or the crushed hat, or whatever it is, you always have to get a little tipsy."

"We're going to get away from it all," Nicole said firmly, but something within her argued: "What a pity—this lovely blue sea, this happy time." What came afterward? Did one just accept a lessening of tension? It was somehow Nelson's business to answer that. His growing discontent that he wasn't getting anywhere ought to explode into a new life for both of them, or rather a new hope and content with life. That secret should be his masculine contribution.

"Well, children, good-by."

"It was a great luncheon."

"Don't forget about getting away from it all."

"See you when—"

The guests walked down the path toward their cars. Only Oscar, just faintly flushed on liqueurs, stood with Nicole on the veranda, talking on and on about the girl he had invited up to see his stamp collection. Momentarily tired of people, impatient to be alone, Nicole listened for a moment and then, taking a glass vase of flowers from the luncheon table, went through the French windows into the dark, shadowy villa, his voice following her as he talked on and on out there.

It was when she crossed the first salon, still hearing Oscar's monologue on the veranda, that she began to hear another voice in the next room, cutting sharply across Oscar's voice.

"Ah, but kiss me again," it said, stopped; Nicole stopped, too, rigid in the silence, now broken only by the voice on the porch.

"Be careful." Nicole recognized the faint French accent of Noel Delauney.

"I'm tired of being careful. Anyhow, they're on the veranda."

"No, better the usual place."

"Darling, sweet darling."

The voice of Oscar Dane on the veranda grew weary and stopped and, as if thereby released from her paralysis, Nicole took a step—forward or backward, she did not know which. At the sound of her heel on the floor, she heard the two people in the next room breaking swiftly apart.

Then she went in. Nelson was lighting a cigarette; Noel, with her back turned, was apparently hunting for hat or purse on a chair. With blind horror rather than anger, Nicole threw, or rather pushed away from her, the glass vase which she carried. If at anyone, it was at Nelson she threw it, but the force of her feeling had entered the inanimate thing; it flew past him, and Noel Delauney, just turning about, was struck full on the side of her head and face.

"Say, there!" Nelson cried. Noel sank slowly into the chair before which she stood, her hand slowly rising to cover the side of her face. The jar rolled unbroken on the thick carpet, scattering its flowers.

"You look out!" Nelson was at Noel's side, trying to take the hand away to see what had happened.

"C'est liquide," gasped Noel in a whisper. "Est-ce que c'est le sang?"

He forced her hand away, and cried breathlessly, "No, it's just water!" and then, to Oscar, who had appeared in the doorway: "Get some cognac!" and to Nicole: "You fool, you must be crazy!"

Nicole, breathing hard, said nothing. When the brandy arrived, there was a continuing silence, like that of people watching an operation, while Nelson poured a glass down Noel's throat. Nicole signaled to Oscar for a drink, and, as if afraid to break the silence without it, they all had a brandy. Then Noel and Nelson spoke at once:

"If you can find my hat—"

"This is the silliest—"

"—I shall go immediately."

"—thing I ever saw; I—"

They all looked at Nicole, who said: "Have her car drive right up to the door." Oscar departed quickly.

"Are you sure you don't want to see a doctor?" asked Nelson anxiously.

"I want to go."

A minute later, when the car had driven away, Nelson came in and poured himself another glass of brandy. A wave of subsiding tension flowed over him, showing in his face; Nicole saw it, and saw also his gathering will to make the best he could of it.

"I want to know just why you did that," he demanded. "No, don't go, Oscar." He saw the story starting out into the world.

"What possible reason—"

"Oh, shut up!" snapped Nicole.

"If I kissed Noel, there's nothing so terrible about it. It's of absolutely no significance."

She made a contemptuous sound. "I heard what you said to her."

"You're crazy."

He said it as if she were crazy, and wild rage filled her.

"You liar! All this time pretending to be so square, and so particular what I did, and all the time behind my back you've been playing around with that little—"

She used a serious word, and as if maddened with the sound of it, she sprang toward his chair. In protection against this sudden attack, he flung up his arm quickly, and the knuckles of his open hand struck across the socket of her eye. Covering her face with her hand as Noel had done ten minutes previously, she fell sobbing to the floor.

"Hasn't this gone far enough?" Oscar cried.

"Yes," admitted Nelson, "I guess it has."

"You go on out on the veranda and cool off."

He got Nicole to a couch and sat beside her, holding her hand.

"Brace up—brace up, baby," he said, over and over. "What are you— Jack Dempsey? You can't go around hitting French women; they'll sue you."

"He told her he loved her," she gasped hysterically. "She said she'd meet him at the same place. . . . Has he gone there now?"

"He's out on the porch, walking up and down, sorry as the devil that he accidentally hit you, and sorry he ever saw Noel Delauney."

"Oh, yes!"

"You might have heard wrong, and it doesn't prove a thing, anyhow."

After twenty minutes, Nelson came in suddenly and sank down on his knees by the side of his wife. Mr. Oscar Dane, reënforced in his idea that he gave much more than he got, backed discreetly and far from unwillingly to the door.

In another hour, Nelson and Nicole, arm in arm, emerged from their villa and walked slowly down to the Café de Paris. They walked instead of driving, as if trying to return to the simplicity they had once possessed, as if they were trying to unwind something that had become visibly tangled. Nicole accepted his explanations, not because they were credible, but because she wanted passionately to believe them. They were both very quiet and sorry.

The Café de Paris was pleasant at that hour, with sunset drooping through the yellow awnings and the red parasols as through stained glass. Glancing about, Nicole saw the young woman she had encountered that morning. She was with a man now, and Nelson placed them immediately as the young couple they had seen in Algeria, almost three years ago.

"They've changed," he commented. "I suppose we have, too, but not so much. They're harder-looking and he looks dissipated. Dissipation always shows in light eyes rather than in dark ones. The girl is *tout ce qu'il y a de chic,* as they say, but there's a hard look in her face too."

"I like her."

"Do you want me to go and ask them if they are that same couple?"

"No! That'd be like lonesome tourists do. They have their own friends."

At that moment people were joining them at their table.

"Nelson, how about tonight?" Nicole asked a little later. "Do you think we can appear at the Goldings' after what's happened?"

"We not only can but we've got to. If the story's around and we're not there, we'll just be handing them a nice juicy subject of conversation. . . . Hello! What on earth—"

Something strident and violent had happened across the café; a woman screamed and the people at one table were all on their feet, surging back and forth like one person. Then the people at the other tables were standing and crowding forward; for just a moment the Kellys saw the face of the girl they had been watching, pale now, and distorted with anger. Panic-stricken, Nicole plucked at Nelson's sleeve.

"I want to get out. I can't stand any more today. Take me home. Is everybody going crazy?"

On the way home, Nelson glanced at Nicole's face and perceived with a start that they were not going to dinner on the Goldings' yacht after all. For Nicole had the beginnings of a well-defined and unmistakable black eye—an eye that by eleven o'clock would be beyond the aid of all the cosmetics in the principality. His heart sank and he decided to say nothing about it until they reached home.

· I I I ·

THERE IS SOME wise advice in the catechism about avoiding the occasions of sin, and when the Kellys went up to Paris a month later they made a conscientious list of the places they wouldn't visit any more and the people they didn't want to see again. The places included several famous bars, all the night clubs except one or two that were highly decorous, all the early-morning clubs of every description, and all summer resorts that made whoopee for its own sake—whoopee triumphant and unrestrained—the main attraction of the season.

The people they were through with included three-fourths of those with whom they had passed the last two years. They did this not in snobbishness, but for self-preservation, and not without a certain fear in their hearts that they were cutting themselves off from human contacts forever.

But the world is always curious, and people become valuable merely for their inaccessibility. They found that there were others in Paris who were only interested in those who had separated from the many. The first crowd they had known was largely American, salted with Europeans; the second was largely European, peppered with Americans. This latter crowd was "society," and here and there it touched the ultimate *milieu*, made up of individuals of high position, of great fortune, very occasionally of genius, and always of power. Without being intimate with the great, they made new friends of a more conservative type. Moreover, Nelson began to paint again; he had a studio, and they visited the studios of Brancusi and Leger and Deschamps. It seemed that they were more part of something than before, and when certain gaudy rendezvous were mentioned, they felt a contempt for their first two years in Europe, speaking of their former acquaintances as "that crowd" and as "people who waste your time."

So, although they kept their rules, they entertained frequently at home and they went out to the houses of others. They were young and handsome and intelligent; they came to know what did go and what did not go, and adapted themselves accordingly. Moreover, they were naturally generous and willing, within the limits of common sense, to pay.

When one went out one generally drank. This meant little to Nicole, who had a horror of losing her *soigné* air, losing a touch of bloom or a ray of admiration, but Nelson, thwarted somewhere, found himself quite as tempted to drink at these small dinners as in the more frankly rowdy world. He was not a drunk, he did nothing conspicuous or sodden, but he was no longer willing to go out socially without the stimulus of liquor. It was with the idea of bringing him to a serious and responsible attitude that Nicole decided after a year in Paris, that the time had come to have a baby.

This was coincidental with their meeting Count Chiki Sarolai. He was an attractive relic of the Austrian court, with no fortune or pretense to any, but with solid social and financial connections in France. His sister was married to the Marquis de la Clos d'Hirondelle, who, in addition to being of the ancient noblesse, was a successful banker in Paris. Count Chiki roved here and there, frankly sponging, rather like Oscar Dane, but in a different sphere.

His penchant was Americans; he hung on their words with a pathetic eagerness, as if they would sooner or later let slip their mysterious formula for making money. After a casual meeting, his interest gravitated to the Kellys. During Nicole's months of waiting he was in the house continually, tirelessly interested in anything that concerned American crime, slang, finance or manners. He came in for a luncheon or dinner when he had no other place to go, and with tacit gratitude he persuaded his sister to call on Nicole, who was immensely flattered.

It was arranged that when Nicole went to the hospital he would stay at the *appartement* and keep Nelson company—an arrangement of which Nicole didn't approve, since they were inclined to drink together. But the day on which it was decided, he arrived with news of one of his brother-in-law's famous canal-boat parties on the Seine, to which the Kellys were to be invited and which, conveniently enough, was to occur three weeks after the arrival of the baby. So, when Nicole moved out to the American Hospital Count Chiki moved in.

The baby was a boy. For a while Nicole forgot all about people and their human status and their value. She even wondered at the fact that she had become such a snob, since everything seemed trivial compared with the new individual that, eight times a day, they carried to her breast.

After two weeks she and the baby went back to the apartment, but Chiki and his valet stayed on. It was understood, with that subtlety the Kellys had only recently begun to appreciate, that he was merely staying until after his brother-in-law's party, but the apartment was crowded and Nicole wished him gone. But her old idea, that if one had to see people they might as well be the best, was carried out in being invited to the de la Clos d'Hirondelles'.

As she lay in her chaise longue the day before the event, Chiki explained the arrangements, in which he had evidently aided.

"Everyone who arrives must drink two cocktails in the American style before they can come aboard—as a ticket of admission."

"But I thought that very fashionable French—Faubourg St. Germain and all that—didn't drink cocktails."

"Oh, but my family is very modern. We adopt many American customs."

"Who'll be there?"

"Everyone! Everyone in Paris."

Great names swam before her eyes. Next day she could not resist dragging the affair into conversation with her doctor. But she was rather offended at the look of astonishment and incredulity that came into his eyes.

"Did I understand you aright?" he demanded. "Did I understand you to say that you were going to a ball tomorrow?"

"Why, yes," she faltered. "Why not?"

"My dear lady, you are not going to stir out of the house for two more weeks; you are not going to dance or do anything strenuous for two more after that."

"That's ridiculous!" she cried. "It's been three weeks already! Esther Sherman went to America after—"

"Never mind," he interrupted. "Every case is different. There is a complication which makes it positively necessary for you to follow my orders."

"But the idea is that I'll just go for two hours, because of course I'll have to come home to Sonny—"

"You'll not go for two minutes."

She knew, from the seriousness of his tone, that he was right, but, perversely, she did not mention the matter to Nelson. She said, instead, that she was tired, that possibly she might not go, and lay awake that night measuring her disappointment against her fear. She woke up for Sonny's first feeding, thinking to herself: "But if I just take ten steps from a limousine to a chair and just sit half an hour—"

At the last minute the pale green evening dress from Callets, draped across a chair in her bedroom, decided her. She went.

Somewhere, during the shuffle and delay on the gangplank while the guests went aboard and were challenged and drank down their cocktails with attendant gayety, Nicole realized that she had made a mistake. There was, at any rate, no formal receiving line and, after greeting their hosts, Nelson found her a chair on deck, where presently her faintness disappeared.

Then she was glad she had come. The boat was hung with fragile lanterns, which blended with the pastels of the bridges and the reflected stars in the dark Seine, like a child's dream out of the Arabian Nights. A crowd of hungry-eyed spectators were gathered on the banks. Champagne moved past in platoons like a drill of bottles, while the music, instead of being loud and obtrusive, drifted down from the upper deck like frosting dripping over a cake. She became aware presently that they were not the only Americans there—across the deck were the Liddell Mileses, whom she had not seen for several years.

Other people from that crowd were present, and she felt a faint disappointment. What if this was not the marquis' best party? She remembered her mother's second days at home. She asked Chiki, who was at her side, to point out celebrities, but when she inquired about several people whom she associated with that set, he replied vaguely that they were away, or coming later, or could not be there. It seemed to her that she saw across the room the girl who had made the scene in the Café de Paris at Monte Carlo, but she could not be sure, for with the faint almost imperceptible movement of the boat, she realized that she was growing faint again. She sent for Nelson to take her home.

"You can come right back, of course. You needn't wait for me, because I'm going right to bed."

He left her in the hands of the nurse, who helped her upstairs and aided her to undress quickly.

"I'm desperately tired," Nicole said. "Will you put my pearls away?"

"Where?"

"In the jewel box on the dressing table."

"I don't see it," said the nurse after a minute.

"Then it's in a drawer."

There was a thorough rummaging of the dressing table, without result.

"But of course it's there." Nicole attempted to rise, but fell back, exhausted. "Look for it, please, again. Everything is in it—all my mother's things and my engagement things."

"I'm sorry, Mrs. Kelly. There's nothing in this room that answers to that description."

"Wake up the maid."

The maid knew nothing; then, after a persistent cross-examination, she did know something. Count Sarolai's valet had gone out, carrying his suitcase, half an hour after madame left the house.

Writhing in sharp and sudden pain, with a hastily summoned doctor at her side, it seemed to Nicole hours before Nelson came home. When he arrived, his face was deathly pale and his eyes were wild. He came directly into her room.

"What do you think?" he said savagely. Then he saw the doctor. "Why, what's the matter?"

"Oh, Nelson, I'm sick as a dog and my jewel box is gone, and Chiki's valet has gone. I've told the police. . . . Perhaps Chiki would know where the man—"

"Chiki will never come in this house again," he said slowly. "Do you know whose party that was? Have you got any idea whose party that was?" He burst into wild laughter. "It was our party—our party, do you understand? We gave it—we didn't know it, but we did."

"*Maintenant, monsieur, il ne faut pas exciter madame—*" the doctor began.

"I thought it was odd when the marquis went home early, but I didn't suspect till the end. They were just guests—Chiki invited all the people. After it was over, the caterers and musicians began to come up and ask me where to send their bills. And that damn Chiki had the nerve to tell me he thought I knew all the time. He said that all he'd promised was that it would be his brother-in-law's sort of party, and that his sister would be there. He said perhaps I was drunk, or perhaps I didn't understand French—as if we'd ever talked anything but English to him."

"Don't pay!" she said. "I wouldn't think of paying."

"So I said, but they're going to sue—the boat people and the others. They want twelve thousand dollars."

She relaxed suddenly. "Oh, go away!" she cried. "I don't care! I've lost my jewels and I'm sick, sick!"

· I V ·

THIS IS THE STORY of a trip abroad, and the geographical element must not be slighted. Having visited North Africa, Italy, the Riviera, Paris and points in between, it was not surprising that eventually the Kellys should go to Switzerland. Switzerland is a country where very few things begin, but many things end.

Though there was an element of choice in their other ports of call, the Kellys went to Switzerland because they had to. They had been married a little more than four years when they arrived one spring day at the lake that is the center of Europe—a placid, smiling spot with pastoral hillsides, a backdrop of mountains and waters of postcard blue, waters that are a little sinister beneath the surface with all the misery that has dragged itself here from every corner of Europe. Weariness to recuperate and death to die. There are schools, too, and young people splashing at the sunny plages; there is Bonivard's dungeon and Calvin's city, and the ghosts of Byron and Shelley still sail the dim shores by night; but the Lake Geneva that Nelson and Nicole came to was the dreary one of sanatoriums and rest hotels.

For, as if by some profound sympathy that had continued to exist beneath the unlucky destiny that had pursued their affairs, health had failed them both at the same time; Nicole lay on the balcony of a hotel coming slowly back to life after two successive operations, while Nelson fought for life against jaundice in a hospital two miles away. Even after the reserve force of twenty-nine years had pulled him through, there were months ahead during which he must live quietly. Often they wondered why, of all those who sought pleasure over the face of Europe, this misfortune should have come to them.

"There've been too many people in our lives," Nelson said. "We've never been able to resist people. We were so happy the first year when there weren't any people."

Nicole agreed. "If we could ever be alone—really alone—we could make up some kind of life for ourselves. We'll try, won't we, Nelson?"

But there were other days when they both wanted company desperately, concealing it from each other. Days when they eyed the obese, the wasted, the crippled and the broken of all nationalities who filled the hotel, seeking for one who might be amusing. It was a new life for them, turning on the daily visits of their two doctors, the arrival of the mail and newspapers from Paris, the little walk into the hillside village or occasionally the descent by funicular to the pale resort on the lake, with its *Kursaal*, its grass beach, its tennis clubs and sight-seeing busses. They read Tauchnitz editions and yellow-jacketed Edgar Wallaces; at a certain hour each day they watched the baby being given its bath; three nights a week there was a tired and patient orchestra in the lounge after dinner, that was all.

And sometimes there was a booming from the vine-covered hills on the other side of the lake, which meant that cannons were shooting at hail-bearing clouds, to save the vineyard from an approaching storm; it came swiftly, first falling from the heavens and then falling again in torrents from the mountains, washing loudly down the roads and stone ditches; it came with a dark, frightening sky and savage filaments of lightning and crashing, world-splitting thunder, while ragged and destroyed clouds fled along before the wind past the hotel. The mountains and the lake disappeared completely; the hotel crouched alone amid tumult and chaos and darkness.

It was during such a storm, when the mere opening of a door admitted a tornado of rain and wind into the hall, that the Kellys for the first time in months saw someone they knew. Sitting downstairs with other victims of frayed nerves, they became aware of two new arrivals—a man and woman whom they recognized as the couple, first seen in Algiers, who had crossed their path several times since. A single unexpressed thought flashed through Nelson and Nicole. It seemed like destiny that at last here in this desolate place they should know them, and watching, they saw other couples eying them in the same tentative way. Yet something held the Kellys back. Had they not just been complaining that there were too many people in their lives?

Later, when the storm had dozed off into a quiet rain, Nicole found herself near the girl on the glass veranda. Under cover of reading a book, she inspected the face closely. It was an inquisitive face, she saw at once, possibly calculating; the eyes, intelligent enough, but with no peace in them, swept over people in a single quick glance as though estimating their value. "Terrible egoist," Nicole thought, with a certain distaste. For the rest, the cheeks were wan, and there were little pouches of ill health under the eyes;

these combining with a certain flabbiness of arms and legs to give an impression of unwholesomeness. She was dressed expensively, but with a hint of slovenliness, as if she did not consider the people of the hotel important.

On the whole, Nicole decided she did not like her; she was glad that they had not spoken, but she was rather surprised that she had not noticed these things when the girl crossed her path before.

Telling Nelson her impression at dinner, he agreed with her.

"I ran into the man in the bar, and I noticed we both took nothing but mineral water, so I started to say something. But I got a good look at his face in the mirror and I decided not to. His face is so weak and self-indulgent that it's almost mean—the kind of face that needs half a dozen drinks really to open the eyes and stiffen the mouth up to normal."

After dinner the rain stopped and the night was fine outside. Eager for the air, the Kellys wandered down into the dark garden; on their way they passed the subjects of their late discussion, who withdrew abruptly down a side path.

"I don't think they want to know us any more than we do them," Nicole laughed.

They loitered among the wild rosebushes and the beds of damp-sweet, indistinguishable flowers. Below the hotel, where the terrace fell a thousand feet to the lake, stretched a necklace of lights that was Montreux and Vevey, and then, in a dim pendant, Lausanne; a blurred twinkling across the lake was Evian and France. From somewhere below—probably the *Kursaal*—came the sound of full-bodied dance music—American, they guessed, though now they heard American tunes months late, mere distant echoes of what was happening far away.

Over the Dent du Midi, over a black bank of clouds that was the rearguard of the receding storm, the moon lifted itself and the lake brightened; the music and the far-away lights were like hope, like the enchanted distance from which children see things. In their separate hearts Nelson and Nicole gazed backward to a time when life was all like this. Her arm went through his quietly and drew him close.

"We can have it all again," she whispered. "Can't we try, Nelson?"

She paused as two dark forms came into the shadows nearby and stood looking down at the lake below.

Nelson put his arm around Nicole and pulled her closer.

"It's just that we don't understand what's the matter," she said. "Why did we lose peace and love and health, one after the other? If we knew, if there was anybody to tell us, I believe we could try. I'd try so hard."

The last clouds were lifting themselves over the Bernese Alps. Suddenly, with a final intensity, the west flared with pale white lightning. Nelson and

Nicole turned, and simultaneously the other couple turned, while for an instant the night was as bright as day. Then darkness and a last low peal of thunder, and from Nicole a sharp, terrified cry. She flung herself against Nelson; even in the darkness she saw that his face was as white and strained as her own.

"Did you see?" she cried in a whisper. "Did you see them?"

"Yes!"

"They're us! They're us! Don't you see?"

Trembling, they clung together. The clouds merged into the dark mass of mountains; looking around after a moment, Nelson and Nicole saw that they were alone together in the tranquil moonlight.

THE HOTEL CHILD

◆

"The Hotel Child" (Saturday Evening Post, 31 January 1931) is a Tender-cluster story that again contrasts the corruption of European society with American innocence. Fitzgerald informed his agent, Harold Ober: "Practically the whole damn thing is true, bizarre as it seems."

Post fiction editor Thomas Costain noted that "it was not a straight-away story" and the "characters will appear shady, to say the least, to American readers"; but he accepted "The Hotel Child" because it was so well written. Nonetheless, the Post found it necessary to bowdlerize the story. Fitzgerald replied to a fan letter about "The Hotel Child": "Frankly the English have long been on my nerves (those were real people + the Post cut the best scene when they kept feeding hashish to the pekinese.)"

Bopes stretched himself out in several chairs and a sofa, took a hasheesh tablet from a silver box which he proffered to the other two and called for the barman. He announced that he had driven from Paris without a stop and was going over the Simplon Pass next morning to meet the only woman he had ever loved in Milan. He did not look in a condition to meet anyone. . . .

The Marquis Kinkallow glanced with tired eyes about the bar.

"Ah, who is that?" he demanded, surreptitiously feeding a hasheesh tablet to the Pekingese, "the lovely Sheeny. And who is that item with her?"

◆

IT IS A PLACE where one's instinct is to give a reason for being there—"Oh, you see, I'm here because——" Failing that, you are faintly suspect, because this corner of Europe does not draw people; rather, it accepts them without too many inconvenient questions—live and let live. Routes cross here—people bound for private *cliniques* or tuberculosis resorts in the mountains, people who are no longer *persona grata* in Italy or France. And if that were all——

Yet on a gala night at the Hotel des Trois Mondes a new arrival would scarcely detect the current beneath the surface. Watching the dancing there would be a gallery of Englishwomen of a certain age, with neckbands, dyed hair and faces powdered pinkish gray; a gallery of American women of a certain age, with snowy-white transformations, black dresses and lips of cherry red. And most of them with their eyes swinging right or left from time to time to rest upon the ubiquitous Fifi. The entire hotel had been made aware that Fifi had reached the age of eighteen that night.

Fifi Schwartz. An exquisitely, radiantly beautiful Jewess whose fine, high forehead sloped gently up to where her hair, bordering it like an armorial shield, burst into lovelocks and waves and curlicues of soft dark red. Her eyes were bright, big, clear, wet and shining; the color of her cheeks and lips was real, breaking close to the surface from the strong young pump of her heart. Her body was so assertively adequate that one cynic had been heard to remark that she always looked as if she had nothing on underneath her dresses; but he was probably wrong, for Fifi had been as thoroughly equipped for beauty by man as by God. Such dresses—cerise for Chanel, mauve for Molyneux, pink for Patou; dozens of them, tight at the hips, swaying, furling, folding just an eighth of an inch off the dancing floor. Tonight she was a woman of thirty in dazzling black, with long white gloves dripping from her forearms. "Such ghastly taste," the whispers said. "The stage, the shop window, the manikins' parade. What can her mother be thinking? But, then, look at her mother."

Her mother sat apart with a friend and thought about Fifi and Fifi's brother, and about her other daughters, now married, whom she considered to have been even prettier than Fifi. Mrs. Schwartz was a plain woman; she had been a Jewess a long time, and it was a matter of effortless indifference to her what was said by the groups around the room. Another large class who did not care were the young men—dozens of them. They followed Fifi about all day in and out of motorboats, night clubs, inland lakes, automobiles, tea rooms and funiculars, and they said, "Hey, look, Fifi!" and showed off for her, or said, "Kiss me, Fifi," or even, "Kiss me again, Fifi," and abused her and tried to be engaged to her.

Most of them, however, were too young, since this little city, through some illogical reasoning, is supposed to have an admirable atmosphere as an educational center.

Fifi was not critical, nor was she aware of being criticized herself. Tonight the gallery in the great, crystal, horseshoe room made observations upon her birthday party, being somewhat querulous about Fifi's entrance. The table had been set in the last of a string of dining rooms, each accessible from the central hall. But Fifi, her black dress shouting and halloing for notice, came in by way of the first dining room, followed by a whole platoon of young men of all possible nationalities and crosses, and at a sort of little run that swayed her lovely hips and tossed her lovely head, led them bumpily through the whole vista, while old men choked on fish bones, old women's facial muscles sagged, and the protest rose to a roar in the procession's wake.

They need not have resented her so much. It was a bad party, because Fifi thought she had to entertain everybody and be a dozen people, so she talked to the entire table and broke up every conversation that started, no matter how far away from her. So no one had a good time, and the people in the hotel needn't have minded so much that she was young and terribly happy.

Afterward, in the salon, many of the supernumerary males floated off with a temporary air to other tables. Among these was young Count Stanislas Borowki, with his handsome, shining brown eyes of a stuffed deer, and his black hair already dashed with distinguished streaks like the keyboard of a piano. He went to the table of some people of position named Taylor and sat down with just a faint sigh, which made them smile.

"Was it ghastly?" he was asked.

The blond Miss Howard who was traveling with the Taylors was almost as pretty as Fifi and stitched up with more consideration. She had taken pains not to make Miss Schwartz's acquaintance, although she shared several of the same young men. The Taylors were career people in the diplomatic service and were now on their way to London, after the League Conference at Geneva. They were presenting Miss Howard at court this season. They were very Europeanized Americans; in fact, they had reached a position where they could hardly be said to belong to any nation at all; certainly not to any great power, but perhaps to a sort of Balkanlike state composed of people like themselves. They considered that Fifi was as much of a gratuitous outrage as a new stripe in the flag.

The tall Englishwoman with the long cigarette holder and the half-paralyzed Pekingese presently got up, announcing to the Taylors that she had an engagement in the bar, and strolled away, carrying her paralyzed Pekingese and causing, as she passed, a chilled lull in the seething baby talk that raged around Fifi's table.

About midnight, Mr. Weicker, the assistant manager, looked into the bar, where Fifi's phonograph roared new German tangoes into the smoke and clatter. He had a small face that looked into things quickly, and lately he had taken a cursory glance into the bar every night. But he had not come to admire Fifi; he was engaged in an inquiry as to why matters were not going well at the Hotel des Trois Mondes this summer.

There was, of course, the continually sagging American Stock Exchange. With so many hotels begging to be filled, the clients had become finicky, exigent, quick to complain, and Mr. Weicker had had many fine decisions to make recently. One large family had departed because of a night-going phonograph belonging to Lady Capps-Karr. Also there was presumably a thief operating in the hotel; there had been complaints about pocketbooks, cigarette cases, watches and rings. Guests sometimes spoke to Mr. Weicker as if they would have liked to search his pockets. There were empty suites that need not have been empty this summer.

His glance fell dourly, in passing, upon Count Borowki, who was playing pool with Fifi. Count Borowki had not paid his bill for three weeks. He had told Mr. Weicker that he was expecting his mother, who would arrange everything. Then there was Fifi, who attracted an undesirable crowd— young students living on pensions who often charged drinks, but never paid for them. Lady Capps-Karr, on the contrary, was a *grande cliente;* one could count three bottles of whisky a day for herself and entourage, and her father in London was good for every drop of it. Mr. Weicker decided to issue an ultimatum about Borowki's bill this very night, and withdrew. His visit had lasted about ten seconds.

Count Borowki put away his cue and came close to Fifi, whispering something. She seized his hand and pulled him to a dark corner near the phonograph.

"My American dream girl," he said. "We must have you painted in Budapest the way you are tonight. You will hang with the portraits of my ancestors in my castle in Transylvania."

One would suppose that a normal American girl, who had been to an average number of moving pictures, would have detected a vague ring of familiarity in Count Borowki's persistent wooing. But the Hotel des Trois Mondes was full of people who were actually rich and noble, people who did fine embroidery or took cocaine in closed apartments and meanwhile laid claim to European thrones and half a dozen mediatized German principalities, and Fifi did not choose to doubt the one who paid court to her beauty. Tonight she was surprised at nothing: not even his precipitate proposal that they get married this very week.

"Mamma doesn't want that I should get married for a year. I only said I'd be engaged to you."

"But my mother wants me to marry. She is hard-boiling, as you Americans say; she brings pressure to bear that I marry Princess This and Countess That."

Meanwhile Lady Capps-Karr was having a reunion across the room. A tall, stooped Englishman, dusty with travel, had just opened the door of the bar, and Lady Capps-Karr, with a caw of "Bopes!" had flung herself upon him: "Bopes, I say!"

"Capps, darling. Hi, there, Rafe——" this to her companion. "Fancy running into you, Capps."

"Bopes! Bopes!"

Their exclamations and laughter filled the room, and the bartender whispered to an inquisitive American that the new arrival was the Marquis Kinkallow.

Bopes stretched himself out in several chairs and a sofa and called for the barman. He announced that he had driven from Paris without a stop and was leaving next morning to meet the only woman he had ever loved, in Milan. He did not look in a condition to meet anyone.

"Oh, Bopes, I've been so blind," said Lady Capps-Karr pathetically. "Day after day after day. I flew here from Cannes, meaning to stay one day, and I ran into Rafe here and some other Americans I knew, and it's been two weeks, and now all my tickets to Malta are void. Stay here and save me! Oh, Bopes! Bopes! Bopes!"

The Marquis Kinkallow glanced with tired eyes about the bar.

"Ah, who is that?" he demanded. "The lovely Jewess? And who is that item with her?"

"She's an American," said the daughter of a hundred earls. "The man is a scoundrel of some sort, but apparently he's a cat of the stripe; he's a great pal of Schenzi, in Vienna. I sat up till five the other night playing two-handed *chemin de fer* with him here in the bar and he owes me a mille Swiss."

"Have to have a word with that wench," said Bopes twenty minutes later. "You arrange it for me, Rafe, that's a good chap."

Ralph Berry had met Miss Schwartz, and, as the opportunity for the introduction now presented itself, he rose obligingly. The opportunity was that a *chasseur* had just requested Count Borowki's presence in the office; he managed to beat two or three young men to her side.

"The Marquis Kinkallow is so anxious to meet you. Can't you come and join us?"

Fifi looked across the room, her fine brow wrinkling a little. Something warned her that her evening was full enough already. Lady Capps-Karr had never spoken to her; Fifi believed she was jealous of her clothes.

"Can't you bring him over here?"

A minute later Bopes sat down beside Fifi with a shadow of fine tolerance settling on his face. This was nothing he could help; in fact, he constantly struggled against it, but it was something that happened to his expression when he met Americans. "The whole thing is too much for me," it seemed to say. "Compare my confidence with your uncertainty, my sophistication with your naïveté, and yet the whole world has slid into your power." Of later years he found that his tone, unless carefully guarded, held a smoldering resentment.

Fifi eyed him brightly and told him about her glamorous future.

"Next I'm going to Paris," she said, announcing the fall of Rome, "to, maybe, study at the Sorbonne. Then, maybe, I'll get married; you can't tell. I'm only eighteen. I had eighteen candles on my birthday cake tonight. I wish you could have been here. . . . I've had marvelous offers to go on the stage, but of course a girl on the stage gets talked about so."

"What are you doing tonight?" asked Bopes.

"Oh, lots more boys are coming in later. Stay around and join the party."

"I thought you and I might do something. I'm going to Milan tomorrow."

Across the room, Lady Capps-Karr was tense with displeasure at the desertion.

"After all," she protested, "a chep's a chep, and a chum's a chum, but there are certain things that one simply doesn't do. I never saw Bopes in such frightful condition."

She stared at the dialogue across the room.

"Come along to Milan with me," the marquis was saying. "Come to Tibet or Hindustan. We'll see them crown the King of Ethiopia. Anyhow, let's go for a drive right now."

"I got too many guests here. Besides, I don't go out to ride with people the first time I meet them. I'm supposed to be engaged. To a Hungarian count. He'd be furious and would probably challenge you to a duel."

Mrs. Schwartz, with an apologetic expression, came across the room to Fifi.

"John's gone," she announced. "He's up there again."

Fifi gave a yelp of annoyance. "He gave me his word of honor he would not go."

"Anyhow, he went. I looked in his room and his hat's gone. It was that champagne at dinner." She turned to the marquis. "John is not a vicious boy, but vurry, vurry weak."

"I suppose I'll have to go after him," said Fifi resignedly.

"I hate to spoil your good time tonight, but I don't know what else. Maybe this gentleman would go with you. You see, Fifi is the only one that can handle him. His father is dead and it really takes a man to handle a boy."

"Quite," said Bopes.

"Can you take me?" Fifi asked. "It's just up in town to a café."

He agreed with alacrity. Out in the September night, with her fragrance seeping through an ermine cape, she explained further:

"Some Russian woman's got hold of him; she claims to be a countess, but she's only got one silver-fox fur, that she wears with everything. My brother's just nineteen, so whenever he's had a couple glasses champagne he says he's going to marry her, and mother worries."

Bopes' arm dropped impatiently around her shoulder as they started up the hill to the town.

Fifteen minutes later the car stopped at a point several blocks beyond the café and Fifi stepped out. The marquis' face was now decorated by a long, irregular finger-nail scratch that ran diagonally across his cheek, traversed his nose in a few sketchy lines and finished in a sort of grand terminal of tracks upon his lower jaw.

"I don't like to have anybody get so foolish," Fifi explained. "You needn't wait. We can get a taxi."

"Wait!" cried the marquis furiously. "For a common little person like you? They tell me you're the laughingstock of the hotel, and I quite understand why."

Fifi hurried along the street and into the café, pausing in the door until she saw her brother. He was a reproduction of Fifi without her high warmth; at the moment he was sitting at a table with a frail exile from the Caucasus and two Serbian consumptives. Fifi waited for her temper to rise to an executive pitch; then she crossed the dance floor, conspicuous as a thundercloud in her bright black dress.

"Mamma sent me after you, John. Get your coat."

"Oh, what's biting her?" he demanded, with a vague eye.

"Mamma says you should come along."

He got up unwillingly. The two Serbians rose also; the countess never moved; her eyes, sunk deep in Mongol cheek bones, never left Fifi's face; her head crouched in the silver-fox fur which Fifi knew represented her brother's last month's allowance. As John Schwartz stood there swaying unsteadily the orchestra launched into *Ich bin von Kopf bis Fuss*. Diving into the confusion of the table, Fifi emerged with her brother's arm, marched him to the coat room and then out toward the taxi stand.

It was late, the evening was over, her birthday was over, and driving back to the hotel, with John slumped against her shoulder, Fifi felt a sudden depression. By virtue of her fine health she had never been a worrier, and certainly the Schwartz family had lived so long against similar backgrounds that Fifi felt no insufficiency in the Hotel des Trois Mondes as cloud and community—and yet the evening was suddenly all wrong. Didn't evenings sometimes end on a high note and not fade out vaguely in bars? After ten o'clock every night she felt she was the only real being in a colony of ghosts, that she was surrounded by utterly intangible figures who retreated whenever she stretched out her hand.

The doorman assisted her brother to the elevator. Stepping in, Fifi saw, too late, that there were two other people inside. Before she could pull John out again, they had both brushed past her as if in fear of contamination. Fifi heard "Mercy!" from Mrs. Taylor and "How revolting!" from Miss Howard. The elevator mounted. Fifi held her breath until it stopped at her floor.

It was, perhaps, the impact of this last encounter that caused her to stand very still just inside the door of the dark apartment. Then she had the sense that someone else was there in the blackness ahead of her, and after her brother had stumbled forward and thrown himself on a sofa, she still waited.

"Mamma," she called, but there was no answer; only a sound fainter than a rustle, like a shoe scraped along the floor.

A few minutes later, when her mother came upstairs, they called the *valet de chambre* and went through the rooms together, but there was no one. Then they stood side by side in the open door to their balcony and looked out on the lake with the bright cluster of Evian on the French shore and the white caps of snow on the mountains.

"I think we've been here long enough," said Mrs. Schwartz suddenly. "I think I'll take John back to the States this fall."

Fifi was aghast. "But I thought John and I were going to the Sorbonne in Paris?"

"How can I trust him in Paris? And how could I leave you behind alone there?"

"But we're used to living in Europe now. Why did I learn to talk French? Why, mamma, we don't even know any people back home any more."

"We can always meet people. We always have."

"But you know it's different; everybody is so bigoted there. A girl hasn't the chance to meet the same sort of men, even if there were any. Everybody just watches everything you do."

"So they do here," said her mother. "That Mr. Weicker just stopped me in the hall; he saw you come in with John, and he talked to me about how you must keep out of the bar, you were so young. I told him you only took lemonade, but he said it didn't matter; scenes like tonight made people leave the hotel."

"Oh, how perfectly mean!"

"So I think we better go back home."

The empty word rang desolately in Fifi's ears. She put her arms around her mother's waist, realizing that it was she and not her mother, with her mother's clear grip on the past, who was completely lost in the universe. On the sofa her brother snored, having already entered the world of the weak, of the leaners together, and found its fetid and mercurial warmth sufficient. But Fifi kept looking at the alien sky, knowing that she could pierce it and find her own way through envy and corruption. For the first time she seriously considered marrying Borowki immediately.

"Do you want to go downstairs and say good night to the boys?" suggested her mother. "There's lots of them still there asking where you are."

But the Furies were after Fifi now—after her childish complacency and her innocence, even after her beauty—out to break it all down and drag it in any convenient mud. When she shook her head and walked sullenly into her bedroom, they had already taken something from her forever.

· II ·

THE FOLLOWING MORNING Mrs. Schwartz went to Mr. Weicker's office to report the loss of two hundred dollars in American money. She had left the sum on her chiffonier upon retiring; when she awoke, it was gone. The door of the apartment had been bolted, but in the morning the bolt was found drawn, and yet neither of her children was awake. Fortunately, she had taken her jewels to bed with her in a chamois sack.

Mr. Weicker decided that the situation must be handled with care. There were not a few guests in the hotel who were in straitened circumstances and inclined to desperate remedies, but he must move slowly. In America one has money or hasn't; in Europe the heir to a fortune may be unable to stand himself a haircut until the collapse of a fifth cousin, yet be a sure risk and not to be lightly offended. Opening the office copy of the Almanack de Gotha, Mr. Weicker found Stanislas Karl Joseph Borowki hooked firmly on to the end of a line older than the crown of St. Stephen. This morning, in riding clothes that were smart as a hussar's uniform, he had gone riding with the utterly correct Miss Howard. On the other hand, there was no doubt as to who had been robbed, and Mr. Weicker's indignation began to concentrate on Fifi and her family, who might have saved him this trouble by taking themselves off some time ago. It was even conceivable that the dissipated son, John, had nipped the money.

In all events, the Schwartzes were going home. For three years they had lived in hotels—in Paris, Florence, St. Raphael, Como, Vichy, La Baule, Lucerne, Baden-Baden and Biarritz. Everywhere there had been schools—always new schools—and both children spoke in perfect French and scrawny fragments of Italian. Fifi had grown from a large-featured child of fourteen to a beauty; John had grown into something rather dismal and lost. Both of them played bridge, and somewhere Fifi had picked up tap dancing. Mrs. Schwartz felt that it was all somehow unsatisfactory, but she did not know why. So, two days after Fifi's party, she announced that they would pack their trunks, go to Paris for some new fall clothes and then go home.

That same afternoon Fifi came to the bar to get her phonograph, left there the night of her party. She sat up on a high stool and talked to the barman while she drank a ginger ale.

"Mother wants to take me back to America, but I'm not going."

"What will you do?"

"Oh, I've got a little money of my own, and then I may get married." She sipped her ginger ale moodily.

"I hear you had some money stolen," he remarked. "How did it happen?"

"Well, Count Borowki thinks the man got into the apartment early and hid in between the two doors between us and the next apartment. Then, when we were asleep, he took the money and walked out."

"Ha!"

Fifi sighed. "Well, you probably won't see me in the bar any more."

"We'll miss you, Miss Schwartz."

Mr. Weicker put his head in the door, withdrew it and then came in slowly.

"Hello," said Fifi coldly.

"A-ha, young lady." He waggled his finger at her with affected facetiousness. "Didn't you know I spoke to your mother about your coming in to the bar? It's merely for your own good."

"I'm just having a ginger ale," she said indignantly.

"But no one can tell what you're having. It might be whisky or what not. It is the other guests who complain."

She stared at him indignantly—the picture was so different from her own—of Fifi as the lively center of the hotel, of Fifi in clothes that ravished the eye, standing splendid and unattainable amid groups of adoring men. Suddenly Mr. Weicker's obsequious, but hostile, face infuriated her.

"We're getting out of this hotel!" she flared up. "I never saw such a narrow-minded bunch of people in my life; always criticizing everybody and making up terrible things about them, no matter what they do themselves. I think it would be a good thing if the hotel caught fire and burned down with all the nasty cats in it."

Banging down her glass, she seized the phonograph case and stalked out of the bar.

In the lobby a porter sprang to help her, but she shook her head and hurried on through the salon, where she came upon Count Borowki.

"Oh, I'm so furious!" she cried. "I never saw so many old cats! I just told Mr. Weicker what I thought of them!"

"Did someone dare to speak rudely to you?"

"Oh, it doesn't matter. We're going away."

"Going away!" He started. "When?"

"Right away. I don't want to, but mamma says we've got to."

"I must talk to you seriously about this," he said. "I just called your room. I have brought you a little engagement present."

Her spirits returned as she took the handsome gold-and-ivory cigarette case engraved with her initials.

"How lovely!"

"Now, listen; what you tell me makes it more important that I talk to you immediately. I have just received another letter from my mother. They have chosen a girl for me in Budapest—a lovely girl, rich and beautiful and of my own rank who would be very happy at the match, but I am in love with you. I would never have thought it possible, but I have lost my heart to an American."

"Well, why not?" said Fifi, indignantly. "They call girls beautiful here if they have one good feature. And then, if they've got nice eyes or hair, they're usually bow-legged or haven't got nice teeth."

"There is no flaw or fault in you."

"Oh, yes," said Fifi modestly. "I got a sort of big nose. Would you know I was Jewish?"

With a touch of impatience, Borowki came back to his argument: "So they are bringing pressure to bear for me to marry. Questions of inheritance depend on it."

"Besides, my forehead is too high," observed Fifi abstractedly. "It's so high it's got sort of wrinkles in it. I knew an awfully funny boy who used to call me 'the highbrow.' "

"So the sensible thing," pursued Borowki, "is for us to marry immediately. I tell you frankly there are other American girls not far from here who wouldn't hesitate."

"Mamma would be about crazy," Fifi said.

"I've thought about that too," he answered her eagerly. "Don't tell her. If we drove over the border tonight we could be married tomorrow morning. Then we come back and you show your mother the little gilt coronets painted on your luggage. My own personal opinion is that she'll be delighted. There you are, off her hands, with social position second to none in Europe. In my opinion, your mother has probably thought of it already, and may be saying to herself: 'Why don't those two young people just take matters into their own hands and save me all the fuss and expense of a wedding?' I think she would like us for being so hard-boiled."

He broke off impatiently as Lady Capps-Karr, emerging from the dining room with her Pekingese, surprised them by stopping at their table. Count Borowki was obliged to introduce them. As he had not known of the Marquis Kinkallow's defection the other evening, nor that His Lordship had taken a wound to Milan the following morning, he had no suspicion of what was coming.

"I've noticed Miss Schwartz," said the Englishwoman in a clear, concise voice. "And of course I've noticed Miss Schwartz's clothes."

"Won't you sit down?" said Fifi.

"No, thank you." She turned to Borowki. "Miss Schwartz's clothes make us all appear somewhat drab. I always refuse to dress elaborately in hotels. It seems such rotten taste. Don't you think so?"

"I think people always ought to look nice," said Fifi, flushing.

"Naturally. I merely said that I consider it rotten taste to dress elaborately, save in the houses of one's friends."

She said "Good-by-e-e" to Borowki and moved on, emitting a mouthed cloud of smoke and a faint fragrance of whisky.

The insult had been as stinging as the crack of a whip, and as Fifi's pride of her wardrobe was swept away from her, she heard all the comments that she had not heard, in one great resurgent whisper. Then they said that she wore her clothes here because she had nowhere else to wear them. That was why the Howard girl considered her vulgar and did not care to know her.

For an instant her anger flamed up against her mother for not telling her, but she saw that her mother did not know either.

"I think she's so dowdy," she forced herself to say aloud, but inside she was quivering. "What is she, anyhow? I mean, how high is her title? Very high?"

"She's the widow of a baronet."

"Is that high?" Fifi's face was rigid. "Higher than a countess?"

"No. A countess is much higher—infinitely higher." He moved his chair closer and began to talk intently.

Half an hour later Fifi got up with indecision on her face.

"At seven you'll let me know definitely," Borowki said, "and I'll be ready with a car at ten."

Fifi nodded. He escorted her across the room and saw her vanish into a dark hall mirror in the direction of the lift.

As he turned away, Lady Capps-Karr, sitting alone over her coffee, spoke to him:

"I want a word with you. Did you, by some slip of the tongue, suggest to Weicker that in case of difficulties I would guarantee your bills?"

Borowki flushed. "I may have said something like that, but——"

"Well, I told him the truth—that I never laid eyes on you until a fortnight ago."

"I, naturally, turned to a person of equal rank——"

"Equal rank! What cheek! The only titles left are English titles. I must ask you not to make use of my name again."

He bowed. "Such inconveniences will soon be for me a thing of the past."

"Are you getting off with that vulgar little American?"

"I beg your pardon," he said stiffly.

"Don't be angry. I'll stand you a whisky-and-soda. I'm getting in shape for Bopes Kinkallow, who's just telephoned he's tottering back here."

Meanwhile, upstairs, Mrs. Schwartz was saying to Fifi: "Now that I know we're going away I'm getting excited about it. It will be so nice seeing the Hirsts and Mrs. Bell and Amy and Marjorie and Gladys again, and the new baby. You'll be happy, too; you've forgotten how they're like. You and Gladys used to be great friends. And Marjorie——"

"Oh, mamma, don't talk about it," cried Fifi miserably. "I can't go back."

"We needn't stay. If John was in a college like his father wanted, we could, maybe, go to California."

But for Fifi all the romance of life was rolled up into the last three impressionable years in Europe. She remembered the tall guardsmen in Rome and the old Spaniard who had first made her conscious of her beauty at the Villa d'Este at Como, and the French naval aviator at St. Raphael who had dropped her a note from his plane into their garden, and the feeling that she had sometimes, when she danced with Borowki, that he was dressed in gleaming boots and a white-furred dolman.

She had seen many American moving pictures and she knew that the girls there always married the faithful boy from the old home town, and after that there was nothing.

"I won't go," she said aloud.

Her mother turned with a pile of clothes in her arms. "What talk is that from you, Fifi? You think I could leave you here alone?" As Fifi didn't answer, she continued, with an air of finality: "That talk doesn't sound nice from you. Now you stop fretting and saying such things, and get me this list of things uptown."

But Fifi had decided. It was Borowki, then, and the chance of living fully and adventurously. He could go into the diplomatic service, and then one day when they encountered Lady Capps-Karr and Miss Howard at a legation ball, she could make audible the observation that for the moment seemed so necessary to her: "I hate people who always look as if they were going to or from a funeral."

"So run along," her mother continued. "And look in at that café and see if John is up there, and take him to tea."

Fifi accepted the shopping list mechanically. Then she went into her room and wrote a little note to Borowki which she would leave with the concierge on the way out.

Coming out, she saw her mother struggling with a trunk, and felt terribly sorry for her. But there were Amy and Gladys in America, and Fifi hardened herself.

She walked out and down the stairs, remembering halfway that in her distraction she had omitted an official glance in the mirror; but there was a large mirror on the wall just outside the grand salon, and she stopped in front of that instead.

She was beautiful—she learned that once more, but now it made her sad. She wondered whether the dress she wore this afternoon was in bad taste, whether it would minister to the superiority of Miss Howard or Lady Capps-Karr. It seemed to her a lovely dress, soft and gentle in cut, but in color a hard, bright, metallic powder blue.

Then a sudden sound broke the stillness of the gloomy hall and Fifi stood suddenly breathless and motionless.

· III ·

AT ELEVEN O'CLOCK Mr. Weicker was tired, but the bar was in one of its periodical riots and he was waiting for it to quiet down. There was nothing to do in the stale office or the empty lobby; and the salon, where all day he held long conversations with lonely English and American women, was deserted; so he went out the front door and began to make the circuit of the hotel. Whether due to his circumambient course or to his frequent glances up at the twinkling bedroom lights and into the humble, grilled windows of the kitchen floor, the promenade gave him a sense of being in control of the hotel, of being adequately responsible, as though it were a ship and he was surveying it from a quarterdeck.

He went past a flood of noise and song from the bar, past a window where two bus boys sat on a bunk and played cards over a bottle of Spanish wine. There was a phonograph somewhere above, and a woman's form blocked out a window; then there was the quiet wing, and turning the corner, he arrived back at his point of departure. And in front of the hotel, under the dim porte-cochère light, he saw Count Borowki.

Something made him stop and watch—something incongruous—Borowki, who couldn't pay his bill, had a car and a chauffeur. He was giving the chauffeur some sort of detailed instructions, and then Mr. Weicker perceived that there was a bag in the front seat, and came forward into the light.

"You are leaving us, Count Borowki?"

Borowki started at the voice. "For the night only," he answered. "I'm going to meet my mother."

"I see."

Borowki looked at him reproachfully. "My trunk and hat box are in my room, you'll discover. Did you think I was running away from my bill?"

"Certainly not. I hope you will have a pleasant journey and find your mother well."

But inside he took the precaution of dispatching a *valet de chambre* to see if the baggage was indeed there, and even to give it a thoughtful heft, lest its kernel were departed.

He dozed for perhaps an hour. When he woke up, the night concierge was pulling at his arm and there was a strong smell of smoke in the lobby. It was some moments before he could get it through his head that one wing of the hotel was on fire.

Setting the concierge at the alarms, he rushed down the hall to the bar, and through the smoke that poured from the door he caught sight of the burning billiard table and the flames licking along the floor and flaring up in alcoholic ecstasy every time a bottle on the shelves cracked with the heat. As he hastily retreated he met a line of half-dressed *chasseurs* and bus boys already struggling up from the lower depths with buckets of water. The concierge shouted that the fire department was on its way. He put two men at the telephones to awaken the guests, and as he ran back to form a bucket line at the danger point, he thought for the first time of Fifi.

Blind rage consumed him—with a precocious Indianlike cruelty she had carried out her threat. Ah, he would deal with that later; there was still law in the country. Meanwhile a clangor outdoors announced that the engines had arrived, and he made his way back through the lobby, filled now with men in pajamas carrying brief cases, and women in bedclothes carrying jewel boxes and small dogs; the number swelling every minute and the talk rising from a cadence heavy with sleep to the full staccato buzz of an afternoon soirée.

A *chasseur* called Mr. Weicker to the phone, but the manager shook him off impatiently.

"It's the commissionaire of police," the boy persisted. "He says you must speak to him."

With an exclamation, Mr. Weicker hurried into the office. " 'Allo!"

"I'm calling from the station. Is this the manager?"

"Yes, but there's a fire here."

"Have you among your guests a man calling himself Count Borowki?"

"Why, yes——"

"We're bringing him there for identification. He was picked up on the road on some information we received."

"But——"

"We picked up a girl with him. We're bringing them both down there immediately."

"I tell you——"

The receiver clicked briskly in his ear and Mr. Weicker hurried back to the lobby, where the smoke was diminishing. The reassuring pumps had been at work for five minutes and the bar was a wet charred ruin. Mr. Weicker began passing here and there among the guests, tranquilizing and persuading; the phone operators began calling the rooms again, advising such guests as had not appeared that it was safe to go back to bed; and then, at the continued demands for an explanation, he thought again of Fifi, and this time of his own accord he hurried to the phone.

Mrs. Schwartz's anxious voice answered; Fifi wasn't there. That was what he wanted to know. He rang off brusquely. There was the story, and he could not have wished for anything more sordidly complete—an incendiary blaze and an attempted elopement with a man wanted by the police. It was time for paying, and all the money of America couldn't make any difference. If the season was ruined, at least Fifi would have no more seasons at all. She would go to a girls' institution where the prescribed uniform was rather plainer than any clothing she had ever worn.

As the last of the guests departed into the elevators, leaving only a few curious rummagers among the soaked débris, another procession came in by the front door. There was a man in civilian clothes and a little wall of policemen with two people behind. The commissionaire spoke and the screen of policemen parted.

"I want you to identify these two people. Has this man been staying here under the name of Borowki?"

Mr. Weicker looked. "He has."

"He's been wanted for a year in Italy, France and Spain. And this girl?"

She was half hidden behind Borowki, her head hanging, her face in shadow. Mr. Weicker craned toward her eagerly. He was looking at Miss Howard.

A wave of horror swept over Mr. Weicker. Again he craned his head forward, as if by the intensity of his astonishment he could convert her into

Fifi, or look through her and find Fifi. But this would have been difficult, for Fifi was far away. She was in front of the café, assisting the stumbling and reluctant John Schwartz into a taxi. "I should say you can't go back. Mother says you should come right home."

·IV·

COUNT BOROWKI TOOK his incarceration with a certain grace, as though, having lived so long by his own wits, there was a certain relief in having his days planned by an external agency. But he resented the lack of intercourse with the outer world, and was overjoyed when, on the fourth day of his imprisonment, he was led forth to find Lady Capps-Karr.

"After all," she said, "a chep's a chep and a chum's a chum, whatever happens. Luckily, our consul here is a friend of my father's, or they wouldn't have let me see you. I even tried to get you out on bail, because I told them you went to Oxford for a year and spoke English perfectly, but the brutes wouldn't listen."

"I'm afraid there's no use," said Count Borowki gloomily. "When they've finished trying me I'll have had a free journey all over Europe."

"But that's not the only outrageous thing," she continued. "Those idiots have thrown Bopes and me out of the Trois Mondes, and the authorities are trying to get us to leave the city."

"What for?"

"They're trying to put the full blame of that tiresome fire on us."

"Did you start it?"

"We did set some brandy on fire because we wanted to cook some potato chips in alcohol, and the bartender had gone to bed and left us there. But you'd think, from the way the swine talk, that we'd come there with the sole idea of burning everyone in their beds. The whole thing's an outrage and Bopes is furious. He says he'll never come here again. I went to the consulate and they agreed that the whole affair was perfectly disgraceful, and they've wired the Foreign Office."

Borowki considered for a moment. "If I could be born over again," he said slowly, "I think without any doubt I should choose to be born an Englishman."

"I could choose to be anything but an American! By the way, the Taylors are not presenting Miss Howard at court because of the disgraceful way the newspapers played up the matter."

"What puzzles me is what made Fifi suspicious," said Borowki.

"Then it was Miss Schwartz who blabbed?"

"Yes. I thought I had convinced her to come with me, and I knew that if she didn't, I had only to snap my fingers to the other girl. . . . That very afternoon Fifi visited the jeweler's and discovered I'd paid for the cigarette case with a hundred-dollar American note I'd lifted from her mother's chiffonier. She went straight to the police."

"Without coming to you first! After all, a chep's a chep——"

"But what I want to know is what made her suspicious enough to investigate, what turned her against me."

Fifi, at that moment sitting on a high stool in a hotel bar in Paris and sipping a lemonade, was answering that very question to an interested bartender.

"I was standing in the hall looking in the mirror," she said, "and I heard him talking to the English lady—the one who set the hotel on fire. And I heard him say, 'After all, my one nightmare is that she'll turn out to look like her mother.' " Fifi's voice blazed with indignation. "Well, you've seen my mother, haven't you?"

"Yes, and a very fine woman she is."

"After that I knew there was something the matter with him, and I wondered how much he'd paid for the cigarette case. So I went up to see. They showed me the bill he paid with."

"And you will go to America now?" the barman asked.

Fifi finished her glass; the straw made a gurgling sound in the sugar at the bottom.

"We've got to go back and testify, and we'll stay a few months anyhow." She stood up. "Bye-bye; I've got a fitting."

They had not got her—not yet. The Furies had withdrawn a little and stood in the background with a certain gnashing of teeth. But there was plenty of time.

Yet, as Fifi tottered out through the lobby, her face gentle with new hopes, as she went out looking for completion under the impression that she was going to the *couturier,* there was a certain doubt among the eldest and most experienced of the Furies if they would get her, after all.

BABYLON REVISITED

◆

"Babylon Revisited" (Saturday Evening Post, *21 February 1931*) is one of Fitzgerald's half-dozen greatest stories. Like all of his best fiction it was intensely personal, expressing his feelings about his alcoholism, his wife's mental collapse, and his responsibility to his daughter. It is a companion work to "One Trip Abroad," another story which assessed the effects of unearned money and expatriation on American character.

Although Fitzgerald revised "Babylon Revisited" for Taps at Reveille, small problems of chronology and detail remain.

◆

"AND WHERE'S Mr. Campbell?" Charlie asked.

"Gone to Switzerland. Mr. Campbell's a pretty sick man, Mr. Wales."

"I'm sorry to hear that. And George Hardt?" Charlie inquired.

"Back in America, gone to work."

"And where is the Snow Bird?" — *coke dealer*

"He was in here last week. Anyway, his friend, Mr. Schaeffer, is in Paris."

Two familiar names from the long list of a year and a half ago. Charlie scribbled an address in his notebook and tore out the page.

"If you see Mr. Schaeffer, give him this," he said. "It's my brother-in-law's address. I haven't settled on a hotel yet."

He was not really disappointed to find Paris was so empty. But the stillness in the Ritz bar was strange and portentous. It was not an American bar any more—he felt polite in it, and not as if he owned it. It had gone back into France. He felt the stillness from the moment he got out of the taxi and saw the doorman, usually in a frenzy of activity at this hour, gossiping with a *chasseur* by the servants' entrance.

Passing through the corridor, he heard only a single, bored voice in the once-clamorous women's room. When he turned into the bar he travelled the twenty feet of green carpet with his eyes fixed straight ahead by old habit; and then, with his foot firmly on the rail, he turned and surveyed the room, encountering only a single pair of eyes that fluttered up from a newspaper in the corner. Charlie asked for the head barman, Paul, who in the latter days of the bull market had come to work in his own custom-built car—disembarking, however, with due nicety at the nearest corner. But Paul was at his country house today and Alix giving him information.

"No, no more," Charlie said, "I'm going slow these days."

Alix congratulated him: "You were going pretty strong a couple of years ago."

"I'll stick to it all right," Charlie assured him. "I've stuck to it for over a year and a half now."

"How do you find conditions in America?"

"I haven't been to America for months. I'm in business in Prague, representing a couple of concerns there. They don't know about me down there."

Alix smiled.

"Remember the night of George Hardt's bachelor dinner here?" said Charlie. "By the way, what's become of Claude Fessenden?"

Alix lowered his voice confidentially: "He's in Paris, but he doesn't come here any more. Paul doesn't allow it. He ran up a bill of thirty thousand francs, charging all his drinks and his lunches, and usually his dinner, for more than a year. And when Paul finally told him he had to pay, he gave him a bad check."

Alix shook his head sadly.

"I don't understand it, such a dandy fellow. Now he's all bloated up—" He made a plump apple of his hands.

Charlie watched a group of strident queens installing themselves in a corner.

"Nothing affects them," he thought. "Stocks rise and fall, people loaf or work, but they go on forever." The place oppressed him. He called for the dice and shook with Alix for the drink.

"Here for long, Mr. Wales?"

"I'm here for four or five days to see my little girl."

"Oh-h! You have a little girl?"

Outside, the fire-red, gas-blue, ghost-green signs shone smokily through the tranquil rain. It was late afternoon and the streets were in movement; the *bistros* gleamed. At the corner of the Boulevard des Capucines he took a taxi. The Place de la Concorde moved by in pink majesty; they crossed the logical Seine, and Charlie felt the sudden provincial quality of the Left Bank.*

* Fitzgerald deleted this paragraph in a marked copy of *Taps at Reveille* because it was "Used in *Tender*." The excision solves the problem of Charlie's puzzling Right Bank–Left Bank–Right Bank–Left Bank itinerary.

Charlie directed his taxi to the Avenue de l'Opera, which was out of his way. But he wanted to see the blue hour spread over the magnificent façade, and imagine that the cab horns, playing endlessly the first few bars of *La Plus que Lent,* were the trumpets of the Second Empire. They were closing the iron grill in front of Brentano's Book-store, and people were already at dinner behind the trim little bourgeois hedge of Duval's. He had never eaten at a really cheap restaurant in Paris. Five-course dinner, four francs fifty, eighteen cents, wine included. For some odd reason he wished that he had.

As they rolled on to the Left Bank and he felt its sudden provincialism, he thought, "I spoiled this city for myself. I didn't realize it, but the days came along one after another, and then two years were gone, and everything was gone, and I was gone."

He was thirty-five, and good to look at. The Irish mobility of his face was sobered by a deep wrinkle between his eyes. As he rang his brother-in-law's bell in the Rue Palatine, the wrinkle deepened till it pulled down his brows; he felt a cramping sensation in his belly. From behind the maid who opened the door darted a lovely little girl of nine who shrieked "Daddy!" and flew up, struggling like a fish, into his arms. She pulled his head around by one ear and set her cheek against his.

"My old pie," he said.

"Oh, daddy, daddy, daddy, daddy, dads, dads, dads!"

She drew him into the salon, where the family waited, a boy and girl his daughter's age, his sister-in-law and her husband. He greeted Marion with his voice pitched carefully to avoid either feigned enthusiasm or dislike, but her response was more frankly tepid, though she minimized her expression of unalterable distrust by directing her regard toward his child. The two men clasped hands in a friendly way and Lincoln Peters rested his for a moment on Charlie's shoulder.

The room was warm and comfortably American. The three children moved intimately about, playing through the yellow oblongs that led to other rooms; the cheer of six o'clock spoke in the eager smacks of the fire and the sounds of French activity in the kitchen. But Charlie did not relax; his heart sat up rigidly in his body and he drew confidence from his daughter, who from time to time came close to him, holding in her arms the doll he had brought.

"Really extremely well," he declared in answer to Lincoln's question. "There's a lot of business there that isn't moving at all, but we're doing even better than ever. In fact, damn well. I'm bringing my sister over from America next month to keep house for me. My income last year was bigger than it was when I had money. You see, the Czechs——"

His boasting was for a specific purpose; but after a moment, seeing a faint restiveness in Lincoln's eye, he changed the subject:

"Those are fine children of yours, well brought up, good manners."

"We think Honoria's a great little girl too."

Marion Peters came back from the kitchen. She was a tall woman with worried eyes, who had once possessed a fresh American loveliness. Charlie had never been sensitive to it and was always surprised when people spoke of how pretty she had been. From the first there had been an instinctive antipathy between them.

"Well, how do you find Honoria?" she asked.

"Wonderful. I was astonished how much she's grown in ten months. All the children are looking well."

"We haven't had a doctor for a year. How do you like being back in Paris?"

"It seems very funny to see so few Americans around."

"I'm delighted," Marion said vehemently. "Now at least you can go into a store without their assuming you're a millionaire. We've suffered like everybody, but on the whole it's a good deal pleasanter."

"But it was nice while it lasted," Charlie said. "We were a sort of royalty, almost infallible, with a sort of magic around us. In the bar this afternoon"—he stumbled, seeing his mistake—"there wasn't a man I knew."

She looked at him keenly. "I should think you'd have had enough of bars."

"I only stayed a minute. I take one drink every afternoon, and no more."

"Don't you want a cocktail before dinner?" Lincoln asked.

"I take only one drink every afternoon, and I've had that."

"I hope you keep to it," said Marion.

Her dislike was evident in the coldness with which she spoke, but Charlie only smiled; he had larger plans. Her very aggressiveness gave him an advantage, and he knew enough to wait. He wanted them to initiate the discussion of what they knew had brought him to Paris.

At dinner he couldn't decide whether Honoria was most like him or her mother. Fortunate if she didn't combine the traits of both that had brought them to disaster. A great wave of protectiveness went over him. He thought he knew what to do for her. He believed in character; he wanted to jump back a whole generation and trust in character again as the eternally valuable element. Everything wore out.

He left soon after dinner, but not to go home. He was curious to see Paris by night with clearer and more judicious eyes than those of other days. He bought a *strapontin* for the Casino and watched Josephine Baker go through her chocolate arabesques.

After an hour he left and strolled toward Montmartre, up the Rue Pigalle into the Place Blanche. The rain had stopped and there were a few people in evening clothes disembarking from taxis in front of cabarets, and *cocottes* prowling singly or in pairs, and many Negroes. He passed a lighted door from which issued music, and stopped with the sense of familiarity; it was Bricktop's, where he had parted with so many hours and so much money. A few doors farther on he found another ancient rendezvous and incautiously put his head inside. Immediately an eager orchestra burst into sound, a pair of professional dancers leaped to their feet and a maître d'hôtel swooped toward him, crying, "Crowd just arriving, sir!" But he withdrew quickly.

"You have to be damn drunk," he thought.

Zelli's was closed, the bleak and sinister cheap hotels surrounding it were dark; up in the Rue Blanche there was more light and a local, colloquial French crowd. The Poet's Cave had disappeared, but the two great mouths of the Café of Heaven and the Café of Hell still yawned—even devoured, as he watched, the meager contents of a tourist bus—a German, a Japanese, and an American couple who glanced at him with frightened eyes.

So much for the effort and ingenuity of Montmartre. All the catering to vice and waste was on an utterly childish scale, and he suddenly realized the meaning of the word "dissipate"—to dissipate into thin air; to make nothing out of something. In the little hours of the night every move from place to place was an enormous human jump, an increase of paying for the privilege of slower and slower motion.

He remembered thousand-franc notes given to an orchestra for playing a single number, hundred-franc notes tossed to a doorman for calling a cab.

But it hadn't been given for nothing.

It had been given, even the most wildly squandered sum, as an offering to destiny that he might not remember the things most worth remembering, the things that now he would always remember—his child taken from his control, his wife escaped to a grave in Vermont.

In the glare of a *brasserie* a woman spoke to him. He bought her some eggs and coffee, and then, eluding her encouraging stare, gave her a twenty-franc note and took a taxi to his hotel.

· I I ·

HE WOKE upon a fine fall day—football weather. The depression of yesterday was gone and he liked the people on the streets. At noon he sat opposite Honoria at Le Grand Vatel, the only restaurant he could think of

not reminiscent of champagne dinners and long luncheons that began at two
and ended in a blurred and vague twilight.

"Now, how about vegetables? Oughtn't you to have some vegetables?"

"Well, yes."

"Here's *épinards* and *chou-fleur* and carrots and *haricots*."

"I'd like *chou-fleur*."

"Wouldn't you like to have two vegetables?"

"I usually only have one at lunch."

The waiter was pretending to be inordinately fond of children. "*Qu'elle
est mignonne la petite? Elle parle exactement comme une Française.*"

"How about dessert? Shall we wait and see?"

The waiter disappeared. Honoria looked at her father expectantly.

"What are we going to do?"

"First, we're going to that toy store in the Rue Saint-Honoré and buy
you anything you like. And then we're going to the vaudeville at the Empire."

She hesitated. "I like it about the vaudeville, but not the toy store."

"Why not?"

"Well, you brought me this doll." She had it with her. "And I've got
lots of things. And we're not rich any more, are we?"

"We never were. But today you are to have anything you want."

"All right," she agreed resignedly.

When there had been her mother and a French nurse he had been inclined
to be strict; now he extended himself, reached out for a new tolerance; he
must be both parents to her and not shut any of her out of communication.

"I want to get to know you," he said gravely. "First let me introduce
myself. My name is Charles J. Wales, of Prague."

"Oh, daddy!" her voice cracked with laughter.

"And who are you, please?" he persisted, and she accepted a rôle immediately: "Honoria Wales, Rue Palatine, Paris."

"Married or single?"

"No, not married. Single."

He indicated the doll. "But I see you have a child, madame."

Unwilling to disinherit it, she took it to her heart and thought quickly:
"Yes, I've been married, but I'm not married now. My husband is dead."

He went on quickly, "And the child's name?"

"Simone. That's after my best friend at school."

"I'm very pleased that you're doing so well at school."

"I'm third this month," she boasted. "Elsie"—that was her cousin—"is
only about eighteenth, and Richard is about at the bottom."

"You like Richard and Elsie, don't you?"

"Oh, yes. I like Richard quite well and I like her all right."

Cautiously and casually he asked: "And Aunt Marion and Uncle Lincoln—which do you like best?"

"Oh, Uncle Lincoln, I guess."

He was increasingly aware of her presence. As they came in, a murmur of ". . . adorable" followed them, and now the people at the next table bent all their silences upon her, staring as if she were something no more conscious than a flower.

"Why don't I live with you?" she asked suddenly. "Because mamma's dead?"

"You must stay here and learn more French. It would have been hard for daddy to take care of you so well."

"I don't really need much taking care of any more. I do everything for myself."

Going out of the restaurant, a man and a woman unexpectedly hailed him.

"Well, the old Wales!"

"Hello there, Lorraine. . . . Dunc."

Sudden ghosts out of the past: Duncan Schaeffer, a friend from college. Lorraine Quarrles, a lovely, pale blonde of thirty; one of a crowd who had helped them make months into days in the lavish times of three years ago.

"My husband couldn't come this year," she said, in answer to his question. "We're poor as hell. So he gave me two hundred a month and told me I could do my worst on that. . . . This your little girl?"

"What about coming back and sitting down?" Duncan asked.

"Can't do it." He was glad for an excuse. As always, he felt Lorraine's passionate, provocative attraction, but his own rhythm was different now.

"Well, how about dinner?" she asked.

"I'm not free. Give me your address and let me call you."

"Charlie, I believe you're sober," she said judicially. "I honestly believe he's sober, Dunc. Pinch him and see if he's sober."

Charlie indicated Honoria with his head. They both laughed.

"What's your address?" said Duncan sceptically.

He hesitated, unwilling to give the name of his hotel.

"I'm not settled yet. I'd better call you. We're going to see the vaudeville at the Empire."

"There! That's what I want to do," Lorraine said. "I want to see some clowns and acrobats and jugglers. That's just what we'll do, Dunc."

"We've got to do an errand first," said Charlie. "Perhaps we'll see you there."

"All right, you snob. . . . Good-by, beautiful little girl."

"Good-by."

Honoria bobbed politely.

Somehow, an unwelcome encounter. They liked him because he was functioning, because he was serious; they wanted to see him, because he was stronger than they were now, because they wanted to draw a certain sustenance from his strength.

At the Empire, Honoria proudly refused to sit upon her father's folded coat. She was already an individual with a code of her own, and Charlie was more and more absorbed by the desire of putting a little of himself into her before she crystallized utterly. It was hopeless to try to know her in so short a time.

Between the acts they came upon Duncan and Lorraine in the lobby where the band was playing.

"Have a drink?"

"All right, but not up at the bar. We'll take a table."

"The perfect father."

Listening abstractedly to Lorraine, Charlie watched Honoria's eyes leave their table, and he followed them wistfully about the room, wondering what they saw. He met her glance and she smiled.

"I liked that lemonade," she said.

What had she said? What had he expected? Going home in a taxi afterward, he pulled her over until her head rested against his chest.

"Darling, do you ever think about your mother?"

"Yes, sometimes," she answered vaguely.

"I don't want you to forget her. Have you got a picture of her?"

"Yes, I think so. Anyhow, Aunt Marion has. Why don't you want me to forget her?"

"She loved you very much."

"I loved her too."

They were silent for a moment.

"Daddy, I want to come and live with you," she said suddenly.

His heart leaped; he had wanted it to come like this.

"Aren't you perfectly happy?"

"Yes, but I love you better than anybody. And you love me better than anybody, don't you, now that mummy's dead?"

"Of course I do. But you won't always like me best, honey. You'll grow up and meet somebody your own age and go marry him and forget you ever had a daddy."

"Yes, that's true," she agreed tranquilly.

He didn't go in. He was coming back at nine o'clock and he wanted to keep himself fresh and new for the thing he must say then.

"When you're safe inside, just show yourself in that window."

"All right. Good-by, dads, dads, dads, dads."

He waited in the dark street until she appeared, all warm and glowing, in the window above and kissed her fingers out into the night.

· I I I ·

THEY WERE WAITING. Marion sat behind the coffee service in a dignified black dinner dress that just faintly suggested mourning. Lincoln was walking up and down with the animation of one who had already been talking. They were as anxious as he was to get into the question. He opened it almost immediately:

"I suppose you know what I want to see you about—why I really came to Paris."

Marion played with the black stars on her necklace and frowned.

"I'm awfully anxious to have a home," he continued. "And I'm awfully anxious to have Honoria in it. I appreciate your taking in Honoria for her mother's sake, but things have changed now"—he hesitated and then continued more forcibly—"changed radically with me, and I want to ask you to reconsider the matter. It would be silly for me to deny that about three years ago I was acting badly——"

Marion looked up at him with hard eyes.

"—but all that's over. As I told you, I haven't had more than a drink a day for over a year, and I take that drink deliberately, so that the idea of alcohol won't get too big in my imagination. You see the idea?"

"No," said Marion succinctly.

"It's a sort of stunt I set myself. It keeps the matter in proportion."

"I get you," said Lincoln. "You don't want to admit it's got any attraction for you."

"Something like that. Sometimes I forget and don't take it. But I try to take it. Anyhow, I couldn't afford to drink in my position. The people I represent are more than satisfied with what I've done, and I'm bringing my sister over from Burlington to keep house for me, and I want awfully to have Honoria too. You know that even when her mother and I weren't getting along well we never let anything that happened touch Honoria. I know she's fond of me and I know I'm able to take care of her and—well, there you are. How do you feel about it?"

He knew that now he would have to take a beating. It would last an hour or two hours, and it would be difficult, but if he modulated his inevitable resentment to the chastened attitude of the reformed sinner, he might win his point in the end.

Keep your temper, he told himself. You don't want to be justified. You want Honoria.

Lincoln spoke first: "We've been talking it over ever since we got your letter last month. We're happy to have Honoria here. She's a dear little thing, and we're glad to be able to help her, but of course that isn't the question——"

Marion interrupted suddenly. "How long are you going to stay sober, Charlie?" she asked.

"Permanently, I hope."

"How can anybody count on that?"

"You know I never did drink heavily until I gave up business and came over here with nothing to do. Then Helen and I began to run around with——"

"Please leave Helen out of it. I can't bear to hear you talk about her like that."

He stared at her grimly; he had never been certain how fond of each other the sisters were in life.

"My drinking only lasted about a year and a half—from the time we came over until I—collapsed."

"It was time enough."

"It was time enough," he agreed.

"My duty is entirely to Helen," she said. "I try to think what she would have wanted me to do. Frankly, from the night you did that terrible thing you haven't really existed for me. I can't help that. She was my sister."

"Yes."

"When she was dying she asked me to look out for Honoria. If you hadn't been in a sanitarium then, it might have helped matters."

He had no answer.

"I'll never in my life be able to forget the morning when Helen knocked at my door, soaked to the skin and shivering, and said you'd locked her out."

Charlie gripped the sides of the chair. This was more difficult than he expected; he wanted to launch out into a long expostulation and explanation, but he only said: "The night I locked her out—" and she interrupted, "I don't feel up to going over that again."

After a moment's silence Lincoln said: "We're getting off the subject. You want Marion to set aside her legal guardianship and give you Honoria. I think the main point for her is whether she has confidence in you or not."

"I don't blame Marion," Charlie said slowly, "but I think she can have entire confidence in me. I had a good record up to three years ago. Of course, it's within human possibilities I might go wrong any time. But if we wait much longer I'll lose Honoria's childhood and my chance for a home." He shook his head, "I'll simply lose her, don't you see?"

"Yes, I see," said Lincoln.

"Why didn't you think of all this before?" Marion asked.

"I suppose I did, from time to time, but Helen and I were getting along badly. When I consented to the guardianship, I was flat on my back in a sanitarium and the market had cleaned me out. I knew I'd acted badly, and I thought if it would bring any peace to Helen, I'd agree to anything. But now it's different. I'm functioning, I'm behaving damn well, so far as——"

"Please don't swear at me," Marion said.

He looked at her, startled. With each remark the force of her dislike became more and more apparent. She had built up all her fear of life into one wall and faced it toward him. This trivial reproof was possibly the result of some trouble with the cook several hours before. Charlie became increasingly alarmed at leaving Honoria in this atmosphere of hostility against himself; sooner or later it would come out, in a word here, a shake of the head there, and some of that distrust would be irrevocably implanted in Honoria. But he pulled his temper down out of his face and shut it up inside him; he had won a point, for Lincoln realized the absurdity of Marion's remark and asked her lightly since when she had objected to the word "damn."

"Another thing," Charlie said: "I'm able to give her certain advantages now. I'm going to take a French governess to Prague with me. I've got a lease on a new apartment——"

He stopped, realizing that he was blundering. They couldn't be expected to accept with equanimity the fact that his income was again twice as large as their own.

"I suppose you can give her more luxuries than we can," said Marion. "When you were throwing away money we were living along watching every ten francs. . . . I suppose you'll start doing it again."

"Oh, no," he said. "I've learned. I worked hard for ten years, you know—until I got lucky in the market, like so many people. Terribly lucky. It didn't seem any use working any more, so I quit. It won't happen again."

There was a long silence. All of them felt their nerves straining, and for the first time in a year Charlie wanted a drink. He was sure now that Lincoln Peters wanted him to have his child.

Marion shuddered suddenly; part of her saw that Charlie's feet were planted on the earth now, and her own maternal feeling recognized the naturalness of his desire; but she had lived for a long time with a prejudice—a prejudice founded on a curious disbelief in her sister's happiness, and which, in the shock of one terrible night, had turned to hatred for him. It had all happened at a point in her life where the discouragement of ill health and adverse circumstances made it necessary for her to believe in tangible villainy and a tangible villain.

"I can't help what I think!" she cried out suddenly. "How much you were responsible for Helen's death, I don't know. It's something you'll have to square with your own conscience."

An electric current of agony surged through him; for a moment he was almost on his feet, an unuttered sound echoing in his throat. He hung on to himself for a moment, another moment.

"Hold on there," said Lincoln uncomfortably. "I never thought you were responsible for that."

"Helen died of heart trouble," Charlie said dully.

"Yes, heart trouble." Marion spoke as if the phrase had another meaning for her.

Then, in the flatness that followed her outburst, she saw him plainly and she knew he had somehow arrived at control over the situation. Glancing at her husband, she found no help from him, and as abruptly as if it were a matter of no importance, she threw up the sponge.

"Do what you like!" she cried, springing up from her chair. "She's your child. I'm not the person to stand in your way. I think if it were my child I'd rather see her—" She managed to check herself. "You two decide it. I can't stand this. I'm sick. I'm going to bed."

She hurried from the room; after a moment Lincoln said:

"This has been a hard day for her. You know how strongly she feels—" His voice was almost apologetic: "When a woman gets an idea in her head."

"Of course."

"It's going to be all right. I think she sees now that you—can provide for the child, and so we can't very well stand in your way or Honoria's way."

"Thank you, Lincoln."

"I'd better go along and see how she is."

"I'm going."

He was still trembling when he reached the street, but a walk down the Rue Bonaparte to the quais set him up, and as he crossed the Seine, fresh and new by the quai lamps, he felt exultant. But back in his room he couldn't sleep. The image of Helen haunted him. Helen whom he had loved so until they had senselessly begun to abuse each other's love, tear it into shreds. On that terrible February night that Marion remembered so vividly, a slow quarrel had gone on for hours. There was a scene at the Florida, and then he attempted to take her home, and then she kissed young Webb at a table; after that there was what she had hysterically said. When he arrived home alone he turned the key in the lock in wild anger. How could he know she would arrive an hour later alone, that there would be a snowstorm in which she wandered about in slippers, too confused to find a taxi? Then the aftermath, her escaping pneumonia by a miracle, and all the attendant horror. They were "reconciled," but that was the beginning of the end, and Marion, who had seen with her own eyes and who imagined it to be one of many scenes from her sister's martyrdom, never forgot.

Going over it again brought Helen nearer, and in the white, soft light that steals upon half sleep near morning he found himself talking to her again. She said that he was perfectly right about Honoria and that she wanted Honoria to be with him. She said she was glad he was being good and doing better. She said a lot of other things—very friendly things—but she was in a swing in a white dress, and swinging faster and faster all the time, so that at the end he could not hear clearly all that she said.

·IV·

HE WOKE UP feeling happy. The door of the world was open again. He made plans, vistas, futures for Honoria and himself, but suddenly he grew sad, remembering all the plans he and Helen had made. She had not planned to die. The present was the thing—work to do and someone to love. But not to love too much, for he knew the injury that a father can do to a daughter or a mother to a son by attaching them too closely: afterward, out in the world, the child would seek in the marriage partner the same blind tenderness and, failing probably to find it, turn against love and life.

It was another bright, crisp day. He called Lincoln Peters at the bank where he worked and asked if he could count on taking Honoria when he left for Prague. Lincoln agreed that there was no reason for delay. One thing—the legal guardianship. Marion wanted to retain that a while longer. She was upset by the whole matter, and it would oil things if she felt that the situation was still in her control for another year. Charlie agreed, wanting only the tangible, visible child.

Then the question of a governess. Charlie sat in a gloomy agency and talked to a cross Béarnaise and to a buxom Breton peasant, neither of whom he could have endured. There were others whom he would see tomorrow.

He lunched with Lincoln Peters at Griffons, trying to keep down his exultation.

"There's nothing quite like your own child," Lincoln said. "But you understand how Marion feels too."

"She's forgotten how hard I worked for seven years there," Charlie said. "She just remembers one night."

"There's another thing." Lincoln hesitated. "While you and Helen were tearing around Europe throwing money away, we were just getting along. I didn't touch any of the prosperity because I never got ahead enough to carry anything but my insurance. I think Marion felt there was some kind of injustice in it—you not even working toward the end, and getting richer and richer."

"It went just as quick as it came," said Charlie.

"Yes, a lot of it stayed in the hands of *chasseurs* and saxophone players and maîtres d'hôtel—well, the big party's over now. I just said that to explain Marion's feeling about those crazy years. If you drop in about six o'clock tonight before Marion's too tired, we'll settle the details on the spot."

Back at his hotel, Charlie found a *pneumatique* that had been redirected from the Ritz bar where Charlie had left his address for the purpose of finding a certain man.

DEAR CHARLIE: You were so strange when we saw you the other day that I wondered if I did something to offend you. If so, I'm not conscious of it. In fact, I have thought about you too much for the last year, and it's always been in the back of my mind that I might see you if I came over here. We *did* have such good times that crazy spring, like the night you and I stole the butcher's tricycle, and the time we tried to call on the president and you had the old derby rim and the wire cane. Everybody seems so old lately, but I don't feel old a bit. Couldn't we get together some time today for old time's sake? I've got a vile hang-over for the moment, but will be feeling better this afternoon and will look for you about five in the sweat-shop at the Ritz.

Always devotedly,

LORRAINE.

His first feeling was one of awe that he had actually, in his mature years, stolen a tricycle and pedalled Lorraine all over the Étoile between the small hours and dawn. In retrospect it was a nightmare. Locking out Helen didn't fit in with any other act of his life, but the tricycle incident did—it was one of many. How many weeks or months of dissipation to arrive at that condition of utter irresponsibility?

He tried to picture how Lorraine had appeared to him then—very attractive; Helen was unhappy about it, though she said nothing. Yesterday, in the restaurant, Lorraine had seemed trite, blurred, worn away. He emphatically did not want to see her, and he was glad Alix had not given away his hotel address. It was a relief to think, instead, of Honoria, to think of Sundays spent with her and of saying good morning to her and of knowing she was there in his house at night, drawing her breath in the darkness.

At five he took a taxi and bought presents for all the Peters—a piquant cloth doll, a box of Roman soldiers, flowers for Marion, big linen handkerchiefs for Lincoln.

He saw, when he arrived in the apartment, that Marion had accepted the inevitable. She greeted him now as though he were a recalcitrant member of the family, rather than a menacing outsider. Honoria had been told she was going; Charlie was glad to see that her tact made her conceal her excessive happiness. Only on his lap did she whisper her delight and the question "When?" before she slipped away with the other children.

He and Marion were alone for a minute in the room, and on an impulse he spoke out boldly:

"Family quarrels are bitter things. They don't go according to any rules. They're not like aches or wounds; they're more like splits in the skin that won't heal because there's not enough material. I wish you and I could be on better terms."

"Some things are hard to forget," she answered. "It's a question of confidence." There was no answer to this and presently she asked, "When do you propose to take her?"

"As soon as I can get a governess. I hoped the day after tomorrow."

"That's impossible. I've got to get her things in shape. Not before Saturday."

He yielded. Coming back into the room, Lincoln offered him a drink.

"I'll take my daily whisky," he said.

It was warm here, it was a home, people together by a fire. The children felt very safe and important; the mother and father were serious, watchful. They had things to do for the children more important than his visit here. A spoonful of medicine was, after all, more important than the strained relations between Marion and himself. They were not dull people, but they were very much in the grip of life and circumstances. He wondered if he couldn't do something to get Lincoln out of his rut at the bank.

A long peal at the door-bell; the *bonne à tout faire* passed through and went down the corridor. The door opened upon another long ring, and then voices, and the three in the salon looked up expectantly; Lincoln moved to bring the corridor within his range of vision, and Marion rose. Then the maid came back along the corridor, closely followed by the voices, which developed under the light into Duncan Schaeffer and Lorraine Quarrles.

They were gay, they were hilarious, they were roaring with laughter. For a moment Charlie was astounded; unable to understand how they ferreted out the Peters' address.

"Ah-h-h!" Duncan wagged his finger roguishly at Charlie. "Ah-h-h!"

They both slid down another cascade of laughter. Anxious and at a loss, Charlie shook hands with them quickly and presented them to Lincoln and Marion. Marion nodded, scarcely speaking. She had drawn back a step toward the fire; her little girl stood beside her, and Marion put an arm about her shoulder.

With growing annoyance at the intrusion, Charlie waited for them to explain themselves. After some concentration Duncan said:

"We came to invite you out to dinner. Lorraine and I insist that all this chi-chi, cagy business 'bout your address got to stop."

Charlie came closer to them, as if to force them backward down the corridor.

"Sorry, but I can't. Tell me where you'll be and I'll phone you in half an hour."

This made no impression. Lorraine sat down suddenly on the side of a chair, and focussing her eyes on Richard, cried, "Oh, what a nice little boy! Come here, little boy." Richard glanced at his mother, but did not move. With a perceptible shrug of her shoulders, Lorraine turned back to Charlie:

"Come and dine. Sure your cousins won' mine. See you so sel'om. Or solemn."

"I can't," said Charlie sharply. "You two have dinner and I'll phone you."

Her voice became suddenly unpleasant. "All right, we'll go. But I remember once when you hammered on my door at four A.M. I was enough of a good sport to give you a drink. Come on, Dunc."

Still in slow motion, with blurred, angry faces, with uncertain feet, they retired along the corridor.

"Good night," Charlie said.

"Good night!" responded Lorraine emphatically.

When he went back into the salon Marion had not moved, only now her son was standing in the circle of her other arm. Lincoln was still swinging Honoria back and forth like a pendulum from side to side.

"What an outrage!" Charlie broke out. "What an absolute outrage!"

Neither of them answered. Charlie dropped into an armchair, picked up his drink, set it down again and said:

"People I haven't seen for two years having the colossal nerve——"

He broke off. Marion had made the sound "Oh!" in one swift, furious breath, turned her body from him with a jerk and left the room.

Lincoln set down Honoria carefully.

"You children go in and start your soup," he said, and when they obeyed, he said to Charlie:

"Marion's not well and she can't stand shocks. That kind of people make her really physically sick."

"I didn't tell them to come here. They wormed your name out of somebody. They deliberately——"

"Well, it's too bad. It doesn't help matters. Excuse me a minute."

Left alone, Charlie sat tense in his chair. In the next room he could hear the children eating, talking in monosyllables, already oblivious to the scene between their elders. He heard a murmur of conversation from a farther room and then the ticking bell of a telephone receiver picked up, and in a panic he moved to the other side of the room and out of earshot.

In a minute Lincoln came back. "Look here, Charlie. I think we'd better call off dinner for tonight. Marion's in bad shape."

"Is she angry with me?"

"Sort of," he said, almost roughly. "She's not strong and——"

"You mean she's changed her mind about Honoria?"

"She's pretty bitter right now. I don't know. You phone me at the bank tomorrow."

"I wish you'd explain to her I never dreamed these people would come here. I'm just as sore as you are."

"I couldn't explain anything to her now."

Charlie got up. He took his coat and hat and started down the corridor. Then he opened the door of the dining room and said in a strange voice, "Good night, children."

Honoria rose and ran around the table to hug him.

"Good night, sweetheart," he said vaguely, and then trying to make his voice more tender, trying to conciliate something, "Good night, dear children."

· V ·

CHARLIE WENT DIRECTLY to the Ritz bar with the furious idea of finding Lorraine and Duncan, but they were not there, and he realized that in any case there was nothing he could do. He had not touched his drink at the Peters', and now he ordered a whisky-and-soda. Paul came over to say hello.

"It's a great change," he said sadly. "We do about half the business we did. So many fellows I hear about back in the States lost everything, maybe not in the first crash, but then in the second. Your friend George Hardt lost every cent, I hear. Are you back in the States?"

"No, I'm in business in Prague."

"I heard that you lost a lot in the crash."

"I did," and he added grimly, "but I lost everything I wanted in the boom."

"Selling short."

"Something like that."

Again the memory of those days swept over him like a nightmare—the people they had met travelling; then people who couldn't add a row of figures or speak a coherent sentence. The little man Helen had consented to dance with at the ship's party, who had insulted her ten feet from the table; the women and girls carried screaming with drink or drugs out of public places——

—The men who locked their wives out in the snow, because the snow of twenty-nine wasn't real snow. If you didn't want it to be snow, you just paid some money.

He went to the phone and called the Peters' apartment; Lincoln answered.

"I called up because this thing is on my mind. Has Marion said anything definite?"

"Marion's sick," Lincoln answered shortly. "I know this thing isn't altogether your fault, but I can't have her go to pieces about it. I'm afraid we'll have to let it slide for six months; I can't take the chance of working her up to this state again."

"I see."

"I'm sorry, Charlie."

He went back to his table. His whisky glass was empty, but he shook his head when Alix looked at it questioningly. There wasn't much he could do now except send Honoria some things; he would send her a lot of things tomorrow. He thought rather angrily that this was just money—he had given so many people money. . . .

"No, no more," he said to another waiter. "What do I owe you?"

He would come back some day; they couldn't make him pay forever. But he wanted his child, and nothing was much good now, beside that fact. He wasn't young any more, with a lot of nice thoughts and dreams to have by himself. He was absolutely sure Helen wouldn't have wanted him to be so alone.

A NEW LEAF

◆

"A New Leaf" (Saturday Evening Post, 4 July 1931) is probably the best of the stories in which Fitzgerald examined the effects of alcoholism on character. Nevertheless, it elicited Harold Ober's criticism—which he was probably relaying from the Post—*that in this and two other recent stories Fitzgerald had "failed to make the reader care about any one of the characters." This complaint can be challenged, particularly for Julia. It would appear that Ober was really concerned that the suicide was strong stuff for the* Post, *whose editors believed that Depression readers wanted to be distracted from harsh reality.*

◆

IT WAS THE first day warm enough to eat outdoors in the Bois de Boulogne, while chestnut blossoms slanted down across the tables and dropped impudently into the butter and the wine. Julia Ross ate a few with her bread and listened to the big goldfish rippling in the pool and the sparrows whirring about an abandoned table. You could see everybody again—the waiters with their professional faces, the watchful Frenchwomen all heels and eyes, Phil Hoffman opposite her with his heart balanced on his fork, and the extraordinarily handsome man just coming out on the terrace.

> ———*the purple noon's transparent might.*
> *The breath of the moist air is light*
> *Around each unexpanded bud*———

Julia trembled discreetly; she controlled herself; she didn't spring up and call, "Yi-yi-yi-yi! Isn't this grand?" and push the maître d'hôtel into the lily pond. She sat there, a well-behaved woman of twenty-one, and discreetly trembled.

Phil was rising, napkin in hand. "Hi there, Dick!"

"Hi, Phil!"

It was the handsome man; Phil took a few steps forward and they talked apart from the table.

"——seen Carter and Kitty in Spain——"

"——poured on to the Bremen——"

"——so I was going to——"

The man went on, following the head waiter, and Phil sat down.

"Who is that?" she demanded.

"A friend of mine—Dick Ragland."

"He's without doubt the handsomest man I ever saw in my life."

"Yes, he's handsome," he agreed without enthusiasm.

"Handsome! He's an archangel, he's a mountain lion, he's something to eat. Just why didn't you introduce him?"

"Because he's got the worst reputation of any American in Paris."

"Nonsense; he must be maligned. It's all a dirty frame-up—a lot of jealous husbands whose wives got one look at him. Why, that man's never done anything in his life except lead cavalry charges and save children from drowning."

"The fact remains he's not received anywhere—not for one reason but for a thousand."

"What reasons?"

"Everything. Drink, women, jails, scandals, killed somebody with an automobile, lazy, worthless——"

"I don't believe a word of it," said Julia firmly. "I bet he's tremendously attractive. And you spoke to him as if you thought so too."

"Yes," he said reluctantly, "like so many alcholics, he has a certain charm. If he'd only make his messes off by himself somewhere—except right in people's laps. Just when somebody's taken him up and is making a big fuss over him, he pours the soup down his hostess' back, kisses the serving maid and passes out in the dog kennel. But he's done it too often. He's run through about everybody, until there's no one left."

"There's me," said Julia.

There was Julia, who was a little too good for anybody and sometimes regretted that she had been quite so well endowed. Anything added to beauty has to be paid for—that is to say, the qualities that pass as substitutes can be liabilities when added to beauty itself. Julia's brilliant hazel glance was enough, without the questioning light of intelligence that flickered in it; her irrepressible sense of the ridiculous detracted from the gentle relief of her mouth, and the loveliness of her figure might have been more obvious if she had slouched and postured rather than sat and stood very straight, after the discipline of a strict father.

Equally perfect young men had several times appeared bearing gifts, but generally with the air of being already complete, of having no space for development. On the other hand, she found that men of larger scale had sharp corners and edges in youth, and she was a little too young herself to like that. There was, for instance, this scornful young egotist, Phil Hoffman, opposite her, who was obviously going to be a brilliant lawyer and who had practically followed her to Paris. She liked him as well as anyone she knew, but he had at present all the overbearance of the son of a chief of police.

"Tonight I'm going to London, and Wednesday I sail," he said. "And you'll be in Europe all summer, with somebody new chewing on your ear every few weeks."

"When you've been called for a lot of remarks like that you'll begin to edge into the picture," Julia remarked. "Just to square yourself, I want you to introduce that man Ragland."

"My last few hours!" he complained.

"But I've given you three whole days on the chance you'd work out a better approach. Be a little civilized and ask him to have some coffee."

As Mr. Dick Ragland joined them, Julia drew a little breath of pleasure. He was a fine figure of a man, in coloring both tan and blond, with a peculiar luminosity to his face. His voice was quietly intense; it seemed always to tremble a little with a sort of gay despair; the way he looked at Julia made her feel attractive. For half an hour, as their sentences floated pleasantly among the scent of violets and snowdrops, forget-me-nots and pansies, her interest in him grew. She was even glad when Phil said:

"I've just thought about my English visa. I'll have to leave you two incipient love birds together against my better judgment. Will you meet me at the Gare St. Lazare at five and see me off?"

He looked at Julia hoping she'd say, "I'll go along with you now." She knew very well she had no business being alone with this man, but he made her laugh, and she hadn't laughed much lately, so she said: "I'll stay a few minutes; it's so nice and springy here."

When Phil was gone, Dick Ragland suggested a *fine* champagne.

"I hear you have a terrible reputation?" she said impulsively.

"Awful. I'm not even invited out any more. Do you want me to slip on my false mustache?"

"It's so odd," she pursued. "Don't you cut yourself off from all nourishment? Do you know that Phil felt he had to warn me about you before he introduced you? And I might very well have told him not to."

"Why didn't you?"

"I thought you seemed so attractive and it was such a pity."

His face grew bland; Julia saw that the remark had been made so often that it no longer reached him.

"It's none of my business," she said quickly. She did not realize that his being a sort of outcast added to his attraction for her—not the dissipation itself, for never having seen it, it was merely an abstraction—but its result in making him so alone. Something atavistic in her went out to the stranger to the tribe, a being from a world with different habits from hers, who promised the unexpected—promised adventure.

"I'll tell you something else," he said suddenly. "I'm going permanently on the wagon on June fifth, my twenty-eighth birthday. I don't have fun drinking any more. Evidently I'm not one of the few people who can use liquor."

"You sure you can go on the wagon?"

"I always do what I say I'll do. Also I'm going back to New York and go to work."

"I'm really surprised how glad I am." This was rash, but she let it stand.

"Have another *fine*?" Dick suggested. "Then you'll be gladder still."

"Will you go on this way right up to your birthday?"

"Probably. On my birthday I'll be on the Olympic in mid-ocean."

"I'll be on that boat too!" she exclaimed.

"You can watch the quick change; I'll do it for the ship's concert."

The tables were being cleared off. Julia knew she should go now, but she couldn't bear to leave him sitting with that unhappy look under his smile. She felt, maternally, that she ought to say something to help him keep his resolution.

"Tell me why you drink so much. Probably some obscure reason you don't know yourself."

"Oh, I know pretty well how it began."

He told her as another hour waned. He had gone to the war at seventeen and, when he came back, life as a Princeton freshman with a little black cap was somewhat tame. So he went up to Boston Tech and then abroad to the Beaux Arts; it was there that something happened to him.

"About the time I came into some money I found that with a few drinks I got expansive and somehow had the ability to please people, and the idea turned my head. Then I began to take a whole lot of drinks to keep going and have everybody think I was wonderful. Well, I got plastered a lot and quarreled with most of my friends, and then I met a wild bunch and for a while I was expansive with them. But I was inclined to get superior and suddenly think 'What am I doing with this bunch?' They didn't like that much. And when a taxi that I was in killed a man, I was sued. It was just a graft, but it got in the papers, and after I was released the impression remained that I'd killed him. So all I've got to show for the last five years is a reputation that makes mothers rush their daughters away if I'm at the same hotel."

An impatient waiter was hovering near and she looked at her watch.

"Gosh, we're to see Phil off at five. We've been here all the afternoon."

As they hurried to the Gare St. Lazare, he asked: "Will you let me see you again; or do you think you'd better not?"

She returned his long look. There was no sign of dissipation in his face, in his warm cheeks, in his erect carriage.

"I'm always fine at lunch," he added, like an invalid.

"I'm not worried," she laughed. "Take me to lunch day after tomorrow."

They hurried up the steps of the Gare St. Lazare, only to see the last carriage of the Golden Arrow disappearing toward the Channel. Julia was remorseful, because Phil had come so far.

As a sort of atonement, she went to the apartment where she lived with her aunt and tried to write a letter to him, but Dick Ragland intruded himself into her thoughts. By morning the effect of his good looks had faded a little; she was inclined to write him a note that she couldn't see him. Still, he had made her a simple appeal and she had brought it all on herself. She waited for him at half-past twelve on the appointed day.

Julia had said nothing to her aunt, who had company for luncheon and might mention his name—strange to go out with a man whose name you couldn't mention. He was late and she waited in the hall, listening to the echolalia of chatter from the luncheon party in the dining room. At one she answered the bell.

There in the outer hall stood a man whom she thought she had never seen before. His face was dead white and erratically shaven, his soft hat was crushed bunlike on his head, his shirt collar was dirty, and all except the band of his tie was out of sight. But at the moment when she recognized the figure as Dick Ragland she perceived a change which dwarfed the others into nothing; it was in his expression. His whole face was one prolonged sneer—the lids held with difficulty from covering the fixed eyes, the drooping mouth drawn up over the upper teeth, the chin wabbling like a made-over chin in which the paraffin had run—it was a face that both expressed and inspired disgust.

"H'lo," he muttered.

For a minute she drew back from him; then, at a sudden silence from the dining room that gave on the hall, inspired by the silence in the hall itself, she half pushed him over the threshold, stepped out herself and closed the door behind them.

"Oh-h-h!" she said in a single, shocked breath.

"Haven't been home since yest'day. Got involve' on a party at——"

With repugnance, she turned him around by his arm and stumbled with him down the apartment stairs, passing the concierge's wife, who peered out at them curiously from her glass room. Then they came out into the bright sunshine of the Rue Guynemer.

Against the spring freshness of the Luxembourg Gardens opposite, he was even more grotesque. He frightened her; she looked desperately up and down the street for a taxi, but one turning the corner of the Rue de Vaugirard disregarded her signal.

"Where'll we go lunch?" he asked.

"You're in no shape to go to lunch. Don't you realize? You've got to go home and sleep."

"I'm all right. I get a drink I'll be fine."

A passing cab slowed up at her gesture.

"You go home and go to sleep. You're not fit to go anywhere."

As he focused his eyes on her, realizing her suddenly as something fresh, something new and lovely, something alien to the smoky and turbulent world where he had spent his recent hours, a faint current of reason flowed through him. She saw his mouth twist with vague awe, saw him make a vague attempt to stand up straight. The taxi yawned.

"Maybe you're right. Very sorry."

"What's your address?"

He gave it and then tumbled into a corner, his face still struggling toward reality. Julia closed the door.

When the cab had driven off, she hurried across the street and into the Luxembourg Gardens as if someone were after her.

· II ·

QUITE BY ACCIDENT, she answered when he telephoned at seven that night. His voice was strained and shaking:

"I suppose there's not much use apologizing for this morning. I didn't know what I was doing, but that's no excuse. But if you could let me see you for a while somewhere tomorrow—just for a minute—I'd like the chance of telling you in person how terribly sorry——"

"I'm busy tomorrow."

"Well, Friday then, or any day."

"I'm sorry, I'm very busy this week."

"You mean you don't ever want to see me again?"

"Mr. Ragland, I hardly see the use of going any further with this. Really, that thing this morning was a little too much. I'm very sorry. I hope you feel better. Good-by."

She put him entirely out of her mind. She had not even associated his reputation with such a spectacle—a heavy drinker was someone who sat up late and drank champagne and maybe in the small hours rode home singing. This spectacle at high noon was something else again. Julia was through.

Meanwhile there were other men with whom she lunched at Ciro's and danced in the Bois. There was a reproachful letter from Phil Hoffman in America. She liked Phil better for having been so right about this. A fortnight passed and she would have forgotten Dick Ragland, had she not heard his name mentioned with scorn in several conversations. Evidently he had done such things before.

Then, a week before she was due to sail, she ran into him in the booking department of the White Star Line. He was as handsome—she could hardly believe her eyes. He leaned with an elbow on the desk, his fine figure erect, his yellow gloves as stainless as his clear, shining eyes. His strong, gay personality had affected the clerk who served him with fascinated deference; the stenographers behind looked up for a minute and exchanged a glance. Then he saw Julia; she nodded, and with a quick, wincing change of expression he raised his hat.

They were together by the desk a long time and the silence was oppressive.

"Isn't this a nuisance?" she said.

"Yes," he said jerkily, and then: "You going by the Olympic?"

"Oh, yes."

"I thought you might have changed."

"Of course not," she said coldly.

"I thought of changing; in fact, I was here to ask about it."

"That's absurd."

"You don't hate the sight of me? So it'll make you seasick when we pass each other on the deck?"

She smiled. He seized his advantage:

"I've improved somewhat since we last met."

"Don't talk about that."

"Well then, you have improved. You've got the loveliest costume on I ever saw."

This was presumptuous, but she felt herself shimmering a little at the compliment.

"You wouldn't consider a cup of coffee with me at the café next door, just to recover from this ordeal?"

How weak of her to talk to him like this, to let him make advances. It was like being under the fascination of a snake.

"I'm afraid I can't." Something terribly timid and vulnerable came into his face, twisting a little sinew in her heart. "Well, all right," she shocked herself by saying.

Sitting at the sidewalk table in the sunlight, there was nothing to remind her of that awful day two weeks ago. Jekyll and Hyde. He was courteous, he was charming, he was amusing. He made her feel, oh, so attractive! He presumed on nothing.

"Have you stopped drinking?" she asked.

"Not till the fifth."

"Oh!"

"Not until I said I'd stop. Then I'll stop."

When Julia rose to go, she shook her head at his suggestion of a further meeting.

"I'll see you on the boat. After your twenty-eighth birthday."

"All right; one more thing: It fits in with the high price of crime that I did something inexcusable to the one girl I've ever been in love with in my life."

She saw him the first day on board, and then her heart sank into her shoes as she realized at last how much she wanted him. No matter what his past was, no matter what he had done. Which was not to say that she would ever let him know, but only that he moved her chemically more than anyone she had ever met, that all other men seemed pale beside him.

He was popular on the boat; she heard that he was giving a party on the night of his twenty-eighth birthday. Julia was not invited; when they met they spoke pleasantly, nothing more.

It was the day after the fifth that she found him stretched in his deck chair looking wan and white. There were wrinkles on his fine brow and around his eyes, and his hand, as he reached out for a cup of bouillon, was trembling. He was still there in the late afternoon, visibly suffering, visibly miserable. After three times around, Julia was irresistibly impelled to speak to him:

"Has the new era begun?"

He made a feeble effort to rise, but she motioned him not to and sat on the next chair.

"You look tired."

"I'm just a little nervous. This is the first day in five years that I haven't had a drink."

"It'll be better soon."

"I know," he said grimly.

"Don't weaken."

"I won't."

"Can't I help you in any way? Would you like a bromide?"

"I can't stand bromides," he said almost crossly. "No, thanks, I mean."

Julia stood up: "I know you feel better alone. Things will be brighter tomorrow."

"Don't go, if you can stand me."

Julia sat down again.

"Sing me a song—can you sing?"

"What kind of a song?"

"Something sad—some sort of blues."

She sang him Libby Holman's "This is how the story ends," in a low, soft voice.

"That's good. Now sing another. Or sing that again."

"All right. If you like, I'll sing to you all afternoon."

· I I I ·

THE SECOND DAY in New York he called her on the phone. "I've missed you so," he said. "Have you missed me?"

"I'm afraid I have," she said reluctantly.

"Much?"

"I've missed you a lot. Are you better?"

"I'm all right now. I'm still just a little nervous, but I'm starting work tomorrow. When can I see you?"

"When you want."

"This evening then. And look—say that again."

"What?"

"That you're afraid you have missed me."

"I'm afraid that I have," Julia said obediently.

"Missed me," he added.

"I'm afraid I have missed you."

"All right. It sounds like a song when you say it."

"Good-by, Dick."

"Good-by, Julia dear."

She stayed in New York two months instead of the fortnight she had intended, because he would not let her go. Work took the place of drink in the daytime, but afterward he must see Julia.

Sometimes she was jealous of his work when he telephoned that he was too tired to go out after the theater. Lacking drink, night life was less than nothing to him—something quite spoiled and well lost. For Julia, who never drank, it was a stimulus in itself—the music and the parade of dresses and the handsome couple they made dancing together. At first they saw Phil Hoffman once in a while; Julia considered that he took the matter rather badly; then they didn't see him any more.

A few unpleasant incidents occurred. An old schoolmate, Esther Cary, came to her to ask if she knew of Dick Ragland's reputation. Instead of growing angry, Julia invited her to meet Dick and was delighted with the ease with which Esther's convictions were changed. There were other, small, annoying episodes, but Dick's misdemeanors had, fortunately, been confined to Paris and assumed here a far-away unreality. They loved each other deeply now—the memory of that morning slowly being effaced from Julia's imagination—but she wanted to be sure.

"After six months, if everything goes along like this, we'll announce our engagement. After another six months we'll be married."

"Such a long time," he mourned.

"But there were five years before that," Julia answered. "I trust you with my heart and with my mind, but something else says wait. Remember, I'm also deciding for my children."

Those five years—oh, so lost and gone.

In August, Julia went to California for two months to see her family. She wanted to know how Dick would get along alone. They wrote every day; his letters were by turns cheerful, depressed, weary and hopeful. His work was going better. As things came back to him, his uncle had begun really to believe in him, but all the time he missed his Julia so. It was when an occasional note of despair began to appear that she cut her visit short by a week and came East to New York.

"Oh, thank God you're here!" he cried as they linked arms and walked out of the Grand Central station. "It's been so hard. Half a dozen times lately I've wanted to go on a bust and I had to think of you, and you were so far away."

"Darling—darling, you're so tired and pale. You're working too hard."

"No, only that life is so bleak alone. When I go to bed my mind churns on and on. Can't we get married sooner?"

"I don't know; we'll see. You've got your Julia near you now, and nothing matters."

After a week, Dick's depression lifted. When he was sad, Julia made him her baby, holding his handsome head against her breast, but she liked it best when he was confident and could cheer her up, making her laugh and feel taken care of and secure. She had rented an apartment with another girl and she took courses in biology and domestic science in Columbia. When deep fall came, they went to football games and the new shows together, and walked through the first snow in Central Park, and several times a week spent long evenings together in front of her fire. But time was going by and they were both impatient. Just before Christmas, an unfamiliar visitor— Phil Hoffman—presented himself at her door. It was the first time in many months. New York, with its quality of many independent ladders set side by side, is unkind to even the meetings of close friends; so, in the case of strained relations, meetings are easy to avoid.

And they were strange to each other. Since his expressed skepticism of Dick, he was automatically her enemy; on another count, she saw that he had improved, some of the hard angles were worn off; he was now an assistant district attorney, moving around with increasing confidence through his profession.

"So you're going to marry Dick?" he said. "When?"

"Soon now. When mother comes East."

He shook his head emphatically. "Julia, don't marry Dick. This isn't jealousy—I know when I am licked—but it seems awful for a lovely girl like you to take a blind dive into a lake full of rocks. What makes you think that people change their courses? Sometimes they dry up or even flow into a parallel channel, but I've never known anybody to change."

"Dick's changed."

"Maybe so. But isn't that an enormous 'maybe'? If he was unattractive and you liked him, I'd say go ahead with it. Maybe I'm all wrong, but it's so darn obvious that what fascinates you is that handsome pan of his and those attractive manners."

"You don't know him," Julia answered loyally. "He's different with me. You don't know how gentle he is, and responsive. Aren't you being rather small and mean?"

"Hm." Phil thought for a moment. "I want to see you again in a few days. Or perhaps I'll speak to Dick."

"You let Dick alone," she cried. "He has enough to worry him without your nagging him. If you were his friend you'd try to help him instead of coming to me behind his back."

"I'm your friend first."

"Dick and I are one person now."

But three days later Dick came to see her at an hour when he would usually have been at the office.

"I'm here under compulsion," he said lightly, "under threat of exposure by Phil Hoffman."

Her heart dropping like a plummet. "Has he given up?" she thought. "Is he drinking again?"

"It's about a girl. You introduced me to her last summer and told me to be very nice to her—Esther Cary."

Now her heart was beating slowly.

"After you went to California I was lonesome and I ran into her. She'd liked me that day, and for a while we saw quite a bit of each other. Then you came back and I broke it off. It was a little difficult; I hadn't realized that she was so interested."

"I see." Her voice was starved and aghast.

"Try and understand. Those terribly lonely evenings. I think if it hadn't been for Esther, I'd have fallen off the wagon. I never loved her—I never loved anybody but you—but I had to see somebody who liked me."

He put his arm around her, but she felt cold all over and he drew away.

"Then any woman would have done," Julia said slowly. "It didn't matter who."

"No!" he cried.

"I stayed away so long to let you stand on your own feet and get back your self-respect by yourself."

"I only love you, Julia."

"But any woman can help you. So you don't really need me, do you?"

His face wore that vulnerable look that Julia had seen several times before; she sat on the arm of his chair and ran her hand over his cheek.

"Then what do you bring me?" she demanded. "I thought that there'd be the accumulated strength of having beaten your weakness. What do you bring me now?"

"Everything I have."

She shook her head. "Nothing. Just your good looks—and the head waiter at dinner last night had that."

They talked for two days and decided nothing. Sometimes she would pull him close and reach up to his lips that she loved so well, but her arms seemed to close around straw.

"I'll go away and give you a chance to think it over," he said despairingly. "I can't see any way of living without you, but I suppose you can't marry a man you don't trust or believe in. My uncle wanted me to go to London on some business——"

The night he left, it was sad on the dim pier. All that kept her from breaking was that it was not an image of strength that was leaving her; she would be just as strong without him. Yet as the murky lights fell on the fine structure of his brow and chin, as she saw the faces turn toward him, the eyes that followed him, an awful emptiness seized her and she wanted to say: "Never mind, dear; we'll try it together."

But try what? It was human to risk the toss between failure and success, but to risk the desperate gamble between adequacy and disaster——

"Oh, Dick, be good and be strong and come back to me. Change, change, Dick—change!"

"Good-by, Julia—good-by."

She last saw him on the deck, his profile cut sharp as a cameo against a match as he lit a cigarette.

· I V ·

IT WAS PHIL Hoffman who was to be with her at the beginning and the end. It was he who broke the news as gently as it could be broken. He reached her apartment at half-past eight and carefully threw away the morning paper outside. Dick Ragland had disappeared at sea.

After her first wild burst of grief, he became purposely a little cruel.

"He knew himself. His will had given out; he didn't want life any more. And, Julia, just to show you how little you can possibly blame yourself, I'll tell you this: He'd hardly gone to his office for four months—since you went to California. He wasn't fired because of his uncle; the business he went to London on was of no importance at all. After his first enthusiasm was gone he'd given up."

She looked at him sharply. "He didn't drink, did he? He wasn't drinking?"

For a fraction of a second Phil hesitated. "No, he didn't drink; he kept his promise—he held on to that."

"That was it," she said. "He kept his promise and he killed himself doing it."

Phil waited uncomfortably.

"He did what he said he would and broke his heart doing it," she went on chokingly. "Oh, isn't life cruel sometimes—so cruel, never to let anybody off. He was so brave—he died doing what he said he'd do."

Phil was glad he had thrown away the newspaper that hinted of Dick's gay evening in the bar—one of many gay evenings that Phil had known of in the past few months. He was relieved that was over, because Dick's weakness had threatened the happiness of the girl he loved; but he was terribly sorry for him—even understanding how it was necessary for him to turn his maladjustment to life toward one mischief or another—but he was wise enough to leave Julia with the dream that she had saved out of wreckage.

There was a bad moment a year later, just before their marriage, when she said:

"You'll understand the feeling I have and always will have about Dick, won't you, Phil? It wasn't just his good looks. I believed in him—and I was right in a way. He broke rather than bent; he was a ruined man, but not a bad man. In my heart I knew when I first looked at him."

Phil winced, but he said nothing. Perhaps there was more behind it than they knew. Better let it all alone in the depths of her heart and the depths of the sea.

A FREEZE-OUT

◆

"A Freeze-Out" (Saturday Evening Post, 19 December 1931) was the last story Fitzgerald wrote in Europe before his return to America in September 1931. In response to the Post's reservations about his recent work, Fitzgerald selected an American setting and ignored the Depression. "A Freeze-Out" represents a return to the mood of his earlier stories in which problems are solved by decency and good breeding.

◆

HERE AND THERE in a sunless corner skulked a little snow under a veil of coal specks, but the men taking down storm windows were laboring in shirt sleeves and the turf was becoming firm underfoot.

In the streets, dresses dyed after fruit, leaf and flower emerged from beneath the shed somber skins of animals; now only a few old men wore mousy caps pulled down over their ears. That was the day Forrest Winslow forgot the long fret of the past winter as one forgets inevitable afflictions, sickness, and war, and turned with blind confidence toward the summer, thinking he already recognized in it all the summers of the past—the golfing, sailing, swimming summers.

For eight years Forrest had gone East to school and then to college; now he worked for his father in a large Minnesota city. He was handsome, popular and rather spoiled in a conservative way, and so the past year had been a comedown. The discrimination that had picked Scroll and Key at New Haven was applied to sorting furs; the hand that had signed the Junior Prom expense checks had since rocked in a sling for two months with mild *dermatitis venenata*. After work, Forrest found no surcease in the girls with whom he had grown up. On the contrary, the news of a stranger within the tribe stimulated him and during the transit of a popular visitor he displayed a convulsive activity. So far, nothing had happened; but here was summer.

On the day spring broke through and summer broke through—it is much the same thing in Minnesota—Forrest stopped his coupé in front of a music store and took his pleasant vanity inside. As he said to the clerk, "I want some records," a little bomb of excitement exploded in his larynx, causing an unfamiliar and almost painful vacuum in his upper diaphragm. The unexpected detonation was caused by the sight of a corn-colored girl who was being waited on across the counter.

She was a stalk of ripe corn, but bound not as cereals are but as a rare first edition, with all the binder's art. She was lovely and expensive, and about nineteen, and he had never seen her before. She looked at him for just an unnecessary moment too long, with so much self-confidence that he felt his own rush out and away to join hers—". . . from him that hath not shall be taken away even that which he hath." Then her head swayed forward and she resumed her inspection of a catalogue.

Forrest looked at the list a friend had sent him from New York. Unfortunately, the first title was: "When Voo-do-o-do Meets Boop-boop-a-doop, There'll Soon be a Hot-Cha-Cha." Forrest read it with horror. He could scarcely believe a title could be so repulsive.

Meanwhile the girl was asking: "Isn't there a record of Prokofiev's 'Fils Prodigue'?"

"I'll see, madam." The saleswoman turned to Forrest.

" 'When Voo——' " Forrest began, and then repeated, " 'When Voo——' "

There was no use; he couldn't say it in front of that nymph of the harvest across the table.

"Never mind that one," he said quickly. "Give me 'Huggable——' " Again he broke off.

" 'Huggable, Kissable You'? " suggested the clerk helpfully, and her assurance that it was very nice suggested a humiliating community of taste.

"I want Stravinsky's 'Fire Bird,' " said the other customer, "and this album of Chopin waltzes."

Forrest ran his eye hastily down the rest of his list: "Digga Diggity," "Ever So Goosy," "Bunkey Doodle I Do."

"Anybody would take me for a moron," he thought. He crumpled up the list and fought for air—his own kind of air, the air of casual superiority.

"I'd like," he said coldly, "Beethoven's 'Moonlight Sonata.' "

There was a record of it at home, but it didn't matter. It gave him the right to glance at the girl again and again. Life became interesting; she was the loveliest concoction; it would be easy to trace her. With the "Moonlight Sonata" wrapped face to face with "Huggable, Kissable You," Forrest quitted the shop.

There was a new book store down the street, and here also he entered, as if books and records could fill the vacuum that spring was making in his heart. As he looked among the lifeless words of many titles together, he was wondering how soon he could find her, and what then.

"I'd like a hard-boiled detective story," he said.

A weary young man shook his head with patient reproof; simultaneously, a spring draft from the door blew in with it the familiar glow of cereal hair.

"We don't carry detective stories or stuff like that," said the young man in an unnecessarily loud voice. "I imagine you'll find it at a department store."

"I thought you carried books," said Forrest feebly.

"Books, yes, but not that kind." The young man turned to wait on his other customer.

As Forrest stalked out, passing within the radius of the girl's perfume, he heard her ask:

"Have you got anything of Louis Arragon's, either in French or in translation?"

"She's just showing off," he thought angrily. "They skip right from Peter Rabbit to Marcel Proust these days."

Outside, parked just behind his own adequate coupé, he found an enormous silver-colored roadster of English make and custom design. Disturbed, even upset, he drove homeward through the moist, golden afternoon.

The Winslows lived in an old, wide-verandaed house on Crest Avenue —Forrest's father and mother, his great-grandmother and his sister Eleanor. They were solid people as that phrase goes since the war. Old Mrs. Forrest was entirely solid; with convictions based on a way of life that had worked for eighty-four years. She was a character in the city; she remembered the Sioux war and she had been in Stillwater the day the James brothers shot up the main street.

Her own children were dead and she looked on these remoter descendants from a distance, oblivious of the forces that had formed them. She understood that the Civil War and the opening up of the West were forces, while the free-silver movement and the World War had reached her only as news. But she knew that her father, killed at Cold Harbor, and her husband, the merchant, were larger in scale than her son or her grandson. People who tried to explain contemporary phenomena to her seemed, to her, to be talking against the evidence of their own senses. Yet she was not atrophied; last summer she had traveled over half of Europe with only a maid.

Forrest's father and mother were something else again. They had been in the susceptible middle thirties when the cocktail party and its concomitants arrived in 1921. They were divided people, leaning forward and backward. Issues that presented no difficulty to Mrs. Forrest caused them painful heat and agitation. Such an issue arose before they had been five minutes at table that night.

"Do you know the Rikkers are coming back?" said Mrs. Winslow. "They've taken the Warner house." She was a woman with many uncertainties, which she concealed from herself by expressing her opinions very slowly and thoughtfully, to convince her own ears. "It's a wonder Dan Warner would rent them his house. I suppose Cathy thinks everybody will fall all over themselves."

"What Cathy?" asked old Mrs. Forrest.

"She was Cathy Chase. Her father was Reynold Chase. She and her husband are coming back here."

"Oh, yes."

"I scarcely knew her," continued Mrs. Winslow, "but I know that when they were in Washington they were pointedly rude to everyone from Minnesota—went out of their way. Mary Cowan was spending a winter there, and she invited Cathy to lunch or tea at least half a dozen times. Cathy never appeared."

"I could beat that record," said Pierce Winslow. "Mary Cowan could invite me a hundred times and I wouldn't go."

"Anyhow," pursued his wife slowly, "in view of all the scandal, it's just asking for the cold shoulder to come out here."

"They're asking for it, all right," said Winslow. He was a Southerner, well liked in the city, where he had lived for thirty years. "Walter Hannan came in my office this morning and wanted me to second Rikker for the Kennemore Club. I said: 'Walter, I'd rather second Al Capone.' What's more, Rikker'll get into the Kennemore Club over my dead body."

"Walter had his nerve. What's Chauncey Rikker to you? It'll be hard to get anyone to second him."

"Who are they?" Eleanor asked. "Somebody awful?"

She was eighteen and a débutante. Her current appearances at home were so rare and brief that she viewed such table topics with as much detachment as her great-grandmother.

"Cathy was a girl here; she was younger then I was, but I remember that she was always considered fast. Her husband, Chauncey Rikker, came from some little town upstate."

"What did they do that was so awful?"

"Rikker went bankrupt and left town," said her father. "There were a lot of ugly stories. Then he went to Washington and got mixed up in the alien-property scandal; and then he got in trouble in New York—he was in the bucket-shop business—but he skipped out to Europe. After a few years the chief Government witness died and he came back to America. They got him for a few months for contempt of court." He expanded into eloquent irony: "And now, with true patriotism, he comes back to his beautiful Minnesota, a product of its lovely woods, its rolling wheat fields——"

Forrest called him impatiently: "Where do you get that, father? When did two Kentuckians ever win Nobel prizes in the same year? And how about an upstate boy named Lind——"

"Have the Rikkers any children?" Eleanor asked.

"I think Cathy has a daughter about your age, and a boy about sixteen."

Forrest uttered a small, unnoticed exclamation. Was it possible? French books and Russian music—that girl this afternoon had lived abroad. And with the probability his resentment deepened—the daughter of a crook putting on all that dog! He sympathized passionately with his father's refusal to second Rikker for the Kennemore Club.

"Are they rich?" old Mrs. Forrest suddenly demanded.

"They must be well off if they took Dan Warner's house."

"Then they'll get in all right."

"They won't get into the Kennemore Club," said Pierce Winslow. "I happen to come from a state with certain traditions."

"I've seen the bottom rail get to be the top rail many times in this town," said the old lady blandly.

"But this man's a criminal, grandma," explained Forrest. "Can't you see the difference? It isn't a social question. We used to argue at New Haven whether we'd shake hands with Al Capone if we met him——"

"Who is Al Capone?" asked Mrs. Forrest.

"He's another criminal, in Chicago."

"Does he want to join the Kennemore Club too?"

They laughed, but Forrest had decided that if Rikker came up for the Kennemore Club, his father's would not be the only black ball in the box.

Abruptly it became full summer. After the last April storm someone came along the street one night, blew up the trees like balloons, scattered bulbs and shrubs like confetti, opened a cage full of robins and, after a quick look around, signaled up the curtain upon a new backdrop of summer sky.

Tossing back a strayed baseball to some kids in a vacant lot, Forrest's fingers, on the stitched seams of the stained leather cover, sent a wave of ecstatic memories to his brain. One must hurry and get there—"there" was now the fairway of the golf course, but his feeling was the same. Only when he teed off at the eighteenth that afternoon did he realize that it wasn't the same, that it would never be enough any more. The evening stretched large and empty before him, save for the set pieces of a dinner party and bed.

While he waited with his partner for a match to play off, Forrest glanced at the tenth tee, exactly opposite and two hundred yards away.

One of the two figures on the ladies' tee was addressing her ball; as he watched, she swung up confidently and cracked a long drive down the fairway.

"Must be Mrs. Horrick," said his friend. "No other woman can drive like that."

At that moment the sun glittered on the girl's hair and Forrest knew who it was; simultaneously, he remembered what he must do this afternoon. That night Chauncey Rikker's name was to come up before the membership committee on which his father sat, and before going home, Forrest was going to pass the clubhouse and leave a certain black slip in a little box. He had carefully considered all that; he loved the city where his people had lived honorable lives for five generations. His grandfather had been a founder of this club in the 90's when it went in for sailboat racing instead of golf, and when it took a fast horse three hours to trot out here from town. He agreed with his father that certain people were without the pale. Tightening his face, he drove his ball two hundred yards down the fairway, where it curved gently into the rough.

The eighteenth and tenth holes were parallel and faced in opposite directions. Between tees they were separated by a belt of trees forty feet wide. Though Forrest did not know it, Miss Rikker's hostess, Helen Hannan, had dubbed into this same obscurity, and as he went in search of his ball he heard female voices twenty feet away.

"You'll be a member after tonight," he heard Helen Hannan say, "and then you can get some real competition from Stella Horrick."

"Maybe I won't be a member," said a quick, clear voice. "Then you'll have to come and play with me on the public links."

"Alida, don't be absurd."

"Why? I played on the public links in Buffalo all last spring. For the moment there wasn't anywhere else. It's like playing on some courses in Scotland."

"But I'd feel so silly. . . . Oh, gosh, let's let the ball go."

"There's nobody behind us. As to feeling silly—if I cared about public opinion any more, I'd spend my time in my bedroom." She laughed scornfully. "A tabloid published a picture of me going to see father in prison. And I've seen people change their tables away from us on steamers, and once I was cut by all the American girls in a French school. . . . Here's your ball."

"Thanks. . . . Oh, Alida, it seems terrible."

"All the terrible part is over. I just said that so you wouldn't be too sorry for us if people didn't want us in this club. I wouldn't care; I've got a life of my own and my own standard of what trouble is. It wouldn't touch me at all."

They passed out of the clearing and their voices disappeared into the open sky on the other side. Forrest abandoned the search for his lost ball and walked toward the caddie house.

"What a hell of a note," he thought. "To take it out on a girl that had nothing to do with it"—which was what he was doing this minute as he went up toward the club. "No," he said to himself abruptly, "I can't do it. Whatever her father may have done, she happens to be a lady. Father can do what he feels he has to do, but I'm out."

After lunch the next day, his father said rather diffidently: "I see you didn't do anything about the Rikkers and the Kennemore Club."

"No."

"It's just as well," said his father. "As a matter of fact, they got by. The club has got rather mixed anyhow in the last five years—a good many queer people in it. And, after all, in a club you don't have to know anybody you don't want to. The other people on the committee felt the same way."

"I see," said Forrest dryly. "Then you didn't argue against the Rikkers?"

"Well, no. The thing is I do a lot of business with Walter Hannan, and it happened yesterday I was obliged to ask him rather a difficult favor."

"So you traded with him." To both father and son, the word "traded" sounded like traitor.

"Not exactly. The matter wasn't mentioned."

"I understand," Forrest said. But he did not understand, and some old childhood faith in his father died at that moment.

· I I ·

TO SNUB ANYONE effectively one must have him within range. The admission of Chauncey Rikker to the Kennemore Club and, later, to the Downtown Club was followed by angry talk and threats of resignation that simulated the sound of conflict, but there was no indication of a will underneath. On the other hand, unpleasantness in crowds is easy, and Chauncey Rikker was a facile object for personal dislike; moreover, a recurrent echo of the bucket-shop scandal sounded from New York, and the matter was reviewed in the local newspapers, in case anyone had missed it. Only the liberal Hannan family stood by the Rikkers, and their attitude aroused considerable resentment, and their attempt to launch them with a series of small parties proved a failure. Had the Rikkers attempted to "bring Alida out," it would have been for the inspection of a motley crowd indeed, but they didn't.

When, occasionally during the summer, Forrest encountered Alida Rikker, they crossed eyes in the curious way of children who don't know each other. For a while he was haunted by her curly yellow head, by the golden-brown defiance of her eyes; then he became interested in another girl. He wasn't in love with Jane Drake, though he thought he might marry her. She was "the girl across the street"; he knew her qualities, good and bad, so that they didn't matter. She had an essential reality underneath, like a relative. It would please their families. Once, after several highballs and some casual necking, he almost answered seriously when she provoked him with "But you don't really care about me"; but he sat tight and next morning was relieved that he had. Perhaps in the dull days after Christmas——Meanwhile, at the Christmas dances among the Christmas girls he might find the ecstasy and misery, the infatuation that he wanted. By autumn he felt that his predestined girl was already packing her trunk in some Eastern or Southern city.

It was in his more restless mood that one November Sunday he went to a small tea. Even as he spoke to his hostess he felt Alida Rikker across the firelit room; her glowing beauty and her unexplored novelty pressed up against him, and there was a relief in being presented to her at last. He bowed and passed on, but there had been some sort of communication. Her look said that she knew the stand that his family had taken, that she didn't mind, and was even sorry to see him in such a silly position, for she knew that he admired her. His look said: "Naturally, I'm sensitive to your beauty, but you see how it is; we've had to draw the line at the fact that your father is a dirty dog, and I can't withdraw from my present position."

Suddenly in a silence, she was talking, and his ears swayed away from his own conversation.

". . . Helen had this odd pain for over a year and, of course, they suspected cancer. She went to have an X ray; she undressed behind a screen, and the doctor looked at her through the machine, and then he said, 'But I told you to take off all your clothes,' and Helen said, 'I have.' The doctor looked again, and said, 'Listen, my dear, I brought you into the world, so there's no use being modest with me. Take off everything.' So Helen said, 'I've got every stitch off; I swear.' But the doctor said, 'You have not. The X ray shows me a safety pin in your brassiere.' Well, they finally found out that she'd been suspected of swallowing a safety pin when she was two years old."

The story, floating in her clear, crisp voice upon the intimate air, disarmed Forrest. It had nothing to do with what had taken place in Washington or

New York ten years before. Suddenly he wanted to go and sit near her, because she was the tongue of flame that made the firelight vivid. Leaving, he walked for an hour through feathery snow, wondering again why he couldn't know her, why it was his business to represent a standard.

"Well, maybe I'll have a lot of fun some day doing what I ought to do," he thought ironically—"when I'm fifty."

The first Christmas dance was the charity ball at the armory. It was a large, public affair; the rich sat in boxes. Everyone came who felt he belonged, and many out of curiosity, so the atmosphere was tense with a strange haughtiness and aloofness.

The Rikkers had a box. Forrest, coming in with Jane Drake, glanced at the man of evil reputation and at the beaten woman frozen with jewels who sat beside him. They were the city's villains, gaped at by the people of reserved and timid lives. Oblivious of the staring eyes, Alida and Helen Hannan held court for several young men from out of town. Without question, Alida was incomparably the most beautiful girl in the room.

Several people told Forrest the news—the Rikkers were giving a big dance after New Year's. There were written invitations, but these were being supplemented by oral ones. Rumor had it that one had merely to be presented to any Rikker in order to be bidden to the dance.

As Forrest passed through the hall, two friends stopped him and with a certain hilarity introduced him to a youth of seventeen, Mr. Teddy Rikker.

"We're giving a dance," said the young man immediately. "January third. Be very happy if you could come."

Forrest was afraid he had an engagement.

"Well, come if you change your mind."

"Horrible kid, but shrewd," said one of his friends later. "We were feeding him people, and when we brought up a couple of saps, he looked at them and didn't say a word. Some refuse and a few accept and most of them stall, but he goes right on; he's got his father's crust."

Into the highways and byways. Why didn't the girl stop it? He was sorry for her when he found Jane in a group of young women reveling in the story.

"I hear they asked Bodman, the undertaker, by mistake, and then took it back."

"Mrs. Carleton pretended she was deaf."

"There's going to be a carload of champagne from Canada."

"Of course, I won't go, but I'd love to, just to see what happens. There'll be a hundred men to every girl—and that'll be meat for her."

The accumulated malice repelled him, and he was angry at Jane for being part of it. Turning away, his eyes fell on Alida's proud form swaying along a wall, watched the devotion of her partners with an unpleasant resentment. He did not know that he had been a little in love with her for many months. Just as two children can fall in love during a physical struggle over a ball, so their awareness of each other had grown to surprising proportions.

"She's pretty," said Jane. "She's not exactly overdressed, but considering everything, she dresses too elaborately."

"I suppose she ought to wear sackcloth and ashes or half mourning."

"I was honored with a written invitation, but, of course, I'm not going."

"Why not?"

Jane looked at him in surprise. "You're not going."

"That's different. I would if I were you. You see, you don't care what her father did."

"Of course, I care."

"No, you don't. And all this small meanness just debases the whole thing. Why don't they let her alone? She's young and pretty and she's done nothing wrong."

Later in the week he saw Alida at the Hannans' dance and noticed that many men danced with her. He saw her lips moving, heard her laughter, caught a word or so of what she said; irresistibly he found himself guiding partners around in her wake. He envied visitors to the city who didn't know who she was.

The night of the Rikkers' dance he went to a small dinner; before they sat down at table he realized that the others were all going on to the Rikkers'. They talked of it as a sort of comic adventure; insisted that he come too.

"Even if you weren't invited, it's all right," they assured him. "We were told we could bring anyone. It's just a free-for-all; it doesn't put you under any obligations. Norma Nash is going and she didn't invite Alida Rikker to her party. Besides, she's really very nice. My brother's quite crazy about her. Mother is worried sick, because he says he wants to marry her."

Clasping his hand about a new highball, Forrest knew that if he drank it he would probably go. All his reasons for not going seemed old and tired, and, fatally, he had begun to seem absurd to himself. In vain he tried to remember the purpose he was serving, and found none. His father had weakened on the matter of the Kennemore Club. And now suddenly he found reasons for going—men could go where their women could not.

"All right," he said.

The Rikkers' dance was in the ballroom of the Minnekada Hotel. The Rikkers' gold, ill-gotten, tainted, had taken the form of a forest of palms, vines and flowers. The two orchestras moaned in pergolas lit with fireflies, and many-colored spotlights swept the floor, touching a buffet where dark bottles gleamed. The receiving line was still in action when Forrest's party came in, and Forrest grinned ironically at the prospect of taking Chauncey Rikker by the hand. But at the sight of Alida, her look that at last fell frankly on him, he forgot everything else.

"Your brother was kind enough to invite me," he said.

"Oh, yes," she was polite, but vague; not at all overwhelmed by his presence. As he waited to speak to her parents, he started, seeing his sister in a group of dancers. Then, one after another, he identified people he knew: it might have been any one of the Christmas dances; all the younger crowd were there. He discovered abruptly that he and Alida were alone; the receiving line had broken up. Alida glanced at him questioningly and with a certain amusement.

So he danced out on the floor with her, his head high, but slightly spinning. Of all things in the world, he had least expected to lead off the Chauncey Rikkers' ball.

· I I I ·

NEXT MORNING HIS first realization was that he had kissed her; his second was a feeling of profound shame for his conduct of the evening. Lord help him, he had been the life of the party; he had helped to run the cotillion. From the moment when he danced out on the floor, coolly meeting the surprised and interested glances of his friends, a mood of desperation had come over him. He rushed Alida Rikker, until a friend asked him what Jane was going to say. "What business is it of Jane's?" he demanded impatiently. "We're not engaged." But he was impelled to approach his sister and ask her if he looked all right.

"Apparently," Eleanor answered, "but when in doubt, don't take any more."

So he hadn't. Exteriorly he remained correct, but his libido was in a state of wild extroversion. He sat with Alida Rikker and told her he had loved her for months.

"Every night I thought of you just before you went to sleep," his voice trembled with insincerity, "I was afraid to meet you or speak to you. Sometimes I'd see you in the distance moving along like a golden chariot, and the world would be good to live in."

After twenty minutes of this eloquence, Alida began to feel exceedingly attractive. She was tired and rather happy, and eventually she said:

"All right, you can kiss me if you want to, but it won't mean anything. I'm just not in that mood."

But Forrest had moods enough for both; he kissed her as if they stood together at the altar. A little later he had thanked Mrs. Rikker with deep emotion for the best time he had ever had in his life.

It was noon, and as he groped his way upright in bed, Eleanor came in in her dressing gown.

"How are you?" she asked.

"Awful."

"How about what you told me coming back in the car? Do you actually want to marry Alida Rikker?"

"Not this morning."

"That's all right then. Now, look: the family are furious."

"Why?" he asked with some redundancy.

"Both you and I being there. Father heard that you led the cotillion. My explanation was that my dinner party went, and so I had to go; but then you went too!"

Forrest dressed and went down to Sunday dinner. Over the table hovered an atmosphere of patient, puzzled, unworldly disappointment. Finally Forrest launched into it:

"Well, we went to Al Capone's party and had a fine time."

"So I've heard," said Pierce Winslow dryly. Mrs. Winslow said nothing.

"Everybody was there—the Kayes, the Schwanes, the Martins and the Blacks. From now on, the Rikkers are pillars of society. Every house is open to them."

"Not this house," said his mother. "They won't come into this house." And after a moment: "Aren't you going to eat anything, Forrest?"

"No, thanks. I mean, yes, I am eating." He looked cautiously at his plate. "The girl is very nice. There isn't a girl in town with better manners or more stuff. If things were like they were before the war, I'd say——"

He couldn't think exactly what it was he would have said; all he knew was that he was now on an entirely different road from his parents'.

"This city was scarcely more than a village before the war," said old Mrs. Forrest.

"Forrest means the World War, granny," said Eleanor.

"Some things don't change," said Pierce Winslow. Both he and Forrest thought of the Kennemore Club matter and, feeling guilty, the older man lost his temper:

"When people start going to parties given by a convicted criminal, there's something serious the matter with them."

"We won't discuss it any more at table," said Mrs. Winslow hastily.

About four, Forrest called a number on the telephone in his room. He had known for some time that he was going to call a number.

"Is Miss Rikker at home? . . . Oh, hello. This is Forrest Winslow."

"How are you?"

"Terrible. It was a good party."

"Wasn't it?"

"Too good. What are you doing?"

"Entertaining two awful hangovers."

"Will you entertain me too?"

"I certainly will. Come on over."

The two young men could only groan and play sentimental music on the phonograph, but presently they departed; the fire leaped up, day went out behind the windows, and Forrest had rum in his tea.

"So we met at last," he said.

"The delay was all yours."

"Damn prejudice," he said. "This is a conservative city, and your father being in this trouble——"

"I can't discuss my father with you."

"Excuse me. I only wanted to say that I've felt like a fool lately for not knowing you. For cheating myself out of the pleasure of knowing you for a silly prejudice," he blundered on. "So I decided to follow my own instincts."

She stood up suddenly. "Good-by, Mr. Winslow."

"What? Why?"

"Because it's absurd for you to come here as if you were doing me a favor. And after accepting our hospitality, to remind me of my father's troubles is simply bad manners."

He was on his feet, terribly upset. "That isn't what I meant. I said I had felt that way, and I despised myself for it. Please don't be sore."

"Then don't be condescending." She sat back in her chair. Her mother came in, stayed only a moment, and threw Forrest a glance of resentment and suspicion as she left. But her passage through had brought them together, and they talked frankly for a long time.

"I ought to be upstairs dressing."

"I ought to have gone an hour ago, and I can't."

"Neither can I."

With the admission they had traveled far. At the door he kissed her unreluctant lips and walked home, throwing futile buckets of reason on the wild fire.

Less than two weeks later it happened. In a car parked in a blizzard he poured out his worship, and she lay on his chest, sighing, "Oh, me too—me too."

Already Forrest's family knew where he went in the evenings; there was a frightened coolness, and one morning his mother said:

"Son, you don't want to throw yourself away on some girl that isn't up to you. I thought you were interested in Jane Drake."

"Don't bring that up. I'm not going to talk about it."

But it was only a postponement. Meanwhile the days of this February were white and magical, the nights were starry and crystalline. The town lay under a cold glory; the smell of her furs was incense, her bright cheeks were flames upon a northern altar. An ecstatic pantheism for his land and its weather welled up in him. She had brought him finally back to it; he would live here always.

"I want you so much that nothing can stand in the way of that," he said to Alida. "But I owe my parents a debt that I can't explain to you. They did more than spend money on me; they tried to give me something more intangible—something that their parents had given them and that they thought was worth handing on. Evidently it didn't take with me, but I've got to make this as easy as possible for them." He saw by her face that he had hurt her. "Darling——"

"Oh, it frightens me when you talk like that," she said. "Are you going to reproach me later? It would be awful. You'll have to get it out of your head that you're doing anything wrong. My standards are as high as yours, and I can't start out with my father's sins on my shoulders." She thought for a moment. "You'll never be able to reconcile it all like a children's story. You've got to choose. Probably you'll have to hurt either your family or hurt me."

A fortnight later the storm broke at the Winslow house. Pierce Winslow came home in a quiet rage and had a session behind closed doors with his wife. Afterward she knocked at Forrest's door.

"Your father had a very embarrassing experience today. Chauncey Rikker came up to him in the Downtown Club and began talking about you as if you were on terms of some understanding with his daughter. Your father walked away, but we've got to know. Are you serious about Miss Rikker?"

"I want to marry her," he said.

"Oh, Forrest!"

She talked for a long time, recapitulating, as if it were a matter of centuries, the eighty years that his family had been identified with the city; when she passed from this to the story of his father's health, Forrest interrupted:

"That's all so irrelevant, mother. If there was anything against Alida personally, what you say would have some weight, but there isn't."

"She's overdressed; she runs around with everybody——"

"She isn't a bit different from Eleanor. She's absolutely a lady in every sense. I feel like a fool even discussing her like this. You're just afraid it'll connect you in some way with the Rikkers."

"I'm not afraid of that," said her mother, annoyed. "Nothing would ever do that. But I'm afraid that it'll separate you from everything worth while, everybody that loves you. It isn't fair for you to upset our lives, let us in for disgraceful gossip——"

"I'm to give up the girl I love because you're afraid of a little gossip."

The controversy was resumed next day, with Pierce Winslow debating. His argument was that he was born in old Kentucky, that he had always felt uneasy at having begotten a son upon a pioneer Minnesota family, and that this was what he might have expected. Forrest felt that his parents' attitude was trivial and disingenuous. Only when he was out of the house, acting against their wishes, did he feel any compunction. But always he felt that something precious was being frayed away—his youthful companionship with his father and his love and trust for his mother. Hour by hour he saw the past being irreparably spoiled, and save when he was with Alida, he was deeply unhappy.

One spring day when the situation had become unendurable, with half the family meals taken in silence, Forrest's great-grandmother stopped him on the stair landing and put her hand on his arm.

"Has this girl really a good character?" she asked, her fine, clear, old eyes resting on his.

"Of course she has, gramma."

"Then marry her."

"Why do you say that?" Forrest asked curiously.

"It would stop all this nonsense and we could have some peace. And I've been thinking I'd like to be a great-great-grandmother before I die."

Her frank selfishness appealed to him more than the righteousness of the others. That night he and Alida decided to be married the first of June, and telephoned the announcement to the papers.

Now the storm broke in earnest. Crest Avenue rang with gossip—how Mrs. Rikker had called on Mrs. Winslow, who was not at home. How Forrest had gone to live in the University Club. How Chauncey Rikker and Pierce Winslow had had words in the Downtown Club.

It was true that Forrest had gone to the University Club. On a May night, with summer sounds already gathered on the window screens, he packed his trunk and his suitcases in the room where he had lived as a boy. His throat contracted and he smeared his face with his dusty hand as he took a row of golf cups off the mantelpiece, and he choked to himself: "If they won't take Alida, then they're not my family any more."

As he finished packing, his mother came in.

"You're not really leaving." Her voice was stricken.

"I'm moving to the University Club."

"That's so unnecessary. No one bothers you here. You do what you want."

"I can't bring Alida here."

"Father——"

"Hell with father!" he said wildly.

She sat down on the bed beside him. "Stay here, Forrest. I promise not to argue with you any more. But stay here."

"I can't."

"I can't have you go!" she wailed. "It seems as if we're driving you out, and we're not!"

"You mean it looks as though you were driving me out."

"I don't mean that."

"Yes, you do. And I want to say that I don't think you and father really care a hang about Chauncey Rikker's moral character."

"That's not true, Forrest. I hate people that behave badly and break the laws. My own father would never have let Chauncey Rikker——"

"I'm not talking about your father. But neither you nor my father care a bit what Chauncey Rikker did. I bet you don't even know what it was."

"Of course I know. He stole some money and went abroad, and when he came back they put him in prison."

"They put him in prison for contempt of court."

"Now you're defending him, Forrest."

"I'm not! I hate his guts; undoubtedly he's a crook. But I tell you it was a shock to me to find that father didn't have any principles. He and his friends sit around the Downtown Club and pan Chauncey Rikker, but when it comes to keeping him out of a club, they develop weak spines."

"That was a small thing."

"No, it wasn't. None of the men of father's age have any principles. I don't know why. I'm willing to make an allowance for an honest conviction, but I'm not going to be booed by somebody that hasn't got any principles and simply pretends to have."

His mother sat helplessly, knowing that what he said was true. She and her husband and all their friends had no principles. They were good or bad according to their natures; often they struck attitudes remembered from the past, but they were never sure as her father or her grandfather had been sure. Confusedly she supposed it was something about religion. But how could you get principles just by wishing for them?

The maid announced the arrival of a taxi.

"Send up Olsen for my baggage," said Forrest; then to his mother, "I'm not taking the coupé; I left the keys. I'm just taking my clothes. I suppose father will let me keep my job down town."

"Forrest, don't talk that way. Do you think your father would take your living away from you, no matter what you did?"

"Such things have happened."

"You're hard and difficult," she wept. "Please stay here a little longer, and perhaps things will be better and father will get a little more reconciled. Oh, stay, stay! I'll talk to father again. I'll do my best to fix things."

"Will you let me bring Alida here?"

"Not now. Don't ask me that. I couldn't bear——"

"All right," he said grimly.

Olsen came in for the bags. Crying and holding on to his coat sleeve, his mother went with him to the front door.

"Won't you say good-by to father?"

"Why? I'll see him tomorrow in the office."

"Forrest, I was thinking, why don't you go to a hotel instead of the University Club?"

"Why, I thought I'd be more comfortable——" Suddenly he realized that his presence would be less conspicuous at a hotel. Shutting up his bitterness inside him, he kissed his mother roughly and went to the cab.

Unexpectedly, it stopped by the corner lamp-post at a hail from the sidewalk, and the May twilight yielded up Alida, miserable and pale.

"What is it?" he demanded.

"I had to come," she said. "Stop the car. I've been thinking of you leaving your house on account of me, and how you loved your family—the way I'd like to love mine—and I thought how terrible it was to spoil all that. Listen, Forrest! Wait! I want you to go back. Yes, I do. We can wait. We haven't any right to cause all this pain. We're young. I'll go away for a while, and then we'll see."

He pulled her toward him by her shoulders.

"You've got more principles than the whole bunch of them," he said. "Oh, my girl, you love me and, gosh, it's good that you do!"

· I V ·

IT WAS TO BE a house wedding, Forrest and Alida having vetoed the Rikkers' idea that it was to be a sort of public revenge. Only a few intimate friends were invited.

During the week before the wedding, Forrest deduced from a series of irresolute and ambiguous telephone calls that his mother wanted to attend the ceremony, if possible. Sometimes he hoped passionately she would; at others it seemed unimportant.

The wedding was to be at seven. At five o'clock Pierce Winslow was walking up and down the two interconnecting sitting rooms of his house.

"This evening," he murmured, "my only son is being married to the daughter of a swindler."

He spoke aloud so that he could listen to the words, but they had been evoked so often in the past few months that their strength was gone and they died thinly upon the air.

He went to the foot of the stairs and called: "Charlotte!" No answer. He called again, and then went into the dining room, where the maid was setting the table.

"Is Mrs. Winslow out?"

"I haven't seen her come in, Mr. Winslow."

Back in the sitting room he resumed his walking; unconsciously he was walking like his father, the judge, dead thirty years ago; he was parading his dead father up and down the room.

"You can't bring that woman into this house to meet your mother. Bad blood is bad blood."

The house seemed unusually quiet. He went upstairs and looked into his wife's room, but she was not there; old Mrs. Forrest was slightly indisposed; Eleanor, he knew, was at the wedding.

He felt genuinely sorry for himself as he went downstairs again. He knew his role—the usual evening routine carried out in complete obliviousness of the wedding—but he needed support, people begging him to relent, or else deferring to his wounded sensibilities. This isolation was different; it was almost the first isolation he had ever felt, and like all men who are fundamentally of the group, of the herd, he was incapable of taking a strong stand with the inevitable loneliness that it implied. He could only gravitate toward those who did.

"What have I done to deserve this?" he demanded of the standing ash tray. "What have I failed to do for my son that lay within my power?"

The maid came in. "Mrs. Winslow told Hilda she wouldn't be here for dinner, and Hilda didn't tell me."

The shameful business was complete. His wife had weakened, leaving him absolutely alone. For a moment he expected to be furiously angry with her, but he wasn't; he had used up his anger exhibiting it to others. Nor did it make him feel more obstinate, more determined; it merely made him feel silly.

"That's it. I'll be the goat. Forrest will always hold it against me, and Chauncey Rikker will be laughing up his sleeve."

He walked up and down furiously.

"So I'm left holding the bag. They'll say I'm an old grouch and drop me out of the picture entirely. They've licked me. I suppose I might as well be graceful about it." He looked down in horror at the hat he held in his hand. "I can't—I can't bring myself to do it, but I must. After all, he's my only son. I couldn't bear that he should hate me. He's determined to marry her, so I might as well put a good face on the matter."

In sudden alarm he looked at his watch, but there was still time. After all, it was a large gesture he was making, sacrificing his principles in this manner. People would never know what it cost him.

An hour later, old Mrs. Forrest woke up from her doze and rang for her maid.

"Where's Mrs. Winslow?"

"She's not in for dinner. Everybody's out."

The old lady remembered.

"Oh, yes, they've gone over to get married. Give me my glasses and the telephone book. . . . Now, I wonder how you spell Capone."

"Rikker, Mrs. Forrest."

In a few minutes she had the number. "This is Mrs. Hugh Forrest," she said firmly. "I want to speak to young Mrs. Forrest Winslow. . . . No, not to Miss Rikker; to Mrs. Forrest Winslow." As there was as yet no such person, this was impossible. "Then I will call after the ceremony," said the old lady.

When she called again, in an hour, the bride came to the phone.

"This is Forrest's great-grandmother. I called up to wish you every happiness and to ask you to come and see me when you get back from your trip if I'm still alive."

"You're very sweet to call, Mrs. Forrest."

"Take good care of Forrest, and don't let him get to be a ninny like his father and mother. God bless you."

"Thank you."

"All right. Good-by, Miss Capo——Good-by, my dear."

Having done her whole duty, Mrs. Forrest hung up the receiver.

SIX OF ONE—

◆

"Six of One—" was published in Redbook *(February 1932); since this story is not mentioned in the Fitzgerald/Ober correspondence, it is impossible to determine why—or if—the* Post *declined "Six of One—." Although the plot is contrived, "Six of One—" merits attention as Fitzgerald's attempt to reevaluate the effects of wealth and privilege on character against the stringent mood of the Thirties. The poor boys turn out better than the rich ones; but Fitzgerald refused to simplify the situation: "Only it was too bad and very American that there should be all that waste at the top. . . ."*

◆

BARNES STOOD ON the wide stairs looking down through a wide hall into the living-room of the country place and at the group of youths. His friend Schofield was addressing some benevolent remarks to them, and Barnes did not want to interrupt; as he stood there, immobile, he seemed to be drawn suddenly into rhythm with the group below; he perceived them as statuesque beings, set apart, chiseled out of the Minnesota twilight that was setting on the big room.

In the first place all five, the two young Schofields and their friends, were fine-looking boys, very American, dressed in a careless but not casual way over well-set-up bodies, and with responsive faces open to all four winds. Then he saw that they made a design, the faces profile upon profile, the heads blond and dark, turning toward Mr. Schofield, the erect yet vaguely lounging bodies, never tense but ever ready under the flannels and the soft angora wool sweaters, the hands placed on other shoulders, as if to bring each one into the solid freemasonry of the group. Then suddenly, as though a group of models posing for a sculptor were being dismissed, the composition broke and they all moved toward the door. They left Barnes with a sense of having seen something more than five young men between sixteen and eighteen going out to sail or play tennis or golf, but having gained a sharp impression of a whole style, a whole mode of youth, something different from his own less assured, less graceful generation, something unified by standards that he didn't know. He wondered vaguely what the standards of 1920 were, and whether they were worth anything—had a sense of waste, of much effort for a purely esthetic achievement. Then Schofield saw him and called him down into the living-room.

"Aren't they a fine bunch of boys?" Schofield demanded. "Tell me, did you ever see a finer bunch?"

"A fine lot," agreed Barnes, with a certain lack of enthusiasm. He felt a sudden premonition that his generation in its years of effort had made possible a Periclean age, but had evolved no prospective Pericles. They had set the scene: was the cast adequate?

"It isn't just because two of them happen to be mine," went on Schofield. "It's self-evident. You couldn't match that crowd in any city in the country. First place, they're such a husky lot. Those two little Kavenaughs aren't going to be big men—more like their father; but the oldest one could make any college hockey-team in the country right now."

"How old are they?" asked Barnes.

"Well, Howard Kavenaugh, the oldest, is nineteen—going to Yale next year. Then comes my Wister—he's eighteen, also going to Yale next year. You liked Wister, didn't you? I don't know anybody who doesn't. He'd make a great politician, that kid. Then there's a boy named Larry Patt who wasn't here today—he's eighteen too, and he's State golf champion. Fine voice too; he's trying to get in Princeton."

"Who's the blond-haired one who looks like a Greek god?"

"That's Beau Lebaume. He's going to Yale, too, if the girls will let him leave town. Then there's the other Kavenaugh, the stocky one—he's going to be an even better athlete than his brother. And finally there's my youngest, Charley; he's sixteen," Schofield sighed reluctantly. "But I guess you've heard all the boasting you can stand."

"No, tell me more about them—I'm interested. Are they anything more than athletes?"

"Why, there's not a dumb one in the lot, except maybe Beau Lebaume; but you can't help liking him anyhow. And every one of them's a natural leader. I remember a few years ago a tough gang tried to start something with them, calling them 'candies'—well, that gang must be running yet. They sort of remind me of young knights. And what's the matter with their being athletes? I seem to remember you stroking the boat at New London, and that didn't keep you from consolidating railroad systems and—"

"I took up rowing because I had a sick stomach," said Barnes. "By the way, are these boys all rich?"

"Well, the Kavenaughs are, of course; and my boys will have something."

Barnes' eyes twinkled.

"So I suppose since they won't have to worry about money, they're brought up to serve the State," he suggested. "You spoke of one of your sons having a political talent and their all being like young knights, so I suppose they'll go out for public life and the army and navy."

"I don't know about that," Schofield's voice sounded somewhat alarmed. "I think their fathers would be pretty disappointed if they didn't go into business. That's natural, isn't it?"

"It's natural, but it isn't very romantic," said Barnes good-humoredly.

"You're trying to get my goat," said Schofield. "Well, if you can match that—"

"They're certainly an ornamental bunch," admitted Barnes. "They've got what you call glamour. They certainly look like the cigarette ads in the magazine; but—"

"But you're an old sour-belly," interrupted Schofield. "I've explained that these boys are all well-rounded. My son Wister led his class at school this year, but I was a darn' sight prouder that he got the medal for best all-around boy."

The two men faced each other with the uncut cards of the future on the table before them. They had been in college together, and were friends of many years' standing. Barnes was childless, and Schofield was inclined to attribute his lack of enthusiasm to that.

"I somehow can't see them setting the world on fire, doing better than their fathers," broke out Barnes suddenly. "The more charming they are, the harder it's going to be for them. In the East people are beginning to realize what wealthy boys are up against. Match them? Maybe not now." He leaned forward, his eyes lighting up. "But I could pick six boys from any high-school in Cleveland, give them an education, and I believe that ten years from this time your young fellows here would be utterly outclassed. There's so little demanded of them, so little expected of them—what could be softer than just to have to go on being charming and athletic?"

"I know your idea," objected Schofield scoffingly. "You'd go to a big municipal high-school and pick out the six most brilliant scholars—"

"I'll tell you what I'll do—" Barnes noticed that he had unconsciously substituted "I will" for "I would," but he didn't correct himself. "I'll go to the little town in Ohio, where I was born—there probably aren't fifty or sixty boys in the high-school there, and I wouldn't be likely to find six geniuses out of that number."

"And what?"

"I'll give them a chance. If they fail, the chance is lost. That is a serious responsibility, and they've got to take it seriously. That's what these boys haven't got—they're only asked to be serious about trivial things." He thought for a moment. "I'm going to do it."

"Do what?"

"I'm going to see."

A fortnight later he was back in the small town in Ohio where he had been born, where, he felt, the driving emotions of his own youth still haunted the quiet streets. He interviewed the principal of the high-school, who made suggestions; then by the, for Barnes, difficult means of making an address and afterward attending a reception, he got in touch with teachers and pupils. He made a donation to the school, and under cover of this found opportunities of watching the boys at work and at play.

It was fun—he felt his youth again. There were some boys that he liked immediately, and he began a weeding-out process, inviting them in groups of five or six to his mother's house, rather like a fraternity rushing freshman. When a boy interested him, he looked up his record and that of his family—and at the end of a fortnight he had chosen five boys.

In the order in which he chose them, there was first Otto Schlach, a farmer's son who had already displayed extraordinary mechanical aptitude and a gift for mathematics. Schlach was highly recommended by his teachers, and he welcomed the opportunity offered him of entering the Massachusetts Institute of Technology.

A drunken father left James Matsko as his only legacy to the town of Barnes' youth. From the age of twelve, James had supported himself by keeping a newspaper-and-candy store with a three-foot frontage; and now at seventeen he was reputed to have saved five hundred dollars. Barnes found it difficult to persuade him to study money and banking at Columbia, for Matsko was already assured of his ability to make money. But Barnes had prestige as the town's most successful son, and he convinced Matsko that otherwise he would lack frontage, like his own place of business.

Then there was Jack Stubbs, who had lost an arm hunting, but in spite of this handicap played on the high-school football team. He was not among the leaders in studies; he had developed no particular bent; but the fact that he had overcome that enormous handicap enough to play football—to tackle and to catch punts—convinced Barnes that no obstacles would stand in Jack Stubbs' way.

The fourth selection was George Winfield, who was almost twenty. Because of the death of his father, he had left school at fourteen, helped to support his family for four years, and then, things being better, he had come back to finish high-school. Barnes felt, therefore, that Winfield would place a serious value on an education.

Next came a boy whom Barnes found personally antipathetic. Louis Ireland was at once the most brilliant scholar and most difficult boy at school. Untidy, insubordinate and eccentric, Louis drew scurrilous caricatures behind his Latin book, but when called upon inevitably produced a perfect recitation. There was a big talent nascent somewhere in him—it was impossible to leave him out.

The last choice was the most difficult. The remaining boys were mediocrities, or at any rate they had so far displayed no qualities that set them apart. For a time Barnes, thinking patriotically of his old university, considered the football captain, a virtuosic halfback who would have been welcome on any Eastern squad; but that would have destroyed the integrity of the idea.

He finally chose a younger boy, Gordon Vandervere, of a rather higher standing than the others. Vandervere was the handsomest and one of the most popular boys in school. He had been intended for college, but his father, a harassed minister, was glad to see the way made easy.

Barnes was content with himself; he felt godlike in being able to step in to mold these various destinies. He felt as if they were his own sons, and he telegraphed Schofield in Minneapolis:

HAVE CHOSEN HALF A DOZEN OF THE OTHER, AND AM BACKING THEM AGAINST THE WORLD.

And now, after all this biography, the story begins. . . .

The continuity of the frieze is broken. Young Charley Schofield had been expelled from Hotchkiss. It was a small but painful tragedy—he and four other boys, nice boys, popular boys, broke the honor system as to smoking. Charley's father felt the matter deeply, varying between disappointment about Charley and anger at the school. Charley came home to Minneapolis in a desperate humor and went to the country day-school while it was decided what he was to do.

It was still undecided in midsummer. When school was over, he spent his time playing golf, or dancing at the Minnekada Club—he was a handsome boy of eighteen, older than his age, with charming manners, with no serious vices, but with a tendency to be easily influenced by his admirations. His principal admiration at the time was Gladys Irving, a young married woman scarcely two years older than himself. He rushed her at the club dances, and felt sentimentally about her, though Gladys on her part was in love with her husband and asked from Charley only the confirmation of her own youth and charm that a belle often needs after her first baby.

Sitting out with her one night on the veranda of the Lafayette Club, Charley felt a necessity to boast to her, to pretend to be more experienced, and so more potentially protective.

"I've seen a lot of life for my age," he said. "I've done things I couldn't even tell you about."

Gladys didn't answer.

"In fact last week—" he began, and thought better of it. "In any case I don't think I'll go to Yale next year—I'd have to go East right away, and tutor all summer. If I don't go, there's a job open in Father's office; and after Wister goes back to college in the fall, I'll have the roadster to myself."

"I thought you were going to college," Gladys said coldly.

"I was. But I've thought things over, and now I don't know. I've usually gone with older boys, and I feel older than boys my age. I like older girls, for instance." When Charley looked at her then suddenly, he seemed unusually attractive to her—it would be very pleasant to have him here, to cut in on her at dances all summer. But Gladys said:

"You'd be a fool to stay here."

"Why?"

"You started something—you ought to go through with it. A few years running around town, and you won't be good for anything."

"You think so," he said indulgently.

Gladys didn't want to hurt him or to drive him away from her; yet she wanted to say something stronger.

"Do you think I'm thrilled when you tell me you've had a lot of dissipated experience? I don't see how anybody could claim to be your friend and encourage you in that. If I were you, I'd at least pass your examinations for college. Then they can't say you just lay down after you were expelled from school."

"You think so?" Charley said, unruffled, and in his grave, precocious manner, as though he were talking to a child. But she had convinced him, because he was in love with her and the moon was around her. "*Oh me, oh my, oh you,*" was the last music they had danced to on the Wednesday before, and so it was one of those times.

Had Gladys let him brag to her, concealing her curiosity under a mask of companionship, if she had accepted his own estimate of himself as a man formed, no urging of his father's would have mattered. As it was, Charley passed into college that fall, thanks to a girl's tender reminiscences and her own memories of the sweetness of youth's success in young fields.

And it was well for his father that he did. If he had not, the catastrophe of his older brother Wister that autumn would have broken Schofield's heart. The morning after the Harvard game the New York papers carried a headline:

YALE BOYS AND FOLLIES GIRLS IN
MOTOR CRASH NEAR RYE

IRENE DALEY IN GREENWICH HOS-
PITAL THREATENS BEAUTY SUIT
MILLIONAIRE'S SON INVOLVED

The four boys came up before the dean a fortnight later. Wister Schofield, who had driven the car, was called first.

"It was not your car, Mr. Schofield," the dean said. "It was Mr. Kavenaugh's car, wasn't it?"

"Yes sir."

"How did you happen to be driving?"

"The girls wanted me to. They didn't feel safe."

"But you'd been drinking too, hadn't you?"

"Yes, but not so much."

"Tell me this," asked the dean: "Haven't you ever driven a car when you'd been drinking—perhaps drinking even more than you were that night?"

"Why—perhaps once or twice, but I never had any accidents. And this was so clearly unavoidable—"

"Possibly," the dean agreed; "but we'll have to look at it this way: Up to this time you had no accidents even when you deserved to have them. Now you've had one when you didn't deserve it. I don't want you to go out of here feeling that life or the University or I myself haven't given you a square deal, Mr. Schofield. But the newspapers have given this a great deal of prominence, and I'm afraid that the University will have to dispense with your presence."

Moving along the frieze to Howard Kavenaugh, the dean's remarks to him were substantially the same.

"I am particularly sorry in your case, Mr. Kavenaugh. Your father has made substantial gifts to the University, and I took pleasure in watching you play hockey with your usual brilliance last winter."

Howard Kavenaugh left the office with uncontrollable tears running down his cheeks.

Since Irene Daley's suit for her ruined livelihood, her ruined beauty, was directed against the owner and the driver of the automobile, there were lighter sentences for the other two occupants of the car. Beau Lebaume came into the dean's office with his arm in a sling and his handsome head swathed in bandages and was suspended for the remainder of the current year. He took it jauntily and said good-by to the dean with as cheerful a smile as could show through the bandages. The last case, however, was the most difficult. George Winfield, who had entered high-school late because work in the world had taught him the value of an education, came in looking at the floor.

"I can't understand your participation in this affair," said the dean. "I know your benefactor, Mr. Barnes, personally. He told me how you left school to go to work, and how you came back to it four years later to continue your education, and he felt that your attitude toward life was essentially serious. Up to this point you have a good record here at New Haven, but it struck me several months ago that you were running with a rather gay crowd, boys with a great deal of money to spend. You are old enough to realize that they couldn't possibly give you as much in material ways as they took away from you in others. I've got to give you a year's suspension. If you come back, I have every hope you'll justify the confidence that Mr. Barnes reposed in you."

"I won't come back," said Winfield. "I couldn't face Mr. Barnes after this. I'm not going home."

At the suit brought by Irene Daley, all four of them lied loyally for Wister Schofield. They said that before they hit the gasoline pump they had seen Miss Daley grab the wheel. But Miss Daley was in court, with her face, familiar to the tabloids, permanently scarred; and her counsel exhibited a letter canceling her recent moving-picture contract. The students' case looked bad; so in the intermission, on their lawyer's advice, they settled for forty thousand dollars. Wister Schofield and Howard Kavenaugh were snapped by a dozen photographers leaving the courtroom, and served up in flaming notoriety next day.

That night, Wister, the three Minneapolis boys, Howard and Beau Lebaume started for home. George Winfield said good-by to them in the Pennsylvania station; and having no home to go to, walked out into New York to start life over.

Of all Barnes' protégés, Jack Stubbs with his one arm was the favorite. He was the first to achieve fame—when he played on the tennis team at Princeton, the rotogravure section carried pictures showing how he threw the ball from his racket in serving. When he was graduated, Barnes took him into his own office—he was often spoken of as an adopted son. Stubbs, together with Schlach, now a prominent consulting engineer, were the most satisfactory of his experiments, although James Matsko at twenty-seven had just been made a partner in a Wall Street brokerage house. Financially he was the most successful of the six, yet Barnes found himself somewhat repelled by his hard egoism. He wondered, too, if he, Barnes, had really played any part in Matsko's career—did it after all matter whether Matsko was a figure in metropolitan finance or a big merchant in the Middle West, as he would have undoubtedly become without any assistance at all.

One morning in 1930 he handed Jack Stubbs a letter that led to a balancing up of the book of boys.

"What do you think of this?"

The letter was from Louis Ireland in Paris. About Louis they did not agree, and as Jack read, he prepared once more to intercede in his behalf.

MY DEAR SIR:

After your last communication, made through your bank here and enclosing a check which I hereby acknowledge, I do not feel that I am under any obligation to write you at all. But because the concrete fact of an object's commercial worth may be able to move you, while you remain utterly insensitive to the value of an abstract idea—because of this I write to tell you that my exhibition was an unqualified success. To bring the matter even nearer to your intellectual level, I may tell you that I sold two pieces—a head of Lallette, the actress, and a bronze animal group—for a total of seven thousand francs ($280.00). Moreover I have commissions which will take me all summer—I enclose a piece about me cut from CAHIERS D'ART, which will show you that whatever your estimate of my abilities and my career, it is by no means unanimous.

This is not to say that I am ungrateful for your well-intentioned attempt to "educate" me. I suppose that Harvard was no worse than any other polite finishing school—the years that I wasted there gave me a sharp and well-documented attitude on American life and institutions. But your suggestions that I come to America and make standardized nymphs for profiteers' fountains was a little too much—

Stubbs looked up with a smile.

"Well," Barnes said, "what do you think? Is he crazy—or now that he has sold some statues, does it prove that I'm crazy?"

"Neither one," laughed Stubbs. "What you objected to in Louis wasn't his talent. But you never got over that year he tried to enter a monastery and then got arrested in the Sacco-Vanzetti demonstrations, and then ran away with the professor's wife."

"He was just forming himself," said Barnes dryly, "just trying his little wings. God knows what he's been up to abroad."

"Well, perhaps he's formed now," Stubbs said lightly. He had always liked Louis Ireland—privately he resolved to write and see if he needed money.

"Anyhow, he's graduated from me," announced Barnes. "I can't do any more to help him or hurt him. Suppose we call him a success, though that's pretty doubtful—let's see how we stand. I'm going to see Schofield out in Minneapolis next week, and I'd like to balance accounts. To my mind, the successes are you, Otto Schlach, James Matsko,—whatever you and I may think of him as a man,—and let's assume that Louis Ireland is going to be a great sculptor. That's four. Winfield's disappeared. I've never had a line from him."

"Perhaps he's doing well somewhere."

"If he were doing well, I think he'd let me know. We'll have to count him as a failure so far as my experiment goes. Then there's Gordon Vandervere."

Both were silent for a moment.

"I can't make it out about Gordon," Barnes said. "He's such a nice fellow, but since he left college, he doesn't seem to come through. He was younger than the rest of you, and he had the advantage of two years at Andover before he went to college, and at Princeton he knocked them cold, as you say. But he seems to have worn his wings out—for four years now he's done nothing at all; he can't hold a job; he can't get his mind on his work, and he doesn't seem to care. I'm about through with Gordon."

At this moment Gordon was announced over the phone.

"He asked for an appointment," explained Barnes. "I suppose he wants to try something new."

A personable young man with an easy and attractive manner strolled in to the office.

"Good afternoon, Uncle Ed. Hi there, Jack!" Gordon sat down. "I'm full of news."

"About what?" asked Barnes.

"About myself."

"I know. You've just been appointed to arrange a merger between J. P. Morgan and the Queensborough Bridge."

"It's a merger," agreed Vandervere, "but those are not the parties to it. I'm engaged to be married."

Barnes glowered.

"Her name," continued Vandervere, "is Esther Crosby."

"Let me congratulate you," said Barnes ironically. "A relation of H. B. Crosby, I presume."

"Exactly," said Vandervere unruffled. "In fact, his only daughter."

For a moment there was silence in the office. Then Barnes exploded.

"*You're* going to marry H. B. Crosby's daughter? Does he know that last month you retired by request from one of his banks?"

"I'm afraid he knows everything about me. He's been looking me over for four years. You see, Uncle Ed," he continued cheerfully, "Esther and I got engaged during my last year at Princeton—my roommate brought her down to a house-party, but she switched over to me. Well, quite naturally Mr. Crosby wouldn't hear of it until I'd proved myself."

"Proved yourself!" repeated Barnes. "Do you consider that you've proved yourself?"

"Well—yes."

"How?"

"By waiting four years. You see, either Esther or I might have married anybody else in that time, but we didn't. Instead we sort of wore him away. That's really why I haven't been able to get down to anything. Mr. Crosby is a strong personality, and it took a lot of time and energy wearing him away. Sometimes Esther and I didn't see each other for months, so she couldn't eat; so then thinking of that I couldn't eat, so then I couldn't work—"

"And you mean he's really given his consent?"

"He gave it last night."

"Is he going to let you loaf?"

"No. Esther and I are going into the diplomatic service. She feels that the family has passed through the banking phase." He winked at Stubbs. "I'll look up Louis Ireland when I get to Paris, and send Uncle Ed a report."

Suddenly Barnes roared with laughter.

"Well, it's all in the lottery-box," he said. "When I picked out you six, I was a long way from guessing—" He turned to Stubbs and demanded: "Shall we put him under *failure* or under *success?*"

"A howling success," said Stubbs. "Top of the list."

A fortnight later Barnes was with his old friend Schofield in Minneapolis. He thought of the house with the six boys as he had last seen it—now it seemed to bear scars of them, like the traces that pictures leave on a wall that they have long protected from the mark of time. Since he did not know what had become of Schofield's sons, he refrained from referring to their conversation of ten years before until he knew whether it was dangerous ground. He was glad of his reticence later in the evening when Schofield spoke of his elder son, Wister.

"Wister never seems to have found himself—and he was such a high-spirited kid! He was the leader of every group he went into; he could always make things go. When he was young, our houses in town and at the lake were always packed with young people. But after he left Yale, he lost interest in things—got sort of scornful about everything. I thought for a while that it was because he drank too much, but he married a nice girl and she took that in hand. Still, he hasn't any ambition—he talked about country life, so I bought him a silver-fox farm, but that didn't go; and I sent him to

Florida during the boom, but that wasn't any better. Now he has an interest in a dude-ranch in Montana; but since the depression—"

Barnes saw his opportunity and asked:

"What became of those friends of your sons' that I met one day?"

"Let's see—I wonder who you mean. There was Kavenaugh—you know, the flour people—he was here a lot. Let's see—he eloped with an Eastern girl, and for a few years he and his wife were the leaders of the gay crowd here—they did a lot of drinking and not much else. It seems to me I heard the other day that Howard's getting a divorce. Then there was the younger brother—he never could get into college. Finally he married a manicurist, and they live here rather quietly. We don't hear much about them."

They had had a glamour about them, Barnes remembered; they had been so sure of themselves, individually, as a group; so high-spirited, a frieze of Greek youths, graceful of body, ready for life.

"Then Larry Patt, you might have met him here. A great golfer. He couldn't stay in college—there didn't seem to be enough fresh air there for Larry." And he added defensively: "But he capitalized what he could do—he opened a sporting-goods store and made a good thing of it, I understand. He has a string of three or four."

"I seem to remember an exceptionally handsome one."

"Oh—Beau Lebaume. He was in that mess at New Haven too. After that he went to pieces—drink and what-not. His father's tried everything, and now he won't have anything more to do with him." Schofield's face warmed suddenly; his eyes glowed. "But let me tell you, I've got a boy—my Charley! I wouldn't trade him for the lot of them—he's coming over presently, and you'll see. He had a bad start, got into trouble at Hotchkiss—but did he quit? Never. He went back and made a fine record at New Haven, senior society and all that. Then he and some other boys took a trip around the world, and then he came back here and said: 'All right, Father, I'm ready—when do I start?' I don't know what I'd do without Charley. He got married a few months back, a young widow he'd always been in love with; and his mother and I are still missing him, though they come over often—"

Barnes was glad about this, and suddenly he was reconciled at not having any sons in the flesh—one out of two made good, and sometimes better, and sometimes nothing; but just going along getting old by yourself when you'd counted on so much from sons—

"Charley runs the business," continued Schofield. "That is, he and a young man named Winfield that Wister got me to take on five or six years ago. Wister felt responsible about him, felt he'd got him into this trouble at New Haven—and this boy had no family. He's done well here."

Another one of Barnes' six accounted for! He felt a surge of triumph, but he saw he must keep it to himself; a little later when Schofield asked him if he'd carried out his intention of putting some boys through college, he avoided answering. After all, any given moment has its value; it can be questioned in the light of after-events, but the moment remains. The young princes in velvet gathered in lovely domesticity around the queen amid the hush of rich draperies may presently grow up to be Pedro the Cruel or Charles the Mad, but the moment of beauty was there. Back there ten years, Schofield had seen his sons and their friends as samurai, as something shining and glorious and young, perhaps as something he had missed from his own youth. There was later a price to be paid by those boys, all too fulfilled, with the whole balance of their life pulled forward into their youth so that everything afterward would inevitably be anticlimax; these boys brought up as princes with none of the responsibilities of princes! Barnes didn't know how much their mothers might have had to do with it, what their mothers may have lacked.

But he was glad that his friend Schofield had one true son.

His own experiment—he didn't regret it, but he wouldn't have done it again. Probably it proved something, but he wasn't quite sure what. Perhaps that life is constantly renewed, and glamour and beauty make way for it; and he was glad that he was able to feel that the republic could survive the mistakes of a whole generation, pushing the waste aside, sending ahead the vital and the strong. Only it was too bad and very American that there should be all that waste at the top; and he felt that he would not live long enough to see it end, to see great seriousness in the same skin with great opportunity—to see the race achieve itself at last.

WHAT A HANDSOME PAIR!

◆

"What a Handsome Pair!" (Saturday Evening Post, 27 August 1932) was a response—as in "Two Wrongs"—to the feelings of competition between Fitzgerald and his wife, as she sought her own career as a dancer, painter, and writer. This story was engendered by the mutual resentment that resulted from the publication of Zelda Fitzgerald's only novel, Save Me the Waltz *(1932). The* Post *apparently accepted this story with reluctance, for Fitzgerald's price was cut to $2,500.*

◆

AT FOUR O'CLOCK on a November afternoon in 1902, Teddy Van Beck got out of a hansom cab in front of a brownstone house on Murray Hill. He was a tall, round-shouldered young man with a beaked nose and soft brown eyes in a sensitive face. In his veins quarreled the blood of colonial governors and celebrated robber barons; in him the synthesis had produced, for that time and place, something different and something new.

His cousin, Helen Van Beck, waited in the drawing-room. Her eyes were red from weeping, but she was young enough for it not to detract from her glossy beauty—a beauty that had reached the point where it seemed to contain in itself the secret of its own growth, as if it would go on increasing forever. She was nineteen and, contrary to the evidence, she was extremely happy.

Teddy put his arm around her and kissed her cheek, and found it changing into her ear as she turned her face away. He held her for a moment, his own enthusiasm chilling; then he said:

"You don't seem very glad to see me."

Helen had a premonition that this was going to be one of the memorable scenes of her life, and with unconscious cruelty she set about extracting from it its full dramatic value. She sat in a corner of the couch, facing an easy-chair.

"Sit there," she commanded, in what was then admired as a "regal manner," and then, as Teddy straddled the piano stool: "No, don't sit there. I can't talk to you if you're going to revolve around."

"Sit on my lap," he suggested.

"No."

Playing a one-handed flourish on the piano, he said, "I can listen better here."

Helen gave up hopes of beginning on the sad and quiet note.

"This is a serious matter, Teddy. Don't think I've decided it without a lot of consideration. I've got to ask you—to ask you to release me from our understanding."

"What?" Teddy's face paled with shock and dismay.

"I'll have to tell you from the beginning. I've realized for a long time that we have nothing in common. You're interested in your music, and I can't even play chopsticks." Her voice was weary as if with suffering; her small teeth tugged at her lower lip.

"What of it?" he demanded, relieved. "I'm musician enough for both. You wouldn't have to understand banking to marry a banker, would you?"

"This is different," Helen answered. "What would we do together? One important thing is that you don't like riding; you told me you were afraid of horses."

"Of course I'm afraid of horses," he said, and added reminiscently: "They try to bite me."

"It makes it so——"

"I've never met a horse—socially, that is—who didn't try to bite me. They used to do it when I put the bridle on; then, when I gave up putting the bridle on, they began reaching their heads around trying to get at my calves."

The eyes of her father, who had given her a Shetland at three, glistened, cold and hard, from her own.

"You don't even like the people I like, let alone the horses," she said.

"I can stand them. I've stood them all my life."

"Well, it would be a silly way to start a marriage. I don't see any grounds for mutual—mutual——"

"Riding?"

"Oh, not that." Helen hesitated, and then said in an unconvinced tone, "Probably I'm not clever enough for you."

"Don't talk such stuff!" He demanded some truth: "Who's the man?"

It took her a moment to collect herself. She had always resented Teddy's tendency to treat women with less ceremony than was the custom of the day. Often he was an unfamiliar, almost frightening young man.

"There is someone," she admitted. "It's someone I've always known slightly, but about a month ago, when I went to Southampton, I was—thrown with him."

"Thrown from a horse?"

"Please, Teddy," she protested gravely. "I'd been getting more unhappy about you and me, and whenever I was with him everything seemed all right." A note of exaltation that she would not conceal came into Helen's voice. She rose and crossed the room, her straight, slim legs outlined by the shadows of her dress. "We rode and swam and played tennis together—did the things we both liked to do."

He stared into the vacant space she had created for him. "Is that all that drew you to this fellow?"

"No, it was more than that. He was thrilling to me like nobody ever has been." She laughed. "I think what really started me thinking about it was one day we came in from riding and everybody said aloud what a nice pair we made."

"Did you kiss him?"

She hesitated. "Yes, once."

He got up from the piano stool. "I feel as if I had a cannon ball in my stomach," he exclaimed.

The butler announced Mr. Stuart Oldhorne.

"Is he the man?" Teddy demanded tensely.

She was suddenly upset and confused. "He should have come later. Would you rather go without meeting him?"

But Stuart Oldhorne, made confident by his new sense of proprietorship, had followed the butler.

The two men regarded each other with a curious impotence of expression; there can be no communication between men in that position, for their relation is indirect and consists in how much each of them has possessed or will possess of the woman in question, so that their emotions pass through her divided self as through a bad telephone connection.

Stuart Oldhorne sat beside Helen, his polite eyes never leaving Teddy. He had the same glowing physical power as she. He had been a star athlete at Yale and a Rough Rider in Cuba, and was the best young horseman on Long Island. Women loved him not only for his points but for a real sweetness of temper.

"You've lived so much in Europe that I don't often see you," he said to Teddy. Teddy didn't answer and Stuart Oldhorne turned to Helen: "I'm early; I didn't realize——"

"You came at the right time," said Teddy rather harshly. "I stayed to play you my congratulations."

To Helen's alarm, he turned and ran his fingers over the keyboard. Then he began.

What he was playing, neither Helen nor Stuart knew, but Teddy always remembered. He put his mind in order with a short résumé of the history of music, beginning with some chords from The Messiah and ending with Debussy's La Plus Que Lent, which had an evocative quality for him, because he had first heard it the day his brother died. Then, pausing for an instant, he began to play more thoughtfully, and the lovers on the sofa could feel that they were alone—that he had left them and had no more traffic with them—and Helen's discomfort lessened. But the flight, the elusiveness of the music, piqued her, gave her a feeling of annoyance. If Teddy had played the current sentimental song from Erminie, and had played it with feeling, she would have understood and been moved, but he was plunging her suddenly into a world of mature emotions, whither her nature neither could nor wished to follow.

She shook herself slightly and said to Stuart: "Did you buy the horse?"

"Yes, and at a bargain. . . . Do you know I love you?"

"I'm glad," she whispered.

The piano stopped suddenly. Teddy closed it and swung slowly around: "Did you like my congratulations?"

"Very much," they said together.

"It was pretty good," he admitted. "That last was only based on a little counterpoint. You see, the idea of it was that you make such a handsome pair."

He laughed unnaturally; Helen followed him out into the hall.

"Good-by, Teddy," she said. "We're going to be good friends, aren't we?"

"Aren't we?" he repeated. He winked without smiling, and with a clicking, despairing sound of his mouth, went out quickly.

For a moment Helen tried vainly to apply a measure to the situation, wondering how she had come off with him, realizing reluctantly that she had never for an instant held the situation in her hands. She had a dim realization that Teddy was larger in scale; then the very largeness frightened her and, with relief and a warm tide of emotion, she hurried into the drawing-room and the shelter of her lover's arms.

Their engagement ran through a halcyon summer. Stuart visited Helen's family at Tuxedo, and Helen visited his family in Wheatley Hills. Before breakfast, their horses' hoofs sedately scattered the dew in sentimental glades, or curtained them with dust as they raced on dirt roads. They bought a tandem bicycle and pedaled all over Long Island—which Mrs. Cassius Ruthven, a contemporary Cato, considered "rather fast" for a couple not yet married. They were seldom at rest, but when they were, they reminded people of His Move on a Gibson pillow.

Helen's taste for sport was advanced for her generation. She rode nearly as well as Stuart and gave him a decent game in tennis. He taught her some polo, and they were golf crazy when it was still considered a comic game. They liked to feel fit and cool together. They thought of themselves as a team, and it was often remarked how well mated they were. A chorus of pleasant envy followed in the wake of their effortless glamour.

They talked.

"It seems a pity you've got to go to the office," she would say. "I wish you did something we could do together, like taming lions."

"I've always thought that in a pinch I could make a living breeding and racing horses," said Stuart.

"I know you could, you darling."

In August he brought a Thomas automobile and toured all the way to Chicago with three other men. It was an event of national interest and their pictures were in all the papers. Helen wanted to go, but it wouldn't have been proper, so they compromised by driving down Fifth Avenue on a sunny September morning, one with the fine day and the fashionable crowd, but distinguished by their unity, which made them each as strong as two.

"What do you suppose?" Helen demanded. "Teddy sent me the oddest present—a cup rack."

Stuart laughed. "Obviously, he means that all we'll ever do is win cups."

"I thought it was rather a slam," Helen ruminated. "I saw that he was invited to everything, but he didn't answer a single invitation. Would you mind very much stopping by his apartment now? I haven't seen him for months and I don't like to leave anything unpleasant in the past."

He wouldn't go in with her. "I'll sit and answer questions about the auto from passers-by."

The door was opened by a woman in a cleaning cap, and Helen heard the sound of Teddy's piano from the room beyond. The woman seemed reluctant to admit her.

"He said don't interrupt him, but I suppose if you're his cousin——"

Teddy welcomed her, obviously startled and somewhat upset, but in a minute he was himself again.

"I won't marry you," he assured her. "You've had your chance."

"All right," she laughed.

"How are you?" He threw a pillow at her. "You're beautiful! Are you happy with this—this centaur? Does he beat you with his riding crop?" He peered at her closely. "You look a little duller than when I knew you. I used to whip you up to a nervous excitement that bore a resemblance to intelligence."

"I'm happy, Teddy. I hope you are."

"Sure, I'm happy; I'm working. I've got MacDowell on the run and I'm going to have a shebang at Carnegie Hall next September." His eyes became malicious. "What did you think of my girl?"

"Your girl?"

"The girl who opened the door for you."

"Oh, I thought it was a maid." She flushed and was silent.

He laughed. "Hey, Betty!" he called. "You were mistaken for the maid!"

"And that's the fault of my cleaning on Sunday," answered a voice from the next room.

Teddy lowered his voice. "Do you like her?" he demanded.

"Teddy!" She teetered on the arm of the sofa, wondering whether she should leave at once.

"What would you think if I married her?" he asked confidentially.

"Teddy!" She was outraged; it had needed but a glance to place the woman as common. "You're joking. She's older than you. . . . You wouldn't be such a fool as to throw away your future that way."

He didn't answer.

"Is she musical?" Helen demanded. "Does she help you with your work?"

"She doesn't know a note. Neither did you, but I've got enough music in me for twenty wives."

Visualizing herself as one of them, Helen rose stiffly.

"All I can ask you is to think how your mother would have felt—and those who care for you. . . . Good-by, Teddy."

He walked out the door with her and down the stairs.

"As a matter of fact, we've been married for two months," he said casually. "She was a waitress in a place where I used to eat."

Helen felt that she should be angry and aloof, but tears of hurt vanity were springing to her eyes.

"And do you love her?"

"I like her; she's a good person and good for me. Love is something else. I loved you, Helen, and that's all dead in me for the present. Maybe it's coming out in my music. Some day I'll probably love other women—or maybe there'll never be anything but you. Good-by, Helen."

The declaration touched her. "I hope you'll be happy, Teddy. Bring your wife to the wedding."

He bowed noncommittally. When she had gone, he returned thoughtfully to his apartment.

"That was the cousin that I was in love with," he said.

"And was it?" Betty's face, Irish and placid, brightened with interest. "She's a pretty thing."

"She wouldn't have been as good for me as a nice peasant like you."

"Always thinking of yourself, Teddy Van Beck."

He laughed. "Sure I am, but you love me, anyhow?"

"That's a big wur-red."

"All right. I'll remember that when you come begging around for a kiss. If my grandfather knew I married a bog trotter, he'd turn over in his grave. Now get out and let me finish my work."

He sat at the piano, a pencil behind his ear. Already his face was resolved, composed, but his eyes grew more intense minute by minute, until there was a glaze in them, behind which they seemed to have joined his ears in counting and hearing. Presently there was no more indication in his face that anything had occurred to disturb the tranquillity of his Sunday morning.

· II ·

MRS. CASSIUS RUTHVEN and a friend, veils flung back across their hats, sat in their auto on the edge of the field.

"A young woman playing polo in breeches." Mrs. Ruthven sighed. "Amy Van Beck's daughter. I thought when Helen organized the Amazons she'd stop at divided skirts. But her husband apparently has no objections, for there he stands, egging her on. Of course, they always have liked the same things."

"A pair of thoroughbreds, those two," said the other woman complacently, meaning that she admitted them to be her equals. "You'd never look at them and think that anything had gone wrong."

She was referring to Stuart's mistake in the panic of 1907. His father had bequeathed him a precarious situation and Stuart had made an error of judgment. His honor was not questioned and his crowd stood by him loyally, but his usefulness in Wall Street was over and his small fortune was gone.

He stood in a group of men with whom he would presently play, noting things to tell Helen after the game—she wasn't turning with the play soon enough and several times she was unnecessarily ridden off at important moments. Her ponies were sluggish—the penalty for playing with borrowed mounts—but she was, nevertheless, the best player on the field, and in the last minute she made a save that brought applause.

"Good girl! Good girl!"

Stuart had been delegated with the unpleasant duty of chasing the women from the field. They had started an hour late and now a team from New Jersey was waiting to play; he sensed trouble as he cut across to join Helen and walked beside her toward the stables. She was splendid, with her flushed cheeks, her shining, triumphant eyes, her short, excited breath. He temporized for a minute.

"That was good—that last," he said.

"Thanks. It almost broke my arm. Wasn't I pretty good all through?"

"You were the best out there."

"I know it."

He waited while she dismounted and handed the pony to a groom.

"Helen, I believe I've got a job."

"What is it?"

"Don't jump on the idea till you think it over. Gus Myers wants me to manage his racing stables. Eight thousand a year."

Helen considered. "It's a nice salary; and I bet you could make yourself up a nice string from his ponies."

"The principal thing is that I need the money; I'd have as much as you and things would be easier."

"You'd have as much as me," Helen repeated. She almost regretted that he would need no more help from her. "But with Gus Myers, isn't there a string attached? Wouldn't he expect a boost up?"

"He probably would," answered Stuart bluntly, "and if I can help him socially, I will. As a matter of fact, he wants me at a stag dinner tonight."

"All right, then," Helen said absently. Still hesitating to tell her her game was over, Stuart followed her glance toward the field, where a runabout had driven up and parked by the ropes.

"There's your old friend, Teddy," he remarked dryly—"or rather, your new friend, Teddy. He's taking a sudden interest in polo. Perhaps he thinks the horses aren't biting this summer."

"You're not in a very good humor," protested Helen. "You know, if you say the word, I'll never see him again. All I want in the world is for you and I to be together."

"I know," he admitted regretfully. "Selling horses and giving up clubs put a crimp in that. I know the women all fall for Teddy, now he's getting famous, but if he tries to fool around with you I'll break his piano over his head. . . . Oh, another thing," he began, seeing the men already riding on the field. "About your last chukker——"

As best he could, he put the situation up to her. He was not prepared for the fury that swept over her.

"But it's an outrage! I got up the game and it's been posted on the bulletin board for three days."

"You started an hour late."

"And do you know why?" she demanded. "Because your friend Joe Morgan insisted that Celie ride sidesaddle. He tore her habit off her three times, and she only got here by climbing out the kitchen window."

"I can't do anything about it."

"Why can't you? Weren't you once a governor of this club? How can women ever expect to be any good if they have to quit every time the men want the field? All the men want is for the women to come up to them in the evening and tell them what a beautiful game they played!"

Still raging and blaming Stuart, she crossed the field to Teddy's car. He got out and greeted her with concentrated intensity:

"I've reached the point where I can neither sleep nor eat from thinking of you. What point is that?"

There was something thrilling about him that she had never been conscious of in the old days; perhaps the stories of his philanderings had made him more romantic to her.

"Well, don't think of me as I am now," she said. "My face is getting rougher every day and my muscles lean out of an evening dress like a female impersonator. People are beginning to refer to me as handsome instead of pretty. Besides, I'm in a vile humor. It seems to me women are always just edged out of everything."

Stuart's game was brutal that afternoon. In the first five minutes, he realized that Teddy's runabout was no longer there, and his long slugs began to tally from all angles. Afterward, he bumped home across country at a gallop; his mood was not assuaged by a note handed him by the children's nurse:

DEAR: Since your friends made it possible for us to play, I wasn't going to sit there just dripping; so I had Teddy bring me home. And since you'll be out to dinner, I'm going into New York with him to the theater. I'll either be out on the theater train or spend the night at mother's.

HELEN.

Stuart went upstairs and changed into his dinner coat. He had no defense against the unfamiliar claws of jealousy that began a slow dissection of his insides. Often Helen had gone to plays or dances with other men, but this was different. He felt toward Teddy the faint contempt of the physical man for the artist, but the last six months had bruised his pride. He perceived the possibility that Helen might be seriously interested in someone else.

He was in a bad humor at Gus Myers' dinner—annoyed with his host for talking so freely about their business arrangement. When at last they rose from the table, he decided that it was no go and called Myers aside.

"Look here. I'm afraid this isn't a good idea, after all."

"Why not?" His host looked at him in alarm. "Are you going back on me? My dear fellow——"

"I think we'd better call it off."

"And why, may I ask? Certainly I have the right to ask why."

Stuart considered. "All right, I'll tell you. When you made that little speech, you mentioned me as if you had somehow bought me, as if I was a sort of employee in your office. Now, in the sporting world that doesn't go; things are more—more democratic. I grew up with all these men here tonight, and they didn't like it any better than I did."

"I see," Mr. Myers reflected carefully—"I see." Suddenly he clapped Stuart on the back. "That is exactly the sort of thing I like to be told; it helps me. From now on I won't mention you as if you were in my—as if we had a business arrangement. Is that all right?"

After all, the salary was eight thousand dollars.

"Very well, then," Stuart agreed. "But you'll have to excuse me tonight. I'm catching a train to the city."

"I'll put an automobile at your disposal."

At ten o'clock he rang the bell of Teddy's apartment on Forty-eighth Street.

"I'm looking for Mr. Van Beck," he said to the woman who answered the door. "I know he's gone to the theater, but I wonder if you can tell me——" Suddenly he guessed who the woman was. "I'm Stuart Oldhorne," he explained. "I married Mr. Van Beck's cousin."

"Oh, come in," said Betty pleasantly. "I know all about who you are."

She was just this side of forty, stoutish and plain of face, but full of a keen, brisk vitality. In the living room they sat down.

"You want to see Teddy?"

"He's with my wife and I want to join them after the theater. I wonder if you know where they went?"

"Oh, so Teddy's with your wife." There was a faint, pleasant brogue in her voice. "Well, now, he didn't say exactly where he'd be tonight."

"Then you don't know?"

"I don't—not for the life of me," she admitted cheerfully. "I'm sorry."

He stood up, and Betty saw the thinly hidden anguish in his face. Suddenly she was really sorry.

"I did hear him say something about the theater," she said ruminatively.

"Now sit down and let me think what it was. He goes out so much and a play once a week is enough for me, so that one night mixes up with the others in my head. Didn't your wife say where to meet them?"

"No. I only decided to come in after they'd started. She said she'd catch the theater train back to Long Island or go to her mother's."

"That's it," Betty said triumphantly, striking her hands together like cymbals. "That's what he said when he called up—that he was putting a lady on the theater train for Long Island, and would be home himself right afterward. We've had a child sick and it's driven things from my mind."

"I'm very sorry I bothered you under those conditions."

"It's no bother. Sit down. It's only just after ten."

Feeling easier, Stuart relaxed a little and accepted a cigar.

"No, if I tried to keep up with Teddy, I'd have white hair by now," Betty said. "Of course, I go to his concerts, but often I fall asleep—not that he ever knows it. So long as he doesn't take too much to drink and knows where his home is, I don't bother about where he wanders." As Stuart's face grew serious again, she changed her tone: "All and all, he's a good husband to me and we have a happy life together, without interfering with each other. How would he do working next to the nursery and groaning at every sound? And how would I do going to Mrs. Ruthven's with him, and all of them talking about high society and high art?"

A phrase of Helen's came back to Stuart: "Always together—I like for us to do everything together."

"You have children, haven't you, Mr. Oldhorne?"

"Yes. My boy's almost big enough to sit a horse."

"Ah, yes; you're both great for horses."

"My wife says that as soon as their legs are long enough to reach stirrups, she'll be interested in them again." This didn't sound right to Stuart and he modified it: "I mean she always has been interested in them, but she never let them monopolize her or come between us. We've always believed that marriage ought to be founded on companionship, on having the same interests. I mean, you're musical and you help your husband."

Betty laughed. "I wish Teddy could hear that. I can't read a note or carry a tune."

"No?" He was confused. "I'd somehow got the impression that you were musical."

"You can't see why else he'd have married me?"

"Not at all. On the contrary."

After a few minutes, he said good night, somehow liking her. When he had gone, Betty's expression changed slowly to one of exasperation; she went to the telephone and called her husband's studio:

"There you are, Teddy. Now listen to me carefully. I know your cousin is with you and I want to talk with her. . . . Now, don't lie. You put her on the phone. Her husband has been here, and if you don't let me talk to her, it might be a serious matter."

She could hear an unintelligible colloquy, and then Helen's voice: "Hello."

"Good evening, Mrs. Oldhorne. Your husband came here, looking for you and Teddy. I told him I didn't know which play you were at, so you'd better be thinking which one. And I told him Teddy was leaving you at the station in time for the theater train."

"Oh, thank you very much. We——"

"Now, you meet your husband or there's trouble for you, or I'm no judge of men. And—wait a minute. Tell Teddy, if he's going to be up late, that Josie's sleeping light, and he's not to touch the piano when he gets home."

Betty heard Teddy come in at eleven, and she came into the drawing-room smelling of camomile vapor. He greeted her absently; there was a look of suffering in his face and his eyes were bright and far away.

"You call yourself a great musician, Teddy Van Beck," she said, "but it seems to me you're much more interested in women."

"Let me alone, Betty."

"I do let you alone, but when the husbands start coming here, it's another matter."

"This was different, Betty. This goes way back into the past."

"It sounds like the present to me."

"Don't make any mistake about Helen," he said. "She's a good woman."

"Not through any fault of yours, I know."

He sank his head wearily in his hands. "I've tried to forget her. I've avoided her for six years. And then, when I met her a month ago, it all rushed over me. Try and understand, Bet. You're my best friend; you're the only person that ever loved me."

"When you're good I love you," she said.

"Don't worry. It's over. She loves her husband; she just came to New York with me because she's got some spite against him. She follows me a certain distance just like she always has, and then——Anyhow, I'm not going to see her any more. Now go to bed, Bet. I want to play for a while."

He was on his feet when she stopped him.

"You're not to touch the piano tonight."

"Oh, I forgot about Josie," he said remorsefully. "Well, I'll drink a bottle of beer and then I'll come to bed."

He came close and put his arm around her.

"Dear Bet, nothing could ever interfere with us."

"You're a bad boy, Teddy," she said. "I wouldn't ever be so bad to you."

"How do you know, Bet? How do you know what you'd do?"

He smoothed down her plain brown hair, knowing for the thousandth time that she had none of the world's dark magic for him, and that he couldn't live without her for six consecutive hours. "Dear Bet," he whispered. "Dear Bet."

· III ·

THE OLDHORNES were visiting. In the last four years, since Stuart had terminated his bondage to Gus Myers, they had become visiting people. The children visited Grandmother Van Beck during the winter and attended school in New York. Stuart and Helen visited friends in Asheville, Aiken and Palm Beach, and in the summer usually occupied a small cottage on someone's Long Island estate. "My dear, it's just standing there empty. I wouldn't dream of accepting any rent. You'll be doing us a favor by occupying it."

Usually, they were; they gave out a great deal of themselves in that eternal willingness and enthusiasm which makes a successful guest—it became their profession. Moving through a world that was growing rich with the war in Europe, Stuart had somewhere lost his way. Twice playing brilliant golf in the national amateur, he accepted a job as professional at a club which his father had helped to found. He was restless and unhappy.

This week-end they were visiting a pupil of his. As a consequence of a mixed foursome, the Oldhornes went upstairs to dress for dinner surcharged with the unpleasant accumulation of many unsatisfactory months. In the afternoon, Stuart had played with their hostess and Helen with another man—a situation which Stuart always dreaded, because it forced him into competition with Helen. He had actually tried to miss that putt on the eighteenth—to just miss it. But the ball dropped in the cup. Helen went through the superficial motions of a good loser, but she devoted herself pointedly to her partner for the rest of the afternoon.

Their expressions still counterfeited amusement as they entered their room.

When the door closed, Helen's pleasant expression faded and she walked toward the dressing table as though her own reflection was the only decent company with which to forgather. Stuart watched her, frowning.

"I know why you're in a rotten humor," he said; "though I don't believe you know yourself."

"I'm not in a rotten humor," Helen responded in a clipped voice.

"You are; and I know the real reason—the one you don't know. It's because I holed that putt this afternoon."

She turned slowly, incredulously, from the mirror.

"Oh, so I have a new fault! I've suddenly become, of all things, a poor sport!"

"It's not like you to be a poor sport," he admitted, "but otherwise why all this interest in other men, and why do you look at me as if I'm—well, slightly gamy?"

"I'm not aware of it."

"I am." He was aware, too, that there was always some man in their life now—some man of power and money who paid court to Helen and gave her the sense of solidity which he failed to provide. He had no cause to be jealous of any particular man, but the pressure of many was irritating. It annoyed him that on so slight a grievance, Helen should remind him by her actions that he no longer filled her entire life.

"If Anne can get any satisfaction out of winning, she's welcome to it," said Helen suddenly.

"Isn't that rather petty? She isn't in your class; she won't qualify for the third flight in Boston."

Feeling herself in the wrong, she changed her tone.

"Oh, that isn't it," she broke out. "I just keep wishing you and I could play together like we used to. And now you have to play with dubs, and get their wretched shots out of traps. Especially"—she hesitated—"especially when you're so unnecessarily gallant."

The faint contempt in her voice, the mock jealousy that covered a growing indifference was apparent to him. There had been a time when, if he danced with another woman, Helen's stricken eyes followed him around the room.

"My gallantry is simply a matter of business," he answered. "Lessons have brought in three hundred a month all summer. How could I go to see you play at Boston next week, except that I'm going to coach other women?"

"And you're going to see me win," announced Helen. "Do you know that?"

"Naturally, I want nothing more," Stuart said automatically. But the unnecessary defiance in her voice repelled him, and he suddenly wondered if he really cared whether she won or not.

At the same moment, Helen's mood changed and for a moment she saw the true situation—that she could play in amateur tournaments and Stuart could not, that the new cups in the rack were all hers now, that he had given up the fiercely competitive sportsmanship that had been the breath of life to him in order to provide necessary money.

"Oh, I'm so sorry for you, Stuart!" There were tears in her eyes. "It seems such a shame that you can't do the things you love, and I can. Perhaps I oughtn't to play this summer."

"Nonsense," he said. "You can't sit home and twirl your thumbs."

She caught at this: "You wouldn't want me to. I can't help being good at sports; you taught me nearly all I know. But I wish I could help you."

"Just try to remember I'm your best friend. Sometimes you act as if we were rivals."

She hesitated, annoyed by the truth of his words and unwilling to concede an inch; but a wave of memories rushed over her, and she thought how brave he was in his eked-out, pieced-together life; she came and threw her arms around him.

"Darling, darling, things are going to be better. You'll see."

Helen won the finals in the tournament at Boston the following week. Following around with the crowd, Stuart was very proud of her. He hoped that instead of feeding her egotism, the actual achievement would make things easier between them. He hated the conflict that had grown out of their wanting the same excellences, the same prizes from life.

Afterward he pursued her progress toward the clubhouse, amused and a little jealous of the pack that fawned around her. He reached the club among the last, and a steward accosted him. "Professionals are served in the lower grill, please," the man said.

"That's all right. My name's Oldhorne."

He started to walk by, but the man barred his way.

"Sorry, sir. I realize that Mrs. Oldhorne's playing in the match, but my orders are to direct the professionals to the lower grill, and I understand you are a professional."

"Why, look here——" Stuart began, wildly angry, and stopped. A group of people were listening. "All right; never mind," he said gruffly, and turned away.

The memory of the experience rankled; it was the determining factor that drove him, some weeks later, to a momentous decision. For a long time he had been playing with the idea of joining the Canadian Air Force, for service in France. He knew that his absence would have little practical bearing on the lives of Helen and the children; happening on some friends who were also full of the restlessness of 1915, the matter was suddenly decided. But he had not counted on the effect upon Helen; her reaction was not so much one of grief or alarm, but as if she had been somehow outwitted.

"But you might have told me!" she wailed. "You leave me dangling; you simply take yourself away without any warning."

Once again Helen saw him as the bright and intolerably blinding hero, and her soul winced before him as it had when they first met. He was a warrior; for him, peace was only the interval between wars, and peace was destroying him. Here was the game of games beckoning him——Without throwing over the whole logic of their lives, there was nothing she could say.

"This is my sort of thing," he said confidently, younger with his excitement. "A few more years of this life and I'd go to pieces, take to drink. I've somehow lost your respect, and I've got to have that, even if I'm far away."

She was proud of him again; she talked to everyone of his impending departure. Then, one September afternoon, she came home from the city, full of the old feeling of comradeship and bursting with news, to find him buried in an utter depression.

"Stuart," she cried, "I've got the——" She broke off. "What's the matter, darling? Is something the matter?"

He looked at her dully. "They turned me down," he said.

"What?"

"My left eye." He laughed bitterly. "Where that dub cracked me with the brassie. I'm nearly blind in it."

"Isn't there anything you can do?"

"Nothing."

"Stuart!" She stared at him aghast. "Stuart, and I was going to tell you! I was saving it for a surprise. Elsa Prentice has organized a Red Cross unit to serve with the French, and I joined it because I thought it would be wonderful if we both went. We've been measured for uniforms and bought our outfits, and we're sailing the end of next week."

· IV ·

HELEN WAS a blurred figure among other blurred figures on a boat deck, dark against the threat of submarines. When the ship had slid out into the obscure future, Stuart walked eastward along Fifty-seventh Street. His grief at the severance of many ties was a weight he carried in his body, and he walked slowly, as if adjusting himself to it. To balance this there was a curious sensation of lightness in his mind. For the first time in twelve years he was alone, and the feeling came over him that he was alone for good; knowing Helen and knowing war, he could guess at the experiences she would go through, and he could not form any picture of a renewed life together afterward. He was discarded; she had proved the stronger at last. It seemed very strange and sad that his marriage should have such an ending.

He came to Carnegie Hall, dark after a concert, and his eye caught the name of Theodore Van Beck, large on the posted bills. As he stared at it, a green door opened in the side of the building and a group of people in evening dress came out. Stuart and Teddy were face to face before they recognized each other.

"Hello, there!" Teddy cried cordially. "Did Helen sail?"

"Just now."

"I met her on the street yesterday and she told me. I wanted you both to come to my concert. Well, she's quite a heroine, going off like that. . . . Have you met my wife?"

Stuart and Betty smiled at each other.

"We've met."

"And I didn't know it," protested Teddy. "Women need watching when they get toward their dotage. . . . Look here, Stuart; we're having a few people up to the apartment. No heavy music or anything. Just supper and a few débutantes to tell me I was divine. It will do you good to come. I imagine you're missing Helen like the devil."

"I don't think I——"

"Come along. They'll tell you you're divine too."

Realizing that the invitation was inspired by kindliness, Stuart accepted. It was the sort of gathering he had seldom attended, and he was surprised to meet so many people he knew. Teddy played the lion in a manner at once assertive and skeptical. Stuart listened as he enlarged to Mrs. Cassius Ruthven on one of his favorite themes:

"People tried to make marriages coöperative and they've ended by becoming competitive. Impossible situation. Smart men will get to fight shy of ornamental women. A man ought to marry somebody who'll be grateful, like Betty here."

"Now don't talk so much, Theodore Van Beck," Betty interrupted. "Since you're such a fine musician, you'd do well to express yourself with music instead of rash words."

"I don't agree with your husband," said Mrs. Ruthven. "English girls hunt with their men and play politics with them on absolutely equal terms, and it tends to draw them together."

"It does not," insisted Teddy. "That's why English society is the most disorganized in the world. Betty and I are happy because we haven't any qualities in common at all."

His exuberance grated on Stuart, and the success that flowed from him swung his mind back to the failure of his own life. He could not know that his life was not destined to be a failure. He could not read the fine story that three years later would be carved proud above his soldier's grave, or know that his restless body, which never spared itself in sport or danger, was destined to give him one last proud gallop at the end.

"They turned me down," he was saying to Mrs. Ruthven. "I'll have to stick to Squadron A, unless we get drawn in."

"So Helen's gone." Mrs. Ruthven looked at him, reminiscing. "I'll never forget your wedding. You were both so handsome, so ideally suited to each other. Everybody spoke of it."

Stuart remembered; for the moment it seemed that he had little else that it was fun to remember.

"Yes," he agreed, nodding his head thoughtfully, "I suppose we were a handsome pair."

CRAZY SUNDAY

◆

"Crazy Sunday" (American Mercury, October 1932) was written after Fitz-gerald's 1931 work at MGM on the screenplay for Red-Headed Woman, *which was not used. While in Hollywood, Fitzgerald, inspired by alcohol, performed a humorous song at a party given by Irving Thalberg and Norma Shearer, and was booed by John Gilbert and Lupe Velez.*

The story was turned down by the Post *because "it didn't get anywhere or prove anything" and because the ending made it "difficult" for them. Hearst's* Cosmopolitan *refused the story because of the risk of offending Hollywood figures, although Fitzgerald insisted that "I had mixed up those characters so thoroughly that there was no character who could have been identified except possibly King Vidor and he would have been very amused by the story." Harold Ober was unable to place it in another mass-circulation magazine because of its sexual material and its length. Fitzgerald declined to provide a different ending and sold it to the* American Mercury *for $200; he included it in* Taps at Reveille.

◆

IT WAS SUNDAY—not a day, but rather a gap between two other days. Behind, for all of them, lay sets and sequences, the long waits under the crane that swung the microphone, the hundred miles a day by automobiles to and fro across a county, the struggles of rival ingenuities in the conference rooms, the ceaseless compromise, the clash and strain of many personalities fighting for their lives. And now Sunday, with individual life starting up again, with a glow kindling in eyes that had been glazed with monotony the afternoon before. Slowly as the hours waned they came awake like "Puppenfeen" in a toy shop: an intense colloquy in a corner, lovers disappearing to neck in a hall. And the feeling of "Hurry, it's not too late, but for God's sake hurry before the blessed forty hours of leisure are over."

Joel Coles was writing continuity. He was twenty-eight and not yet broken by Hollywood. He had had what were considered nice assignments since his arrival six months before and he submitted his scenes and sequences with enthusiasm. He referred to himself modestly as a hack but really did not think of it that way. His mother had been a successful actress; Joel had spent his childhood between London and New York trying to separate the real from the unreal, or at least to keep one guess ahead. He was a handsome man with the pleasant cow-brown eyes that in 1913 had gazed out at Broadway audiences from his mother's face.

When the invitation came it made him sure that he was getting somewhere. Ordinarily he did not go out on Sundays but stayed sober and took work home with him. Recently they had given him a Eugene O'Neill play destined for a very important lady indeed. Everything he had done so far had pleased Miles Calman, and Miles Calman was the only director on the lot who did not work under a supervisor and was responsible to the money men alone. Everything was clicking into place in Joel's career. ("This is Mr. Calman's secretary. Will you come to tea from four to six Sunday—he lives in Beverly Hills, number——.")

Joel was flattered. It would be a party out of the top-drawer. It was a tribute to himself as a young man of promise. The Marion Davies' crowd, the high-hats, the big currency numbers, perhaps even Dietrich and Garbo and the Marquise, people who were not seen everywhere, would probably be at Calman's.

"I won't take anything to drink," he assured himself. Calman was audibly tired of rummies, and thought it was a pity the industry could not get along without them.

Joel agreed that writers drank too much—he did himself, but he wouldn't this afternoon. He wished Miles would be within hearing when the cocktails were passed to hear his succinct, unobtrusive, "No, thank you."

Miles Calman's house was built for great emotional moments—there was an air of listening, as if the far silences of its vistas hid an audience, but this afternoon it was thronged, as though people had been bidden rather than asked. Joel noted with pride that only two other writers from the studio were in the crowd, an ennobled limey and, somewhat to his surprise, Nat Keogh, who had evoked Calman's impatient comment on drunks.

Stella Calman (Stella Walker, of course) did not move on to her other guests after she spoke to Joel. She lingered—she looked at him with the sort of beautiful look that demands some sort of acknowledgment and Joe drew quickly on the dramatic adequacy inherited from his mother:

"Well, you look about sixteen! Where's your kiddy car?"

She was visibly pleased; she lingered. He felt that he should say something more, something confident and easy—he had first met her when she was struggling for bits in New York. At the moment a tray slid up and Stella put a cocktail glass into his hand.

"Everybody's afraid, aren't they?" he said, looking at it absently. "Everybody watches for everybody else's blunders, or tries to make sure they're with people that'll do them credit. Of course that's not true in your house," he covered himself hastily. "I just meant generally in Hollywood."

Stella agreed. She presented several people to Joel as if he were very important. Reassuring himself that Miles was at the other side of the room, Joel drank the cocktail.

"So you have a baby?" he said. "That's the time to look out. After a pretty woman has had her first child, she's very vulnerable, because she wants to be reassured about her own charm. She's got to have some new man's unqualified devotion to prove to herself she hasn't lost anything."

"I never get anybody's unqualified devotion," Stella said rather resentfully.

"They're afraid of your husband."

"You think that's it?" She wrinkled her brow over the idea; then the conversation was interrupted at the exact moment Joel would have chosen.

Her attentions had given him confidence. Not for him to join safe groups, to slink to refuge under the wings of such acquaintances as he saw about the room. He walked to the window and looked out toward the Pacific, colorless under its sluggish sunset. It was good here—the American Riviera and all that, if there were ever time to enjoy it. The handsome, well-dressed people in the room, the lovely girls, and the—well, the lovely girls. You couldn't have everything.

He saw Stella's fresh boyish face, with the tired eyelid that always drooped a little over one eye, moving about among her guests and he wanted to sit with her and talk a long time as if she were a girl instead of a name; he followed her to see if she paid anyone as much attention as she had paid him. He took another cocktail—not because he needed confidence but because she had given him so much of it. Then he sat down beside the director's mother.

"Your son's gotten to be a legend, Mrs. Calman—Oracle and a Man of Destiny and all that. Personally, I'm against him but I'm in a minority. What do you think of him? Are you impressed? Are you surprised how far he's gone?"

"No, I'm not surprised," she said calmly. "We always expected a lot from Miles."

"Well now, that's unusual," remarked Joel. "I always think all mothers are like Napoleon's mother. My mother didn't want me to have anything to do with the entertainment business. She wanted me to go to West Point and be safe."

"We always had every confidence in Miles." . . .

He stood by the built-in bar of the dining room with the good-humored, heavy-drinking, highly paid Nat Keogh.

"—I made a hundred grand during the year and lost forty grand gambling, so now I've hired a manager."

"You mean an agent," suggested Joel.

"No, I've got that too. I mean a manager. I make over everything to my wife and then he and my wife get together and hand me out the money. I pay him five thousand a year to hand me out my money."

"You mean your agent."

"No, I mean my manager, and I'm not the only one—a lot of other irresponsible people have him."

"Well, if you're irresponsible why are you responsible enough to hire a manager?"

"I'm just irresponsible about gambling. Look here——"

A singer performed; Joel and Nat went forward with the others to listen.

· II ·

THE SINGING reached Joel vaguely; he felt happy and friendly toward all the people gathered there, people of bravery and industry, superior to a bourgeoisie that outdid them in ignorance and loose living, risen to a position of the highest prominence in a nation that for a decade had wanted only to be entertained. He liked them—he loved them. Great waves of good feeling flowed through him.

As the singer finished his number and there was a drift toward the hostess to say good-by, Joel had an idea. He would give them "Building It Up," his own composition. It was his only parlor trick, it had amused several parties and it might please Stella Walker. Possessed by the hunch, his blood throbbing with the scarlet corpuscles of exhibitionism, he sought her.

"Of course," she cried. "Please! Do you need anything?"

"Someone has to be the secretary that I'm supposed to be dictating to."

"I'll be her."

As the word spread the guests in the hall, already putting on their coats to leave, drifted back and Joel faced the eyes of many strangers. He had a dim foreboding, realizing that the man who had just performed was a famous radio entertainer. Then someone said "Sh!" and he was alone with Stella, the center of a sinister Indian-like half-circle. Stella smiled up at him expectantly—he began.

His burlesque was based upon the cultural limitations of Mr. Dave Silverstein, an independent producer; Silverstein was presumed to be dictating a letter outlining a treatment of a story he had bought.

"—a story of divorce, the younger generators and the Foreign Legion," he heard his voice saying, with the intonations of Mr. Silverstein. "But we got to build it up, see?"

A sharp pang of doubt struck through him. The faces surrounding him in the gently molded light were intent and curious, but there was no ghost of a smile anywhere; directly in front the Great Lover of the screen glared at him with an eye as keen as the eye of a potato. Only Stella Walker looked up at him with a radiant, never faltering smile.

"If we make him a Menjou type, then we get a sort of Michael Arlen only with a Honolulu atmosphere."

Still not a ripple in front, but in the rear a rustling, a perceptible shift toward the left, toward the front door.

"—then she says she feels this sex appil for him and he burns out and says 'Oh go on destroy yourself'——"

At some point he heard Nat Keogh snicker and here and there were a few encouraging faces, but as he finished he had the sickening realization that he had made a fool of himself in view of an important section of the picture world, upon whose favor depended his career.

For a moment he existed in the midst of a confused silence, broken by a general trek for the door. He felt the undercurrent of derision that rolled through the gossip; then—all this was in the space of ten seconds—the Great Lover, his eye hard and empty as the eye of a needle, shouted "Boo! Boo!" voicing in an overtone what he felt was the mood of the crowd. It was the resentment of the professional toward the amateur, of the community toward the stranger, the thumbs-down of the clan.

Only Stella Walker was still standing near and thanking him as if he had been an unparalleled success, as if it hadn't occurred to her that anyone hadn't liked it. As Nat Keogh helped him into his overcoat, a great wave of self-disgust swept over him and he clung desperately to his rule of never betraying an inferior emotion until he no longer felt it.

"I was a flop," he said lightly, to Stella. "Never mind, it's a good number when appreciated. Thanks for your coöperation."

The smile did not leave her face—he bowed rather drunkenly and Nat drew him toward the door. . . .

The arrival of his breakfast awakened him into a broken and ruined world. Yesterday he was himself, a point of fire against an industry, today he felt that he was pitted under an enormous disadvantage, against those faces, against individual contempt and collective sneer. Worse than that, to Miles

Calman he was become one of those rummies, stripped of dignity, whom
Calman regretted he was compelled to use. To Stella Walker, on whom he
had forced a martyrdom to preserve the courtesy of her house—her opinion
he did not dare to guess. His gastric juices ceased to flow and he set his
poached eggs back on the telephone table. He wrote:

> DEAR MILES: You can imagine my profound self-disgust. I confess
> to a taint of exhibitionism, but at six o'clock in the afternoon, in broad
> daylight! Good God! My apologies to your wife.
>   Yours ever,
>   JOEL COLES.

Joel emerged from his office on the lot only to slink like a malefactor to
the tobacco store. So suspicious was his manner that one of the studio police
asked to see his admission card. He had decided to eat lunch outside when
Nat Keogh, confident and cheerful, overtook him.

"What do you mean you're in permanent retirement? What if that Three
Piece Suit did boo you?

"Why, listen," he continued, drawing Joel into the studio restaurant.
"The night of one of his premiers at Grauman's, Joe Squires kicked his tail
while he was bowing to the crowd. The ham said Joe'd hear from him later
but when Joe called him up at eight o'clock next day and said, 'I thought
I was going to hear from you,' he hung up the phone."

The preposterous story cheered Joel, and he found a gloomy consolation
in staring at the group at the next table, the sad, lovely Siamese twins, the
mean dwarfs, the proud giant from the circus picture. But looking beyond
at the yellow-stained faces of pretty women, their eyes all melancholy and
startling with mascara, their ball gowns garish in full day, he saw a group
who had been at Calman's and winced.

"Never again," he exclaimed aloud, "absolutely my last social appearance
in Hollywood!"

The following morning a telegram was waiting for him at his office:

> You were one of the most agreeable people at our party. Expect you
> at my sister June's buffet supper next Sunday.
>   STELLA WALKER CALMAN.

The blood rushed fast through his veins for a feverish minute. Incredulously he read the telegram over.

"Well, that's the sweetest thing I ever heard of in my life!"

· III ·

CRAZY SUNDAY again. Joel slept until eleven, then he read a newspaper to catch up with the past week. He lunched in his room on trout, avocado salad and a pint of California wine. Dressing for the tea, he selected a pin-check suit, a blue shirt, a burnt orange tie. There were dark circles of fatigue under his eyes. In his second-hand car he drove to the Riviera apartments. As he was introducing himself to Stella's sister, Miles and Stella arrived in riding clothes—they had been quarrelling fiercely most of the afternoon on all the dirt roads back of Beverly Hills.

Miles Calman, tall, nervous, with a desperate humor and the unhappiest eyes Joel ever saw, was an artist from the top of his curiously shaped head to his niggerish feet. Upon these last he stood firmly—he had never made a cheap picture though he had sometimes paid heavily for the luxury of making experimental flops. In spite of his excellent company, one could not be with him long without realizing that he was not a well man.

From the moment of their entrance Joel's day bound itself up inextricably with theirs. As he joined the group around them Stella turned away from it with an impatient little tongue click—and Miles Calman said to the man who happened to be next to him:

"Go easy on Eva Goebel. There's hell to pay about her at home." Miles turned to Joel, "I'm sorry I missed you at the office yesterday. I spent the afternoon at the analyst's."

"You being psychoanalyzed?"

"I have been for months. First I went for claustrophobia, now I'm trying to get my whole life cleared up. They say it'll take over a year."

"There's nothing the matter with your life," Joel assured him.

"Oh, no? Well, Stella seems to think so. Ask anybody—they can all tell you about it," he said bitterly.

A girl perched herself on the arm of Miles' chair; Joel crossed to Stella, who stood disconsolately by the fire.

"Thank you for your telegram," he said. "It was darn sweet. I can't imagine anybody as good-looking as you are being so good-humored."

She was a little lovelier than he had ever seen her and perhaps the unstinted admiration in his eyes prompted her to unload on him—it did not take long, for she was obviously at the emotional bursting point.

"—and Miles has been carrying on this thing for two years, and I never knew. Why, she was one of my best friends, always in the house. Finally when people began to come to me, Miles had to admit it."

She sat down vehemently on the arm of Joel's chair. Her riding breeches were the color of the chair and Joel saw that the mass of her hair was made up of some strands of red gold and some of pale gold, so that it could not be dyed, and that she had on no make-up. She was that good-looking——

Still quivering with the shock of her discovery, Stella found unbearable the spectacle of a new girl hovering over Miles; she led Joel into a bedroom, and seated at either end of a big bed they went on talking. People on their way to the washroom glanced in and made wisecracks, but Stella, emptying out her story, paid no attention. After a while Miles stuck his head in the door and said, "There's no use trying to explain something to Joel in half an hour that I don't understand myself and the psychoanalyst says will take a whole year to understand."

She talked on as if Miles were not there. She loved Miles, she said—under considerable difficulties she had always been faithful to him.

"The psychoanalyst told Miles that he had a mother complex. In his first marriage he transferred his mother complex to his wife, you see—and then his sex turned to me. But when we married the thing repeated itself—he transferred his mother complex to me and all his libido turned toward this other woman."

Joel knew that this probably wasn't gibberish—yet it sounded like gibberish. He knew Eva Goebel; she was a motherly person, older and probably wiser than Stella, who was a golden child.

Miles now suggested impatiently that Joel come back with them since Stella had so much to say, so they drove out to the mansion in Beverly Hills. Under the high ceilings the situation seemed more dignified and tragic. It was an eerie bright night with the dark very clear outside of all the windows and Stella all rose-gold raging and crying around the room. Joel did not quite believe in picture actresses' grief. They have other preoccupations— they are beautiful rose-gold figures blown full of life by writers and directors, and after hours they sit around and talk in whispers and giggle innuendoes, and the ends of many adventures flow through them.

Sometimes he pretended to listen and instead thought how well she was got up—sleek breeches with a matched set of legs in them, an Italian-colored sweater with a little high neck, and a short brown chamois coat. He couldn't decide whether she was an imitation of an English lady or an English lady was an imitation of her. She hovered somewhere between the realest of realities and the most blatant of impersonations.

"Miles is so jealous of me that he questions everything I do," she cried scornfully. "When I was in New York I wrote him that I'd been to the theater with Eddie Baker. Miles was so jealous he phoned me ten times in one day."

"I was wild," Miles snuffled sharply, a habit he had in times of stress. "The analyst couldn't get any results for a week."

Stella shook her head despairingly. "Did you expect me just to sit in the hotel for three weeks?"

"I don't expect anything. I admit that I'm jealous. I try not to be. I worked on that with Dr. Bridgebane, but it didn't do any good. I was jealous of Joel this afternoon when you sat on the arm of his chair."

"You were?" She started up. "You were! Wasn't there somebody on the arm of your chair? And did you speak to me for two hours?"

"You were telling your troubles to Joel in the bedroom."

"When I think that that woman"—she seemed to believe that to omit Eva Goebel's name would be to lessen her reality—"used to come here——"

"All right—all right," said Miles wearily. "I've admitted everything and I feel as bad about it as you do." Turning to Joel he began talking about pictures, while Stella moved restlessly along the far walls, her hands in her breeches pockets.

"They've treated Miles terribly," she said, coming suddenly back into the conversation as if they'd never discussed her personal affairs. "Dear, tell him about old Beltzer trying to change your picture."

As she stood hovering protectively over Miles, her eyes flashing with indignation in his behalf, Joel realized that he was in love with her. Stifled with excitement he got up to say good night.

With Monday the week resumed its workaday rhythm, in sharp contrast to the theoretical discussions, the gossip and scandal of Sunday; there was the endless detail of script revision—"Instead of a lousy dissolve, we can leave her voice on the sound track and cut to a medium shot of the taxi from Bell's angle or we can simply pull the camera back to include the station, hold it a minute and then pan to the row of taxis"—by Monday afternoon Joel had again forgotten that people whose business was to provide entertainment were ever privileged to be entertained. In the evening he phoned Miles' house. He asked for Miles but Stella came to the phone.

"Do things seem better?"

"Not particularly. What are you doing next Saturday evening?"

"Nothing."

"The Perrys are giving a dinner and theater party and Miles won't be here—he's flying to South Bend to see the Notre Dame-California game. I thought you might go with me in his place."

After a long moment Joel said, "Why—surely. If there's a conference I can't make dinner but I can get to the theater."

"Then I'll say we can come."

Joel walked his office. In view of the strained relations of the Calmans, would Miles be pleased, or did she intend that Miles shouldn't know of it?

That would be out of the question—if Miles didn't mention it Joel would. But it was an hour or more before he could get down to work again.

Wednesday there was a four-hour wrangle in a conference room crowded with planets and nebulae of cigarette smoke. Three men and a woman paced the carpet in turn, suggesting or condemning, speaking sharply or persuasively, confidently or despairingly. At the end Joel lingered to talk to Miles.

The man was tired—not with the exaltation of fatigue but life-tired, with his lids sagging and his beard prominent over the blue shadows near his mouth.

"I hear you're flying to the Notre Dame game."

Miles looked beyond him and shook his head.

"I've given up the idea."

"Why?"

"On account of you." Still he did not look at Joel.

"What the hell, Miles?"

"That's why I've given it up." He broke into a perfunctory laugh at himself. "I can't tell what Stella might do just out of spite—she's invited you to take her to the Perrys', hasn't she? I wouldn't enjoy the game."

The fine instinct that moved swiftly and confidently on the set, muddled so weakly and helplessly through his personal life.

"Look, Miles," Joel said frowning. "I've never made any passes whatsoever at Stella. If you're really seriously cancelling your trip on account of me, I won't go to the Perrys' with her. I won't see her. You can trust me absolutely."

Miles looked at him, carefully now.

"Maybe." He shrugged his shoulders. "Anyhow there'd just be somebody else. I wouldn't have any fun."

"You don't seem to have much confidence in Stella. She told me she'd always been true to you."

"Maybe she has." In the last few minutes several more muscles had sagged around Miles' mouth, "But how can I ask anything of her after what's happened? How can I expect her—" He broke off and his face grew harder as he said, "I'll tell you one thing, right or wrong and no matter what I've done, if I ever had anything on her I'd divorce her. I can't have my pride hurt—that would be the last straw."

His tone annoyed Joel, but he said:

"Hasn't she calmed down about the Eva Goebel thing?"

"No." Miles snuffled pessimistically. "I can't get over it either."

"I thought it was finished."

"I'm trying not to see Eva again, but you know it isn't easy just to drop something like that—it isn't some girl I kissed last night in a taxi! The psychoanalyst says——"

"I know," Joel interrupted. "Stella told me." This was depressing. "Well, as far as I'm concerned if you go to the game I won't see Stella. And I'm sure Stella has nothing on her conscience about anybody."

"Maybe not," Miles repeated listlessly. "Anyhow I'll stay and take her to the party. Say," he said suddenly, "I wish you'd come too. I've got to have somebody sympathetic to talk to. That's the trouble—I've influenced Stella in everything. Especially I've influenced her so that she likes all the men I like—it's very difficult."

"It must be," Joel agreed.

·IV·

JOEL COULD NOT get to the dinner. Self-conscious in his silk hat against the unemployment, he waited for the others in front of the Hollywood Theatre and watched the evening parade: obscure replicas of bright, particular picture stars, spavined men in polo coats, a stomping dervish with the beard and staff of an apostle, a pair of chic Filipinos in collegiate clothes, reminder that this corner of the Republic opened to the seven seas, a long fantastic carnival of young shouts which proved to be a fraternity initiation. The line split to pass two smart limousines that stopped at the curb.

There she was, in a dress like ice-water, made in a thousand pale-blue pieces, with icicles trickling at the throat. He started forward.

"So you like my dress?"

"Where's Miles?"

"He flew to the game after all. He left yesterday morning—at least I think—" She broke off. "I just got a telegram from South Bend saying that he's starting back. I forgot—you know all these people?"

The party of eight moved into the theater.

Miles had gone after all and Joel wondered if he should have come. But during the performance, with Stella a profile under the pure grain of light hair, he thought no more about Miles. Once he turned and looked at her and she looked back at him, smiling and meeting his eyes for as long as he wanted. Between the acts they smoked in the lobby and she whispered:

"They're all going to the opening of Jack Johnson's night club—I don't want to go, do you?"

"Do we have to?"

"I suppose not." She hesitated. "I'd like to talk to you. I suppose we could go to our house—if I were only sure——"

Again she hesitated and Joel asked:

"Sure of what?"

"Sure that—oh, I'm haywire I know, but how can I be sure Miles went to the game?"

"You mean you think he's with Eva Goebel?"

"No, not so much that—but supposing he was here watching everything I do. You know Miles does odd things sometimes. Once he wanted a man with a long beard to drink tea with him and he sent down to the casting agency for one, and drank tea with him all afternoon."

"That's different. He sent you a wire from South Bend—that proves he's at the game."

After the play they said good night to the others at the curb and were answered by looks of amusement. They slid off along the golden garish thoroughfare through the crowd that had gathered around Stella.

"You see he could arrange the telegrams," Stella said, "very easily."

That was true. And with the idea that perhaps her uneasiness was justified, Joel grew angry: if Miles had trained a camera on them he felt no obligations toward Miles. Aloud he said:

"That's nonsense."

There were Christmas trees already in the shop windows and the full moon over the boulevard was only a prop, as scenic as the giant boudoir lamps of the corners. On into the dark foliage of Beverly Hills that flamed as eucalyptus by day, Joel saw only the flash of a white face under his own, the arc of her shoulder. She pulled away suddenly and looked up at him.

"Your eyes are like your mother's," she said. "I used to have a scrap book full of pictures of her."

"Your eyes are like your own and not a bit like any other eyes," he answered.

Something made Joel look out into the grounds as they went into the house, as if Miles were lurking in the shrubbery. A telegram waited on the hall table. She read aloud:

CHICAGO.

Home tomorrow night. Thinking of you. Love.

MILES.

"You see," she said, throwing the slip back on the table, "he could easily have faked that." She asked the butler for drinks and sandwiches and ran upstairs, while Joel walked into the empty reception rooms. Strolling about he wandered to the piano where he had stood in disgrace two Sundays before.

"Then we could put over," he said aloud, "a story of divorce, the younger generators and the Foreign Legion."

His thoughts jumped to another telegram.

"You were one of the most agreeable people at our party——"

An idea occurred to him. If Stella's telegram had been purely a gesture of courtesy then it was likely that Miles had inspired it, for it was Miles who had invited him. Probably Miles had said:

"Send him a wire—he's miserable—he thinks he's queered himself."

It fitted in with "I've influenced Stella in everything. Especially I've influenced her so that she likes all the men I like." A woman would do a thing like that because she felt sympathetic—only a man would do it because he felt responsible.

When Stella came back into the room he took both her hands.

"I have a strange feeling that I'm a sort of pawn in a spite game you're playing against Miles," he said.

"Help yourself to a drink."

"And the odd thing is that I'm in love with you anyhow."

The telephone rang and she freed herself to answer it.

"Another wire from Miles," she announced. "He dropped it, or it says he dropped it, from the airplane at Kansas City."

"I suppose he asked to be remembered to me."

"No, he just said he loved me. I believe he does. He's so very weak."

"Come sit beside me," Joel urged her.

It was early. And it was still a few minutes short of midnight a half-hour later, when Joel walked to the cold hearth, and said tersely:

"Meaning that you haven't any curiosity about me?"

"Not at all. You attract me a lot and you know it. The point is that I suppose I really do love Miles."

"Obviously."

"And tonight I feel uneasy about everything."

He wasn't angry—he was even faintly relieved that a possible entanglement was avoided. Still as he looked at her, the warmth and softness of her body thawing her cold blue costume, he knew she was one of the things he would always regret.

"I've got to go," he said. "I'll phone a taxi."

"Nonsense—there's a chauffeur on duty."

He winced at her readiness to have him go, and seeing this she kissed him lightly and said, "You're sweet, Joel." Then suddenly three things happened: he took down his drink at a gulp, the phone rang loud through the house and a clock in the hall struck in trumpet notes.

Nine—ten—eleven—twelve——

· V ·

IT WAS SUNDAY again. Joel realized that he had come to the theater this evening with the work of the week still hanging about him like cerements. He had made love to Stella as he might attack some matter to be cleaned up hurriedly before the day's end. But this was Sunday—the lovely, lazy perspective of the next twenty-four hours unrolled before him—every minute was something to be approached with lulling indirection, every moment held the germ of innumerable possibilities. Nothing was impossible—everything was just beginning. He poured himself another drink.

With a sharp moan, Stella slipped forward inertly by the telephone. Joel picked her up and laid her on the sofa. He squirted soda-water on a handkerchief and slapped it over her face. The telephone mouthpiece was still grinding and he put it to his ear.

"—the plane fell just this side of Kansas City. The body of Miles Calman has been identified and——"

He hung up the receiver.

"Lie still," he said, stalling, as Stella opened her eyes.

"Oh, what's happened?" she whispered. "Call them back. Oh, what's happened?"

"I'll call them right away. What's your doctor's name?"

"Did they say Miles was dead?"

"Lie quiet—is there a servant still up?"

"Hold me—I'm frightened."

He put his arm around her.

"I want the name of your doctor," he said sternly. "It may be a mistake but I want someone here."

"It's Doctor—Oh, God, is Miles dead?"

Joel ran upstairs and searched through strange medicine cabinets for spirits of ammonia. When he came down Stella cried:

"He isn't dead—I know he isn't. This is part of his scheme. He's torturing me. I know he's alive. I can feel he's alive."

"I want to get hold of some close friend of yours, Stella. You can't stay here alone tonight."

"Oh, no," she cried. "I can't see anybody. You stay. I haven't got any friend." She got up, tears streaming down her face. "Oh, Miles is my only friend. He's not dead—he can't be dead. I'm going there right away and see. Get a train. You'll have to come with me."

"You can't. There's nothing to do tonight. I want you to tell me the name of some woman I can call: Lois? Joan? Carmel? Isn't there somebody?"

Stella stared at him blindly.

"Eva Goebel was my best friend," she said.

Joel thought of Miles, his sad and desperate face in the office two days before. In the awful silence of his death all was clear about him. He was the only American-born director with both an interesting temperament and an artistic conscience. Meshed in an industry, he had paid with his ruined nerves for having no resilience, no healthy cynicism, no refuge—only a pitiful and precarious escape.

There was a sound at the outer door—it opened suddenly, and there were footsteps in the hall.

"Miles!" Stella screamed. "Is it you, Miles? Oh, it's Miles."

A telegraph boy appeared in the doorway.

"I couldn't find the bell. I heard you talking inside."

The telegram was a duplicate of the one that had been phoned. While Stella read it over and over, as though it were a black lie, Joel telephoned. It was still early and he had difficulty getting anyone; when finally he succeeded in finding some friends he made Stella take a stiff drink.

"You'll stay here, Joel," she whispered, as though she were half-asleep. "You won't go away. Miles liked you—he said you—" She shivered violently, "Oh, my God, you don't know how alone I feel." Her eyes closed, "Put your arms around me. Miles had a suit like that." She started bolt upright. "Think of what he must have felt. He was afraid of almost everything, anyhow."

She shook her head dazedly. Suddenly she seized Joel's face and held it close to hers.

"You won't go. You like me—you love me, don't you? Don't call up anybody. Tomorrow's time enough. You stay here with me tonight."

He stared at her, at first incredulously, and then with shocked understanding. In her dark groping Stella was trying to keep Miles alive by sustaining a situation in which he had figured—as if Miles' mind could not die so long as the possibilities that had worried him still existed. It was a distraught and tortured effort to stave off the realization that he was dead.

Resolutely Joel went to the phone and called a doctor.

"Don't, oh, don't call anybody!" Stella cried. "Come back here and put your arms around me."

"Is Doctor Bales in?"

"Joel," Stella cried. "I thought I could count on you. Miles liked you. He was jealous of you—Joel, come here."

Ah then—if he betrayed Miles she would be keeping him alive—for if he were really dead how could he be betrayed?

"—has just had a very severe shock. Can you come at once, and get hold of a nurse?"

"Joel!"

Now the door-bell and the telephone began to ring intermittently, and automobiles were stopping in front of the door.

"But you're not going," Stella begged him. "You're going to stay, aren't you?"

"No," he answered. "But I'll be back, if you need me."

Standing on the steps of the house which now hummed and palpitated with the life that flutters around death like protective leaves, he began to sob a little in his throat.

"Everything he touched he did something magical to," he thought. "He even brought that little gamin alive and made her a sort of masterpiece."

And then:

"What a hell of a hole he leaves in this damn wilderness—already!"

And then with a certain bitterness, "Oh, yes, I'll be back—I'll be back!"

MORE THAN JUST A HOUSE

◆

*"More than Just a House" (Saturday Evening Post, 24 June 1933) brought
an appreciative letter from John O'Hara:*

> *Miss Jean Gunther, of the More Than Just a House Gunthers, was one
> of those girls for the writing about of whom you hold the exclusive
> franchise. . . . It was really all told when she told Lew Lowrie, "Well,
> at least you've kissed one Gunther girl." . . . the second thing you've
> done so well: Lowrie, the climber; and I wonder why you do the climber
> so well. Is it the Irish in you? . . . And another thing you did was to
> take a rather fantastic little detail—the girl wearing bedroom slippers
> with Jodhpurs—and put it across by timing it just right.*

*Fitzgerald responded with an admission of his "two cylinder inferiority com-
plex" resulting from the conflict between his "black Irish" and "old American" roots.*

Fitzgerald's work continued to appear in the Post *until 1937, but "More
than Just a House" is the last important story he wrote for the magazine
with which his career had been intimately and complexly connected.*

◆

THIS WAS THE sort of thing Lew was used to—and he'd been around a
good deal already. You came into an entrance hall, sometimes narrow New
England Colonial, sometimes cautiously spacious. Once in the hall, the host
said: "Clare"—or Virginia, or Darling—"this is Mr. Lowrie." The woman
said, "How do you do, Mr. Lowrie," and Lew answered, "How do you
do, Mrs. Woman." Then the man suggested, "How about a little cocktail?"
And Lew lifted his brows apart and said, "Fine," in a tone that implied:
"What hospitality—consideration—attention!" Those delicious canapés.
"M'm'm! Madame, what are they—broiled feathers? Enough to spoil a
stronger appetite than mine."

But Lew was on his way up, with six new suits of clothes, and he was getting into the swing of the thing. His name was up for a downtown club and he had his eye on a very modern bachelor apartment full of wrought-iron swinging gates—as if he were a baby inclined to topple downstairs—when he saved the life of the Gunther girl and his tastes underwent revision.

This was back in 1925, before the Spanish-American——No, before whatever it is that has happened since then. The Gunther girls had got off the train on the wrong side and were walking along arm in arm, with Amanda in the path of an approaching donkey engine. Amanda was rather tall, golden and proud, and the donkey engine was very squat and dark and determined. Lew had no time to speculate upon their respective chances in the approaching encounter; he lunged at Jean, who was nearest him, and as the two sisters clung together, startled, he pulled Amanda out of the iron pathway by such a hair's breadth that a piston cylinder touched her coat.

And so Lew's taste was changed in regard to architecture and interior decoration. At the Gunther house they served tea, hot or iced, sugar buns, gingerbread and hot rolls at half-past four. When he first went there he was embarrassed by his heroic status—for about five minutes. Then he learned that during the Civil War the grandmother had been saved by her own grandmother from a burning house in Montgomery County, that father had once saved ten men at sea and been recommended for the Carnegie medal, that when Jean was little a man had saved her from the surf at Cape May —that, in fact, all the Gunthers had gone on saving and being saved for the last fifty years and that their real debt to Lew was that now there would be no gap left in the tradition.

This was on the very wide, vine-curtained veranda ["The first thing I'd do would be tear off that monstrosity," said a visiting architect] which almost completely bounded the big square box of the house, circa 1880. The sisters, three of them, appeared now and then during the time Lew drank tea and talked to the older people. He was only twenty-six himself and he wished Amanda would stay uncovered long enough for him to look at her, but only Bess, the sixteen-year-old sister, was really in sight; in front of the two others interposed a white-flannel screen of young men.

"It was the quickness," said Mr. Gunther, pacing the long straw rug, "that second of coordination. Suppose you'd tried to warn them—never. Your subconscious mind saw that they were joined together—saw that if you pulled one, you pulled them both. One second, one thought, one motion. I remember in 1904——"

"Won't Mr. Lowrie have another piece of gingerbread?" asked the grandmother.

"Father, why don't you show Mr. Lowrie the apostles' spoons?" Bess proposed.

"What?" Her father stopped pacing. "Is Mr. Lowrie interested in old spoons?"

Lew was thinking at the moment of Amanda twisting somewhere between the glare of the tennis courts and the shadow of the veranda, through all the warmth and graciousness of the afternoon.

"Spoons? Oh, I've got a spoon, thank you."

"Apostles' spoons," Bess explained. "Father has one of the best collections in America. When he likes anybody enough he shows them the spoons. I thought, since you saved Amanda's life——"

He saw little of Amanda that afternoon—talked to her for a moment by the steps while a young man standing near tossed up a tennis racket and caught it by the handle with an impatient bend of his knees at each catch. The sun shopped among the yellow strands of her hair, poured around the rosy tan of her cheeks and spun along the arms that she regarded abstractedly as she talked to him.

"It's hard to thank a person for saving your life, Mr. Lowrie," she said. "Maybe you shouldn't have. Maybe it wasn't worth saving."

"Oh, yes, it was," said Lew, in a spasm of embarrassment.

"Well, I'd like to think so." She turned to the young man. "Was it, Allen?"

"It's a good enough life," Allen admitted, "if you go in for wooly blondes."

She turned her slender smile full upon Lew for a moment, and then aimed it a little aside, like a pocket torch that might dazzle him. "I'll always feel that you own me, Mr. Lowrie; my life is forfeit to you. You'll always have the right to take me back and put me down in front of that engine again."

Her proud mouth was a little overgracious about being saved, though Lew didn't realize it; it seemed to Amanda that it might at least have been someone in her own crowd. The Gunthers were a haughty family—haughty beyond all logic, because Mr. Gunther had once been presented at the Court of St. James's and remained slightly convalescent ever since. Even Bess was haughty, and it was Bess, eventually, who led Lew down to his car.

"It's a nice place," she agreed. "We've been going to modernize it, but we took a vote and decided to have the swimming pool repaired instead."

Lew's eyes lifted over her—she was like Amanda, except for the slightness of her and the childish disfigurement of a small wire across her teeth—up to the house with its decorative balconies outside the windows, its fickle gables, its gold-lettered, Swiss-chalet mottoes, the bulging projections of its many bays. Uncritically he regarded it; it seemed to him one of the finest houses he had ever known.

"Of course, we're miles from town, but there's always plenty of people. Father and mother go South after the Christmas holidays when we go back to school."

It was more than just a house, Lew decided as he drove away. It was a place where a lot of different things could go on at once—a private life for the older people, a private romance for each girl. Promoting himself, he chose his own corner—a swinging seat behind one of the drifts of vines that cut the veranda into quarters. But this was in 1925, when the ten thousand a year that Lew had come to command did not permit an indiscriminate crossing of social frontiers. He was received by the Gunthers and held at arm's length by them, and then gradually liked for the qualities that began to show through his awkwardness. A good-looking man on his way up can put directly into action the things he learns; Lew was never again quite so impressed by the suburban houses whose children lived upon rolling platforms in the street.

It was September before he was invited to the Gunthers' on an intimate scale—and this largely because Amanda's mother insisted upon it.

"He saved your life. I want him asked to this one little party."

But Amanda had not forgiven him for saving her life.

"It's just a dance for friends," she complained. "Let him come to Jean's debut in October—everybody'll think he's a business acquaintance of father's. After all, you can be nice to somebody without falling into their arms."

Mrs. Gunther translated this correctly as: "You can be awful to somebody without their knowing it"—and brusquely overrode her: "You can't have advantages without responsibilities," she said shortly.

Life had been opening up so fast for Lew that he had a black dinner coat instead of a purple one. Asked for dinner, he came early; and thinking to give him his share of attention when it was most convenient, Amanda walked with him into the tangled, out-of-hand garden. She wanted to be bored, but his gentle vitality disarmed her, made her look at him closely for almost the first time.

"I hear everywhere that you're a young man with a future," she said.

Lew admitted it. He boasted a little; he did not tell her that he had analyzed the spell which the Gunther house exerted upon him—his father had been gardener on a similar Maryland estate when he was a boy of five. His mother had helped him to remember that when he told her about the Gunthers. And now this garden was shot bright with sunset, with Amanda one of its own flowers in her flowered dress; he told her, in a rush of emotion, how beautiful she was, and Amanda, excited by the prospect of impending hours with another man, let herself encourage him. Lew had never been so happy as in the moment before she stood up from the seat and put her hand on his arm lightly.

"I do like you," she said. "You're very handsome. Do you know that?"

The harvest dance took place in an L-shaped space formed by the clearing of three rooms. Thirty young people were there, and a dozen of their elders, but there was no crowding, for the big windows were opened to the veranda and the guests danced against the wide, illimitable night. A country orchestra alternated with the phonograph, there was mildly calculated cider punch, and an air of safety beside the open bookshelves of the library and the oil portraits of the living room, as though this were one of an endless series of dances that had taken place here in the past and would take place again.

"Thought you never would cut in," Bess said to Lew. "You'd be foolish not to. I'm the best dancer of us three, and I'm much the smartest one. Jean is the jazzy one, the most *chic*, but I think it's *passé* to be jazzy and play the traps and neck every second boy. Amanda is the beauty, of course. But I'm going to be the Cinderella, Mr. Lowrie. They'll be the two wicked sisters, and gradually you'll find I'm the most attractive and get all hot and bothered about me."

There was an interval of intervals before Lew could maneuver Amanda to his chosen segment of the porch. She was all radiant and shimmering. More than content to be with him, she tried to relax with the creak of the settee. Then instinct told her that something was about to happen.

Lew, remembering a remark of Jean's—"He asked me to marry him, and he hadn't even kissed me"—could yet think of no graceful way to assault Amanda; nevertheless he was determined to tell her tonight that he was in love with her.

"This'll seem sudden," he ventured, "but you might as well know. Please put me down on the list of those who'd like to have a chance."

She was not surprised, but being deep in herself at the moment, she was rather startled. Giving up the idea of relaxing, she sat upright.

"Mr. Lowrie—can I call you by your first name?—can I tell you something? No, I won't—yes, I will, because I like you now. I didn't like you at first. How's that for frankness?"

"Is that what you wanted to tell me?"

"No. Listen. You met Mr. Horton—the man from New York—the tall man with the rather old-looking hair?"

"Yes." Lew felt a pang of premonition in his stomach.

"I'm engaged to him. You're the first to know—except mother suspects. Whee! Now I told you because you saved my life, so you do sort of own me—I wouldn't be here to be engaged, except for you." Then she was honestly surprised at his expression. "Heavens, don't look like that!" She regarded him, pained. "Don't tell me you've been secretly in love with me all these months. Why didn't I know? And now it's too late."

Lew tried a laugh.

"I hardly know you," he confessed. "I haven't had time to fall in love with you."

"Maybe I work quick. Anyhow, if you did, you'll have to forget it and be my friend." Finding his hand, she squeezed it. "A big night for this little girl, Mr. Lew; the chance of a lifetime. I've been afraid for two days that his bureau drawer would stick or the hot water would give out and he'd leave for civilization."

They were silent for a moment; then he asked:

"You very much in love with him?"

"Of course I am. I mean, I don't know. You tell me. I've been in love with so many people; how can I answer that? Anyhow, I'll get away from this old barn."

"This house? You want to get away from here? Why, this is a lovely old house."

She was astonished now, and then suddenly explosive:

"This old tomb! That's the chief reason I'm marrying George Horton. Haven't I stood it for twenty years? Haven't I begged mother and father on my knees to move into town? This—shack—where everybody can hear what everybody else says three rooms off, and father won't allow a radio, and not even a phone till last summer. I'm afraid even to ask a girl down from school—probably she'd go crazy listening to the shutters on a stormy night."

"It's a darn nice old house," he said automatically.

"Nice and quaint," she agreed. "Glad you like it. People who don't have to live here generally do, but you ought to see us alone in it—if there's a family quarrel you have to stay with it for hours. It all comes down to father wanting to live fifty miles from anywhere, so we're condemned to rot. I'd rather live in a three-room apartment in town!" Shocked by her own vehemence, she broke off. "Anyhow," she insisted, "it may seem nice to you, but it's a nuisance to us."

A man pulled the vines apart and peered at them, claimed her and pulled her to her feet; when she was gone, Lew went over the railing with a handhold and walked into the garden; he walked far enough away so that the lights and music from the house were blurred into one entity like a stage effect, like an approaching port viewed from a deck at night.

"I only saw her four times," he said to himself. "Four times isn't much. Eeney-meeney-miney-moe—what could I expect in four times? I shouldn't feel anything at all." But he was engulfed by fear. What had he just begun to know that now he might never know? What had happened in these moments in the garden this afternoon, what was the excitement that had blacked out in the instant of its birth? The scarcely emergent young image of Amanda—he did not want to carry it with him forever. Gradually he realized a truth behind his grief: He had come too late for her; unknown to him, she had been slipping away through the years. With the odds against him, he had managed to found himself on solid rock, and then, looking around for the girl, discovered that she had just gone. "Sorry, just gone out; just left; just gone." Too late in every way—even for the house. Thinking over her tirade, Lew saw that he had come too late for the house; it was the house of a childhood from which the three girls were breaking away, the house of an older generation, sufficient unto them. To a younger generation it was pervaded with an aura of completion and fulfillment beyond their own power to add to. It was just old.

Nevertheless, he recalled the emptiness of many grander mansions built in more spectacular fashions—empty to him, at any rate, since he had first seen the Gunther place three months before. Something humanly valuable would vanish with the break-up of this family. The house itself, designed for reading long Victorian novels around an open fire of the evening, didn't even belong to an architectural period worthy of restoration.

Lew circled an outer drive and stood quiet in the shadow of a rosebush as a pair of figures strolled down from the house; by their voices he recognized Jean and Allen Parks.

"Me, I'm going to New York," Jean said, "whether they let me or not. . . . No, not now, you nut. I'm not in that mood."

"Then what mood are you in?"

"Not in any mood. I'm only envious of Amanda because she's hooked this M'sieur, and now she'll go to Long Island and live in a house instead of a mouse trap. Oh, Jake, this business of being simple and swell——"

They passed out of hearing. It was between dances, and Lew saw the colors of frocks and the quick white of shirt fronts in the window-panes as the guests flowed onto the porch. He looked up at the second floor as a light went on there—he had a conception of the second floor as walled with crowded photographs; there must be bags full of old materials, and trunks with costumes and dress-making forms, and old dolls' houses, and an overflow, everywhere along the vacant walls, of books for all generations—many childhoods side by side drifting into every corner.

Another couple came down the walk from the house, and feeling that inadvertently he had taken up too strategic a position, Lew moved away;

but not before he had identified the pair as Amanda and her man from New York.

"What would you think if I told you I had another proposal tonight?"

". . . be surprised at all."

"A very worthy young man. Saved my life. . . . Why weren't you there on that occasion, Bubbles? You'd have done it on a grand scale, I'm sure."

Standing square in front of the house, Lew looked at it more searchingly. He felt a kinship with it—not precisely that, for the house's usefulness was almost over and his was just beginning; rather, the sense of superior unity that the thoughtful young feel for the old, sense of the grandparent. More than only a house. He would like to be that much used up himself before being thrown out on the ash heap at the end. And then, because he wanted to do some courteous service to it while he could, if only to dance with the garrulous little sister, he pulled a brash pocket comb through his hair and went inside.

· II ·

THE MAN WITH the smiling scar approached Lew once more.

"This is probably," he announced, "the biggest party ever given in New York."

"I even heard you the first time you told me," agreed Lew cheerfully.

"But, on the other hand," qualified the man, "I thought the same thing at a party two years ago, in 1927. Probably they'll go on getting bigger and bigger. You play polo, don't you?"

"Only in the back yard," Lewis assured him. "I said I'd like to play. I'm a serious business man."

"Somebody told me you were the polo star." The man was somewhat disappointed. "I'm a writer myself. A humani—a humanitarian. I've been trying to help out a girl over there in that room where the champagne is. She's a lady. And yet, by golly, she's the only one in the room that can't take care of herself."

"Never try to take care of anybody," Lew advised him. "They hate you for it."

But although the apartment, or rather the string of apartments and pent-houses pressed into service for the affair, represented the best resources of the New York sky line, it was only limited metropolitan space at that, and moving among the swirls of dancers, thinned with dawn, Lew found himself finally in the chamber that the man had spoken of. For a moment he did not recognize the girl who had assumed the role of entertaining the glassy-eyed citizenry, chosen by natural selection to personify dissolution; then, as she issued a blanket invitation to a squad of Gaiety beauties to come south and recuperate on her Maryland estates, he recognized Jean Gunther.

She was the dark Gunther—dark and shining and driven. Lew, living in New York now, had seen none of the family since Amanda's marriage four years ago. Driving her home a quarter of an hour later, he extracted what news he could; and then left her in the dawn at the door of her apartment, mussed and awry, yet still proud, and tottering with absurd formality as she thanked him and said good night.

He called next afternoon and took her to tea in Central Park.

"I am," she informed him, "the child of the century. Other people claim to be the child of the century, but I'm actually the child of the century. And I'm having the time of my life at it."

Thinking back to another period—of young men on the tennis courts and hot buns in the afternoon, and of wistaria and ivy climbing along the ornate railings of a veranda—Lew became as moral as it was possible to be in that well-remembered year of 1929.

"What are you getting out of it? Why don't you invest in some reliable man—just a sort of background?"

"Men are good to invest money for you," she dodged neatly. "Last year one darling spun out my allowance so it lasted ten months instead of three."

"But how about marrying some candidate?"

"I haven't got any love," she said. "Actually, I know four—five—I know six millionaires I could maybe marry. This little girl from Carroll County. It's just too many. Now, if somebody that had everything came along——" She looked at Lew appraisingly. "You've improved, for example."

"I should say I have," admitted Lew, laughing. "I even go to first nights. But the most beautiful thing about me is I remember my old friends, and among them are the lovely Gunther girls of Carroll County."

"You're very nice," she said. "Were you terribly in love with Amanda?"

"I thought so, anyhow."

"I saw her last week. She's super-Park Avenue and very busy having Park Avenue babies. She considers me rather disreputable and tells her friends about our magnificent plantation in the old South."

"Do you ever go down to Maryland?"

"Do I though? I'm going Sunday night, and spend two months there saving enough money to come back on. When mother died"—she paused —"I suppose you knew mother died—I came into a little cash, and I've still got it, but it has to be stretched, see?"—she pulled her napkin cornerwise—"by tactful investing. I think the next step is a quiet summer on the farm."

Lew took her to the theater the next night, oddly excited by the encounter. The wild flush of the times lay upon her; he was conscious of her physical pulse going at some abnormal rate, but most of the young women he knew were being hectic, save the ones caught up tight in domesticity.

He had no criticism to make—behind that lay the fact that he would not have dared to criticize her. Having climbed from a nether rung of the ladder, he had perforce based his standards on what he could see from where he was at the moment. Far be it from him to tell Jean Gunther how to order her life.

Getting off the train in Baltimore three weeks later, he stepped into the peculiar heat that usually preceded an electric storm. He passed up the regular taxis and hired a limousine for the long ride out to Carroll County, and as he drove through rich foliage, moribund in midsummer, between the white fences that lined the rolling road, many years fell away and he was again the young man, starved for a home, who had first seen the Gunther house four years ago. Since then he had occupied a twelve-room apartment in New York, rented a summer mansion on Long Island, but his spirit, warped by loneliness and grown gypsy with change, turned back persistently to this house.

Inevitably it was smaller than he had expected, a small, big house, roomy rather than spacious. There was a rather intangible neglect about it—the color of the house had never been anything but a brown-green relict of the sun; Lew had never known the stable to lean otherwise than as the Tower of Pisa, nor the garden to grow any other way than plebeian and wild.

Jean was on the porch—not, as she had prophesied, in the role of gingham queen or rural equestrienne, but very Rue-de-la-Paix against the dun cushions of the swinging settee. There was the stout, colored butler whom Lew remembered and who pretended, with racial guile, to remember Lew delightedly. He took the bag to Amanda's old room, and Lew stared around it a little before he went downstairs. Jean and Bess were waiting over a cocktail on the porch.

It struck him that Bess had made a leaping change out of childhood into something that was not quite youth. About her beauty there was a detachment, almost an impatience, as though she had not asked for the gift and considered it rather a burden; to a young man, the gravity of her face might have seemed formidable.

"How is your father?" Lew asked.

"He won't be down tonight," Bess answered. "He's not well. He's over seventy, you know. People tire him. When we have guests, he has dinner upstairs."

"It would be better if he ate upstairs all the time," Jean remarked, pouring the cocktails.

"No, it wouldn't," Bess contradicted her. "The doctors said it wouldn't. There's no question about that."

Jean turned in a rush to Lew. "For over a year Bess has hardly left this house. We could——"

"What junk!" her sister said impatiently. "I ride every morning."

"——we could get a nurse who would do just as well."

Dinner was formal, with candles on the table and the two young women in evening dresses. Lew saw that much was missing—the feeling that the house was bursting with activity, with expanding life—all this had gone. It was difficult for the diminished clan to do much more than inhabit the house. There was not a moving up into vacated places; there was simply an anachronistic staying on between a vanishing past and an incalculable future.

Midway through dinner, Lew lifted his head at a pause in the conversation, but what he had confused with a mutter of thunder was a long groan from the floor above, followed by a measured speech, whose words were interrupted by the quick clatter of Bess' chair.

"You know what I ordered. Just so long as I am the head of——"

"It's father." Momentarily Jean looked at Lew as if she thought the situation was faintly humorous, but at his concerned face, she continued seriously, "You might as well know. It's senile dementia. Not dangerous. Sometimes he's absolutely himself. But it's hard on Bess."

Bess did not come down again; after dinner, Lew and Jean went into the garden, splattered with faint drops before the approaching rain. Through the vivid green twilight Lew followed her long dress, spotted with bright red roses—it was the first of that fashion he had ever seen; in the tense hush he had an illusion of intimacy with her, as though they shared the secrets of many years and, when she caught at his arm suddenly at a rumble of thunder, he drew her around slowly with his other arm and kissed her shaped, proud mouth.

"Well, at least you've kissed one Gunther girl," Jean said lightly. "How was it? And don't you think you're taking advantage of us, being unprotected out here in the country?"

He looked at her to see if she were joking, and with a swift laugh she seized his arm again. It was raining in earnest, and they fled toward the house—to find Bess on her knees in the library, setting light to an open fire.

"Father's all right," she assured them. "I don't like to give him the medicine till the last minute. He's worrying about some man that lent him twenty dollars in 1892." She lingered, conscious of being a third party, and yet impelled to play her mother's role and impart an initial solidarity before she retired. The storm broke, shrieking in white at the windows, and Bess took the opportunity to fly to the windows upstairs, calling down after a moment:

"The telephone's trying to ring. Do you think it's safe to answer it?"

"Perfectly," Jean called back, "or else they wouldn't ring." She came close to Lewis in the center of the room, away from the white, quivering windows.

"It's strange having you here right now. I don't mind saying I'm glad you're here. But if you weren't, I suppose we'd get along just as well."

"Shall I help Bess close the windows?" Lew asked.

Simultaneously, Bess called downstairs:

"Nobody seemed to be on the phone, and I don't like holding it."

A ripping crash of thunder shook the house and Jean moved into Lew's arm, breaking away as Bess came running down the stairs with a yelp of dismay.

"The lights are out up there," she said. "I never used to mind storms when I was little. Father used to make us sit on the porch sometimes, remember?"

There was a dazzle of light around all the windows of the first floor, reflecting itself back and forth in mirrors, so that every room was pervaded with a white glare; there followed a sound as of a million matches struck at once, so loud and terrible that the thunder rolling down seemed secondary; then a splintering noise separated itself out, and Bess' voice:

"That struck!"

Once again came the sickening lightning, and through a rolling pandemonium of sound they groped from window to window till Jean cried: "It's William's room! There's a tree on it!"

In a moment, Lew had flung wide the kitchen door and saw, in the next glare, what had happened: The great tree, in falling, had divided the lean-to from the house proper.

"Is William there?" he demanded.

"Probably. He should be."

Gathering up his courage, Lew dashed across the twenty feet of new marsh, and with a waffle iron smashed in the nearest window. Inundated with sheet rain and thunder, he yet realized that the storm had moved off from overhead, and his voice was strong as he called: "William! You all right?"

No answer.

"William!"

He paused and there came a quiet answer:

"Who dere?"

"You all right?"

"I wanna know who dere."

"The tree fell on you. Are you hurt?"

There was a sudden peal of laughter from the shack as William emerged mentally from dark and atavistic suspicions of his own. Again and again the pealing laughter rang out.

"Hurt? Not me hurt. Nothin' hurt me. I'm never better, as they say. Nothin' hurt me."

Irritated by his melting clothes, Lew said brusquely:

"Well, whether you know it or not, you're penned up in there. You've got to try and get out this window. That tree's too big to push off tonight."

Half an hour later, in his room, Lew shed the wet pulp of his clothing by the light of a single candle. Lying naked on the bed, he regretted that he was in poor condition, unnecessarily fatigued with the exertion of pulling a fat man out a window. Then, over the dull rumble of the thunder he heard the phone again in the hall, and Bess' voice, "I can't hear a word. You'll have to get a better connection," and for thirty seconds he dozed, to wake with a jerk at the sound of his door opening.

"Who's that?" he demanded, pulling the quilt up over himself.

The door opened slowly.

"Who's that?"

There was a chuckle; a last pulse of lightning showed him three tense, blue-veined fingers, and then a man's voice whispered: "I only wanted to know whether you were in for the night, dear. I worry—I worry."

The door closed cautiously, and Lew realized that old Gunther was on some nocturnal round of his own. Aroused, he slipped into his sole change of clothes, listening to Bess for the third time at the phone.

"——in the morning," she said. "Can't it wait? We've got to get a connection ourselves."

Downstairs he found Jean surprisingly spritely before the fire. She made a sign to him, and he went and stood above her, indifferent suddenly to her invitation to kiss her. Trying to decide how he felt, he brushed his hand lightly along her shoulder.

"Your father's wandering around. He came in my room. Don't you think you ought to——"

"Always does it," Jean said. "Makes the nightly call to see if we're in bed."

Lew stared at her sharply; a suspicion that had been taking place in his subconscious assumed tangible form. A bland, beautiful expression stared back at him; but his ears lifted suddenly up the stairs to Bess still struggling with the phone.

"All right. I'll try to take it that way. . . . P-ay-double ess-ee-dee— 'p-a-s-s-e-d.' All right; ay-double you-ay-wy. 'Passed away?' " Her voice, as she put the phrase together, shook with sudden panic. "What did you say—'Amanda Gunther passed away'?"

Jean looked at Lew with funny eyes.

"Why does Bess try to take that message now? Why not——"

"Shut up!" he ordered. "This is something serious."

"I don't see——"

Alarmed by the silence that seeped down the stairs, Lew ran up and found Bess sitting beside the telephone table holding the receiver in her lap, just breathing and staring, breathing and staring. He took the receiver and got the message:

"Amanda passed away quietly, giving life to a little boy."

Lew tried to raise Bess from the chair, but she sank back, full of dry sobbing.

"Don't tell father tonight."

How did it matter if this was added to that old store of confused memories? It mattered to Bess, though.

"Go away," she whispered. "Go tell Jean."

Some premonition had reached Jean, and she was at the foot of the stairs while he descended.

"What's the matter?"

He guided her gently back into the library.

"Amanda is dead," he said, still holding her.

She gathered up her forces and began to wail, but he put his hand over her mouth.

"You've been drinking!" he said. "You've got to pull yourself together. You can't put anything more on your sister."

Jean pulled herself together visibly—first her proud mouth and then her whole body—but what might have seemed heroic under other conditions seemed to Lew only reptilian, a fine animal effort—all he had begun to feel about her went out in a few ticks of the clock.

In two hours the house was quiet under the simple ministrations of a retired cook whom Bess had sent for; Jean was put to sleep with a sedative by a physician from Ellicott City. It was only when Lew was in bed at last that he thought really of Amanda, and broke suddenly, and only for a moment. She was gone out of the world, his second—no, his third love— killed in single combat. He thought rather of the dripping garden outside, and nature so suddenly innocent in the clearing night. If he had not been so tired he would have dressed and walked through the long-stemmed, clinging ferns, and looked once more impersonally at the house and its inhabitants—the broken old, the youth breaking and growing old with it, the other youth escaping into dissipation. Walking through broken dreams, he came in his imagination to where the falling tree had divided William's bedroom from the house, and paused there in the dark shadow, trying to piece together what he thought about the Gunthers.

"It's degenerate business," he decided—"all this hanging on to the past. I've been wrong. Some of us are going ahead, and these people and the roof over them are just push-overs for time. I'll be glad to leave it for good and get back to something fresh and new and clean in Wall Street tomorrow."

Only once was he wakened in the night, when he heard the old man quavering querulously about the twenty dollars that he had borrowed in '92. He heard Bess' voice soothing him, and then, just before he went to sleep, the voice of the old Negress blotting out both voices.

· III ·

LEW'S BUSINESS took him frequently to Baltimore, but with the years it seemed to change back into the Baltimore that he had known before he met the Gunthers. He thought of them often, but after the night of Amanda's death he never went there. By 1933, the role that the family had played in his life seemed so remote—except for the unforgettable fact that they had formed his ideas about how life was lived—that he could drive along the Frederick Road to where it dips into Carroll County before a feeling of recognition crept over him. Impelled by a formless motive, he stopped his car.

It was deep summer; a rabbit crossed the road ahead of him and a squirrel did acrobatics on an arched branch. The Gunther house was up the next crossroad and five minutes away—in half an hour he could satisfy his curiosity about the family; yet he hesitated. With painful consequences, he had once tried to repeat the past, and now, in normal times, he would have driven on with a feeling of leaving the past well behind him; but he had come to realize recently that life was not always a progress, nor a search for new horizons, nor a going away. The Gunthers were part of him; he would not be able to bring to new friends the exact things that he had brought to the Gunthers. If the memory of them became extinct, then something in himself became extinct also.

The squirrel's flight on the branch, the wind nudging at the leaves, the

cock splitting distant air, the creep of sunlight transpiring through the immobility, lulled him into an adolescent trance, and he sprawled back against
the leather for a moment without problems. He loafed for ten minutes before
the "k-dup, k-dup, k-dup" of a walking horse came around the next bend
of the road. The horse bore a girl in Jodhpur breeches, and bending forward,
Lew recognized Bess Gunther.

He scrambled from the car. The horse shied as Bess recognized Lew and
pulled up. "Why, Mr. Lowrie! . . . Hey! Hoo-oo there, girl! . . . Where
did you arrive from? Did you break down?"

It was a lovely face, and a sad face, but it seemed to Lew that some new
quality made it younger—as if she had finally abandoned the cosmic sense
of responsibility which had made her seem older than her age four years
ago.

"I was thinking about you all," he said. "Thinking of paying you a visit."
Detecting a doubtful shadow in her face, he jumped to a conclusion and
laughed. "I don't mean a visit; I mean a call. I'm solvent—sometimes you
have to add that these days."

She laughed too: "I was only thinking the house was full and where would
we put you."

"I'm bound for Baltimore anyhow. Why not get off your rocking horse
and sit in my car a minute."

She tied the mare to a tree and got in beside him.

He had not realized that flashing fairness could last so far into the
twenties—only when she didn't smile, he saw from three small thoughtful
lines that she was always a grave girl—he had a quick recollection of Amanda
on an August afternoon, and looking at Bess, he recognized all that he
remembered of Amanda.

"How's your father?"

"Father died last year. He was bedridden a year before he died." Her
voice was in the singsong of something often repeated. "It was just as well."

"I'm sorry. How about Jean? Where is she?"

"Jean married a Chinaman—I mean she married a man who lives in China.
I've never seen him."

"Do you live alone, then?"

"No, there's my aunt." She hesitated. "Anyhow, I'm getting married next
week."

Inexplicably, he had the old sense of loss in his diaphragm.

"Congratulations! Who's the unfortunate——"

"From Philadelphia. The whole party went over to the races this afternoon. I wanted to have a last ride with Juniper."

"Will you live in Philadelphia?"

"Not sure. We're thinking of building another house on the place, tear down the old one. Of course, we might remodel it."

"Would that be worth doing?"

"Why not?" she said hastily. "We could use some of it, the architects think."

"You're fond of it, aren't you?"

Bess considered.

"I wouldn't say it was just my idea of modernity. But I'm a sort of a home girl." She accentuated the words ironically. "I never went over very big in Baltimore, you know—the family failure. I never had the sort of thing Amanda and Jean had."

"Maybe you didn't want it."

"I thought I did when I was young."

The mare neighed peremptorily and Bess backed out of the car.

"So that's the story, Lew Lowrie, of the last Gunther girl. You always did have a sort of yen for us, didn't you?"

"Didn't I! If I could possibly stay in Baltimore, I'd insist on coming to your wedding."

At the lost expression on her face, he wondered to whom she was handing herself, a very precious self. He knew more about people now, and he felt the steel beneath the softness in her, the girders showing through the gentle curves of cheek and chin. She was an exquisite person, and he hoped that her husband would be a good man.

When she had ridden off into a green lane, he drove tentatively toward Baltimore. This was the end of a human experience and it released old images that regrouped themselves about him—if he had married one of the sisters; supposing——The past, slipping away under the wheels of his car, crunched awake his acuteness.

"Perhaps I was always an intruder in that family. . . . But why on earth was that girl riding in bedroom slippers?"

At the crossroads store he stopped to get cigarettes. A young clerk searched the case with country slowness.

"Big wedding up at the Gunther place," Lew remarked.

"Hah? Miss Bess getting married?"

"Next week. The wedding party's there now."

"Well, I'll be dog! Wonder what they're going to sleep on, since Mark H. Bourne took the furniture away?"

"What's that? What?"

"Month ago Mark H. Bourne took all the furniture and everything else while Miss Bess was out riding—they mortgaged on it just before Gunther died. They say around here she ain't got a stitch except them riding clothes. Mark H. Bourne was good and sore. His claim was they sold off all the best pieces of furniture without his knowing it. . . . Now, that's ten cents I owe you."

"What do she and her aunt live on?"

"Never heard about an aunt—I only been here a year. She works the truck garden herself; all she buys from us is sugar, salt and coffee."

Anything was possible these times, yet Lew wondered what incredibly fantastic pride had inspired her to tell that lie.

He turned his car around and drove back to the Gunther place. It was a desperately forlorn house he came to, and a jungled garden; one side of the veranda had slipped from the brick pillars and sloped to the ground; a shingle job, begun and abandoned, rotted paintless on the roof, a broken pane gaped from the library window.

Lew went in without knocking. A voice challenged him from the dining room and he walked toward it, his feet loud on the rugless floor, through rooms empty of stick and book, empty of all save casual dust. Bess Gunther, wearing the cheapest of house dresses, rose from the packing box on which she sat, with fright in her eyes; a tin spoon rattled on the box she was using as a table.

"Have you been kidding me?" he demanded. "Are you actually living like this?"

"It's you." She smiled in relief; then, with visible effort, she spurred herself into amenities:

"Take a box, Mr. Lowrie. Have a canned-goods box—they're superior; the grain is better. And welcome to the open spaces. Have a cigar, a glass of champagne, have some rabbit stew and meet my fiancé."

"Stop that."

"All right," she agreed.

"Why didn't you go and live with some relatives?"

"Haven't got any relatives. Jean's in China."

"What are you doing? What do you expect to happen?"

"I was waiting for you, I guess."

"What do you mean?"

"You always seemed to turn up. I thought if you turned up, I'd make a play for you. But when it came to the point, I thought I'd better lie. I seem to lack the S.A. my sisters had."

Lew pulled her up from the box and held her with his fingers by her waist.

"Not to me."

In the hour since Lew had met her on the road the vitality seemed to have gone out of her; she looked up at him very tired.

"So you liked the Gunthers," she whispered. "You liked us all."

Lew tried to think, but his heart beat so quick that he could only sit her back on the box and pace along the empty walls.

"We'll get married," he said. "I don't know whether I love you—I don't even know you—I know the notion of your being in want or trouble makes me physically sick." Suddenly he went down on both knees in front of her so that she would not seem so unbearably small and helpless. "Miss Bess Gunther, so it was you I was meant to love all the while."

"Don't be so anxious about it," she laughed. "I'm not used to being loved. I wouldn't know what to do; I never got the trick of it." She looked down at him, shy and fatigued. "So here we are. I told you years ago that I had the makings of Cinderella."

He took her hand; she drew it back instinctively and then replaced it in his. "Beg your pardon. Not even used to being touched. But I'm not afraid of you, if you stay quiet and don't move suddenly."

It was the same old story of reserve Lew could not fathom, motives reaching back into a past he did not share. With the three girls, facts seemed to reveal themselves precipitately, pushing up through the gay surface; they were always unsuspected things, currents and predilections alien to a man who had been able to shoot in a straight line always.

"I was the conservative sister," Bess said. "I wasn't any less pleasure loving but with three girls, somebody has to play the boy, and gradually that got to be my part. . . . Yes, touch me like that. Touch my cheek. I want to be touched; I want to be held. And I'm glad it's you; but you've got to go slow; you've got to be careful. I'm afraid I'm the kind of person that's forever. I'll live with you and die for you, but I never knew what halfway meant. . . . Yes, that's the wrist. Do you like it? I've had a lot of fun looking at myself in the last month, because there's one long mirror upstairs that was too big to take out."

Lew stood up. "All right, we'll start like that. I'll be so healthy that I'll make you all healthy again."

"Yes, like that," she agreed.

"Suppose we begin by setting fire to this house."

"Oh, no!" She took him seriously. "In the first place, it's insured. In the second place——"

"All right, we'll just get out. We'll get married in Baltimore, or Ellicott City if you'd rather."

"How about Juniper? I can't go off and leave her."

"We'll leave her with the young man at the store."

"The house isn't mine. It's all mortgaged away, but they let me live here—I guess it was remorse after they took even our old music, and our old scrapbooks. They didn't have a chance of getting a tenant, anyhow."

Minute by minute, Lew found out more about her, and liked what he found, but he saw that the love in her was all incrusted with the sacrificial years, and that he would have to be gardener to it for a while. The task seemed attractive.

"You lovely," he told her. "You lovely! We'll survive, you and I because you're so nice and I'm so convinced about it."

"And about Juniper—will she survive if we go away like this?"

"Juniper too."

She frowned and then smiled—and this time really smiled—and said: "Seems to me, you're falling in love."

"Speak for yourself. My opinion is that this is going to be the best thing ever happened."

"I'm going to help. I insist on——"

They went out together—Bess changed into her riding habit, but there wasn't another article that she wanted to bring with her. Backing through the clogging weeds of the garden, Lew looked at the house over his shoulder. "Next week or so we'll decide what to do about that."

It was a bright sunset—the creep of rosy light that played across the blue fenders of the car and across their crazily happy faces moved across the house too—across the paralyzed door of the ice house, the rusting tin gutters, the loose-swinging shutter, the cracked cement of the front walk, the burned place of last year's rubbish back of the tennis court. Whatever its further history, the whole human effort of collaboration was done now. The purpose of the house was achieved—finished and folded—it was an effort toward some commonweal, an effort difficult to estimate, so closely does it press against us still.

AFTERNOON OF·AN AUTHOR

◆

"Afternoon of an Author" (Esquire, August 1936) has been classified as a story and as an essay. It is included here to demonstrate the change in the form and material of Fitzgerald's work after the disappointing reception of Tender Is the Night. His best nonfiction appeared in Esquire—notably the 1936 "Crack-Up" essays, which "Afternoon of an Author" extends.

◆

WHEN HE WOKE UP he felt better than he had for many weeks, a fact that became plain to him negatively—he did not feel ill. He leaned for a moment against the door frame between his bedroom and bath till he could be sure he was not dizzy. Not a bit, not even when he stooped for a slipper under the bed.

It was a bright April morning, he had no idea what time because his clock was long unwound but as he went back through the apartment to the kitchen he saw that his daughter had breakfasted and departed and that the mail was in, so it was after nine.

"I think I'll go out today," he said to the maid.

"Do you good—it's a lovely day." She was from New Orleans, with the features and coloring of an Arab.

"I want two eggs like yesterday and toast, orange juice and tea."

He lingered for a moment in his daughter's end of the apartment and read his mail. It was an annoying mail with nothing cheerful in it—mostly bills and advertisements with the diurnal Oklahoma school boy and his gaping autograph album. Sam Goldwyn might do a ballet picture with Spessiwitza and might not—it would all have to wait till Mr. Goldwyn got back from Europe when he might have half a dozen new ideas. Paramount wanted a release on a poem that had appeared in one of the author's books, as they didn't know whether it was an original or quoted. Maybe they were going to get a title from it. Anyhow he had no more equity in that property—he had sold the silent rights many years ago and the sound rights last year.

"Never any luck with movies," he said to himself. "Stick to your last, boy."

He looked out the window during breakfast at the students changing classes on the college campus across the way.

"Twenty years ago I was changing classes," he said to the maid. She laughed her débutante's laugh.

"I'll need a check," she said, "if you're going out."

"Oh, I'm not going out yet. I've got two or three hours' work. I meant late this afternoon."

"Going for a drive?"

"I wouldn't drive that old junk—I'd sell it for fifty dollars. I'm going on the top of a bus."

After breakfast he lay down for fifteen minutes. Then he went into the study and began to work.

The problem was a magazine story that had become so thin in the middle that it was about to blow away. The plot was like climbing endless stairs, he had no element of surprise in reserve, and the characters who started so bravely day-before-yesterday couldn't have qualified for a newspaper serial.

"Yes, I certainly need to get out," he thought. "I'd like to drive down the Shenandoah Valley, or go to Norfolk on the boat."

But both of these ideas were impractical—they took time and energy and he had not much of either—what there was must be conserved for work. He went through the manuscript underlining good phrases in red crayon and after tucking these into a file slowly tore up the rest of the story and dropped it in the waste-basket. Then he walked the room and smoked, occasionally talking to himself.

"Wee-l, let's see—"

"Nau-ow, the next thing—would be—"

"Now let's see, now—"

After awhile he sat down thinking:

"I'm just stale—I shouldn't have touched a pencil for two days."

He looked through the heading "Story Ideas" in his notebook until the maid came to tell him his secretary was on the phone—part time secretary since he had been ill.

"Not a thing," he said. "I just tore up everything I'd written. It wasn't worth a damn. I'm going out this afternoon."

"Good for you. It's a fine day."

"Better come up tomorrow afternoon—there's a lot of mail and bills."

He shaved, and then as a precaution rested five minutes before he dressed. It was exciting to be going out—he hoped the elevator boys wouldn't say they were glad to see him up and he decided to go down the back elevator where they did not know him. He put on his best suit with the coat and trousers that didn't match. He had bought only two suits in six years but they were the very best suits—the coat alone of this one had cost a hundred and ten dollars. As he must have a destination—it wasn't good to go places without a destination—he put a tube of shampoo ointment in his pocket for his barber to use, and also a small phial of luminol.

"The perfect neurotic," he said, regarding himself in the mirror. "By-product of an idea, slag of a dream."

· I I ·

He went into the kitchen and said good-by to the maid as if he were going to Little America. Once in the war he had commandeered an engine on sheer bluff and had it driven from New York to Washington to keep from being A.W.O.L. Now he stood carefully on the street corner waiting for the light to change, while young people hurried past him with a fine disregard for traffic. On the bus corner under the trees it was green and cool and he thought of Stonewall Jackson's last words: "Let us cross over the river and rest under the shade of the trees." Those Civil War leaders seemed to have realized very suddenly how tired they were—Lee shriveling into another man, Grant with his desperate memoir-writing at the end.

The bus was all he expected—only one other man on the roof and the green branches ticking against each window through whole blocks. They would probably have to trim those branches and it seemed a pity. There was so much to look at—he tried to define the color of one line of houses and could only think of an old opera cloak of his mother's that was full of tints and yet was of no tint—a mere reflector of light. Somewhere church bells were playing "*Venite Adoremus*" and he wondered why, because Christmas was eight months off. He didn't like bells but it had been very moving when they played "*Maryland, My Maryland*" at the governor's funeral.

On the college football field men were working with rollers and a title occurred to him: "Turf-keeper" or else "The Grass Grows," something about a man working on turf for years and bringing up his son to go to college and play football there. Then the son dying in youth and the man's going to work in the cemetery and putting turf over his son instead of under his feet. It would be the kind of piece that is often placed in anthologies, but not his sort of thing—it was sheer swollen antithesis, as formalized as a popular magazine story and easier to write. Many people, however, would consider it excellent because it was melancholy, had digging in it and was simple to understand.

The bus went past a pale Athenian railroad station brought to life by the blue shirted redcaps out in front. The street narrowed as the business section began and there were suddenly brightly dressed girls, all very beautiful— he thought he had never seen such beautiful girls. There were men too but they all looked rather silly, like himself in the mirror, and there were old undecorative women, and presently, too, there were plain and unpleasant faces among the girls; but in general they were lovely, dressed in real colors all the way from six to thirty, no plans or struggles in their faces, only a state of sweet suspension, provocative and serene. He loved life terribly for a minute, not wanting to give it up at all. He thought perhaps he had made a mistake in coming out so soon.

He got off the bus, holding carefully to all the railings and walked a block to the hotel barbershop. He passed a sporting goods store and looked in the window unmoved except by a first baseman's glove which was already dark in the pocket. Next to that was a haberdasher's and here he stood for quite a while looking at the deep shade of shirts and the ones of checker and plaid. Ten years ago on the summer Riviera the author and some others had bought dark blue workmen's shirts, and probably that had started that style. The checkered shirts were nice looking, bright as uniforms and he wished he were twenty and going to a beach club all dolled up like a Turner sunset or Guido Reni's dawn.

The barbershop was large, shining and scented—it had been several months since the author had come downtown on such a mission and he found that his familiar barber was laid up with arthritis; however, he explained to another man how to use the ointment, refused a newspaper and sat, rather happy and sensually content at the strong fingers on his scalp, while a pleasant mingled memory of all the barbershops he had ever known flowed through his mind.

Once he had written a story about a barber. Back in 1929 the proprietor of his favorite shop in the city where he was then living had made a fortune of $300,000 on tips from a local industrialist and was about to retire. The author had no stake in the market, in fact, was about to sail for Europe for a few years with such accumulation as he had, and that autumn hearing how the barber had lost all his fortune he was prompted to write a story, thoroughly disguised in every way yet hinging on the fact of a barber rising in the world and then tumbling; he heard, nevertheless, that the story had been identified in the city and caused some hard feelings.

The shampoo ended. When he came out into the hall an orchestra had started to play in the cocktail room across the way and he stood for a moment in the door listening. So long since he had danced, perhaps two evenings in five years, yet a review of his last book had mentioned him as being fond of night clubs; the same review had also spoken of him as being indefatigable. Something in the sound of the word in his mind broke him momentarily and feeling tears of weakness behind his eyes he turned away. It was like in the beginning fifteen years ago when they said he had "fatal facility," and he labored like a slave over every sentence so as not to be like that.

"I'm getting bitter again," he said to himself. "That's no good, no good—I've got to go home."

The bus was a long time coming but he didn't like taxis and he still hoped that something would occur to him on that upper-deck passing through the green leaves of the boulevard. When it came finally he had some trouble climbing the steps but it was worth it for the first thing he saw was a pair of high school kids, a boy and a girl, sitting without any self-consciousness on the high pedestal of the Lafayette statue, their attention fast upon each other. Their isolation moved him and he knew he would get something out of it professionally, if only in contrast to the growing seclusion of his life and the increasing necessity of picking over an already well-picked past. He needed reforestation and he was well aware of it, and he hoped the soil would stand one more growth. It had never been the very best soil for he had had an early weakness for showing off instead of listening and observing.

Here was the apartment house—he glanced up at his own windows on the top floor before he went in.

"The residence of the successful writer," he said to himself. "I wonder what marvelous books he's tearing off up there. It must be great to have a gift like that—just sit down with pencil and paper. Work when you want —go where you please."

His child wasn't home yet but the maid came out of the kitchen and said:
"Did you have a nice time?"

"Perfect," he said. "I went roller skating and bowled and played around with Man Mountain Dean and finished up in a Turkish Bath. Any telegrams?"

"Not a thing."

"Bring me a glass of milk, will you?"

He went through the dining room and turned into his study, struck blind for a moment with the glow of his two thousand books in the late sunshine. He was quite tired—he would lie down for ten minutes and then see if he could get started on an idea in the two hours before dinner.

FINANCING FINNEGAN

♦

"Financing Finnegan" (Esquire, January 1938) was written in Hollywood. After Fitzgerald went on the MGM payroll in the summer of 1937, his studio chores did not allow him time or energy for extended independent writing projects, and this was the only story he published in 1938. He continued writing for Esquire to keep his name before the public and because he did not enjoy screenwriting. "Financing Finnegan" is one of Fitzgerald's self-warning stories, this time combined with an inside joke. The agent and editor in the story who "had entered into a silent conspiracy to cheer each other up about Finnegan" are clearly Harold Ober and Maxwell Perkins.

♦

FINNEGAN AND I have the same literary agent to sell our writings for us—but though I'd often been in Mr. Cannon's office just before and just after Finnegan's visits, I had never met him. Likewise we had the same publisher and often when I arrived there Finnegan had just departed. I gathered from a thoughtful sighing way in which they spoke of him—

"Ah—Finnegan—"

"Oh yes, Finnegan was here."

—that the distinguished author's visit had been not uneventful. Certain remarks implied that he had taken something with him when he went—manuscripts, I supposed, one of those great successful novels of his. He had taken "it" off for a final revision, a last draft, of which he was rumored to make ten in order to achieve that facile flow, that ready wit, which distinguished his work. I discovered only gradually that most of Finnegan's visits had to do with money.

"I'm sorry you're leaving," Mr. Cannon would tell me, "Finnegan will be here tomorrow." Then after a thoughtful pause, "I'll probably have to spend some time with him."

I don't know what note in his voice reminded me of a talk with a nervous bank president when Dillinger was reported in the vicinity. His eyes looked out into the distance and he spoke as to himself:

"Of course he may be bringing a manuscript. He has a novel he's working on, you know. And a play too."

He spoke as though he were talking about some interesting but remote events of the cinquecento; but his eyes became more hopeful as he added: "Or maybe a short story."

"He's very versatile, isn't he?" I said.

"Oh yes," Mr. Cannon perked up. "He can do anything—anything when he puts his mind to it. There's never been such a talent."

"I haven't seen much of his work lately."

"Oh, but he's working hard. Some of the magazines have stories of his that they're holding."

"Holding for what?"

"Oh, for a more appropriate time—an upswing. They like to think they have something of Finnegan's."

His was indeed a name with ingots in it. His career had started brilliantly and if it had not kept up to its first exalted level, at least it started brilliantly all over again every few years. He was the perennial man of promise in American letters—what he could actually do with words was astounding, they glowed and coruscated—he wrote sentences, paragraphs, chapters that were masterpieces of fine weaving and spinning. It was only when I met some poor devil of a screen writer who had been trying to make a logical story out of one of his books that I realized he had his enemies.

"It's all beautiful when you read it," this man said disgustedly, "but when you write it down plain it's like a week in the nut-house."

From Mr. Cannon's office I went over to my publishers on Fifth Avenue and there too I learned in no time that Finnegan was expected tomorrow.

Indeed he had thrown such a long shadow before him that the luncheon where I expected to discuss my own work was largely devoted to Finnegan. Again I had the feeling that my host, Mr. George Jaggers, was talking not to me but to himself.

"Finnegan's a great writer," he said.

"Undoubtedly."

"And he's really quite all right, you know."

As I hadn't questioned the fact I inquired whether there was any doubt about it.

"Oh no," he said hurriedly. "It's just that he's had such a run of hard luck lately——"

I shook my head sympathetically. "I know. That diving into a half-empty pool was a tough break."

"Oh, it wasn't half-empty. It was full of water. Full to the brim. You ought to hear Finnegan on the subject—he makes a side-splitting story of it. It seems he was in a run-down condition and just diving from the side of the pool, you know—" Mr. Jaggers pointed his knife and fork at the table, "and he saw some young girls diving from the fifteen-foot board. He says he thought of his lost youth and went up to do the same and made a beautiful swan dive—but his shoulder broke while he was still in the air." He looked at me rather anxiously. "Haven't you heard of cases like that—a ball player throwing his arm out of joint?"

I couldn't think of any orthopedic parallels at the moment.

"And then," he continued dreamily, "Finnegan had to write on the ceiling."

"On the ceiling?"

"Practically. He didn't give up writing—he has plenty of guts, that fellow, though you may not believe it. He had some sort of arrangement built that was suspended from the ceiling and he lay on his back and wrote in the air."

I had to grant that it was a courageous arrangement.

"Did it affect his work?" I inquired. "Did you have to read his stories backward—like Chinese?"

"They were rather confused for a while," he admitted, "but he's all right now. I got several letters from him that sounded more like the old Finnegan—full of life and hope and plans for the future——"

The faraway look came into his face and I turned the discussion to affairs closer to my heart. Only when we were back in his office did the subject recur—and I blush as I write this because it includes confessing something I seldom do—reading another man's telegram. It happened because Mr. Jaggers was intercepted in the hall and when I went into his office and sat down it was stretched out open before me:

WITH FIFTY I COULD AT LEAST PAY TYPIST AND GET HAIRCUT AND PENCILS LIFE HAS BECOME IMPOSSIBLE AND I EXIST ON DREAM OF GOOD NEWS DESPERATELY FINNEGAN

I couldn't believe my eyes—fifty dollars, and I happened to know that Finnegan's price for short stories was somewhere around three thousand. George Jaggers found me still staring dazedly at the telegram. After he read it he stared at me with stricken eyes.

"I don't see how I can conscientiously do it," he said.

I started and glanced around to make sure I was in the prosperous publishing office in New York. Then I understood—I had misread the telegram. Finnegan was asking for fifty thousand as an advance—a demand that would have staggered any publisher no matter who the writer was.

"Only last week," said Mr. Jaggers disconsolately, "I sent him a hundred dollars. It puts my department in the red every season, so I don't dare tell my partners any more. I take it out of my own pocket—give up a suit and a pair of shoes."

"You mean Finnegan's broke?"

"Broke!" He looked at me and laughed soundlessly—in fact I didn't exactly like the way that he laughed. My brother had a nervous—but that is afield from this story. After a minute he pulled himself together. "You won't say anything about this, will you? The truth is Finnegan's been in a slump, he's had blow after blow in the past few years, but now he's snapping out of it and I know we'll get back every cent we've—" He tried to think of a word but "given him" slipped out. This time it was he who was eager to change the subject.

Don't let me give the impression that Finnegan's affairs absorbed me during a whole week in New York—it was inevitable, though, that being much in the offices of my agent and my publisher, I happened in on a lot. For instance, two days later, using the telephone in Mr. Cannon's office, I was accidentally switched in on a conversation he was having with George Jaggers. It was only partly eavesdropping, you see, because I could only hear one end of the conversation and that isn't as bad as hearing it all.

"But I got the impression he was in good health . . . he did say something about his heart a few months ago but I understood it got well . . . yes, and he talked about some operation he wanted to have—I think he said it was cancer. . . . Well, I felt like telling him I had a little operation up my sleeve too, that I'd have had by now if I could afford it. . . . No, I didn't say it. He seemed in such good spirits that it would have been a shame to bring him down. He's starting a story today, he read me some of it on the phone. . . .

". . . I did give him twenty-five because he didn't have a cent in his pocket . . . oh, yes—I'm sure he'll be all right now. He sounds as if he means business."

I understood it all now. The two men had entered into a silent conspiracy to cheer each other up about Finnegan. Their investment in him, in his future, had reached a sum so considerable that Finnegan belonged to them. They could not bear to hear a word against him—even from themselves.

· II ·

I SPOKE MY mind to Mr. Cannon. "If this Finnegan is a four-flusher you can't go on indefinitely giving him money. If he's through he's through and there's nothing to be done about it. It's absurd that you should put off an operation when Finnegan's out somewhere diving into half-empty swimming pools."

"It was full," said Mr. Cannon patiently—"full to the brim."

"Well, full or empty the man sounds like a nuisance to me."

"Look here," said Cannon, "I've got a talk to Hollywood due on the wire. Meanwhile you might glance over that." He threw a manuscript into my lap. "Maybe it'll help you understand. He brought it in yesterday."

It was a short story. I began it in a mood of disgust but before I'd read five minutes I was completely immersed in it, utterly charmed, utterly convinced and wishing to God I could write like that. When Cannon finished his phone call I kept him waiting while I finished it and when I did there were tears in these hard old professional eyes. Any magazine in the country would have run it first in any issue.

But then nobody had ever denied that Finnegan could write.

· I I I ·

MONTHS PASSED before I went again to New York, and then, so far as the offices of my agent and my publisher were concerned, I descended upon a quieter, more stable world. There was at last time to talk about my own conscientious if uninspired literary pursuits, to visit Mr. Cannon in the country and to kill summer evenings with George Jaggers where the vertical New York starlight falls like lingering lightning into restaurant gardens. Finnegan might have been at the North Pole—and as a matter of fact he was. He had quite a group with him, including three Bryn Mawr anthropologists, and it sounded as if he might collect a lot of material there. They were going to stay several months, and if the thing had somehow the ring of a promising little house party about it, that was probably due to my jealous, cynical disposition.

"We're all just delighted," said Cannon. "It's a God-send for him. He was fed up and he needed just this—this—"

"Ice and snow," I supplied.

"Yes, ice and snow. The last thing he said was characteristic of him. Whatever he writes is going to be pure white—it's going to have a blinding glare about it."

"I can imagine it will. But tell me—who's financing it? Last time I was here I gathered the man was insolvent."

"Oh, he was really very decent about that. He owed me some money and I believe he owed George Jaggers a little too—" He "believed," the old hypocrite. He knew damn well—"so before he left he made most of his life insurance over to us. That's in case he doesn't come back—those trips are dangerous of course."

"I should think so," I said—"especially with three anthropologists."

"So Jaggers and I are absolutely covered in case anything happens—it's as simple as that."

"Did the life-insurance company finance the trip?"

He fidgeted perceptibly.

"Oh, no. In fact when they learned the reason for the assignments they were a little upset. George Jaggers and I felt that when he had a specific plan like this with a specific book at the end of it, we were justified in backing him a little further."

"I don't see it," I said flatly.

"You don't?" The old harassed look came back into his eyes. "Well, I'll admit we hesitated. In principle I know it's wrong. I used to advance authors small sums from time to time, but lately I've made a rule against it—and kept it. It's only been waived once in the last two years and that was for a woman who was having a bad struggle—Margaret Trahill, do you know her? She was an old girl of Finnegan's, by the way."

"Remember I don't even know Finnegan."

"That's right. You must meet him when he comes back—if he does come back. You'd like him—he's utterly charming."

Again I departed from New York, to imaginative North Poles of my own, while the year rolled through summer and fall. When the first snap of November was in the air, I thought of the Finnegan expedition with a sort of shiver and any envy of the man departed. He was probably earning any loot, literary or anthropological, he might bring back. Then, when I hadn't been back in New York three days, I read in the paper that he and some other members of his party had walked off into a snowstorm when the food supply gave out, and the Arctic had claimed another sacrifice.

I was sorry for him, but practical enough to be glad that Cannon and Jaggers were well protected. Of course, with Finnegan scarcely cold—if such a simile is not too harrowing—they did not talk about it but I gathered that the insurance companies had waived *habeas corpus* or whatever it is in their lingo, and it seemed quite sure that they would collect.

His son, a fine looking young fellow, came into George Jaggers' office while I was there and from him I could guess at Finnegan's charm—a shy frankness together with an impression of a very quiet brave battle going on inside of him that he couldn't quite bring himself to talk about—but that showed as heat lightning in his work.

"The boy writes well too," said George after he had gone. "He's brought in some remarkable poems. He's not ready to step into his father's shoes, but there's a definite promise."

"Can I see one of his things?"

"Certainly—here's one he left just as he went out."

George took a paper from his desk, opened it and cleared his throat. Then he squinted and bent over a little in his chair.

"*Dear Mr. Jaggers,*" he began, "*I didn't like to ask you this in person—*" Jaggers stopped, his eyes reading ahead rapidly.

"How much does he want?" I inquired.

He sighed.

"He gave me the impression that this was some of his work," he said in a pained voice.

"But it is," I consoled him. "Of course he isn't quite ready to step into his father's shoes."

I was sorry afterwards to have said this, for after all Finnegan had paid his debts, and it was nice to be alive now that better times were back and books were no longer rated as unnecessary luxuries. Many authors I knew who had skimped along during the depression were now making long-deferred trips or paying off mortgages or turning out the more finished kind of work that can only be done with a certain leisure and security. I had just got a thousand dollars advance for a venture in Hollywood and was going to fly out with all the verve of the old days when there was chicken feed in every pot. Going in to say good-by to Cannon and collect the money, it was nice to find he too was profiting—wanted me to go along and see a motor boat he was buying.

But some last-minute stuff came up to delay him and I grew impatient and decided to skip it. Getting no response to a knock on the door of his sanctum, I opened it anyhow.

The inner office seemed in some confusion. Mr. Cannon was on several telephones at once and dictating something about an insurance company to a stenographer. One secretary was getting hurriedly into her hat and coat as upon an errand and another was counting bills from her purse.

"It'll be only a minute," said Cannon, "it's just a little office riot—you never saw us like this."

"Is it Finnegan's insurance?" I couldn't help asking. "Isn't it any good?"

"His insurance—oh, perfectly all right, perfectly. This is just a matter of trying to raise a few hundred in a hurry. The banks are closed and we're all contributing."

"I've got that money you just gave me," I said. "I don't need all of it to get to the coast." I peeled off a couple of hundred. "Will this be enough?"

"That'll be fine—it just saves us. Never mind, Miss Carlsen. Mrs. Mapes, you needn't go now."

"I think I'll be running along," I said.

"Just wait two minutes," he urged. "I've only got to take care of this wire. It's really splendid news. Bucks you up."

It was a cablegram from Oslo, Norway—before I began to read I was full of a premonition.

AM MIRACULOUSLY SAFE HERE BUT DETAINED BY AUTHORITIES PLEASE WIRE PASSAGE MONEY FOR FOUR PEOPLE AND TWO HUNDRED EXTRA I AM BRINGING BACK PLENTY GREETINGS FROM THE DEAD.

FINNEGAN

"Yes, that's splendid," I agreed. "He'll have a story to tell now."

"Won't he though," said Cannon. "Miss Carlsen, will you wire the parents of those girls—and you'd better inform Mr. Jaggers."

As we walked along the street a few minutes later, I saw that Mr. Cannon, as if stunned by the wonder of this news, had fallen into a brown study, and I did not disturb him, for after all I did not know Finnegan and could not whole-heartedly share his joy. His mood of silence continued until we arrived at the door of the motor boat show. Just under the sign he stopped and stared upward, as if aware for the first time where we were going.

"Oh, my," he said, stepping back. "There's no use going in here now. I thought we were going to get a drink."

We did. Mr. Cannon was still a little vague, a little under the spell of the vast surprise—he fumbled so long for the money to pay his round that I insisted it was on me.

I think he was in a daze during that whole time because, though he is a man of the most punctilious accuracy, the two hundred I handed him in his office has never shown to my credit in the statements he has sent me. I imagine, though, that some day I will surely get it because some day Finnegan will click again and I know that people will clamor to read what he writes. Recently I've taken it upon myself to investigate some of the stories about him and I've found that they're mostly as false as the half-empty pool. That pool was full to the brim.

So far there's only been a short story about the polar expedition, a love story. Perhaps it wasn't as big a subject as he expected. But the movies are interested in him—if they can get a good long look at him first and I have every reason to think that he will come through. He'd better.

THE LOST DECADE

◆

"The Lost Decade" (Esquire, December 1939) is the most remarkable of Fitzgerald's late elliptical sketches, which convey the effects of fully developed stories. It has been described as haunting, *a term easier to demonstrate than to explain. In eleven hundred words "The Lost Decade" develops a controlled, understated impression of a man trying to renew his responses to experience after a ten-year drunk.*

◆

ALL SORTS OF people came into the offices of the news-weekly and Orrison Brown had all sorts of relations with them. Outside of office hours he was "one of the editors"—during work time he was simply a curly-haired man who a year before had edited the Dartmouth *Jack-O-Lantern* and was now only too glad to take the undesirable assignments around the office, from straightening out illegible copy to playing call boy without the title.

He had seen this visitor go into the editor's office—a pale, tall man of forty with blond statuesque hair and a manner that was neither shy nor timid, nor otherworldly like a monk, but something of all three. The name on his card, Louis Trimble, evoked some vague memory, but having nothing to start on, Orrison did not puzzle over it—until a buzzer sounded on his desk, and previous experience warned him that Mr. Trimble was to be his first course at lunch.

"Mr. Trimble—Mr. Brown," said the Source of all luncheon money. "Orrison—Mr. Trimble's been away a long time. Or he *feels* it's a long time—almost twelve years. Some people would consider themselves lucky to've missed the last decade."

"That's so," said Orrison.

"I can't lunch today," continued his chief. "Take him to Voisin or 21 or anywhere he'd like. Mr. Trimble feels there're lots of things he hasn't seen."

Trimble demurred politely.

"Oh, I can get around."

"I know it, old boy. Nobody knew this place like you did once—and if Brown tries to explain the horseless carriage just send him back here to me. And you'll be back yourself by four, won't you?"

Orrison got his hat.

"You've been away ten years?" he asked while they went down in the elevator.

"They'd begun the Empire State Building," said Trimble. "What does that add up to?"

"About 1928. But as the chief said, you've been lucky to miss a lot." As a feeler he added, "Probably had more interesting things to look at."

"Can't say I have."

They reached the street and the way Trimble's face tightened at the roar of traffic made Orrison take one more guess.

"You've been out of civilization?"

"In a sense." The words were spoken in such a measured way that Orrison concluded this man wouldn't talk unless he wanted to—and simultaneously wondered if he could have possibly spent the thirties in a prison or an insane asylum.

"This is the famous 21," he said. "Do you think you'd rather eat somewhere else?"

Trimble paused, looking carefully at the brownstone house.

"I can remember when the name 21 got to be famous," he said, "about the same year as Moriarity's." Then he continued almost apologetically, "I thought we might walk up Fifth Avenue about five minutes and eat wherever we happened to be. Some place with young people to look at."

Orrison gave him a quick glance and once again thought of bars and gray walls and bars; he wondered if his duties included introducing Mr. Trimble to complaisant girls. But Mr. Trimble didn't look as if that was in his mind—the dominant expression was of absolute and deep-seated curiosity and Orrison attempted to connect the name with Admiral Byrd's hideout at the South Pole or flyers lost in Brazilian jungles. He was, or he had been, quite a fellow—that was obvious. But the only definite clue to his environment—and to Orrison the clue that led nowhere—was his countryman's obedience to the traffic lights and his predilection for walking on the side next to the shops and not the street. Once he stopped and gazed into a haberdasher's window.

"Crêpe ties," he said. "I haven't seen one since I left college."

"Where'd you go?"

"Massachusetts Tech."

"Great place."

"I'm going to take a look at it next week. Let's eat somewhere along here—" They were in the upper Fifties "—you choose."

There was a good restaurant with a little awning just around the corner. "What do you want to see most?" Orrison asked, as they sat down. Trimble considered.

"Well—the back of people's heads," he suggested. "Their necks—how their heads are joined to their bodies. I'd like to hear what those two little girls are saying to their father. Not exactly what they're saying but whether the words float or submerge, how their mouths shut when they've finished speaking. Just a matter of rhythm—Cole Porter came back to the States in 1928 because he felt that there were new rhythms around."

Orrison was sure he had his clue now, and with nice delicacy did not pursue it by a millimeter—even suppressing a sudden desire to say there was a fine concert in Carnegie Hall tonight.

"The weight of spoons," said Trimble, "so light. A little bowl with a stick attached. The cast in that waiter's eye. I knew him once but he wouldn't remember me."

But as they left the restaurant the same waiter looked at Trimble rather puzzled as if he almost knew him. When they were outside Orrison laughed: "After ten years people will forget."

"Oh, I had dinner there last May—" He broke off in an abrupt manner.

It was all kind of nutsy, Orrison decided—and changed himself suddenly into a guide.

"From here you get a good candid focus on Rockefeller Center," he pointed out with spirit "—and the Chrysler Building and the Armistead Building, the daddy of all the new ones."

"The Armistead Building," Trimble rubber-necked obediently. "Yes—I designed it."

Orrison shook his head cheerfully—he was used to going out with all kinds of people. But that stuff about having been in the restaurant last May . . .

He paused by the brass entablature in the cornerstone of the building. "Erected 1928," it said.

Trimble nodded.

"But I was taken drunk that year—every-which-way drunk. So I never saw it before now."

"Oh." Orrison hesitated. "Like to go in now?"

"I've been in it—lots of times. But I've never seen it. And now it isn't what I want to see. I wouldn't ever be able to see it now. I simply want to see how people walk and what their clothes and shoes and hats are made of. And their eyes and hands. Would you mind shaking hands with me?"

"Not at all, sir."

"Thanks. Thanks. That's very kind. I suppose it looks strange—but people will think we're saying good-by. I'm going to walk up the avenue for awhile, so we *will* say good-by. Tell your office I'll be in at four."

Orrison looked after him when he started out, half expecting him to turn into a bar. But there was nothing about him that suggested or ever had suggested drink.

"Jesus," he said to himself. "Drunk for ten years."

He felt suddenly of the texture of his own coat and then he reached out and pressed his thumb against the granite of the building by his side.

"BOIL SOME WATER—LOTS OF IT"

♦

" 'Boil Some Water—Lots of It' " (Esquire, *March 1940) was the third of the seventeen stories about Pat Hobby. These stories have been incorrectly classified as autobiographical and are therefore misread. Pat is an untalented, dishonest movie hack; and the Pat stories are properly read as satire or burlesque. Fitzgerald wrote this series (for $250 and $300 each) to pay his bills while he was working on* The Last Tycoon, *his unfinished novel about Hollywood.*

♦

PAT HOBBY SAT in his office in the writers' building and looked at his morning's work, just come back from the script department. He was on a "polish job," about the only kind he ever got nowadays. He was to repair a messy sequence in a hurry, but the word "hurry" neither frightened nor inspired him for Pat had been in Hollywood since he was thirty—now he was forty-nine. All the work he had done this morning (except a little changing around of lines so he could claim them as his own)—all he had actually invented was a single imperative sentence, spoken by a doctor.

"Boil some water—lots of it."

It was a good line. It had sprung into his mind full grown as soon as he had read the script. In the old silent days Pat would have used it as a spoken title and ended his dialogue worries for a space, but he needed some spoken words for other people in the scene. Nothing came.

"Boil some water," he repeated to himself. "Lots of it."

The word boil brought a quick glad thought of the commissary. A reverent thought too—for an old-timer like Pat, what people you sat with at lunch was more important in getting along than what you dictated in your office. This was no art, as he often said—this was an industry.

"This is no art," he remarked to Max Leam who was leisurely drinking at a corridor water cooler. "This is an industry."

Max had flung him this timely bone of three weeks at three-fifty.

"Say look, Pat! Have you got anything down on paper yet?"

"Say I've got some stuff already that'll make 'em—" He named a familiar biological function with the somewhat startling assurance that it would take place in the theater.

Max tried to gauge his sincerity.

"Want to read it to me now?" he asked.

"Not yet. But it's got the old guts if you know what I mean."

Max was full of doubts.

"Well, go to it. And if you run into any medical snags check with the doctor over at the First Aid Station. It's got to be right."

The spirit of Pasteur shone firmly in Pat's eyes.

"It will be."

He felt good walking across the lot with Max—so good that he decided to glue himself to the producer and sit down with him at the Big Table. But Max foiled his intention by cooing "See you later" and slipping into the barber shop.

Once Pat had been a familiar figure at the Big Table; often in his golden prime he had dined in the private canteens of executives. Being of the older Hollywood he understood their jokes, their vanities, their social system with its swift fluctuations. But there were too many new faces at the Big Table now—faces that looked at him with the universal Hollywood suspicion. And at the little tables where the young writers sat they seemed to take work so seriously. As for just sitting down anywhere, even with secretaries or extras—Pat would rather catch a sandwich at the corner.

Detouring to the Red Cross Station he asked for the doctor. A girl, a nurse, answered from a wall mirror where she was hastily drawing her lips, "He's out. What is it?"

"Oh. Then I'll come back."

She had finished, and now she turned—vivid and young and with a bright consoling smile.

"Miss Stacey will help you. I'm about to go to lunch."

He was aware of an old, old feeling—left over from the time when he had had wives—a feeling that to invite this little beauty to lunch might cause trouble. But he remembered quickly that he didn't have any wives now—they had both given up asking for alimony.

"I'm working on a medical," he said. "I need some help."

"A medical?"

"Writing it—idea about a doc. Listen—let me buy you lunch. I want to ask you some medical questions."

The nurse hesitated.

"I don't know. It's my first day out here."

"It's all right," he assured her, "studios are democratic; everybody is just 'Joe' or 'Mary'—from the big shots right down to the prop boys."

He proved it magnificently on their way to lunch by greeting a male star and getting his own name back in return. And in the commissary, where they were placed hard by the Big Table, his producer, Max Leam, looked up, did a little "takem" and winked.

The nurse—her name was Helen Earle—peered about eagerly.

"I don't see anybody," she said. "Except oh, there's Ronald Colman. I didn't know Ronald Colman looked like that."

Pat pointed suddenly to the floor.

"And there's Mickey Mouse!"

She jumped and Pat laughed at his joke—but Helen Earle was already staring starry-eyed at the costume extras who filled the hall with the colors of the First Empire. Pat was piqued to see her interest go out to these nonentities.

"The big shots are at this next table," he said solemnly, wistfully, "directors and all except the biggest executives. They could have Ronald Colman pressing pants. I usually sit over there but they don't want ladies. At lunch, that is, they don't want ladies."

"Oh," said Helen Earle, polite but unimpressed. "It must be wonderful to be a writer too. It's so very interesting."

"It has its points," he said . . . he had thought for years it was a dog's life.

"What is it you want to ask me about a doctor?"

Here was toil again. Something in Pat's mind snapped off when he thought of the story.

"Well, Max Leam—that man facing us—Max Leam and I have a script about a Doc. You know? Like a hospital picture?"

"I know." And she added after a moment, "That's the reason that I went in training."

"And we've got to have it *right* because a hundred million people would check on it. So this doctor in the script he tells them to boil some water. He says, 'Boil some water—lots of it.' And we were wondering what the people would do then."

"Why—they'd probably boil it," Helen said, and then, somewhat confused by the question, "What people?"

"Well, somebody's daughter and the man that lived there and an attorney and the man that was hurt."

Helen tried to digest this before answering.

"—and some other guy I'm going to cut out," he finished.

There was a pause. The waitress set down tuna fish sandwiches.

"Well, when a doctor gives orders they're orders," Helen decided.

"Hm." Pat's interest had wandered to an odd little scene at the Big Table while he inquired absently, "You married?"

"No."

"Neither am I."

Beside the Big Table stood an extra. A Russian Cossack with a fierce moustache. He stood resting his hand on the back of an empty chair between Director Paterson and Producer Leam.

"Is this taken?" he asked, with a thick Central European accent.

All along the Big Table faces stared suddenly at him. Until after the first look the supposition was that he must be some well-known actor. But he was not—he was dressed in one of the many-colored uniforms that dotted the room.

Someone at the table said: "That's taken." But the man drew out the chair and sat down.

"Got to eat somewhere," he remarked with a grin.

A shiver went over the near-by tables. Pat Hobby stared with his mouth ajar. It was as if someone had crayoned Donald Duck into the *Last Supper*.

"Look at that," he advised Helen. "What they'll do to him! Boy!"

The flabbergasted silence at the Big Table was broken by Ned Harman, the Production Manager.

"This table is reserved," he said.

The extra looked up from a menu.

"They told me sit anywhere."

He beckoned a waitress—who hesitated, looking for an answer in the faces of her superiors.

"Extras don't eat here," said Max Leam, still politely. "This is a—"

"I got to eat," said the Cossack doggedly. "I been standing around six hours while they shoot this stinking mess and now I got to eat."

The silence had extended—from Pat's angle all within range seemed to be poised in mid-air.

The extra shook his head wearily.

"I dunno who cooked it up—" he said—and Max Leam sat forward in his chair—"but it's the lousiest tripe I ever seen shot in Hollywood."

—At his table Pat was thinking why didn't they do something? Knock him down, drag him away. If they were yellow themselves they could call the studio police.

"Who is that?" Helen Earle was following his eyes innocently, "Somebody I ought to know?"

He was listening attentively to Max Leam's voice, raised in anger.

"Get up and get out of here, buddy, and get out quick!"

The extra frowned.

"Who's telling me?" he demanded.

"You'll see." Max appealed to the table at large, "Where's Cushman—where's the Personnel man?"

"You try to move me," said the extra, lifting the hilt of his scabbard above the level of the table, "and I'll hang this on your ear. I know my rights."

The dozen men at the table, representing a thousand dollars an hour in salaries, sat stunned. Far down by the door one of the studio police caught wind of what was happening and started to elbow through the crowded room. And Big Jack Wilson, another director, was on his feet in an instant coming around the table.

But they were too late—Pat Hobby could stand no more. He had jumped up, seizing a big heavy tray from the serving stand nearby. In two springs he reached the scene of action—lifting the tray he brought it down upon the extra's head with all the strength of his forty-nine years. The extra, who had been in the act of rising to meet Wilson's threatened assault, got the blow full on his face and temple and as he collapsed a dozen red streaks sprang into sight through the heavy grease paint. He crashed sideways between the chairs.

Pat stood over him panting—the tray in his hand.

"The dirty rat!" he cried. "Where does he think—"

The studio policeman pushed past; Wilson pushed past—two aghast men from another table rushed up to survey the situation.

"It was a gag!" one of them shouted. "That's Walter Herrick, the writer. It's his picture."

"My God!"

"He was kidding Max Leam. It was a gag I tell you!"

"Pull him out . . . Get a doctor . . . Look out, there!"

Now Helen Earle hurried over; Walter Herrick was dragged out into a cleared space on the floor and there were yells of "Who did it?—Who beaned him?"

Pat let the tray lapse to a chair, its sound unnoticed in the confusion.

He saw Helen Earle working swiftly at the man's head with a pile of clean napkins.

"Why did they have to do this to him?" someone shouted.

Pat caught Max Leam's eye but Max happened to look away at the moment and a sense of injustice came over Pat. He alone in this crisis, real or imaginary, had *acted*. He alone had played the man, while those stuffed shirts let themselves be insulted and abused. And now he would have to take the rap—because Walter Herrick was powerful and popular, a three thousand a week man who wrote hit shows in New York. How could anyone have guessed that it was a gag?

There was a doctor now. Pat saw him say something to the manageress and her shrill voice sent the waitresses scattering like leaves toward the kitchen.

"Boil some water! Lots of it!"

The words fell wild and unreal on Pat's burdened soul. But even though he now knew at first hand what came next, he did not think that he could go on from there.

LAST KISS

♦

"Last Kiss" is closely related to The Last Tycoon; *Pamela Knighton and Kathleen Moore were both based on Fitzgerald's companion, Sheilah Graham. The story was declined in 1940 by* Cosmopolitan: *". . . we cannot see our way clear to adding this one to our crowded story line-up." Fitzgerald changed the title to "Pink and Silver Frost" and may have submitted it to other magazines under the pseudonym John Darcy. He then withdrew the story and stripped it for* The Last Tycoon, *noting on the typescript: "Unpleasant as hell except the end. Break up."*

It was published posthumously as "Last Kiss" by Collier's *(16 April 1949), which awarded it a $1,000 bonus as the best story in that issue. But* Collier's *was sent an early version. The text published here for the first time is Fitzgerald's latest revision.*

♦

IT WAS A FINE pure feeling to be on top. One was very sure that everything was for the best, that the lights shone upon fair ladies and brave men, that pianos dripped the right notes and that the young lips singing them spoke for happy hearts. All these beautiful faces, for instance, must be absolutely happy.

And then in a twilit rhumba, a face passed Jim's table that was not quite happy. It had gone before Jim decided this, but it remained fixed on his retina for some seconds thereafter. It belonged to a girl almost as tall as he was, with opaque brown eyes and cheeks as delicate as a Chinese tea-cup.

"There you go," said his hostess, following his glance. She sighed. "It happens in a second and I've tried for years."

Jim wanted to answer:

—But you've had your day—three husbands. How about me? Thirty-five and still trying to match every woman with a lost childhood love, still finding in all girls the similarities and not the differences.

The next time the lights were dim he wandered through the tables toward the entrance hall. Here and there friends hailed him—more than the usual number of course, because his contract as a producer had been noticed in the *Hollywood Reporter* that morning, but Jim had made other steps up and he was used to that. It was a charity ball and by the bar ready to perform was the man who imitated wall paper and Bob Bordley with a sandwich board on his back which read:

AT TEN TONIGHT

IN THE HOLLYWOOD BOWL

SONJA HEINE

WILL SKATE ON

HOT SOUP

Nearby Jim saw the producer whom he was displacing tomorrow, having an unsuspecting drink with the agent who had contrived his ruin. Next to the agent was the girl whose face had seemed sad as she danced by in the rhumba.

"Oh, Jim," said the agent, "Pamela Knighton—your future star."

She turned to him with professional eagerness. What the agent's voice had said to her was: "Look alive! This *is* somebody."

"Pamela's joined my stable," said the agent. "I want her to change her name to Boots."

"I thought you said Toots," the girl laughed.

"Toots or Boots. It's the oo-oo sound. Cutie shoots Toots. Judge Hoots. No conviction possible. Pamela is English. Her real name is Sybil Higgins."

Jim felt the deposed producer looking at him with an infinite something in his eyes—not hatred, not jealousy but a profound and curious astonishment that asked "Why? Why? For God's sake, why?" More disturbed by this than by enmity, Jim surprised himself by asking the English girl to dance. As they faced each other on the floor he felt a rising exultation.

"Hollywood's a good place," he said, as if to forestall any criticism from her. "You'll like it. Most English girls do—they don't expect too much. I've had luck working with English girls."

"Are you a director?"

"I've been everything—from press agent on. I've just signed a producer's contract that begins tomorrow."

"I like it here," she said after a minute, "You can't help expecting things. But if they don't come I could always teach school again."

Jim leaned back and looked at her—the impression was of pink and silver frost. She was so far from a school marm, even a school marm in a Western, that he laughed. But again he saw that there was something sad and a little lost within the triangle formed by lips and eyes.

"Who are you with tonight?" he asked.

"Joe Becker," she answered naming the agent. "Myself and three other girls."

"Look—I have to go out for half an hour. To see a man—this is not phoney. Believe me. Will you come along for company and night air?"

She nodded.

On the way they passed his hostess who looked inscrutably at the girl and shook her head slightly at Jim. Out in the clear California night he liked his big new car for the first time, liked it better than driving himself. The streets through which they rolled were quiet at this hour and the limousine stole silently along the darkness. Miss Knighton waited for him to speak.

"What did you teach in school?" he asked.

"Sums. Two and two are five and all that."

"It's a long jump from that to Hollywood."

"It's a long story."

"It can't be very long—you're about eighteen."

"Twenty." Anxiously she asked: "Do you think that's too old?"

"Lord, no! It's a beautiful age. I know—I'm twenty-one myself and the arteries are only beginning to harden."

She looked at him gravely, estimating his age and keeping it to herself.

"I want to hear the long story," he said.

She sighed.

"Well, a lot of old men fell in love with me. Old, old men—I was an old man's darling."

"You mean old gaffers of twenty-two?"

"They were between sixty and seventy. This is all true. So I became a gold-digger and dug enough money out of them to come to New York. I walked into Twenty-one the first day and Joe Becker saw me."

"Then you've never been in pictures?" he asked.

"Oh yes—I had a test this morning."

Jim smiled.

"And you don't feel bad taking money from all those old men?" he inquired.

"Not really," she said, matter-of-fact. "They enjoyed giving it to me. Anyhow it wasn't really money. When they wanted to give me presents I'd send them to a jeweler I knew and afterwards I'd take the present back to the jeweler and get four fifths of the cash."

"Why, you little chiseller!"

"Yes," she admitted placidly, "Somebody told me how. I'm out for all I can get."

"Didn't they mind—the old men I mean—when you didn't wear their presents?"

"Oh, I'd wear them—once. Old men don't see very well, or remember. But that's why I haven't got any jewelry." She broke off. "I understand you can rent jewelry here."

Jim looked at her again and then laughed.

"I wouldn't bother about it. California's full of old men."

They had twisted into a residential district. As they turned a corner Jim picked up the speaking tube.

"Stop here." He turned to Pamela, "I have some dirty work to do."

He looked at his watch, got out and went up the street to a building with the names of several doctors on a sign. He went past the sign walking slowly, and presently a man came out of the building and followed him. In the darkness between two lamps Jim went close, handed him an envelope and spoke concisely. The man walked off in the opposite direction and Jim returned to the car.

"I'm having all the old men bumped off," he explained. "There're some things worse than death."

"Oh, I'm not free now," she assured him. "I'm engaged."

"Oh." After a minute he asked, "To an Englishman?"

"Well—naturally. Did you think—" She stopped herself but too late.

"Are we that uninteresting?" he asked.

"Oh, no." Her casual tone made it worse. And when she smiled, at the moment when an arc light shone in and dressed her beauty up to a white radiance, it was more annoying still.

"Now you tell *me* something," she said. "Tell me the mystery."

"Just money," he answered almost absently. "That little Greek doctor keeps telling a certain lady that her appendix is bad—we need her in a picture. So we bought him off. It's the last time I'll ever do anyone else's dirty work."

She frowned.

"Does she really need her appendix out?"

He shrugged.

"Probably not. At least that rat wouldn't know. He's her brother-in-law and he wants the money."

After a long time Pamela spoke judicially.

"An Englishman wouldn't do that."

"Some would," he said shortly, "—and some Americans wouldn't."

"An English gentleman wouldn't."

"Aren't you getting off on the wrong foot," he suggested, "if you're going to work here."

"Oh, I like Americans all right—the civilized ones."

From her look Jim took this to include him, but far from being appeased he had a sense of outrage.

"You're taking chances," he said. "In fact I don't see how you dared come out with me. I might have had feathers under my hat."

"You didn't bring a hat," she said placidly. "Besides Joe Becker said to. There might be something in it for me."

After all he was a producer and you didn't reach eminence by losing your temper—except on purpose.

"I'm *sure* there's something in it for you," he said, listening to a stealthy treacherous purr creep into his voice.

"Are you?" she demanded. "Do you think I'll stand out at all—or am I just one of the thousands."

"You stand out already," he continued on the same note. "Everyone at the dance was looking at you."

He wondered if this was even faintly true. Was it only he who had fancied some uniqueness?

"You're a new type," he went on. "A face like yours might give American pictures a—a more civilized tone."

This was his arrow—but to his vast surprise it glanced off.

"Oh, do you think so?" she cried. "Are you going to give me a chance?"

"Why certainly." It was hard to believe that the irony in his voice was missing its mark. "Except, of course, after tonight there'll be so much competition that—"

"Oh, I'd rather work for you," she declared; "I'll tell Joe Becker—"

"Don't tell him anything," he interrupted.

"Oh, I won't. I'll do just as you say."

Her eyes were wide and expectant. Disturbed, he felt that words were being put in his mouth or slipping from him unintended. That so much innocence and so much predatory toughness could go side by side behind this gentle English voice.

"You'd be wasted in bits," he began. "The thing is to get a fat part—" He broke off and began again, "You've got such a strong personality that—"

"Oh don't!" He saw tears blinking in the corners of her eyes. "Let me just keep this to sleep on tonight. You call me in the morning—or when you need me."

The car came to rest at the strip of red carpet in front of the dance. Seeing Pamela, the crowd bulged forward grotesquely in the spilt glare of the drum lights. They held their autograph books at the ready, but failing to recognize her, they sighed back behind the ropes.

In the ballroom he danced her to Becker's table.

"I won't say a word," she whispered. From her evening case she took a card with the name of her hotel penciled on it. "If any other offers come I'll refuse them."

"Oh no," he said quickly.

"Oh yes." She smiled brightly at him and for an instant the feeling Jim had had on seeing her came back. There was an impression in her face, at least, of a rich warm sympathy, of youth and suffering side by side. He braced himself for a final quick slash to burst the scarcely created bubble.

"After a year or so—" he began. But the music and her voice overrode him.

"I'll wait for you to call. You're the—you're the most civilized American I've ever met."

She turned her back as if embarrassed by the magnificence of her compliment. Jim started back to his table—then seeing his hostess talking to someone across his empty chair, he turned obliquely away. The room, the evening had gone raucous—the blend of music and voices seemed inharmonious and accidental and his eyes covering the room saw only jealousies and hatreds—egos tapping like drum beats up to a fanfare. He was not above the battle as he had thought.

He started for the coat-room thinking of the note he would dispatch by waiter to his hostess: "You were dancing so I——" Then he found himself almost upon Pamela Knighton's table, and turning again he took another route toward the door.

· II ·

A PICTURE EXECUTIVE can do without creative intelligence but not without tact. Tact now absorbed Jim Leonard to the exclusion of everything else. Power should have pushed diplomacy into the background, leaving him free, but instead it intensified all his human relations—with the executives, with the directors, writers, actors and technical men assigned to his unit, with department heads, censors and "men from the East" besides. So the stalling off of one lone English girl, who had no weapon except the telephone and a little note that reached him from the entrance desk, should have been no problem at all.

Just passing by the studio and thought of you and of our ride. There have been some offers but I keep stalling Joe Becker. If I move I will let you know.

A city full of youth and hope spoke in it—in its two transparent lies, the brave falsity of its tone. It didn't matter to her—all the money and glory beyond the impregnable walls. She had just been passing by—just passing by.

That was after two weeks. In another week, Joe Becker dropped in to see him.

"About that little English girl, Pamela Knighton—remember? How'd she strike you?"

"Very nice."

"For some reason she didn't want me to talk to you." Joe looked out the window. "So I suppose you didn't get along so well that night."

"Sure we did."

"The girl's engaged, you see, to some guy in England."

"She told me that," said Jim, annoyed. "I didn't make any passes at her if that's what you're getting at."

"Don't worry—I understand those things. I just wanted to tell you something about her."

"Nobody else interested?"

"She's only been here a month. Everybody's got to start. I just want to tell you that when she came into Twenty-one that day the barflies dropped like—like flies. Let me tell you—in one minute she was the talk of Cafe Society."

"It must have been great," Jim said dryly.

"It was. And LaMarr was there that day too. Listen—Pam was all alone, and she had on English clothes I guess, nothing you'd look at twice—rabbit fur. But she shone through it like a diamond."

"Yeah?"

"Strong women wept into their vichysoisse. Elsa Maxwell—"

"Joe, this is a busy morning."

"Will you look at her test?"

"Tests are for make-up men," said Jim, impatiently. "I never believe a good test. And I always suspect a bad one."

"Got your own ideas, eh."

"About that. There've been a lot of bad guesses in projection rooms."

"Behind desks too," said Joe rising.

A second note came after another week.

When I phoned yesterday one secretary said you were away and one said you were in conference. If this is a run-around tell me. I'm not getting any younger. Twenty-one is staring me in the face—and you must have bumped off all the old men.

Her face had grown dim now. He remembered the delicate cheeks, the haunted eyes, as from a picture seen a long time ago. It was easy to dictate a letter that told of changed plans, of new casting, of difficulties which made it impossible. . . .

He didn't feel good about it but at least it was finished business. Having a sandwich in his neighborhood drugstore that night, he looked back at his month's work as good. He had reeked of tact. His unit functioned smoothly. The shades who controlled his destiny would soon see.

There were only a few people in the drugstore. Pamela Knighton was the girl at the magazine rack. She looked up at him, startled, over a copy of the *Illustrated London News*.

Knowing of the letter that lay for signature on his desk, Jim wished he could pretend not to see her. He turned slightly aside, held his breath, listened. But though she had seen him, nothing happened, and hating his Hollywood cowardice he turned again presently and lifted his hat.

"You're up late," he said.

Pamela searched his face momentarily.

"I live around the corner," she said. "I've just moved—I wrote you today."

"I live near here too."

She replaced the magazine in the rack. Jim's tact fled. He felt suddenly old and harassed and asked the wrong question.

"How do things go?"

"Oh very well," she said. "I'm in a play—a real play at the New Faces Theatre in Pasadena. For the experience."

"Oh, that's very wise."

"We open in two weeks. I was hoping you could come."

They walked out the door together and stood in the glow of the red neon sign. Across the autumn street newsboys were shouting the result of the night football.

"Which way?" she asked.

—The other way from you, he thought, but when she indicated her direction he walked with her. It was months since he had seen Sunset Boulevard, and the mention of Pasadena made him think of when he had first come to California ten years ago, something green and cool.

Pamela stopped before some tiny bungalows around a central court.

"Good night," she said. "Don't let it worry you if you can't help me. Joe has explained how things are, with the war and all. I know you wanted to."

He nodded solemnly—despising himself.

"Are you married?" she asked.

"No."

"Then kiss me goodnight."

As he hesitated she said, "I like to be kissed good night. I sleep better."

He put his arms around her shyly and bent down to her lips, just touching them—and thinking hard of the letter on his desk which he couldn't send now—and liking holding her.

"You see it's nothing," she said, "just friendly. Just good night."

On his way to the corner Jim said aloud, "Well, I'll be damned" and kept repeating the sinister prophecy to himself for some time after he was in bed.

· III ·

On the third night of Pamela's play Jim went to Pasadena and bought a seat in the last row. He entered a tiny auditorium and was the first arrival except for fluttering ushers and voices chattering amid the hammers backstage. He considered a discreet retirement but was reassured by the arrival of a group of five, among them Joe Becker's chief assistant. The lights went out; a gong was beaten; to an audience of six the play began.

Jim watched Pamela; in front of him the party of five leaned together and whispered after her scenes. Was she good? He was sure of it. But with pictures drawing upon half the world for talent there was scarcely such a phenomenon as a "natural." There were only possibilities—and luck. He was luck. He was maybe this girl's luck—if he felt that her pull at his insides was universal. Stars were no longer created by one man's casual desire as in the silent days, but stock girls were, tests were, chances were. When the last curtain dropped, domestically as a Venetian blind, he went backstage by the simple process of walking through a door on the side. She was waiting for him.

"I was hoping you wouldn't come tonight," she said. "We've flopped. But the first night it was full and I looked for you."

"You were fine," he said shyly.

"Oh no. You should have seen me then."

"I saw enough," he said. "I can give you a little part. Will you come to the studio tomorrow?"

He watched her expression. Out of her eyes, out of the curve of her mouth gleamed a sudden and overwhelming pity.

"Oh," she said. "Oh, I'm terribly sorry. Joe brought some people over and next day I signed up with Bernie Wise."

"You did?"

"I knew you wanted me and at first I didn't realize you were just a sort of supervisor. I thought you had more power—" She broke off and assured him hastily, "Oh, I like you better *per*sonally. You're much more civilized than Bernie Wise."

He felt a stab of pain and protest. All right then, he was civilized.

"Can I drive you back to Hollywood?" he asked.

They rode through an October night soft as April. When they crossed a bridge, its walls topped with wire screens, he gestured toward it and she nodded.

"I know what it is," she said. "But how stupid! English people don't commit suicide when they don't get what they want."

"I know. They come to America."

She laughed and looked at him appraisingly. Oh, she could do something with him all right. She let her hand rest upon his.

"Kiss tonight?" he suggested after a while.

Pamela glanced at the chauffeur, insulated in his compartment.

"Kiss tonight," she said.

He flew East next day, looking for a young actress just like Pamela Knighton. He looked so hard that any eyes with an aspect of lovely melancholy, any bright English voice, predisposed him. It seemed rather a desperate matter that he should find some one exactly like this girl. Then when a telegram called him impatiently back to Hollywood, he found Pamela dumped in his lap.

"You got a second chance, Jim," said Joe Becker. "Don't miss it again."

"What was the matter over there?"

"They had no part for her. They're in a mess. So we tore up the contract."

Mike Harris, the studio head, investigated the matter. Why was a shrewd picture man like Bernie Wise willing to let her go?

"Bernie says she can't act," he reported to Jim. "And what's more she makes trouble. I keep thinking of Simone and those two Austrian girls."

"I've seen her act," insisted Jim. "And I've got a place for her. I don't even want to build her up yet. I want to spot her in this little part and let you see."

A week later Jim pushed open the padded door of Stage III and walked anxiously in. Extras in dress clothes turned toward him in the semi-darkness; eyes widened.

"Where's Bob Griffin?"

"In that bungalow with Miss Knighton."

They were sitting side by side on a couch in the glare of the make-up light, and from the resistance in Pamela's face Jim knew the trouble was serious.

"It's *nothing*," Bob insisted heartily. "We get along like a couple of kittens, don't we, Pam?"

"You smell of onions," said Pamela.

Griffin tried again.

"There's an English way and an American way. We're looking for the happy mean—that's all."

"There's a nice way and a silly way," Pamela said shortly. "I don't want to begin by looking like a fool."

"Leave us alone, will you Bob?" Jim said.

"Sure. All the time in the world."

Jim had not seen her in this busy week of tests and fittings and rehearsals, and he thought now how little he knew about her and she of them.

"Bob seems to be in your hair," he said.

"He wants me to say things no sane person would say."

"All right—maybe so," he agreed. "Pamela, since you've been working here have you ever blown up in your lines?"

"Why—everybody does sometimes."

"Listen, Pamela—Bob Griffin gets almost ten times as much money as you do—for a particular reason. Not because he's the most brilliant director in Hollywood—he isn't—but because he never blows up in his lines."

"He's not an actor," she said puzzled.

"I mean his lines in real life. I picked him for this picture because once in a while I blow up. But not Bob. He signed a contract for an unholy amount of money—which he doesn't deserve, which nobody deserves. But he earns it because smoothness is the fourth dimension of this business and Bob has learned never to say the word 'I'. People of three times his talent —producers and troopers and directors—go down the sink because they can't learn that."

"I know I'm being lectured to," she said uncertainly. "But I don't seem to understand. An actress has her own personality—"

He nodded.

"And we pay her five times what she could get for it anywhere else—*if* she'll only keep it off the floor where it trips the rest of us up. You're tripping us all up, Pamela."

—I thought you were my friend, her eyes said.

He talked to her a few minutes more. Everything he said he believed with all his heart, but because he had twice kissed those lips he saw that it was support and protection they wanted from him. All he had done was to make her a little shocked that he was not on her side. Feeling rather baffled, and sorry for her loneliness he went to the door of the bungalow and called:

"Hey, Bob!"

Jim went about other business. He got back to his office to find Mike Harris waiting.

"Again that girl's making trouble."

"I've been over there."

"I mean in the last five minutes," cried Harris. "Since you left she's made trouble! Bob Griffin had to stop shooting for the day. He's on his way over."

Bob came in.

"There's one type you can't seem to get at—can't find what makes them that way."

There was a moment's silence. Mike Harris, upset by the situation, suspected that Jim was having an affair with the girl.

"Give me till tomorrow morning," said Jim. "I think I can find what's back of this."

Griffin hesitated but there was a personal appeal in Jim's eyes—an appeal to associations of a decade.

"All right, Jim," he agreed.

When they had gone Jim called Pamela's number. What he had almost expected happened but his heart sank none the less when a man's voice answered the phone.

· I V ·

EXCEPTING a trained nurse, an actress is the easiest prey for the unscrupulous male. Jim had learned that in the background of their troubles or their failures there was often some plausible confidence man, who asserted his masculinity by way of interference, midnight nagging, bad advice. The technique of the man was to belittle the woman's job and to question endlessly the motives and intelligence of those for whom she worked.

When Jim reached the bungalow hotel in Beverly Hills where Pamela had moved, it was after six. In the court a cold fountain plashed senselessly against the December fog and he heard Major Bowes' voice loud from three radios.

When the door of the apartment opened Jim stared. The man was old—a bent and withered Englishman with ruddy winter color dying in his face. He wore an old dressing gown and slippers and he asked Jim to sit down with an air of being at home. Pamela would be in shortly.

"Are you a relative?" Jim asked wonderingly.

"No, Pamela and I met here in Hollywood, strangers in a strange land. Are you employed in pictures, Mr.——Mr.——"

"Leonard," said Jim. "Yes. At present I'm Pamela's boss."

A change came into the man's eyes—the watery blink became conspicuous, there was a stiffening of the old lids. The lips curled down and backward and Jim was gazing into an expression of utter malignanty. Then the features became old and bland again.

"I hope Pamela is being handled properly?"

"You've been in pictures?" Jim asked.

"Till my health broke down. But I am still on the rolls at Central Casting and I know everything about this business and the souls of those who own it—"

He broke off. The door opened and Pamela came in.

"Well hello," she said in surprise. "You've met? The Honorable Chauncey Ward—Mr. Leonard."

Her glowing beauty, borne in from outside like something snatched from wind and weather, made Jim breathless for a moment.

"I thought you told me my sins this afternoon," she said with a touch of defiance.

"I wanted to talk to you away from the studio."

"Don't accept a salary cut," the old man said. "That's an old trick."

"It's not that, Mr. Ward," said Pamela. "Mr. Leonard has been my friend up to now. But today the director tried to make a fool of me and Mr. Leonard backed him up."

"They all hang together," said Mr. Ward.

"I wonder—" began Jim. "Could I possibly talk to you alone."

"I trust Mr. Ward," said Pamela frowning. "He's been over here twenty-five years and he's practically my business manager."

Jim wondered from what deep loneliness this relationship had sprung.

"I hear there was more trouble on the set," he said.

"Trouble!" She was wide-eyed. "Griffin's assistant swore at me and I heard it. So I walked out. And if Griffin sent apologies by you I don't want them—our relation is going to be strictly business from now on."

"He didn't send apologies," said Jim uncomfortably. "He sent an ultimatum."

"An ultimatum!" she exclaimed. "I've got a contract, and you're his boss, aren't you?"

"To an extent," said Jim, "—but of course making pictures is a joint matter—"

"Then let me try another director."

"Fight for your rights," said Mr. Ward. "That's the only thing that impresses them."

"You're doing your best to wreck this girl," said Jim quietly.

"You can't frighten us," snapped Ward. "I've seen your type before."

Jim looked again at Pamela. There was exactly nothing he could do. Had they been in love, had it ever seemed the time to encourage the spark between them, he might have reached her now. But it was too late. He seemed to feel the swift wheels of the industry turning in the Hollywood darkness outside. He knew that when the studio opened tomorrow, Mike Harris would have new plans that did not include Pamela at all.

For a moment longer he hesitated. He was a well-liked man, still young, and with a wide approval. He could buck them about this girl, send her to a dramatic teacher. He could not bear to see her make such a mistake. On the other hand he was afraid that somewhere people had yielded to her too much, spoiled her for this sort of career.

"Hollywood isn't a very civilized place," said Pamela.

"It's a jungle," agreed Mr. Ward. "Full of prowling beasts of prey."

Jim rose.

"Well, this one will prowl out," he said. "Pam, I'm very sorry. Feeling like you do, I think you'd be wise to go back to England and get married."

For a moment a flicker of doubt was in her eyes. But her confidence, her young egotism, was greater than her judgment—she did not realize that this very minute was opportunity and she was losing it forever.

For she had lost it when Jim turned and went out. It was weeks before she knew how it happened. She received her salary for some months—Jim saw to that—but she did not set foot on that lot again. Nor on any other. She was placed quietly on that black list that is not written down but that functions at backgammon games after dinner, or on the way to the races. Men of influence stared at her with interest at restaurants here and there but all their inquiries about her reached the same dead end.

She never gave up during the following months—even long after Becker had lost interest and she was in want, and no longer seen in the places where people go to be looked at. It was not from grief or discouragement but only through commonplace circumstances that in June she died.

· V ·

WHEN JIM heard about it, it seemed incredible. He learned accidentally that she was in the hospital with pneumonia—he telephoned and found that she was dead. "Sybil Higgins, actress, English. Age 21."

She had given old Ward as the person to be informed and Jim managed to get him enough money to cover the funeral expenses, on the pretext that some old salary was still owing. Afraid that Ward might guess the source of the money he did not go to the funeral but a week later he drove out to the grave.

It was a long bright June day and he stayed there an hour. All over the city there were young people just breathing and being happy and it seemed senseless that the little English girl was not one of them. He kept on trying and trying to twist things about so that they would come out right for her but it was too late. That pink and silver frost had melted. He said good-by aloud and promised that he would come again.

Back at the studio he reserved a projection room and asked for her tests and for the bits of film that had been shot on her picture. He sat in a big leather chair in the darkness and pressed the button for it to begin.

In the test Pamela was dressed as he had seen her that first night at the dance. She looked very happy and he was glad she had had at least that much happiness. The reel of takes from the picture began and ran jerkily with the sound of Bob Griffin's voice off scene and with prop boys showing the number blocks for the takes. Then Jim started as the next-to-last one came up, and he saw her turn from the camera and whisper:

"I'd rather die than do it that way."

Jim got up and went back to his office where he opened the three notes he had from her and read them again.

. . . *just passing by the studio and thought of you and of our ride.*

—just passing by. During the spring she had called him twice on the phone, he knew, and he had wanted to see her. But he could do nothing for her and could not bear to tell her so.

"I am not very brave," Jim said to himself. Even now there was fear in his heart that this would haunt him like that memory of his youth, and he did not want to be unhappy.

Several days later he worked late in the dubbing room, and afterwards he dropped into his neighborhood drugstore for a sandwich. It was a warm night and there were many young people at the soda counter. He was paying his check when he became aware that a figure was standing by the magazine rack looking at him over the edge of a magazine. He stopped—he did not want to turn for a closer look only to find the resemblance at an end. Nor did he want to go away.

He heard the sound of a page turning and then out of the corner of his eye he saw the magazine cover, *The Illustrated London News*.

He felt no fear—he was thinking too quickly, too desperately. If this were real and he could snatch her back, start from there, from that night.

"Your change, Mr. Leonard."

"Thank you."

Still without looking he started for the door and then the magazine closed and dropped to a pile and he heard someone breathe close to his side. Newsboys were calling an extra across the street and after a moment he turned the wrong way, her way, and he heard her following—so plain that he slowed his pace with the sense that she had trouble keeping up with him.

In front of the apartment court he took her in his arms and drew her radiant beauty close.

"Kiss me goodnight," she said. "I like to be kissed goodnight. I sleep better."

—Then sleep, he thought as he turned away—sleep. I couldn't fix it. I tried to fix it. When you brought your beauty here I didn't want to throw it away, but I did somehow. There is nothing left for you now but sleep.

DEARLY BELOVED

◆

"Dearly Beloved" was rejected by Esquire *in 1940—one of editor Arnold Gingrich's lapses in judgment. Apart from the interesting circumstance that it is the only Fitzgerald magazine piece in which a black character is treated seriously, "Dearly Beloved" is delicately and movingly written. Beauty Boy has obvious connections with the philosophical black fisherman in* The Last Tycoon. *This 850-word sketch was first published by the* Fitzgerald/Hemingway Annual *in 1969—twenty-nine years after Fitzgerald's death.*

◆

O MY BEAUTY BOY—reading Plato so divine! O, dark, oh fair, colored golf champion of Chicago. Over the rails he goes at night, steward of the club car, and afterwards in the dim smoke by the one light and the smell of stale spittoons, writing west to the Rosecrucian Brotherhood. Seeking ever.

O Beauty Boy here is your girl, not one to soar like you, but a clean swift serpent who will travel as fast on land and look toward you in the sky.

Lilymary loved him, oft invited him and they were married in St. Jarvis' church in North Englewood. For years they bettered themselves, running along the tread-mill of their race, becoming only a little older and no better than before. He was loaned the Communist Manifesto by the wife of the advertising manager of a Chicago daily but for preference give him Plato— the Phaedo and the Apologia, or else the literature of the Rosecrucian Brotherhood of Sacramento, California, which burned in his ears as the rails clicked past Alton, Springfield and Burlington in the dark.

Bronze lovers, never never canst thou have thy bronze child—or so it seemed for years. Then the clock struck, the gong rang and Dr. Edwin Burch of South Michigan Avenue agreed to handle the whole thing for two hundred dollars. They looked so nice—so delicately nice, neither of them ever hurting the other and gracefully expert in the avoidance. Beauty Boy took fine care of her in her pregnancy—paid his sister to watch with her while he did double work on the road and served for caterers in the city; and one day the bronze baby was born.

O Beauty Boy, Lilymary said, here is your beauty boy. She lay in a four bed ward in the hospital with the wives of a prize fighter, an undertaker and a doctor. Beauty Boy's face was so twisted with radiance; his teeth shining so in his smile and his eyes so kind that it seemed that nothing and nothing could ever.

Beauty Boy sat beside her bed when she slept and read Thoreau's Walden for the third time. Then the nurse told him he must leave. He went on the road that night and in Alton going to mail a letter for a passenger he slipped under the moving train and his leg was off above the knee.

Beauty Boy lay in the hospital and a year passed. Lilymary went back to work again cooking. Things were tough, there was even trouble about his workman's compensation, but he found lines in his books that helped them along for awhile when all the human beings seemed away.

The little baby flourished but he was not beautiful like his parents; not as they had expected in those golden dreams. They had only spare-time love to give the child so the sister more and more and more took care of him. For they wanted to get back where they were, they wanted Beauty Boy's leg to grow again so it would all be like it was before. So that he could find delight in his books again and Lilymary could find delight in hoping for a little baby.

Some years passed. They were so far back on the tread-mill that they would never catch up. Beauty Boy was a night-watchman now but he had six operations on his stump and each new artificial limb gave him constant pain. Lilymary worked fairly steadily as a cook. Now they had become just ordinary people. Even the sister had long since forgotten that Beauty Boy was formerly colored golf champion of Chicago. Once in cleaning the closet she threw out all his books—the Apologia and the Phaedo of Plato, and the Thoreau and the Emerson and all the leaflets and correspondence with the Rosecrucian Brotherhood. He didn't find out for a long time that they were gone. And then he just stared at the place where they had been and said "Say, man . . . say man."

For things change and get so different that we can hardly recognize them and it seems that only our names remain the same. It seemed wrong for them still to call each other Beauty Boy and Lilymary long after the delight was over.

Some years later they both died in an influenza epidemic and went to heaven. They thought it was going to be all right then—indeed things began to happen in exactly the way that they had been told as children. Beauty Boy's leg grew again and he became golf champion of all heaven, both white and black, and drove the ball powerfully from cloud to cloud through the blue fairway. Lilymary's breasts became young and firm, she was respected among the other angels, and her pride in Beauty Boy became as it had been before.

In the evening they sat and tried to remember what it was they missed. It was not his books, for here everyone knew all those things by heart, and it was not the little boy for he had never really been one of them. They couldn't remember so after a puzzled time they would give up trying, and talk about how nice the other one was, or how fine a score Beauty Boy would make tomorrow.

So things go.